Dedicat

I would like to dedicate this book to all
being told that they are not able to do so
do it.

MAP 1
TARRACONENSIS AND GALIA GOTHICA

INDEX OF PLACES AND PEOPLE

PLACE NAMES

7th CENTURY	TODAY
Ausona	Olot
Barcino	Barcelona
Caesaragusta	Zaragoza
Castrum de Caucoliberi	Colliure
Castrum Libiae	Llivia
Clausurae	Les Cluses
Dertosa	Tortosa
Egara	Terrassa
Gallia Gothica	Area north of the Pyrenees. (Septimania)
Gerunda	Girona
Hispalis	Sevilla
Ilerda	Lleida
Narbo	Narbonne
Nemausus	Nimes
Pampaelo	Pamplona
Port area	Serrallo
Tarrraco / Tarraconense	Tarragona
Toletum	Toledo

TARRACO	
Duke Ranosindus (wife- Heva)	
Amalaswinth:	his housekeeper
Marcus:	Son of Duke Ranosindus
Pere:	Arms instructor of Marcus
Antonia:	Pere's wife
CLERGY	
Cyprianus:	Metropolitan Bishop (Tarraco)
Maria:	his housekeeper
JEWS	
Rebecca:	Daughter of Jacob

Saul:	Rabbi of Tarraco
Abraham:	Chief rabbi based in Barcino
Zachery :	Elder of Tarraco
Hillel :	New rabbi

GALLIA GOTHICA

Count Hilderic:	Count of Nemausus
Chlodoswintha:	Wife of the Count
Avina:	Daughter of the Count

GALLIA GOTHICA MILITARY

General Wittimir

FRANKS

Chlothar

GALLIA GOTHICA CLERGY

Gunhild:	Bishop of Maguelonne
Argebaud:	Metropolitan Bishop of Narbo
Abbot Ranimiro	
Aregio:	Bishop of Elna

ROYAL FORCES

King Wamba	
Egica:	Nephew of Wamba

GENERALS

Flavius Paulus

Hermenguild

Kunimund

Alaric

THE BARONS

Teodofred	
Gelvira	Baron's daughter
Ervigius	
Cixilona	Baron's daughter

SOLDIERS

Centurion Milo

Caius

TOLETUM

Quiricus:	Bishop of Barcino, then first bishop of Toletum
Taio:	Bishop of Caesaragusta.
Julian:	Leading Bishop of Toletum

Iulianus:	Bishop of Hispalis

VASC
Aitziber
Arantxa
Eztebeni

"I really hate fish."

The no longer slim, religious figure all but pushed past his host in order to get out of the stifling heat and stench.

"It never used to be so bad, your Grace. It's the decline, it affects us all."

The intruder stopped to inspect the area that was affording shade from the blistering outside sun. It must have been a great deal grander in previous times, he mused. Still it bore some echoes of its more glorious past. Some particularly fine pieces of ceramics lined the entrance hall and decorously fabric hung from its walls. However, not even the quality of these pieces could hide the fact that what they decorated was and had been for some time in disrepair.

"The fish, sadly, are much more abundant than the potential buyers, thus they stay longer than they should on sale on the quayside. And, most unfortunately for you, your Grace, what wind there is, seems to be headed in our direction. I do apologise most profusely. Unfortunately, I can do nothing about the hurrying of the sale of the fishermans' ware nor the direction of the breeze, however, if you would be so kind as to step farther into my most humble abode, the unfortunate effects of both would be somewhat diminished."

The sweating suffering bulk allowed himself to be lead into an interior courtyard, which again, in its day, would have been a sight to be held. There was only one chair which Bishop Cyprianus took full advantage of.

"I do so hate fish."

The body was now at rest, unlike the perspiration pores which were working as fast as they could to shed excess body fluid.

"Nasty creatures. They taste of dirty salt water, try to assassinate you with their sharp little bones and they, no other word for it, stink. Why God ever put them on this earth is well beyond me. And to make His own son mix with fishermen throughout His life, well...."

He began to shake his head in a clear sign of bewilderment. This also gave flight to some of the rivulets that were pouring down his face, causing the newly arrived drink bearer to take a step back in an act of self-protection.

The sudden movement caused the bishop to raise his head. What his fading blue eyes saw, gave him great pleasure and stopped his pondering on idle inexplicable quirks of a superior being who would want to create something as malicious as sea creatures.

"Would your Grace care for some ale? We do have some local wine but given the heat of the day I thought ..."

" Oh my my my, what, or should I say who, do we have here, Jacob?"

He took a long draught of the proffered ale not letting his eyes and attention move from the ale server. Suddenly his face, one second open-eyed in appreciation, creased into a scowl. "Oh, even the ale tastes a bit fishy."

A little too quickly, over defensively and certainly not showing due deference, Jacob continued, "some refreshment would be in order." Changing the direction of his voice he added "That will be all, Rebecca."

*

"How is that possible?" King Wamba paced violently up and down the confines of the campaign tent. Even though it was the King's official residence for the duration of the conflict, it didn't afford him much space to vent his anger this despite his comparatively little marching step,"

"Froia you say. That just is not possible. He's dead. I saw him executed myself. And now you are telling me that he is back. Has he risen from the dead like Our Lord Jesus? Hallowed be his name. Are you saying that he has become a new saviour? Come to oppose those who fight in the name of the Lord. Us, the righteous…"

The rant was in full swing now. Those present had learnt to their considerable pain that the only possible thing to do was grunt agreement, say absolutely nothing and wait until it was spent.

The tirade was relatively short, barely getting to ten minutes with almost no fits of apoplectic anger and only one goblet hurled in rage.

The King was generally an extremely mild-manner considerate person who genuinely seemed to care about those inferiors around him.

However, there were moments when a sort of demon entered his thin almost saintly looking form.

This was one of those.

A lull or the end?

General Kunimund wagered on the latter. "Not in person, sire."

"What? What the devil are you talking about Kunimund?"

A wager won. "Froia."

"Of course not. I realise that but you say that they use his name as some sort of rallying or battle cry."

King Wamba, the considerate and contemplative was back. An almost audible sigh blew through the tent.

"It has been used as such since we have arrived here in the Vasconia."

"Well, it's up to us to stop it, and finally bury that nasty traitorous incompetent Froia."

"Not the slightest bit incompetent. The man, with little help from real soldiers, just the ferocious Vascones, who we know fight bravely, but are no match for an organised force, actually made it as far as Ceasaragusta." The welcome breeze from the tent flap brought these words and the appearance of a handsome very self-assured young man in full battle dress.

"Ah Falvius, so good of you to join us….eventually. We've all been here for quite some time. I presume it was something vitally important that caused your delay?" Wamba's words were stern and delivered with an air of rebuke trying to hide a sly knowing grin.

"Gathering vital information behind lines, Sire. You know nought else would prevent my attendance."

"And did the extent of this information get to the point where you actually found out her name this time?"

"Sire! I was labouring for the good of the campaign."

The King looked amused. The others were stony faced not understanding what power this youth had over the king that he indulged him so.

"Actually, I can tell you that the use of Froia's name is not in any great deference or hero worship of that traitor, more due to the fact that it's the only slight victory the Vascones have had for years. Not since the Roman led forces were they so successful. So, by invoking his name, it's like a premature victory chant. In reality most of them despise him for rebelling against his own. They value blood, family and tribal loyalty above all. He didn't, nor was he, one of them, and never would have been. If we hadn't got to him first, they would have. It's a generation, twenty years, since his partial victory, the little details get lost and forgotten. Now they just remember getting to Caesaragusta under him, nothing else. Oh, and Aitziber."

The grin became an all out smile.

"It would appear that your labour was fruitful. Try to get things done faster next time. You have kept some important generals waiting. Ceasaragusta? That is that awful dump we spent the night in last week? If it weren't for the memory of what it was under Roman times and its strategic position, I would let them have it. Imagine being proud of getting there. More of a place to leave than one to go to, I would say."

"You won't find much disagreement here with that sentiment" Offered Kunimund, tentatively trying to get into the conversational spotlight."Decidedly smelly."

The King cast a glance in Kunimund's direction, then, as usual, dismissed him and his opinions.

Hermenguild, another general, the eldest and most experienced, looked pained. "Actually Sire, my family originally hail from there. I can trace our lineage back to when we took over from the Romans. Admittedly, it wasn't much at any time but we have always been loyal and been at the forefront of the empire keeping those tribes, our distant cousins, or the uncouthed unwashed Vascones at bay. Every king has appreciated our efforts. King Reccesvinth, when he was here, complemented us on our stoic valour. I was there when he did it, fighting by his side to destroy and capture the traitor Froia."

"Terribly sorry General Hermenguild." The considerate and contemplative version of the King was definitely back in control of his emotions again. "I really didn't mean to offend. My appreciation of your home town has never wavered. Your personal sacrifice of decades of service is also held in the highest of esteem. Quite how the kingdom would have fared without you and your likes, I really don't know. Your campaign twenty years ago was masterful. We need a repetition now." The smoothing of ruffled feathers was vital to the unity and harmony of the armed forces. In fact, since Wamba had come to power a couple years ago he had done his best to remodel and reorganise what had become a lazy flabby top-heavy force that hadn't seen any real action for far too long. Hermenguild was typical of all that was wrong; slow, arrogant, overweight and anything but decisively incisive. He certainly was one of the main reasons that the war was dragging on despite their overwhelming numbers and firepower. He was the last of the old guard to be cleared out. This task would take time and skill as Hermenguild had a large and loyal following.

*

Wamba had come to the throne with great reluctance. He didn't want, nor had ever wanted the role/job. He was quite happy as he had always been, moderately important without too many ties or obligations. God Almighty, in all His wisdom knew that he had not sought the position. Instead, it was foisted upon him; the compromise candidate. Isn't it always the way? He didn't want it and nobody really wanted him. God knows the sons of the last king, Reccesvinth, had tried to assert what right they thought they had. The Goths, in either of their forms - not that distinction had come to mean much since the Ostrogoths had saved the bacon of the Visigoths back in the days when the Franks were a force to be reckoned with had always elected their kings. Hereditary rights were rarely taken into accounts. Dynasties were to be avoided. It was, and hopefully, always would be, the way with the tribes of the Rhine. However, the result of this lack of clarity of succession leads to bizarre facts being taken into account. Wamba thought he was safely out of the running. He remembered raising his ale cup to propose the toast of "Let them squabble and may God select the best man." God was certainly due to take more than a passive part in the proceedings as the bishops were now the main electing force, taking the role once performed by the tribal elders. Sadly for him, the toast was made around an iron table.

That fact, combined with Goth mythology and new ecclesiastical predominance, sealed his fate. His was the chosen one.

Buggered.

*

"Another loan can most certainly be arranged your Grace." Jacob squirmed in his richly upholstered high-backed chair, placed at a strategically lower level than the Bishop's own which, both in use and size, resembled a throne.

This was going to cost a lot, thought Jacob.

"I do hesitate to mention it, and I'm sure such a little trifling matter must have slipped your Grace's mind, however, there is the matter of the two previous, ermm, dealings we have had. Their repayment date is well passed. I wondered whether… "

"Jacob, Jacob, Jacob, you do well to remind me. The first, when was it? It seems to have slipped my mind. Oh no, I do remember. It was when I was introduced to your daughter. What was her name again?"

The squirming instantly turned to turmoil.

"Rebecca." His ashened face managed to whisper as if mentioning her name too loud would make this increasingly dire situation even worse.

"Such a lovely thing, and such a splendidly Jewish name. How old is she now? Just a slip of a thing the last time. She must be quite some woman by now. You must be SO proud of her."

"I am your Grace."

There was silence, not a long gap of no words, sufficient, verbal communication was totally unnecessary, the triumphal grin of recollection and future pleasure was eloquent enough.

"The amount you asked for will take some time to get together. It should be possible by the end of the month though."

"Excellent, excellent, excellent." The bishop was never a man to use one word when three would do as well.

"Also, Jacob. There is that other matter we alluded to in the past. There is only so much I can do. After all the Eighth Concilium at Toledo was eight years ago. My word, what a lot of eights. Never liked that number, I regard more than four letters to express one number as, well, excessive, don't you? Such a waste. Now, nine, that's much more concise, just IX. Neat. Where was I? Oh yes, very precise it was. Though, as you well know, I voted against the strictures of the last concilium, I was invited to in the hope that moderation and reconciliation could prosper. It seems the wind will not blow that way. In the years between the two, positions have hardened. My vote and that of Dertosa carried little sway."

"A pity, a pity, a pity." These words were accompanied by a head shaking lament.

The turmoil inside Jacob had now grown into fear bordering on panic. The conversation had taken a turn for the worse. No, this wasn't a turning, mulling uncomfortable Jacob, this was him facing a gaping abyss. A chasm was opening, albeit slowly, beneath his feet. For so long had he had been dreading this moment. His policy of low profile subservience had served him and his well, for decades, now for the sake of his big mouth and desire to recover his money, he had put everyone and everything in danger.

*

"Shield wall!" Hermenguild ordered. As senior General he marshalled his troops from the relative height, and safety, of his white horse. Attired in his best battle dress his armour shone in the early morning sun. He looked the part, a figure to be respected and feared.

His troops, well-organised, superbly trained and equipped for the battle, locked shields in their rehearsed and efficient manner.

The Goths had been fighting like this, successfully for centuries. At one time they were just any other Germanic type tribe living a settled relatively peaceful existence near the shores of the Baltic.

The unrelenting eastward drive of the unstoppable Hun put pay to that type of existence. They had moved; all of them, a massive uprooting to, well, anywhere the Hun wasn't. They trudged and fought and survived until they hit the borders of the Roman Empire.

Huns behind, Romans in front. Some sort of deal had to be done. It took years, setbacks, changes in fortune, more setbacks, more years, eventually the Goths had become the backbone of the Roman army. The tactics were Roman, the orders; Roman, the uniforms; Roman, the pay, a mixture of Roman and Goth coins, but they remained Goths.

That was all a very long time ago.

Rome withered. The Goths prospered. For the best part of three centuries the Iberian Peninsula had been theirs to hold and defend, something that needed doing constantly. Nowadays, quite how much of them could be compared with that escaping Goth tribe was debatable. Purity was the mantra that had sustained them and their clan structure for centuries. All that tradition was fading away. People were choosing Hispano-Roman names and ways. Certainly this melt down had become clearer since the law recognising what was already widespread; the inter-marriage and breeding with the locals.

Four men deep, the line stretched from the river to the trees. A picture of ordered fighting elegance, beautifully organised and in total symmetry. Hermenguild looked rightly proud.

In front were about a thousand ill-dressed, ill-kempt Vascones. They hadn't formed their own shield wall, which was unusual, as they had learnt the terrifying efficiency of such formations in many previous battles, and knew that a similar formation was their only possible defence. Instead, they were jeering and chanting making no attempt to move in any direction. It wasn't just the usual pre-battle banter used to gear up all, the feint-hearted and battle-hardened, for the bloody mess that was about to ensue. No, they were taunting to the point of laughing.

A speeding chestnut mare disturbed this temporary stalemate. Flavius Paulus was aboard. Coming to an abrupt halt in front of General Hermenguild, he yelled at his superior ignoring all the required niceties of rank and privilege, "Re-form into a square!"

Hermenguild was purple with rage at this clear case of insubordination in front of his officers and men. The little whippersnapper may enjoy Wamba's favour, this time though, he had gone too far.

"Guards, remove this man from his horse and secure him tightly."

Paulus looked shocked at the response. The men around Hermenguild reacted with speed and efficiency. Within seconds the rider was horseless and trussed tight.

"I have information…"

"Gag him if necessary."

The guards had more problems complying with this order as gags are not high on the list of necessary items when one is about to fight the enemy. While they searched for something suitable, Paulus took his opportunity, "It's an ambush, they are.." An armour cleansing rag had been found. At that moment, the attack began.

Firstly from the trees; spears from height and men from behind the trunks, simultaneously, the jeers stopped and voice owners charged forward with their blood curdling yells. And most surprisingly, as if monsters were rising from the deep, men wielding short swords with breathing reeds being spat from their mouths attacked on the left flank.

A three pronged assault on a wall designed for a full frontal battle. Hermenguild sat in shock and awe seemingly incapable of reaction.

"Cut me lose, you idiot." Paulus had spat out his gag and was offering tied hands to the equally surprised guard.

Once lose, Paulus rode to the carnage. The shield wall was being destroyed from both unprotected flanks.

"Kunimund, wheel to the right. Alaric to the left." He yelled trying to be heard over the dim of screaming men, clashing metal and the agony of death.

The two experienced commanders had already worked out that this was the manoeuvre that needed to be performed, but the instructions were necessary to know who was to go which way.

Hurriedly, but not without great loss in spite of the clear abandonment of some to their own fate, the line performed the practised drill of becoming a square. This defensive re-alignment would save the bulk of the force. Those left out of the square did their best to get back in. This would not be permitted by their former comrades as it would mean opening up the square to the enemy as well. They were left outside, hopelessly outnumbered and fighting until their inevitable death.

It was bloody and difficult for those in the square to watch. Their discipline held as the slaughter continued.

Hermenguild had finally reacted. He led all of his horsed men, about two dozen, down to join the fray to try to salvage some honour.

Paulus couldn't believe his eyes. A poor battle was rapidly becoming a total disaster. Clearly these horsemen were insufficient to drive the Vascons back. The loss of the men, and worse, the horses, would be the inevitable result of this brave but foolhardy charge.

The only thing to do was get the square with its back to the water, setting free the men that previously were needed for the fourth flank of the wall. A three-sided water backed defence was much more agile and allowed a whole side to march forward to take on the enemy also giving a rallying point and refuge to those not yet butchered.

Paulus gave the orders. Again, Alaric and Kunimund were well ahead of the game. They reacted with their men in perfect unison and double quick time.

Kunimund led out his men to take the fight to the enemy. It took all of his strength and commanders' skill to contain the desire of his men to fight back. A badly led attack has been the undoing of many a battle. Paulus watched in relief and happiness as the disciplined attack started moving slowly forward driving back the ill organised blood frenzied enemy. That, though, was the last thing Paulus did see.

*

"That's not fair!" Her indignation was palpable. Her hands were firmly planted on her hips and her full lips quivered.

"Marcus, the honourable nobleman, cheats!"

The object of her wrath was smirking with obvious delight.

"It wasn't *cheating,* just a slight alteration of the game."

"Alteration my foot. If you look when you're supposed to be blindfolded, that is not an alteration… it's cheating. And that Sr. Roman, makes you nothing but a cheat."

"No longer noble , am I?" with that he discarded the blindfold completely and ran towards Rebecca at full speed. Seeing his predictable reaction, she took flight taking refuge behind some coiled rope and waiting-to-be-repaired nets on the quayside.

"Predictable, slow and a cheat" she taunted him from her position of relative safety. When he moved left, she moved right. When he feigned a right shift, she stood her ground. Her slim, nimble form was perfectly adapted to this sort of pursuit

"Not only a cheat, but totally useless even at catching *a girl.*"

Marcus was beginning to get annoyed, one thing is a game, and quite another to shout these "playful" allegations in the cramped streets of the port area. Anyone could hear them, and his or his father's reputation would be stained. He took a massive lurching dive over the rope managing to grab the material of her tunic. Her resulting squeal was mostly in delight with just a tinge of fear which made it all even more exciting.

A crab pot was handy. She used it to release herself from his grip and dashed off in the direction of home as fast as she could, leaving Marcus rubbing his painfully throbbing wrist and sullenly silently reflecting on how that girl could really affect him.

Decided, he stood up, shook off some of the dirt and mustered all the dignity and pride he could. No more! At sixteen he should no longer be playing these sorts of games in the streets and especially not with that little Jewess. Definitely, no more!

*

"How many dead?"

"Eighty-three and eight horses, Sire."

"Such a waste. Enemy?"

"Perhaps a couple of dozen. They were carried away quickly as they all left the field. Not one body was recovered."

This wasn't the cup throwing uncontrolled Wamba, nor was it the considerate and contemplative mode either. Pained hand wringing, sweat filled furrows of the confused brow and a frighteningly whispered voice was the order of the day. The merciless warmth of the midday sun spared no-one from the intense heat within the tent. The stillness of the royal response increased the temperature yet further.

The steely blue eyes looked down on the two kneeling report givers, both with their hands tied behind their backs, still in their blood-splattered armour, stinking of old and new body fluids.

"Now, let me understand this. You Kunimund and you Alaric, both senior generals in one of the most effective fighting forces the world has ever seen, were ambushed and lost a battle to a …rabble. Losing eighty-three men and eight horses dead, an undisclosed number of wounded, the enemy receiving almost no losses and you start your report by telling me, your king, that you all fought bravely, did honour to the name of Goth, and in fact, it was, what was your expression; "on the face of it" quite a victory as things could have been so much worse?"

"Sire, …"

"No, no, no don't speak. I need to absorb all this information and then decide whether both of you, or just one of you, shall be executed."

The king slumped into a chair on a raised platform.

The Goths traditionally had never held with the whole concept of "thrones". The king was all powerful but he was still only the first among equals. This raised platform chair was a new invention and a piece of furniture that Wamba detested. He avoided its use as much as possible. He was assured it "had" to be there as much as the royal standard had to fly outside. It didn't mean that he had to use it.

All thoughts of protocol had disappeared and his use of it was completely accidental. There was nowhere else to slump. Disaster. Actually, was it a disaster? The losses were considerable, not great. The majority of the army was still intact. From the sketchy reports from his own personal guard, who were present at the debacle, had clearly stated that these two cowed figures in front of him, had actually acquitted themselves with distinction by performing a difficult training ground manoeuvre with great skill. There was another positive.

*

"Don't let your father catch you looking and *smelling* like that. You stink of old fish! What have you been doing?"

Marcus had been waylaid in the outer courtyard while trying to sneak back in.

"Your mother, may the Lord rest her soul, will be turning over in her grave. A fine young gentleman in such a state. Whatever would she think?"

The waylayer had a strong hold onto the material at the neck of his tunic with no intention of letting go anytime soon. Furthermore, it was quite likely with the volume of her admonitory remarks that his father would be alerted to his "lamentable presence", which would be a most undesirable meeting.

"Amalaswinth, please let go of me. I am no longer five years old to be bullied around by you." For the second time in an hour he was made to feel just an insignificant *little* boy. No more.

"Bullied!" The shriek was audible enough to be heard in the court in Toletum, never mind the inner courtyard of this palace in Tarraco. "This is how you treat me?" The dam of the eye ducts were well and truly broken. Tears first trickled, then streamed down her face anything but silently. Amalaswinth didn't do weeping. Her grip didn't loosen in the slightest though.

"After all I have done for you. I didn't experience the birth pains to bring you into this world, that was your saintly mother's function, god rest her soul. Everything else I did do. Cleaning your bottom…"

"Amalaswinth, please. I am seventeen. I am a man. I am the next duke. You can no longer speak to me like this." Marcus pleaded as quietly as he could. Considerable pain stopped him.

"Not too old for a clip on the ear though." It was a left-handed backhand delivered with much practised skill while her right kept her vicelike grip. "Listen to me, young *master*, to your room now. I will send up hot water and a newly cleaned set of clothes." With anything but a delicate push she set him on his way. Marcus stumbled, got to his feet and slowly, with as much dignity as he could muster- he was getting a great deal of practice at this today walked slowly, very slowly in the direction of his room.

*

He woke. He was in a tent. Not his tent. Not the king's but quite a large one. Everything hurt. How did he get here? Where was he? What had happened? All these thought questions made his head hurt more. Gingerly he moved his right arm. It hurt. He managed to lift it up to his face. There was nothing familiar there. No skin, no hair just a great wad of mud type stuff.

"So, you have decided, finally, to wake up. Late again Flavius. If this was, what was her name? .. Aitziber? I suggest most strongly that you give her up. She's too rough for a gentle Greek. Not only is your tardiness becoming a bad habit, but this time I am told that I have to come to you. Me, your king!"

"Sire.." Paulus managed to stammer. It hurt.

"In pain are we? That's good. It means you are alive and that you will probably mend though your good looks may have been…altered."

Paulus fondled that wad. It seemed to encase most of his skull and all of the right-side of his face down to his neck.

"That Greek doctor you swear by, stuck that on you. It was either that or we chopped off the whole head as there was only a bit of it left. It was a close thing."

"I have been close to death before it's nothing …"

"Oh no, not you dying, us killing you. We had a vote on it. Apparently, you showed immense insubordination to General Hermenguild, and, on a battle field, in front of his men no less. We can't have that, can we? The vote was close. In the end we decided to let your Greek quack do his business, then, if you ever woke, we would sound out opinion anew."
He didn't believe that he could hurt even more, but this information caused pain where there was none.
"At the moment I am trying to decide what to do with Alaric and Kunimund."
Barely audibly Paulus managed to whisper "They fought well, bravely."
"So they tell me. It doesn't detract from the fact that they lost. The name Froia has gained considerably in volume I am told. It must be stopped. My question is, if I do the right thing and execute both and your head is demanded, who will I have left to lead the army?"
With the greatest of effort and righteous indignation he spat out "You have that fool, Hermenguild."
"Oh Flavius, Flavius, this *is* the problem, your total lack of respect. Armies, as you well know, can only work if the hierarchy is respected and obeyed without question. Your outburst has not helped your cause. I must think." Wamba the contemplative, wandered off to consider while Paulus just hurt.

*

"Your Grace, His Grace the Bishop of Dertosa has arrived to see you."
"Don't keep him waiting, send him in immediately" The Bishop of Tarraco en functions was relieved to get a break from the paperwork that was mounted on his desk in neat piles.
"Your Grace, may I present his Grace …"
"Enough graces! Anyone would think it's dinnertime."
A thin wizened elderly man with very sparse grey hair shuffled in looking anything but a picture of robust health. Then, when surrounded in the warm portly embrace of the host, he disappeared from view completely.
"My dear Cecilius, such an unexpected pleasure. Why didn't you let me know that you were coming? You know that you are always welcome, but I could have laid on a special meal. You will be staying for dinner I presume. I'm afraid that you'll have to take potluck and just have to share my poor meagre daily fare."
Emerging from the folds of fat and cassock, the Bishop of Dertosa looked winded from the effusive crushing he had suffered. "You look and *feel* very well Cyprianus. I somewhat doubt that dinner will be meagre. As for the quality, I know the hospitality of this house."

"You are so right, my dear colleague. Lent is gone we must have something decent to celebrate your presence. I will call the servants and tell them to do their best. Do you have any preferences? I am sure that they can rustle up something passable in a couple of hours."

" Fish would be a treat as we are here in Tarraco. I do so love a nice fresh fish, don't you Cyprianus?"

The big Bishop's face fell. "Fish. Yes, fish. Fish it shall be. If fish was good enough for our Lord, then, we should have it also. Yes fish… "

The servant, who had shown the visitor in, was still at the door. "Did you hear that? His Grace would like fish. Go immediately to the Port area and get the freshest and most succulent that there is."

The servant's face tried not to register the surprise it felt knowing his master's opinions on this question. Normally, those creatures were not allowed within a couple of hundred yards of the Bishop's palace. "Yes, your Grace. However, if the boats haven't returned yet and only yesterday's fish is available, should I buy it anyway? In this heat it.."

Cyprianus's face lightened. What a splendid servant. What was his name? He was relatively new as old Ebrimuth was no longer with them. These days he had problems retaining names and he was beginning to forget all types of things. His memory used to be prestigious. Actually, it was something that used to be remarked upon in all the concilia he had attended. Perhaps that was the problem that he had too much information stored, he wasn't getting any younger and these little details now escaped him.

Getting old, what a terrible thought, he mused. He had always been the youth, the little one, in age, not size. He was the youngest of three brothers, hence the Church being his lot, not the family name and lands. Thanks to these connections, his rise to Bishop en functions had been meteoric. He had attended the fourth Ecumenical Council at the age of twenty –two. By far the youngest. Marius!

"Marius, I hope that you wouldn't dare to serve such an esteemed guest *old* fish. Only the freshest will do. If that is not possible, then something else suitable will have to suffice. Thank you, Marius. You may go Marius, ermm yes Marius."

Cecilius smirked. He had enjoyed this performance. Cyprianus's thoughts on fish were the stuff of legend. His reaction when presented one at a conference was a source of much merriment. Not to his face of course, though rarely did any of the bishops of the area let the opportunity pass to "fish" him. He would tell this particular story with great glee when he got to Gerunda.

"You are most considerate Cyprianus. I am most grateful for your hospitality. As I was passing by, I couldn't let up the opportunity of seeing my old friend."

"Not so much of the old if you please, Cecilius. I am but a spring chicken compared to you! And just why are you travelling anywhere at your age? Normally a shoehorn is needed to prise you out of Dertosa."

"Oh, so true. I'm off to Gerunda for a meeting."

"A meeting in Gerunda? Of whom and about what? Am I to go as well?" Perplexed and distracted by all this talk of fish and secret meetings, the Metropolitan Bishop of Tarraco, en functions, had completely forgotten his manners and the age of his guest.

"May we be seated, I am feeling a …."

"Oh, I am SO sorry. Please come and sit here." Led by the elbow, Cecilius, looking all of his eighty years plonked himself down wearily. "Sometimes I think it is a curse living to this age. The only way I know I am alive each morning is that I find a different part of my body that hurts. And I can tell you, without the slightest doubt, that there are an awful lot of body parts. It's not as if the previous hurters give up on their pain giving, it's just the new ones are more strident in their need of attention. A little like the political / religious situation we are living through."

"I thought everything had calmed since the election of Wamba to the throne," Cyprianus dragged up another chair to sit close to his friend.

"Oh, were that so. Rumblings have been heard. My purpose in going to Gerunda is a meeting of bishops.."

"But I …"

"Cyprianus, please let me finish."
Looking like a child who hasn't been invited to the party, the Metropolitan Bishop of Tarraco, en functions, rested his still boyish, chubby face on the fist which was on the armrest closest to the speaker, trying his best not to look as miffed as he felt. He was failing totally in this endeavour. The Bishop of Dertosa took note and continued slowly and with great care, choosing his words after consideration, which did nothing for the flow of the imparted information, thus annoying the listener even more.

"There is a certain amount of discontent as you well know, how long have you been "en functions" now, forty years?" He didn't wait for a verbal answer, instead accepting the forward movement of the head. "Tarraconensis' slide into marginalisation has been in process for the whole of my lifetime. It seems as though this tendency is to be accelerated under Wamba. Not necessarily at his behest. The Court at Toletum sees their chance to dominate, even further, when the incumbent is new, and the that said-person is busy putting down rebellion in Vasconia. Do you think I could have something to drink?"

"I am so SORRY. All my manners have been found wanting today. Ebrimuth!"

"I think you said, various times, that his name was Marius."

"So it is, you're right, yes, Marius!!"

The servant appeared at the door clearly in no haste. "Sire, the fish has proved.."

"Fish, fish, fish? What's this with fish?"

Marius, who thought he was doing the right thing announcing the unavailability of the fish, looked confused. "We don't want nor need fish. My guest needs refreshment. Bring ale."

Cecilius sat quietly licking his lips in order to stop them cracking while waiting patiently. It had been a long hot journey, and now all this talking was taking all the saliva out of him.

Cyprianus waited quietly too but with considerably less patience. As his right arm was still busy in the face supporting duty it had started a few minutes earlier, this only gave him the option of finger drumming with his left hand. Apart from this less than rhythmic noise, there was silence until Marius bustled in with two large jugs of ale.

Half a jug later Cecilius continued.

"As I was saying, four decades without confirming the Metropolitan Bishop of Tarraco, there can be no excuse for this neglect. The same policy is enforced elsewhere in Tarraconensis/ Gallia Gothica. We are regularly excluded from the meeting of bishops wherever they are held. This attitude to centralise all power in Toletum has got to be stopped. We here in Tarraconensis, the most important province, boasting the capital of Roman Iberia, deserve more respect. Perhaps with all these centuries of Goth rule, we both come from this proud race, it is inevitable that the old should diminish in importance, but to the extent that it has, is intolerable."

Cyprianus's fist had become unemployed and his still baby blue eyes were wide open giving the speaker his rapt attention.

"This is why I have been dragged from my beloved Dertosa and travel, the much in need of repair roads, to Gerunda."

Jumping to his feet, as much as he could jump at all, Cyprianus announced "I will make preparations immediately to travel with you."

"Cyprianus, don't. You are not invited.. " There was a loud spluttering from the now completely vertical figure. ".. because of your importance. I am relatively minor. Nobody will notice my movements, and more to the point, nobody will care what this old man does. However, if you are seen in Gerunda meeting with the bishops from Elna and Narbo, then Toletum would be alerted." Another sip of ale. "We have always seen eye to eye on all the major matters of doctrine from the old faith to the treatment of the Jews. So, it'll be my job to represent us both. I am here to collect your thoughts and on the way back I will report to you any decisions that have been made. We need you included, just not physically, yet"

A mollified bishop, mug in hand, took a deep drowning swig of ale.

Panting with delight Rebecca sprinted into the house. She knew that Marcus wasn't following; it was just that she really enjoyed running, especially running fast and when you were getting away from someone else, it was even more fun. To run quickly in a long tunic wasn't easy, so to aid her progress, and so as not to trip, she hitched her tunic above the knee level. It was in this bare kneed panting gleeful looking over her shoulder state that she actually ran full pelt into her father. He clattered to the ground.

"Oh papa, sorry. Are you alright?"

She dropped her hem and set about picking up her father. He was shaken. Most wobbly and holding onto her arm, he managed to get up.

"Rebecca, tell me that you are being chased by the Egyptian army and the Red Sea wouldn't part, for that is the only explanation I can think of for what you have just done to me."

She could hear that he was annoyed, indulgently so.

"You see papa, I was making a dash for it looking back to see how far the Egyptian army was behind me. Which is why…" She stopped clearly seeing her father's annoyance dissipate and his indulgence increment. An oh-what-am-I-going-to-do with- you-smile crept slowly across his face. Rebecca stopped her story and instead just hugged the man.

"Now you're crushing the bruises that you have just inflicted. Good policy. Why make your father suffer once when you can do it twice, and in the same places? Excellent. Please let me go before I die of pain."

"How you do exaggerate!"

"Would you mind telling me who or what was following you for you to be moving at that speed in that state of undress?"

"No, nothing really, just keen to get back home to you, favourite papa." She shone her most convincing coy smile.

"You knock me over half killing me, you then crush the living daylights out of me, tell me bare face sweetly smiled lies and worst of all, you treat me like the naïve village idiot. In general ranking terms, I think that last part of the treatment is the worst." His indulgence had now dissipated. Rebecca knew she had gone just that little too far. The truth though, had to be avoided at all costs, that is what would probably cause him most pain.

"God, you were fast. I couldn't keep up with you at all." A slight boy, about her age who, by his looks, could not have been anything else than Jewish, panted his way into the hall. "His face was a picture after you.."

"David, I beat you again. You are going to have to try to get faster, you know."

The boy looked most confused.

Rebecca opened her mouth to speak, the look on her father's now stern face, silenced her.

"David, welcome. How's your father? Well I trust."

"Yes uncle. He said he'd be over shortly."

"Now answer me just one question, whose face looked " a picture"?"

Rebecca was sending her cousin as many eye messages as she could. Sadly though, he was just a boy and didn't understand anything of what she wanted of him. Instead he set about answering the question truthfully. Once the information was out, David was further confused as Rebecca was ordered to her room and tearfully, certainly not silently, she went.

*

The messenger was cowed and humbled as he knelt at his king's seated knees. His eyes were studying the King's feet.

"I believe you have a message for me. Please don't tell me that I need new sandals. The Queen is forever harping on about them. I certainly do NOT want to hear her opinions reinforced. I like them and that's it."

The young lad was completely flummoxed now. He'd only ever seen the king from a distance, a long distance. He had never thought that he would actually get to speak to the king. Having been at the front, watching the hordes of Vascones gathering, he was chosen because of his proximity to the General rather than any merit on his part. And now here he was having a conversation about the propriety of the king's sandals.

Seeing the boy's utter discomfort, Wamba decided he wasn't up to a little banter and got down to business.

"What does the General say?"

The boy let out an audible sigh, which made Wamba chuckle, he was on safer ground now. "The General says, Sire, compliments Sire, that an attack from the vascones looks imminent. Sire."

"I see. Thank you. Are you sure that he didn't have anything to say about the sandal question?"

"No, no Sire, no, nothing, Sire."

Leaving a flustering confused messenger still kneeling the king stood up and headed from the tent towards the adjacent stockade area where some livestock was kept. At the back, there was a small stone shepherd's hut that must have been built pre-roman times, a circular dry wall construction with a small door you'd have to crouch very low to get through.

Kings shouldn't crouch remembered Wamba as he thought about entering. Instead, he addressed the very stiff straight figure of the guard.

"Bring out the prisoners."

The two previous Generals; Kunimund and Alaric, were escorted gently out. This was more like house arrest rather than prison. They both dropped to their knees the moment they saw the king.

"NO, stand. Stand up. I couldn't bare another sandal conversation."

Confused but grateful, the two stood. They knew that standing men were never ordered to be executed.

"How long have you served in the army?"

"Twenty-five years, Sire." "Sixteen years, Sire." They each snapped an answer in the most military way.

"Let's see, you have served under three kings, General Kunimund. You are capable of making a comparison. So, how do you think I am doing?"

The military figure was completely flabbergasted. Kings don't think, nor ask, questions like that. And generals don't answer them, certainly not truthfully. He opened his mouth, not to speak, more to allow the gasp of surprise to get out.

"That bad, eh? Guard, could you possibly leave me to have a chat with my generals?"

If there had been a wager on who was the most confused person the King had spoken to this morning, it would have been a very close run thing. Feeling most unhappy about abandoning his post, and not being able to listen into what promised to be an extremely interesting conversation, the guard marched away, but not too far.

"I think, guard, you can leave me safely in the company of these generals, remove yourself from the area completely."

"Shall we sit, gentlemen? There are some most comfortable looking boulders over there."

The three of them wandered slowly up the fairly steep stony hill and perched on a set of stones, strategically the generals choose the ones lower down from the King. Settled, Wamba the most considerate and utterly contemplative, started,

"In order, we have King Chindaswinth, then his son, King Recceswinth, and now, me. I know you probably think this is some sort of trap to get you to say something inappropriate or worse still, you think that I am fishing for compliments, but really it isn't. Think about it, how many people can I have this sort of conversation with? If I spoke to the barons or the bishops like this, they would immediately think that I was weak and should either be replaced or more likely dominated. It's common knowledge that I didn't seek this role, it was rather foisted upon me. Now I am "en situ" I would like to know how I am doing from your point of view, as you are capable of comparing. Alaric, you are not excluded from this conversation, it's just that Kunimund has served one king more than you."

Alaric looked relieved. Kunimund looked genuinely frightened. It was only a couple of days ago that he was threatened with execution by this man, for doing nothing wrong. What could happen to him now? He wasn't very good at masking his emotions and his dilemma was written, in capital letters, all over his face.

"Come on, let's start with Chindaswinth. We'll get to me later."

"I was very young, Sire," was the slow, clear, full of trepidation reply.

"That I know. And believe it or not, we all were once. I also know that in our formative years our opinions tend to be stronger. Most things appear to be, no, are, simple and clear. So, what did you think?"

"It was the end of quite a terrible time, Sire." The voice was much more secure. "So many nobles had been... *found wanting* in their support for King Chindaswinth. It was bloody, very bloody. As I say, Sire, I just caught the end of the reign. Word in the army was to keep a very low profile, make sure that you were allied to someone close to the king and ignore the status of the old nobility. It was said that some of those families formed part of the inner core dating back centuries, as far back as King Reccared and from when he changed from the old religion."

"Yes, I saw with my own eyes families lose...everything."

"The number spoken about in the army, and it was us who had to install the new order, was about seven hundred."

"That high? That's not a purge, it's a slaughter."

"I have no opinions on the matter, Sire, it just was. Perhaps it was necessary. Perhaps not. It certainly made King Recceswinth's reign extremely peaceful. There was great relief within the army, we were no longer used against our own. In fact, we were hardly used at all."

"Yes, that was my experience" Alaric felt confident enough to join in. "Except for the Froia trouble, I never saw any action whatsoever, which may explain why we aren't performing so well at the moment. We've got rusty and flabby. No amount of training and drills prepare the men for the real thing. A shield wall is the most frightening place in the world. It's impossible to explain in words and impossible to recreate on the training ground."

"That was the reason for the debacle the other day?"

"Ermm, no, not really but it must have been a great part of it." Alaric had become tentative and nervous again.

"I sense you have more to say but you are reluctant to say it. Spit it out. I want to hear." Wamba's voice had taken a steely edge. Alaric's face changed. It showed that caution was going to be thrown to the wind.

"We were badly led! That's the truth of it. Hermenguild hadn't prepared properly. He was far too slow to react to the change in circumstances. Thankfully, Dux Paulus had all but assumed power by then. It was his orders we listened to. Thanks to them and our training, the day wasn't a total disaster,"

"I heard Hermenguild fought bravely not stinting in his duty."

"When he did react, "Alaric couldn't be stopped now, he knew that he had already said too much for his own protection, so he may as well go whole hog. He moved to stand up to deliver the rest of his report, because this is what it had become, Wamba signalled for him to be re-seated. "it was too little, too late and totally inappropriate. He had put the whole cavalry in as much danger as he had placed us in the shield wall."

"Let me get this clear, you are saying that General Hermenguild, the esteemed, leading officer of the whole army, is exceptionally incompetent."

Alaric was back on the defensive. "Well, I wouldn't use those words, Sire. Nor.."

"Oh dear. He would be most upset to hear those words. Oh yes, he certainly would."

Defiance had come back to Alaric's face. He had said his piece. It was more than likely going to be his death sentence but he had been true to the soldiers he had led, and most of all to himself. Then something strange happened, strange even for this strange day, Wamba began to chuckle.

"Oooh yes, most upset he would have been. He was very proud of all his achievements and battles fought and won. In fact, it made up for most of what he called conversation. God, I loathed those campaign meals. Not for the food quality, but for the quantity and quality of Hermenguild's conversation. A few cups of ale and he couldn't be stopped. And now I hear from you, Kunimund, that besides the killing of our own people the only major action was against Froia, and from you Alaric, that he was mega incompetent. Splendid. It's a shame though we won't be able to have another meal together, I would so love to inform him of your views, but it won't be so. You'll be sad to hear that he succumbed to his injuries early this morning."

As Wamba continued his chuckle, the other two looked both surprised and relieved.

"I don't suppose that I can execute either of you now, as it would leave me frightfully short of leading military figures. No, not advisable." With that he stood and starting wandering back to the centre of the camp, he looked over his shoulder, "By the way, the funeral is later this afternoon. I suggest you get cleaned up to attend looking like your role."

*

"Isaac, Trudy, Shabbat shalom."

The brothers embraced warmly. The in-laws exchanged cheek kisses. "Where is David?" asked his mother. "He said that he'd make his own way here."

"He arrived a couple of hours ago. I believe he's out back."

"Ehh these children. They go where they want, when they want. Do they listen to their mother? Of course not. They always know better. What is to be done! I always respected everything that my parents said to me when I was a child. Now! They choose to do the opposite. I say to him, David, wait for your father, he will be but a short time. But as you know "a short time" with Isaac, can be any amount of time. Is this a reason not to wait, I ask? No, it's not good enough for his son. So, off he goes saying he wanted to see his cousin. His cousin! As if we stop him from seeing her. He must see her every day, probably more than his mother. Ehhh. I suppose he's with Rebecca now."

"No. She's in her room."

"Just what can he be up to? I must go and find out. He'll be the death of me, that child." With much head shaking and tut tutting she headed towards the back of the house.

"Rebecca is in her room and David out back, what has happened Jacob? Now that Trudi has gone perhaps we can have a conversation before dinner as we both know, we won't get much chance to say too much over dinner when my dearest wife starts."

 The brothers walked to a side room which was used as an office. A sideboard, a couple of not very comfortable chairs and a table strewn with a great number of disorganized papers were the room's contents. Jacob claimed that he knew where everything was, and it was all where it should be. Everybody else in the house, which basically meant Rebecca and the part-time house keeper, were actively discouraged from entering here as they would only upset his balanced dis-organised organised order. While Jacob filled two cups of sweet wine, Isaac sat himself down in the only unpapered chair. He was sorely tempted to pick up or at least straighten some of the mess, instead he sat on his hands to stop the urge. His big brother had always been this way and it was too late to change him now.

The proffered wine was accepted with gratitude. For the first time in quite a while Isaac looked at his brother's face. When did he get so old? He wasn't an old man. Forty-five may be passed your prime, it wasn't old. It was written that Noah had lived to nine hundred! Jacob's face was deeply lined. He looked as if he hadn't slept in a week with those massive bags under his eyes. He still had a full head of thick dark hair which was a source of envy because it was more than could be said for others in the family. It wasn't just the physical impression though, there was an atmosphere about him. What was it? Depression? Or perhaps even defeat?

"I see your filing system still works very well. How you ever find anything I really don't know."

The brothers had inherited their father's import / export business. It was true that Tarraco was in a steady decline and would never get back to the heady days of one of the busiest ports in the Roman Empire, but it was still very important. Most commerce still left or entered from the port. The fact of the matter was that there just wasn't as much international trade as there used to be. Pirates, wars and the lack of stability had forced most areas of the Mediterranean to look inwards and do with less, meaning the brothers business wasn't thriving.

They had divided the business a few years back because it made more economic sense for them to specialise in different areas. Isaac had taken the perishable section and Jacob stayed with ceramics. On a minor scale, they both lent some of their accumulated cash at not extortionate rates of interest. All in all, they both made a tidy if shrinking amount of money, nothing new to be worried about there, even with Jacob's mess of papers.

They sat in silence nursing their wine. It wasn't the sort of comfortable silence that they had enjoyed at other points in their life together.

"When are you going to tell me? Will I need a new cup of wine? This one is about finished. Silence is a thirsty business. Jacob, what *is* the matter?"

"Nothing."

Another silence lasting two minutes, feeling like three weeks.

"Everything."

Another silence, shorter.

"There's quite a big gap between those two words."

"There's an ill wind and it's blowing this way. It'll affect us all. I am worried. Worried for us all, Rebecca, you and yours, the rest of the community…"

Isaac waited, not very patiently fidgeting with his empty cup. Eventually he stood up and filled it, bringing the jug to top up Jacob's half empty. Before he could get to him, Jacob drained his in one gulp then stretched out his arm for more. Once filled, Jacob repeated the process of draining and stretching. This time it wasn't filled, instead, Isaac removed the cup so as to hold his brother's hand.

"Tell me. Is it about us as God's *chosen* people in general, or one of us in particular?"

*

"The Venison is most tender, don't you think, Marcus?"

Father and son were the only diners at the top of a huge table. Everything in the room was large. Once the most opulent villa in Roman Tarraco it had hosted emperors, Augustus had even been a relatively long term resident. The centuries had taken their toll, as they had with the whole of the city. Once a thriving bustling city full of energy, life, games in the amphitheatre, a spectacular circus to rival any, it now wore the clothes of a down-at-heel-aged decrepit senator barely covering the parts that no one wanted to see.

Ranosindus, the Duke of Tarraco, tried his best to revitalise the city by encouraging events, commerce and religious devotion, to no avail. His efforts were ignored by the diminished population, they just didn't seem to care, and were positively stopped, or shunned by the powers in Toletum. Even the Metropolitan Bishop, in place for decades, had yet to be confirmed.

The actual ethnic Goth population in the city was very small, it always having been so, there was little change there. Nearly everyone in Tarraco that wasn't a Jew was of Hispano-Roman in origin. The Goths that had settled, had been more or less assimilated into the existing melting pot since the laws on Goth only being able to marry Goth were relaxed last century. The ethnic tension, which seemed so rife throughout most of the country, didn't apply here, nor in the vast majority of Tarraconensis/Gallia Gothica. The hatred and vilification of the Jews wasn't practised much either. The laws against Jews were there, and had to be put into force at times, but there was no great appetite for them. This wasn't because of any great empathy for the Hebrews, most people found them arrogant, aloof and insular, though not to the point of the hatred, bile and persecution imposed by Toletum.

"Yes, father."

"As tender as your ear?"

Startled and blushing bright pink Marcus looked up at his smiling father. Marcus did not find the situation at all amusing.

"Amalaswinth goes too far. I shouldn't be treated that way. Not by her, nor anyone!"

"I heard her justification was that you had come back stinking of fish and you showed her no respect. You well know that a man, if that is what you say you now are, shows respect and courtesy to women in general, and family members in particular. I know you will say that Amalaswinth is not family, and you're right, not blood. She is the woman who brought you up which is as good as…nearly."

Marcus whose face remained red, no longer through embarrassment, it was now anger that was rushing to his head ready to contest his father's words. His father stopped him with a hand movement.

"Wait Marcus, I haven't finished. It has also come to my hearing that the reason for your *fishiness* was that you were seen down in the port area being bested by a pretty young lady."

Marcus' anger disappeared faster than it had arrived. His defence hackles and antennae were up. This was dangerous ground. This was a conversation he really didn't want to have with his father.

"Who was she? And what were you doing together?"

"No one. Just a girl. It was part of a game. There were quite a few of us there."

"Does this *no-one* have a name?"

"Rebecca." Amalaswinth had entered baring another dish.

"What! Jacob the ceramics merchant's daughter?"

"That's the one. A rare beauty she is, I am told. Forever flirting with all the young men and then exposing herself while running away just to entice more" The dish was on the table and it was being served with great relish.

"She doesn't *expose* herself and she doesn't flirt with *all* the young men! She …"

"Only has eyes for you? Is that what you think? And you think yourself all grown and you know the ways of women. That girl is fishing. She knows what to use as bait and she sure as hell knows just what she is fishing for. Or am I bullying you again by pointing out the ways of the world?"

"Father, this really is not true. Amalaswinth, you are just stirring the pot. We are just *friends* that's all. Part of a group."

"Stop, both of you! Marcus, I have been hearing these rumours for some time, not just from Amalaswinth, various people have come to me informing me of things that they think I should know about my son. You know well that I am not anti-Semitic, I don't really care one way or another. However, there are very clear laws in this country which could cause you problems if you get any closer to this girl. Her father has yet to renounce his faith publicly, many others have already made that step. At least he doesn't flaunt his faith, which is prudent. Nevertheless, consorting with his daughter can bring you, and this family nothing but trouble."

Marcus was now looking down. He wasn't going to win this battle. He had been taught in arms training that battles you can't win, you don't fight. By looking compliant he thought perhaps it would all blow over. Wrong.

"So, I have taken steps. Your arms instructor, Pere, says that you are more than competent; in fact he says you are quite a talent. To further that talent I have arranged for you to take a small company of soldiers to help King Wamba in his fight against the Vascones. He has been insisting that all the Dukes of all of the provinces share the weight of the defence of the country. You will leave at the weekend."

*

"God knows that I really do not like the Jews and I agree they must be kept in their place. After all, they were responsible for killing our Lord Jesus Christ and for that they must pay. And the way they hoard money, and are so mean about the lending of it. They have the monopoly, and don't they know it. I had a conversation with one the other day, Jacob, who by the way has a very pretty daughter, I was practically cap in hand asking him for a new loan. If only we could go to other Christians." Cyprianus paused momentarily, just long enough for Cecilius not to get a word in.

"The Church's strictures on usury are most inconvenient at times. Jesus was right to drive those money lenders from the temple. Back then, that's what the Jews had come to, using a place of worship as a sort of bank. Disgraceful. Disgraceful, yes disgraceful. He was also very clear on *love thy neighbour,* which I suppose means the Jews as well. It is our duty to try to convert them and to make them see the errors of their ways. How we should do this, must have limits, otherwise it becomes a farce."

"Yet again, we agree brother." Cecilius finally squeezed into the monologue which had been masquerading as a conversation for the best part of half an hour. Cecilius had been listening intermittently, drifting in and out of the monotone. Quite a lot of the time he spent being thankful to God. Praise should be given that he would be gone very shortly, and that he only saw Cyprianus rarely, and above all, he never had to listen to one of his sermons in mass. The Christians of Tarraco had always been a long-suffering lot going back to the martyrdom of Saint Fructuosus. It seemed as if their pain would never cease. Being stoned to death at least was relatively quick!

Cyprianus managed to continue, "We have never applied the law of 654 here in Tarraconensis. It's excessive, and worse, impractical, as is the way with every impractical edict issued since Chintilla. If we took everything they said in Toletum seriously, we would have to excommunicate ourselves for not applying them. Ridiculous. Furthermore, we would need a specialised army to enforce it. It's all well and good saying the Jews shouldn't circumcise their boys, a brutish practice but,..."

"Celebrating the Passover when there is Easter is an abomination." Cecilius had left a gap while he was thinking.

"Yes, I was just about to say.."

"But what they eat, and when they eat it, should be up to them. It doesn't affect me in the slightest, as long as it's not Christian children."
Cecilius sat back with resigned patience. How much of a sin would the Lord consider it when you wish that a fellow clergyman would be harmed, not too seriously, by say, a lightning bolt? His mission here had been a success in that Cyprianus had been persuaded not to come, and wasn't too perturbed. The other bishops would receive Cecilius as a hero for not bringing the esteemed fish-hater, who they all loved to avoid as much as they liked to talk and laugh about. It made the proposed meeting possibly one of action and not just hot air.

*

This was one of the best times of the day. Away from the rest of the village, the inane uninteresting chatter of daily life. To be alone. Thankfully he wasn't there either, off playing important with the other men.
When the sun was at its hottest and everyone else was hiding from its blistering baking power, she liked her longish walk down to the lake. To be able to run into those cold clear waters to wash off the grime and sweat of all those around her was liberating. Her sister-in-law came at the beginning. Her constant complaining about the "trudge", the heat, the coldness of the water and how dirty your feet became when coming out onto the muddy sand, finally made her revalue the whole exercise much to Aitziber's relief.
She never worried about being alone despite all the warnings, often quite dramatic and dire, which the other women felt it necessary to deliver, usually, upon her return to the village. Her little sister, nearly two years younger, Arantxa, pleaded to come and, nice though she was, Aitziber wanted to be alone. She had never seen anyone else and the animals had more sense than to be out in the midday sun.
Today was different. Today was not the same. There was a horse tied to the trees closest to the lake. It was comfortably in the shade and wasn't startled when she almost bumped into it. A very attractive, strong chestnut mare. A war horse. Now Aitziber was on her guard. She froze. Nobody in the village had a horse like this, in fact, nobody in the village had a horse.. This could only belong to one of the invading Goth-Romans.
As she moved very quietly forward she could see what she could only presume was the owner. He had his back to her. He was admiring the view of the lake with sheer incline of the grey rock of the mountains at the end. A pretty view it was, she never tired of it.

Horse quiet, her, well-hidden, it was decision time. To quietly creep back out the way she had come was the most sensible thing to do. Not her style. This was an opportunity. She would wait a bit longer, she was sure that the owner was going to go into the water. Once there, she could unhitch the horse and ride in back to the village.

Undoubtedly she would be treated as a heroine. No, THE heroine of the village. Songs would be sung about her exploit. Everyone would look up to her and treat her with the respect she deserved, respect she wasn't getting now. A great plan with only a tiny hitch, she couldn't ride, actually, she'd never even sat on a horse, but, just how difficult could it be? She was sure it was a matter on sitting on the, well, very big thing, and pointing it in the right direction while giving it a considerable heel kick into its ribcage. Easy.

While her brain buzzed with her future fame, the horse owner, the enemy, took off his shirt. Ohh. Her daily pretty view had just been improved. Broad-shouldered, with a slim muscled torso was enhancing the foreground. A third option had just presented itself. She could watch. She had been married at fourteen, five long years ago to a friend of her father's. He wasn't a *bad* man but he looked nothing like what was in front of her. He was fat, flabby and grey. The sight in front of her made parts of her swell and tingle. She had never felt anything like that with her husband. Perhaps she could watch a bit more, she had to wait for him to go into the water anyway if she wanted the heroine option.

Off came the bottom part. Ohh dear. More tingling. What firm buttocks! Her husband's sagged. She would stay a bit longer. Him turning around would be a bonus. The danger of that made her excited as well because it would mean that he might be able to see her.

"Come on out and join me." The buttocks spoke. "The horse won't leave without me, and if I come back there then I will have to go running. In this heat that would be too much."

Aitziber wondered how it was possible that he had seen her. He was still looking at the view, at no point had she made a noise, nor had he turned around. Her choice of options had diminished if not vanished, to quietly creep away; gone, heroine horse stealer; gone, voyeur in the bushes; gone. He didn't sound aggressive or even threatening. He didn't shout. He had a confidence that his *invitation* would be accepted. There was no other choice, she abandoned her inadequate hiding place and confidently, fearlessly, well that was the effect she was trying for, even though her insides were jelly, walked onto the not yet muddy shore.

He turned. Ohhh dear, oh dear. Tingling jelly. He was handsome, very handsome.

"Flavius Paulus." He held out his hand. She had been concentrating on those blue eyes. Now she had to move her vision down to his hand. Ooooh!

"I fear I have taken your usual bathing spot. I am sorry. It's just so gorgeous here; the lake, the mountain and now you. Nobody told me about all this extreme beauty."

Ooooooh.

"I do apologise. Do you speak Latin? I just presumed.."

"Some. Better than most in this area, which as you probably know isn't much. My father had insisted."

"Splendid. Would you like to join me in the water? It is hot and I can see that you must be suffering as you are all flushed."

Ummmm.

*

"Most troubling I have to agree. I understand now why you look so haggard." Isaac twirled his empty cup distractedly.

"I'm not sure, which is the worst part of the story, nor for whom. That fact that we Jews are living on the knife edge of disaster is nothing new. Did you hear what the Rabbi had to say about what's happening in the south? Shocking, but what can we do?"

Jacob remembered back to what he had just told Isaac, the Bishop's insinuation. Protection came at a price; free loans and Rebecca was his. "Please not a word of this to Trudy."

"Brother, how stupid do you think I am? She leaves your house and only visits occasionally. She lives in mine! We have a drama of Torah proportions when David does something she hasn't sanctioned. Imagine what she would say to all this. And worse, how much!"

"Since her mother died I have tried hard to bring Rebecca up correctly. I know I get a lot of criticism especially from the women of the community."

Isaac was shaking his head ready to make protestations to the contrary.

"Yes brother. I have heard with my own ears though nobody has actually said it to my face. The women saying that it wasn't *right* a man bringing up a girl by himself. That it was my *duty,* both to her and the memory of her mother, for me to marry again. Rebecca's actual Jewishness was at stake. Nothing but bad would come of me not doing it." Jacob didn't look up.

" Perhaps I was selfish. Perhaps I haven't done the right thing. The fact that Rebecca is now in trouble is entirely my fault." His eyes raised to meet his brother's whose were full of compassion.

"I loved Sarah. I didn't, nor do I, want her replaced." His eyes were beginning to fill. "To tell you the truth, I actually thought I was doing a *good* job of bringing up Rebecca."

"Not bad. Quite a bit of room for improvement, I would say." Rebecca was standing in the doorway. Neither of the brothers had heard the door open, which was as Rebecca had wanted it. These two had been closeted in here for ages. Aunt Trudy's wails of lament could be heard in Jerusalem. Rebecca had to avoid her and her noise, the only safe place was with the hiding men.

"Why do you think you are not, papa? Because you sent her to her room, totally unjustifiably without giving her a chance to explain her side of the story, perhaps?"

"How long have you been listening, young lady? You know this room is out of bounds for you. Is it not possible to have a private conversation with my own brother, in my own house?"

"It would seem not."

"You see what I mean, Isaac. Wilful, disobedient and not an ounce of respect."

Rebecca launched herself from the doorway, sprang across the room and planted herself on her father's lap. She smothered his left cheek with kisses until she had to come up for air.

"Heaps of respect and boatloads of love. You are the best papa in the world. You don't listen to the synagogue women for anything else, why bother listening to their opinions on marriage and child rearing? I think you are doing a *great* job. "

"Aren't you a bit old for lap sitting? You are certainly too heavy. I'm not sure if you have broken one of my legs, or both of them."

Slowly and reluctantly she shifted her weight off him, not before giving him a loud smacking kiss on top of his head. "Always exaggerating." Then her bottom elegantly hit the floor like some faithful obedient old dog next to its master's chair, arranging her legs underneath her while demurringly covering them with her pulled down tunic.

"I missed the beginning of the conversation, so you'll have to fill me in."

"Rebecca! Please! This conversation is for adults. You are not invited."

"But I seem to be a large part of the content. Also papa, you may not have noticed, I am an adult now. In fact, I believe that that is *the* problem here. The fact that the bishop thinks I am a woman, and you think Marcus's thoughts may be running along the same lines. So, as I am integral to the topic, I am staying. Remember papa, this is the way you have always taught me to be, and why I love and respect you for it."

"Isaac, you are lucky you have a boy."

"The fish-faced fat priest doesn't want to marry me. I am a Jew, remember? He would only need to be with me for an hour before he realised that converting my soul would be *far* too much trouble. He didn't even like the extra little welcoming detail he got the last time. Who wouldn't appreciate a sardine being dipped in his ale before serving? Ungrateful chap!"

"You didn't?!"

"Now to Marcus, he is just a boy. A rich boy. Again, a Christian. An heir. His father will have a heart attack if he even finds out that Marcus has spoken to me, never mind anything else. So, problem solved. Next item on the agenda?"

*

"Brothers, let's bring this meeting to order. As this is not official, no records will be kept. As far as all other aspects of formality, they will be kept the same. So try to respect the speaker's right to speak and wait until you have been signalled to start your interventions, and please, try to err on the side of brevity, as today we would like to finish at a reasonable time so that we can eat an evening meal rather than an early breakfast." There was a general murmur of agreement from the ten elderly men seated around the table, everyone believing that everyone else spoke too much and they too little.

"The primary question before us is, how *do* we move from the talking agreement stage to its implementation? It has been six long years since the ecumenical council of 675 when we were saying pretty much the same thing. Then we tried to restrict numbers to a minimum, just seventeen, if my memory serves me right, in the hope of avoiding yet another talking shop. To that end, the diverging, dissenting and frankly distracting views of our colleagues from Tarraconensis were not heard, mainly due to the fact that they were not invited. This is true again today. As ex-bishop of Barcino, I will act as the voice of that region."

The speaking figure was stood, robed and commanded complete respect. Bishop Quiricus, in the five years as first bishop of Toletum, and therefore the whole of the country, had consolidated his hold on power. It was his hand that had anointed King Wamba last year. He had supported his appointment believing he was the right person for the role, which meant, as far as Quiricus was concerned, controllable by the power of the bishops and a blow against those, not in the clergy, who believed that they should have a greater voice in the running of the state. In all but name this was, and would continue to be, a theocracy with a titular non religious leader called king. The state existed for a purpose, and that purpose was for the glory of God here on earth. His values, the values of the Church, would and should be paramount. This is why it was most galling to all those present that the will of the Church expressed through the laws of the state was not being enforced, and lamentably, in some cases, actively thwarted.

Quiricus' predecessor had King Recceswinth's ear and there was complete agreement back at the time of the tenth Ecumenical Council to further restrict and contain the rights the Jews had in the Kingdom. Jews were an abomination, and should be driven out, or forced to live correctly, that is to say, as Christians, in this *Christian* country. The laws laid out, clearly, with no room for misinterpretation, that Jewish celebrations like Passover and observation of Shabbat had to cease, Jewish rites such as caixer and circumcision were banned. In fact, the practising of this so called religion, which through many decades of restrictions and curtailments, had encouraged its believers of the necessity and righteous to come to the one true faith, had to be stopped once and for all. There were those Jews, over the last hundred years, who had pretended, for self-protection or gain, to convert, instead of keeping to their original beliefs. They were dealt with in the same law. They would be burnt or stoned to death at the hands of their ex- brethren.

Yet eight years later, and to the consternation of all those present in this meeting these righteous laws were having little effect. Jews in some areas still openly practised their poisonous perversion, this being particularly true in the region of Tarraconensis/ Gallia Gothica where the bishops did their best to ignore the clear orders sent from the Court in Toletum.

Their oft spouted claims of the adverse effect on commerce, joined with their selective reading of history when they stated the old Arian view of Christianity, which they claimed never spoke of converting or destroying the Jews, did not hold water. They should come into line, seeing the Jews for the vermin that they really are.

Quiricus recognised the hand that shot up demanding to speak as a very safe option to start the proceedings; Julian was an intellectual, respected by all as such and his views were akin to the lead bishop's.

"Speak, brother."

"Thank you, your Grace. I do not think we should waste too much time setting out the reasons for our holy crusade for the purity of the kingdom, we all know of at least one of our own flocks who has been directly affected by these perverts. The kidnapping and murder for consumption of Christian babies for the religious rites of Jews are well-documented facts. We surely need no more evidence to condemn this *sect*. Yet they, as you so rightly point out, are still among us practising openly, seemingly without fear. The council is aware that prior efforts have been frustrated by lack of compliance among authorities on the local level. This, despite the written warnings that anyone — including nobles and clergy — found to have aided Jews in the practice of Judaism were to be punished by seizure of one quarter of their property and excommunication. An exemplary law passed by you good people here present." He paused for effect, not quite long enough to be interrupted, "Has this law of the State been applied anywhere I ask? Has there been one land seizure? What is the use of having these laws if they are not enforced?"

"Well said Julian and I think remarkably similar to my opening words. What we are looking for here is practical solutions to this chasm of intentions and results."

"An armed force." The Bishop of Caesaragusta, Taio, was brief. Quiricus thought that Taio would continue. There was silence. Evidently, he had taken the call to brevity to heart.

Julian filled the void.

"Whose? It's something that needs to be addressed. I believe the King is having his own problems in this area as we speak. He is woefully short of troops to put down this rebellion in Vasconia."

"That tribe needs to be taught a lesson once and for all. Every generation they come back with more men and more sophistication. The people of Caesaragusta live in constant fear of when they are going to be attacked next." Taio was getting into the swing of it now. "Before the King set out, I said he needed more men. This should not be just a quick punishment sortie. They should be driven deep back into their land or across to their brothers in Frankia, raise their villages, destroy their crops and enslave as many as we can. These people cannot be negotiated with. They only understand the sword. They are the major external threat we have. I agree the Jews are an internal problem. However, the priority must be securing our borders."

"Whereas I view the Jew question as more important as it is more insidious. It undermines our very existence."

"Easy to say when you are hundreds of miles away here in Toletum, Julian. But…"

"Brothers, brothers let's not play the blame game here. I believe that both problems have the same solution." Restoring the fractious bubble of noise to order, Quiricus laid out his plans.

"The barons have too much power. They keep their armies for their own use not for the good of the Kingdom, not even when we are threatened from without and within. I know King Wamba has ambitious plans of reform, forcing the barons to give a proportion of their forces anytime they are demanded."

"How? This is not the first time I've heard this in my lifetime. Actually, if I had a solidus for every time, I would be a rich baron myself." A shrivelled old man in a habit which must have fitted him once, toned his opinion with resignation.

"Now we are getting to the nub of the problem. Money. Where does money and power come from? Land ownership. We, as the Church need to acquire as much land as possible, then, we need to create our own armed forces to fight on the side of good whenever and wherever it is necessary, both externally and internally." Julian's flow was interrupted. "VERY long term brother and totally right. What we have to devise is a way of enforcement that sees the forfeit of land of all the Jew helpers immediately."

More voices were joining in without waiting for the previous speaker to finish thus requiring everyone to speak louder in order to be heard by someone other than themselves.

"Expel the Jews now. All of them."

"Force them to convert. Take their children away from them to be brought up true Christians"

"That's already the law!"

"Is it? See, I have never seen it done in my parish."

"We all know they keep hoards of money stashed away. Expropriate it. They have lived at our expense for too long."

"Yes, that would allow us to form our own Christian army."

The discussion rumbled on in circles for the next two days. Tired and frustrated, Quiricus had decided that nothing could be achieved until the King returned. They needed his titular authority; Wamba owed his position to them, so it would be a quid pro quo type of arrangement. If, however, he proved "difficult", then they would set about replacing him.

"Brothers, I think we are agreed that ALL the solutions like total Jewish expulsion proposed by our esteemed brother Julian, will have to wait until the end of this campaigning season and, hopefully, the destruction of the threat from the Vascones. We need though, to keep the pressure up on those vermin. I propose we issue an edict along the lines mentioned by my brother Taio."

Tired agreement was the general noise.

"I will leave the exact wording to the brother who proposed it, but it will read something like; all those former Jews who have converted to the true faith should, no, *have to*, celebrate ALL the festivals of Christianity in the church presided over by the Bishop of the area. Their names will be logged and checked. Those not fulfilling their Christian obligations will be publicly flogged that very same day."

*

Marcus had never seen so many men. Tarraco was a large place with a decent sized population spread out over quite a large area, spreading from the port area up to where his house was behind the old circus and then stretching out along the coast all the way to Els Munts. Except for important church services, never did the whole population come together. Anyway, that would have included mainly women and children. This was a sea of men he was being lead through.

He had had to leave his own group - how small they seemed in this expanse of masculinity - at the perimeter, and now he was following an officer, who didn't look much older than himself, through the masses to some large more opulent tents in what must be the epicentre of operations.

Awed, he waited outside the flap. Voices using military type vocabulary were audible from inside.

"Yes, sir! Immediately, sir!"

Marcus was escorted in. It took his eyes a few seconds to adjust to the relative darkness after the bright blinding sunshine. It was also considerably cooler than standing outside, a welcome relief, allowing him to relax a little.

"And you are who?" A not unpleasant voice coming from a non-uniformed tuniced man asked.

"Marcus, son of Duke Ranosindus of Tarraco."

"Sir."

Marcus was confused. Why was this older clearly more important man calling him sir? He thought it probably better not to say anything. Nothing appropriate for the situation came to mind. It was then he received a flat of the sword slap in the back delivered by the boy who had been his escort just a few minutes ago. It was a shock and it hurt although not that much force had been used.

"You address General Kunimund as "sir".

"Oh, yes, sorry. " Flustered Marcus, "Sir," taking the opportunity to straighten his hurting back.

The General looked on the young specimen in front of him. This is what he was given to forge a fighting force. Perhaps it would be not so bad if they were back in training camp and his junior officers were given time to lick these raw babies into something resembling an army, instead he was chronically short of experienced men while at the same time receiving intelligence reports saying that the local tribes were gathering again.

"Take the Duke's son to the General Paulus section."

*

"Does it hurt?" She traced her finger down the scarred side of his face with great tenderness.

"Oh, no. Real men don't.."

"Seriously." She scowled at him.

"Seriously? Well, only when I laugh, or I am smacked by a spearpoint."
She leant over him slightly more and administered a long, long, long kiss.
"So doing that is alright?"
"Except for the fact that I have found breathing helps my condition of being alive .. greatly!"
"Such a complaining baby. Real man? Huh!" She repeated her previous move except this time extending the length.
He eventually managed to push back from the super human suction and, gasping for air, managed to say "This is how the you intend to kill the invading force! You have lured me here into this cave to deprive me of air."
"Oh, no! That's not true!" She pouted seductively with a determined look in her eyes.
"My orders were to exhaust you to death." With that she hitched up her tunic and
moved her left leg so that she was now straddling him.
They hadn't arranged to meet again. It was an accident. An accident that both were hoping would happen. Aitziber had come every day at the same time hoping to see the chestnut mare. Some days she came twice. It was easier to get away these days as everyone was distracted by the great celebrations that were taking place to honour the men who had outwitted and defeated the Goth-Romans so convincingly.
She was torn between joining the fun and worrying about what had happened to her tender handsome strong *firm* young man. She hoped he hadn't been part of the mass slaughter that the village talk was abuzz with.
She had never experienced anything like that afternoon with Flavius. He was considerate, caring and impressively virile. Walking home would have been extremely difficult if she had had to walk. She didn't, she floated. She didn't realise she could be so..alive. Every part of her sang. The body section was united in a collective joy. The mind was not so unified. There were moments when she realised that she was going against, some might say; betraying, her people, family friends and everything else she had ever known. Then, there was the infinitely pleasurable glow that thoughts of him brought. Feelings that no-one, at no time, in all her years in the village had ever come close to evoking. She seriously felt she was living in a different world with different rules. Every day had been a disappointment until today. When she saw the horse her heart had leapt. Arrangement for other meetings were never made. Her new world, besides a couple of glorious afternoons, was only in her head until she saw his back again, a repeat of the magnificent view from two angles.
"You're not going to play that hiding game again, are you, Aitziber?"

He remembered her name. How far is it possible for a heart to leap before it jumps out of the body? She would keep her mouth shut for a bit longer just in case it tried to escape from there.

Slowly, he turned. Her heart and face fell as she let out a wail of concern. "Oh, no! Flavius. Are you alright? Oh, no!" She ran up to him stopped in front of the disfigured face.

"Your people thought I was too pretty." His piercing blue eyes smiled. She melted into his arms. "You're not any longer." She breathed into his chest causing him to guffaw with laughter.

"Owww! That hurts!" He held her with one arm and his injured face with the other.

*

"Well I never! You go weeks without seeing one bishop, then you get two for the price of one."

The room was elegantly decorated, statues, fine ceramic work, all clearly visible in the candlelight and the warmth of an unnecessarily blazing fire. The two clerics were standing very close to each other looking into the burning logs jumped obviously startled by this interruption from their evidently intense conversation which could have been interpreted in a couple of ways, either romantic, or conspiratorial, as their heads were so close.

"Checking out what the flames of hell would look like for you or your sinners?"

"It always does well to beware of God's fate for some."

"Did you have anyone in particular in mind? I know I haven't been to confession for quite some time but there are extenuating circumstances, like neither of you being in the province for an age, and don't you think that's more than a little harsh for such a minor crime?"

"Missing confession is no minor crime as you well know Count. Baring one's soul to God through his representatives on earth, in the hope of forgiveness, is fundamental to our faith."

"And to whom, dear Bishop Argebaud, should I do this when the two highest representatives of the Church are off gallivanting around the state?"

"Gallivanting? I would hardly call it that." The younger of the two fire watchers moved forward to clasp the Count in a warm embrace "It's good to see you, Hilderic. I trust you've been well in our absence, despite your lack of ecclesiastical care."

"Splendid, however, I will endeavour to put my besmirched soul into your hands before mass in the hope of avoiding that particular heat." He murmured in mocking servility. "Although if you make room, a little bit of it would be appreciated right now, the evenings still have a considerable chill."

The three men huddled close to the massive fireplace, Count Hilderic stretching his arms and rubbing his hands together.

"If you haven't been gallivanting Gunhild, what have you been up to for the last few months?"

Gunhild was in his mid forties and looked all of his age and some more. His hair was thinning, instead of lines on his face, he had deep crevasses, his brow was continuously creased, all of which contrasted with the sharp bright intelligent blue eyes which darted around causing a major distraction from the rest of the weather-beaten surroundings. It was difficult to ascertain just how the face had become so. It certainly wasn't due to any hard toil in the fields, he had been born into a most privileged family and had spent all his life in comfort, still his face resembled more a galley slave that had been exposed to sun and salt water for far too long.

"We have had a most dreadful journey and tiresome sojourn in the capital. Toletum is just SO provincial when compared to here in Argebaud's Narbo. Even my humble town of Maguelonne feels more cosmopolitan."

"Argebaud's Narbo? My dear bishop, I hadn't realised that Bishop Argebaud here," slapping the Bishop heartily on the shoulder, "had actually taken control of the town, and province, that I am nominally Governor, is this why you have invited me here this evening, to inform with that you have taken over in some sort of ecclesiastical coup?"

Much flustered, Gunhild repeated his negations faster than their fellow bishop from Tarraco, Cyprianus, would spit out fish.

"What I was trying to say is that as we are standing next to the fire in the dining room of Bishop Argebaud's palace…"

"Don't worry Gunhild. I know what you mean. So, it was that bad in the capital, was it?"

"Worse." Having been unaccustomedly quiet for such a long time, the older man joined in the conversation. "When was the last time you were in Toletum, Count?"

"Haven't been there for years. As with you, I found it dreary, tedious and full of whispering groups in quiet corners."

"Well, it hasn't changed much though the conspiratorial dissenting voices are no longer heard, not even in whispers. Total control is held by a few leading bishops. The King hardly seems to matter. True, he was away campaigning against the forever troublesome Vascones. However, it was as if he didn't really exist in any real sense of power."

"I always said he was too weak for the role. I can't understand why he was ever appointed."

"For exactly that reason, Count. Whether he is really as weak as he's painted I'm not totally convinced, but this is the perception of all and sundry. Real power and command lies in the hands of the few bishops who selected and elected him into that position, the most influential of whom is without a doubt Julian."

"That revolting, beak nosed scarecrow of a man who is forever scurrying or scribbling?"

"That's the one. A wretched man. No breeding , no history, yet he has wheedled his way into a position of predominant power. How he has done it, nobody knows. It might be his continuous writing, perhaps he keeps notes on everyone and uses them against them. Without a doubt, there is an undisputed feeling of fear, not awe, whenever he is in the room."

It was the younger man's turn to rejoin the conversation. "This is why we proposed having a meal together this evening, to *discuss* the situation and our response to it."

*

"Stand at ease, Flavius. No, better still, let's be seated around the table." Wamba got out of his "raised chair", he so hated being in that place. Either you have authority or you don't. Lifting a chair a few inches off the ground really does not affect that state of the perception of others. He indicated a smallish table which had five rudimentary chairs around it and was decorated with a map.

"Who's your new "assistant"?"

"Yes, Sire! Greetings Sire! Oh this is .."

"Marcus, son of Duke Ranosindus of Tarraco, Sire"

Marcus felt another blow on his back. Surprised again, he stifled an expletive and began rubbing away the pain. It was then he received another, slightly higher up than last time. Being in the army was proving a more painful business than he had imagined and the source not coming from where he'd imagined it.

"You don't speak to unless requested to do so. Furthermore, you ALWAYS stand to attention in the presence of the King. Stop rubbing your back like some pained little girl."

Marcus opened his mouth to speak until he saw the look on General Flavius's face, a quick calculation was enough to realise that swallowing his words and indignation about the unfairness of the situation would be less painful than what would follow, if he did speak.

"Apologies, Sire! He has yet to get used to military discipline."

"Well, he should he'll fit in perfectly with your staff then." Wamba smiled, then looking at Marcus for the first time, he addressed him directly. "Tarraco, you say?"

Unsure whether to answer or not Marcus plumped for silence.

Oww. A slap on the neck this time.

"When your King asks you a question, you answer it."

Marcus thought that this was all most confusing. It didn't sound like a real question. It was more like confirmation of what he had said earlier. He really wanted to say this, he was sure that he was right. The proximity of Flavius' hands and the strange etiquette of this, his new world, kept him silent.

Another blow.

Flavius exhaled with a tone of expiration of patience. "Answer!"

The utterly confused look that Marcus was wearing, evidently trying not to say or express his feelings made Wamba laugh.

"Definitely. He will fit superbly well in your personal guard." Wamba looked on almost paternally. "Let's try again, shall we?"

Marcus hesitated. Was that a real question? Should he answer? He shot a sideways glance in the direction of the hitting hands. They hadn't moved. Thankfully, King Wamba continued talking.

"I remember meeting your father in Tarraco. Beautiful house you have. I wasn't King then. Your father was most hospitable. I have always thought of Tarraco as one of the jewels of the kingdom. We must try to restore some of its former glory. Well, I doubt our hospitality here will be quite so opulent or comfortable. I am sure that General Paulus will endeavour to make it as *painless* as possible. However, for the moment, if you wouldn't mind waiting outside, I would like a few words in private."

As the King had switched the focus of his vision away from him, Marcus was a little confused. Who was going to get the private audience? A kick on his calf answered that question. "Yes, Sire. Thank you, Sire." He did his best to exit militarily.

Wamba laughed, quietly again, sat down and indicated the fuming general to do the same.

"He's young. Give him a chance."

"Sire, if this is the best the barons can send us, we may as well give up now and head off back to Toletum."

"Don't rubbish their contribution so quickly. He is the eldest son, not expendable, so, a sacrifice from that baron. Also, all the men he has brought with him, admittedly not many, are experienced, disciplined fighters. Though I don't suppose that you know that, as you spend so little time in camp these days. *Reconnaissance* isn't that what you told Kunimund it was?"

"And that's what it is, Sire. It was this source of information that helped turn the last battle from a major disaster to a minor defeat."

"I believe that to be true, which is why you are both alive and a still a general. What was her name again?"

"Aitziber."

"Quite. She's also the reason why I am not able to give you overall command."

Flavius started to speak. Wamba's hand rose. "Remember the military discipline you have just beaten into that boy? You don't speak until I have finished! As I was saying, I believe you most capable of command, you have a natural talent and you are well loved by the men. However, giving you overall control would cause too many problems. Firstly, Kunimund and Alaric would both feel hard done by. Resentment simmering below your command is not something you want. Believe me. It's something I am all too familiar with. And, secondly, you are always on *reconnaissance.*

Therefore you will serve Kunimund and Alaric loyally and with respect. We will review the situation at the end of the campaign."

"I am your servant, Sire. I am here to serve."

"That was almost convincing. Keep it up!"

They both laughed.

"Onto business. You have drawn this map, I am told it's the fruit of all these *reconnaissance* missions. It's a bit rough. Is it accurate?"

"I believe it to be. The villages are certainly in the right place and not moving. Their troop concentration, as you would expect, is quite a fluid situation. For the most part it remains stable as the enemy is organised in bands under one village headman, so their inclination is to stay near their own village. Only when they are gathering to attack, or they fear we are about to attack them, do they bring all their forces together."

"If I understand what you're saying, it means that attacking these groups/ villages would be a waste of time. Instead, it would be better to provoke them into one big battle, which we would win. So, how do we persuade them to fight on our terms or are you suggesting we should wait for them to attack us?"

"Well, I have this idea which could possibly work…."

Their planning meeting lasted half an hour.

"It could work. I will suggest it to Kunimund as my idea, if that is acceptable to you. He may be more amenable if it comes from me as it is quite an ambitious plan, and he is the most cautious of Generals. Thank you, Flavius. On your way out, could you ask young Marcus, was that his name? to come back in. I'd like a word with him. That is, if you can spare him."

"I'm fairly sure that the army will survive without him, as long as you do not keep him too long, Sire."

Both men smiled. Flavius remembered to bow before taking his leave. Wamba liked that man. He could become one of his most trusted advisors in the future.

"Arrh, Marcus. I have a little job for you to do. I do hope I can rely on your TOTAL discretion."

Ramrod straight Marcus snapped a "Yes, Sire."

"You see I want you to follow General Paulus when he goes on his *reconnaissance* mission. You MUSTN'T be seen. Every time it happens, you come to report to me. This will require immense skill and cunning. I am putting a great deal of trust in you, Marcus. Don't defraud me."

*

Bishop Argebad's household had really pushed the boat out for the meal. Count Hilderic wasn't a big fan of eating at the ecclesiastical palace as the Bishop was old-school religious; eating frugally and drinking infrequently. Tavern fare was considerably better than the hunk of bread, cheese and water that was normally served. This evening was evidently different, various starters culminating in a magnificently presented, wonderfully succulent duck. The cook had been let off her leash and was showing just what she was capable of doing if only her employer would let her. Even the wine cellar had been raided, a superb red that needed no adulterating with water or spices was on the table.

Despite all the alluring aromas, the Count suspected he smelt a rat. Something was afoot and he was being buttered up, almost literally, for some reason. So far no obvious hand had been shown with conversation limited to family health and welfare.

As he was being served yet another glass of the young fruity wine his reasoning made it increasingly evident; that if he didn't broach the subject soon, he would be incapable of any coherent conversation, and his guard would be lowered to a dangerous depth, so he threw his hat into the ring.

"Alright, which one of you is going to start?"

"Start what?" The weather-beaten face innocently chirped.

The host looked up and instantly became alert, serious and dominant, ordering the serving staff out of the room. Once the door was heard to close he commenced, "The Hispani have taken over the state completely. There is not one Gali anywhere the centre of power, fact. We, in Gallia Gothica, have been gradually eased out for decades. It started with Tarraco not being invited to the Concilia. We are all now in the same boat - excluded, discarded, unimportant appendages to power of Toletum. Our existence can be happily ignored as long as the border is secure and no marauding threatening bands of Franks cross it."

The Count had suspected the whole evening was connected to the bishops' recent trip, what he hadn't expected was the venom and hatred that the bishop had used. It wasn't spat out, instead it was with quiet, clear menace.

"And we propose that something should be done about it," added the blue eyes.

"You don't have to tell me these things, I know. I was treated as a leper the last time I was there. Also, I don't even remember meeting Wamba *ever*. He must have been there, it was in the last years of King Recceswinth. He was so unimportant, or inconsequential that I have no recollection of his face never mind his voice. Yet, within a couple of years he is elected King. This role, that of choosing who should rule, was, and has always been, the pejorative of counts and barons, then it moved to counts and bishops, and now it's exclusively you, bishops."

"Not the majority of us, just a few Hispani"

"I agree with you gentlemen, it is a sad truth that if the King of the realm were to walk through that door, none of us would recognise the man."

"Perhaps his clothes might give him away, though I have heard that he doesn't bother greatly with the trappings of State. Actually, what I did hear, time and again, on our trip was that Wamba was a good man. "Humble" was often used when I asked for opinions of him. Nobody had a bad word to say against him, and it sounds as if his now lofty status was thrust upon him rather than him seeking it, which may explain your lack of memory of him."

"I agree with Gunhild, I heard exactly the same, however, this to me, makes him *more* dangerous rather than less, if it's true that he is nought but a puppet in the hands of a few who secretly hold the reins of power."

After taking another sip of wine, the Count came to the conclusion that the bishops should hear what they had been less than subtlety nudging him to, "We ought to do something about this situation."

"Our thoughts, precisely."

"But what can we do?"

Allowing the elder bishop to sit back and look stately, the younger took up the mantle.

"Scouting and observing were the main purposes of our trip. It was clear to us that the Hispani were actively seeking our exclusion from the inner Circle of power, and that no longer was there any place for us. Therefore, if we can't fight the system from within, our only conclusion is to do so from without."

*

Every day she had been leaving the village a little earlier. He nearly always arrived when the sun was directly above. She wanted to make things *nicer*. Their cave was sheltered, cool and close to the lake. Her sister, Arantxa had accompanied her for many years spending many hours of their "free" time exploring caves around the village, so she had an extensive knowledge of all great number of the caves of the area. To describe this one, comfortable it wasn't. No, that was wrong. It was extremely comfortable for a cave. As a love nest, it needed some help. This is what she'd set about doing before his arrival, putting down bedding. The rock floor had a number of sharp edges, which could be painful and distracting for whoever was on the bottom.

She couldn't transport straw from the village. That would be far far too dangerous. She did what she could. Cutting and drying grasses, pulling up reeds from the lake edge, using some of the larger not yet dried leaves. It wasn't comfortable but..

One afternoon they had stayed on the lakeside which was so much better, despite the heat. The problem there being they were too exposed, too vulnerable. Every noise from the bushes, every gush of wind through the trees was potential disaster. It had to be the cave. Their cave.

She had found a patch of exceptionally high thick fairly dry grass and she set about pulling up as much as she could. Taking a knife or sickle from home wouldn't have been plausible. So she pulled. This gave her time to reflect on what was happening. When she was with him, she lived all these moments with such intensity that reflecting never came into the equation. It had been five consecutive days!

When she was back in the village, this world of happiness and pleasure did not exist. They were two separate parallel universes that could never meet without cataclysmic results.

Showing anything different in the village would have been noticed straight away. Instead, she went about her daily drudge doing everything that was expected of her with the resigned expression she had worn throughout her married life. She cooked, cleaned, gathered, chatted as if there were no cave life.

The only time she allowed thoughts of Flavius to creep into her village world was when her husband decided that he would avail himself of his conjugal rights.

This was usually after drinking too much while reliving battle exploits with the other village men. The results of his *efforts* shouldn't have caused the need for any comparison. Oh, but they did! Her husband was either physically incapable, professing great desire, which was a limp affair, despite his insistence on her trying harder, or he suffered from over-enthusiasm when he did actually manage to get it up. At least then it didn't last too long until he rolled off and started his usual loud snoring. Either way, it was not pleasant.

That had been her lot until very recently and she had not known it could be any different. Some other women had, bawdily, made comments and expressed great satisfaction in their husbands and the *act*. Not many, it must be admitted. Most stayed quiet. Actually, she often wondered what these women were talking about. She could see no pleasure in what had to happen. She knew differently now.

The bliss of the other world was without measure. Two hours, sometimes less, of total pleasure. It is what she imagined Heaven to be like. In the her people's beliefs, there wasn't really a heaven type place with most of their gods inhabiting the earth. This sky-living Christian god had been introduced to her tribe by missionaries. Most, didn't bother much with their teachings, as He seemed a god full of wrath and the "Hell place" that was often mentioned or threatened, didn't sound much fun. Eternal damnation and the fires! Their own gods Mari, Sugaar, Odei, and the others, were MUCH better, even Basajaun, the bad boy of their deity, did some good as well as doing his best to upset people.

She felt that even in silly Christian religion eyes, her life had been without blemish, and thought that all her suffering and acceptance would ensure her a place with these missionary promised angels in paradise, if it and they actually existed. However, what she was doing now threw all those previous calculations into doubt. She was definitely breaking at least one of the commandments. She didn't need a justification as it wasn't her religion, but you never know whether those missionaries might be right, so, when she did think about this, she tried to bear in mind those strange people saying things like; Jesus was the God of love, so, what she was doing, experiencing love for the first time, had to be right. It couldn't be wrong to feel this good, could it? Furthermore, she hadn't neglected any of her duties in the other, village, world. This was *extra*. However, it didn't matter how many times she repeated this to herself, there was always a niggling sensation, a feeling, which interfered with, and intruded on, her blissful happiness. Not today though. She could hear his horse coming. She shivered with excitement and anticipation.

She all but pulled him off his horse.

They had agreed that the lakeside was too dangerous. Sometimes the best laid plans and intentions come unstuck.

Late, later than the other days. As they played together swimming underwater, under each other, washing off the sand and bodily fluids, she came to the definite conclusion; Jesus, this love god, He would approve.

*

Marcus knew where he was going, he didn't have to follow too closely. He had dismounted half a mile back so as to not make much noise. The first day had been the most difficult. He had tracked deer and wolf many times with his father's huntsmen, he was therefore confident of his abilities. None of which were stretched in this case. The path was well ridden. It was a matter of not being seen and trying to work out where the final destination was. Again, this wasn't taxing as female squeals of delight were clearly audible.

Settling into what had become his favourite viewing site, he waited for his favourite moment. Apart from the first day, when he wasn't in the best position to see, this pivotal moment normally had to be waited for. About an hour was the norm. Today, was so much better . No sooner had he arrived than he realised that they were already in the water. Now it was just seconds he had to wait. Making sure he was comfortable with hands at the ready, out they came. The "they" wasn't important to Marcus, out *she* came. What a sight! What a beauty! What a body! Heaven.

His imagination, before these days, had run wild with the thoughts of some of the Tarraco girls like this; naked, dripping, wet bodies. All he had been permitted to see were bare knees with flashes of thigh. Here, this *vision* was walking slowly, oh so slowly, occasionally jumping the piddling little excuses for waves. Oh, when she jumped! They bounced. Oh, my God. Is there any more exciting, beautiful sight on this world than two full, firm breasts bouncing completely free? If there was, he hadn't seen it. Her skin. Oh, her skin! So white, almost translucent, setting off the jet black of her long dripping hair. Magnificent.

When delivering his reports to King Wamba, he rather skipped over these parts. They were kept for individual, personal consumption. The King had paid keen attention to all of the report he provided, asking about minute details. The way in which he said "Is there anything you have left out?" he clearly knew that Marcus was holding back on some information.

*

"What month is it today?"
"The fifth, Your Grace.
"Remind me what year it is?"
"673."
"You started on this project, when?"
The chief mason was clearly out of his depths. He knew exactly where this was going.
"There have been many technical and logistical problems. The good stone from the costal quarry has been exhausted. We have had to transport material in by sea."
"From Egypt, I presume. I'm sure the Egyptians took less time building one of their pyramids than you on this one relatively small church."

"All the initial work of last decade had to be replaced because the specifications had not been followed. Repairing that damage was both costly in time and money."

"Master mason, you and your predecessors have been coming to me with these excuses throughout my time as bishop. A life time! You promised it would be ready for the feast day of Saint Fructuous. A church dedicated to the martyr should have its first mass on his feast day. We all agreed on that last year. His feast day is in which month?"

"The first."

"At least you haven't forgotten that." Completely exasperated Cyprianus nearly broke the chair he had dumped his great weight on to. It creaked badly but remained in one piece. "What lame excuses have you come to give me now?"

"Actually, your Grace, I have come to announce that we shall be finished sometime this month, or at the very latest, the beginning of the next. We are doing the final touches. The altar should be finished by the time this conversation is over."

Pushing down on the chair while trying to "spring" up in his surprise, the chair finally gave up on its utilitarian wooden existence. The bishop stumbled and would have hit the floor if it hadn't been for the quick intervention of the mason's strong arms.

"Thank you, my son. That could have been quite nasty. It was the shock. No, the excitement. Altar finished before this conversation, you say?"

Still holding on to the unsteady bulk, the mason nodded.

"Then, goodbye."

Cyprianus shook himself free of the sweaty clasp and set about looking for a better-built chair.

A woman about the same age as Cyprianus flustered in, bearing ale.

"I heard that you'd had a fall, your Grace."

He gratefully received the refreshment and only after quaffing half the content did he answer while wiping the excess from around his mouth with his sleeve.

"Not quite. Find the carpenter. I want all the chairs in the palace checked. It could be a disaster if someone who is actually *heavy* sat in one of the wonky excuses for horizontal stability. Do it right away, yes right away, right away." He set about finishing what was left of the ale. "And bring another one of these and a little something to settle my empty upset stomach. Dinner isn't for at least an hour. I feel like a martyr being starved to death."

The housekeeper departed anything but quietly, leaving the chief representative of the Christian church in Tarraco to reflect.

It really must have been tough in those early days. Imagine having so much faith to face a hungry lion; he could identify with the lion more than the meal, or perhaps even worse, like good old Fructuous, burned to death and all in front of a happy, paying for the privilege of watching, audience. How did they do it? Not the audience, the unfortunate protagonists.

He personally felt that he had always had faith. What was there not to accept and believe? It all made perfect sense.

Well, sort of.

His family, he could trace his ancestors back hundreds of years, were Goths. Proud Goths. The superior nation. The people who sustained the Roman Empire for decades leading into centuries, and who were their natural successors in maintaining the civilised way of life this part of the world had come to expect.

Reports from the other side of the Mediterranean spoke of chaos. Barbarians taking over. New religions springing up. In short, Iberia was lucky the Goths ended here. It could have been so much worse. Just at the end of Gallia Gothica there were those uncouthed Franks. He and his forefathers had kept civilisation safe.

His family had never embraced the change that Reccared brought about. In fact, until but a generation ago, they kept to the old faith. Last century it was the norm for most areas to have two Bishops; one Arian and the other Catholic.

From his point of view, Arianism was so much more logical. Not something he'd been able to say to anyone other than Cecilius, the Bishop of Dertosa, in fact Dertosa was one of the last places in the Kingdom that had this dual authority. The logical consistency of Arianism was proved and supported in the first Ecumenical Council in Nicaea, only for what is now considered Christian orthodoxy to gain the upper hand.

He had never found it easy explaining just who or what role the Holy Spirit was, or played. Also, Maria being a virgin. That was a tough one to sell. Only so many "You have to have faith." or " We don't understand how God works," can be dished out until eyes remain raised.

The Arian acceptance that there was, and could be only one God was so much easier. If Jesus was the son of God and therefore had some sort of beginning, then he wasn't an eternal timeless everlasting god, was he? Begotten or not begotten. He was son of. Just like he, Cyprianus, was the youngest son of. Sadly, his position in the family did not entitle him to the family land, instead he became a man of the cloth, despite his less than rock solid *calling*.

The housekeeper came in with the requested items, placing them on the large solid table.

"Will that be all, your Grace"

He stood up from his corner seat and maudlin thoughts of incorrect career choice heading towards his snack.

"Thank you, Maria."

She passed him, moving towards the door. He gave her a hard playful slap on the bottom which caused her to give him a doleful accepting glance before continuing on her way.

Cyprianus sat, chewed, and lamented.

There was a time, not so long ago, when that slap would have been met with a simpering giggle and led to an afternoon of sweaty pleasure. No longer. Since Maria had stopped her monthly bleeding, she had also lost what inclination or acceptance she had. It would still happen, but more in earnest duty rather than delighted participation. Her interest had all dried up, both figuratively and literally.

He had to have a new outlet for his *needs*.

Throughout his life, he had been encouraged by family, friends and others in the clergy to take a wife. He never felt he was the marrying kind. He liked women. Oh yes, did he like them! Just didn't feel the need to have one around ALL the time.

There was a sector of the church that believed that all clergy shouldn't marry, not just monks, but all. That was plain daft.

There were those who wanted to cut themselves off from the rest of society and devote their lives to prayer and the contemplation of God. Fair play to them. Each to their own and all that. But it wasn't *normal*.

If you wanted to exist in society, you ought to abide by the same norms of that society which meant having sex. Another long draft of ale was necessary. Hopefully this silly tendency will never have more than the few celibate zealots it has now.

Coming back to the point, a new willing enthusiastic outlet, where could she be found?

Now, there was Jacob's daughter. A fine looking wench was she. He was sure she'd be more than pleased to accommodate him. The problem was that she was a Jew. The parishioners wouldn't accept that, no matter how quiet he kept it. It would leak out and eventually undermine his authority. Furthermore, there were all those laws that Toletum was forever passing. No, the way things stood, it wasn't going to be possible. Damned shame, she'll have to miss out, poor girl.

Conversion? That was the solution. Then he could save her both body and soul.

That may take time though.

An outlet was more urgent than that.

"Maria!"

*

The attack, when it came, was completely out of the blue and caught Marcus with his trousers down, literally.

There were six, yes six, he was sure there were six. No, there was another behind the others. They were armed, axes mainly, some pretty rudimentary looking swords. They were in no hurry. There was no yelping, nor war cry. Slowly moving towards their prey that was on the water's edge, stealth was their approach.

Seeing what was appearing on the shore, the woman and Flavius headed back into deeper water, their only protection was the depths. The woman had covered her breasts, the water covering the rest.

"This is where you go and what you do, *wife*. Whore! There is no point in covering yourself modestly. They have all seen."

Flavius moved closer to her.

"And the skinny little runt, I presume he is a Goth. Don't worry, he won't be able to protect you now." His head was shaking in disbelief, anger and indignation.

"Whoring with the enemy, does your shame know no limits?" Having spoken calmly until this moment, his anger was beginning to move upstage.

"If you come out of the lake now, I will be lenient. The boy will be maimed, not killed, and sent on his way back to camp of the invading scum."

"And my fate, dear husband?"

"Once the boys here have had their fill of you, you clearly don't mind who you open your legs for, you will be taken to face justice in the village."

Aitziber's face and stance was defiant, her voice strong, not trembling, showing little of the way in which she felt inside.

Flavius had been quiet too long. The conversation was in an incomprehensible tongue. The elderly man obviously wanted them to come out of the water to make his task easier.

"I'm not sure we are going to comply with any of your wishes. However, if you would care to join us in the water, you'd be made most welcome."

The amount of Latin the men had between them barely came to a dozen words. Having no idea what he said, they were impressed by the way he addressed them in voice of authority and supreme confidence.

Fully clothed and seeing this dreadful situation, it was decision time for Marcus. Riding onto the beach would surprise the attackers and he was sure he could cut down at least three. That still left four. His tutor had despaired of his lack of understanding of anything resembling mathematics, this sum though was easy; seven minus three equalled suicide.

Marcus observed the couple retreating farther back into the water so they were safe. Swimming while swinging a sword - his arms instructor never specifically mentioned the difficulties involved in this action, but Marcus felt totally sure that he wouldn't have recommended it.

The question then was, did he have enough time to get back to camp to bring reinforcements? The usual journey time was the best part of an hour at a gentle trot. Galloping there and back, he reckoned, he would be able to do it in half that time. Still that left at least an hour for the assailants to think of something else. Perhaps they had a boat nearby.

Dilemma.

Waiting to see was a possibility, probably the worst one. His lack of decisiveness and inaction was beginning to annoy himself.

Aitziber wasn't sure how close she actually wanted him. She was very frightened. Jesus had made His decision. She would have to pay for her *sins*. That didn't mean that Flavius would have to, he didn't have to share this punishment, prepared and imposed by this foreign Christian god.

Flavius had done nothing wrong, in fact, he had done everything wonderfully right. He was even unaware of her marital state. If he came physically closer to her; the guilty party, it would surely infuriate them more and they would likely make Flavius suffer for longer.

"He's my husband." She whispered.

"Ah. That explains why he's so mad. I imagine his shouting earlier was not awfully complimentary to you. What else did he have to say?"

She repeated her husband's offer.

"Decent chap. I do hope you are considering the offer. Most reasonable it sounds.."

She made a pained sound. "Chopping off my manhood and you being stoned to death, is that the usual procedure for adulteresses? In the Circumstances, not bad at all."

She looked at him in complete horror while he tried to show the face of a potential buyer.

"Nah. Let's see if he can offer anything a bit better. I am most attached to my manhood and you gave me the impression that you rather liked it as well."

Surprising themselves, and all involved, they began to laugh.

This infuriated all the war party, especially the cuckolded. Unable to understand what they were saying, and then laughing at *him*, he presumed, made him dash for the water. Two of the men held him back. "Not yet." They pleaded. "We will skin him alive and see he is still laughing then, just a bit of patience, uncle."

Flavius took Aitziber's elbow from under the water and started to guide her to an outcrop of rocks. She was both surprised and relieved at his touch.

"Aitziber, you know me, we are family. This is just an indiscretion and at the moment has a solution. If you don't come out of the water though, it will be worse for you." the younger man shouted in his most solicitous tone.

"How can this get any worse for me? I'd rather swim out and drown myself in the water than face the village justice."

"I presume their initial opening offer has been withdrawn and a considerably less enticing one has replaced it."

"That's about the size of it. Flavius, before this goes any further I want to put into words things I presume you already know."

"Let's not get dramatic here, Aitziber!"

She laughed again.

She tried to move her arm to stroke his face. He held it tightly under water. This caused her to feel complete confusion.

"Don't annoy them any more than they already are."

She felt this rejection keenly.

"See that outcrop of rocks to our left?"

Still feeling deeply hurt she reluctantly nodded.

"We are starting to edge that way, slowly. At some point, they will cotton on to what we are doing. When that happens, swim as fast as you can to the rocks."

The family were arguing among themselves as to the best plan of action. There was a great deal of parallel talking and little listening. Still, a conclusion was reached rapidly; a boat looked as if it was the only realistic solution. One of their number was dispatched to get one, and perhaps a couple more of the extended family.

Still waiting and seeing Marcus's inaction was getting chronic. He was just about to lead his horse away when he heard laughter. She had a beautiful laugh, as well as all her other attributes. Was there no end to this woman's perfection? One of the natives departed at a trot, leaving only six. The decision was made for him, he was staying. Quietly he mounted, unsheathed his long sword and waited. This was not like the previous undecided dithering, this was waiting, choosing the correct timing.

When the one had left, the others turned in unison to see what was going on in the water.

"Uncle, I think they have moved to the right. They may be headed to those rocks."

"Shit! Come on, let's get there first."

"Swim! They're on to us. Quick." They both were reasonably comfortable in water though she was by far the superior swimmer. The rocks were but twenty or thirty yards away. It would be much quicker to run, mused Flavius, while swallowing about three quarters of the lake. Aitziber arrived first and clambered up onto the end rock farthest from the shore. She wasn't quite sure how getting out of the water would help their plight, all she could do was trust. Flavius spluttered his way towards her. She helped him up. He was breathing hard, almost gasping for breath. She held him and kissed him deeply. He eventually managed to push her away without pushing her off. They both slipped.

"You're trying to do their job for them! You are forever trying to deprive me of air." She laughed. They were two stark-naked lovers, trying to stay upright waiting to be butchered, and she laughed again.

"You never know when it'll be the last." She said eyes aglow. If Jesus wanted this finished then they would go together, let Him decide where the guilt lay.

"What I was trying to say to you earlier was that I LOVE YOU!" She hadn't thought through what effect these previously unsaid words would have, but she certainly didn't expect that he would throw himself back in the water, do a few movements that on previous days he claimed were elegant strokes, only to emerge and pull himself up the rock again about fifteen yards farther to shore.

She looked at him. She couldn't believe what had just happened. She said she loved him and he abandoned her. Now she felt her nakedness even more starkly.

"What..?"

He held up a bundle of what looked like rags from which he extracted a long dagger or was it a short sword?

It was his favourite shield wall fighting weapon. In the melee of sweat, blood and spilled guts that is the close quarter fighting of a shield wall, a big sword or an axe is only useful if you have room to swing it. The Roman short sword, which was used by most, was extremely effective. His long exceptionally sharp dagger was superb. With a quick jab, or flick of a wrist, he could remove an eye or pierce a throat.

He brandished it so she could see it. The reflection of the sun was dancing off the blade.

"You always need to be prepared. Stay there out of the way."

While he was instructing her, he saw the flash of another blade coming out of the bushes.

Marcus dug his heels hard into the flanks of the mare. With great speed, he covered the first couple of hundred yards between him and the lagging enemy. With a swooping motion, as he had been taught, his sword sliced through what was a living body. He had only ever done it with dummies before. This felt totally different. It jarred his arm back not being pliable like the targets in Tarraco. It hurt. Also, it was louder and messier. Blood and screams filled his vision and ears. His adrenalin pumping, he kicked the horse on. The second man had turned, hearing what was going on. He was not to be taken by surprise and cut down from behind. He stood his ground. What he wasn't ready for was the speed of the horse. Before he had even begun to swing; the horse knocked him off balance. Marcus shooting by, managed a backhand swipe, which more by luck than skill, gashed the man's face deeply. Marcus was still looking back when he realised the third man's axe was high and swinging. The aim was low. The objective was one the horse's legs. The horse duly buckled. This was going to be the end of Marcus if he went down with the animal. Stuck underneath, he would be easy to slaughter. It wasn't an elegant move. His horse-master had insisted that he practiced this manoeuvre daily for about a year until it had become one of his party pieces, earning lots of applause from appreciative friends and family. No applause would have rung out for what he had done. Like a sack of turnips being thrown from a cart, he landed softly in the wet sand. True to form when you are a pile of root vegetables, you are not holding a sword.

The uncle and the two nephews had reached the rocks and had made their way along to where the naked man was standing.

"Our argument is not with you, it's with her." said the first to arrive. As Flavius could only understand the nod of the head towards Aitziber, he wasted no time conversing, instead, he leant forward and pushed the boy off the rock. Moving swiftly to the next target, his favourite piece of metal hit home, catching the young man in the throat. This brought a shocked sound from his female relative. It was lightening fast. Nobody actually saw it, only the deadly results. The boy dropped his cheap sword and held his gushing throat, his eyes showed total disbelief. Everyone was stunned. Everyone except the husband, who pushed past the dying boy and struck at Paulus. A dagger was no match for a sword. Although Paulus had seen it coming and used his dagger to its best effect to stop the blow, it wasn't enough. Instead the sword slid down the blade removing one of the defender's fingers instantly.

Aitziber let out another gasp.

Both fighters were precariously balanced sliding on lake weeds, water and blood. Strangely, Paulus didn't feel any pain. He concentrated on the sword wielder who was clearly experienced, much older, and to Paulus' advantage, much slower.

The thud missed him by inches. Marcus managed to roll to the side behind the horse which gave him time to prepare his trusted short sword. He faced the axe with confidence. This was the part of his training he had liked the most. Admittedly, they had practiced with wooden weapons, the principle was the same though, weave, dodge and jab. They circled each other as if they were about to start dancing.

Suddenly the air was pierced by a woman's scream. The first boy, who had been pushed into the water, emerged behind Aitziber and rested his knife in his right hand against her throat while holding her hair roughly and extremely firmly in his other.

"Drop the weapon or she dies, Goth."

The distraction almost cost Marcus his life. It was only out of the corner of his eye did he see the axe coming. Instinctively, he moved to his left, crouched and thrusted, burying his sword deep into the man's guts. Flavius didn't understand the words, nor did he understand the sight of Marcus scrambling over the rocks, unarmed, behind the husband. Stupid boy, where was his sword?

They had no common language so no meaningful negotiation was possible. It was clear he had to get to Aitziber as quickly as possible, hoping Marcus could distract the sworded husband, who had heard him coming whose calculations ran along the lines of - the baby swordless Goth would be dispatched first, then they would deal with the affront to his honour, turning supremely confidently to face the negligible threat the moment he saw the naked Goth go in vain towards his whore wife. Marcus hadn't been able to pull his sword out. It was stuck in bone and gut on the beach. He knew, even without a weapon, he could cause enough distraction to help Flavius. Both of the naked bodies would be dead, if he couldn't. He definitely saw this swing coming. The way he told the story later, he nimbly ducked under its path, in reality, he slipped on the wet rock. The result was the same. The swinger had put so much force into the movement expecting it to be stopped by solid flesh, that he too lost balance and tumbled into the sea.

Menacingly, Flavius approached the struggling cousins.

"Aitziber, tell him he's the only one left. We will let him go, if he releases you."

Having understood his cousin's name and the approach of this armed naked man he thought there could be no way out of this except by water. He pulled the knife across the inclined white neck and jumped into the water, swimming away as fast as he could.

"Me, no swim." The husband did have some Latin then. Marcus stamped on the hands trying to hold onto the rock while the little waves lapped around him.

"Should have thought of that before you jumped in."

The man was weakening and his grasps were getting more desperate. He tried to speak again, instead, his mouth filled with water making him splutter. It was then he lost all contact with land going under the water with his arms waving.

Pleased with himself, Marcus looked at the end of the causeway to see the expected the negotiating three. Surprisingly, one was swimming away. There was a lot of blood. Marcus wasn't sure whose until he had managed to scramble closer. One full hand and the three bleeding fingers of the other were trying to stem the flow gushing from her no longer white throat. Flavius was also attempting to cradle her head on his lap. It flopped too much. The cut had sawed through so much that it was still connected to the body only by a part of the neck.

"I knew you loved me. I am SO sorry I never told you so."

*

"Don't look so glum, paps, worse things have happened at sea. Come on, let's compare notes. What time is Uncle Isaac due?"

"He sent a message saying he had some urgent problems with a shipment of figs. He'll arrive when he can."

Rebecca had prepared a few things to "pick at"- olives, muscles, not caixer, but they were SO good cooked in a garlic sauce. She poured some cool, white wine into both of their cups.

It was another warm day.

So far this year they had had nothing but heat. No rain, just heat, either blazing hot or disgustingly unpleasant sticky humidity. Today fell in the latter category. The worst sort of day. It was difficult to believe that a body could leak from so many different places all at once. This sensation of a never dry body was *so* unpleasant.

Living down by the port made it even worse than the rest of Tarraco. Their chairs were damp. Their walls were damp and the smell was rank.

"Sit, papa. Have something to drink."

"It has got to rain soon. It can't go on like this. I don't remember a worse year. It's been hot since.." Jacob didn't finish his sentence. Rebecca did.

"Since the fat bishop was here. The point that you think all our troubles started. Papa- that wasn't the beginning, get that out of your head, we are JEWS. We always have some problems."

"Nothing like now. Expulsion from Egypt, or the Holy land, imprisonment in Babylon, admittedly, were worse, but it hasn't been this bad for hundreds of years. There seems to be no end to their bile and hatred. Why do they hate us so? Traditionally, the Goths never used to be like this. We have had relative peace and harmony here for centuries."

"We are JEWS, papa."

"That's no reason. We don't do anything bad to them. They try to convert us, we never try with them. We are discreet in our traditions and celebrations, not causing them any inconvenience. They probably don't even know when we celebrate nor how."

"True. But we do eat Christian babies at Passover. You must admit that that causes some resentment."

"Rebecca!"

"We haven't had a good one since mama died. My favourite used to be the roasted version. Sooo tender." Rebecca started smacking her lips in savoury memories.

"Rebecca!!!"

"Really, papa, how can you rationalise with people who actually believe things like that?"

As their house wasn't in a traditional Jewish area, most Jews lived in the quarter, the Call, in the cooler up town, behind the circus, most of Rebecca's playmates were Christian. The ones that were allowed to play with her that is. She had had a very good friend, Tecla. They went hand in hand everywhere, not to each other's houses though. They skipped, played hop-scotch, hide and seek throughout the port until one day when they were about seven when Tecla's mother found them playing near the quay. Upon introducing her best friend by name, the mother's face fell saying, " Her name is Rebecca? That's a Jewish name. Oh, the Lord be praised, I have found and saved my daughter in time." She dragged Tecla off, telling her not to cry but to be happy as neither she nor her little sister would be eaten.

This had a profound effect on Rebecca. It didn't make her stop playing with gentiles, it just made her very wary of them.

"Have something to eat. The muscles are really fresh. You'll have to wait a bit for the baby as it isn't quite cooked yet."

"Rebecca stop! How can you laugh at these sorts of things?"

"Papa, the question should be, how can you NOT laugh at these sorts of things. Their ignorance is not our fault."

"It is the price we pay that worries me. I'll tell you about the meeting with the rabbi and the elders in a minute. First tell me what you have found out."

"Well it looks as if Marcus has gone off to play soldiers. He was no good at blind man's bluff, I do hope he's better at his new game. I'm told it was at the instigation of the housekeeper, that witch, Amalaswinth. She'd heard that Marcus had been playing with a Jewish temptress, me! She persuaded the Duke that Marcus had to be protected, removed from my insidious-all-encompassing grasp. He needed to be kept safe. The solution; send him to fight in a war. Splendid logic. You'll be pleased to know that your daughter is more dangerous than an army of Vascones!"

Despite the whole situation, despite the absolute danger in the Duke situation with all its implications, despite everything, Jacob laughed. This girl had this ability. She told stories that made listeners laugh.

What he went on to relate was not a laughing matter.

The Rabbi had called a meeting of elders, all the *nasi,* to update them on what was happening. The rabbinical network worked well in Tarraconensis/ Gallia Gothica as they were still above ground. The

Jewish structures in the rest of the state had been destroyed and could not be seen by the authorities to be working, though it did, after a fashion, in an underground sort of way. If anyone was caught, the punishments were severe. News was sporadic and unreliable.

The information from Gallia Gothica was that there was something afoot. It was going to be big. The Christians were squabbling, even more than usual. For some time there had been great resentment about the new centralised authoritarian structures being imposed from Toletum - no respect for the traditional Goth structure nor the Hispano-Roman way of doing things. Rebellion was in the air.

The Jewish community had been sounded out as to how they felt. Would they support a new order?

Fearing a trap or just yet another inter-Christian bun fight, the Jewish council's response had been lukewarm. They had been given assurance that the whole of Tarraconensis/ Gallia Gothica would rise as one. The epicentre was in the north, around Narbo. Strangely enough, the bishops, not the usual suspects of the barons, were leading the call to arms.

"That's great news papa."

"I'm not so sure. I think we need to err on the side of caution."

"Papa, things are getting worse all the time, you said so yourself. What are we supposed to do? Leave the country? Convert to Christianity? We don't have many realistic options. A new state could be a good thing."

*

"So, how and what do you propose by your statement " fighting the system from without?"

The younger man, who had been the conversation leader suddenly looked down as though a strong emotion was weighing down his head. The older man looking every bit the leader of men and souls he had spent his life doing announced, "We will leave the kingdom."

Count Hilderic had been expecting something stern like a total boycott of all calls to meetings, or perhaps, a refusal to send finances to Toletum until the question of their representation could be addressed. He was aghast at the idea. Recovering as best as he could, he knew he should have drunk less.

"How can we all leave the kingdom, where would we go?"

Argebaud's surprise and impatience showed, as he enunciated the words more slowly.

"We will leave the kingdom of the Hispani and start our own here."

"You can't."

"Why can't we? We are a viable state. We have resources in terms of money, men and infrastructure."

"You're bishops! You don't have any of those things!"

"True, very true, my son, but you and the other aggrieved dukes do. There is a considerable feeling for the idea."

"And just who would lead this *rebellion*? Not Ranosindus from Tarraco I hope?"

"Not a rebellion, a separation of states. The Hispani can stay the other side of Tarraconensis and us, Gali, will be happily here under King Hilderic."

*

"Oh, dear Flavius. It feels like most of my regal duties involve visiting you while you are recovering." Wamba was genuinely moved by the physical state of his general, and he heard rumours that his mental state was far worse.

"Every time I come, there is less of you. I truly believe that you should leave *reconnaissance* to someone else."

Paulus winced.

"Did I say something out of place?"

No reaction.

"It looks as if I have. I do apologise for whatever it might be."

Paulus still remained tight-lipped.

Wamba was beginning to lose his patience.

"It's cards on the table time Flavius. Let's start with some things that should not need to be said. I am king. I am your king. I have made the effort to come to see you - not a normal thing for a king to do. The usual procedure is the other way round, with great dollops of humility and deference given to my position. You remain silent. I will give you one last chance, if you choose not to speak, then, you will be dispatched from whence you came."

"Sire. I do not mean to be disrespectful or rude. It's just that I am not ready to talk."

"I'm afraid I can't give you that luxury. I need a report back on what happened, and now is the appropriate time."

"Sire, you already know. You must have heard Marcus's version. After all you did send him to spy on me."

"I know that you came back to camp riding the same horse as Marcus, completely naked, you that is, not the boy, minus a finger and a great deal of blood, you were delirious for a couple of days but now the fever has passed. As to the accusation of spying, thank your lucky stars that he was there, otherwise you wouldn't be here."

Flavius started to choke. He was trying not to show his emotion, trying to stop himself from crying, trying to look sullen, not devastated. His efforts sent saliva down the airways instead of the throat. He was doubled up gasping for breath.

"Marcus, Marcus!"

The young man entered at a fast marching pace.

"I believe your General needs a good slapping on the back, would you be so kind."

Seeing Paulus beginning to change colour he set to his task with evident gusto.

"Don't kill him or break him in two. Just.."

Flavius took in a massive amount of air, only air, then breathed out.

"Enough, Marcus."

Wamba had noticed the cause and the result. Perhaps he ought to give him a little more time to recover. He hadn't realised that the general had been affected so. He had been led to believe it was just a bit of fun in the hay with a local floozy. Evidently not. Wamba retired from the tent without another word.

He re-entered his own tent and headed for the map table where Kunimund and Alaric were huddled.

"Not sure that General Paulus is quite ready to join us. More recuperation time will be necessary. So, what do you think of my plan?"

"Dangerous, Sire."

"In my experience, limited as it is, war tends to be. It is, after all, the very nature of the beast."

"We could be opening ourselves up to a counterattack that we wouldn't have the numbers or terrain to defend. I would say that it is all too risky"

Kunimund's head was shaking from side to side accompanied by numerous *tuts*.

"Do you have an alternative plan, General?"

"The day before Paulus's *adventure,* we had news of an overture to talks."

Kunimund believed that given the state of the terrain, especially these hills, there was no way that the army could ever fight, never mind win, a decisive battle. They could be camped here skirmishing for weeks, months or even years. The enemy knew the land far too well, and they were overtly supported by the local population; a recipe for defeat and disaster in any military engagement. Make a deal and cut the losses, was his opinion. He dared not say it. He would be seen as weak, and perhaps a coward after the loss in the last battle.

"I believe the statement we received went something like "if you leave, we won't harass you on your way home". I am not sure if they added "with your tail between your legs" or not. Do you honestly believe we should accept those conditions? The kingdom's largest and best fighting force, which just happens to have the king leading it, should meekly melt away?"

"NO Sire, I wasn't saying that. I imagine what they sent was the opening gambit to serious talks later, not their final definitive offer."

"Kunimund. General Kunimund, we need a victory. A decisive one if possible."

"Perhaps I, no, we, might be able to assist in that endeavour, Sire." Paulus supported heavily by Marcus, made his way in.

"Always late, perhaps this time, better late than never."

*

Flavius and Marcus led a troop of twenty soldiers. They both knew the path to the lake well. The scouts reported back that there was no sign of an enemy ambush or protective scouts. Wheeling quietly, as quietly as twenty armed marching men could, it was to the left, away from the water they went.

"Shouldn't we be in more of a stealth mode, sir?"

Flavius looked directly at the young man for the first time in quite a while. He had grown up. The childish arrogant insecure boy had been replaced by a hardened, wary matured boy. Nothing would change that fact, he was a boy. A boy Flavius owed his life to, but as yet remained a boy unthanked.

"This is not one of your spying missions. Our role is decidedly different. By the way, how many days had you been watching?"

Marcus coloured. His sexual thoughts of the woman had been replaced by blood lolling heads and death. His report back to the king was, as usual, factual, playing down his part in the fight and showing the general in the best light possible, though unable to avoid the fact that the general had fought naked as that was how he returned to the camp. He did try to emphasise that Paulus was prepared even though he was in the water with a woman.

"Five, sir."

"Your own initiative? Did you come to see the show?"

"Sir! That is grossly unfair." Marcus had blushed redder still, any more and his head would explode from the built up pressure. "The king issued the orders on the day we were in the tent. The day you hit me so many times ... for my own good."

"Wiley old fox."

Flavius knew that he should apologise and thank the boy. It was difficult. The only way that he had of dealing with all that had happened that day was not to. Not to think of what she had said, what he hadn't said. Not to think of her as he last saw her, a severed head, lying in his lap. Not to regret. Not to repeat over and over again..*if only*.

Marcus's aggrieved, trying- so- hard to be stony face finally persuaded him into action.

"You fought well."

The change was much more dramatic than day-to-night or vice versa, that was a gradual process requiring fading and time. This was instant. Dead of night to bright midday sunshine.

"Thank you, sir" Marcus tried hard to curtail his beaming smile. He failed.

"Though next time you should try not to leave your sword inside the enemy."

The noon sun was replaced by the glow of a red setting one.

When they had got back to the beach, Marcus doing his best to chivvy along his grieving commander by telling him that one of the survivors had gone for reinforcements before the fight had been enjoined. This caused Paulus to stop and look at one of the dead ones who still had a short Roman sword protruding from his abdomen area. He kicked the body, hurting his foot considerably more than the dead body.

"They will pay heavily for her. Bastards." He thought about kicking it again, the throbbing in his foot advised against.

"You seem to have left something." He pointed with the slightly damaged foot to the sword.

Marcus bent and tugged, to no avail. He tried to get leverage by placing one of his feet on the body, yanking with all his might. Foul air was emitted from the body, the sword hardly budged. Sweating and getting more fraught by the second, Marcus gave up and suggested moving as time was really of the essence.

Flavius leant over and, almost effortlessly, removed the sword.

"You might need it later."

The smoke from cooking fires was becoming visible

"As my second in command, I am going to inform you of the plan."

It didn't take long. It wasn't complicated. It was somewhat risky, especially to this vanguard.

"From what you have said, basically, we are bait."

"That's the size of it."

Marcus' face could never hide what he was thinking. He tried. He had tried especially with Rebecca. She, however, always knew and how to take the cruellest advantage of it.

"Don't worry so. This is not a suicide mission. It will give us time for a considerable amount of payback to Aitziber's village before the party really begins. Oh, by the way, twist and turn."

"What?"

"When you bury your sword in someone, a flick of the wrist will help its extraction."

The setting sun was back. So much so that Marcus felt he should turn to the men to instruct them to be as quiet as mice from now on.

It was Flavius's first smile in a long time since..

*

Word was out. A big catch of tuna had been hauled in. It wasn't often that tuna was caught, and certainly, if rumours were to be believed, not in the quantity of last night.

Rebecca joined the group of women waiting at the dockside.

"Who's the last?" She chimed the set phrase that was the substitute for queuing.

Jacob particularly liked a tuna steak. There were those who claimed that it wasn't caixer and others who pointed out that it had scales and fins, therefore, must be caixer and, in any case, if it is prepared to the rules of caixrut, then there is no discussion.

Rebecca didn't bother herself with these silly little rules. They kept the main strictures of caixrut avoiding the fine points and smaller fish bones! The fact of the matter was that her father liked it, and it was available at a good price. End of story.

The "queue" was moving slowly, all the women wanted to congratulate the fishermen's wives and they, in turn, wanted to, mixing metaphors slightly, milk the moment.

After what felt like a lifetime, it was now Rebecca's turn.

"I want five large steaks. Put it on the duke's account."

"Hey, wait. I am next."

Amalaswinth who had arrived that moment, didn't accept that the duke's food should be queued for. It was her right to take when she wanted, and, furthermore, was entitled to the best of anything that was available.

"And make sure that they are the best cuts."

"I'm afraid that they will be the last five. I have no more."

"This really is NOT good enough."

"I can't invent any more fish, my husband.."

"I will take them. Next time your husband is lucky, I want you to bring the whole fish up to the palace first. We will decide what we want and the rest you may sell afterwards."

A general murmur of disagreement rose from the huddle of women which Amalaswinth silenced with a much practiced look that could wither plants from forty paces.

"I said I was next."

For the first time Amalaswinth took in who was next to her. She turned her bulky, domineering form to face the speaker full on. The tried and tested look was in place and on maximum power.

"What did you say?"

"I said, twice, that it isn't your turn, it is mine." Rebecca was not withered nor cowed.

It was more than a murmur, it was almost a collective gasp.

Ignoring the look, the women, and the exhaling, Rebecca shifted her attention to the fishwife. "I'd like two steaks please."

Quandary, fluster, dither, the usual loud and vocal seller was flabbergasted and speechless. No-one had ever challenged Amalaswinth before. Universally hated for her airs and graces, this nothing more than a glorified servant had ruled without question for at least a decade.

The fishmonger set about cutting. The knife wavered after slicing two.

"Don't take any notice of this *Jewess*. Nobody ever does, and the sooner we remove this illness from Tarraco the better."

"That's correct just the two steaks. How much will that be?"

What was an orderly scrum full of daily chatter had become totally silent. Many of the waiting women were Jews. A collective dilemma was in place. Did they watch this to the end, or, take the prudent well trodden path of avoidance of conflict and its inherent possibilities of collateral damage. Some were edging to the perimeter.

The fishwife's bloodless face took on a harder aspect. She knew Rebecca. Her husband sometimes did some fair-paid, part –time work for Jacob when the sea didn't permit boats to sail on it. She wrapped the fish and her voice shakily set the price, adding to nobody and everybody "It was her turn."

Initially there was a hush, the sort of calm before a storm. Amalaswinth was stunned, unable to react as words and thoughts fought to get out, she managed to say nothing. It was then that the applause started. Not a riotous affair, more genteel appreciation.

Rebecca paid, took her wrapped prize and as nonchalantly as she could, extracted herself from the crowd. No more than two or three steps out of the crowd she was tugged back by her elbow.

"You Jewish whore! Don't think I don't know what you were trying to do to my little Marcus. Parading and enticing him with your naked wanton flesh, and him just a young innocent boy, all in the hope of catching and perverting him."

"Actually we were playing Blind Man's bluff."

Spitting in rage, she eventually managed to hurl numerous abusive remarks and insults at a walking serenely away back. Rebecca did not react, she continued on her way home.

The crowd was shocked and excited… would they have a story to tell! All those who weren't present would wish that they had been. Amalaswinth had lost face but she promised revenge. To regain some of her lost stature, she pushed herself back to the fishwife.

"Give me all that is left. And I promise you as well, you will pay for this."

A timid voice from a very petite woman was heard "I think it's my turn." Amalaswinth dispensed with the withering look approach, and slapped the woman hard in the face.

"I do NOT think so."

*

They entered the village, the small retribution party split in two. Marcus from the north and Paulus from the south.

The pre- fight instructions were simple; kill, capture and wreak as much havoc as possible. Spare no-one or thing.

The village evidently was taken by surprise by the silently entering force. There was no organised resistance. People were doing what people normally do in a village in summer. Upon seeing troops with weapons, what men there were, sped to their huts to gather up their rudimentary fighting implements. Despite overwhelming numbers on the defending side, there was no way it could have been a fair fight. Men were butchered with or without trying to defend themselves, screaming women and children were dispatched swiftly. Very soon there was nothing but strewn bodies either dead or dying decorating the spaces between the huts.

Once the silent entry had been broken, Flavius was uncontrollably wild. He could be heard yelling "This is for Aitziber!" Many fell to his sword. At one point an elderly man with rudimentary Latin came out of a hut, apparently in no hurry or panic, to ask "Why my daughter's name?" This caused Flavius to pause in his one man massacre mission. He looked the man in the eyes he recognised all too well, they were the same as his daughter's. The swish of the sword was heard rather than seen. The man buckled and fell. His leg had been severed slightly above the knee.

"You won't die so quickly. I'll be back."

Flavius marched on, relentlessly slashing to both left and right until the two forces met in the middle.

"Burn the huts. Raze this village to the ground, it will exist no more. Slaughter the animals as well."

Huddled in a whimpering group were a number of women with some toddlers.

"What shall we do with them?" Marcus asked.

Jarred from his blood letting reverie, Flavius looked at the Circle of combined fear.

At that moment a man, the man, pelted out of the back of a burning hut heading for the trees. Marcus spurred into action by his face set off, only to be yanked back.

"Let him go."

"But that was him, the murderer."

"I know."

Marcus was speechless. He had watched a one man killing machine slaughtering all; men, women and children in his path, in the name of his lost lover. These people were guilty by association being his motivation. And now, the author of her death was visible, and he allows him to go free. Unbelievable!

"We need someone to escape, remember?"

"Yes, but him?"

"Don't worry, we'll meet him again very soon and until then he can live with the pain of death and destruction that his actions have brought on his village, his family, his friends."

The bloodletting anger of a few minutes before was less frightening than the cold calculating pent up hatred and fury which showed in Flavius' eyes.

"We are not taking prisoners. You know that very shortly we will be attacked. Keep some of the younger women for entertainment for the men while we wait and possibly, if we get out, they can be sold as slaves. The others, dispatch." With that moved back to where he had left the one-legged father.

Moaning on the ground, trying to staunch the flow of served arteries, he didn't have long left in this world, he was bleeding out.

"Her father! You ordered her death." It wasn't a question. It didn't need an answer. It was more like the sentence from a judge.

"Whore. She dishonoured me and all her family."

Swish. Off came the bottom of the arm that was cradling the first wound. The old man tipped sideways.

"The whole of the family is now dead. The village is no longer. This is the price you pay for your honour. She knew how to love. That was her only crime."

"Whore! May the worms eat her!!"

Flavius thought about finishing the job and then, looking down on this bloody mess, rejected the idea. Let him bleed and suffer.

He left him shouting and screaming in his own tongue with nobody to understand him.

The whole village was alight. There were more dead bodies where the Circle had been, all of them either children or elderly. The massacre had been brutal and quick. The majority of the men had hung back letting the one real enthusiast, Caius, take the lead. For him this was great sport. The elderly got one chop after being commanded to kneel, if it took two, he was most unpleased. His favourite part was ripping a baby from the mother's arms, throwing it high enough with his left hand so he could slash it with his right. Sadly, there were only a few to hone his skill. Toddlers tended to move or be pushed away to what the mothers hoped would be safety, a couple of lolloping strides and a swish could make two pieces where there was one. Caius laughed and marvelled at his skill, often inviting the reluctant to appreciate the beauty of his work.

Sounds of screaming women could be heard in the northern end of the village.

Answering the puzzled look, Marcus spoke as militarily as possible, trying to cover his revulsion and shock of what he had just seen, and worse still, what he had ordered to be done.

"I deemed that to be the safest area until their attack starts."

"Good. Go and check that disputes don't break out, sometimes one woman is desired by a number of men. Once they have had their fill, tie up and corral the women in that animal pen." He indicated a fenced off area with various animal carcasses.

Hoping that he had finished for the day, receiving this order caused Marcus significant anxiety. Pained at just hearing the abuse from a distance, the prospect of seeing it up close and having to act as a referee dismayed him.

The sight was appalling. Some women had chosen the sensible path of least resistance and were being enthusiastically humped. Others fought back and received many pitiless blows delivered by an assortment of instruments ranging from branches to flat swords.

True to the Flavius prediction there was a standoff. Caius held a woman roughly by her hair and had a dagger pointed at the throat of one of his companions who Marcus couldn't for the life of him remember the name of.

"I said I'm taking her and that's all there is to it."

"I had her first, so she's mine."

This was about to get bloody. The force could ill afford to lose any member with any injury.

Marcus steeled himself. These men were twice his age, experienced and ruthless fighters, somehow he had to impose his authority. Deeming that the unsheathing of his sword would only make things worse, he physically inserted his small wiry form between these two brutes.

"As senior officer present, I believe custom dictates that I have prior claim to either of you, I will take her. There are plenty of others over there."

This plan occurred while it was happening. As he stood his ground, he reflected that this was possibly the worst situation he could have opted for. If he had favoured one or other of the angry lumps of muscle, at least he would have had one ally, as it stood he had two sweaty heaps of testosterone glowering at him

"Unhand her!"

What followed was one of those *long* moments when any and all outcomes were possible. Trying as hard as he could to remember that he was from vastly superior stock, the son of a duke no less, and also attempting not to actually lose control to the quaking and shaking that was beginning to engulf him physically, he returned the intensity of the looks he was being given.

The woman fell to the ground when Caius released his grip.

Marcus pulled her up roughly, leading her to a clump of trees some distance from the

others.

*

"Maria, this cut of meat is not as tender or thick as usual." The Bishop looked up from his plate to see a storm brewing. "Wonderfully cooked though." He quickly added in the hope of reducing the force eight warning signs to nothing more than a squall.

"Your Grace may be interested to know that some of the traders, the better ones, are refusing to extend anymore credit to this household until some/ all of the outstanding bills have been settled."

"Ahh." Not a storm, nor squall, it felt like that persistently ill wind was about to increase in strength.

"I know your Grace is preoccupied with the matters of the next world and it is, and should be, your priority to care for the souls of your flock, and there are none who would dispute the amount of time and effort you dedicate to this task. However, there are bodily matters that need attention as well."

"Ermm, yes. Pretty dire, are they?"

Maria went from a slow lamenting shake of the head to a determined nodding movement.

"The stipend is well overdue. Furthermore, my brother has had a number of capital outlays of late and has asked us to be patient. His portion will arrive. Perhaps if these factors were explained to the suppliers, then they would not be so demanding."

"I have been using this line of explanation since the Christ Mass."

"I see. And they are being told that I am fervently interceding for them with their Maker?"

"That is always my second line. The butcher pointed out that flesh and blood are paid for in this life as there will be little use for it in the next."
"A fair point. While I do my best to chew through this..." He looked down in disgust at his plate then lifting his eyes he realised his error, " Beautifully cooked, rather elderly animal, could you send a message to the Jew that I would like to see him urgently?" His face brightened somewhat when he added "Tell him to bring his daughter."
It was now Maria's turn to look disgusted. "The daughter? Whatever for?"
Thinking as quickly as he could, and in the hope of avoiding another censor-ish scowl, he trotted out one of his set phrases.
"The ways of the Lord are not always understood."

*

After finishing his sweet wine with figs, he strolled out into the evening cool of the courtyard to see the waiting Jew.
"Ah, Jacob, so good of you to come so quickly."
Jacob felt that he hadn't had too much choice in the matter. Furthermore, the request had been made by two of the Bishop's armed guards which made dallying a less attractive way of answering. The whole situation made Jacob sweat and worry, both the manner in which the "request" was delivered, as well as the order in itself.
"I see you are by yourself." The Bishop was peeved and disappointed. Peeved that his order had not been obeyed, the reason for which, yet to be offered, will have to be convincing. Disappointed, at not seeing the beauty, especially at a time that her father would be so vulnerable. It might have made her more...forthcoming.
Surprisingly, there was a movement from behind the pillar on his right. It was the said beauty. His memory had not deceived him, she was truly stunning. More so than at their last meeting, she had *developed,* becoming, how should he put it? more *womanly,* considerably so. This evening was improving. Moving from jaw exercises on indigestible, old meat to agile, lithe, soft young flesh is undoubtedly a move in the right direction.
"But he's not, your Grace. I do believe you requested my presence also." Rebecca's finger was delicately poised near her chin as she barely whispered her coquettish entrance. Jacob's heart dropped. This was going to be even worse than he feared. He had *ordered* her to stay in bed and feint illness. She would have nothing of it, speaking loudly, certainly within earshot of the messenger, saying that she'd be delighted to go. having never seen the inside of the palace, the invitation did her a great honour.

"What an impressively attractive house, your Grace. Such style. Such workmanship."

Seductively she caressed the carved stonework she had been admiring. "Yes, magnificent, isn't it? Sadly, I can't take much credit for it, or the work involved. The Romans really did know how to build. As you probably know, it is said that Emperor Augustus actually used this building back in the day. I am just its latest and the most humble caretaker. As you can imagine, it takes a considerable amount of money to keep it in its pristine condition." Reluctantly he moved his eyes to the father. "Which brings me directly to the point of our little meeting."

Jacob had been thunderously angry with Rebecca's rebellious stance all the way up town to the palace, eventually calming down enough to explain that their tactics would be simple - agreement to the bishop's monetary request would be speedy, not overenthusiastic, only making a slight play on haggling about the rate of interest. After all, what did it matter? The money was never going to come back anyway. She was to remain totally silent. She was a woman, and women did not intervene in the affairs of men. He repeated himself several times. Finally asking her whether she understood, her head was demurely nodded as they entered the side entrance to the courtyard.

Another order disobeyed, Jacob was beginning to despair. Her upbringing was rightly questioned, and to be disobeyed in such a manner, so *wantonly*. She was too young to realise just how much fire she was playing with. Jacob was now in a quandary, should he remain where he was in the hope of the bishop coming over to talk business, or should he go to stand next to, no, in front, of his daughter to shield her from the leering look of the fat Christian..

The first.

"I quite understand, your Grace the outgoings on such a building must be considerable and the income, as you were good enough to inform me in our last meeting, can be precarious in its arrival. Perhaps I could be of assistance in helping you in that unfortunate time gap."

The bishop was moving towards him, indicating with his head that they both should be seated.

"Jacob, as always, most perceptive of you, you have outlined the nub of the problem."

Having the bishop close to him, and seated, made Jacob more comfortable in the greater scheme of things. The smarmy approach of the Bbshop produced a feeling of wariness. This was going to be expensive. The only question was how much poorer was he shortly going to be.

"It would be an honour if you allowed me to be of assistance."

"As the shortfall is larger than I had expected.."

Considerably poorer.

"I expect I may be able to survive for this short period of time, on about double of the previous loan."

Teetering-on-the-edge-of-bankruptcy poor.

"Clearly, I would expect the level interest to be higher than before. I know that you are a business not a charity. The Church would not like to be seen to be abusing its situation. No, we all should pay the required amount. That would be fair. Yes, fair. Yes, yes, appropriate and fair."

Jacob did his best not to splutter or cry. This would be the end of him. Isaac would help, which would inevitably put both of the businesses into a perilous state. The *short period of time* was the most worrying part. It made matters clearer than a glass of water, like an insatiate, overgrown leech, he would leave his victim only momentarily to return again and again, until the victim can bleed no longer. Disaster loomed.

"Your Grace must realise that to collect such an amount of money will take some considerable time and effort."

"Jacob, Jacob, Jacob, what you perceptively understood earlier, is that time is of the essence. I would require this money immediately." The bishop's tone had hardened, clearly more than money matters were in the air.

Rebecca had sauntered across to the chairs, the bishop's eyes taking any and every swish of the best outfit. She moved to a place directly behind her father. She leant forward to rest her head on top of his, at the same time allowing a more than slight spillage of breast to escape the top of her dress.

"I can think of a solution to this problem of amount and immediacy."

Cyprianus straightened. His eyes were agog. Unconsciously, but noticed by all else in the room, he licked his lips.

"It's very good of you to join our conversation, young lady. I can't quite remember your name."

"Rebecca." She almost purred. Jacob could not see what she was doing either physically or objectively. He had to put a stop to whatever it was. Losing money is a setback, a daughter, would be catastrophic. He made to get up, Rebecca's hand firmly planted on his shoulders impeded any movement.

"What is the *solution* you propose?" another moistening movement on the ecclesiastical mouth, and more downward gravity enhancing force by her.

"I don't think it appropriate…"

"Jacob, Jacob, Jacob, do let the girl speak. I know it really is not a norm for negotiations to be conducted this way, however, I am intrigued by just what *Rebecca* has to *offer* to help our impasse."

"Instalments."

"What?" was the unified response of both males.

"Papa could send what he can, as soon as he can. Then, as he is able to acquire more, the amount and frequency would steadily increase until the required sum is met. This would allow you, your Grace, to solve the immediacy problem in the quiet confidence that the other instalments would arrive in due course."

"Young lady, I really do not think.."

"Furthermore, *I could* deliver the money, thus enabling me to see more of this wonderful building."

*

"King who?"

"Hilderic."

"You are insane. I thought I had drunk too much." Hilderic took in the two sets of eyes that were scrutinising his every movement, there was no hint that this might be a post dinner jest, they were serious and this for him could prove dead-ly serious.

"Count, we are agreed that there is nothing that can be done with Toletum. They are beyond reform. We are different to them. We do not feel the need to hate the Jews so much, nor suffocate the Goth traditions that have held us in good stead for centuries like for example, the king being first among his peers, not a puppet in the hands of some meddling behind-the-scenes people as it is now. It's time we asserted ourselves. And as you rightly pointed out, we bishops do not have our own men at arms. Furthermore, we are not interested in the new state becoming a theocracy. In all but name that is what the Toletum kingdom is now. We believe there is a role, a dominant role, for religion in the state, but we wield power of souls not bodies."

"But.."

"Count, you know there are always buts, always reasons for inaction. Excuses are forever found. However, we honestly believe that it's time for action. Don't think that we came to this conclusion lightly. It has been brewing for decades. You know that and you also know that something should have been done about it before. Still though, it's not too late, in fact it may be an excellent moment as a whole number of disparate factors are joining together and they all lead in one direction; a new state."

Gunhild who had been nodding his head sagely throughout the discourse decided an echo was needed, "a new state, a new beginning." Upon gaining his voice, he thought that he could give vent to his poetic tendency, "Chop away the dead wood, prune the branches and let the tree thrive and blossom in the new light.."

"Yes, quite. Most agricultural, Gunhild, but if it goes wrong it'll be my head that will be chopped."

"Count, Count, what could go wrong? The bishops of Tarraconense/ Gallia Gothica have met and are as one, the Jews are meeting to decide on their support, we believe it will be a favourable outcome , and there has been some tentative contacts with both the Vascones and Franks, both of whom look upon our venture with favourable eyes."

"Eyes are not swords. When push comes to shove who will actually be beside us?"

*

"This tuna is truly excellent, Amalaswinth. Wonderfully fresh and excellently cooked, do give my compliments to cook. She has really excelled herself. We should have served this last night, my guest would have been rightfully impressed. I know this is most gluttonous of me, please don't tell anyone, if I could have just one more slice ..

The duke readied himself.

"There is no more."

"What, no more? What a shame. So succulent. Now I see why it was not on the bill of fare last night, insufficient quantity. Next time Amalaswinth, do buy more. A treat like this should be shared."

This was her moment. Deliberately she had restricted the duke to one, rather large, slice. The other two were to be shared among the domestic service later.

"I did my best to get more. It seems that preference is given to the Jews these days."

"What?"

"I queued just like any other goodwife waiting my turn and along came a Jewess demanding various slices. For some reason, unknown, you know some of these Jews have magical ways and can use curses against normal people, the fishwife stopped serving me mid order and instead catered to the needs of this *person* who she obviously feared."

"This is intolerable. You are well known as the representative of this household. How could anyone usurp, your, and therefore, my, authority in such a brazen way?"

The duke had forgotten his hunger. Shock and righteous indignation now filled his belly.

"You know sir, that I am not one to impose my authority because of my relation to this household, but I *was* upset. I had been waiting quite some time until it was my turn. The other women supported my claim of unfair treatment, one even confronted the Jewess and was roundly slapped for her intervention. It wasn't just the fear of physical violence, no, this

Jewess had the general populous shaking, perhaps quaking, would be a better word, too frightened to challenge her authority."

"Well I never. Did you not point out that you were on the duke's errands?"

"I most certainly did, directly to her face. Her response shocked me to the core. Her words were something like; *And who is he? He doesn't control me and never will.* Then she turned on her heel and flounced away."

Steam was now rising from the duke's head. He stood with such violence that his chair fell backwards nearly taking him with it. Amalaswinth dashed to his aid to restore equilibrium of furniture and employer. Steadied, his voice dropped to a deeper pitch to intone authority and gravitas.

"Do we know the name of this …insulter of authority?"

"Rebecca, daughter of Jacob, sir."

"The same as the one who was trying to ensnarl my son?

"The very same."

"A word with her would be in order."

*

"I believe that we have everyone who said that they would attend."

They were in a smallish unadorned side room of the synagogue in the town of Barcino, chosen not for its importance, it didn't have any, all the other towns represented carried more weight, instead, it was its central location that was the attraction.

Most of Tarraconensis/Gallia Gothica was represented, from Dertosa in the south to Narbo in the north, the missing elements were those farther inland.

"In an effort to be discreet we have limited numbers. As most of you know each other from other rabbinical meetings, there is no need to waste time introducing everyone. The only two who are "new" are, over here on my right, Isaac, who is representing Tarraco as Rabbi Saul has some health problems. Isaac is here on business. He is not a rabbi, nor, he assures me, is he a leader of the community."

"My only qualification is that I am here."

"You are too modest, Isaac. Rabbi Saul assures me that Isaac has his full confidence. Furthermore, his family is one of the most influential in Tarraco."

There was a generalised nodding of heads and quiet shaloms.

"The other guest is, again, here on business. Having made his way throughout the kingdom selling off his slaves, he is in a unique position to tell us how things are. We are privileged to have David from Betica."

More of the same warmth that had been previously afforded to Isaac, was extended to the new comer at the end of the table.

Abraham let the greetings peter out before moving on.

"The main order of business is for us to discuss what is going on among the Christians, and what our stance should be. Do we think it is pertinent to become embroiled in their affairs, or do we stand aside awaiting the outcome? However, before getting to that point, I would like to ask David to tell us about his trip from the far south to here. It's rare that we get firsthand accounts of the turmoil and oppression faced by our brethren in the rest of the kingdom."

David, who was clearly not unused to public speaking, held his audience in awe, shock and disbelief for the best part of half an hour explaining the lot of the Jews.

"We have all of these laws here as well, but no one, except very occasionally, in a case of personal vengeance, ever bothers enforcing them. Are you telling us that they are universally applied throughout the rest of the kingdom?" The rabbi from Narbo, Ariel, was open mouthed in his disbelief. "I had heard rumours of it getting more difficult, but to this extent?"

"I hate to be the messenger of doom. It can be said no other way. It has been coming for a long time. We have avoided contact, kept our heads down, ceased any overt trade with the Christians as they requested. Many of us have gone through the baptism process which seems to make them happy for a while."

"You are baptised? Are you a *converse*?" asked the incredulous rabbi from Narbo.

"Yes. Most other ways have been tried and failed. The community in Toletum believed it was possible to buy, or perhaps bribe, their way into some peace. It cost them 3000 solidi to find out that this policy doesn't work."

There was a general gasp, not at the attempt of bribery but at the massive quantity of money involved.

"The Christians were emboldened, and richer, once this was paid. There seems to be no end to the persecution. There is genuine concern as to the future of the community. Those not baptised are hunted, or stunted in business, those couples who ostensibly *convert* but who are found out, lose their children to Christian adoption and face stoning or public burning, not by the Christians, no, other Jews who are forced to do it! I have heard tell in Toletum that one of their most important ideologues, Julian, is openly proposing a *final solution* which involves mass expulsion or death. "

Another lamenting gasp filled the room with all heads shaking in unison and despair.

Abraham felt it pertinent to point out a doctrine at this moment.

"It has been decided that Jews may go through this water ceremony, if it helps in their survival. We all know it is not a real conversion. It's expedient. As long as the person involved keeps to our ceremonies and ways, albeit secretly, we have no problems with it. Sometimes appearing to give in is more effective than all out futile confrontation."

This doctrine was not universally supported.

The forever vocal Narbo rabbi, Ariel, demanded to be heard.

"It is clear then that the Christians will not accept us here even if we are nominally part of their church. As I see it, it leaves us few options."

He had the complete attention of the whole room.

"In Tarraconensis/Gallia Gothica we have been fortunate. We pay, we suffer. This is true in other Christian kingdoms, we are not unique. Frankia, just across our border, is looking to the Goth lead. Byzantium is reported to be imposing anti Jewish laws. All of which begs the question, if we *are* expelled, where to?"

"It is the lot of God's chosen people to be hounded in this world." chimed an elderly rabbi. This intervention made Ariel thump the table.

"Enough already!"

"Please, Ariel, keep your temper. Shouting will not help as we all can hear you clearly anyway."

"I apologise, Abraham." Meekly he continued "If we can do nothing to appease them, the only option is to fight back. We can't do this by ourselves which is why this dispute between Christian central authority and this region of Hispanias is a godsend. We have to ensure a victory."

"Why do you think that the Goths here will be any different to those in power in Toletum? As you said previously, a Christian is a Christian." The long suffering elderly rabbi had found his voice again.

"Fair point. All I can say is that we need to look at their record. They have not enforced these instructions from Toletum. Relatively, we are free. Buildings like this are still open." He indicated the small, secure synagogue.

" None of which guarantees a bright future for us. It does give us a slight amount of hope, something, from what David has told us, is in very short supply in the rest of the kingdom."

The control of the meeting had been lost with the participants talking to those who were close by. The noise level rose as conversations became more animated. The only two people not talking were Abraham and Isaac. Abraham was gesticulating, trying to wrest control from a chaos. Isaac was dumbfounded. He had no idea that things were SO bad. The future surely did look incredibly bleak. He stood quite brusquely, knocking over some things that were on the table which fell to the floor in a huge clatter. This sudden movement brought quiet and gave Isaac a moment of unexpected and unsolicited attention.

He felt he had to speak, "Can I just ask one question?"

The quiet in the room continued.

"The rabbi from Narbo, David?"

"No, Ariel."

"Sorry. So many new names and faces, I'm getting confused. What I would like clarity on, is, who has asked for our support and what are they promising?"

*

"Why did you do it? You practically offered yourself to him, along with all my money. I will be penniless, with a daughter who gives herself away for ….what? "

Rebecca brought her crumpled father a drink. He waved it away preferring his despairing thoughts delivered with a dry mouth.

"A cup of wine is never a bad thing."

His eyebrows raised, no other comment was necessary. She tried again to put it in his hands, only to meet a clenched fist. Giving up on the giving approach, the wine was lifted to her lips and the cup was drained in one. The eyebrows searched for heights unknown.

"Waste not, want not."

Lowering herself to the floor, she found a comfortable spot and held on to his knees.

"Do you remember when I was little, I used to sit in this position? You always tried to pull me up, to sit on your lap, or next to you, saying that this spot was for dogs not daughters. For me though, it felt so secure, so safe. Nothing bad could happen while I held on to you. "

Jacob didn't reply. His memory zoomed back a decade. They were alone, the two of them against the world. He felt the tears begin to well. He had failed her. Her security had evaporated. The danger was present, real and from many quarters. Not understanding her then, when she preferred the floor, he sure as hell didn't understand her now. How did this girl think and work? Her mother had been a simple hard working soul who had succumbed to illness while pregnant with what would have been Rebecca's younger sibling. She had never been complicated. She never sat on the floor, and it would never have occurred to her to flirt disgracefully with a Christian, a bishop no less.

They held this position, each lost in their own thoughts and memories, for quite some time. Breaking the reverie quite suddenly, Rebecca, without moving position said, "So how much shall we give him in the first instalment? As you know, I don't understand money nor the ways of business, but I think ten percent would be a reasonable start if I deliver it quickly. It would show good intention."

Realising he was being played, Rebecca was an excellent business woman, she ran all the household expenses more than competently, and had offered various innovative ideas to his business: one which had changed Isaac's approach to the export of figs completely. He waited patiently to see if there was more, or if he would have to react first. He had taught her to read, write and do her numbers, something which had been frowned upon by ALL the community, not just the synagogue women. It was standard practice to teach boys to read Hebrew from the Torah, and as such, all men were literate in the Word of God. As a language for communication, Hebrew was not used, with only some exceptions - in the written form; commerce and religion, orally clearly, all the prayers and orations were in their ancestral language. The community spoke and worked in the version of Latin that the others in the city used. Very few knew how to write in Latin as it wasn't that necessary. Rebecca had learnt written Latin, as well as Hebrew, nobody knowing how she had done it as she steadfastly refused to explain. Language skills came easy to her. Her Hebrew was a million times better than her cousin David's, who was a competent scholar, often lauded by the old rabbi, Saul. In fact once when David was being praised he let slip that his cousin, who was much better than him, had helped him with his *homework*. The result was that all hell was let loose with the whole community, spearheaded by the rabbi, queuing up to reprimand Jacob, for which he received a period of, if not quite total cherem, excommunication - certainly an extended period of shunning.

Eventually he broke the long silence, a small victory for her as he was forced to show his opposition.

"You know that I will not allow you to take any amount of money anywhere near that palace."

"Papa, let's look at this coldly, not emotionally."

Here it comes, whatever she's been working up to.

"No Rebecca. For once you are going to listen to me. I am your father, you are my daughter." This caused her to change her gaze from the vastly interesting mosaic floor to his struggling to control face.

"Stop looking at me like that! I know that I am stating the obvious. It's just that sometimes it needs to be said. I will not allow you to risk..." There was a pause while he tried to find the right words, "..anything for the sake of money."

"Papa. That is emotion, not business."

"Some things are more important than business!"

"I totally agree, just don't allow these *details* to cloud your judgement. Firstly, let's talk about money. Have you got the amount he is asking for?"

"You well know I haven't."

"Without bankrupting yourself, Uncle Isaac and throwing me into destitution, can you get it?"

"The community could.."

"Papa, answer the question."

"Improbable."

"I am not going to become a servant in someone else's house, nor marry a moderately affluent minor trader who is doing you a favour by taking me off your hands."

"You'd prefer to be a ….. to a bishop?"

"A what, papa? A wife would be impossible, I'm a Jew, remember? A consort? A kept- woman on the side? A glorified whore? A *sota*?"

Jacob's face had paled. She was using language she had never used in his presence before and she was outlining his worst nightmares.

"None of those things will happen. He's arrogant, not very bright, fat, and above all thinks with something that hangs between his legs."

"Rebecca!"

"This will be an unfair fight which will cost us some money. That's all. Now, let me explain how this is going to work and don't "Rebecca!" me until I get to the end, please."

*

It smelled pretty good. The large pot that had been left cooking, by its now deceased cooks, was steaming. Flavius ladled a small portion into a bowl, smelt it again and trying not to burn his tongue, tasted it. It was excellent. Much better than the stuff they got in camp. Filling the bowl to the brim, he passed it to a squatting near the fire Marcus.

"No thanks. I'm not really hungry."

The bowl was pushed harder into his hands giving him no choice but to take it. A wooden spoon was thrown at him as he sat cradling the food.

"Marcus, you will need the energy later. This may be your last meal, eat it. That's an order."

Reluctantly and delicately he put a small morsel in his mouth. Whether he would be able to keep it down was his biggest fear. His stomach was churning with revulsion at what he had seen and done. Until the steaming bowl appeared, he was proud that he hadn't shown how he felt. Nobody else was showing signs of disgust. The majority of the men could be seen at another campfire near some charred huts eating heartily, laughing and taking it in turns with the young women, who no longer had voices with the amount of screaming they had already done, nor hope, after the brutal incessant pounding they were receiving. His losing face by vomiting was something that had to be avoided.

Flavius joined him on the floor. There was nothing delicate about the way he was eating, he was positively shovelling the stuff into his mouth.

"Really good. These people do know how to cook." Because he was talking with his mouth full, Marcus misheard him.

"I'm not sure they are given a chance to show how well they fuck."

Swallowing hard and trying not to choke with the combination of food and laughter, "Cook, Marcus. Cook."

Noticing the white, getting whiter, face for the first time, Flavius' merriment came to a sudden halt.

"Sorry. I forgot this was your first real exposure to war. That skirmish, when you left your sword in that body, didn't really count, did it? That was spontaneous do or die stuff. This time it was more calculated and *brutal.*"

"Was it really necessary to slaughter all – women and children? I'm all in favour of, and well-trained for, a fight, but this..." He indicated the body - strewn space between the two cook fires.

His spoon suspended in mid air, Flavius was debating with himself how to conduct the rest of this conversation. Marcus was a good soldier, a good person, both had to be maintained. Everyone remembers their first battle. In fact, from what he knew of conversations with other veterans, most relived it in their minds continually. The adrenalin, the blood, the screams of fallen comrades, the smell of fear, the stink of shit as men evacuated themselves in panic, or death throes, the post battle high when you realise that you have survived, the joy. That this scene is repeated time and time again by further battles, never replaces that first time.

Sadly, Marcus' ever abiding memories wouldn't be a titanic struggle of will, skill and strength pitted against an equal or superior foe, instead he would forever recall the cries of unarmed helpless women and children.

"Marcus, this is not the norm, but it is part of a fight against an enemy. You point out the defenceless, and you are right to, however, if you had been in charge what would you have done?

Marcus shrugged.

"We are about to be attacked by half a nation. We are twenty soldiers. Should I delegate two, three, four of our force to keeping these *defenceless* under control, who left to their own devices, are quite capable of finding and using pitch forks, knifes and other sharp domestic instruments, to attack us from behind, while we are facing the male armed and primed enemy? Under normal circumstances we would take prisoners, later selling them for slaves, making all the men a tidy little amount of money. Again, I ask, as commander, what would you do?"

Another, more resigned shrug.

His shoulders were then roughly pushed and held.

"That's NOT an option. As a commander, you order. And your first obligation is to the safety of your men! They will only follow you into the hell that is battle, if they trust you. If, as in this case, that means, an appalling massacre, then so be it. Nobody enjoys this work."

His head now pulled up. He looked as if he was about to cry.

"Eat Marcus, and then we will discuss tactics and probably our death. Furthermore, I have been told that you have reserved a woman for your personal use. Caius was most perturbed. I gave him short shrift. Now, go and enjoy your prize."

Marcus headed for the trees where he had left the girl tied.

Since removing her from the clutches of the potential duellists, he had tried not to think of her, or what he was going to do with her, which naturally meant that he didn't stop thinking about it. Something had to be done. She couldn't just be added back to the group untouched, that would make her easy prey for whoever was to follow.

He approached her with leaden feet. Her head was twisted unnaturally in the opposite direction, showing that she had either seen, or heard his coming. Bending down, he untied her. She was no longer attached to the tree and had hands and feet free. Still not turning, she took in her unshackled self, then the horizon.

"If you run, I'll catch you and return you to the men who wanted you before." Marcus suddenly realised that his idiocy knew no bounds. He had freed the woman with a dire warning in a language she had no understanding of. He may as well have said nothing as he very much doubted his tone had transmitted his intent.

"Why do you free me?" she turned head and body. The torn rags that were once her clothes covered little. Marcus gasped. She was probably about fourteen or fifteen, very clearly a woman, not a girl.

"You want to feel that you are not a rapist?"

Moving his gaze to her glare, he was struck by the fact that she was speaking acceptably good Latin.

"You speak my language?"

"Not all of us are uneducated barbarians. Compared to you and what you have just done, we are the advanced society even though Latin is not our mother tongue."

This was not what he had expected. As he hadn't had a plan, it wasn't so much a case of changing plans, as making one on the hoof. They were some distance from the main *activity,* but still close enough to see and hear what was happening.

"Would you mind following me up to that cave up there?" he indicated with his head trying to stop himself looking at her partially covered parts.

"You are too shy to *fuck* me in public?"

"Please."

Not knowing what else to do, she obeyed by slowly rising to her feet and led the way.

The exposed rear of her was now in his sights. Oh, lovely! No glowering, glaring, angry eyes to deal with, he could feast himself. Magnificent. The way the buttocks of the small firm arse rose and fell with the walking movement. Magic.

Upon reaching the cave entrance, she plonked herself on the jagged stone floor.

"Did you enjoy the show? I felt your eyes burning into me."

Marcus blushed. Trying SO hard to avoid staring at the now completely exposed breasts, he risked the wrath of her eyes. To his surprise, he found familiarity there.

*

Sauntering uptown, she was lost deep in thought, hardly acknowledging the greetings she was getting from friends, acquaintances or just fellow Jews. She had left the house a picture of gaiety and confidence, which was a show to try to decrease the furrows on her father's brow.

"If those lines get any deeper, papa, we'll be able to plant vegetables there," were the last words that she threw over her shoulder, which at least made him smile, if somewhat lopsidedly as his face fought the contradictions he was feeling.

She had managed to mollify his fears to some extent with a ridiculous idea which had occurred to her at that moment. There was no way that plan could work. She would have to play the whole thing by ear, hope and pray. Another thing her father shouldn't know, she wasn't big on praying. She found it all a bit hard to take and believe. Who would make their chosen people suffer SO much? Not much of a god that one.

The distance from the port had been covered without her even noticing and she found herself in front of the massive wooden doors to the palace. They were ajar. First decision, to walk in like the Queen of Sheba, full of arrogance and confidence, or use the side entrance for suppliers, supplicants and the occasional Jew?

After a few seconds of doubt, in she marched, well perhaps not marched, more like strode like an imposter, a wealthy with something to offer imposter, the money was secreted in her dress, which made her powerful and exceptionally frightened.

Not seeing anyone in the hall, she carried on deeper into the palace. She vaguely remembered her way to the inner courtyard where the previous negotiations had taken place. On her way she heard some grunting type sounds coming from one of the side rooms, again, the door was slightly open. She stopped at the door to spy in. What she saw surprised, shocked and it must be said, amused her.

It was a magnificent banqueting room. The tapestries, mosaics and furniture were out of this world. Such opulence she had never seen. However, she took all these factors in as a by product of the most amazing sight, the bishop groaning and penetrating a pair of wrinkled saggy naked buttocks, which were spread-eagled over the enormous dining table. It was like a bloated whale humping a wizened old stork, quite disgusting. She could make out the sides of their faces; nobody seeming to be having fun. The stork had a resigned bored face, the whale seemed to be in a hurry to get it over and done with.

Despite her amusement at the sight, Rebecca did not want anyone to see her. She headed back to the big doors, found the knocker and gave it a few almighty belts, which produced a deep satisfying demanding sound. The flustered stork arrived remarkably quickly. Her red face didn't betray any frustration at being interrupted, relief, could have been a more accurate description of her face. When she saw who was causing the commotion, she was not best pleased.

"Trade, supplicants and Jews to the side door."

A few minutes ago that would have been Rebecca's first choice, now though she felt superior, not one to be ordered around by some housekeeping semi-whore.

"I am here to see the bishop."

"I told you, to the side."

Queen of Sheba, eat your heart out.

"If he does not want the money I am carrying, then he'll have to come down to the port area to fetch it himself. My name is Rebecca. You may tell him that I called and you barred my entrance."

Maria struggled with her thoughts. She hated Jews; filthy, smelly money grabbing baby-eaters. She had never allowed one through the front door, by doing so would have bestowed on them some sort of undeserved importance. The father of this one in front of her, knew his place, automatically coming in the side, how she would like to teach this one. Rebecca turned to move away.

Maria knew how desperate the bishop was for the money. She'd be able to go shopping with a head held high, not grovelling for favour or tick tomorrow. She also knew how entranced the man was with this young beauty. His anger would be monumental, if he found out that she would not allow the bitch in.

"Wipe your feet and wait in the hall."

The bishop was hunched over the very same table doing something as pleasurable as before and even more satisfying. He turned feeling similar to the way he did when the door knocked, unfulfilled and frustrated.

"This is all?"

"Your Grace, it's a beginning. It is but one day since we undertook to service your needs. This is ten percent of the required amount, a considerable sum given the time."

For the first time since she'd entered he took in what he was seeing. Clearly, she had made an effort to look good, a same quality dress as yesterday's, which, thankfully, he knew through experience, was immodest when used in the correct way.. Her jet black, loosely curled hair was no longer tied back, it fell in great contrast to the whiteness of the skin of her neck. Her deep dark eyes smouldered for him, they held so much promise. He was excited. His hardly decreased member since the interruption was beginning to re-swell.

"*Service my needs*. I like that."

Rebecca was truly frightened, perhaps she'd overplayed her hand. Plan A, had been rejected. Plan B, obviously was backfiring. Plan C? Did she have a plan C?

*

"Here."

They were standing next to an outcrop of rocks to the south of the village. Flavius looked around.

"You really think so?"

"I read about a battle like this. My tutor used to make us study old Roman tactics. I can't remember where or when it was. I wasn't the most attentive student, but I do remember that the most important part of the fight was the narrowness of the gorge in which they were fighting. By placing a shield wall at the narrowest point and leaving a few in rearguard, the Romans were able to hold off a much superior force."

Flavius reviewed his previous scepticism without looking any less convinced. The boy was much more upbeat today. That girl must have done him a lot of good, probably got rid of gallons of pent up tension.

"Marcus, if there's only one narrow entrance, how do we retreat?"

"We don't."

"Oh I see. By the way, what happened in this battle, who won?"

"It was epic, the stuff of legends. In the overall war the Romans trounced the barbarians."

"And in this little *epic* defence?"

"That was the downside of the story. They fought bravely, holding the hordes at bay for various days until the main force could arrive, in turn blocking the exit of the enemy, then setting about the total slaughter of thousands."

"Were there any survivors from the heroic narrow pass defenders to join in the celebrations of victory."

"In spirit and honour, they were all present."

"Physically, bodily?"

"None."

"You read, and are taught, too much heroic shit. Being dead is not good. Fighting to the death is one thing. Giving up on life is something quite different. I told you this was not a suicide mission. Difficult, fraught with danger, yes. Let's take your plan and modify, so a happy ending is plausible, shall we?"

After their little chat, Marcus headed towards the cave where he kept his girl. Flavius smiled to himself. Rumour had it that the girl remained untied and hadn't attempted to leave the cave. She must be enjoying some young, virile, Roman flesh.

"May I sit?"

"The cave's not mine, and I remind you that I am your *guest,* not the other way around."

Marcus sat. Words didn't come. What could he say, *don't worry your ordeal will be over soon enough as it seems that we are about to die, or perhaps; things aren't as bad as they seem.*

Silence was the much better option.

No physical contact had been made as yet. Marcus didn't want to admit that he was a virgin, neither did he want his first sexual experience to be a rape. His first battle was a slaughter of women and children, not the heroic battle of strength and will he had been taught for. If, as was likely, death would arrive shortly, he would rather face it a full time virgin than a onetime rapist.

"When you are not looking at my breasts, and you actually look at me, I get the impression that you feel as if you think know me. Do I remind you of a girl at home? Or your sister perhaps?"

At the mention of the breast ogling, began his face colouring again, so, his discreet glances weren't quite so discreet. Trying to recover his poise, he started processing what she was saying. Who was it she reminded him of?

"I have no sisters, and no, you don't look like anyone back in Tarraco. You are familiar though."

"Perhaps all undressed girls look the same to you!" Her voice had taken on a gentler tone, she was less vitriolic. She was almost taunting in a teasing way.

"Shit!! You're right! That's who! You must be related."

"To who?"

"Another girl, a village girl, I saw, accidently saw, naked. Aitziber."

"Aitziber? Were you her Roman-Goth lover?"

"No, that was Flavius. That's why he was screaming her name yesterday in the village. He really did love her and wanted to wreak vengeance for her death."

The girl went deathly quiet.

"So that's why our village was chosen?"

Marcus nodded.

"And why were you looking at my naked sister?"

Marcus's gentle blush had become deep rose red. He stuttered a start of a sentence a couple of times before rejecting them to try another.

"It's a long story."

"I'm not going anywhere." A subtle power shift had taken place. The man with the sword no longer had control.

"Well, I was asked to keep an eye on Flavius."

"You were spying? Without the knowledge of either. A little voyeur!"

"It was a military mission! It was lucky I was there. I helped save Flavius. Your sister, we couldn't get to in time."

Silence returned. It wasn't the empty variety nor the comfortable one. It was more like a pause for reflection.

"I know her throat was slit by Iñaki, our cousin, my future husband. He boasted to everyone in the village how he had saved the honour of the family. That day I lost the one person who I really loved in this world. Aitziber was more than my big sister, she brought sunshine, fun, and love into our lives. Now because of his bravery and service to the family, I have been promised in marriage to him. There's no end to the sorrow, her death, me having to marry her murderer, and your destruction of my village, our lives, all in her name."

For the first time in the ordeal of her life since Iñaki's announcement, tears flowed, they flowed uncontrollably, her shoulders began to shake with the outpouring of emotion.

Marcus didn't know what to do though he was quite fascinated by the way the breasts wobbled almost with a life of their own. Fascinating.

*

The Bishop had sidled up to her, not so much like a snake slithering s-wardly towards an unsuspecting prey, more like an overweight slime-excreting slug heading towards a succulent cabbage leaf.

One of his fat, smooth, manicured, clammy hands was placed squarely on the upper part of where he suspected the bottom to be under the bilious dress. Rebecca froze.

"I do hope that I am not interrupting anything."

The new face was most pleased by everything, his timely entrance, the amount of horror showed by the Bishop, matched by an equal amount of evident relief from the stunningly attractive girl.

"OH Duke Ranosindus. What a surprise!"

Cyprianus's frustration knew no bounds. Heaven was there in the grasp of his right hand, he had felt it with his fingertips. No *needs* would be serviced now. Doing his best to look composed and hide the protruding tent pole that he had wanted noticed earlier, he moved awkwardly behind the nearest high-backed chair.

"Yes, quite a surprise, a lovely surprise, nevertheless, a surprise." He babbled not knowing quite what to do in the situation.

God does exist. Rebecca had a new found faith.

"I must be off."

"Please, don't go on my account. My business with the bishop is but a moment. I am sure he'd be happy to continue where you left off before my *lovely surprise* visit."

"I am pleased to say that *my business* with the bishop, which had taken up too much of his precious time and energy, doesn't need any further action."

"Yes, over, over, yes, over. No more time needed."

Bowing, Rebecca tried not to run out. Her heart pounding ready to burst, she had to slow to a stop just outside the doorframe in order to breathe.

"You old rascal, Cyprianus."

"It's not what it seemed. Nothing unto-wards was happening."

"Only because I arrived too soon for your liking."

"It was nothing more than a business deal." The bishop couldn't move from his hiding position until the swelling went down.

"You give her money and she gives you pleasure. That's the exchange you were negotiating."

"Totally wrong, my dear duke. She was giving me money."

Ranosindus collapsed laughing.

"What a rogue! I suppose your job was to give her pleasure. Cyprianus, I am sure that you were a fine looking charming man in your day, but that day is well past. You now have wealth and position. She has the beauty. Her paying you…"

He started laughing again. So much so that he began almost to choke. Cyprianus rejected the thought of rushing to his friend's aid as his extended self would probably cause even more merriment. Instead, he stayed and tried to make himself look impervious and above all this frivolity. When eventually things calmed, he set about correcting the misunderstanding.

"The fact is that she brought the first instalment of a loan I have taken out with the Jew from the port."

This piqued the interest of both listeners, the now seated Duke and the breathing normally Rebecca.

"That girl is the rebellious witch who flaunts my authority and tries to capture the interest of my son?"

That's unfair. I've done neither. Rebecca nearly said out loud, and I am no witch!

"Insufficient information to say whether she is those things, but she certainly is the daughter of Jacob the Jew."

"Apparently she insulted me while queue jumping and offending Amalaswinth yesterday. Poor Marcus was so enthralled with her, I had to dispatch him off to fight with Wamba's forces. Furthermore, she's a Jewess. You are playing with fire there, my dear bishop."

Thanks to you, I'm not playing with anyone mused the now-descending, almost decently deflated cleric.

"She is most definitely a beauty. Never having entered into one of these financial arrangements with Jews, I'm not totally sure how the system works, I've heard that you're supposed to pay interest, however, I don't think it's in the way you were attempting." The duke chortled at his own jest. "Seriously though, Cyprianus, what do you propose doing with her? She's a beauty who's not going to do anything with you unless you can threaten her in some way."

"Firstly, her soul needs saving."

"Your hands were more interested in the body and blood part from what I saw. We have many measures we can use against the Jews. I know there are those who think that we are too lenient. It's oft heard that they are far too uppity, and if they, especially this one, believes we can allow them to insult my authority in public, perhaps they should be taught a lesson."

Rebecca was transfixed and hadn't noticed that she was no longer alone.

"Listening in on our betters are we, Jew!" with that she was pushed back into the room with the two most important men in Tarraco.

"Look what I caught spying at the door!"

The bishop looked horrified at her re-entrance, whereas the duke felt verified.

"What did I say? Uppity! Explain yourself, girl."

Perhaps God had a busy schedule and had to be elsewhere, or rescues were limited to a maximum of one, without doubt she had been abandoned. In for a penny.. may as well be hung for a sheep as a lamb, all proverbs pointed her in one direction. Take the bull by the horns was the one that finally caused her to speak.

"Firstly, I was NOT spying, I was catching my breath. However, when I heard these baseless, slanderous comments about me, I did stop to listen."

The slap across her left cheek was a total surprise.

"Don't you dare speak to your betters like that girl!"

Slowly, coldly, deliberately Rebecca faced her slapper.

"I was asked by the duke to explain myself, I am doing so. I would ask you not to interfere with the instructions of *your* betters, and kindly keep your hands to yourself."

A backhand swung her way which Rebecca managed to block and then take hold of the wrist.

"You let go, you Jewish whore!"

Rebecca increased her grip and whispered quietly so the men wouldn't hear, "Whore? It wasn't me who had her legs open on the table just a while ago."

This made Maria explode with anger, the duke felt duty bound to jump from his seat to separate them. Taking a firm hold of Rebecca's hair, he dragged her across the room in the direction of the bishop. Letting go, he pushed her into a seat.

"I will tie you up, if you cause anymore problems."

Rebecca wanted to cry. Her scalp really hurt.

There were four strong emotions in the room, fumingly angry, apprehension, sulkiness and indignation. The latter broke the silence.

"How dare you listen in on a private conversation?"

The sulk replied, "As you were talking about me, I thought my input to correct some of the lies you have been told was necessary."

There was a rush of potential slappers. Rebecca cowered and sought to protect her face without being silent, "Beating me won't make me any less right."

"It might teach you some manners, you disrespectful little bitch!" Maria was the first to arrive with hand primed. She was stopped by the other hand which was ready to strike.

"This girl needs punishing correctly and severely, not just a gentle slap. With your permission, bishop," Ranosindus's gaze moved around the room clockwise, from Rebecca, passing past Maria to rest on the highest representative of the Church in Tarraco. "I will ask Maria to leave us to deal with this."

That permission would not have been given by the housekeeper. Her employer though nodded his agreement. She firmly extracted her arm from the duke's grip, used it to flatten some non-existent bunching, made sure she gave an example of respect by bowing to both men, turned, and seethed her way to the door.

"Close it behind you, if you could please, Maria." The bishop had finally found his unusually quiet voice.

The sulk was gradually changing to abject fear. Alone with the two most powerful men in Tarraco, neither of whom could be described as a major Rebecca fan, she feared the worst. Caution had been thrown to the wind a good time ago. She was not going to meekly grovel, no matter the consequences. The bravery of youth, which didn't consider, or weigh up the consequences of actions, was flowing through her veins.

"So, will you allow me to speak before you decide on my fate?" Her arm, no longer being used as a shield, moved to the edge of the chair to help her adjust her posture to a straight backed confident poise she most certainly didn't feel.

Both men were dumbfounded by this show of defiance that they had never seen the likes of before. Rebecca took full advantage of this momentary lull.

"I didn't jump any queue, it was my turn for the fish. I didn't insult anyone. I have never been interested in any *boy* called Marcus and I am not a witch." She blurted out as fast as she could.

The men's silence continued until the most unexpected reaction occurred. The duke began to laugh. It wasn't the deep belly kind, it was more a surprised giggle.

"That *boy* is my son, and he is away defending the kingdom from invasion."

"I wish him well, honestly I do. I just hope he is less clumsy than he was when playing games down by the port."

The laugh moved to hearty.

"Perhaps you ought to tell me about your version of the fish story."

She started by saying that there was only one version, and that version was the truth, then continued to relate events as they had happened without embellishments.

"Tell me, why I should believe you?"

"Because I tell the truth to important people like yourselves and to everyone else."

Ranosindus had fallen under her spell. Looking at her was a total pleasure, listening to her fire, amused and interested him. He could well understand his son's bewitchment and he fully believed that she would not be interested in a *boy* as she said. He also saw the opportunity to have some fun.

"The woman who never tells lies, eh? Tell me, what were you about to do with the bishop when I, *unfortunately*, entered the room?"

Cyprianus, who had been taking a disinterested interest in matters until that moment, was now totally and uncomfortably interested. Rebecca contemplated for a few seconds before replying.

"The truth can only be told from one point of view, and when no exchange of opinions has taken place." The duke was amazed at how well and confidently this girl spoke. "What I was about to do, was, to leave the room before .."

"Before what?" Ranosindus smirked encouragingly.

The bishop had turned a deep shade of Cardinal purple

"Matters of religious doctrine were discussed. I didn't want to get wet in any Christian ceremony."
The Duke exploded in delight.

*

"Sire, is this wise? The force we are readying will leave nothing but a rearguard consisting of your personal protection and little else. You will be vulnerable to attack. I would advise most strongly that no more than half of the army be dispatched on this *endeavour*."
"Not keen on this plan are you, Kunimund?"
Kunimund had kept quiet while they had talked about this before Paulus left, in the hope that sense would be seen. The plan was fraught with danger, had more holes than a fisherman's net, and, in his opinion, was doomed from the very start. Wars were not fought and won on foolish adventures. Their success was a matter of slow, steady progress wearing down the enemy by persistent well-chosen confrontations with the minimum of losses.
"Sire, my opinion is that even if we win this..., whatever it is, we will sustain considerable losses, and given that no reinforcements from Toletum, or anywhere else, are due, we may have to abandon the whole campaign, which would be an unacceptable loss for the kingdom."
"What if we win?"
"I believe the objective of any commander is to win. Not to gamble. Risk games should be confided to fireside entertainment."
Wamba started pacing and chin stroking. His own misgivings had come to the fore of late. When the badly injured Flavius made his case for this attack, his enthusiasm was contagious. The way in which it was presented, gave no room for any doubt to creep in. It would be over in a jiffy; attack, bait, trap, destroy. What could be easier?
Flavius, along with the boy Marcus, had set off with such high spirits and such a piddling little force that success seemed assured. Despite his own injuries, which he hadn't fully recovered from, he insisted no more men were needed. The army just needed to be readied in time to save their bacon when the time came.
Readying that had been less than speedy. There had been a great deal of faffing, preparing, and re-preparing, so much so, that Wamba feared that the timing was already off. If they didn't swing into action now, there would be no point in doing anything. The bait will have been consumed, and the army, if it were dispatched, perilously vulnerable in terrain not of their choosing. Kunimund could be right. It could be an ignominious end. Crawling back to the capital with his tail between his legs, one year into the job of being king, and already defeated. Stakes were high.

He could see but two courses of action. The Kunimund push for caution, which now at this stage would mean the abandonment of the expeditionary force of twenty men and two officers. This would ensure the continuation of the war, with an inevitable victory, his crown being secured and a long reign. Or, a roll of the dice.

Walking helped him think. Lifting the tent flap, he headed for a moving contemplation. While weighing up the advantages and drawbacks, he was beginning to be aware of the state of preparations of the army. It seemed to him, not a vastly experienced military man, well… quiet. Not a lot was happening, or had happened, men were idling. Could this be a case of subtle undermining of policy? Kunimund wouldn't openly oppose, but he was capable of sabotage by inertia. Decision made, he wandered no more, with a determined turn on the heel and purposeful stride he got back to his command tent in very little time and only slightly out of breath.

Addressing his patiently waiting, supremely confident looking commander, "We leave now! We can wait no longer."

"Sire, that's not possible. The army isn't ready to march. A couple more days are necessary."

"Why?"

"Why, what, Sire?"

"Is it necessary to repeat? Why are you not ready to go?"

"Getting this size of force is no easy task."

"Exactly what is the problem?"

"It's the central phalanx. Both the flanks have been ready to march for a day or so, the middle, which includes some of the more difficult to move parts, needs a little more time."

"I suggest, very strongly, that you get out there and get that *difficult to move* part ready to roll as soon as possible."

Kunimund was most pleased with this outcome. He was trying not to show it, when he heard the King announce.

"With the assistance of Alaric, I will lead the flanks out of camp in the next few minutes. Send out that order, and get my horse saddled. "

*

"May the Lord forgive her, she is but a heathen and knows not what she is saying." The bishop had found a voice with a strong imperative to regain and redirect this conversation.

"Holy is the sacrament of baptism and should not be offered up for ridicule," he shot a quick glance in the direction of the duke, " nor should it be taken lightly. Girl, you were correct in your assumption that that was where our conversation was leading. Firmly, I do believe in your salvation."

The bishop was pleased he had reasserted himself even pushing himself up to the high moral ground, smugly from his new lofty position, he viewed all around.

"Rebecca, this is worse than I feared. Your soul was about to be saved and you were relieved at my entrance, your excuse, to move away from the Glory of the Lord through the personification of the Bishop of Tarraco." The stern rebuking voice was looking at Rebecca, and there was a significant mismatch between the words and their tone, and the way in which a smile played around the corners of the Duke's mouth. He was having fun.

This concept of figures of authority having light fun, had never occurred to her before. If she ever thought of these people, which was not often, as they moved in a different world to hers, she imagined them to be austere, serious men spending their days on important matters with no time for frivolity. Without a doubt though, the duke was laughing *at* the bishop, with sex and body being substituted for religion and soul. To use his own words about the bishop; *the old rogue.* The bishop was too full of his own pomposity and self-worth to realise what was happening, or was it because he was a bit thick?

The unchanged horizon, much to her relief, showed that she hadn't said anything out loud. Sometimes she did that. When she was convinced it was an internal reflection, she looked up to see angry, or astonished faces, as she'd let it slip out whatever uncomplimentary thing she was thinking. It had been a day of choices. Like flipping a coin, heads or tails, she had chosen correctly about as many times as she hadn't. This time the game was serious, the stakes were high. It was packed with real danger. Heads, she follows the conversation with the words said, shows contrite humility while trying to extract herself out of the christening waters the best she could. Or tails, she plays the duke's game.

"My knowledge, as a Jewish heathen, of Christian practices is somewhat vague. May I ask, where on, or, in the human body, is the *soul*?"

"You see, my dear duke, such confusion and ignorance, it would be a negation of my role of Christian evangelist NOT to try to help in these situations. Your soul lies deep within in you. It is your very essence." Ranosindus´s glee was welling. He could hardly keep himself from jumping up and down on his seat with the prospect of future pleasure. To him it was clear on which path the girl was leading the bishop. He needed to savour this. It could be payback for the hundreds of hours in church when he had had to listen to this self-important, fat cleric drone on about righteousness, and not falling into the temptations of sin, in his interminably long sermons.

"And, can this be accessed *physically,* your Grace?"

Wearily, the dispenser of religious doctrine denied this approach, recommending the road of prayer.

"Isn't it true Cyprianus that when you anoint, physical contact is both recommendable and necessary?" The duke and Rebecca threw each other conspiratorial half grins.

"A thumb marked cross on the forehead is the set procedure."

Setting her face to totally innocent, young girl mode, Rebecca puzzled a contemplative "Ohh."

"Encouragement to religious fervour can take on a physical aspect." The duke wasn't letting go, ostensibly only seeking to clarify matters for the possible convertee, he was doing his best to stoke the fires.

"So, at no time is the grabbing and holding of buttocks, singular or plural, at all required?"

Rebecca looked as if butter wouldn't nor couldn't ever melt in her mouth, the bishop's face was back to playing cardinal colours, and Ranosindus couldn't keep his mirth in any longer. He exploded with a peel of laughter and thigh slapping that could probably have been heard in Rome. It caused so much commotion that Maria reappeared at the door full of solicitous enquires into the duke's well-being. Splutteringly, he managed to reassure her that all was well, and he was learning a great deal about how to spread the faith in new and novel ways. Maria gave a death look to Rebecca, re-establishing herself next to the slightly open outside door frame.

"Maria, close the door completely, will you?" The bishop sought refuge in ordering around those he could. "And you, young lady, I think it's time that you left so that we can decide on your fate."

Rebecca stood casting one last look at the eye-drying duke. Should she deliver a last salvo of her hope for more religious instruction in the near future? For once, common sense prevailed. She moved slowly, and meekly, towards the door as she turned to bow, she definitely caught the Duke both wink and smile at her like true co-conspirators.

Waiting for her was the housekeeper. All servility disappeared in a second, Rebecca straightened herself to her true height and brushed past without a look or a word, trying to give the impression that women like her didn't stoop to acknowledge the presence of the lowly. Maria growled at her back, "You've not heard the last of this, bitch!"

The bishop was on his feet, stomping around the room.

"The punishment for that Jewess should be exemplary. And not just her, her father should be made to suffer as well as he is primarily responsible for such a jezebel. Spare the rod and spoil the child. Quite what sort of education and upbringing she was given doesn't bear thinking about. She needs to be taken away from that influence and shown the true path. A spell in a convent would do her the power of good. As for the father, flogging is a minimum. Yes, flogging in public, flogging, yes."

The dry-eyed duke was enjoying the show, the discomfort, the stomping and the upper-ward spiralling rhetoric.

"I'll have it arranged for tomorrow in the square by the lower forum. Forty lashes should be enough. She can watch, then be dragged to the Saint Magdalena's church in the port area to be baptised and dispatched immediately to a convent."

"What will be the charge?"

"Does it matter? They are Jews."

"True, very true. If this is the way you would like to proceed, count on me to do all I can to help, though I can't help thinking that it would be a waste. You would lose the rest of your loan. I'm sure he hasn't got the amount of money that you are asking for and he must be in negotiations to acquire it. Thus, if he should die or be too severely injured, you may find yourself out of pocket. Her? Well, there's sport there for another day."

The calming down bishop saw the logic in what his friend was counselling. It would be longer, and more painful for a Jew to lose all of his money. It was well known that the Jews don't feel pain the way a Christian does. To prove that, one need go no further than the fact that while being burned at the stake, the Jew often refuses the help of Our Lord, despite the fact that they had, in theory, been converted, and were being burned as a heretic, not a Jew. Decided; demanding the rest of the money would be more satisfying.

"I believe that your advice is sound, my dear friend. Furthermore, tomorrow will be a busy day as Cecilius is due back from Gerunda"

"Cecilius travelling to and from Gerunda, why ever would he do that? I don't think he has left Dertosa more than a handful of times in the last twenty years and never farther than coming here."

Cyprianus didn't realise his error until too late. Flustered again, with a bit of inconsequential hand waving he muttered something about an ecumenical conference.

"What! Without the most important bishop in Tarraconensis?"

More fobbing and muttering wasn't shaking the duke off his tail.

"Cyprianus, is this about rebellion? Some rumours have come to the palace in the last few weeks which I gave little credence to. There's always a plot a foot in Toletum, but not here! Tell me what you know."

*

"The men are tired, General."

Marcus, himself looking haggard, not like his youthful, energetic self, reported the obvious. They had expected an attack during the night. The watch was four men alternating every three hours. The result was that nobody had actually got any decent sleep. Yesterday's village-found-leftovers were served for breakfast, again, eaten sullenly in shifts. Camp fires could be seen in the middle distance, quite a number of them, quite a few more than yesterday. They were gathering. Even if they had only half a dozen around each fire, they would have more than enough men to overwhelm the small force despite their well chosen defensive position. The gorge entrance allowed four or five men, at the very most, to stand abreast, which meant that the defenders would have a shield wall of four deep with replacements available. The result of which would be bloody, very bloody. The attackers would lose, at the very least, double the number of men that they might be able to kill in an attack. Perhaps it was that prospect that made the enemy hesitate, even though their inevitable victory was assured.

Flavius had asked for volunteers for this mission, explaining its complexity and likely outcome to all beforehand. It was most gratifying that a selection had to be made as so many men were prepared to follow him. La crème de la crème were chosen, as well as some enthusiastic out and out killers like Caius. He was an animal, but you wanted him as your animal, not somebody else's. All in all, they were the best, most experienced fighting force that the kingdom could field, well, not quite field, more like stick between two massive rock cliffs.

Tiredness affected all though. Perhaps that's what the enemy was awaiting for; an easier fight against already exhausted men.

Strangely, there had been no taunting. No displays of individual bravado, silly faces and predictions of the dire fate that awaited the losers, in fact, no individual appearance whatsoever. A fact considered most unusual by the experienced hands.

Those women who had been kept alive were trussed up at the back of the cave, no longer used for sport as nobody had the extra energy. They huddled and whimpered for communal comfort as they knew that their fate would be sealed shortly, either lifelong slavery, or hope against hope, a return to …not their men, children or village, that had all been destroyed in front of their eyes, but maybe, to a *normal* life with distant relatives in other villages. Nothing would ever be normal again. The future looked bleak or bleaker. However, none could afford the luxury of looking forward, no-one wanted to look back, tear ducts were too dry and empty to cry for the present. All they could do was hold each other, they were the only ones they had, the only ones who would or could understand the pain and suffering that they had had to endure in the last couple of … days? This eternity of hell.

"When do you think they will attack? This waiting is the worst. I would like it all to be over one way or another. I can't stand the waiting."

"Marcus, don't speak like that, and NEVER show these sorts of emotions in front of the men. Patience isn't just a virtue in this case. Their inactivity is a godsend, a potential lifeline. We have to transmit that to the men. The more time they dawdle, the better. It gives the army time to ready itself and come to our salvation."

"Actually, I would have thought that we would have heard something from the main force by now. Our signal fire has been burning night and day, and the only thing it has attracted is a hundred more enemy cooking fires."

This was the same thought that wouldn't leave Flavius' mind. Where were they? The main force had to remain hidden, that was part of the plan, as was the communication of their presence in the area by pigeon or human messenger. Something had gone awry. Had they been sacrificed by design or ineptitude?

Kunimund was an excellent commander, Flavius counted him among his friends, not enemies. His cautionary approach to warfare was the stuff of legend; battle was never sought, only enjoined when victory was all but certain, he was a true disciple of Hermenguild. This respectable approach was extremely popular among the men he led. Lives were not wasted. Fighting for Kunimund meant victories, wealth and life. None of this made Flavius feel any better or secure about his timely arrival though.

Marcus on the other hand was another worry. He wasn't showing any traits of a leader; fretting, voiced negative thoughts, wandering around camp as if he had the world on his shoulders. His whole persona and demeanour was inappropriate of an official. This was excusable due to his youth and lack of experience, but it could not be allowed to continue. Thinking defeat was a contagious disease that would undermine moral and discipline much more effectively than any superior enemy.

There was no way of ordering or shouting this approach into a junior officer. They had to be led by example. To this end, Flavius purposely set about the camp jovially passing time, sharing jokes and relating sexual exploits at all the different campfire shifts. He gave the impression of never sleeping and was always on hand for consultation and advice. Marcus did see this, realising that it was his role as well. He really did envy Flavius and so wanted to try to emulate him. Much as he tried though, his bon joie never lasted long. The lively step and quick witted remark with a constant smile was replaced by a sag of the shoulder, a drag of the foot and an unappealing scowl. This was compounded by any time he spent with the girl. He had found this out on his last visit, which was kept brief, as she made it clear that his presence was not welcome. He had led her to be with the others tied together at the back of a cave.

"They are coming!" a yell from the watchers was heard, spurring all to put on what body protection they had, pick up their trusted shield, razor sharp sword and any spear that was handy. There were lots of those left over from the village armaments.

*

"Welcome, brother. Please take a seat. When did you get back?"
"Thank you, Jacob." Lowering himself into a chair, Isaac gave off an exhausted defeated air. "It was a long, arduous and disturbing journey."
"So bad? You do that trip at least a couple of times a year. Are you getting old, little brother?"
"I am, I most definitely am."
"Uncle, you look terrible." Rebecca brought her disquieting brand of honesty into the room.
"I really should visit this house more often. It's so *uplifting* being here. Such pleasantries and kind statements are hard to take. Sometimes, I wonder whether all these compliments are being used to hide something bad you are reluctant to say!"
"I'm always getting into trouble these days for telling the truth. The same thing happened with .." She realised she had said what she didn't intend to say.
"With who, daughter?"
"No, nothing, it's always happening, that's all."
" Evidently, you are hiding something. Once you have brought your uncle some refreshment, we will get to the bottom of it."
Rebecca busied her way out hoping that her bottom didn't actually appear in her tale. She all but ran as she didn't want to miss anything Isaac had to say.
"Is business worse than we suspected?"
"This Christian ban is not helping trade. Some are not prepared to be seen doing business with us anymore. They do, it's just they don't want to be seen, which makes things more difficult *and* expensive. Insurmountable it hasn't become yet, though the trend is there."
"I brought you ale. I forgot to ask you what you wanted." Rebecca had broken all previous records of getting to the kitchen and back.
"Thank you, that's most kind and quick of you."
Handing him the cup which had obviously slopped over the side "Always keen to hear my favourite uncle."
"Rebecca, we are talking business, you really don't need to be present."
"Papa, we've had.."
"Let her stay, Jacob. What I have to say isn't just about business. It's something that will affect us all, we need to be prepared, so, better she

hears it firsthand today rather than a distorted market version in a few days time."

"That bad?" Jacob took up his chair and Rebecca moved into her faithful dog role.

"I'm afraid it is. You know that my trip to Gerunda was planned. Perhaps what you didn't know was that rabbi Saul asked me to do him a favour while I was there. In his stead, I attended a meeting of a great number of the rabbis in the area."

"Becoming religious, are you now, brother? Fancy a change of profession?"

"I wish it were that simple. There were rabbis from all the towns from Narbo to Dertosa, the only non rabbis were me and some bloke from somewhere in the south, Betica, I think he said. His name was Ariel, or was that David? I can't remember, there were so many new faces, they all had names, and everyone wanted to speak. This whatever his name was, gave us a report on what he had seen on his business trip throughout the kingdom."

Isaac took along slurp of ale, going on to relate the dire state of Jewry under the Goth rule.

"You're saying that things are getting much worse and it's coming our way?"

"That was the nub of what *he* was saying, yes."

Rebecca moved from listening mode, "We can't be passive. We need to do *something*."

"Daughter, what can we do? They have the power."

"Let me finish my story ,and you will see that the very same point was raised there by the rabbi from, Narbo I think. He may have been the Ariel."

After finishing, Rebecca looked vindicated, so much so, she felt she had to move to the same height as the other participants. She pulled a chair so she was in the middle of the brothers.

"I see nothing but disaster, and yet more sorrow for our people." Jacob, hearing the furniture moving, kept his head down shaking it in a slow lament.

"Papa, what should we do? Convert? The bishop was proposing to baptise me when I went there."

Jacob's head shot up. "You told me that everything went very smoothly, no problems, money delivered. You said you were in and out because the duke was just arriving."

Yet another error. Rebecca promised herself that she would try to think before speaking in the future.

"No, there weren't any problems, honest, Papa."

"Rebecca!"

"Well, he sort of thought that he ought to save my soul. His Christian duty or something like that. The duke facilitated my exit. He was actually quite funny."

"Rebecca!"

"Papa, you are getting repetitious. I really do know my name. *Nothing* happened!

Uncle Isaac, tell us more about this inter-Christian trouble and who is asking for our help."

"Exactly the question I asked. From what I understand , Tarraconensis/Gallia Gothica feel marginalised from decision making, which, as we all know, has become centralised in previously unheard of proportions in Toletum. The bishops and barons down there want to rule. They're inextricably; I think that was the word that was used, moving away from the traditional Goth practices of first among equals, to an authoritarian central power. The bigwigs here are seething and want to do something."

"Are they proposing a new kingdom separate from Toletum? Or fighting to take over the present kingdom?"

"Good question, Rebecca, and one which is fundamental to our participation, I feel.

From what Narbo said, the objective is to break away, not usurp, or replace. If that is true, then our role could be crucial, and decisive, as we have both money and people."

"And, hopefully," she shot a quick look at her father, "a desire to fight. Fight for something, not against. Imagine a safe state for us Jews. All the others from the kingdom would rush to join us. This is really exciting."

"Disaster. That's what is going to happen."

*

"What's the word from the scouts, general?"

Alaric set out a most unpromising panorama. He explained that the Vascones were camped a couple of miles away. The only way to get there would be through a narrow ravine. Beyond the enemy camp was a tiny gorge which boasted a dead end and the twenty defending Goths. The only good news was that access for the attack was via a tiny mountain path, no more than four men wide.

"How large is the enemy force?"

"The scouts estimate, never easy in these situations when the primary objective is not to be seen, at about the same number as us. It is important to put into that calculation that they are men who will fight, whereas all our forces are fighting men, which is a significant difference when push comes to shove."

"Thank you, Alaric. The trouble is that we will not be fighting in formation in these hills. Our superior training will count for less when it's not two forces meeting on the field of battle."

"True, Sire."

A thinking silence reigned.

"I believe that we are both thinking the same thing, aren't we?"

"Yes Sire, and General Kunimund would have saved us the thinking time by telling us so."

Wamba laughed.

"Actually, I think he would have taken us one step back by pointing out that we should never have been in this position in the first place!"

It was Alaric's turn to laugh.

"So, skipping the absent general's reproach, the correct logical thing to do would be to lay our troops behind these rocks, wait for the victoriously happy, returning enemy and ambush them here. Alaric, you and I would enter the annals of Goth military history as the leaders who lay to waste the pride of the Vasconis nation."

Alaric was nodding unenthusiastically in agreement.

"Do I detect a reluctance to write your name in history, general?"

"No, Sire.."

"But.."

"Condemning comrades to death, even for the greater good, doesn't sit well with me. Especially, as in this case, I know and appreciate every one of those men who volunteered for a risky mission, not a suicidal one. General Paulus may be impetuous, but he is also brave. It was his unorthodoxy that saved us in the last battle. If it weren't for him, we wouldn't be here discussing his fate. Somehow, to me, it feels wrong, though logically the plan you have outlined is superb with the guarantee of a war changing massacre."

Wamba took in the earnest words and sincere face in front of him. He felt exactly the same, the problem being that he was king, the overall commander, whose job it was to consider the bigger picture. Would the valiant death of twenty-two be that high a price to pay for striking a decisive blow in bringing this war to an end? Surely Paulus would both accept and understand the sacrifice he was being asked to make.

"A right royal pickle, eh?"

Despite himself and the situation Alaric couldn't help but snigger.

"I reckon the best place to wait, would be just up there. As they turn the bend, there would be no chance of them seeing us. We could hit them from right, left and perhaps even behind, if we leave a smaller force farther down the valley."

The King surveyed the scene. "Excellent. Let's deploy. Send a messenger back to Kunimund explaining where we are and what we are about to do.

Not even he could fault our strategy. We'll need scouts closer to the beginning of the valley to tell us when they are about to arrive. I believe we will have some time. How long do you think it'll take them to, er, defeat Paulus?"

"It depends, Sire. From what we know they cannot just send in numbers, they would just get in each other's way. Waves would be what we would do in this sort of situation. The first group go in hard for a very short period of time, retreat, second wave again with equal force, retreat and so on. The strength of the defenders will sap quickly and by the tenth or eleventh wave, the wall will begin to fold. It could be a matter of an hour after the assault starts."

"So, we should just wait?"

"There is the possibility of sending a small group of soldiers to the enemy rear to harry and distract them which would only delay the inevitable and probably alert them to the possibility of our presence."

"So be it. We wait.

*

The bishop sat. Today hadn't gone well at all. Just as he got his hands on that floozy Jewess, oh, the buttock felt heavenly, firm and round, the duke's appearance spoilt it. He had spoken far too much afterwards, found himself in such a sticky situation, so much so, that he felt he'd trodden in jam and couldn't clean his sandals.

"Ranosindus, I tell you the truth when I say I know next to nothing about what is afoot."

"So, there is something."

"It is not in my nature to speculate. Experience has taught me that nought good comes from that. I will tell you what I know for certain to be true."

"I would ask no more than that from an honourable man of the cloth as yourself."

"Well, Cecilius passed by here for rest and refreshment on his way to Gerunda. He, as a matter of courtesy, informed me that there was a gathering of bishops to talk about our the increasing isolation."

"There's nothing new in that. We here in Tarraco are treated shockingly. As if that provincial town of Toletum could ever compete with the architectural majesty and history of Roman Iberia. And Cecilius has never really given up the old faith, an Arian till his death, that one. What makes this meeting different?"

"Well, from what I understand it, I have not been told, and I really do not know for certain, however, I believe armed insurrection is being mooted."

"What! Why haven't I been told?"

*

"Much as we feared, it's a wave formation General."

"Wedged or straight?"

Marcus checked yet again. "Straight."

General Paulus raised his voice, "You all know what is going to happen at the start of this fight. Play your role, dispatch the enemy with speed. To be victorious we need to be unified. Shield wall!"

The attackers were already set up in shield walls two deep; the idea being, shallow fast engagement, followed by a retreat and replacement. Marcus, whose contribution was not needed, made sure that they were matched like for like. Stealthily the wall marched tidily forward grunting each pace. The first sword blows hit the defenders' shields without being met by a corresponding reply, then as the second strike was about to hit, the shields parted, allowing the surprised attackers through. Immediately the defenders moved beyond the attackers to reform leaving a whole number of literally behind enemy lines where in their confused disorientated state they were quickly set upon by Marcus and his grouping. Within seconds there were eight dead bodies on the floor.

Not realising what had happened to their comrades, the second wave attacked with exactly the same result. The third wave was about to follow suit until it was halted by a rock stood commander who had a higher perspective. Nevertheless, all they could do was watch as the Goth frontline, without a bloodied sword among them, fell back behind a dozen or so corpses, which were earnestly being piled by Marcus' section to form a defensive barrier two bodies deep and two high.

The scenery had changed. The Goths had moved back twenty paces leaving various dead bleeding bodies and a low human flesh wall. The next attack would have to come over their dead bodies.

The attack was halted. The warriors retreated for consultations and a tactical review. Marcus was ecstatic. *His* plan had worked a treat. All those not in the frontline keeping a wary eye out, congratulated him, except Caius, who had made a point of turning his back and clearing his throat in noisy glob which he spat less than delicately on one of the dead bodies. Flavius had told everyone in the briefing that the tactics had been chosen by their new young officer. At the time they had complained about the couple of hours of practice that they had put in, now, nobody minded that "wasted" energy.

They had bought themselves more time.

Flavius indicated that Marcus should disentangle himself from his "fans" and follow him. When they were a good distance behind the battle site, Flavius handed over a scrap of cloth. Marcus read;

Rescue not possible

"It arrived by pigeon. We're on our own."

"But your plan was simple and good. Why has it changed? We're doing well. Why are we being sacrificed?"

"Your guess is as good as mine. Don't tell the men, yet. And if you have any more of those tactics from previous battles you have studied, don't keep them to yourself." He smiled indulgently, adding, " I don't think we'll be attacked again today. I suppose they will come at us with sheer force of numbers tomorrow, accepting any, and all the casualties that they have to. For the moment, take it easy."

It was, as predicted, a quiet afternoon and evening. Nothing except the rank smell of dead bodies changed.

*

"Isaac, I'm worried. No, I am very worried."

"We all are, brother, these are trying times. The fate of our brethren and the whole of Judaism in this country is in doubt. I didn't understand a lot of what the rabbis were saying, everyone was speaking, many at the same time and everyone knew more than me about the topic, referencing it to the historical events I'd never heard of, and then outlining the future consequences of us making a decision, or, conversely not making one. It was really terribly difficult to understand their finer points of, if this happened, then this other thing would. And some of the accents! It was hard to believe that they were speaking Latin, especially that man from the south, David, or was it Ariel? My memory is definitely going. Dreadful, hardly pronounced any part of the word, it would have been easier for me, if he had written it down in Hebrew. Still, despite my failings as a representative, this is an enormous and unwanted responsibility that has been given to our family, something as simple traders, we are not used to. Yes, brother, I do understand your preoccupation. Anyway, I have to be off now as Trudy awaits."

"I'll see you out."

"No, Rebecca, let me walk with my brother."

Jacob felt a stab of guilt, truth be known the macro scheme of politico-religious events was not what was uppermost in his mind. Instead his thoughts revolved around just one thing, or better said, person; Rebecca. Sending her to deliver the first instalment was not his idea, she had insisted. The capitulation to her, was just the latest of a long, long line. Was she spoilt as vox populous would have it? Of course she was. If there was anything, besides love, that characterized their relationship it was his constant caving into to any of her whims, or convictions. It couldn't be helped. His firmness of conviction was forever undermined by her coaxing, wheedling and outright manipulation. Until recently, he was quite proud of the woman that she had become. Now, she was in trouble and his neglect of authority was to blame.

It was well known that the bishop had a roving eye. "Lock up your daughters" was a warning that oft precipitated his arrival in an area, some even went to the extent of adding wives to the advice. His power was immense. Force was never resorted to. It wasn't necessary, as most Christians were all too willing to help with the bishop's endeavours until they found out what it actually involved. Rumour had it, that many a young female had visited the palace to be *blessed*. Few spoke of the experience explicitly as they believed that their souls were in danger of eternal damnation if they revealed the secrets of their *blessing*. However, they did return to their families with a different air about them which was hard to describe as saintly.

The moment she had left with the money, he regretted it. Since then, he had done nothing but torment himself about what had happened, or what could have happened. The fact that she was Jewish and headstrong should have been enough to keep her safe even though it was acknowledged that she was a true beauty. No self-respecting bishop would want it known that he was *blessing* a Jewess, and Rebecca wasn't a girl who would have acquiesced willingly to Christian beliefs or *sainthood*. The possibility that the bishop would want to force her into conversion and baptism, had not occurred to him.

Why was he SO stupid?

To add yet more wood to the blaze, the duke had become involved as well. Any and every power that the bishop didn't posses, the other had. The two most important men in Tarraco were alone with his daughter, and he had allowed it to happen.

It was his duty to protect her from now on, but how?

"Has Trudy thought about anyone for marriage?"

"Jacob, what are you talking about? Here we are talking about the future of our religion and you want to know whether *my* wife is thinking about marriage to anyone else. Please, concentrate."

"No, not marriage for Trudy, for David."

"David? "

*

Various women had already been extracted from the trussed up group for *use* by the celebrating soldiers, so, it wasn't any surprise when Marcus yanked *his* unwilling one away.

It wasn't dragging, nor was it a light sprightly step. There was reluctance. Marcus suspected and hoped that it was for show. She couldn't be seen to be going willing in front of the other women.

Once out of sight, actually there wasn't that much space that could be described as anywhere resembling private, Marcus was heading for *their* tree, when she nudged him in another direction, towards a slight opening to another cave. After squeezing through the gap, they found themselves in a large cavernous area almost of church proportions.

"Impressive. Look at the way those rocks hang down!"

"Beautiful, isn't it? Aitziber loved rocks and caves. I tagged along not because I shared her passion, actually, often I found the spaces claustrophobic, but just to be with her." Her eyes had taken on a wistful air. "I miss her."

Still being at a complete loss at how to respond to all this emotional stuff and not to be tempted to stare at her body parts, he made out as if he was testing the strength of the rock by knocking on it.

She wandered up behind him.

"Why haven't you *fucked* me? Isn't that what conquering *heroes* are supposed to do to their prizes? It's certainly what is happening to the other girls. Nobody actually mentions anything, the blood and bruising are testimony enough, plus the fact that some never come back. Dorote's body was seen strangled after an encounter with that brute Caius. "

She was close, not touching distance, but close. Having this conversation without looking at each other was appropriate. She had been both relieved and confused by the actions of this boy in military uniform, who so obviously lusted after her. She certainly wasn't angling for any change in the situation, it was fine the way it was, she just wanted to know why.

Since reading the note and having come to the conclusion that death was imminent, he'd been reviewing his stance of leaving this world a virgin or a rapist. He would like to know what sex with someone else, was like. Would he find out if he forced her into it? This would be his last chance. He turned determined to act not speak. However, upon seeing her, he couldn't. Instead, he moved to a ledge to sit down. She followed and sat at his feet rather than at the same level, wanting to carry on with the candid non-eye contact conversation.

"I was taught that taking women against their will is not the lot of a gentleman. Being in a position of power which my father is, brings many benefits, one of which is that willing women are plentiful. Having a duke's son, even if he is illegitimate, is no bad thing, as it usually implies a meal ticket for life. I've seen how it works. These women are not official but they are not forced, either."

How much more should he say? She didn't encourage nor discourage.

"Today I was determined it would be different…"

From her submissive, seated position, she straightened her back defensively.

"So, you thought today I would happily open my legs for this important man who had helped destroy my village and way of life, in some sort of gratitude at him for not acting like an animal?" Her indignation was close to shrill.

"No!" he spoke slowly and firmly, "Firstly, I would like to know your name, mine is Marcus."

Surprised, defensively so, she almost automatically said, "Arantxa."

"Well, Arantxa, today I thought I would actually go through with the idea of forcing you!"

She deflated physically and mentally, her defiance wilted. She had, in some way, come to think that she was sort of *safe* with him. In spite of all the provocation of rebellion and nakedness she had given, he had not raised his voice, nor struck her once. Both of those things she had suffered many times at the hand of her father and future husband. These new words came as a shock, how ridiculous was that? A scantily clad female prisoner alone with a warrior, shocked at his words.

"However, I don't think I can."

As she was hurt, she wanted to hurt back, "You are impotent, is that the problem?"

Now glaring into his eyes, she saw him wince. Good. Her aim was true. His hands moved to his face in some sort of distracting face rub, as his eyes closed. Little more than whispering, "No Arantxa, I don't think I am. I don't know for sure, the thing is, I am still a virgin."

The gasp that this produced was loud and profound.

Opening his eyes looking at nothing in the middle distance, he continued, "Today we had word that we will not be rescued. For whatever reason, the main army that was supposed to extract us from this baiting exercise, will not be arriving. This means that either tonight or tomorrow morning, we will be slaughtered by your kinfolk, who are massed in vast numbers just the other side of this gorge."

She searched his face. He didn't change, slowly explaining the way in which a teacher would to a slow student.

"My choice was, or is, to die a virgin, or to force someone, no, not someone, you, into an unknown act because it would be my last chance. I decided a couple of moments ago that I cannot do that. I hope that answers your original question as to why I haven't *fucked* you."

Of all the possible explanations that had gone through her head, this one had not occurred. It made her feel *tender* towards him. Not enough to want to change his virginal status at her expense, though.

Resuming her slump at his feet, the safe silence gave her time to reflect. Without a doubt, all men were animals; to call them pigs would be an insult to the animal. They functioned through power and brute force. Her father had beaten her and her sister for the slightest offence, sometimes she thought their only crime was that they were daughters not sons. They were never shown any respect by any men. They were there to be used; pack animals or breeding sows, in the village, or now, as playthings and sperm receptacles by the conquerors.

Aitziber was the only woman she had ever heard say a good thing about a man, look at all the sorrow and trouble that caused. One night, as they lay together in the hut, while her husband was off fighting, she whispered how happy she was. She recounted her experiences with the Roman. It seemed that she was floating in a surreal world of pleasure.

When the captured, *lucky* to still be alive, women were huddled together, no-one had talked about her personal raping, but a number had questioned what would happen to them if they were ever set free to return. The consensus was that they would be shunned, treated as pariahs, as if their received abuse had, in some way, been their fault. They would be the lowest of the low in the eyes of other women, and fair game to any sort of attack by a man, as they were already dirty by *giving* themselves to the enemy.

It was then an idea occurred to her. While Marcus was sullen, she weighed up the pros and cons of her proposal. She had something to offer, but she was not going to give it away for free. Her internal debate was how much she could demand in return.

Shockingly to him, his face was grasped in her two hands, she made him look at her. "Marcus, go and get your senior officer, the one who loved my sister. I want to have you both here to hear my offer."

Totally confused by this turn of events, he asked what she was proposing. Her reply was enigmatic, claiming that she could give both of them something they dearly wanted but it had to be together. Having heard of situations like this, Marcus was intrigued and a little excited.

"Be quick before I change my mind."

*

Duke Ranosindus was truly shocked. How could an armed insurrection be so far advanced in planning without his knowledge? His family was one of the most important in the kingdom, both now, and when they had crossed the Pyrenees hundreds of years ago. Admittedly, then they were under nominal command of Rome, however, in reality it was a force made up of primarily Goths, with some other smaller Barbarian tribes represented, that dominated some parts of the command. This didn't detract from the fact that Rome was the all-encompassing power in those days, which was ironic, as practically the only ethnic grouping that was missing, and they were conspicuous by their absence, were the Romans themselves.

It had got to the stage when Romans were particularly good at squabbling among themselves, with anyone and everyone calling themselves Emperor, whether they held sway in Rome itself, or massed armies in any part of the empire. Most of Iberia, one of the jewels of the empire, had gradually been lost to the Vandals, Suevi and Alani who had crossed the Pyrenees, then with considerable ease dominated and settled in Roman Iberia.

Duke Ranosindus could trace his family back to the repopulating and re-conquest of Gallia Gothica, after the initial defeat of the Visigoths by the Franks. This was a low in Visigoth history, when they were all but destroyed and wiped out by a superior, better organised Frank force. As part of the reinforcements sent to help their kinsmen by the Ostrogoths, his family had played a major role in reuniting Goths and re-entering the Iberian Peninsula. Since then, his family had controlled what was the most important area, town and port, Tarraco. Nearly two hundred years of history. kings had come and gone. None of these kings lasted more than a decade or so, until there was an excuse for an assassination or overthrow, and yet another election to replace him. His family never sought, or had the highest office, thrust upon them. Their area was safe, secure and prosperous.

Over the last century though there had been a steady ebbing of power and influence away from all that had been the norm. The centre had shifted to Toletum. Since the shift from Arianism to Catholicism, the influence and power of the bishops had risen with the corresponding decrease wielded by the dukes and barons, traditionally the only source of power in the nation. It was the clergy who now held sway in the election of the king. In all but name the kingdom had become a theocracy. Bishops like Julian, a man with no historical roots in the nation of Goth, made the decisions of state which the, now, lowly barons, were expected to implement and support. This extended to providing armed forces, paid for by the barons not the Church, when necessary, which left the Church to carry accumulating land, wealth and power for itself.

All in all, Tarraco and his family were a shadow of what they had been. His stock in terms of land and commerce had diminished as well. The port, once the door and corridor to the nation, and the world, did less trade each year. Gone were the days when ships would queue to enter the harbour bringing luxurious goods for the east and taking back the immense wealth of the kingdom. The population of the city, once significant, thriving and dynamic, was diminishing. People were moving back to live off the land, or work for others with land. The urban dwellers were now restricted to basically two parts of the city.

All of this decline could and should be stopped and reversed in Ranosindus's opinion. However, while the small-minded insular power remained in Toletum, this was never going to happen. Their self aggrandisement and navel gazing, revolved around an ever changing different bottom on the throne, a throne! Goths had never had such ridiculous adornments in the good old days, and the continual persecution of Jews, a necessary internal enemy.

If a new outlook was impossible, then a new state could be the answer. His views were well known, so why had he been excluded from this movement of reassertion?

"Who is actually behind this insurrection?"

Cyprianus, still flustered by the day's happenings, shook his head slowly. "I honestly don't know. I feel excluded."

"Well, I intend to find out. If you hear anything please let me know as soon as it happens." With that, the duke gathered up his things and all but rushed through the door accidently knocking the door-listener backwards. "Cyprianus, invite Maria in next time. It must be uncomfortable to be crouched in a draft for such a long time!"

*

The officers arrived slightly out of breath. Marcus had convinced Flavius to come only by stating that the girl was Aitziber's sister, and wanted to give them something before their imminent deaths. Flavius imagined that the sisters had shared information and there would be a message from the dead, whereas Marcus imagined an altogether different scenario.

She stood as they entered. While they were away, her internal debate was raging; should she or shouldn't she? Would it be the ultimate act of betrayal or just taking advantage of a gods given opportunity? The only thing that she was sure of, was that, after, it would be others who pronounced judgement on her decision. Whatever her arguments, opinions and conscience would never be factored into the equation of whether what she was about to do was good or bad.

Flavius was not an inexperienced boy, he was a man. He looked her up and down, if she had been a horse, she would have fully expected to have her teeth inspected. There was no blushing or stuttering, just the eye of an appreciative audience. This emboldened her as well, she covered nothing, bearing all proudly.

"Without a doubt you certainly look like her."

"Sadly for you, I am not her, nor her replacement."

"You speak like her as well."

"My offer has nothing to do with what you see. I am prepared to save your lives."

"Shall we sit? I was, and am, not the slightest bit interested in a replacement or substitute. Aitziber was unique and will forever be so." When the girl started a long story about sisters and a dog, Marcus was confused and lost quite a bit of interest, in fact at one point he stopped listening. This was not heading in the direction he had imagined.

"…it was in this very cave we followed the stupid hound. It loved the game, and didn't want to be caught, but kept us close enough to make it interesting for him."

That was it? Thankfully Marcus hadn't been listening to such little girl drivel. Guilt was his overriding feeling now, he had pushed his commanding officer, who had at least a million other more important things to do, into a cave to hear a shaggy dog story from a young girl. He opened his mouth to speak but was beaten to it.

"So, from what I understand from this convoluted tale, is that this cave has another exit."

"Precisely. Not easy to find and very very narrow but I am prepared to be your guide…. for a price."

"Name it."

"No more assaults on the women. They are allowed to choose, either to stay, or follow. The ones that follow, will be set free, not sold into slavery."

"NO. They will alert their kinfolk, and we will be captured in these tunnels."

"I'm not sure how many will decide to stay, their futures will not be good back in the village. I agree, they will have to be bound, not as a security risk to you, but for their own safety. If they were perceived to be complicit in this venture, their lives will be worth nothing. If they are seen to have not collaborated, then, their lives might be somewhat better."

"Agreed. What else?"

Unsure whether her resolve stretched this far, she hesitated, "I want one life."

"What?"

"I demand the death of one of your number."

"Negotiation over. I cannot forfeit the life of anyone under my command. They are *my* men, My job is to ensure the safety of them all. What we could do, is force you to tell us where this exit is."

"Try." Her arms folded with all the determination she could muster.

"How about if I brought the other women in here, one at a time, and slit their throats until you reconsidered?"

"My sister could never have loved a man who was capable of such an action. Furthermore, our futures are shit, or really shit, you may, actually, be doing us all a favour. That's certainly what I would tell each woman you brought in!"

Flavius was taken aback by the matter of fact way in which she said this. There was no spit or venom, just as two plus two equalled four, this is what would happen.

Reluctantly he asked the question, "Whose life?"

" I believe, they called him, Caius. He sliced babies in two, tortured old women, brutalised and murdered young women. I cannot save that man's life."

"Marcus, a word."

The men moved towards the opening and started whispering.

"I can't agree to this."

"I have been talking to her for days now. I *know* that you won't be able to force her to tell you the way out."

"She certainly looks like her sister, if she's anything like her in character, I am inclined to agree with you."

"The man *is* subhuman."

"If you are in a tight spot, you will want that *subhuman* by your side. It's men like him who win wars. He's universally hated by all the others, but not one would like to be without him."

"It's twenty lives against one."

"Marcus be serious, what is your /her proposal? Should we tell him, appealing to his better nature by saying that his sacrifice would be for the good of the kingdom or something similar? Should we slit his throat while he's sleeping? Challenge him to armed combat?"

Marcus remained quiet. The two of them were in deep thought and didn't notice that the girl had joined them.

"Is the morality, or the logistics, the problem?"

They chimed together "Both."

"I have a proposal. My sister said something about you being Greek, is that true?"

Flavius nodded.

Turning to the younger officer she asserted, with knowledge he didn't know she had, that all his antecedents must have been Roman. "Both from ancient cultures who believed in many gods. These days you both believe in just one God, but you still have some customs and laws based in the old ways. You Goths still have trial by ordeal. Why not submit the pig to that?"

"How can we..?"

"I will be the ordeal. Leave me a dagger. Tell him you have finished with me, and it's his turn. Whoever emerges will be your destiny."

*

"David, that chap I couldn't understand from the south? Why would Trudy be worrying about his marriage prospects? She doesn't know him. None of us do.

Sometimes, Jacob…"

"No, not that David, your David."

"My David? Oh you mean *my* David. Marriage? He's too young yet. Plenty of time for that."

After hearing the men speaking conspiratorially in the distance Rebecca took it upon herself to get somewhat closer. She was making a habit of listening in to men's conversations. Once within hearing distance, her ears picked up.

"It may solve a whole number of problems."

"Jacob, I'm finding it incredibly difficult to follow you today. How can David solve the problem of kings, rebellion and Jewish persecution by marriage, when he's only fifteen?"

"Brother, we are thinking along parallel lines. You have the affairs of state in mind, I have the state of affairs in my house."

"You are not making yourself much clearer."

Leaning forward and in almost a whisper he mouthed "Rebecca"

"Rebecca!"

"Ssshh, she will hear. I am worried about her. This thing with the bishop and the duke is a looming disaster for all of us in the family. She needs to be removed from it, physically, and emotionally. Her and David have always got on very well. It would be a way of bringing the business back together. The more I think about it, the better the idea becomes."

"They are first cousins. You know that that isn't allowed."

"It's happened before. If you could smooth the way by gently broaching it to Trudy …"

"And when might my opinion be sought!"

Rebecca had entered, standing in a defiant hands on hips pose she faced her father. Jacob looked guiltier than a child caught stealing honey from the pantry. Rallying, he found voice, "Rebecca, I am your father. My duty to you and your deceased mother, is to keep you safe."

"I am safe. By incestuously marrying me off to a little boy will not make me any safer. Sorry, uncle Isaac but David isn't.."

"Don't worry Rebecca, I agree with you entirely. I am not quite sure what has come over my big brother. I am sure that he hasn't thought it through. No one will agree to this merger. Not me, you, nor David, and God alone knows how Trudy will react. I wouldn't even want to be in the room, never mind be the broacher."

Crest-fallen Jacob was beginning to brim. Rebecca had never seen him cry, and didn't want to start now. She softened her stance, hands came off hips followed by a gradually lowering indignant tone .

"Papa, nothing bad is going to happen to me. We really need to concentrate on what is going to happen to us all. We are all in danger, and need to react decisively, which means politically, if necessary, with arms. Then, danger will be everywhere, and will not be solved by a marriage within the family."

*

The Count stomped around the room, his wont was not a gentle stroll stroking his chin in a contemplative manner, a man of action and noise was more his style. The hound by the fire eyed him suspiciously, it knew these moods all too well. The solid oak table shuddered as a cup was thumped down upon it with enormous force.

"Darling, could you please make a decision sooner rather than later, I do really like most of our furniture?" There was an almighty yelp as the big beast lollopped to comparative safety under a sideboard, pushing its nose out to check whether its master was approaching.

"And the hound is certainly not responsible for your indecisiveness. If you really must destroy something, I have always despised that side table that your mother had made for you. She claims it's beautifully carved and ornate, whereas, I think it's an eyesore that wouldn't look out of place in a brothel. Not that I have seen the inside of a brothel, nor for that matter been consulted on its furnishings..."

"Oh do stop your nattering will you, woman, I'm trying to.." The Count looked up to see the pained expression on his wife's face. "Ohh I'm sorry, I didn't mean to be quite so harsh, but I AM trying to make a decision which will affect all of our lives greatly."

Her face softened, she put down her embroidery and glided over to where he was stood with the rustling of her elegant gown, the only sound. With a gentle, loving stroke of his bristly face she spoke in a calm smoothing voice. "*I* know how much you are suffering. The dog doesn't."

Stung into action, the Count headed to the sideboard. The hound was wary, unsure whether to run or accept the consequences of whatever it had done to upset the master. It cringed as a hand moved towards its head, and was delighted when a stroke not a hit came its way.

"Sorry, boy."

Relieved, the animal crawled out and nuzzled the crouching figure, who in turn responded scratching it in its favourite place just behind the ears.

"What do you think, boy, should I lead this rebellion?"

"That's interesting. You kick the dog and then ask it for advice. Do I have to be kicked before you consult me?"

Looking round from his squatting position, he realized that his behaviour today had been less than exemplary towards those closest to him. Thankfully, his daughter was not around.

"I know you have sought the opinion of Geberic as head of your household, and I'm sure he was the right person to ask about relative troop strength, horses and the like. However, as you mentioned earlier, the decision you make will affect greatly my future and that of my daughter. Although I am not suggesting that you should act upon whatever we think, it would be nice to at least be allowed to make some sort of contribution towards our destiny."

Evidently it wasn't just today that his behaviour had been amiss, he straightened and joined her standing by the ugly table. His anger had dissipated, remorse held sway.

"Chlodoswintha, I am truly troubled."

"That much is abundantly clear. Ask the dog." On cue the animal smuggled its head into his master's crotch.

"I am, and always have been decisive. Not always making the correct decisions, but decisions were always made, be it in the heat of battle, or on crop rotation on the estate."

"Heat of battle? You haven't even put armour on in the last decade!"

"Untrue. What about when we drove the Franks back over the border?"

"That was a skirmish with a sheep raiding party, hardly a battle."

"Chloda, you are really NOT helping here, and you wonder why I don't consult you about things!"

"Sorry, husband," as contritely as possible she added, "please continue. I won't interrupt again" Pulling the meekest face she could, she returned to her seat to find the most demure and attentive pose.

"Good position. I almost believe you."

The dog removed its nose to see what all the movement was about and decided that a better position would be lying at the mistress' feet.

"See, we are both listening and waiting for more battlefield stories."

This made the Count laugh as he moved over to cuff her gently on the side of the head while lowering himself to perch on the arm of her chair. This playful violence made the dog open a watchful, slightly perturbed eye.

"To have a loyal supportive attentive submissive wife is a great thing. I do wish I had one!"

This produced a gentle slap and an ear to ear smirk. The dog had both eyes open and readied itself.

Taking the slapping hand, he held it in both of his.

"The thing is that there will be plenty of these battlefield anecdotes, if I do decide to lead the revolt. What is not so clear, is the ending, will we all live happily ever after or … not?"

"Hilderic, whatever decision you come to, you will always be my king, with or without escapades in armour. If you think that we have a strong probability of winning, then, to tell you the truth, I wouldn't mind too much being called Queen Chlodoswintha. It has such a lovely ring to it, don't you think?"

*

"I hear you have tired of boys and would like a real man." After struggling to get through the cave opening, he swaggered across towards where she was waiting. Playing the visual plan in her head for the umpteenth time, not saying a word, she enticed him to a rock behind which the dagger was hidden.

The slap came in with immense speed and accuracy, smack across the face, she hadn't even seen the slightest hand movement. The next thing she felt rather than saw as well, was the tearing off of the rags that had scarcely covered her body.

"Better. Now I can see what I am getting, a bit skinny for my tastes." Feeling, instead of seeing, his hand movements was becoming a norm. "Call these tits! I've seen young goats with bigger and better." It was a backhand not meant to brush but to bruise. It hurt. It really hurt. The scream in her throat, she managed to stifle with just an expulsion of breath.

"No noise eh? You think you are a tough one. Don't worry, I promise you that noise will come."

Her resilience was wilting. The plan didn't involve this. It was supposed to be her playing tease, and finally stabbing him. His control was absolute. A slight movement towards the rock brought another crashing blow which literally knocked her off her feet. Sprawled on the floor, she could see his penis beginning to swell. Evidently this, not her nakedness, was what excited him. Wondering whether fighting back or being passive would make him more pliable, was interrupted by another loud whooshing sound coming involuntarily out of her, as his foot sunk into her belly.

Pride comes before a fall, breathless, she realised she had overestimated herself, and underestimated him. This was going to be a long and painful death. She was sure she would not be left alive, her body would be found in a similar state to Dorote.

"Get up girl, I didn't say you could lie yet." With a strong grip of a bunch of hair, she was yanked with so much force that her feet left the floor. Then pulled close to him, she could feel his, what felt like, enormous penis, at full thickness.

A vision of Marcus passed quickly through her mind. She wasn't a virgin, and had seen a number of erections before, this one was a beast. In spite of herself, she laughed at the ridiculousness of the situation.

The noise infuriated him. God alone knew what he imagined she was laughing at because he didn't communicate it in words, choosing instead to thump hard with his free fist, then throw her by her held hair.

Landing face down on a rock outcrop, she was ordered to stay there, and open her legs. She heard his sword belt fall to the floor with a clang, followed by his menacing steps.

Judging him to be no closer than a couple of steps behind her, she spun dagger in hand, to slice the most outstanding feature closest to her.

His face registered the shock at about the same time as the throbbing blood hit the rock ceiling. Torn between stemming the flow, and grabbing at her, he chose the former.

"Bitch! I'm going to kill you."

Severed private part grasped in one hand, he reached for the sword on the floor.

Arantxa recovering from the shock of doing something she had not intended, sprang into action kicking the sword farther away.

Scenes of life / death situations can be seen as comical, if you are not the one whose life is threatened. This would have been the case here, if there had been any audience. A badly-bleeding naked warrior was holding onto to life, and a prized body part with his right hand, while trying to catch a naked young woman who swung a dagger at him whenever he got close. A most peculiar dance. Fortunately, for the female, the dance floor was large, affording space for manoeuvre and avoidance. The amount of blood loss was copious, squirting through his fisted hands, it covered quite a lot of the ground, and it was on this slippery sticky surface that Arantxa came a cropper. For a big man with half a penis and massive blood loss, he pounced with considerable agility, pinning her down. His free hand was enormous, in fact, both were. This one was easily big enough to hold her small white throat. She started struggling to breathe as his bad breath was emitted with a smile.

In Marcus's armaments training, his tutor stressed every day, to the point of complete annoyance, that when fighting one should always know and predict where the opponent's weapon was. Poor soldiers never had personal tutors, their trade was picked up on the job, as it were. This was much to Caius's regret, as he felt the dagger piercing his chest with his own weight as he flopped onto the girl. The strength in his hand began to wilt.

*

"Do come in, your Grace, the duke awaits you in the dining room."
Amalaswinth was in her best obsequious mode, her bow giving her
creaking back more than a bit of grief which she stoically accepted as
God's price for her life on this earth, and her entry into the next. Being
respectful and doing everything possible to make God's representatives
happy, certainly earned her more points for the celestial chamber. "If
there's anything you want or need, I would be most honoured to get it for
you."

Even Cecilius, who was used to people grovelling in front of him, found
this display completely over the top.

"No, no, I'm sure that Duke Ranosindus has everything under control."
Cecilius's age and frame didn't lend itself to marching haughtily away, at
best, what he achieved was no more than a dignified shuffle.

How he loved this palace. Even in its dilapidated state, it was
magnificent. It must have looked quite something in its heyday. It crossed
his mind that perhaps that was what the housekeeper might be thinking
about him.

"My dear duke, most kind of you to invite me to your hospitality." They
clasped hands and luke-warmly embraced. "How you knew I was here, is
something of a mystery, as I arrived late this morning and I am due to
leave at the crack of dawn tomorrow."

"It is my good fortune to be able to have you here. I do thank you for
coming."

Actually, Cecilius had been given little choice in the matter having been,
if not ordered, at least chivvied by the captain of the town guard, in the
direction of the palace.

"And, I must assure you that the pleasure is mine to be able to sup with
you this evening. It is a matter of common knowledge that the fare served
here rates as the best in the province."

"Most kind of you to say, and for you, to be my guest."

"Do we not dine alone? I see the table is set for three."

"I have sent word for Cyprianus to join us. As there was an abundance of
excellent fish in the market this morning, my housekeeper got a little
carried away and bought what seems and smells like half of the Mare
Nostrum, I thought there would be plenty to go around."

The reality of the situation was that Amalaswinth had been in the process
of buying a small amount of mackerel, when she eyed Rebecca joining
the back of the queue. The bitch wouldn't eat decent fish today she swore
to herself. To the fishmonger's confusion she dramatically increased her
order calculating that nothing of any consequence or quality would be left
by the time it came around to the Jewess' turn.

"I'm sure that my fellow Bishop will be delighted when he hears." They
shared a sly smirk while a glass of wine was served.

"Delightful. Not often you get wine like this these days. Where is it from?"

"A boat from Sardinia docked yesterday. Sweet and refreshing I find."

"Soo sorry I am late but ..."

"Do sit, Cyprianus, before you fall. Really there was no need to hurry so, we would have waited. It's time you admitted to yourself that you are not the young athlete that you once were."

The legs of the chair didn't so much creak as scream. Sweat was pouring from the finely over-dressed clergyman. He had obviously put on his best for the occasion. The effect would have been impressive, if it weren't for the great puddles, and stains of body fluid decorating the elegant cloth. Doing his best to mop up as much as he could with a massive handkerchief, which a young child could easily have used as a bed sheet, he sighed, gratefully accepting the proffered drink.

"Ohh, quite nasty! I think this glass of wine might be off. Do you have anything else?"

Amalaswinth quickly replaced it with a mug of ale. Downing the contents in one caused yet more sweat to leak.

"Much better. I find some of this local wine a little, well, I'm not sure how to describe it, just not like we used to import in the good old days."

"That's exactly what Cecilius and I were just saying! It's most pleasing to have a man of such exquisite taste here to appreciate and share the finer things of life. I'm sure that you will enjoy and appreciate what my cook has been able to prepare in your honour."

"It's getting dark. I'll go in and find out what is happening."

"You have to let a trial by ordeal take its natural course. That's the Goth way."

"But sir, if we don't make a move, one way or another, then there will be no possibility of escape."

"True. All right, we'll both go. If you interrupt him by yourself, he's quite capable of turning on you and killing you."

What met their eyes upon entering the cave nosily, not wanting to take any one by surprise, was *unexpected*. Face down in an enormous pool of blood was a naked Caius, clearly dead, like a beached whale. The girl, though, was nowhere to be seen.

"Looks as if we've been cheated, clever girl. It never occurred to me that she would do that, escape by herself, and leave us to our fate."

Trying not to get his sandals too covered in blood, he approached the big man, "Let's turn him over."

One side was jammed fast against the rock so pushing wasn't an option. Pulling wouldn't be easy either. They positioned themselves, senior officer at the shoulder, lower ranks at the lower regions.

"One, two, three."

The scene that met them was not just *unexpected,* it was totally shocking. With the movement, the body's left arm thudded to the floor, revealing a tight fist. From the chest the hilt of a dagger could be seen. Farther down, there was only part of what normally should be there. The force of the movement of the sprawled arm had caused the fist to open, revealing the missing section. All of this they took in with little more than a blink of the eye, because Arantxa's unconscious naked body was there as well.

"She's still breathing."

Struggling gently, she wasn't particularly heavy, but neither was he that strong, Marcus managed to lift her body out of the mess, moving it to some dripping water near the back of the cave. Breathing heavily from the exertion, he cradled her head into his body. By cupping his hand to catch a few drops, he was able to rub some moisture around her lips. She began to stir.

"Good, we need her alive." Flavius had joined them, then looking back at his most feared soldier he said, "It seems to have been quite an ordeal!"

*

"That's the best I have eaten in a long time! Superb! Up in the north they have absolutely no idea what to do with fish. They have a theory that as long as it's not actually flopping around on the plate, then it is edible. The way this has been charred and delicately rolled in honey, gives it that sharp edge of flavours which contrast and compliment. Do pass on my congratulations to the chef."

"I certainly will, Cecilius. She was a slave I picked up in the market last year. From Asia minor somewhere. It was a good buy."

There were just a few well-sucked fish bones piled on two plates. The other had barely been touched. The fish had clearly been on a tour, as parts of it were smeared all over the serving dish, the animal itself remained very close to its original serving state. Conspiratorial glances had been exchanged between duke and elderly bishop at the evident horror and disgust displayed by Cyprianus as he pushed the fish around in the hope of finding some edible part.

"Oh, yes, splendid. It's just a shame that I have no appetite. I've been a little under the weather of late, not being able to manage a bite for days now. The little I managed to eat was splendid. Yes, splendid."

"You should be careful, my dear Cyprianus, you will waste away, if you eat so little. I have always found that filling up on bread is the best way to try to rekindle an appetite. It causes no irritation to the stomach. Would you like some more? I'm sure cook would be able to find something, even if, you've exhausted all of today's provision."

Teasing the bishop was fun - predictable, yes, easy, yes - but fun nevertheless. Normally, Ranosindus had to make do with just the inner pleasure he got from giving the fat pompous bishop discomfort, having an audience, or collaborator improved the sport greatly. Cecilius was on the same wave length. Actually, with that Jewess the other day it was surprisingly fun. She was not at all inhibited about playing the game and was very good at it. Bright, smart and beautiful girl. He could definitely see why his son was smitten, sad that she was a Jew.

"To business. Cecilius, spill the beans."

"I imagine the "beans" you want spilled is a report back from where I have just returned."

"Precisely."

"Well, there are a couple of things I ought to make clear, as a sort of preface, as I am not sure how much you know. Firstly, the conference I attended was strictly ecumenical, therefore I cannot, nor will I, divulge the contents to a man who is not of the cloth."

"Cecilius .."

"Wait a moment, Ranosindus, please let me finish, as I think I will be answering some of the questions you want to ask by my next point. There were three parallel meetings held. The one I attended, in Gerunda, which was called and presided over by Gunhild, Bishop of Maguelonne, with the able assistance of Abbot Ranimiro. A second was full of rabbis from the province held in Barcino. A certain Abraham, I have not had the pleasure of meeting him personally, though he is held in high esteem by our northern colleagues, was in charge there in the local synagogue. And the third, which I believe will interest you the most, was of nobility and the higher clerics. Metropolitan bishop Argebaud held sway there, and Hilderic, the Count Nemausus was in attendance. From that gathering I was entrusted with a letter for you."

Searching in a sleeve pocket, he pulled out the correspondence sealed with a great glob of wax.

"I have no idea of its contents, my job was to deliver, which I intended to do by messenger until you so kindly invited me to sup with you."

*

"Attack!"

The Goth army sprung out of its hiding place, catching the band of Vascones completely by surprise. Hit from left, right and rear they had little time to respond. They fought bravely, but were overwhelmed by the superior numbers. It didn't last long. King Wamba approached the now quieter scene, a few men were moaning, about fifty enemy were slain, his troops taking few casualties. Turning to Alaric who had left what had been the middle of the fray, "Not the army we had expected, no?"

"Clear up here, send a party to pick up the bodies of our fallen in General Flavius' command and we'll meet back at camp."

*

The bishops maintained a respectful silence while the duke, who had removed himself from the table to sit closer to a candelabra, read, then re-read, and then read again, the not overly long message from his fellow nobles.

"Well, at least one thing has been cleared up by this."

The bishops had hoped for more. To Cecilius it was now excruciatingly evident how frustrating it could be to know about something, without knowing about it. Realising that he would have to trade to find out, he started the ball rolling.

"I imagine that all three conferences were about the same thing. I, for one, am very much in favour of the proposal. It's time to break off the yoke of the repressive over centralised system imposed on us by Toletum. That Julian is a dreadful man. I have known him for years. Plays humble, but is the biggest power grabber I have seen in my long life; a most dangerous man."

"I do believe that is going a little too far. I have met him as well and a perfectly respectful intellectual, almost saintly character, I found him."

"That certainly was the appearance he wants to give off. Unlike us, who were born into good families, families with history and weight, he is an upstart, and typical of those sorts, has a chip on his shoulder. In fact, I think the man has so many chips he could become a carpenter."

"Cecilius!"

"No, I am serious. Forever scribbling down what he, or anyone else, says then trying to pass it off as philosophy, or something akin to cannon law. Doesn't fool me. Furthermore, his rabid out of control and context persecution of Jews is decidedly un-Goth. We had no history of that until the sad day we converted to Catholicism, and started listening to Julian and his ilk. Did you know that he is of Jewish origin? His grandparents were "encouraged" to convert, I believe. Quite an irony, as the logic of that law that Toletum has enacted recently, is that it would be difficult to accept that any Jew could actually successfully convert. According to our leading law-making lights, the Jews are always under suspicion for being nominally Christians but covertly practisers of their own faith. I think this is why Julian wants to show he is at the forefront of removing Judaism from the kingdom, to show to all and sundry, that HE, and his family, are true converts. I have had the misfortune to hear him espouse what he calls the "final solution" , which would mean the expulsion, or death, of every Jew, converted or not. That this man, *the intellectual*, has made his niche and the fact that he is a rising star, is symptomatic of everything that is putrid down there. We need to break away, and the sooner the better."

Ranosindus looked up from his letter quite shocked at the energy and bile with which these comments were spoken. Flecks of spit were still evident around the old man's mouth.

"Oh, come on, Cecilius, stop being the diplomat, tell us what you really think of the man."

This caused laughter and broke the tension somewhat.

"I'm sorry. It's just that I don't like the man."

"We got the drift of that. However, the question is what we are going to do."

"I have already said that I am in favour of sedition. No, I would go further, outright rebellion. A new state; a new beginning. I am old, so I have less to lose. If this goes wrong or fails in any way, then the retribution will be severe. I can only tell you my opinion. I will not divulge what agreements our conference came to."

"Worry not, I already know. It's here, along with the results of the Jewish conference and the nobles' conclusion."

The part of the message that Ranosindus had had to read and re-read, wasn't the conclusion, but the reason for his exclusion. It had been assumed that the Duke of Tarraco would have a conflict of interests. It was widely known that Ranosindus had sent troops to bolster Wamba's campaign in the north, a contingent which included his only son. It was therefore accepted that his loyalty lay with the status quo king.

He was only being contacted now, because it was felt that the uprising would be doomed to failure without his presence. With his support there was a strong probability of success, without it, they would not even try. He was the lynchpin and he was being invited to go to see them in person, the decision to continue, or not, would be arrived at during that conversation.

*

Every part of her hurt, body, soul and mind. Sitting next to the water she felt totally exhausted. Raising her head to see the re-entering Marcus was a considerable effort, pleasing though it was.

Placing a red cape by her side, he explained that that they needed to leave very shortly, she ought to cover herself the best she could and make herself ready.

"I can't. I can't even move."

"*Arantxa,* you must. Once it's completely dark, we move. I'll be back shortly."

With that he was gone again. Perhaps it was too much to expect him to ask how she was. After all, she was still a prisoner, and he her captor. The tiny gap which was the escape route beckoned. What was to stop her leaving by herself. Her complete lack of energy made this consideration short. It was inevitable that they would catch up to her in no time. There was no real choice. By leaning on the rock, she pulled herself to her feet. It was then that the body came into view. Even now, white, drained of blood, he looked menacing. A shudder ran through her making her acutely aware of her nakedness, she snatched at the cloth pulling the cloak tightly around her.

Flavius and Marcus had divided forces. The senior commander took the bulk of the troop to explain the situation, whereas Marcus joined the four men on guard duty.

It was quite a relaxed affair with three seated behind the body wall, and one stood spear in hand looking out into the fading light. At Marcus's approach the three jumped up and did their best to look soldiery.

"Take it easy. I have some news."

Everyone relaxed. Actually, they didn't take Marcus' authority very seriously anyway. " Firstly, there have been some problems, the result of which is that we are not being relieved by the main force."

Their faces dropped with the implication, further re-enforcing their negative opinion of this "officer" boy.

Sounding as upbeat as possible, "It's not quite so bad" doing a fair impression of a puppy wanting to be liked, "we believe that there is a secret way out through the cave- system." A beaming smile, adding quickly as the expected positive reaction didn't happen, "one of the prisoners is prepared to guide us."

Realising that he was not winning this audience, and his popularity rating hadn't increased a jot, he tried his best to sound authoritarian.

"We have to sneak away under the cover of darkness, however, the enemy can't suspect, so we need to maintain four guards here."

This changed their demeanour towards him "Why us?" There was a general clamour of agreement and mutiny was in the air.

Marcus' calming quelling slightly raised voice continued, "Nobody is asking you to do anything other than get out of here with the rest of us. We need to make it look as if there are four guards here. Quietly, in absolutely no hurry, and as surreptitiously as possible, I want you to replace yourselves with a dead body - one of these dead bodies." He pointed to the half a dozen or so that weren't incorporated into the wall. "Give them your helmets, and seat them back to the wall as informally and slovenly as you were when I arrived. Don't do it all at once. We are not leaving quite yet, so you have time. Withdraw one at a time. Do a good job. The whole operation depends on you doing this part convincingly."

This time he found her wrapped in his red cloak much in the way that women do with towels after bathing.

"The colour suits you."

"Do you think? It certainly matches my face." Her hands caressed the welts and cuts. "Can I borrow your dagger?" She saw the mistrust in him as his eyes took in the mutilated form close by. "Don't worry, I do not intent to do the same to you. At least not yet." Her smile was lopsided because of the distortion to her mouth had endured in the beating, still he found it enticing.

Taking the proffered dagger, she slit the cloak material to its end, which was close to her ankles. "I wouldn't be able to walk if not." She answered his confused look.

She had had the experience of moving when she returned to the women. It was nearly as uncomfortable as the conversation they had had.

After explaining the situation, and giving the choice of staying or going, she was met by a barrage of abuse hurled spitefully at her. Words like; "whore" an" traitor", punctuated every line spat at her. They were angry and incredulous at her proposed rescue of these baby slaughterers. Some demanded to be killed there and then after pointing out that the deal would save their lives. Dejected, she turned being unable to take any more of their hatred.

"I'll come with you," it was a young woman of about twenty. She was chubby and unattractive, "I'm not sure they will want me, it's easy to see why they want to take you, but me…"

"No, Eztebeni, you're .."

She indicated herself. "Arantxa, I know what I am," there was a pause as it looked as if Eztebeni was about to cry, " I am …. unable to speak their language."

Both women laughed.

It was then Eztebeni's turn to receive all the abuse and name-calling. Once untied, Eztebeni took in the rest, making sure that her eyes met any that wanted to abuse her "My life in this village, your village, since I was given in marriage two summers ago to Etor, has been hell. You, the pretty girls, you never tried to make me welcome. Your opinion that I was not good enough for one of your men was made clear. And you," she indicated a particular viciously spoken woman at the back, "my dear sister-in-law, you actively encouraged my husband to beat me, even more than he already did. Did you want him to beat me pretty? Well, it wasn't going to happen. I am glad to be shot of the lot of you. Whatever happens, my life cannot be *much* worse than with you."

The women were stunned at the tongue lashing that they had just received, one started to deny the accusations without much conviction, her efforts petering out within a couple of unfinished sentences. Most looked abashed, not the sister-in-law though, "You were never good enough for my courageous beautiful little brother. Get out of here now, you useless dried up infertile bitch!"

Nobody saw the branch while it was on the floor, nor how it got into Eztebeni's hand, everyone did see it land squarely on her relative's back. The sound alone of the hit was startling, when accompanied by one of the loudest yelps of the day, and there were quite a few in the running for that title, it caused a collective gasp of shock and surprise.

"You don't tell me what to do *any more*. That's what you encouraged him to do to me daily. How does it feel? You say your little brother, oh how true that was... very little and completely useless, as a man. He should have stayed fucking his sister."

The sister-in-law raised a tearful face only to be met with another gigantic bash.

"I dearly hope that you, who have been so publicly spoilt by these uncouthed Goths, will be rejected by your husbands. I'm sure the sheep and goats of the village will have more attraction than you!"

"Enough, Ezte."

"True, they are not worth any more of my time or energy. Agur."

Making their way through tiny gaps, crawling between rocks and sliding down scree

hadn't been easy, and it had taken hours, but finally the spaces were getting wider and running water could clearly be heard. It was still dark when they finally emerged.

"Arantxa, well done. Where are we?"

"I don't know. We never made it to the end. I just hoped that there would be one."

*

"Dearly beloved, we are gathered here today in the memory..."

Ranosindus was in the front pew, denoting the privilege and honour due to him. How he wished he were farther back, more anonymous, and completely inconspicuous. The mass had already dragged on for the best part of two tedious hours, and now, the worst was about to begin; Cyprianus's sermon. On a normal Sunday, these words of wisdom and religious passion delivered by God's representative in Tarraco could last for an age, today's was shaping up to rival the length of the Roman empire!

True, it was a special occasion, this church had been in construction for most of his lifetime but did that give the bishop the right to make martyrs out of the congregation? Also, another of the horrors of being so close, besides the fact that you can't just nod off to sleep while he droned on, was that you got covered in spittle. Every, and any, crescendo of implored reverence, was accompanied by a shower of saliva. At times the duke thought that it was deliberately aimed at him as he seemed to be the main recipient.

"Fructuosus, and his deacons, Augurius and Eulogius, were burned alive! Burned alive! Burned alive for their faith. A faith, we now all share. The Romans were yet to see God's light. The Emperor Valerian was an unknowing pagan, and it took the example of Fructuosus and the hundreds of martyrs that followed him to eventually …"

It really must have been tough to be burned alive for your faith, Ranosindus mused, but at least it was relatively short, admittedly more painful. This homily had all the hallmarks of being excruciatingly long. Trying not to do it too obviously, the duke attempted to take in all his surroundings. It was the first time he had entered the building. It gave the appearance of being, well, basic. When he had entered his first thoughts were of size. How could they have spent sooo long building this tiny little *chapel*? The Romans, before they were Christians, had decorated Tarraco with magnificence, the amphitheatre, the temple, the Circus, forums both up and down town, palatial buildings, including the one where he lived, making it one of the most beautiful cities outside Rome itself. In fact it had been called a second Rome, with more than one Emperor setting up residence for protracted periods. And here, after decades of construction, actually stealing the stones from the theatre rather than hewing them for themselves from a quarry, the Christians of today had produced this basic little building to honour their first martyrs. Was this progress?

"Burned slowly alive, yes…"

Ranosindus's thoughts turned away from the *good* old days to the very serious and real problems of today. What should he do? Who should he back? What would happen to Marcus?

A mental list is what he needed of pros and cons, and, as he was sure he had plenty of time to contemplate, his mind was allowed to ponder. If one starts with the negative one can always end on a positive note, the oft repeated phrase of his Greek philosophy teacher came trickling back. The man had had a phrase for every occasion, and if you took a little notice of what he was saying, which wasn't that often in Ranosindus's case, it was easy to see that there was no consistency in what was being said, as that day's wisdom was often in direct contradiction to the one used previously. Perhaps that was how to sound wise and knowledgeable; say a lot, while you say nothing. To do nothing was certainly an attractive option, which he'd allow himself to dwell on after the balancing process. "As the flame licked around his frail human form, he raised his eyes and saw Jesus looking down upon him with open arms ready to embrace..." Negative. They would lose, and Wamba's vengeance would be terrible. In King Chindaswinth's time, even without a serious rebellion, he had slaughtered hundreds of noble men to enforce his control and power. In this case, Marcus could end up paying a double price if he backed his father - his military future and his life. By all the accounts he'd received from the front, which were admittedly sparse, Marcus was doing exceptionally well as a highly regarded assistant to some general called Paulus, who Ranosindus had never heard of before, his family being Greek or something like that. Another Greek. Apparently this one was more decisive than his philosopher, and if rumours were to be believed, he was Wamba's favourite.

Certainly by joining the rebellion Ranosindus's family and its heritage would be put in the greatest of dangers.

"Lord take my soul!" he was heard to shout as the flames.."

To go out in a blaze, sorry Fructuous, would that be better than the slow strangulation that Toletum was imposing on him now. A backwater nobody is how he'd describe himself under the current regime. Law after law, power after power, he'd been stripped of any role on the national stage. Decision making WITHOUT the Duke of Tarraco would have been unthinkable just few decades ago. Was the fate of his proud family to be a slow slide into insignificant obscurity?

"Saint Peter beamed as he took Fructuous's hand and led him..."

If, however, Tarraconensis/Gallia Gothica could establish itself as a separate kingdom, then his family would be re-established in their central role. Tarraco would be the natural site for the centre of the kingdom. It was true that Narbo held an emotional tug in Goth history, and Nemausus' Roman structures were impressive, nearly on a par with Tarraco itself, but they were too close to the Franks, and too vulnerable to attack. History had shown that fact time and again. It would be foolish to have either of those places as the seat of power. No, it must return to Tarraconensis.

The forces aligned were impressive. Furthermore, with Jewish financing and the considerable disenchanted Jewish population more than willing to fight for the cause, this was his/ their chance. Future generations would never forgive him for not taking this opportunity.

"A martyr, no, our first martyr, he had the courage of his convictions, his faith didn't waver, he looked death directly in the face while others

around him spurned and renounced the Lord, and it is for this noble act that he will always be remembered. While time lasts here on this earth, his name will be exalted, praised, and thanked, yes thanked, thanked for blazing the path to everlasting life in heaven which each of us…"
Ranosindus had actually heard that last part. *Blazing the path,* a bit unfortunate that choice of words! How would history remember him? Not at all? An increasingly unimportant minor noble in a city whose heyday was well gone? Or perhaps the man who did have similar courage to Fructuous, in a lay way, not blazing at all, but being able to restore greatness lost?

*

King Wamba was standing outside his tent, contemplating. Pacing up and down, inside hadn't given him any clarity in his thoughts. A flawed plan it most certainly was. Flavius was reckless. The loss of his twenty men would be keenly felt in terms of wasted numbers and lack of clarity of command. Kunimund's role was not quite reprehensible, not quite sabotage, neither was it loyalty and obedience without question. What should he do? After the demise of the exceptionally popular Paulus, he couldn't risk upsetting the men further by more replacements. Hermenguild was gracious enough to die without causing military unrest. It would be too much to expect the same of Kunimund. Besides, he was so cautious that he would never willingly put himself in harm's way. On the other hand, he was a dam good general in a set battle. Alaric was capable, loyal and available. His experience and popularity were somewhat limited. What to do?
Perhaps all generals that take overall control become less adventurous; Hermenguild was, Kunimund is, there was no clear alternative, whatever way he looked at it he had to continue relying on Kunimund. He would send for him, let his displeasure be known, warn him that his conduct is under review and…nothing. Everything would be the same.
Suddenly the camp was astir. Cheering was getting louder and some sort of procession was winding itself through the lower tented areas.
"General Paulus reporting back sir!"
Wamba was astounded. In front of him was a worse for wear dead man, not alone either, in his wake he had, what looked like all of his command and a couple of sparsely clad females. Marching fast, staying most military-like, still some way behind came Kunimund with his entourage.
"Flavius, well I never.. Perhaps you ought to come into the tent for a debriefing. Dispatch your men for food and drink. Those women can be kept in the pen with the other slaves."
"They will not, sir!"

Marcus had found himself directly in front of the king and directly contradicting him.

Not thinking that he could be yet more astounded, Wamba took in the defiant face in front of him. Was this a direct challenge to his authority? Fortunately, there were only three people to hear it. Wamba weighed his options for the second time this day. Having the boy taken away to be tried and probably executed was his first, and most instinctive. Second, was to look weak and listen to the possible reasons for this remarkable show of disrespect.

An impressive clout on the back of the legs of the rebel which brought him to his knees in front the king delivered by Paulus, resolved the matter temporarily.

"What my second in command, in his clumsy way, was trying to say is that we have already made a pact with these natives which we would like to explain, and if you would be so kind as to extend our Goth hospitality to these women while YOU, Sire, decide their fate, once all the facts pertaining to the case have been presented, we would be most grateful as we are greatly in debt to these ladies."

Wamba looked down on the ashamed looking Marcus as Flavius stood over him in a both menacing and paternal manner. What a pair these two made. Who was the worst for being impetuous?

"I see, there are extenuating circumstances for the boy's outburst. I'm not sure this actually makes his impertinence and disrespect forgivable. Have him locked in with the slaves and the females can be escorted by the rest of your men."

While this exchange was taking place Arantxa had made her way to the front of the group.

"Whoever you are, presumably some sort of chief, leave him alone. He's the reason why your men are not dead at the hands of my people."

Wamba's astonishment knew no depths. Everyone was getting annoyed at him without the slightest fear or respect. Surely kings should get a better deal than this? Exploding to exert his authority, he knew, was the appropriate response. Something, though, in the elegant defiance of the woman who was so forthright that she'd allowed a naked breast to escape from the soldier's cloak that barely covered the rest of her nakedness, made him hold back.

Arantxa, suddenly aware of her state of undress, coloured, "This is not my normal clothing, I lost my clothes while being raped by one of your men!"

Wamba was totally lost for words and protocol to deal with this situation. Thankfully, Flavius intervened again.

"Arantxa, do not address the king in any way, and certainly not in that tone. Get back to Ezte and await your fate."

"King? Oh, my gods! I only wanted to…"

"Move, Arantxa, now!"

She did as ordered, and her place at the front of the proceedings was taken by Kunimund.

"What is going on here? General Paulus, explain yourself."

Flavius's reluctant and slow coming to attention in the presence of his superior officer was accompanied by an obvious look of utter disdain for the man.

"Perhaps you ought to explain *yourself,* General Kunimund. We were left to be slaughtered by the enemy as you failed to follow through on a clearly agreed plan!"

Wamba came back to authoritative life.

"Generals, please join me inside now! Boy, take care of those women. Make sure they are clothed and then come back here with a very good story to explain yourself."

*

They were all seated around the map table, the King at the top and glowering generals opposite each other.

"I demand to know.."

"No, General Paulus, you demand nothing in here. That shameful episode outside will be dealt with later. Here and from now on, the only person doing the demanding is me, your rightful king. Is that clear? I will not accept any outburst whatsoever. The questions will be asked by me, and explanations will be given by you two."

Neither general looked abashed. Resignation and inner seething were there to be seen by anyone who looked. Thankfully, Wamba didn't. He concentrated on his fingers which were intertwined and twitching slightly.

"The first thing we need to know is how you escaped as we were assured that it was an impossibility."

Flavius, trying to regain his calm, related the story of the cave escape omitting any reference to Caius and his death.

"Most, most interesting. The question that springs to mind is, why? Why would they abandon their people and why would they want to save you after you had just destroyed their village killing most of its inhabitants?"

"To tell you the truth, Sire, I am not completely sure. The girl that *spoke* to you is Aitziber's sister."

"Who?"

"The local girl I was … getting information from, and who was killed by her family. However, that doesn't explain her, well, treachery to her own people. Only Marcus could give you a full explanation. The other girl just tagged along as it wasn't her village and her life was a misery there."

"When the boy comes it should be an interesting story, though I do feel it is up to you, Flavius, to teach the boy restraint and respect."

"I do most humbly apologise for that. I assure you that he will be dealt with in a manner he will not forget in the near future."

"Why? What did he do? Sounds to me as if he saved the whole expedition."

"Which is more than you tried to do.."

Swords weren't drawn because of the king's presence, visual daggers were exchanged instead.

"Flavius, no outbursts. The reason we were not there to support you is that we were slow taking the field. Inexcusably slow. I, personally, led an advance party without the numbers to challenge the Vascones who were already in the field. I took the decision that we would have lost more men than we would have saved. I take full responsibility for that decision. I believe you would have done the same in my place.

However, the question I address to you, General Kunimund, is why were we so slow when the plan had been previously agreed before dispatching the advanced troop?"

"Sire, there were unforeseen circumstances which .."

"General, part of your job is foresee ALL those circumstances and deal with them in a quick, efficient and effective manner."

Wamba felt that now Flavius was back he had more of an opportunity to give vent to his feeling about Kunimund's behaviour without the fear of decapitating his military force.

Kunimund fidgeted and was struggling to come up with an explanation for his deliberate inaction. He had disagreed with the whole stupid venture. It made no sense at all. It could not have worked, and would have led to an unnecessary diminishing of his already under-strength force. Losing Paulus would not have been an insurmountable loss, in fact despite his clear bravery and decisive action in the previous battle, which had saved the day, he was far too unpredictable to have as a commander. None of this could he voice. Instead, his only choice was look less than competent.

"The culprits of the delay will be found, Sire. I will assure you nothing of its type will ever happen again."

"I do hope not. You are both dismissed."

There was a getting to feet saluting and purposeful striding to the tent flap.

*

Gunhild and Argebaud arrived together deep in conversation. They spent most of their time together and in a place neither of them could call home. Although Nemausus was a large bustling town full of commerce due to the fact that it was the meeting point of the Frankish empire and the Visigoth kingdom, it still felt, acted and was, very provincial. The fact that a metropolitan bishop and a bishop, neither of whom belonged there, visited with such frequency had set tongues wagging. It also hadn't escaped the notice of the gossipers that these clerics spent nearly all of their time with the lay rather than the Church authorities. Aregio, the actual Bishop of Nemausus, had been informed of their comings and goings was a fact both men knew.

"We are going to have to talk to him. It can't be put off too much longer."

"My dear bishops back again? Just who is it that you are neglecting? Certainly not us, your visits are so frequent that I was wondering whether we should make up rooms for you here. All the travelling that you do must be so tiresome."

"Lady Chlodoswintha, I didn't see you there."

"Not too surprising, Bishop Gunhild, you were so conspiratorially in conversation I am surprised that you even realised that you were in my house."

"I do regret my neglect. My manners are appalling. It's *just that*, well, I'm not quite sure what it is, that's, *just that*, besides being a terrible way of behaving. Actually, we were discussing another of our shocking lacks of decorum; not having been to see Bishop Aregio on our visits up here."

"Yes, I have heard talk. Perhaps you ought to rectify the situation after speaking to my husband. I presume that's why you are here and not to have a little chit chat with me."

"It's always a pleasure.."

"Yes, bishop. I'm sure it is. I'll take you to him, he's out back supervising armour cleaning, I believe." The bishops exchanged knowing glances. Chlodoswintha led them through a bustling house. Everyone was fully employed doing something. The verve and energy was a sight to be seen.

"We don't have this much action in a month in Maguelonne."

"Hilderic says preparation is the key, so we are all busy preparing, quite what for we don't know."

"None of us do, Lady. The Lord's plans have not been revealed to any of us as yet."

"Perhaps your Lord ought to get on with it then. My *lord* is chivvying everyone to do something. Ah, there you are, darling. I have a couple of unprepared bishops who wish to see you."

Chlodoswintha made to leave the men to their talk, knowing that she wouldn't be wanted. Women usually clean up and deal with the consequences of war and are not involved in the decisions to start it. Hilderic held her lightly by the arm.

"Don't go. This affects you, so you should be here."

Metropolitan Bishop Argebaud's shock was plain to be seen by all present.

"Do you think that wise, count? After all, this really is the work of men." Chlodoswintha, being impressed by her husband's inclusion, had resolved to remain meek, mild and most ladylike with interventions only if asked. This resolution lasted all of ten seconds.

"Work of men? What exactly is this work of men? I don't see either of you wearing armour or wielding a sword, so , is it the decision-making process that only men can be involved in?"

"My dear," The count was clearly taken aback by this intervention and it's sarcastic delivery, "I'm sure that the metropolitan bishop wanted nought else but to spare you from some of the more tedious and perhaps gruesome details of the planning."

"The planning of what exactly? If it is to be armed conflict, will I be spared the sight of dead or broken bodies? Will I be spared the consequences of failure?"

"It is for those reasons I would like you present. And please, let's not talk of *failure* quite yet."

Gliding to a seat close, but not too close to the men, she sat and settled her skirts.

"It'll be as if I were not here. Except for any consultation, you may want to make of a mere woman."

This produced a smirk on one face and a scowl on another. The third, Gunhild, ushered the others to chairs near a table.

"Gentlemen, we need to make some decisions. The first has to be from you, count. As we mentioned in our last meeting, nothing can proceed without your explicit acceptance of the crown. So, what say you?"

Looking directly into the blue eyes of the anything but meek and mild, he saw her unenthusiastically but determinedly nod her head.

"Who said something like; some seek fame and greatness while others have it thrust upon them?"

"You just did, darling, nobody else."

*

While Kunimund marched militarily away from the tent with his retinue in tow, Flavius shuffled shading his eyes from the blinding light after the relative darkness of the interior. While watching Kunimund's group disappear he set about wondering just why he had done it. Clearly, it was a deliberate decision to sacrifice him and his men but the why, and the when these decisions were taken was what concerned him most. Kunimund had always been , if not a friend, a kindred spirit. They had shared similar views on the campaign about Hermenguild's leadership and perhaps even the overall state of the kingdom, so the timing of him being thrown to the wolves, or Vascones in this case, was paramount in how he should treat Kunimund from now on. Wamba's version of events made sense and it was completely acceptable that given the military conditions in which he found himself then, a commander's role is to make tough decisions to benefit the bigger picture. Wamba was right, he himself would have made exactly the same decision. Had he not done something remarkably similar? The *situation* with Caius, fell, more or less, into the same type of bracket -the sacrifice of fewer, for the sake of more. The real problem lay in the fact that Wamba was there, and was late. A king should not have been leading a relatively small force with the most experienced general chivvying up the rest of the army. There was no military logic in that. Flavius was leading himself to one conclusion; Kunimund's tardiness was deliberate, Wamba had realised this, and had tried to rectify the situation. If this was the only conclusion, the question of why remained. What had caused Kunimund to see *him* as an enemy? His musings were interrupted by a shadow.

"Troubled?"

A fully-dressed Arantxa set herself between him, the sun, and a long disappeared head of the army.

"I thought that you'd be happy back among your people, readying yourself to go off to slaughter more women and children. Instead, you seem more worried now than back in the cave."

She really did look like her sister especially when her dander was up. The hands were on the hips in an identical stance and the scorn in the voice before it mellowed brought back memories that straddled the divide of pain and pleasure.

"Now I know why I'm feeling out of sorts, I haven't chopped up a baby all morning. I was wondering whether it was because I hadn't had breakfast. Your explanation is so much better. Thank you for reminding me, I'll set about looking for a baby, or perhaps a toddler will do, immediately."

Despite herself, Arantxa laughed. She could see what had attracted her sister. The moment she was touched returned her to the present. He held her arm, not aggressively, lightly if anything. Noticing her recoil, Flavius slowly let go.

"Arantxa, I would like you to believe this, though I doubt you ever will, it was not the intention to kill any woman or child in our raid. Things, well, got out of hand." Seeing the beginning of a reaction, he continued quickly. "I know I was the commanding officer, so I MUST take the responsibility for what did happen and no amount of apology will bring those people back. However, I cannot tell you how sorry I really am. I did not join the army to kill unarmed innocent women and children."

"Enslaving them is alright though?" Her creased eyes of merriment had turned to a glower.

"Actually, yes. That's the way with war. Don't tell me that your people don't do that! Your raids against the other tribes are legendary. In fact, it's because of one such attack on the settlement of Caesaragusta that we are here."

"My people.."

"Arantxa, they are no longer *your* people. I don't pretend to know why you did what you did to save us, you must have your reasons, but I very much doubt those reasons will convince *your* people to take you back in with open arms. It'll be seen as a betrayal and you know what happened to your sister for a lot less."

Wamba had asked, and he'd had no answer. Why would someone betray their own people? He had never questioned Aitziber's actions, nor his own. What they did and felt, would that come under the heading of betrayal? Her family clearly thought so. For the first time he began to wonder whether she had been conscious or conflicted by their meetings. In reality, he couldn't remember any on his part. She was beautiful, he loved being with her and that was that. Yes, he thought he did love her, but enough to betray his own people? He couldn't even imagine that. Yet both sisters had done it.

All defiance and anger evaporated from Arantxa in one big sag. For the first time what she had actually done hit her. Until now there had been the adrenaline of the fight against Caius, the escape among the rocks, that pushed her forward without physically or emotionally looking back. Flavius' words laid out the stark reality all too clearly. Dirty feet was the only thing she could see and the only thing she wanted to see.

"Your feet really need washing, you know."

It was his turn to laugh. After pointing out the dire situation she found herself in, the last response he had expected was that he needed to bathe.

"What's so funny?" Marcus had joined them.

"Apparently, I'm not clean enough to talk to our *guest*."

"And you're even worse. Look at the state of you! Mud to your knees and your face, when was the last time that saw water? I thought that you Goth/ Romans had a reputation for baths and spas."

"I have a quite splendid bathing pool inside my house back in Tarraco."

"Do you ever use it?"

Arantxa was enjoying giving discomfort. It was also a way to delay facing the home truths that Flavius had made her only too well aware of.

"Of course. A little inconvenient at the moment as it just happens to be a three week march away. Perhaps you are suggesting that I pop home, have a quick scrub to be able to converse with you."

"Actually..

"She's not wrong, Marcus. The river awaits you. I still have a couple of things I must attend to, then I will join you, so we can make ourselves presentable."

Marcus did feel quite disgusting and yearned to be clean, what he didn't like was to be told so, by anyone, especially a woman. It reminded him of the bad old days of the reign of terror of Amalaswinth. What a dreadful woman she was! She would make any centurion wilt under her power. Quite often he felt a little "homesick". Being away was exciting sometimes, tedious most of the time, and occasionally, well, not like being at home. The thought of Amalaswinth stopped any tender recollections.

"And Marcus, we have to have a serious conversation about the lack of respect you showed the King. An exemplary punishment will be enforced once you are clean."

Now home, even with Amalaswinth scouring his back, seemed a pleasant prospect. He mustered his pride, gave an enthusiastic salute, and headed for the river.

"You, Arantxa, we must decide what to do with you. The king is aware of your role in our escape and it's now up to him to judge your actions and your fate."

*

"It's so good of you to pay me a call, and *SO* unexpected. I had no idea that you were both in town together."

Seated uncomfortably in the drawing room of the Bishop of Narbo's residence in Nemausus, metropolitan bishop Argebaud listened to the false pleasantries of its present resident while taking in the room itself. It had never really occurred to him before that this palace really was palatial, unlike his, back in Narbo. Who wouldn't, given a place like this to stay? And this wasn't even the bishop's city. It was justified, so he said, if he ever felt the need to justify it, which he never did, as the place where he spent a great deal of his time. Imagine! Furthermore, it was reported, that the Bishop of Narbo's real home was pretty impressive as well. Although Argebaud's was much newer, it didn't boast a quarter of the style elegance and sheer opulence of this building. It was if the ability to build with grace and elegance had somehow been lost. Perhaps it was just a case of money and grandeur though he suspected that the whole apprentice system was in chaos, with the youth of today uninterested in learning their trade to the standards demanded before. They were content to produce something quick and reasonably functional. The beauty of construction had been sacrificed on the altar of limited budgets of time and money. And this was just a bishop's residence, he was an metropolitan bishop and deserved of so much better.

This set about a chain of thoughts about his ungodliness. It wasn't correct that he should be hankering after worldly comforts, foregoing those of spiritual enlightenment. Surely he was better than these petty jealousies that were gnawing at him as his vision settled on yet another exquisitely carved arch. Upon hearing his name, he returned to the empty nonsense that was being spouted.

"Metropolitan Bishop Argebaud, if you had given me a little notice, I'm sure my cook could have provided something suitable."

"Worry not, Bishop Aregio, we were but passing after seeing the count, and thought that we would like to ask your valued opinion on certain matters."

Gunhild answered, paying little attention to either the words or their content. It was his turn to wonder as he mouthed formalese. Rather than dallying on the surroundings, he was taking in the resident himself. Bishop Aregio was a massive man, more like a stone labourer than a man of the cloth. However, unlike most of the huge men that he knew, this man was not a gentle giant. His well-earned reputation was one of a bullying, aggressive, arrogant man whose intellect left more than a little to be desired. In all the meetings that they had had as bishops of the area, his was always the note of disaccord. Opinions made of bluster rather than thought out reasoning, delivered in booming tones of one convinced of his own importance, was his wont. Nobody had a good word for the man. The obvious, but verbally unmentioned struggle, not to sit near him at meal times was always desperately fought. This is why they had chosen a time when a meal could not have been served and had not given notice of their arrival, the objective was to spend as little time as politely possible in his company while informing him of what was about to happen.

The discussion with the count had proven most harmonious, with all present quickly agreeing on all the main points. Surprisingly, it was Chlodoswintha who had developed the approach policy to the boisterous bishop. She proposed a considerable amount of buttering up to play to his ego, followed by getting him to tacitly agree to supporting the uprising without actually playing a leading role. His presence in any such venture would cause many more problems than it would solve. The ego-pampering role was Gunhild's, and he set about it with no gusto, but with an awful lot of application. It was a role he was fairly used to, being a young minor bishop forever in the presence of his elders and "·betters", who he sought to impress to enhance his progression in the Church hierarchy.

After what seemed like an eternity of hearing arse cleaning, and with no more beauty to get envious about, metropolitan bishop Argebaud felt that he had to join in the conversation to hasten their exit.

"So brother, what is your opinion on this most blessed course of action?"
The big man, who had been listening with incredulity, but without surprise to the discourse - his sources had pre-warned him of just what and why his *brother* bishops were spending so much time in Nemausus - stood as if he were addressing the congregation on a Sunday.

"I am shocked." he boomed, "King Wamba was chosen by God to lead the Goth kingdom. It is NOT our job to remove him from his very sacred role even if you think, with some legitimacy, that our region has been mistreated and marginalised."

He was warming to his haranguing task when Gunhild in a voice that was a good fifty decibels lower mentioned, "Actually, it was Julian who chose Wamba."

"And without doubt his Holy hand must have been guided by Our Lord."
"I suspect it had more to do with consolidating his, and Toletum's, centralised power than any spiritual intervention."

"Gunhild, you now question the ways of the Lord?"
"Aregio, do stop shouting. Firstly, your position in the Church is lower than mine, and although I do not profess to know quite what our Lord thinks on this matter, I do know that Julian, who ranks but equal to me, chose Wamba for his ability to be manipulated, not because of his divine right to rule. What we are proposing is a sub- division of the kingdom, not the deposing of Wamba. He may remain in his position without having direct control here. Our ancestors divided the nation into different kingdoms at various times in the past. This is an administrative split, not a cleaving of the Goth nation. It is our intention of having brotherly harmonious, neighbourly relations with Toletum, and hopefully we will achieve this objective. What we seek from you is your support in this endeavour."

"And you will NOT have it!"

*

Sitting on a rock with her feet dangling in the river she could see Marcus swimming way out in the distance. No choice now, no dirty feet conversation to distract her, she had to face her thoughts. Why did she do it? What would she do from now on?

Not having one complete answer for her life-changing past decision, she clutched at straws; the murder of her sister by her own family, the mistreatment and unhappy life with her father, the proposed marriage to an elderly relative which was changed to marrying her off to her sister's murderer, and the awful life that would follow, similar to Aitziber's miserable, hated existence. Try as she might, she couldn't nail enough of a reason. All the stuff about a dreadful life was the norm, and wouldn't be any better, and most probably a great deal worse, under a foreign Goth man. And she had chosen to save the very men who had slaughtered children, elderly, women, as well as the men of the village. How could she have done that? Despite the respect and politeness she'd received at the hands of the two officers, they were still murderers who deserved death. The blood of her neighbours, their unavenged deaths, was now on her hands as much as the Goths.

*

On her way down to the river she'd bumped into Ezte, who wasn't suffering any homesickness, quite the opposite - she was exuberant as she had found some distant relative among the camp followers.
Whenever an army went to war, along came a group of followers; women and children mainly, some slaves. It didn't matter, whatever the conflict, men and women found each other. Some of the women were Goths who had come from the different parts of the Iberian Peninsula. The vast majority were from the different tribes that had been subdued by the Romans with the help of the Goths, a few were Franks from the other side of the mountains. All had one thing in common; they had nothing else, nowhere better to be, which generated a surprising amount of sisterly camaraderie. Ezte excelled in it. Although she had only just joined the collective, she had been made to feel welcome. When communication proved to be difficult due to her lack of even the most basic Latin, other local women were found to translate for her. It was then that she realised one of those was a relative from her original village, who had hooked up with a soldier serving in the Goth army. Her soldier wasn't Goth, originally he was an Alan, who, after being captured a few years back, saw the sense in joining the enemy. Ezte told Arantxa that they'd had a great natter, catching up on all those they had in common and her relative explaining life as a camp follower with all its hardships but relative freedoms compared to village life. She had a small child in tow and stated, with no room for doubt, that she would never return to her village, not because she couldn't, but because she didn't want to, life was better here.
Would this be her lot, following a group of men, whose sole purpose was domination of others through their presence or fighting? It wasn't an enticing prospect even when painted in the rosiest forms by Ezte.

"Could you pass me the towel?"

Having been so lost in her dark thoughts of past and future she hadn't noticed Marcus' arrival. Standing waist deep in the shallows his request was bordering on a plea rather than a demand.

"You have seen me naked, are you too shy to show yourself?" To her own surprise her reply was sing-song flirtatious.

"Please pass the towel." No more bordering, an outright cry for help. Clambering none too elegantly off the rock, her long robe almost tripped her up. Moving to the water's edge she held the cloth he called a towel.

"If I throw it, it'll probably land in the water. I'm not coming in any farther than I already have as my borrowed dress will get wet.... Looks as if we have an impasse."

As she held his eyes, she noticed his body shiver; cold or emotion? She took pity on him.

"Compromise. I'll hold the cloth open and at the same time I'll have my eyes closed."

Having never exposed his nakedness to any woman other than Amalaswinth, and she didn't count, he was reluctant to leave the safety of the depths but could see few other options. Trying to swagger in water isn't easy, strolling nonchalantly was a better choice. He did his best. Reaching about half way, she suddenly and very brazenly opened her eyes. "Not bad." Screwing up the towel, she turned and ran up the short, muddy beach towards the bushes.

Not swagger, nor stroll, this was now a sprint. Upon getting close. he launched himself into a flying tackle catching her around the thighs. She came down with an almighty thump, striking her head on the trunk of a tree. Sprawled and inert with the towel at her side, she wasn't moving. Marcus jumped up preparing to chastise her in a playful way, when he realised what had happened.

Gingerly he crept to her side. Kneeling close to her head he could see the wound, it was already beginning to swell. Not knowing what he should do, he did nothing. She was breathing, he could see that.

Remaining in this frozen state his thoughts zoomed back to the port in Tarraco when Claudius had tripped over a coil of rope and had fallen badly on his head. It was Rebecca who had reacted the fastest and most decisively. Rebecca. It had been a long time since he had thought of her! She had gently lifted the boy's head, propping it on her thigh and rubbed water onto his face until he regained consciousness. Sitting next to her, he decided to do the same thing. Slowly, and with as much care as he could, he rested her head on his leg. As he was still wet, it was easy to wring a little water from his hair to pat onto her . Repeating the moisturising motion a few times, she began to stir. It was then he began to think of the consequences of her waking up on his naked body while caressing her face.

As her eyes began to flutter open, consecutively accepting and rejecting the light they afforded, he pondered. Gently replacing her head on the floor was his best bet. Moving his hands ready to take the weight, once he'd extracted his leg.

"Continue with the water please."

Shit. Too late. He did as was requested. One of her eyes was now fully open and looking intently at him.

"You play rough."

"I'm sorry. It was an accident. I didn't .."

"It hurts."

For the first time he took in the detail of the damage that had been done, quite a deep gash which surprisingly wasn't bleeding, surrounded by a swelling dis-colouring which was spreading by the second. Carefully, he attempted to remove the strands of hair that were almost embedded.

"Owww."

"Sorry, I was trying to .."

Instinctively, she turned her head away from the pain to be faced by his penis. His movement was exceptionally fast, grabbing the towel at their side to cover himself. Unfortunately, his movement, also dislodged her head, which thudded none too quietly or slowly, to the ground.

"Owwwwwwwwwwww!"

Now, kneeling with the towel in his hands he was panicking.

"I'm *SO* sorry." His turn to react instinctively, his arms went back to her head just as she was moving it off the ground making direct contact with the injury she was trying to protect.

"OOwwwwwwwwwwwwwwwww!!"

Recoiling from the yet more pain he had caused, he knelt next to her looking totally dejected. She moved away from him, pulling herself up into a seated position.

"You really are a clumsy oaf." Surprising, he thought, her voice wasn't filled with anger, it was more the way a loving mother would chastise her ungainly son. In her position, his reaction would have been so different. When anyone hurt him, be it accidently or not, his automatic failsafe response, was to lash out either physically, or verbally. Sinking back on his kneeling position, feeling less like a duke's son and more like a brutish commoner, he managed to say in little more than a whisper, "I was only trying.."

"I know what you were trying to do." How was it possible, she was getting even mellower instead of angrier. "Not a great success though , was it? And you still haven't managed to cover your body."

Realising that the towel was still in his hands, he dumped it, still fairly screwed up across his midriff.

Leaning over, she took the towel. He wanted to react but feared he would cause yet more pain, he let her do it. Gently and fairly slowly, she untangled it and replaced it flat so it actually covered more of him. "Quite why you are embarrassed about your body, I don't know. It's not bad. I've seen a great deal worse." Looking up, he caught her grin. "And some much better!"

His reaction was to blush. From the soles of his feet to the roots of his hair he felt himself going red.

Finding his reaction both sweet and appealing, she touched his stubbly still acned cheek tenderly causing him to deepen his colour to puce.

"I *do* hope that I am not interrupting anything."

Flavius' jovially delivered comment made Arantxa withdraw her hand faster than a snake strike and Marcus unnecessarily re-adjust the towel while glowing beetroot.

The tone changed when the young woman swivelled her head towards the towel bearing commanding officer.

"MARCUS! This is TOO much. Disrespecting the king and now beating a female guest. Stand to attention when you are being spoken to!"

Marcus fumbled and stumbled to his feet, trying to both salute and keep his towel in place. Arantxa also rose. In contrast to the young, red man, she was serene and almost stately. She moved between the two men hoping to give time and cover for Marcus to cover all essentials.

"Oh, my saviour! A general come to protect the honour of a poor girl." Paulus was taken aback by her mocking tone.

"You allow a whole village to be murdered and raped, but you are on hand when I need you ….least."

"Arantxa, don't speak to an officer in that way."

"What way? I am just expressing my profound gratitude for him coming to my aid when I don't need it, and not coming to my aid when it was necessary."

"Young lady, your tone and …"

"And what? Attitude? What are they, disrespectful? Respect, general is earned. You have failed to do that in my eyes, and no amount of shouting or coercion will change that situation." She put up her hand to stop him interrupting. "What you see here is not what you imagine. What happened was that I fell and hit my head and this shy, naked *boy* was doing his best to help me. Ineffective though it was, I was grateful for his attempt."

Paulus was unsure how to react. Jumping to conclusions he had assumed the worst in one of his trusted men. The girl had made him look both bullying and inept. Trying to restore his authority, he barked at Marcus.

"Be that as it may, Marcus, King Wamba requires your presence immediately. Get back to camp this second."

Glad of an escape route, Marcus all but ran, then suddenly stopped. He had forgotten to salute, he turned and did so, while at the same time the loosely tied towel gave into the forces of gravity.

Arantxa's peel of laughter was the last thing he heard as he ran on without the towel. She looked on after him, appreciating what she saw.

"I do apologise for.."

"So do I for speaking so harshly. I didn't mean to use that tone. I still think what I said is true. What happened isn't as black and white as I tried to make it."

She slumped back to the ground feeling somewhat dizzy after all the rapid movement. Paulus moved solicitously towards her only being stopped for the second time in the last couple of minutes by her raised hand.

"I'll be alright. I just need to sit quietly by myself for a few minutes then I'll head back to camp."

"If there's anything I can.."

"No, please just leave me be for a while."

Accepting the situation, Paulus backed away turning towards the nearby river. Removing his clothes, he sauntered into the water. Arantxa watched. What a difference in attitude between the man and the boy. From her privileged position, there was no denying that the general was ALL man, quite a beautiful specimen. Her sister must have enjoyed that. She felt no tingle of desire, just appreciation, the way she might a lush landscape. The boy's running naked buttocks on the other hand, well, that was quite a different story. Could this be the key to her earlier inconclusive musings?

*

The Jews of Tarraco made up a sizeable proportion of the city's population and had done so for many many years. At one point in its history, Tarraco was known as a "Jewish" city. The city dwellers in general though, had been in steady decline over the years with the Hispanic -Romans finding more plentiful food and work on the land. As they had drifted away, it had left fewer potential buyers for the commerce that the Jews traded in. As a consequence, the numbers of buyers and sellers had diminished correspondingly.

Most of the less well-off believers were gathered in and around the building which served as their temple down near the port, their *call*. Despite the Shabbat services having concluded some time since, people, mainly the men, were in little huddles exchanging gossip and waiting for the promised meeting.

Isaac was nervous, very nervous. Weaving their way purposefully through the chattering circles, he felt as if he were leading the phalanx of an attack, with him forced to be at its spearhead. Having never come close to ever being described as a brave man - to date his most valiant action had been opposing Trudi's desire for their son, David, to study to become a rabbi, he found all the attention excruciating. Nodding as nonchalantly as possible, he fought to keep all his body parts in order. Whenever he was nervous, or had to do something in public, his head would, well, wobble is the only word. It would lose all its usual stability and become more akin to a set jelly. It was as if the tendons or muscles or whatever it was that gave it rigidity, suddenly decided en-masse to have, a, "break" would be the wrong word - more like, a relaxing moment, might be more accurate. The second it was all over, he and they would return to their normal reliable stable function. Moving farther down his body, the next area demanding a change of role was the stomach. Some people described this feeling as having butterflies. Personally, he felt that a clutch of newly hatched chicks had set up residence there. The flapping was accompanied with what could only be described as pecking, scratching and sibling squabbling. To vomit the lot out would be such a relief. The final area of concern and potentially the most embarrassing was his hands. They shook. It was a family trait. His father, brother and others all had a bit of a tremble. This was a constant in their lives and they lived with it. At times of stress, the barely noticeable movement hardly worth mentioning, became all too obvious to ignore. Little daily actions like eating became a torment with it being hit and miss whether the food actually arrived safely to its destination, the mouth.

Moving on, flanked by people he normally lived in the shadow of, his big brother Jacob, the wife, Trudi, and even the young but supremely confident niece, Rebecca, he was a quivering mess. They were headed to an improvised podium-type thing made of coiled fishing rope. It didn't boast sturdiness, it was not even flat, nor did it look remotely easy to stand on. This would do nothing for his security.

"Let me help you up." Jacob was solicitous, knowing full well the terror that Isaac was experiencing.

The dithering was clear to be seen, "Couldn't you .."

"Just get on with it, Isaac. Your meddling has dragged us all into this, now say your piece and we can all get off home." Trudi's high pitched voice transparently transmitted the emotion she was feeling, supreme annoyance at her "man". She glanced over to Rebecca for female solidarity as if to say, "look at what men get us into!" She got none.

Rebecca dismissed her aunt, moving past her to help her uncle both physically and emotionally.

"You can do it." She gently nudged him up. "Be firm and brief. Make the statement. Everyone else will then want to talk and you won't have to do any more."

Isaac's eyes met Rebecca's. Some of her undoubted strength steeled into him. Turning, he clambered up more determinedly than he imagined possible and boomed out.

"Brothers, sisters, could I have your attention for a moment?"

Slowly, the clumps moved towards him, an expectant babble came over what had been a cacophony of sound seconds before.

Finding a reasonably flat part on which to stand, then clearing his throat various times, he held out a scroll. Seeing the thing move so in his hands as if the sea wind had suddenly picked up and decided to blow exclusively on the parchment, he knew he would not be able to read the Hebrew statement on it. His newly found confidence drained away quicker than it had arrived, he would not be able to continue. Finding some sort of face-saving exit was his only worry now. The crowd had become totally silent. The belly chicks were all practising flying at the same time. Seeking in vain to stabilise his head by moving his neck, in what could be confused with a neck exercise, he realised Rebecca was standing next to him. Looking as submissive and as unimportant as she possibly could, she stage whispered "May I hold the scroll for you, uncle?"

Fortified again, Isaac started. He actually hardly glanced at the written words as he had committed it to memory. "The Jewish Council would like to …"

*

"How did you get in? What are you doing here? Guards!!"

In rushed the two fully uniformed-spear-carrying men sweeping the tent flap aside. Marcus who had changed into his best dress uniform, stood totally bemused as the spears jabbed towards his throat.

"I, I, I…"

King Wamba looked most distraught. Scroll in hand, he had been pacing up and down not noticing that Marcus had entered. When he did register his presence, then he started shouting as if Marcus was an assassin wielding a dagger.

"Sire, you left instructions that the officer was to be shown in."

"I did, did I? Oh, yes. I now remember. Thank you guards, please leave us."

Wamba was visibly trying to regain control of himself and the situation. Placing the scroll on the table, then rethinking, picking it back up, he strode over to and very close to Marcus.

"Your insubordination…why did you feel you could speak to your king in such a manner?" Not leaving enough time for Marcus to even start a reply, he continued.

"Is it that you have no respect for me? For the office I hold?"

Marcus was totally taken aback by the words and delivery. He struggled to say "Sire.." before Wamba continued. "Were you sent here as a spy, or worse still, a challenge to my authority?"

"Sire, my father sent me to serve you and the kingdom."

"Aha! I didn't ask for reinforcements, but you appeared anyway. Why?"

Marcus's voice was barely above a whisper. Coming here, he had wondered why he had been summoned. It made no sense if it was for insubordination, those sorts of matters are not dealt with by a king, usually it was a general, or someone much lower down the chain of command would dole out his punishment.

"Apparently, you engineered the escape of General Paulus with the help of that local girl. Why did she do it? Was it part of a bigger scheme to lull us into trusting both you and her, getting into our camp?"

Marcus was completely nonplussed. The confusion he felt was clear to see on his face. For good or bad, Marcus had never been able to hide his feelings. Rebecca, she was back in his thoughts again, was a past-master. She was inscrutable. He had admired her for it and had practiced alone in his bedroom, only to fail spectacularly when the moment of truth arrived. Perhaps for the very first time since the boy had entered the tent, Wamba looked at him. What he saw convinced him that the boy had absolutely no idea what he was talking about. Always priding himself on his judgement of character, he knew he was way off the mark accusing the boy of all these things. What he had read had caused a misjudged attack. Calming himself and his tone he sought to rectify.

"Sit, boy. Let's start again, shall we?"

Pale, shaken, Marcus sat alert to any new accusation.

"Why did the girl…what's her name?"

"Arantxa."

"Help you? She was blatantly betraying her people."

"I really don't know, Sire. She was very upset about the murder of her sister by her own family and she wanted revenge on Caius."

"Caius?"

Realising that he had said totally the wrong thing, his pallid complexion flushed red, yet again today. Feeling the rush of blood, he knew that Wamba had noticed, so there was no way he could invent a lie. The truth and all its consequences would out. Stumbling over his words rather than choosing them carefully, he retold Arantxa's request for a trial by ordeal and its outcome.

"I believe what you are saying, boy, two questions immediately spring to mind." Wamba's tone was back to his norm - calm, considerate and interested. "Firstly, why did she choose Caius? I have a vague memory of a colossal, brutal soldier. And, secondly, why did you allow it to happen?"

Regaining his emotions Marcus explained the deal they had struck; her escape route knowledge for an attempt to bring justice to a baby-slayer.

"I'm intrigued as to how a slip of a girl got the better of one of our best soldiers. What is more, I'm still not sure that the whole story is enough for betrayal of one's people, though that appears to be an easy thing to do these days. What would it take for you to betray your own people?"

The atmosphere of the tent had changed, the tone was different but Marcus felt he was in more danger now from this softly spoken approach than before.

"I would NEVER betray my people!!"

Stroking his chin and looking directly into the blazing eyes of the boy Wamba slapped his palm with the parchment he was holding.

"Again, I believe you, boy, but surely it all depends on who you regard as your *people*."

Marcus could not understand the turn of events. Was he being interrogated, softly and ineptly as it was, for being a traitor, either potential or real? Their escape was now viewed as a plot. It didn't make any sense. Why or how could it be seen that way? He was sure that he would never be able to understand Arantxa's motives, which taken at face value could be interpreted as unbelievable; the abandoning of her people …but there was no way in the world that it could be part of some complex master plan to infiltrate the king's camp, With a view to what? Gaining information? Assassination? It was all too preposterous to consider. Even so, there was little doubt the king was gripped, and definitely troubled by it all.

"Your father. Tell me about your father. As Duke of Tarraco, I should know him. I don't. I don't even remember ever seeing him at Toletum."

Marcus' confusion deepened, didn't Wamba say something about going to Tarraco before he became king? Why was his family being brought into this little incident?

"My father doesn't like to travel. He hardly ever leaves the province."

"Despite it being his duty as one of the leading dukes of the realm, he is never seen at Court."

"I do remember him going once Sire, and upon his return he vowed not to go back."

Wamba's interest was now complete upon hearing this information. Marcus again wondered if his mouth had let him and the family down. "Why, pray, might he have such a *violent* reaction to Toletum? A place full of intrigue and inaction, I agree it most certainly is, but to *vow* never to return, what did we do to him?"

What should he say, and how much should he say? Despite his youth, Marcus remembered well the monumental anger that his father expressed to the bishop and other leading members of Tarraco's elite at a meeting. Marcus wasn't officially there, he just happened to be in the far corner of the dining room, and nobody had thought to clear him out. His father had fumed, thumped the table and raised his voice to re-tell the slight and disrespect he had endured at the hands of the centralised state. The whole room was indignant at the treatment he had received. It devalued all of them that the highest representative of the once most powerful province was treated with disdain, as if he were little better than a country yokel who had found himself in the presence of royalty. He could hardly tell Wamba about how they had all seethed.

"Do I note a reluctance to answer your king's question?"

Shit. His transparent face and dithering had made things yet worse.

"No, Sire. Absolutely not. I was just trying to recall the event. It was quite a few years ago, I was quite young at the time and my memory of it is somewhat hazy." Perhaps lying or moving around the truth was like everything else, a matter of practice. He had delivered the statement without a hint of hesitation.

"I believe that he felt that King Reccesvinth had, well, not afforded enough time to him. After travelling all that way, he found himself sidelined, his counsel was not sought, and he was excluded from most of the more important meetings. He left early and no one even noticed this fact. All in all, he felt that Toletum preferred to live without Tarraco."

"Most interesting. I agree those days were not the most enlightened. Do you think he still feels this way?"

Marcus could smell a trap.

"Absolutely not, Sire. He was delighted at your ascension to the throne. I remember him clearly stating that the right man had got the job and things would be much better from now on. In fact, that was one of the main reasons he sent me here, as a sort of bridge to reconciliation." All said without the slightest colouring to show it for what it was, a pack of lies.

"Tell me a little about your family history. Make it brief. I want an over-view, not who married who, when and why."

"We are an ancient family, Sire. We trace our roots back, without interruption, to the leading families who decided to make the trek south to Roman lands away from the marauding hordes. Centuries of leadership and service is what defines our family. We were among one of the first families to put roots down in this part of the Roman Empire. We led the fight back after nearly being wiped out by the Franks with our cousins from the east. And, as one of the leading families, we were rewarded with Tarraco and that is where we have been ever since, over two centuries."

"However, I believe you are not one hundred percent Goth."

"No, Sire. As you know, there was quite an amount of intermingling with the local Roman population even before King Reccesvinth officially allowed all those years ago. Our family remained pure-bloods until my father's marriage. I am the first to be of mixed stock."

*

"So, I think everyone has said their piece and it's time to start bringing things to a conclusion before it gets any darker, or I get too much older," Jacob boomed out to the already quietening mass. The reason for the lull was clear; exhaustion. The brief meeting started by Isaac's statement reading, had now been going on for FIVE hours. The brothers had presumed that there would be quite a kerfuffle as it's not every day that the Jewish community decides to rebel. The community had been swallowing ignominy and pride after every Christian ecumenical council for over a century now. They had seen their role as reasonably equal citizens descend into what it was today; a people with few rights and an enormous number of legal constraints. It had got to the point when they were never sure if they were transgressing the law because there were so many of them. Laws of prohibition, starting with ownership of slaves thus making any landowner's life totally impossible, moving through limiting who they could trade with, followed quickly by laws denoting who they could marry, *logically,* then, being told how they could / should bring up their children, and ending up with whether they had the right to actually have a different religion in this newly Catholicised country.

Goaded, pushed and prodded, there seemed like there was no alternative to either submission or conversion. However, every cornered animal at some point, fights back no matter how big the hunter. Still though, there was a considerable minority who refused to accept the logic of the path of rebellion. The now weary participants had swung between the two major opinions, the, we-have-nothing-else-to-lose side and the how-bad-will-things-be–if –we–do-lose group.

Jacob had joined his brother and his daughter on the rope platform near the beginning of the *debate*, trying to restore some sort of order and cohesion to the competing loud voices. His role as moderator had been accepted, not because of any authority he had in the community, but because the silent majority wanted to hear something and not just various people shouting at the same time. There had been moments of great tension and, at one point, even a scuffle had broken out. A couple of elderly men, who had hated each other since childhood, took advantage to support the opposing camps to come to blows. Thankfully, their more sensible children restored peace rather than support their undignified, almost brawling parents.

After this marathon, Jacob was the only one left on the rope stage. Isaac took the first opportunity to get off as soon as his brother joined him. His relief was short-lived as he barged straight into Trudi's tirade "Look what you have started..". Again, he was saved by his niece, who had descended with him so as not to undermine her father's adopted role. It would not have looked good, a woman, worse, a daughter, to have a leading role.

"Uncle, you don't look so well. Let's sit here over in the shade. I will fetch you a drink." Taking his arm, she guided him away from her aunt who hardly seemed to notice as she was expressing her opinions, loudly, to the only other woman in the area who was nodding vigorously.

Once seated with a cup of cool water, Isaac began to breathe less rapidly. His heartbeat had dropped to something resembling normal, order was being restored among the chickens, neck muscles had come back from their break, and his hands no longer needed hiding. "Thank you, Rebecca. Your support and help was invaluable. My brother is a lucky man to have such a daughter."

"I'm not sure he thinks that, Uncle."

"Well, I do. Do you remember when he was suggesting that you should marry my David? The thought of having a daughter-in-law ally like you is becoming a most attractive idea."

Concern turned to incredulity on Rebecca's face. Her hands were heading towards her hips to take up her familiar combative stance, when her uncle almost choked spluttering water everywhere while laughing. It took time and more solicitations on her part to bring him back under enough control for him to look at her, still with tears in his eyes from the effort expended, still, with a smile playing around his lips to say, "Just thought I'd try." Playfully, she slapped his arm and kissed him on the head.

They stopped speaking as they vaguely heard her father's voice in the distance loudly shout, "Agreed". In their stillness, they could now hear more, "... unnecessary to go through with the mechanics of voting. To me, and I suppose to everyone else, even you, Jeremiah, that there *is* a clear majority, so, we will join in this Christian-led rebellion along with our brethren in the north."

"And we will all live, no, *die*, to regret it." shouted the unconvinced Jeremiah from a place nearer to Rebecca and Isaac.

There was a chorus of hushing and booing, "Please, let's not start again. The decision is made and when my brother, Isaac, or Rabbi Saul, who with the grace of God will have recovered from his illness, has more instructions we will stand ready. Thank you everyone for.."

"*Recovered from his illness*? How do you recover from dying of old age? Shit. This leaves me still in the spotlight. I don't want to be there. Why should I be there? I'm no rabbi. I'm no leader of men, I'm.."

"Uncle, don't worry yourself, I'm sure everything will work out fine." Rebecca assured him without a great deal of conviction, which diminished further, as she saw her aunt heading in their direction.

*

"Sire, General Paulus asks permission to enter." The tent flap had slapped open revealing a cautious guard who spoke without the conviction of his role.

"What? I told you to show him in the moment he arrived, what's all this about asking permission? Do as you were told, soldier!"

The admonished face came close to answering that exactly those were the instructions that they had received about the officer Marcus, and when they did let him in, they got chewed out. Judiciously closing his mouth, thinking that it was a shit job to be a guard, he saluted and left hastily. Flavius sauntered in still with a bathing towel in his hands, looking supremely confident, happy and delightfully clean. His salute was perfunctory rather than sharply military. Wamba bristled, was he to be treated without respect by everyone?

"Stand to attention, General."

Surprised by the tone, Flavius did so, while taking in the happenings of the tent. Marcus was not at his best, ashen faced and his body in a crumpled, submissive pose. This, both did and didn't surprise him. He knew that Marcus was here to give information about his relationship with the girl and the resulting escape, and he also knew that Marcus had not shown due respect when addressing the king. However, he didn't expect the king himself to deal with that fact, it wasn't his role to administer minor punishment. This, and the perplexing attitude of the guards outside, made for a most confusing situation.

"You've taken your time to get here, I sent for you quite a while ago. Dallying takes preference over an audience with your king, does it?"

So, Wamba was in one of those moods, thought Flavius. It wasn't the first one he had seen nor, he supposed, would it be the last. Tried and tested policy was to humour and weather until it blew over which could be seconds or days.

"Sire, I came as soon as I received the order." He held up the towel as evidence.

"Sadly, due to the fact that I was quite far into the water, the messenger couldn't actually deliver it for some time. I do most humbly apologise for the delay."

"Do put that bloody sopping thing outside, you are making everything in here wet."

Over. That was quick. Perhaps it was something of a record. While completing the latest order, Paulus couldn't help reflect that Wamba was essentially a good man, even if he was anything but stable.

"Now, sit down. We're having an interesting chat about Marcus's family. Did you know that everyone in Tarraco hates Toletum?"

"Sire, I didn't say .."

"Sit down, boy! I know you didn't say it but it was written all over your face and now I have evidence of the fact." He brandished the parchment he had been using for everything but reading since the beginning of the conversation.

The seated officers waited as Wamba returned the rolled up parchment to its previous role of palm slapper, while he paced deep in thought. The wait went on and on. Marcus stole a glance at his senior officer, who saw it and returned the gesture with one raised eyebrow. This was an often used trait. Marcus had observed it various times and wondered yet again on his ability. It was clever, and effective, and Marcus so wanted this skill. So much so that, like many other skills, he had practised for considerable periods when he was alone with no desirable results. It appeared that he could raise both, or neither, not one. Once, he had tried it out in a conversation with Arantxa only for her to ask whether he had stomach cramps.

The pacing suddenly stopped.

"General Paulus, you are to lead a force to Tarraconensis/Gallia Gothica leaving at the earliest possible moment. And you boy, you will accompany him as second-in-command and possessor of local knowledge."

The silence and complete look of astonishment on both men's faces told Wamba that he had neglected to impart some of the essential information. "This document from Bishop Aregio, gives news of the stirrings of a rebellion in that area, led from Gallia Gothica by various nobles and clergy with some sort of support from Tarraco."

*

"Amalaswinth, it's good to see a happy face. Everyone is looking so glum and earnest these days. I suppose the duke is expecting me. Where may he be found?"

The duke's servant looked much as she always did, which no one had ever described as the cheerful sort, full of bonhomie and a quick laugh. She did dour to perfection and seldom wavered from this achievement.

"Ah, good day to you, Bishop Cyprianus, His lordship is…"

"Splendid, splendid, splendid, I'm sure I'll find him in his study. Thank you so much."

Only a deft, backward move saved her from actually being shunted out of the way as the in a hurry chubby form brushed past her, letter in hand. Receiving the message but an hour previous, he felt he had to talk to someone of his own status. Obviously, he had squealed about it to Maria, the cheek of it, summoning him to Nemausus. Him, a metropolitan bishop, being summoned! If she had offered an opinion, it wouldn't have been listened to. She hadn't. She knew her role. Which was to prepare the metropolitan bishop's best robes for him to go out in.

"Cyprianus, do sit down before you fall or burst. You are beginning to make quite a habit of these entrances into this house. You must calm down before you do yourself some sort of injury. Amalaswinth, be so kind as to bring some ale, would you?"

The wind being taken from his sails, Cyprianus lowered himself gently into the nearest proffered chair.

"Ranosindus, do you know about..?"

The duke cut his paper waving short by holding up his own hand.

"Breathe, Cyprianus, breathe. Wait until you have had a drink. Whatever it is, will keep for a couple of minutes more."

Ranosindus knew exactly why the bishop was so disturbed and flustered as he had received a message at about the same time informing him of events. He was as upset by the contents but for entirely different reasons. The drink arrived and was quaffed immediately. "Amalaswinth, do bring another and one for me as well this time,"

"My dear duke, I have been summoned to attend a meeting in Nemausus! Summoned, not invited - quite shocking, summoned! Not even Toletum order, they invite. I must admit to being quite put out by the audacity of it. Me, the Metropolitan Bishop of Tarraco."

"I'm sure it was a clerical error. I have been requested to attend the same meeting and the message mentions you in glowingly respectful terms. It states quite clearly here," he took up the parchment which was lying next to him and pretended to read from it, " Blah blah blah, and if the esteemed Metropolitan Bishop of Tarraco would be so kind as to accompany you to this meeting, we would be so grateful."

Mollified, Cyprianus accepted his second ale and began to sip from it. "Well, that's a completely different story, isn't it? I suppose it's about this rebellion thing. Not sure about that at all."

Amalaswinth was just delivering the duke his ale when Cyprianus realised his error. "Oh, dear, sorry. It's supposed to be all hush hush , isn't it? Shouldn't have mentioned it in front of servants."

"Amalaswinth is much more than a servant, my dear bishop. What is more I would wager a considerable amount that she probably knows more about it than we do. Is that true, Amalaswinth?"

"As you know, Sire, I am not one to gossip or have an opinion on what my betters are talking about, if it be secret, but t'ain't much of a secret when the Jews are having a public meeting about it down in the port."

The duke hesitated as he was about to take a deep draft, "Is that a fact? Well, I never."

"Quite an argy bargee it were to, by all accounts, went on for hours."

"You don't happen to know the outcome, do you?"

"Oh yeah. They're in favour. Think that it'll help them in their defiance of the will of God in that dreadful blasphemous heretical religion of theirs."

"Most interesting. Thank you for the information. However, if you could leave us now to talk through this, I would be most grateful." Reluctantly, she moved to the door to take up her usual listening post. "Also, if you could shut the door completely, it would stop that nasty little draft that so plagues the bishop."

As the door closed anything but quietly, the bishop set down his ale and started muttering that he'd never mentioned anything about a draft. In fact, it was so warm out he'd welcome a little air.

"The Jews on side, our trip to Nemausus, all in all, it would appear that this rebellion is going to take place. Quite a prospect."

"It most certainly is, as is our joint journey. When shall we set off?"

This was the part that had been upsetting the duke when the bishop had blustered in - the prospect of spending days in the company of this man, days there, and then, days coming back!

*

"What's this, your father has become a traitor, has he?" Leaving Wamba's tent they were strolling back to the main body of the force slightly farther down in the valley.

"General, I know this can't be true. Why would he have sent me here if he were contemplating such an action? It must be a mix up, a confusion, or an invention of this bishop. What was his name?"

"I think he said it was Aregio." Marcus was deeply troubled whereas Flavius was amused. "What I can't understand is why the King still trusts you. In his place, I would have had you clapped in irons, either as a precaution or as a hostage. Not even sure I should be seen with you. You may be planning to do away with the best general in the service of the king or convert him to the other side."

Marcus stopped in his tracks, his face registering genuine surprise tinged with more than a little apprehension. Flavius roared with laughter, clapping the boy on the back. "Come on, you little traitor, we have some organising to do."

Flavius almost skipped with joviality all the way back to his tent while Marcus dragged himself deep in thought, which was continually interrupted by slaps on the back or shoulder of varying degrees of force. "Marcus, snap out of it. I need your help and you need to give me your complete and undivided attention. I have never been to that part of the country. Well, I say never, that's not quite true, my parents hail from a place called Emporias, somewhere on the coast I think. Big Greek community there. We moved to Toletum when I was very young so I have absolutely no recollections of the place. They always made it out as some sort of paradise on earth, forever harping on about returning one day, never did though. Ever been there?"

Marcus was still dazed, gratefully accepted the proffered seat as Flavius wittered on with family memories while digging in a box of scrolls. "Here it is, a map, I knew I had one." Weighing it down with unlit candles at either end, he uncoiled it. From Marcus's view point it looked rudimentary at best. "Bought this from a map maker in Toletum. Best in the business I was told. Cost me a pretty penny I can tell you."

"You were robbed. When you see the man again, ask for your money back or better still, cut off his hands before he can cheat anyone else."

"What do you mean? He came highly recommended."

Marcus stood and approached the table and laughed at what he saw. "By whom? Unless they are already blind, I seriously recommend that you maim them as well. How can Dertosa, which is a good day's ride to the south, be next to Tarraco? I have never been to Narbo or Nemausus, but I can tell you, they are not south of Gerunda." Crestfallen, Flavius was unsure whether to trust the boy or his significantly expensive acquisition. Seeing his dilemma, Marcus retook his seat. "Yes, you're right. I wouldn't trust me either, especially as my father is a traitor."

Spurred into action, Flavius ripped the document in half. Intending to go further, he stopped. "No, I will save these for our little map maker to eat before I do him serious injury." Taking in the dejected, slumped form, he resumed his previous bonhomie, "Ok, son of a traitor, give me some information. Where should we go first and how long will it take us?"

Marcus knew that the best approach would be to head for the heart of the rebellion in Gallia Gothica, but he really had to find out what his father knew, and how much he was involved, so he suggested going to Tarraco first, which he knew from experience would take the best part of a week's journey.

"Not sure that is the best approach, but you seem to want to go home and I cannot possibly proceed without my local guide, so to Tarraco we go."

At that moment General Kunimund barged through the tent flap almost shouting, "I hear rumours, nothing but rumours. General Paulus, could you kindly inform me as to what is going on? The king says that you have all the pertinent information and will inform *me*. Would you kindly do so, as *I* still remain the superior officer."

"General Kunimund, so good of you to join us. We were just discussing the best way to Tarraco. Perhaps you have an opinion."

"Opinions? I have lots. Also, I own a map which would give us more informed information. Before any of that, I need to know why you are preparing to abandon camp."

"We are not leaving you voluntarily, Kunimund, we are being sent to put down a small rebellion which is brewing. This map you've got, did you buy it in Toletum in a small shop on the corner, at the end of the main street?"

"I did, but I don't see.."

"That shop keeper should die very slowly with his body parts scattered to all the points on one of his bogus maps."

Flavius explained the whole situation to his fellow general. Kunimund went into thinking pose. It were as if the whole universe had been put on pause. Nothing moved, the breeze had died down, the flies, usually at their annoying busiest at this time of day, decided to have a break while Kunimund contemplated. The time stretched and so did Flavius's patience. If the general were like this in the confines and safety of a tent, what must he be like on a battlefield, he mused.

Hand movement started, head was scratched, chin was stroked, and the flies went back to doing whatever flies feel the need to do, which required Kunimund to wave them away from his face.

"All in all then, we know precious little."

So much time to come to this conclusion! "Kunimund, you really have hit the nail on the head there. A superb summary of the situation in which we find ourselves."

The generals eyed each other. Kunimund was unsure whether he was being made fun of. Irony and sarcasm were not his longest suits.

Actually, it was hard to tell what his redeeming traits were, some might venture loyalty and steadfastness.

"We don't know how serious this is, nor how many people it involves, nor their military strengths. It's difficult to estimate what size force you need to take with you. However, as you are nothing but a dissuasive gesture, perhaps half a cohort will be enough."

"Marcus, we are a *dissuasive gesture*, I have never been one of those before, have you?"

"General Paulus, we cannot leave our forces under strength, it would be an invitation to the Vascones to attack, and we can hardly go on the offensive, if we have been depleted. May be we could spare half with three centurions."

"A half? To put down a rebellion which encompasses one of the biggest and most prosperous regions of the kingdom? Surely that is far too many. I think it might be better if just Marcus and I went. He could go to the south, and I could deal with all those northerners, with a bit of luck I may be able to go on a quick excursion into Frankia to smite them as well."

"Just the two of you? No, I'm not sure that would work."

"Kunimund, think about it, I can be most dissuasive when I put my mind to it. And Marcus would be playing on home ground, so.."

"No, I really feel that you need a few more to back you up."

"My opinion, exactly. We will take the men that Marcus arrived with, plus all the men who escaped with us from the village fight, and add them to a whole cohort with six centuriae."

"What! I will not allow.."

"General, the king told me to take as many I deemed necessary. He stated that as you were not attacking *anyone,* with or without the forces you have got, then you can hold a defensive position until those reinforcements from Toletum arrive in a couple of weeks."

*

It felt as if autumn had arrived early in Gallia Gothica and without much notice. It wasn't one of those seasons fading in and out moments, the change was drastic and brutal. Literally, one day saw meltingly energy sapping temperatures, the next it was time to cover parts for warmth not modesty . The cold wind blew heartily as they entered Narbo. This gave yet more ammunition to Bishop Cyprianus's complaining.

Duke Ranosindus's patience had been stretched to the limit, and beyond, by the last few days. It was now so taut that a drum beat could be played on it. On the journey as the bishop whinged, moaned, complained and whined about anything and everything, Ranosindus had contemplated all sorts of measures; abandoning him, gagging him and even killing him, all of which he would have done either separately or as a combined package had it not been an explicit instruction in the letter that he had received that Bishop Cyprianus arrive safely and in his company. For some reason the rebellion instigators needed him. It was beyond Ranosindus's imagination why *anyone* would need this useless, unpleasant lump of blubber dressed as a bishop.

"Feel that wind, dear duke. I feel chilled to the bone. How am I to survive such adverse conditions? I have but summer clothes. All my warm winter wools are back in Tarraco. I do feel the cold so, I'm not built for it, you know."

Ranosindus implored God to strike the man dumb, or failing that, to make himself, if not completely deaf, at least very hard of hearing. The exact same wailing lament tone and sentence had been used to describe the heat. Instead of impaling him on the end of his long sword, he chose the less messy option of sympathy and a spurt on the horse.

"I'm sure that the local bishop will be able to loan you the use of something suitable to ward off the wind. Oh, I can see some people in the distance. They must be our welcoming party."

"But you don't..." The rest of the words were lost as the duke sped off to be greeted by the fictitious welcoming party.

Narbo was a pretty little town, certainly one of the most pleasant they had come across on their journey. Though provincial, it had an air of importance beyond its size.

Surprisingly and happily, this was their destination. Initially, Ranosindus had been told that they would be meeting in Nemausus, which would have been at least another day's travel, a ride that he was sure that his patience would not survive.

The metropolitan bishop's palace wasn't hard to find. Ranosindus didn't wait for the chilled cleric to catch up. Jumping off his horse, he almost ran into the great hall where there was a group waiting to greet him. The count he knew, the metropolitan bishop himself he recognised and the other bishop he had never seen.

"Welcome brother duke," started the metropolitan bishop Argebaud, "you're alone? I thought that Bishop Cyprianus was to.."

"He is and will be here shortly." Hands were shaken "I need sanctuary. Four days
AND nights on the road, I can take NO more."

While the two elder men looked both amused and surprised by the duke's forthright opinions and total lack of diplomacy, it was the younger man who answered, "We, as fellow bishops, know what you mean. It would be hard to describe Bishop Cyprianus as an easy travelling companion. I'm sure God will reward you for all your suffering. By the way, I don't think we have met, despite me spending some time in your magnificent city. My name is Bishop Gunhild."

"Pleased to meet you. Be prepared. At the moment it is your bitter wind which is his chief complaint, though many other minor causes of great discomfort and dissatisfaction will be heard shortly. If you have something warm to wrap him in, it may save a lot of bloodshed."

The younger man chuckled deeply. "I'm fairly sure that we do not possess swaddling clothes of that size. Perhaps a fur coat, with a hood, might suffice?" He left the room in search of the article mentioned.

"Do be seated, duke." The metropolitan bishop set about playing host. "Drinks will arrive shortly. Normally, at this juncture of the greeting one would ask about your journey, perhaps it would be better to dispense with this formality, as I have the feeling that that is something you would rather forget than dwell upon."

"Thank you. However, if you don't mind I would rather stand and even walk around a little. After sitting so long on a horse, my legs have lost the habit."

Turning abruptly he bumped into the entering figure of Lady Chlodoswintha. Both surprised and confused by the accident, they were a tangle of bodies and profuse apologises on both sides.

"Well, that is a novel way of being introduced to my wife. Duke Ranosindus, meet Lady Chlodoswintha."

They took a step back to see each other better, both appreciating the sight in front of them. It was the female who recovered quickest, "You do have an *interesting* way of making your presence known to a Lady, duke."

"I must apologise again.."

"Metropolitan Bishop, there you are. I can't tell you just how cold I feel. The wind you have is so bitterly chilled, it gets to.."

"I'm most pleased to see you as well, Cyprianus."

"Ohh, yes, very happy to see you metropolitan bishop and.."

"I'm Count Hilderic, the lady in the arms of your duke, I believe, is my wife; Lady Chlodoswintha."

"Bishop Cyprianus, I do hope you find another way of warming yourself from our chill autumn air which doesn't involve embracing the first lady that you meet, which seems to be the duke's solution. I am the only lady present, I would find myself lacking both in body mass and arms."

Ranosindus coloured. A strange experience having not blushed since probably his teen years, he had to add this to another, he thought, long lost sensation he had felt in the accidental arms of the count's wife.

Cyprianus, unused to humour of any sort, found this statement doubly confusing as it came from someone who was clearly most aristocratic and female. Women do not make jokes. Never having heard one, he felt he had to accept the statement at face value even though it made little sense.

"Yes, erm, I can see that you have but two arms, My Lady. Body size is a relative concept as you can see from me, I am well built, and I don't think that you should worry about not being sturdy enough, to me you seem.."

"A cloak for you, my brother bishop." Gunhild's entrance was hurried from the moment he realised that Cyprianus was being moved into the unknown territory of flirtatious humour. Catching the count's eyebrows zooming up his forehead, he did his best to wrap the bishop up.

"Careful, man, do you want to truss me up like the infant Jesus in the manger?"

"Ranosindus, if you could unhand my wife, my sympathy for you and your recent suffering would be plentiful."

Chlodoswintha and the Duke were no longer touching but the distance between them wasn't great, nor was it what was normally required, or accepted, as a norm when different genders shared space. Neither felt the need to be farther away. Stung into action, they both took a speedy step backwards, wife towards husband and duke into a small stool causing him to losing his balance and almost hitting the floor.

It was Gunhild, the man for all crises, who steadied the duke by taking a firm grip of his arm. "I venture to suggest that our guests are tired from their journey and I will escort them to their rooms and we can talk more over dinner."

*

General Kunimund had exited with considerably more bluster than he had entered, which was quite a feat given that there was only the canvass of the tent to make noise with, Marcus dreaded to think what the man could do with solid wood .

"The general appears to have left us. Didn't hear him say goodbye, nor wish us good luck. Perhaps he's one of these emotional sorts that hates long, drawn-out farewells. I do wish he'd taken a few of the flies with him though."

Staying quiet and as still as possible had been Marcus' policy throughout the general's spat. He'd come in for collateral damage on previous occasions back home, when his father had rows with people of a similar social standing. He never worried if it had been someone further down the food chain, they would get all the volume, bile and sometimes violence, however, when his father couldn't resort to his bullying directly, it was he who received whatever was going. His, successful, policy was to believe that he wasn't there, take no notice at all of what was happening and remain statue-like drawing NO attention to himself. As he was deep into this state it took some time for him to realise that Flavius was talking to him.

"What?"

"Marcus, where are you? You are worse than Kunimund, at least he's physically present. I said go and inform your men and the group we had when we were running from the Vascones. I'll make sure the other centuriae are told. Go man, don't stand there looking like a fish out of water."

"Yes," Marcus was startled into action, " I'm going."

"By the way Marcus, in case it has escaped your notice, we are in the army and we are supposed to follow a sort of protocol." Marcus registered perplexity. Flavius threw the nearest thing to hand which was a candlestick that he had been using as a weight for his duff map, a perfect shot smacked into Marcus' temple. "You address me as *sir* and you salute!"

"Ohh, yes. I mean oh, YES SIR!" With a pathetic attempt at a salute he left the tent rubbing his head.

Making his way down to the side of the main encampment where his troops were billeted again lost in his thoughts, he literally bumped into Arantxa. She had seen his approach and was keen to rekindle whatever was interrupted down by the river. Standing her ground, she knew a collision was inevitable.

"I'm so sorry," his head moved from its downward thinking position to take in the girl he was in the process of bundling over, "Oh, it's you." Sensing no emotion in his voice, Arantxa felt she needed to provoke some. "You almost kill me, and now you knock me over. Is there no end to your violence towards me?"

Stung by this accusation Marcus began his denials and offered profuse apologies.

"Don't worry, it doesn't matter. I am used to much worse."

"Arantxa, no, I mean, sorry, I really didn't see you. I was lost in thought about the journey and what it all means to my family and.."

"What journey? What's wrong with your family?"

"I'm to join General Paulus's troop going to Tarraconensis. We will be leaving tomorrow."

"And just when were you going to inform me of this?"

Seeing her bristling with indignant anger, he thought it not wise to tell her that it had never even crossed his mind that he should inform her about this decision, or anything else for that matter.

"I haven't told the troops yet. I was on my way there now."

"When you nearly caused me serious harm."

"I was thinking, you see."

"No, it's you who doesn't see. Walking, thinking and looking where you are going are too much for you to handle all at the same time?"

"Noo.."

"And what's this big red mark on your head?"

"The general threw a candlestick at me for not listening."
To stop herself from laughing, she slapped the other side of his head with more force than would be normal in a playful gesture.
"OWW."
"That's for not talking … to me." With that, she stomped off, her straight back displaying all the displeasure that she actually didn't feel. If he could have viewed her from the front, her conflicting emotions of tenderness and vulnerability were in plain sight.

*

It was quite a spectacular meal.
Ranosindus glowed with satisfactory pleasure. If only Amalaswinth could cook or even organise a meal to this standard, he would be a happy man. Furthermore, he had been seated opposite the only female at the table, the Lady Chlodoswintha, Chloda, as he had heard her called by the count. Such an attractive woman. Her blonde hair, occasionally escaping from its bound state on her head, promising length and shining beauty, swept casually back in a semblance of order in an unconcerned whisk of the hand causing pangs of something inside the duke. Unsure as to what these spasms meant, he knew it wasn't indigestion. Despite trying his level best to be discreet, at times he found himself almost staring at a face that must have been truly beautiful in her youth and had aged into a sort of handsomeness found in few middle-aged women. Lost in wonderment of what age she might be now, he lingered too long, only to find inquisitive blue eyes meeting his. Exposed, he flustered a signal to a servant to pour more wine while he reddened yet again.
Cyprianus didn't glow, he glowered. The food was too rich for his liking. There was plenty of it, which as far as he was concerned was a good thing, but it was too fancy. He hankered after some plainer fare, at a loss to understand why people had to mess around with making things that tasted fine as they were taste like something else by dipping, smothering or marinating it. Furthermore, he had been seated at the far end of the table away from the maximum dignitaries, next to a couple of Frankish Bishops he had never met before and who insisted on waxing about the glory of the food. There was some Abbot, who had been attempting to make polite conversation, who had turned his attention to the other end of the table once Cyprianus mentioned, *ever so slightly*, some of the discomfort and woes he had experienced on the journey. Thankfully though, the never ending parade of food had ceased and the meal was drawing to a close. Feeling tired and chilled again, as he was placed farthest from the roaring fire, he looked forward to the warm bedroom

with many covers to bury himself under. So, it came as something of a surprise when the count cleared his throat demanding the attention of all by stating that they ought to move onto business. What could anyone want to talk about at this hour after so much wine and food, surely the only civilised thing to do would be to bed with or without female company?

"We all know why we have gathered." Cyprianus wanted to raise his objection as he had but the vaguest notion of the reason for the meeting. However, seeing all the other heads nod in agreement, even the Franks, he felt he couldn't show his ignorance.

"It is a matter of great urgency that we proceed with our proposal as I believe that Wamba has received word, forewarning him."

"By whom? About what?" Cyprianus regretted the words as soon as they had left his mouth. All heads turned to him, irritation and annoyance was etched on each one. And to compound his humiliation it was the woman, quite what a female was doing at the table if business was to be spoken about, was beyond him, who answered him in a tone that might be used to a backward, very slow on the uptake, five-year-old.

"My dear Bishop Cyprianus, as you know full well, our plans to secede from the kingdom, are not supported by your fellow resident bishop, Aregio. And it is he who has taken it upon himself to send a messenger to Wamba's camp."

All of this was news to Cyprianus, "Oh yes, of course, it's just a little difficult to actually hear what is being said down here at this end of the table." Feeling eminently proud of this face-saving response, which also acted as veiled complaint at the seating arrangement, he sat back in an air of dissatisfied disdain.

"Thus, I am proposing the consecration for the day after tomorrow. I know it will require a considerable feat of organisation. Thankfully, Lady Chlodoswintha is here and has already, quietly, discreetly and efficiently managed to gather most of the material necessities. And now we have all the personnel required." The Count's arm expansively included all at the table, settling on the cleric close to Cyprianus "Abbot Ranimiro, do you have all you need?"

"I can hear you perfectly from down here, count," the cleric glanced at Cyprianus,   " and I would like to state quite categorically that I have all I need and I am prepared for this great honour you are about to bestow on me."

"Oww." Cyprianus had actually drawn blood as he bit so hard on his lip to stop himself from displaying yet more ignorance. Luckily, he was ignored as Metropolitan Bishop Argebaud had started speaking.

"It is all a trifle unorthodox, Cecilius's absence will be sorely missed both as an enthusiastic supporter and his rank in the Church. Cannon law,

Aregio was most vocal on this question, quoting article nineteen, I believe he said about a thousand times, of the 633 Ecumenical council of Toletum, which references the council of Nicaea, does state that there should be three bishops from the same province present and we have but two in the Bishops of Maguelonne and Tarraco. However, the law does not categorically state that I, as presiding authority, do not count in that number. It's something that has never been questioned before as there are usually a surfeit of bishops attending these events. Furthermore, in case anyone would like to quibble on this point, we do have our two dear Frank colleagues in attendance."

"Splendid, metropolitan bishop. Thus we will remove Aregio from his post as Bishop of Narbo and replace him with Abbot Ranimiro."

The scales fell from Cyprianus's eyes, he was being used, used, use!

*

Unlike the generals' tent, his didn't afford enough room to stand, sitting uncomfortably was a possibility, his preference was to lie. It was true that the ground was bumpy and unpleasant, not anything that caused objection as it reflected his thoughts fairly accurately.

The Tarraco group of soldiers he'd arrived with were delighted by the prospect of returning home. They had never really integrated into the main force. Their different accents and habits caused them to be marginalised to the point of being shunned by the others who all hailed from the middle / south of the kingdom. The sum total of their exposure to fighting, ostensibly the reason for their presence, was zero. A life of hanging around, drills and awful rations was draining. The only Vascones they had seen were the two women who Marcus had brought back, the pretty,aloof one and the chubby friendly one.

Their reception of the returning home news was boisterous, which contrasted sharply with that of the ambushed group. Marcus had a good working relationship with them. The fact that his *contacts* had saved them, made up for his complete lack of military leadership or ability. It was true that there were a couple who resented his role in Caius's demise. The others though, were happy to be shot of the big bully and even more so at the hands of a slip of a girl. The general feeling towards Marcus was that he was a nice, friendly, if a useless sort of bloke, so when he told them that they would be going to put down a rebellion under his leadership, there were mixed reactions. The negative ones were allayed greatly when Marcus explained that General Paulus would be in overall charge. And their reluctance was almost completely relieved when he explained that it wouldn't be arduous, in fact, it would be little more than a reconnaissance mission. The pairing of the words *Paulus* and *reconnaissance* always caused much merriment, the soldiers knowing that was how his fucking trips were described. Still, they were being dragged to the far end of the kingdom full of people with strange accents and Jews - not really an enticing prospect, there was more glory in the slaughtering of the Vascones.

Feeling quite pleased with himself and what he had achieved in his messenger role he wasn't thrilled to spy Arantxa coming from a distance with evident intention of intersecting his trajectory. The fact that both sides of his head were marked red had caused a lot of fun and speculation among the two sets of troops he'd spoken to. He was certainly not keen to add another visible injury, so as subtly as he could, he wielded to the right heading away from the camp and her. After a while of wrong direction walking, he risked a sneak glance over his shoulder, no female in sight, his step slowed slightly.
"Going anywhere interesting? I mean besides to war."
How did she do that? She was behind him, well behind, and quite some way away. It was physically impossible that she could be standing next to the path leaning on a stubby excuse for a tree in front of him.
"Surprised to be seeing me again? At least this time you didn't try to bowl me over. Ezte has just told me that you have informed the men of your departure. Tomorrow, she said."
"I've only just, how could she, and how –here – you - behind…?"
"It's supposed to be me that is bad at Latin, not you. Would you prefer to communicate in my language as I'm not sure what you actually said. It sounded like a lot of ideas rolled into one without there being one complete sentence."
She had reduced the distance between them while speaking and he flinched when she moved her hand towards his face. Braced for the blow, he was relieved when it resulted in a stroke of his face rather than another whack.
"I'm sorry about that. It was meant to be much softer."
Allowing himself to be stroked like some injured animal, he eyed her warily while trying to think of what to say. The recent and distant past were difficult areas and the future was completely out of bounds.
"I said I was sorry, what more do you want me to do? There's no need to sulk."
"I'm not sulking, I'm just thinking."
"Doing a lot of that these days, aren't you? And it seems that whenever it happens no other activity, walking / talking is possible."
Still stumped for words and a safe area in which to put them, he remained silent. Meanwhile her stroking hand stopped its movement, and was joined by the other, on the other side of his face. She gripped, not in a

tender way, more as if she were guiding a horse. "At what time are we leaving tomorrow, the early morning I presume? It doesn't give me much time to get things ready. *Actually*, thinking about it, I haven't got *anything* to get ready. So whatever time you get all the others into marching formation, I'll tag along at the back."

"We?"

"Yes. Oh, I didn't mention, did I? Ezte has decided to stay. She thinks that there is a decent chance that she could have a future here. Good luck to her, I say. I definitely wouldn't want to be stuck in this camp with all these men without my protector." It was double handed stroking, followed by a doubled-handed, very gentle slap and peck on the forehead and she was on her way back to the camp.

The bumpy, unpleasant and protrudingly sharp rock surface he was lying on was the perfect place for him to reflect. How could he tell her that she wasn't allowed to come? Or how would he tell the general that she was coming?

Arantxa had arrived back down at the river, upstream, away from the main bathing area where it was normally busy with splashing men, water gathers or other camp- follower women washing clothes. *Other camp follower women*, the thought had come into her head this way. Is this how she now thought of herself, a female follower?

Her chat with Ezte had been brief and to the point, that girl was always blunt and very much to the point. Since their previous conversation, only a couple of days before, Ezte's Latin had progressed rapidly under the tutelage of her relative. Also, this relative, Arantxa had never actually heard a name used, it was simply *my relative*, whose *man* was the Alun / Goth, had introduced her to one of his friends. According to Ezte, this new man wasn't unkind. She cackled that there was no way he would ever be entered, never mind win, any beauty contest, but when it came to that, she was conscious that neither would she, but he was more attentive and pleasant to her than her husband had ever been. Apparently, their conversation wasn't what anyone might call deep or profound, based instead on pointing at things and saying the word in one language and then the other. They both enjoyed the game and were comfortable in each other's company playing it. Given this, she stated clearly that she appreciated everything that Arantxa had done for her, but she saw no reason to give up this potentially interesting situation to go gallivanting to unknown lands just to keep her company.

This came as something of a blow to Arantxa. Her presumption had been that her only *friend* would make the journey with her. She never contemplated the fact that Ezte wouldn't come. After her conversation with Marcus, it was now clear that *he* hadn't considered her welfare either. Perhaps she was guilty of building a few castles in the air, reality on this rock next to the rushing water was dawning; she was alone. Her future didn't look good at all.

It was weighing options time. The first was to stay, make the most of the camp, find a man. It was true what Ezte had mentioned, there were an awful lot to choose from, and settle down to her lot. Option two, to leave the camp, she was not a prisoner, head back to her *people,* not her village, another, farther away and see what happens. Or option three, follow Marcus, despite the fact that he doesn't want her, to a faraway place to start again.

*

"I feel I must whole heartedly congratulate you, Lady Chlodoswintha." Duke Ranosindus was stood in the hall dressed for his journey as the lady of the house swept from the kitchen area clearly still in full organisational mode. She took in the elegantly attired noble from Tarraco and placed herself extremely close to him, fighting with that rebellious wisp of blond hair as she did.

"With all your heart, duke, really do you mean that?"

Ranosindus, who had been loitering with intent to speak to his hostess alone before setting off, had practised what he was going to say, choosing his words carefully hoping to leave innuendo and doubt in the lady's mind. Instead her response and proximity flustered him. "I mean that, I truly believe that the job you did yesterday was magnificent. Everything went so smoothly, not a hitch in the whole event." Not actually stammering, the words left his mouth haltingly rather than eloquently.

"Oh, duke, I believe that I really do know what you mean." She looked deeply into his eyes and it was he that had to break the contact by pretending to adjust the ties on his cloak as, yet again, she made him blush to the roots of his hair. No woman, not even his dearly loved dead wife, had ever been able to affect him so.

"As you may have ascertained, I am ready for the trip back to Tarraco, so, I suppose I must be off, though the whereabouts of Cyprianus remain a mystery. I suppose he's waiting down by the horses as I saw him leave quite some time ago."

"Duke, because I have enjoyed your *attention*, I decided that you deserve to be rewarded. So, I would like to offer you something as a parting gift. Something, I know will earn me a place in your thoughts." She closed the already short distance towards him and moved her mouth in the direction of his ear. Not only was her lavender perfume enveloping him, but he could actually feel her body warmth.

"Arh, there you are. I have been searching for you all over. I thought that maybe you would be down in the stables where your horse is saddled ready to go, but again I find you in the arms of my wife. You do seem to be making a habit of this and it is something I would not like to encourage." The count's tone was jovial but there was a definite undercurrent of displeasure.

"Oh, husband, you ruined the moment! I was just about to tell him of our little present to him."

"Chloda, ours? No, it was your idea and as always I do as you bid. However, I am sure the duke will be most grateful to you, as I will be, if he unhands you for a moment."

Smartly Ranosindus stepped back firstly checking to see if there were any potential ambushing stools.

"What I was going to tell you before my husband's untimely appearance," her eyes twinkled at him " was, that I, we, have arranged for Cyprianus to stay here for a few more days to try his diplomatic best to instruct the new Bishop of Narbo, Ranimiro, in his duties."

The Duke's face brightened like the sun breaking through the mist of a cold winter's morn. "Really? Oh wonderful! How did you manage to do that? Yesterday evening after the service, he spent the whole time chewing my ear off complaining about how cheated and used he felt and couldn't wait to get home to warm weather and proper food."

"Our food is not up to your standards in Tarraco, is it not?" The lady's eyebrows arched.

"This is not my opinion, it's…"

"If your food is so good perhaps I, we, should come down to visit you." The eyebrows remained questioningly high while the piercing, blue eyes bored into him. "Anyway, we managed to convince him that only his expertise, being a bishop of decades of experience, would allow the ex-abbot to cope in his new role. Flattery tends to resolve even the thorniest of doubts. Talking of which, we have yet to decide a time and date for the coronation of my husband."

"Coronation?"

"My dear duke," she took his arm and lead him in the direction of her husband and the door, "The new kingdom, will need a figurehead."

*

"You sent for me, sir?" Marcus accompanied that stress on the *sir* with a sharp most military salute.

"Yes. You didn't report back on the tasks I delegated to you."

"Didn't I? Should have I? I didn't think.."

"*Marcus*, you really are a disaster at this army way of life, aren't you? I thought, and have been told, that my attitude is a bit wayward however, compared to you…"

Marcus began to formulate a denial when he realised that he had no arguments to refute the accusation, the fact that he managed to salute and remember to say "sir" didn't really cut the mustard. Also, if he just said *nooo* the way Rebecca would, with pleading sincerity, then he would sound exactly like her, a little girl, which would help his military bearing not one jot.

As it was clear that Marcus wasn't going to say anything without prompting Flavius prompted, "So…"

"Well, I did remember to salute.."

"MARCUS! I want a report back.

"Yes, sir. Sorry, sir! Everything done, sir. Both groups were receptive or enthusiastic, well, one was receptive and one enthusiastic."

"Marcus, I don't care about their emotional response to an order. Will everyone be ready to set off at first light?"

"First light? Actually, I didn't mention that we would be leaving quite so early. I just said tomorrow."

"Oh Marcus, Marcus, Marcus…"

"Sorry." Completely deflated Marcus wanted to get back in the general's good books. "I'll run back and tell them now."

"Officers don't run! And don't go back, you'll lose face. Send a messenger with another order, like the amount of rations they will be expected to take, and within that order mention the time of departure."

Marcus's face lit up, "That's a good idea, I'll do that straight away." He turned to leave.

"You have not been given permission to go! It is the commanding officer who decides when conversations are finished! Marcus, get a grip. I think that I will have to recommend to the king that you terminate your military career once we settle this problem in north-east as you just don't seem suited to it."

Unsure if he thought this a good or a bad thing, Marcus found it difficult to react. On the one hand, nobody enjoys being told that they aren't any good at something and being rejected, it spurs them to want to do better. However, on the other, he really did not enjoy all the paraphernalia that went with serving in the army. The fighting bit was quite exciting; the rest was either tedious or boring. It wouldn't be a bad thing to be back home, though his father might be peeved. *His father.* Who knows what he was up to, was he really involved in this rebellion? It seemed most improbable. If he were, then it would be a very good thing that he was discharged from the army.

Expecting, well quite what he was expecting in response to his threat, Flavius wasn't sure, but he didn't think that it would be met with thoughtful silence. Perhaps resignation and silence was an option, but not what he was seeing which was a young man contemplating the pros and cons of being discharged, dishonourably to boot. The lad really wasn't cut out for this life, and the sooner he was left in his father's home in Tarraco the better.

"I apologise for interrupting your thoughts, Marcus," Flavius started sarcastically.

"Don't worry about it. I.."

"Marcus, you really are a total disaster." Flavius sighed. He found it difficult to stay annoyed with such innocence. The boy wasn't trying to be wilful, disobedient and disrespectful; he did them all quite, separately or collectively, naturally.

"I think Arantxa has the same opinion. In fact, it's becoming fairly unanimous among most of the people I have contact with. The list is quite long, starting with my father, which is why I am here, and then Rebecca, another reason I am here, leading through you all the way up to the King."

"We can't all be wrong," Flavius wasn't trying to be cruel, in fact, he was attempting to make light of the evidently dire depths that the boy was wallowing in. Marcus's once sad expression turned to deeply hurt, told him he had made a mistake, so in a friendly tone he continued, " Rebecca, who's she, an old flame? And Arantxa, have you told her we are leaving? I think it would be a matter of courtesy to do so."

Marcus spluttered, "An old flame? Hardly! Just a Jewish girl of the neighbourhood who liked everyone to hear her views. And Arantxa, well, I wanted to talk to you about her. What do you think that I should do about her?"

"I didn't know that the rich and powerful of Tarraco mixed with Jews, that's something that would certainly be frowned upon in Toletum." It suddenly occurred to Paulus that he could raise the boy's spirits, "Actually, Marcus I think that is admirable. I never found the Jews to be either good or bad, whether individually or as a nation. In my experience, they are pretty much like any other group, be they Hispano-Romans, Goths or Greeks, some good, and some bad. This Rebecca seems to be something of a character, and has obviously had a great deal of influence on you. You'll have to introduce us when we reach Tarraco."

"Nooo, she wouldn't like you." Flavius's raised eyebrows made it clear that he'd said the wrong thing yet again, "I mean, I'm not sure you'd like her …very much of a Tomboy who is forever telling you what you've done wrong."

Flavius decided not to make an issue of it, instead moving back to the other female mentioned. "So, what's the problem with Arantxa?"

"She says she's coming with us."

"Marcus, you do get yourself into such muddles. Why should she come? She helped us in the valley, but she was paid back with freedom for herself and her friend. She is no longer your responsibility...unless you have started some sort of romantic attachment."

"Oh no! Not that! It's just that.."

"It's nothing of the sort. Go and tell her straight that she will not be coming and get that messenger sent to the troops about first light." Marcus dithered. " Now!"

Marcus turned and slouched towards the exit. "And Marcus, salute when you leave!!!"

*

Still seated on her rock with bare feet dangling in the water, she felt much like the little fish that circled her toes, confused. They were trying to decide whether this apparition represented danger or a potential new food source. Her conflict was between boring stability of camp life, or the danger of unknown parts with nobody she knew and not considered important by the person she'd saved. Lost in her maudlin thoughts she hadn't noticed that she was no longer alone, it was only after a discreet throat clearance that she was startled enough to look around.

"Sorry to disturb you." Her feet were out of the water and ready to be put to sprinting use on dry land, "It's just that Ezte said that I would find you here."

The use of her friend's name made her relax somewhat though she remained tense and prepared to make a dash for it. For the first time she took in the face of the speaker. He was familiar; she had seen him around the camp. He had some sort of rank, centurion or something like that she supposed because he was forever shouting at others. By appearances he looked as if he were in his late twenties, powerfully built, not unhandsome despite the long badly healed scar that ran down the left side of his face, an uglier deeper version of Flavius's facial feature. His demeanour, normally so severe, was bordering on bashfully timid, clearly not a real threat. Tucking her sopping feet under her body, she turned, inviting him to continue speaking.

"Ezte is, erm, well, with my brother," he hadn't reverted to his usual shouting volume but he was gathering more confidence with every word. "and she was just saying that you were unsure whether you wanted to stay in the camp or go on this expedition."

"Yes, that's true."

"Well, I shall be the leading centurion of the group and Ezte thought that, if you were determined to go, then I should offer you my protection. You see, there will be a small group of women and some children who will follow. However, you do not know any of these and most are *attached* to a soldier in my group. So, Ezte thought.."

"That girl seems to be thinking a great deal. And you, your name is .."

"Milo. Centurion Milo"

"You, *Centurion* Milo, will give me *protection* at what cost to myself?"

"Well, clearly it would be understood.."

It was at that moment that Arantxa spotted Marcus. Having rounded the last tree he was evidently still in one of his thinking strides, only looking up at the last moment to take in the scene of Arantxa giving her whole-hearted attention to one of Flavuis's centurions.

Her voice, which had been wary and distant suddenly became sweet and almost sensual, "Oh, that would be *lovely*. Such a generous offer! As this has come completely out of the blue, may a confused girl have a just a few moments to consider it."

About to inform her that it was a damn good offer and she should be honoured to grasp it with both hands, he became aware of a senior officer next to him. Snapping to attention he followed a crisp salute with a barked, "Sir!"

"Hello Milo, what are you doing here? I thought you would be preparing for the off, you know we are leaving at first light and there are many things to attend to." Marcus's tone was more solicitous than threatening.

"Yes, sir, right away, sir." With a last, confused enquiring glance at Arantxa he performed an exquisite about face, and marched most militarily off, much to the envy and admiration of Marcus. When he was out of earshot, Marcus turned his attention to the wet dress sodden sight.

"Splendid soldier that man, as honest as the day is long. Whatever he's offering, you can bet it is a fair price. Not a man to take advantage, that."

"You don't think he would take advantage of a situation? Interesting. Perhaps I should call him back and agree straight away, then."

"As I say, I have always found him totally trustworthy. What was he offering to sell you?"

"There was no money involved. He has just offered to put me under his *protection* among the women who will follow you to war."

The penny dropped. Marcus felt a lurch in his stomach. His emotions were in turmoil and then he found himself saying, "Actually, that is why I am here. The general says it's perfectly fine if you want to join the group of women following. You have his permission, which would mean that the *protection* of one soldier would not be necessary if you did choose to come."

"It was that trip up north, twice not once, twice, twice in the space of a few months that I think did for him. Never travelled, unless he had to. Hardly ever did he even come up to Tarraco. Getting him out of Dertosa was like trying to prise a particularly stubborn, and well-stuck, mussel from a rock. Yet he made those long journeys, twice, yes twice. It was too much. He should never have been asked to do so much. If he hadn't, I am sure that he would still be with us here today."

"Attending his own funeral? Difficult that, even for a bishop." It wasn't the appropriate time and place to laugh, and it never looks good when you laugh at your own jokes but Ranosindus couldn't help it, he chortled. Many of the still milling post- service congregation looked askance and shocked by the misplaced merriment. One local Dertosian dignitary was about to admonish the culprits when he realised just who they were. Instead, he and others showed their disapproval by murmuring words like *disrespect* and *decorum*.

"You know what I mean, duke. Metropolitan Bishop Argebaud should never have involved Cecilius, given his age and frailty, in this half-baked, hare-brained scheme of Hilderic's, which in my opinion is doomed to failure. Once to Nemausus, then almost immediately back up to Gerunda. Long trips for anyone. Twice was just too much."

Ranosindus was thoroughly fed up of the bishop with his more than twice repeating sentences. True, he had managed, thanks to the skill and manoeuvring of Lady Chlodoswintha, not to have his company on the return journey, which was a massive relief, even though it showed a little more of the true nature of the count's wife, which was something that did travel with him every step of the trip back.

Now, having spent a week in the bishop's company, travelling down to Dertosa, making sure that the preparations were right and the service itself went to plan, he was heartily sick to his back teeth of the man. It didn't help that he had known it would be like this, and he had actually volunteered. A great deal of thought had been put into the weighing of options, seriously thinking about not coming because of the inevitable overbearing irritating presence of Cyprianus. The obligation of paying his last respects to Cecilius, a man he had always liked and appreciated, one he often thought longingly and wishing profoundly he had been the Bishop of Tarraco, instead of Dertosa, had won out - a decision that at times like these he utterly regretted.

"So, you're against Hilderic?"

"No, no, no, not against the man, though I do find him a trifle on the arrogant side. And that wife of his, well, seems a bit of a jezebel to me, no, it's the whole rebellion thing. It's rather, well, drastic, wouldn't you say? I am pro Tarraconensis as much, if not more, than the next man. After all, it's my, no, I should say, the power of the position I hold, that has been diminished more than any other." Seeing the duke's eyebrows raising, he quickly added, "Well, in tandem with the overall importance of the whole province, and it is most definitely wrong that some backwater like Toletum should have acquired importance well beyond its size and history. However, I am not sure that we have totally exhausted the negotiated option."

Exasperated, the duke did all he could to maintain his calm taking into account exactly where he was, and the nature of the occasion. How would it look if he exploded at the stupid fool mouthing all these idiocies? Especially, as people were still muttering about his laughter. Luckily for them, they didn't know the man, he wasn't their bishop. If they did, he was sure that he would probably receive a round of applause and encouragement to continue shouting at, and insulting, the half-wit, but as it was, all they saw was the clothes he was wearing which denoted importance deserving respect. Silently Ranosindus reached twenty even though his intention was to count only to ten."When was the last time you went to the capital, my dear bishop?"

"Not for ages," was the jovial reply. Cyprianus was beginning to think that he might be sent on some sort of ambassadorial type mission.

"Why do you think that you have not received an invitation for such a long time? Also, have you been visited here by anyone of importance from the capital in the last, let's say twenty years?" Not giving the cleric time to answer, he continued, "It's because you, your role, the power that you mentioned, are no longer. The backwater is *here,* not Toletum. As far as they are concerned, we do not exist except to defend their northern border, send taxes for them to spend trying to make that poxy little town look a little more grandiose. If you can make them see this and relinquish some or any of the central power, then, good luck to you. I, personally, think that the talking time is over. Our action may not succeed fully, but it will make them sit up and take notice of us, perhaps move to us towards a more equal status, rather than this vassal state role we have now."

"At what price dear Duke? Your...My... head?"

"Pride and honour have NO price, bishop, and we shall receive our rewards either in this world or the next."

While they were so involved in their increasingly animated-heating-up conversation, one of the chief mutterers had sidled into almost touching position.

"Sires, I know it is most presumptuous of me to address you without prior invitation, but I must inform you that the content of your discussion is being followed by every soul here in the plaza. I'm sure that you do not intend for everyone to hear some of these *details*."

"What! Who the hell are you?" Ranosindus spun to face the now slightly less resolute man in what must be his best finery. Taking in the cringing form, a flicker of recognition occurred - he knew this man from somewhere. Clearly he was of some wealth. Every year the duke hosted all of the minor nobles and heads of the larger land-owning families to a meal in the palace, ostensibly as a social gathering, which in reality served as way for him to keep his finger on the pulse of the province. Most useful it proved as he was able to stop incidents before they became problems and foster a whole network of obsequious, dependent, minor authorities throughout the territory. It must have been from one of these events that the face brought back memories. Ranosindus used to pride himself on his memory, he never forgot a name, or a face, and putting the two together was simple. However, of late, this task was getting harder and harder and he found himself using all sorts of tactics to not show his forgetfulness. In a considerably softer tone he continued "Soo, sorry! I was startled by your interruption, I am most sorry. How are you? Splendid to see you, we haven't met since last Christ Mass and the meal at the palace. I do hope you are well."

The cowering man beamed with pleasure, being remembered by the duke was no mean feat. It took a considerable effort to trek all the way to Tarraco in mid winter to attend Christ Mass. Everyone of importance did it. Last year the delegation from Dertosa was ten strong with him being no more than middle ranking in that group and the duke remembered him!

"And the wife and children are fine, I trust."

Ranosindus saw the cloud pass across the man's face. Evidently this tried and trusted statement had failed. Moving on quickly he added, "Thank you so much for your timely advice. You are right, these topics should not be shouted about in public." The man's face had coloured to an angry red glow, the family question must have been a massive miscalculation. Further effort needed to be made not to lose this man's trust, especially in these times when all of the province could be called to arms. "As you are here and I value your opinion, do give us your thoughts on the matter."

The man was mightily confused; *valued opinion* and asking about a wife and children who had been cruelly taken by disease last year, the only conversation he had had with the duke at Christ Mass was when he had received what he had believed to be heartfelt condolences. Did this man actually remember him or not?

"It is not my place to give an opinion; I rely on you, my betters, for leadership."

"Well put, young man." The bishop had remained silent far too long, he thought. "It's time we moved on as we have the details of our journey back tomorrow to deal with."

"Cyprianus, I am really interested in what this man has to say. I do apologise but at the moment I can't recall your name." Sometimes honesty is the only policy.

"Blasius, Sire. I am with you, as I believe are all of the families here in the south. The insults from Toletum have gone on too long. We often had meetings with our late and dearly beloved bishop about this situation and how it had to be rectified. Bishop Cecilius often stated that he had tried talking to the bishops and former king years ago, to no avail. Now it's time for action, not yet more conversation."

"So when push comes to shove, Blasius, I may count on the assistance of the whole of the south?"

"That you may, Sire."

"Thank you so much, Blasius. You hear that, Cyprianus? Time for action, which I shall take as a point of inspiration. I'll be leaving back to Tarraco directly."

"If you give me an hour, I'll be ready. Together the journey will seem less odious."

"No, you take your time, Cyprianus. I feel that I should get back at speed and your horse doesn't like cantering, never mind galloping. We'll meet back in the capital. Thank you so much, Blasius."

*

The straight rigid back of the general was clearly visible from Marcus's marching position ahead of his contingent. Even from here, it still looked angry. Despite the reason for the anger, they had made good time. Given it wasn't a forced march, a steady pace was being maintained. The last big settlement passed was called Turiaso according to some fairly local soldier, who was in the group behind being led by Centurion Milo, another whose sullen obedient responses showed that Marcus wasn't his flavour of the month.

Marcus had been told that he, as second in command, was entitled to a horse, not of the colour and stature of the general's white stallion, nevertheless a horse. It had been refused, not because he was uncomfortable with or on the animals. No, he loved messing around on the beautiful beasts his father had stabled near their aristocratic villa or smaller summer house in a place the locals called Els Munts. Instead, he felt that it was somehow unfair that he should ride while his men, who he had walked with to war, would be walking home while he rode. This decision was met with scorn and derision by all; the general, the stable-master, and even his own troop, rather than the respect he hoped to foster. There were moments, especially when they were slogging up a particularly steep incline, when he regretted his decision. On the whole though, he felt he was where he wanted to be; with the men not looking down on them.

While they marched, he couldn't help reflect and feel proud of the Roman part of his family. They certainly knew how to build. The roads, where they existed, were straight and easy to walk on despite their evident lack of repair. The Goth administration in Toletum didn't seem to value the infrastructure inheritance they had been given, as it was clear to see that no investment in maintenance or update had been made in many decades in this part of the kingdom. Although costly in both time and money, his father had insisted that the main roads north, south and west be kept in good stead. Many a time he had heard his father's lament, "It can't have cost THAT much," addressed to engineers.

The Hiberus valley road was in a woeful state, due, probably, to the sheer amount of transit. The paving slabs, once one piece were now little more than crumbled sharp rocks which had a tendency to wedge themselves between the sole of your foot and the sandal, causing many a soldier to briefly lose step with his colleagues while clearing out the offending article. They continued apace, with any other traveller quickly clearing out of their way, even if it meant having to move one's heavy wagon onto the sinking soft earth at the side.

Word came down the line that the general wanted a word with Marcus. Doubling his pace, but not running, *officers don't run*, he tried to close the gap between them. Not wanting to upset the general anymore than he had already done, his speed had reached the maximum, it couldn't possibly go any quicker without the dreaded, to be avoided, category change of walk to run. Thinking that this was probably more ridiculous than actually running, he didn't notice a larger, almost boulder-sized piece of slab that had become totally dislodged from the road. The metal of the armour, shield and sword made quite a clatter, only drowned out by the raucous peel of laughter from the soldiers he was trying to overtake, as he went head over heels. Most of his body landed on stone, his face, fortunately, hit the soft mud at the side of the road. Feeling remarkably stupid and pulling his head up, the first thing he saw were the white legs of a horse. He had no desire to look any farther up.

"Don't dawdle! March on. Centurions increase the pace."

"Marcus, light is falling. Evidently, we will not reach Caesaragusta as we had planned. The scouts inform me that there is a suitable place to camp next to a tributary stream of the Hiberus about an hour away. Perhaps you could get yourself cleaned up and meet me in my tent there as I wish to speak to you. I will be riding ahead."

Pulling the reins to the left, his horse obeyed the dig in its sides to canter away leaving Marcus looking and feeling a mess. By that time, his detachment had caught up to him. They had stopped. They were silent, their over-riding emotion was embarrassment. Their leader was a laughing stock and they knew that by association they would become so too as soon as camp was established.

*

"You really are an arrogant saucy little bitch, aren't you? What the hell are you doing here?"

"And a very good morning to you, Amalaswinth, I do hope this fine day finds you in robust health and happiness."

The duke's housekeeper was taken aback by such an effusive, happily delivered without any apparent trace of sarcasm greeting. Her silence was but temporary. "Jewish whores do not use the main door as you well know. And, anyway, the duke is not here, even if he were to make the mistake of summoning you."

"Well, I didn't know that. The duke has a separate entrance for whores? He uses them so much that they have their own door? Amazing! Most enlightening, Amalaswinth, I can't wait to tell all the women in the market."

"He doesn't, and I didn't mean that, as you well know and stop using my name. Scum like you are not allowed to use good-honest Christian words."

"Terribly sorry, *Amalaswinth*, when are you expecting him back?"

"I said stop using my name! That sort of information doesn't concern people like you."

"So, you don't know. You weren't informed, were you, *Amalaswinth*? Well, I'll just have to call back every day until he does actually arrive. That'll be fun as we can renew this little chat every day. I'm sure people will start talking about what great buddies we have become."

"You cheeky little Jewish whore. If only the duke would apply some of the directives against you and your kind, I'd love to see you burn in the public plaza. Hearing your screaming, renouncing that abomination of a religion…"

"Good morning, ladies. Having a pleasant little chin-wag, are you? That's nice, it's good to see you getting on so well these days. Amalaswinth, would you be so kind as to show this young lady in? I'll join you in a moment, once I am changed out of these dirty riding clothes."

Having left his horse with the groom near the stables, the duke had made his way on foot to the house apparently unseen and unheard. However, he did catch nearly all of the exchange between the women. He knew his housekeeper was territorial and protective of him, and that some of her opinions were not the most liberal, but he hadn't realised just how aggressively vindictive and downright unpleasant she actually was. As a counter-balance to this negative discovery, he was yet again so positively impressed by the comportment of this young lady. He had been so while she was under predatory attack by the Bishop, and here was further evidence that she was a most competent orator and defender of herself. He actually found himself looking forward to the upcoming meeting with her. It would certainly make a change from conversing with that pompous arse, the bishop. The journey back from Dertosa had been wet and dirty, it having rained nearly the whole way. Still, he felt it was so much more pleasant than the sun filled outward ride. The one factor that outweighed all others was - it was Cyprianus-less.

No feeling of anticipation had accompanied Rebecca on her trek up town. She knew there would be a problem with the stupid servant, which added to the fact that it really wasn't her job to be dealing with the male authority figures in Tarraco, all made for trepidation rather than excitement. Uncle Isaac had been all of a jitter about the prospect of liaisoning with these hyper important Christians, and her aunt's loud oft voiced opinions that it wasn't his job and absolutely no good would come of the whole venture, were of no help. To save his mental health and probably his marriage too, she had volunteered to take the message of the Jews of Tarraco's willingness to lend whatever support needed to the duke. Hoping that she could probably have got away with a quick word at the doorway or in the hall, she found herself wondering whether she should sit waiting for the changing duke. Having been ordered by that so unpleasant crow not to even think about sitting, or touching anything in the room, before stomping out saying something to the effect that she wasn't going to spend time breathing the same air as a Jew, she was most tempted.

"I told you.."

Temptation had won, Rebecca was seated playing with some sort of strange ornament type thing that had been on the side table.

"Glad to see you have made yourself at home," both servant and master had entered together. Clearly understanding what the servant was about to continue with, she was less sure whether the duke was being sarcastic or not. His second statement removed the doubt, "Amalaswinth, could you bring us *both* some refreshments, please? Interesting little trinket that, isn't it? Rumour has it that it belonged to Caesar August when he spent time here six hundred or so years ago. And in all that time nobody has satisfactorily been able to explain to me just exactly what it is and what it's used for."

"I believe it might be some kind of sun dial though part is obviously missing."

"A sun dial, eh? Never heard that explanation. Pass it over." Turning it round and round in his small white, Rebecca mused, female like hands, he ummed and arrhed, finally giving the verdict that it was improbable. Plonking himself in a chair fairly close and adjacent to hers, he looked directly into her eyes, making her so conscious of where she was, and who she was talking to, that she felt like getting up and making a run for it.

His eyes were penetrating into her, despite her having broken the contact and settling on the vision of her own worn down, inadequate sandals.

"I think I remember that your name is Sarah, isn't it?"

"Rebecca."

"Oh, yes, so sorry, I used to be good at names, old age is a terrible thing. Anyway, Rebecca, I'd like to apologise for my housekeeper. I would make her apologise to you herself, if I thought that it would do any good. Something I very much doubt. She would mouth it because she had been asked to do so, but there wouldn't be a shred of sincerity. And, actually, it might make things worse the next time I am not around."

Rebecca was astounded, a duke apologising to her for being insulted as a Jew, something that was par for the course for most Christians, and nobody EVER thought about apologising about. Unbelievable. Perhaps this alliance wouldn't be such a bad thing if it led to people like him actually ruling the country.

The door creaked open and a servant boy came bearing two mugs of ale. They were both relieved it wasn't Amalaswinth. "Perhaps while we drink you can tell why you wanted to risk your life trying to get past the guard dog to see me."

Lifting her head to re-meet his intense stare, she let out a peal of laughter and relaxed.

*

Arantxa was at the back of the following group. They had lost sight of the men quite some time before, their pace being dictated by the slow sure plod of the oxen pulling the supply wagons.

If she had hoped to find female solidarity among this group, she had been sorely mistaken. An outsider she was, and made to feel so. Nobody enquired after her, or her needs, nor did they include her when making the light-hearted chatter intermixed with admonishments to the children to stop doing something, or to keep up, which was the backing track of the amble. She had tried to befriend a pre-teenage girl, only to have her mother pounce, ordering her child to stay away from strangers.

Initially, she lingered close in the hope that she would be included in the content of their chatter. As that wasn't to be, she decided that it would be better to maintain her distance.

A tight-knit group, who had spent many campaigns together, they were, and intended to continue being. The Tarraco military party had not included females. The big unifying factor of this outfit was that they all spoke with the same accent denoting their similar geographical background. Not being able to distinguish between differing types of Latin, she wasn't sure exactly from where they hailed. She did know that it was distinctly different from anything spoken around her area, or the way Marcus spoke. Also, they made it abundantly plain that they knew that their area was vastly superior to any other, and it was their men's' duty and obligation to fight to instil this God-given fact on the others. They insulted every manner of locals they had come across, each being compared to some lowlife animal. Her people were usually referred to as chickens, because they made a lot of noise but ran whenever they were challenged. How she had wanted to refute and defend her nation. For the want of a better option she bit her tongue, swallowed her pride, and allowed herself to become more detached from the group. This, however, was not before hearing the women's version of why they were going to re-establish order in that part of the country. Popular opinion had it that the Jews had taken over, dispossessing and murdering all the good Christians, eating a fair proportion of the children and setting up their own kingdom. Arantxa was shocked, both at the content of the information and at the hatred with which it was spat out. In their outlook on life, Jews were less than vermin, given the choice of a nest of rats, or a synagogue of Jews in the neighbourhood, they all expressed a strong preference for the former. Back in her *homeland* there weren't many, or any, Jews, in fact she'd never met one, so, she'd never heard a strong view about them one way or another, though quite obviously there couldn't be much good about a tribe that had crucified what the missionaries said was the son of God. Any act like that wouldn't make you popular either in this world, or the next, would it? All in all, they sounded a blood thirsty nasty group of people these Jews, hopefully she wouldn't have to have any contact with them.

*

They were seated around the table with candles lit when Rebecca made her entrance, all eyes turned to her and there was immediate silence. The different eyes expressed varying feelings: her father, concern, Uncle Isaac, guilt, Aunt Trudi, petulance and cousin David, total disinterest. "Sorry I'm late. Shabbat Shalom."

They all chorused the reply. Jacob started to mumble an apology for starting the Sabbath meal without her until he was interrupted by Trudi. "It was I who insisted we start without you. Everything that I had spent hours upon hours preparing and cooking was going cold. We had no idea what time you would return from your traipsing about uptown with goy toffs. Actually, I wasn't even sure that you would come back to us lowly Jews, after all you have been gone for hours.."

"Enough Trudi!" Isaac was forceful and loud in his rebuke, something which shocked everyone, most of all his still open-mouthed, venom-spouting wife, who was about to shout back when she suddenly, and unexpectedly, decided against that course of action as the whole table seemed to be nodding in agreement with Isaac's expressed wishes. Experience had taught her to pick a fight when she could win, storing away this slight, to be re-visited another day, she busied herself setting a place for her interfering niece, who, in her opinion had airs and graces well above her station. Women were women. They took a back seat to men. The torah, their religion, their very essence, said that men should lead, and women follow or at least they should give the impression that the man is leading. Women could, should and the Lord be praised, give wise guidance, but strictly in private within the confines of the house, never outside and NEVER as the public face of Judaism to the gentiles. She was shocked at the way in which Jacob had brought her up, and now treated her as an equal in public. She was horrified that her husband didn't have the backbone to do a duty he volunteered himself for, and she was distraught by Rebecca's acceptance and revelling in her unwomanly role, for the moment she would keep quiet, the day of reckoning would come and so would her revenge.

"Tell us how it went." Her father's voice betrayed all the concern that he felt.

Getting herself comfortable in her seat, she felt anything but comfortable. Everyone was looking at her and waiting for her to speak and her aunt was serving her food, something that she hadn't done in this house since Rebecca was a little girl. It was usually Rebecca's job to serve all the others. Finding her voice, she managed to say "Well."

The silence that followed was deafening. There wasn't even the normal shared meal sound of David's open-mouthed, noisy chewing.

"I think we can trust these people. They seem.."

"Trust Christians! Sweet Moses, the girl is more naïve than I actually thought!" The being quiet and waiting approach hadn't lasted long. A stern rebuking glare from her husband quietened Trudi for a second time in as many minutes.

"Perhaps I am." Rebecca turned the thought and the memory of her conversation with the duke over in her head. She had spent the whole afternoon there. Their conversation had been really most enjoyable, starting on the state of Jewry, passing through various topics like the decline of Tarraco, the power of Toletum, the vision for a new state and finally ending on the personal; their different relations with Marcus, on which, they both expressed concerns as to his future.

Rather than relating any or all of their conversation, she chose only to tell the story of the housekeeper and the apology. It was enough as it surprised and shocked all, including the back to loud chomping David.

"He actually said sorry to you for the behaviour of Amalaswinth!" Aunt Trudi being truly impressed had found her voice again . "That old crow. She's forever trying to lord it over everyone, Christians and Jews. Years and years, I wouldn't be able to count the number of times I have heard her insulting Jews. And what do people do? Nothing! I tell you years, and nothing. The times I wanted to slap her and didn't dare, nobody dared even to say anything. And you see those other spineless goya bitches nodding and murmuring in agreement, when before she'd arrived, they had been as nice as pie to us, well, as nice as any Christian ever gets. And you say the duke himself apologised for her?"

Rebecca nodded smugly.

"Well I never, not in all my born days…"

Still worrying about his role in the whole affair Isaac interrupted, he didn't actually stop Trudi's lament, which was running its own course and would do, they all knew, for some considerable time yet. His choice was to run parallel by enquiring as to what the next move would be.

"Apparently, there will be another meeting in the north, not sure whether he said Narbo or Nemausus, but up there, to decide on who and how this new state shall be ruled. From inference, rather than actual words, it sounds as if there is some indecision on who should rule and where from. Someone called Count Hilderic is the main mover and shaker."

*

It was a pretty little spot. It reminded Marcus of a little curve in the Tulcis river just outside Tarraco. Washed, and spruced up, he was now in the commanding officer's tent waiting for him to finish giving instructions to the scouting party he was sending ahead.

"Right, explain what happened this morning." The others having left, General Paulus bore down on the seated figure. Marcus remained silent trying to think, as he had been doing all day, of a suitable excuse. The truth was that he had none.

"When one part of the army leaves the other, there are always watching and judging eyes. The king, Kunimund, and Uncle Tom Cobbly and all, were there to see how we conducted ourselves as a tight-knit fighting unit sent to represent the kingdom in a war. What do you think they saw?"

The silence remained as Marcus took in the ground the tent had been pitched on. To his way of thinking it was a bit too grassy at this point, comfortable now but it'd be covered in dew come the morn.

"As you won't tell me, I'll tell you. A shambles. Late, slovenly, no order, total confusion and you, you, *running*, yes an officer *running*, from one point to another like some headless chicken being ignored by everyone. Marcus, we were made to look even worse than we are. Can you imagine how the generals are going to laugh over supper tonight? And, who do you think that they will be laughing at? ME!!!!"

It had been clear at the time that the general had been angry but Marcus wasn't quite sure why. Admittedly, it was a bit of a mess when the group all set off at the same time bumping into each other, but they were quickly untangled, thanks to Milo's loud voiced interventions, and on their way in no time. He had no idea that they were being observed and judged.

"I'm sorry, it's just.."

"It's just not good enough is what it is! I would relieve you of your command now if it were not for the fact that I might actually need you when we get to Tarraco."

The bluster had blown out of his voice leaving a sigh of resignation. "And what pray were you doing face down in the mud this afternoon?"

"Trying not to run."

Despite the situation and himself Flavius laughed. "Excellent. A complete success, in that position nobody could ever have accused you of running."

"No, it was when.."

"Also, Marcus, I have a clear recollection of telling you that the girl was not to come on this trip, but lo and behold, just a couple of minutes ago I received a cheery "hello" from her as I was about to enter this tent. Explain."

"Well, it's quite a long story, which involves Centurion Milo and.."

"Enough. Get out before I make up my mind to strangle you where you sit."

*

The camp fires were lit. Sentries were posted. Milo had reminded Marcus, in a tone of a father with a backward child who he would very much like to disown and wishes had been strangled at birth, that he ought to see to it as it was his job. When Milo was asked for advice on how many he ought to post and how often they should be changed, the centurion's eyeballs rolled up and back into his skull accompanied by an audible, from twenty paces, sigh of disgust, then a salute, an off-hand remark saying that he, himself, would see that it was done.

Marcus was at a loss as where to go. Unwanted by the general, laughed at by the main body of the force, he thought about sneaking into the camp of his men from Tarraco. When he was about to appear from behind one of their tents, he heard the topic of conversation. They were not being nasty about him, their attitude towards the backward child, was more of an ashamed father, who was nevertheless indulgent. Knowing that his physical presence would make the whole group awkward, he slinked off towards the trees and the stream. To his surprise he found he wasn't the only waterfront resident. Arantxa was already there seated cross legged near the water's edge.

"By yourself? May I join you?"

Arantxa had barely looked at just who was disturbing her solitude, perhaps it would have been sensible of her to have taken precautions, after all she was right next to a camp of men whose foremost qualities were not chivalry and politeness towards women. However, she was past caring. She couldn't remember ever feeling this sad, depressed and alone. Back in the village, while, and after, it was being burned and people murdered and raped, there was no time to think. Almost dying at the hands of that smelly pig Caius, the adrenalin had been pumping and no thinking was necessary.

Now, she no longer had Ezte or anyone else who spoke nor understood her language, she was headed farther away to a place controlled by people who ate babies, all she had left to do was think.

At least back in the camp the women were all more or less friendly, accepting each other for whoever or whatever they were. Here, this group didn't like ANYONE who was different, and they especially disliked her as they believed that she had spurned the advances of one their best loved and respected men, Milo.

The scene, once camp had been made, was clear. No place had been left for her in their circle. Initially she had thought that the problem was that they all wanted some sort of intimacy as their "men" would call in on the camp, so she tried to be discreet. It soon became clear that discretion was not something sought nor practised as furtive coupling became a regular sight. Trying to look away from one pair, she bumped directly into another. The man looked up with interest thinking that today might be his lucky day when he'd have two at the same time, only to have his head yanked down to the task at hand with the woman stating the he stood no chance with that frigid bitch who thought she was too good for a centurion.

Not understanding, she went directly across to a woman who was momentarily by herself. She was one of a small group that had no *stable* man, instead offering comfort and release to those that sought it; for a price, to seek some clarification. She was told in no uncertain terms that Milo was a good man, a great catch and a much aspired to commodity of many of the females in camp, and when they had been told that he hankered after foreign flesh, initially their reaction was disgust, which quickly changed its target and form from him to her. Their unmentioned, but clear to hear envy, had been replaced with anger that this unworthy foreign bitch, her exact words, had felt too haughty and important to accept his advances. Arantxa's protestations of innocence as she had not rejected anyone, in fact she had not even been given a chance to answer, did nothing to change the attitude of the woman, whatever her name was. "Marta, stay away from her. You never know what you'll catch from that heathen."

So, the name was Marta, who immediately became a back and not face. Arantxa was guilty as charged, and thus was shunned, despised and rejected from the group and over her shoulder was asked to move away, in no uncertain words, as another client was approaching.

Bewildered and dejected she headed to the stream.

"Come to cause me more problems, have you?" the words were spat out while she maintained her concentrated vigil of the water.

The ferocity of the statement took him aback, from surprise as much as anything else. "You as well? I really can't see why it should affect you that I am such a terrible soldier. Okay, I forget to salute and say sir, I run, when I should walk, I make a pig's ear of leading the troops out of camp when I should be putting on a show, and I have no idea how to picket sentries nor for how long. For all of those sins *and* for falling face down in the mud, I am sorry, truly sorry."

The surface of the water had lost its allure. Raising her head she was confronted with a most distraught young man, practically on the point of crying. She, however, was not in the mood to play mother comforter to anyone, least of all to him, the author of a great deal of her confusion. "What the hell are you babbling about?"

Realising that perhaps he had misjudged her words and the situation, an attempt at re- composure was in order. Pulling his shoulders back, standing more erect and with an unwavering tone he said, "I was just suggesting that perhaps I do not think a military calling is my future."

"And why the hell do you think that I should be interested in this information? I never asked you to join the ranks. I wouldn't encourage you to stay. I don't care AT ALL. Now, if you could just leave me alone, I have my own problems to dwell upon."

Another rejection, enough of rejection, he wasn't going to walk away tail between his legs from this one. No, he would make a stand, well, perhaps a sit down would be better. Plonking himself a short distance from her, he managed to say, more childishly than he had intended, "It's not your river and I shall sit here if I want!"

Her sarcastic retort of "That was said like a true officer," made him wish he had chosen not to make his *sit.*

*

Although the meeting was billed as informal, all the participants wore the finery of their office. The re-splendid count sat at the top of the table, the finely adorned duke had the opposite end, and in the middle there were the various bishops, Gunhild of Maguelonne, the pair of regularly attending nameless Franks, the newly anointed, ex- abbot, Ranimiro and Metropolitan Bishop Argebaud. The recently demoted Aregio hadn't been invited, not because there was any bad blood on either side, the power exchange was logical, Aregio couldn't support the rebellion though he had great sympathy for its aims. So, stepping - temporarily he thought - aside was the correct thing to do, and the others believed that this well-meaning bishop, happened to be, in all likelihood, the source of Wamba's information from their camp.

They had all been ushered gracefully and ceremoniously in by Chlodoswintha, who didn't have a place at the table, playing the role of wife, not rebellion organiser in chief, which is what the duke believed to be her true part in the proceedings. Ranosindus had been wary and distant to her obvious tactile charming greeting a few hours earlier. His trust in her had diminished. His previously thought through policy was to keep a clear head throughout the whole of his stay, which meant rejecting excess alcohol, and above all, staying away from the flirtatious hostess.

"Gentlemen, welcome. I have called this meeting so that we can coordinate the final details of our *venture.* Sadly, we are a couple of bishops light. Cyprianus, is I believe, indisposed and the untimely death of Cecilius, the Bishop of Dertosa, who will be sorely missed, both as an excellent person and as one of the main instigators of the new state." Everyone, except the Franks, voiced warm praise for Cecilius, who had been much liked and appreciated. Nobody, including the Franks, mentioned anything about the absence of the Bishop of Tarraco. Most, in fact, knew that no invitation, for various reasons, had been afforded to Cyprianus. The new Bishop Ranimiro, who had spent more than a week being instructed in his new job by the man from Tarraco, had stated in no uncertain terms that if he had to spend any more time with him in any near future that he would not be responsible for his actions, the consequence of which, was that Tarraconense would be looking for a new bishop. Also, Duke Ranosindus had point blank refused to travel with the man again. Thus, it was thought expedient that the invitation be sent so late that he would not arrive in time for the meeting.

"I trust everyone has had time to settle in and is comfortable, if not, please take your complaints to the true power of the house, my dearest wife." Most chortled politely knowing that this was actually the truest statement that they would hear this day. "I thought that this little get together would be better suited to a period of time without the interruption of servants entering and exiting with food and drink, therefore the food will be served after this *chat.*"

This was a departure from previous meetings, and one which was met with varying degrees of agreement, the Franks being the most negative. They were hungry, it was past their usual eating time as here in the south people tended to eat much later than the northerners. Most others accepted the departure from the norm with eyebrow- raised curiosity.

"The reason why I have decided to proceed this way is mainly to do with security. I suspect rather than know that Wamba has ALL the details of our previous meetings, because I know, not suspect, that he has already dispatched a column of troops. By limiting the numbers of us involved in the meeting and by preventing indiscreet ears from entering the room, I hope that this time, everything we say remains between us. So, I would urge maximum restraint on your part once you leave this room." He paused for affect, quickly continuing when he saw mouths opening to refute or agree with his proposals, "I know, I know, nothing we say here is actually secret and everyone will get to know everything sooner or later, but I would prefer that enemies learnt it later."

"I really do not think we should describe the king as an enemy, we are all Goths when All is said and done." The duke's statement was intended to show his disdain at the presence of the Franks. "We may be in dispute with the regime, something which is undeniably true, and also the reason we are here. However, to call our legitimate, up until now, king, an enemy, is taking it a little too far. We are political rivals and want a change of status, that is all. We are all hoping that this does not become an armed conflict."

The count was visibly taken aback, his presumption was that everyone was into this up to the hilt. Before he could express his simmering rage, Gunhild came to his aid.

"Extremely well put, duke. I think we all hope and believe the same as you," He shot a warning glance at the count, "However, the fact of the matter is that there is an armed column heading our way, we know for sure they are nearing Caesaragusta. I believe what the count is saying is that *they,* our political adversary, if you will, do not need to know exactly what we are planning. So, discretion is counselled."

Somewhat cooler in tone than it would have been a few seconds earlier, the count continued, "We are not sure if they are heading here, or whether they will first go to Tarraco, we believe it will be Tarraco, as your son, duke, is second in command."

"What! How…?"

"The force is not large, and does not pose any real military threat. It's led by General Flavius Paulus with your son, Marcus, aiding him. We believe their role is dissuasive, not hostile."

"I need to get home as quickly.."

"Sit, my dear duke. They will not reach Tarraco for days. Today we need to make some decisions, then we will eat, and tomorrow you may return and be back in time to greet your son, if in fact the troop is heading there."

"How do you know all this information?" The duke was genuinely shocked by all he had learned; troops heading to Tarraco, led by his son. Would he be forced to confront his son on the field of battle?

"The Jews are great allies to have. They have commercial contacts throughout the land and their network of communication is second to none. Sadly, we have nobody in the general's camp, which is why we are not sure as to their intent. The only thing left for us to do, is to track their movements. Don't look so worried, duke, this will not be a fight. I believe their job is to engage us in dialogue, to persuade us of the folly of our ways. However, as Paulus will be powerless to grant any real concessions, I imagine his role will be to listen, report back, making his military presence a threat, nothing else."

The duke who was bursting seconds earlier, slouched, silently stricken.

"So, onto business; how and when shall we proclaim the new kingdom?"

"And who, count, shall be king?" One of the Franks had asked the question which nobody wanted to bring up but everyone knew had to be addressed.

*

The General had set the pace and Milo made sure that it was enforced throughout the whole troop. There was no chivvying of potential slackers or potential stragglers, this was a forced march intent on showing who was boss and that they were a military force not a group of Sunday strollers. The two men had planned this strategy, without the presence of the nominal second in command, the previous night. There had been total agreement in the fact that this group of men needed to be beaten, physically if necessary, into shape. Their exit from the camp was now a matter of history, nevertheless, it was a running sore that both men felt continuously. It would never happen again, not while they were in charge.

Marcus's past present and future role was not discussed even though it was the elephant in the room. He was to blame, they both knew. However, he wasn't going to be held responsible, he wouldn't be the one with a blemish on his career, they would be.

Going close to Caesaragusta, the men thought that there would be a temporary halt to resupply, it didn't happen, they were forced to pass at pace seeing and smelling the cooking fires. Their appetites were whet only to be disappointed, a deception that was to last hours as they marched and marched, increased the pace, and marched again. After having set off efficiently at first light and not having stopped all day except for a couple of liquid breaks, the sun was beginning to set when they finally were told to stop and set up camp near a stream. One of Marcus's men had informed the others that by his calculations, they were close to Ilerda, not very close but it was the next big settlement. Apparently when he was little, he used to accompany his father, a haulier from the port of Tarraco, to this area. It was clear that they were deep into Tarraconensis . Even this important revelation didn't matter too much as wherever they were, they were glad of the rest.

Marcus tried to busy himself by informing and imposing the sentry duty roster only to find out that it had already been seen to by Milo. He felt miffed and wondered whether he should assert his authority without making himself look petulant and infantile. He couldn't. Everything was working like clockwork, and he felt sure that if he tried to issue some orders they would clog up the system, or worse still, be ignored. At a loss as to what to do, he went to the general's tent. Not sure what sort of reception he would receive, he was prepared for anything, and what he got was nothing. Smartly saluting and remembering to snap out a *sir* on the sentence endings, he reported that everything was under control; camp being pitched, sentries on post and the men relaxing, only to get a "very good, that'll be all" type reply.

On his way back from this briefest of visits, he felt as if all eyes were checking him out, taking in his removal from the hierarchy of orders, knowing that he was a failure. Obviously, they weren't, as everyone was busy doing something; pitching tents, collecting wood for fires, drawing water from a natural fountain in the rocks, preparing things to cook. He, though, had nothing to do. Wanting desperately to go to help the men who were in the process of pitching his tent, the last to be put up, he knew he couldn't, it was work below his station. He desperately wished that he'd had a higher priority on the shelter front, as he was totally and completely knackered and would have loved to lie down in his own unobserved space. Young and fit he was, but today had been hard, very hard. More than once he had regretted not taking the horse option he had been offered at the start of the trip. The men had kept themselves going with banter and singing aided by Milo's barking, chastisement and physical slaps with his crop. He had slogged along, slightly in front of his group, a bit behind the main body, on his own, nobody to chat, joke and whinge with, lost in his own maudlin thoughts and gnawing hunger. The thoughts were two-pronged; his failure as an officer, and Arantxa.

As they had sat in silence by the river the previous night, he did not want to be the first to make a move after making his triumphal sit down. The "sit-off" lasted for ages, hours he thought. Then, finally, there was movement, she got up and without a word of goodbye or a glance in his direction, she headed back to the women's camp leaving him to feel silly and hungry. By the time he made it back to the Tarraco area of camp all the food had been finished and men were sat around the fires drinking. No one had mentioned that he hadn't been there and there was nothing "saved" for him. This morning, there had been such a rush to get on the road that no proper breakfast had been served, Milo had ensured that there was no time for fire re-kindling. The men were to nibble, gnaw or chew on what dry rations they all carried individually. Marcus didn't have his own supply. He was really hungry and very tired and craved to lie down. None of these options was a available. The proverbial spare prick in a brothel he was, and felt. Not wanting this role, he strode purposefully out of the camp to…somewhere.

Arantxa had fared little better. Theirs wasn't a forced march, it was much more like a faster than usual amble. Their speed was always dictated by the oxen pulling the supply wagons, who were very much one-pace animals despite all the encouragement in the world there was no making them go faster than they wanted. Trying to keep within sight of the troop for their own safety, and the not unimportant fact that they were carrying the food supplies the men would need to eat, was their aim, a target imparted to, though not necessarily shared by the oxen. Despite their best efforts, they were well over a couple hours late entering in the camp where the men were sprawled near fires waiting impatiently to put something on them. Some game had been gathered along the way, rabbits mainly, by those whose job it was to catch these things and they were roasting on spits but there weren't many, and the staples to go with them weren't there.

The entrance caused the stir of activity and admonishments for their tardiness. Meek and mild these women were not, they gave as good as they got in verbal abuse while the supplies were unloaded.

It wasn't the job of the women to cook for the men, they had their separate camps, so once the men had taken what they needed from the wagons, the women started setting up their camp. Arantxa went into the wood to get some wood for the fire. After gathering quite a bundle, she enquired where she should leave it, she was ignored. There was a great deal of noise, the children were hungry and making their feelings, persistently, known to all. Lacking a clear leader, all the women spoke in parallel repeating instructions. It was chaotic, well it looked that way, in fact, despite appearances, it was extremely efficient with everyone doing everything quickly but most definitely not quietly.

This communal effort didn't overtly exclude her, it just carried on, a pace, without her, much like today's journey when nobody turned their back on her, if she asked a question it was monosyllabically replied to, if she made a comment about the countryside, the children, the trudge, it was ignored as if she had said nothing. Nobody told her that she wasn't welcome but everything did. Dumping her pile of wood, although she was belly-rumblingly hungry not having eaten last night, nor this morning, nor during the slog; she had been offered nothing by anyone, she thought it best to wait, out of the way somewhere, until everything calmed down.

Upon arriving at the edge of this stream, the familiar form of Marcus was there. It was the same situation as the previous night, except the other way round. Dithering, not sure what to do, she hadn't been spotted by the hunched back, so moving away was an option but going to … where/ who? She was also unwilling to repeat last night's farce of silent sitting.

"Are you going in?"

"What?"

"It's been a hot horrible dusty day," She had already taken half of her clothes off, "I want to cool off and clean up. I thought you were here for the same reason." Finishing disrobing, into the not terribly deep water she dived.

Completely taken aback by her unexpected appearance and then total, if briefly viewed, nakedness, he felt he had no option but to get in the water himself. Undressing to almost nothing and not feeling particularly shy as she had disappeared swimming mostly under the water down river, he took off the last piece of cloth just as her head appeared from the water right next to the bank where he was standing. Instinctively his hands raced down to cover his *parts*, bringing a squeal of giggling laughter before disappearing back to the depths. Rather ungainly, he jumped in to find that it was shallow enough to stand with his neck and shoulders not getting wet. This upright position was maintained for all of five seconds or so, until he was tackled, his legs being taken away from under him. Spluttering back for air and wiping his face he found her face very close to his. She looked deeply into his eyes, causing all manner of sensations to course through his body, not being as tall as him she was comfortably treading water. This situation remained stable for a while, him not knowing what to do, pondering inactively, feeling that he should respond to the tackle. The rest of his body wouldn't move as his eyes locked in contact with hers dominated everything and caused a pause in all movement, until, all of a sudden, he was faced not with two eyes but two breasts coming out of the water accompanied by yell of pleasure as she pushed his head far under the water and then immediately swam off at pace.

*

The meeting had been going for more than two hours, conclusions were multiple and widely accepted, however, the nitty gritty was elusive, and the tone, which had started well, had taken a decisively negative turn. The Franks were at a loss as to why the count didn't just impose his will. Clearly he wanted to be king and crowned without delay. Gunhild was the main orator furthering the count's cause. Hilderic himself tried his best to stay aloof, superior and most statesman like throughout.

The duke led the resistance to a complete walkover by the northerners. He was not jumping out of one pan into another, or worse still, the fire. Tarraco WAS important. He would muster at least half of any potential military force, yet here was the Nemausus/ Narbo clan, trying to frog march him to *their* tune, which consisted of a proclamation of a new kingdom with Hilderic as its king to be crowned forthwith.

The Franks' irritation, fuelled by stomach-growling hunger pains, boiled over, "It looks to us that the southern Goths are afraid to commit. Perhaps this is due to their dislike of violence."

The duke's reaction left little doubt that violence was something he was prepared to use. The meal prepared plats and knives clattered hitting the floor about the same time as his hands wrapped themselves around the speaker's throat. There was pandemonium. The second Frank was trying to stop the attack by wielding a candelabra in the direction of the attacker's head, the ex-abbot was doing his best to impede the conversion of an ornamental instrument to a deadly weapon. The count was yelling "Gentlemen, gentlemen," at men who were determined to be anything but gentle. Undoubtedly, the scene would have got worse and blood would have been spilled, if it hadn't been for the entrance of Lady Chlodoswintha banging an over large gong with great gusto. The squabblers paused in surprise more than anything else, giving her time to calmly and firmly state that dinner was about to be served. Seeing a posse of platter carrying servants in her wake, the violent protagonists took a step back en masse. A great amount of silent clothing readjustment followed.

"I do apologise for not bringing the food earlier. It has been ready for quite some time, it was just that I didn't want to interrupt anything transcendental. However, hearing the slight commotion, I took it upon myself to decide that perhaps everyone needs a break and some refreshment. It's late."

There was an air of embarrassment as everyone righted their seats to use them for their intended purpose; the candelabra also found its way back to the middle of the table, put there by a servant who held a taper to light the no longer present candles.

*

The heightened expectation that had permeated the Call for days after the public meeting had subsided, a lull ensued. Jeremiah, the nay sayer, never tired of painting a future of death destruction akin to hell on earth, or the years of slavery and torment under the Babylonians, or Egyptians. While no news, good or bad, filtered through, his opinions were gaining favour among others, nowhere near the majority, but a significant minority. The power vacuum after the death of Rabbi Saul didn't help.

A rudderless, leaderless community being scared by rumours had asked neighbouring areas for help as there had developed so many cliques that not one person had sufficient support of the whole community to lead them. They needed a nasí, an intellectual, versed in political matters who would provide the beacon of light they craved.

Hillel's arrival caused quite a stir, appearing in the port area without warning, he sauntered up to a group of market queuing women to ask directions to the synagogue.

"Another Jew, that's all we need. Your sort are not wanted around here. Go back to where you came from."

The bishop's servant Maria turned back to her nodding audience.

"My good lady, I would not be addressing you at all if I could see a man around. However, as there are none, I thought I would lower myself and deign to converse with you. I now realise the error of my ways. I should have been more patient and waited for a man."

The women were, temporarily, dumbfounded and then started mimicking his tone adding comments like "look at him with his airs and graces."

"Has an opinion of himself, that one." Thinks he's the duke, him." etc

All said mockingly though, without spite as in reality nearly all were impressed by his words, his demeanour and above all by his looks. He was impressively handsome, swooningly so. Thick wavy black hair framed an exquisite face, squared chinned, slightly high prominent check bones, luxuriously heavy eyebrows topping deep penetrating dark, dark, dark eyes with full promising lips, all set in a light reflecting pale olive skin. He was the real deal, the like that Tarraco hadn't seen, if ever, in a long time.

Rebecca felt the magnetism from another queue across the plaza and was drawn towards it. Wearing her usual clothes with the fringed edges which denoted her religion, she placed herself in front of him.

"May I be of some assistance?"

Looking directly into her eyes, he liked what he saw though it wasn't the male he was seeking. "Is there not a man of our persuasion close at hand?"

Rebecca felt the rejection sharply, "You're looking for a Jewish man in a market stall? You ought to re-think your approach, not the brightest strategy, stranger."

Realising that he had made a significant mistake which had been made obvious by the tongue of this girl, he re-considered his options.

"I suppose you will do. Guide me to the synagogue. As it is unseemly for an unmarried man to be seen with a woman who is not his sister or mother, you may walk a couple of paces behind and tell me which way to go."

Rebecca was speechless, nobody applied these religious rules in Tarraco and she wasn't going to start adhering to them now. Once over her loss for words, her initial and instinctual reaction was to tell this pompous arse where to go. However, as all the market had stopped to listen and all of them were gentiles, she allowed her better judgement to prevail.

"As I am not totally sure I can give you what you are looking for, I will bid you goodbye." With that she turned on her heel and headed back to her place in the recently abandoned queue for vegetables.

*

The reasonably gentle audible knock on the solid oak door took the duke by surprise.

Sitting, mulling over the happenings of the evening, the only conclusion that could be drawn was that things hadn't gone well. He couldn't say that they hadn't gone to plan, as he never had one. His presence and participation were as a reaction to events, at best described as circumstantial, rather than a planned set of actions. Not sure just what he had expected, nor the way he wished things to go, he found himself in a quandary. Joining the "plot", as it had been referred to throughout the evening, was right, it was a feeling deep within him that if Tarraco didn't make a stand sooner rather than later, then there would be no Tarraco, just a small relatively unimportant port; all that former glory lost and on his watch. What would his ancestors think? They were the proud rightful rulers of the most important province in Hispania. It was his moral duty to defend the role and status of this area, his area, and his son's birthright to inherit power and a title which actually meant something. However, what hovered on the horizon of the near future, was an armed conflict with a king he had no animosity to. Transferring his loyalties to Nemausus and Narbo with little in return for his family, or Tarraco itself, wasn't an appealing or luring prospect, no clear way forward nor backwards offered itself.

Standing, he shambled his way to the door, it was probably a servant asking what time to have his horses ready in the morn. His intention was to leave at first light. Getting back to Tarraco before Marcus' military force arrived was imperative. Yanking the door open in a determined show of authority, he was most surprised to see Lady Chlodoswintha standing smiling sweetly with a platter in one hand and a jug in the other.

"As you ate almost nothing at supper, I thought that perhaps you might be hungry."

The duke stood taking in the whole scene; the Lady of the house bringing food and wine, looking divine in what he presumed must be her bed going attire.

"Are you going to invite me in or send me away? Whichever it is, I would ask you make the decision fairly quickly as it is not really the best thing for someone of my status to be seen delivering food and wine to another man's room."

"Sorry, sorry, do please come in. Let me help you with that." He took the platter of food to place it carefully on the small table near the window. She breezed in picking up the one cup that was by the bed emptying its contents, water, into a bowl at the foot of the bed, she then proceeded to fill the cup with wine.

"Do sit, my dear Ranosindus."

There was only one chair in the room, the one by the table which he had previously used for moping. Unsure what to do, should he offer it to the lady or would that be too presumptuous? It would be like inviting her to stay when she was probably only delivering. Also, just where would he sit if she did agree to be seated? He lowered himself hesitantly onto the chair as if he were trying not to disturb a deer in the forest.

"Here," she proffered the cup, "I'm sure you need a drink after all that has gone on this evening. I did notice that you touched not a drop during supper."

"I felt that I should keep a clear head."

"Unlike most of the others! Those Franks really are quite boorish, dreadful manners, hard to believe that they are considered to be among the elite in Frankia. I meet Franks relatively often, it does to have at least cordial relations with our neighbours, after all, you never know when they will take it upon themselves to try to invade again, a most restless ill-mannered people. Still, we have to live with them."

The duke, who had been craving some mind dulling alcohol, took a deep draft. Hearing the swish of skirts he found the jug near his head ready to refill. He offered up the cup, she took it, finished the little that was left and replenished it to almost the brim. Back in his hand trying not to spill any, he lifted it to his lips his eyes noticing the wine-giver plonking herself on the side of the bed exposing more flesh than she had obviously intended; a naked thigh and the whole edge of her very full rounded right breast were visible over the rim of the cup.

"Isn't that better?"

Nearly spilling his drink, it was all the duke could do to nod and blink his agreement.

Looking slightly above her head, so not to cause any embarrassment to the lady, he managed to say as calmly as he could that the food at supper was beautiful to look at, but he just felt as if he couldn't eat any of it, it wasn't that he wasn't hungry, he was, it was just that it didn't feel right.

"Well, hopefully everything is still as attractive now, and your desire has returned."

Looking back down expecting to see the clothes readjusted, he saw that the breast was clinging onto the last bit of cloth before popping out completely. Immediately averting his eyes, he picked up the half a chicken which sat in a pool of grease on the platter. Taking a big chunk, and conscious that he was talking with his mouth very full, he managed to incoherently say something to the effect that it was lovely and just what he needed.

The duke's experience with women was extremely limited. His marriage had been prearranged when he had been young and completely innocent. She was a few years older than him, from a very good family without claim to any title. It was thought, and generally accepted in all quarters, that it was politically, a good match. She brought wealth and more lands to the Duke's family, and her family received an entrance into the nobility of the land. He, personally hadn't had a view on the negotiations, it was something that had to be done and his parents were there to do it. Actually, the couple had got on extremely well straight from the start, they didn't have to grow into each other. His youth and inexperience helped a great deal. His views, thoughts and habits were ill defined, she defined them for him. Compliant and content is how they spent their seven years together until she died in childbirth of what would have been their second son. The son didn't survive its first week, enough to be baptised but no more. He was devastated. He had lost his wife, mother-figure. All this fourteen years ago, the wounds remained not completely closed with the part that had healed leaving a considerable scar tissue. Despite many offers, and well meaning advice from plenty of others, he had never seriously thought about remarrying. Pretty girls, comely girls,

girls with great fortunes had been pushed his way, but never was any kindred spirit relit or fostered in him. An heir he had, so there was no imperative to breed with another.

There was another slight problem as well. Although he found sex enjoyable even if it were a brief affair, he was more than a bit embarrassed by his, well, equipment; more of a dagger than a sword. Growing up, he had seen what other boys had and what he lacked. All the jokes about sex made him squirm rather than laugh, though he did, and often laughed the loudest, it was to cover his shame. His wedding night was fraught with danger instead of delight. Heva, the woman he married, made everything feel alright. She coaxed, cajoled and eventually smothered him with so much love and affection that it never really mattered to either of them... that much. It was always there, the elephant, or worm, in the room that nobody talked about. Once he did try to bring the topic up, only to be shushed with mollifying statements like it was the only one she had ever known, or wanted to know, and it was him, something she wouldn't change for the world, or words to that effect. How could he replace her? She was an angel, his angel, now God's. He could not, nor did he want to. Sex was still a necessity though. He found relief in a number of maids. Their role was to be bent over a table, accept the little they got, and be off on their way directly after. One had got with child and was quickly dispatched to a position in a minor landowner's household staff in return for a favour owed. He felt he needed no more than the relief that these ejaculations offered.

Now in the presence of this, undeniably from what was in front of him, very much of a woman, he felt stirrings, sensations which he hadn't felt for such a long, long time, if ever. The woman oozed sensuality. She had flirted with him the last time that he was here, using her power for her own ends, or those she deemed in her husband's interest. Surely though, she wasn't here in this disarray of clothing to make her husband happy about being the future king. What would be the point in being the most powerful man in the land, if you have no control over your wife? His reasoning led him to believe that she must be here of her own accord. Swallowing the last piece of chicken while he wiped his hands on a scrap of cloth that was handy, he looked round. The breast was free of all shackles. He stared.

"Don't do that!" He averted his eyes. "You have dirtied the embroidery I have been working on for weeks." She left her semi inclined position to dash across the room to retrieve the recently discarded cloth from the floor, picking it up, she placed it back on the table attempting to flatten it out. This required her to be in a bent over pose right in front of him. Now there wasn't one free breast, there were two, furthermore there was a clear view to farther down the body. Finding breath hard to come by, he managed to stammer, "Sorry I didn't realise. I wasn't looking at what I was doing."

"Oh yes, you were! And you seem to like what you were seeing." Her twinkling eyes locked on his as she slid gently onto his lap. He dithered, she took control. Moving her lips to his, she pressed, forcing him to respond. In seconds she was totally naked writhing on top of him, he was moving as well but floundering rather than passionately gyrating, he was trying his best to respond to her lead and not coming close to succeeding, she was way out of his league having never ever experienced anything like this before in his life. This wasn't the sweet gentle loving provided by Heva, nor was it his quick dip into a servant. He was gasping for air, it being taken both by the sight of her incredible body and her long deep kisses. Having disposed of all her clothes, she was setting about doing the same to him, pulling, ripping and yanking until she got to flesh. Rubbing her hands across his broad slightly hairy chest she sighed with evident pleasure. This was only a slight delay in her quest. Moving on and down she busied herself.

"Oh."

*

"They are vermin, I tell you. Once you have one in the area you suddenly find lots more swarming about."

Amalaswinth was in the courtyard shopping basket in hand, standing close to a similarly dressed and equally basketed Maria, the bishop's housekeeper, who was nodding enthusiastically.

"And that little bitch, Rebecca, I don't even like using her name, thinks she's the queen bee. You know she always uses mine, trying to make out that we are equals or friends of some kind."

"Her? So, you've had problems with her as well?"

"Insulted me in the fish market, she did, and then ran telling tales to the duke that I had *slighted* her, slighted was the word she used, the cheek of the little whore."

"Unbelievable. She's forever coming to the Metropolitan Bishop's palace, using the front door, a Jew! Treats me like dirt, and thinks she can get away with it because she brings money for the Metropolitan Bishop. A loan, I am told, it's a disgrace that good Christians have to take money from the Christ killers."

"Burning is too good for her!"

"The sooner we cleanse the whole kingdom of their likes the better!"

"I couldn't agree more. I'm not sure it's going to happen any time soon though."

Maria looked even more interested in their usual conversation now. They met fairly regularly as you would expect, Tarraco not being such a large place anymore, and being women of a certain status, they didn't mix with the common hoi polloi, a nod and a civil exchange about the weather was as much as they deemed necessary. So, when they did meet, they shared the local gossip and always complained about the Jews.

"Why do you say that? I thought that Toletum was finally getting serious about them."

"Ohh they are, but our masters seem to think differently."

Maria arched an eyebrow.

"I'm not sure if I should tell you."

Maria was both intrigued and peeved, why didn't she have this information, now she would have to feel inferior to that arrogant Amalaswinth.

"Oh you mean all this to-ing and fro-ing? Up and down to Narbo like rabbits going down a hole. The bishop is forever complaining about the journey. In fact, he has just left on yet another one."

"Yes, yes, yes, but do you know what it is all about? Did you know that they are in league with the Jews against the king?"

"Never !" The surprise was too much for Maria, she hadn't wanted to show ignorance.

"Oh, yes. That's why we get to see that bitch up here so often. She's the go between. There's a plot afoot that will take Tarraco out of the kingdom. Our masters are as thick as thieves with the Jews."

"Well I.." Maria was totally dumbstruck, her mouth open like a stuck fish.

 "Good afternoon, Amalaswinth. If you could ask Maria to close her mouth and be off, then, join me inside, we need to plan an evening meal with the Metropolitan Bishop."

"He's not here, Sire. He left two days ago to go back north."

"Maria, I think you will find your master at home wondering just where you are as I have just left him there."

Without another word the Metropolitan Bishop's housekeeper quickly turned and did an unsightly attempt at a run. It would have been comical, if it weren't quite so pathetically awful, and, if the duke were in anything resembling a good mood.

Once inside, the duke set about removing his riding attire. Amalaswinth moved past him at speed, it was clear that her master was not best pleased, heading in the direction of the kitchen.

"Bring me an ale, as soon as you've put those things down."

The journey back was truly terrible. From Nemausus to Gerunda his mind played the bedroom scene back time and again, it got no better with repetition. Then in Gerunda he met Cyprianus going the other way. When told that the meeting was already over the bishop was fumingly angry, the Lord's name was taken in vain a whole number of times. Furthermore colourful and creative language was found to describe their fellow conspirators from the north, with special reference being placed on the personage of Lady Chlodoswintha, who the bishop accused of being a viper and a Jezebel among other things, insults that the duke didn't try to refute or rebuke the bishop for using. Once he had calmed down, Cyprianus informed the duke that he was in luck as he wouldn't have to make the rest of the tedious journey back to Tarraco alone. Surprisingly, Ranosindus was actually pleased by this information. It would reduce the ability and time to brood on the *events*.

The ale arrived with a most contrite looking housekeeper.

A long slurp quenched his immediate thirst without taking off any of the edge to his negative feelings towards the world in general, and this woman in front of him in particular.

"Do sit."

"I couldn't possibly, I do know my place, sire."

"If you do, then obey my instruction."

Some of Amalaswinth's self-assurance was beginning to evaporate as she took the chair in front of the Duke's, not allowing herself a comfortable posture, she perched on the edge.

"How long have you been with this household?"

"Sire, you know that I came with Lady Heva." She paused to make mental calculations. "That would be nay on twenty years ago."

"Have you always been treated with respect?"

"OF course, Sire."

"You were kept on even after my wife's death, despite you not being actually from MY household."

"Yes, Sire. Looking after little Marcus was what my Lady Heva asked me to do on her deathbed, and I have endeavoured to do it to the best of my abilities. Marcus is my life's work and most proud of him, I am. The running of the whole household I didn't take on until the death of the previous housekeeper, Amelina, five or so years ago. Sire, you know all this, why are you making me repeat it?"

Ranosindus didn't answer twirling the now empty ale mug, he was deep in thought. Amalaswinth was now beginning to get truly worried. The master had shown displeasure with her before, not overtly, more expressed through disappointed glances rather than raised voices, he was not a man to shout, and it was an unspoken fact that she had only been kept on because of the deathbed wish of his late wife.

Finally he spoke in a low slow deliberate tone, "Marcus is a man now, he's off fighting for the kingdom, so he is no longer in need of a nursemaid."

Worry was moving quickly to panic. She kept statue-like still, not wanting to agree or disagree.

"Now, if you were me, a head of a household and you had a former nursemaid who had no charge to take care of, but who had been in the house for so long, taking on other roles, that she could be regarded as something like family, then you found that this person was being disloyal, what would you do?"

"Disloyal? I would never dream.."

"Then how would you describe giving out household secrets and being openly critical of them?"

Totally flustered and in extreme panic Amalaswinth tried to deny everything passing it off as idle gossip with her true friend Maria.

"So, if you were me, you would see it as just a little jolly jest, ignore it, and carry on as if it hadn't happened?"

There was light at the end of the tunnel. She nodded vigorously. The duke mused a few seconds longer. "As I mentioned, the bishop has invited himself for supper, please ensure there is plenty of food and if you could make it fish, so much the better."

*

It was late morning, very late morning when Rebecca finally made it back with the ingredients she needed to make lunch, she would have to hurry to get everything prepared on time. Bustling and fussing with all her wares she failed to notice the male voices coming from the "best" room. The voices evidently heard her clattering and banging as her father called out, "Rebecca, come and join us."

Wondering who the "us" could be at this time of day when it was most unusual to pay social calls and by the direction of the voice, it was unlikely to be a business meeting, as they are rarely held in the house, and never in that room. A moment of dread passed over her, could it be the bishop? The second instalment was well overdue; perhaps he'd lowered himself to return to their house. While fixing her hair into some sort of order as she headed towards the voices, she came to the conclusion that it couldn't be, that fat slimebag would have just sent a couple of soldiers with a "message".

"Come and meet our new rabbi."

It was him; the handsome arrogant stranger sat straight backed and imperious in her father's favourite chair, holding one of their best goblets. His face registered no recognition of Rebecca.

"Oh, we've met. Lunch will be a bit late, the market was very full today and I had to wait for an age to get some cheese. Is he staying for lunch?" She nodded in the direction of the now sipping man.

"It's been completely remiss of me, I haven't asked him. Rabbi Hillel, would you do us the honour of staying to break bread with us?" The sipper looked lazily over the rim clearly weighing his options.

"I presume you keep strict caixer."

"Well, we do the best…"

"The question is simple, the answer should be so too. Whether you are the lowest, aniim or the highest guebirim, the dietary laws of our religion are clear and precise and should be followed at all times."

Jacob flushed, they did keep caixer in a sort of more relaxed form, with various prohibited items finding their way onto the menu, especially sea food, living next to the sea it was difficult to avoid shellfish ALL the time.

Rebecca's dislike for this man intensified as her father's face changed colour, hers was doing the same with a different emotion. His, embarrassment, hers anger.

"Well, as we are neither aniim nor guebirim, perhaps we make it just to benonim, I am sure that whatever I cook will not be up to standard. Also, maybe, I should mention that I am having my period today, so the food provided will be from one who is unclean."

Both men looked askance, Jacob's head moved from side to side while his mouth repeated one word; "Rebecca" in a slow lament. The sipper looked horrified, down went the best cup with a thump and up he got with great energy.

"I shall be leaving. Jacob, I do hope to see you…..under *better* circumstances in the near future."

Moving determinedly to the door he took the longer route around the back of the chairs in order to stay as far away from the source of impurity as possible. Stepping a pace closer as he squirmed by, she cheerily boomed "See you around, Hillel, it's been lovely meeting you!" to an all but running broad-shouldered back.

Jacob's still moving somewhat slower head was bent low. "Should I ask why you did that? You have never mentioned ..*womanly* matters before. Why now, in front of the new rabbi, who clearly is a nasrí? Someone, and something, the community has been searching for since Saul's illness and death."

"He's a prick!"

"Rebecca! You can't say that!"

"No, you're right, I should say he's an arrogant prick."

"You go TOO far, I am your father, how dare you use that sort of language in front of me, and about a rabbi. I shall have to think of some fitting punishment for this disgraceful behaviour and lack of manners. He's a stranger and anyone in MY house deserves to be treated with curtsey."

Realising that she had gone too far, she set about trying to rectify the matter by explaining how the man had mistreated and humiliated her in public for the crime of being a woman when she was trying to help.

"Still Rebecca, he was a guest."

"And I am a woman, I was only informing him of matters he needed to know about before I made him food. Imagine if he had found out after? He would have felt cheated or hoodwinked in some way, with his spiritual purity compromised. He dislikes and treats me abominably for one reason; my gender, so he needed to know ALL about this inferior impure creature."

"You will apologise."

"What for? Having a period? Mentioning I have periods? For not being a man? No, Papa, I will not."

"By all Halakhà, there can't ever have been a father so blessed as I!" The bent head shake was back.

"Glad to be finally appreciated. Food will be ready as soon as it is, that's unless you object to.."

His head shot up, "Please don't say it again."

*

"Amalaswinth, lovely to see you. Why are you looking so glum? Maria tells me that you are in fine form quite brimming with new information."

In contrast to the booming bishop, her voice was little above a murmur, "Good evening, Your Grace. Let me take your cloak. I'm sure that Maria exaggerates. You'll find the duke already in the dining room."

The house smelled of cooking. With whetted appetite, he strode happily in the familiar direction. The duke didn't rise. They say familiarity breeds contempt. Although he had certainly spent a great deal of time in this man's company over the last couple of months, he wasn't sure whether the contempt had been bred or just propagated from an already large stock.

"I would say that it is good to see you, Cyprianus, but I feel as if I see you more than anyone else in the world of late."

"And splendid it is, isn't it? It was so good of you to invite me for supper, I'm sure that Maria would have struggled to provide a decent fare given that she was not expecting me back for at least a couple more days. She needs her time, does that one. Getting on a bit now, I suppose that's why. We all get set in our ways, don't we? Well, you probably saved me from a cheese and bread meal."

"I didn't invite you, you invited yourself."

"So I did. A damn good job too as you can now give me, as you promised, the details of what I missed up there in Nemausus. You seemed most reluctant to talk on the ride down. Arh, here is the food, most punctual. Splendid. What have you managed to rustle up for us, dear Amalaswinth?"

"Mackerel. May I serve you some white wine, your Grace?"

"Fish, thank you so much, that can't have been easy to get at such short notice. Wine, yes please."

"No, your Grace, had to send the boy down to port area especially. He said he was extremely fortunate to pick up these last ones."

"Yes, I'm sure, lucky, very lucky indeed."

The duke came close to smiling for the first time this day as he saw a mega polite subservient housekeeper provide a bloated hungry clergyman with exactly what he didn't want.

Pushing the two medium sized fish around the plate didn't make them look any better. Besides the repulsive smell and taste of fish, Cyprianus also despised the reproachful way in which the one visible eye told its sad tale of how it ended up unappreciated in this ignominious state being shoved unceremoniously to and fro, when but yesterday, it had a whole ocean in which to move. Turning it over produced the exact same attitude from the other eye. Starting to eat at the tail only meant that the remorseful rejection had to be faced later.

Bread and cheese was so under-rated and had been scorned too soon.

"How kind of you to go to so much trouble. Ranosindus, you are very quiet, do tell me everything I missed in Nemausus."

"I prefer to wait until the meal has been served and we are by ourselves." This most pointed of comments hit its mark.

"So as not to disturb you gentlemen any longer, all the food is on the table. We," she indicated the young serving girl, "will take our leave. If you need more, or to be served please ring the bell and we will return forthwith." With that Amalaswinth and the girl hurried out of the room.

"What was that all about?"

"The fewer people who know exactly what is happening the better. When I returned home this afternoon, my housekeeper was telling yours how we were about to attack the king with an army of Jews. Where she got such an idea from I don't know. However, wherever it comes from, it does our cause no good."

"Amalaswinth? Can't be true! The woman.."

"Is in my service, and the information she should not have in whatever distorted form, which furthermore should not have been shared to anyone. Eavesdropping is rife."

"I'm sure.."

"I truly doubt that you are. Cyprianus, the only thing I am saying, is that we need to be more careful than *we* have been in the past."

Knowing that he was backing a loser, if he continued to plead any of the trusted servants' innocence, he chose to move on. "I take it that things didn't go so smoothly in Nemausus."

"In that you can be very sure. To start with, you really need one very important piece of information. Wamba has dispatched a military column and it's probably headed this way first. Apparently, Marcus is its second in command."

"The army? Coming here? Marcus in command?" it was a raised voice of incredulity.

"Yes, I do think you've boomed ALL the salient points. Did you get them all, Amalaswinth?" A scurrying noise behind the door confirmed the duke's suspicions.

"What are we to do? Will the count be sending his own forces? Will there be a battle? Should I take up residence outside the city to ensure that all the leaders are not in the same place?"

"Calm yourself, Cyprianus, there's no need for you to run anywhere yet."

"Run, run? No, a prudent dis- concentration of forces is what I had in mind."

The mental agility of this fat coward forever surprised the duke, "Your military awareness and instant strategic thinking will come in very handy during this conflict, I am sure. *Dis- concentration*, what an excellent idea. Actually, we do not know what they want, nor exactly where they are heading. What we do know is that the force isn't large, and my son is second in command, so one would presume that their intentions are not overly or immediately hostile. We believe it's more of a fact finding mission with future intent written all over it."

The cleric's relief was palpable.

The duke went on to explain how he had found himself in a group of one in Nemausus, with all the others pushing for the announcement of Hilderic as the King. He did not, and would not yield. On a head count it was fairly evident that Tarraco would provide about half of the forces that could be marshalled in favour of the new kingdom, and from that position of strength, he maintained that the capital of the new state should not be in either Narbo or Nemausus.

"The meeting broke up inconclusively," he finished saying with the bishop uncharacteristically quiet throughout.

"Upon my soul, well done you, can't have been easy. We can't be ruled from that backwater Nemausus. It would nearly be as bad as the power in Toletum. Hilderic, if he is the consensus person for the role of king, certainly won't, and can't, rule from here, and I know for sure that you do

NOT want that role thrust on you, so, where could a compromise come from? I can't see any."

Nor had Ranosindus when he retired to his room, yet again his mind went back to what it had never left.

Chlodoswintha had laughed. There are many ways of laughing, and many reactions to being laughed at. Her hand –over- mouth burst, clearly said – what-the-hell- do –you – call-that. His reaction could best be described as hedgehog like; rolled up in a ball with spines protruding for defensive protection. Immediately, she realised her mistake, grabbed hold of the object of amusement, which was becoming less stiff with every second, not any less large, as it maintained a constant in the length field, and dragged him squealing by it to the bed, whereupon she got to work. It didn't take long, a blob of white sat on her hand. Standing, she reached over to wipe it off on the embroided cloth. He lay mortified, all hedgehog concepts had dissolved into little more than an out-of-sea jellyfish impression.

She returned to the bed, changed her focus of attention to his head, which she lay gently on her ample breasts. "Every time I sew from now on I'll be able to think of sowing in another way."

This attempt at humour had no effect on her audience. Instead, she caressed his face tenderly. "You are one very attractive and sweet man. I have been wanting to be close to you, *physically,* almost from the first time I saw you."

"And now I disappoint you," came his mumbled into erect nipple reply.

"Well, I must admit that it wasn't quite how I'd fantasised it. Still, I am a married woman and if things had gone too well in this field, we would have had an enormous, sorry wrong word, problem!" She felt him cringe. "Come on, Ranosindus, snap out of it. We have some planning to do."

"So that's why you have come here, to use me!"

She held him closer, "You could say that. Also, you could say that I had a dual mission. I did, no, I do, fancy you greatly. You make me feel all, well, I don't know how to describe it. I have never felt that way in the presence of a man before. No, not even Hilderic, who I have come to love after our years of marriage. Our *arranged* marriage has been a successful union, we get along fine, we've produced a healthy child and I would venture to say that neither of us has been desperately unhappy. I am not his dream woman, he is forever off trying different ones out for size, he always comes back in the end. And, as I said, he doesn't make me all of a tremble inside the way looking at you does. That brings me to the second strand. You don't want Hilderic to be king."

"And you are here to flatter me into accepting this?"

"Ranosindus, please allow me to finish."

"I cannot and will not accept that the king is based here in Nemausus. That's my final point in this discussion."

"As we heard at infinitum downstairs. What I want to do is make it your first point, not your last."

"How do you propose doing that, by having sex with me?"

"Ranosindus, again, please. And by the way the only one to have had sex so far, is you!" before he could say anything else she continued. "From what I can see, your objection is twofold. You don't object to Hilderic per se, it's more the geographical location and the fact that Tarraco, in your opinion has more history and therefore more right to be the seat of power in the new kingdom."

"The *kingdom* wouldn't last two months. You just have to look at those ghoulish preying, not praying, Franks. They would invade almost immediately or perhaps they would wait until there's another dispute of leadership in the Frankish kingdom which is usually resolved by some invasion adventure. How many times have they come across the border in this century alone?"

"In that you are totally right. We need therefore an inventive solution."

"Like?"

"You eventually allow yourself to accept Hilderic as king and me as queen. Let me finish! But this role would be temporary, until we have settled the problems with Wamba and everything has settled down; a period of a few years maximum. Meanwhile we join our two houses in matrimony."

"What, you and me?"

"No, silly. Our liaisons must remain top secret. There is no way the Church would allow us to be together. I'm talking about your son and my daughter. "

"What?"

"Stop saying *what,* and listen. My daughter had her first bleeding last month so she is more or less ready to be married off. Your son is off gaining *experience*, I hear."

"Military."

"I've been told of a Vasconis girl."

"What!"

"There you go again. If we can arrange a marriage, then they would live in Tarraco and all problems will be solved."

"And your husband would agree to this or was it his idea?"

"*What?* Now, you've got me doing it. No, he knows nothing about me being here nor about what I am proposing. He doesn't really want the responsibility of being king. It would curtail a lot of his *fun* activities. He would play the role for a while, leave, then it would be up to our offspring."

Ranosindus forgot about *the happenings* for the first time, mulling the idea over in his head, only for them to be brought sharply back into focus. "Let's see what we can do with this thing of yours so that we can say that we have both had sex tonight."

Clearly none of what happened, the conspiratorial conversation, the other part he presumed would go no further than the participants, could ever become public knowledge, so he had to find a way of letting people in general, and the Metropolitan Bishop in particular, know, what might be the solution to the impasse.

"Cyprianus, I do agree, the situation is not ideal but I think we should remain flexible. Another possibility that we have not considered might suddenly appear. Until that time we have agreed to act together without an official visible head."

"Which means that the decisions will still be made in Nemausus."

"It does."

"Well, I think we need to counterbalance their power. To that end, I propose calling a meeting of all the bishops of Tarraconensis; Gerunda, Emporiae, Ilerda, and Ausona. Dertosa is sadly orphaned by the loss of Cecilius and I DO NOT propose informing that Toletum lackey Quirico, so Barcino, will be excluded. Perhaps, if you summon all the nobles to a parallel meeting, if we were all in one place, it would be like a henhouse, there are a number of our leading elite who like the sound of their own voices far too much, then, without Quirico, the fighting forces of Barcino could be included. "

"Cyprianus, your military leadership skills are in full bloom!"

*

It had been a long slow tedious incident filled *march*. It had taken them over a week to get from Ilerda. Despite Paulus insisting on speed and the centurion's constant chivvying, the pace had been slow and interrupted. Two river crossings had proved most difficult as the recent rains farther upstream had swollen the course of the water so much that the bridge had been partially washed away and the fords unusable. The Roman roads were in such a state of disrepair that their constructors must be turning in their graves thinking about how the inheritance they had left had been squandered by the lack of upkeep.

Marcus didn't mind the amble, stop, amble, journey as he wasn't that keen on arriving back home. From his point of view it was impossible to see how he could come out of this confrontation well. If, and that was a big if, his father had rebelled, as was thought, then which side should/ would he be on? Whichever side he landed on, he would be thought of as a traitor by the other. Hopefully, it will prove to be nothing more than a big misunderstanding, a storm in a winecup that will easily be washed away with some nice words and a bit more understanding of the Tarraconensis position.

There was also Arantxa. What was to be done with her? Although he felt she was not his responsibility, he found himself in the position of caring. The axle on one of the wagons had snapped, yet another of their many mishaps. Being sent back by the general to sort it out as quickly as possible, he was quite looking forward to seeing Arantxa having not seen her since she showed him her breasts and swam away. The scene that met him was unpleasant and chaotic. Apparently, Arantxa had fallen sick and had been unable to walk, so as an act of kindness, despite a considerable minority arguing that she should be abandoned at the roadside to make her own way in life, she had been put onto a wagon to ride until she recovered. As luck would have it, it was this wagon's axel that snapped as they were crossing some off road terrain. The hostile minority became more vocal, with accusations like; it was her witchlike state that had caused the wagon, which had now developed its own personality, way of thinking, and preference for riders, to breakdown in protest at it being forced to carry her.

What a sight she was. The perky breast showing strong character was nothing more than a broken ragdoll half lying, half sitting, slumped against a tree. It was obvious that she had dragged herself there, all the other women were giving her a wide berth. After setting his repair party to work, exhorting them to speed, he went over and crouched down beside this half conscious form.

"Go away. Leave me alone. Just let me die here. I don't need no Roman charity."

"Good afternoon to you as well."

"Marcus, please go away. I want to die. It's punishment for betraying my people. I deserve no better than to die in, the gods knows where, alone."

"Gosh, a bit melodramatic today, aren't we?"

"Piss off, Roman."

"And foul mouthed. Technically I am both Roman and Goth, so that'll give you a little more scope to insult me. My friend Rebecca found endless ways to insult me about either or both. I am sure you could compete."

"I am not competing for *you*, with any other bitch, Roman or Goth."

"Actually she's Jewish." He'd removed the canteen of water he had strapped to his side, poured some onto his finger tips and rubbed them gently on her dry cracked parched lips. Her tongue reacted instinctively, immediately licking the precious liquid.

"When was the last time you drank or ate anything?"

"How many times do you need to be told? Bugger off."

Filling the cap of the canteen he proceeded to tip the water gently into her mouth, she swallowed greedily. "Slowly, don't rush it. Once when I went hiking with.. "

"Marcus, shut the fuck up." She managed to say and almost killing herself as the water went down the wrong way causing her to splutter and come out with a hacking cough.

Looking down with obvious concern, he stated the obvious, "You're not well."

Leaving her with the canteen, with the best authoritative tone he could muster, he gave stern instructions on how she should take little sips. Leaving her to continue the state of uninterested in Marcus and his instructions, he went to check on his work crew and find out who was responsible for the female group.

The first task was simple, "All will be done in a jiffy. It's relatively easy to replace that bit that snapped. When we arrive, the whole of this wagon needs to be reviewed, it's only a matter of time until it'll become beyond repair."

Leaving the "engineer" muttering about a stitch in time, he accosted the first woman he met, "Who's in charge of the women's section?"

"In charge? What, do you think we are part of the army?" she chortled and shouted out to a group of women who were gathering berries from a fortunately placed by the side of the road bush, "Hey, are there any officers among you lot?" Being met by confused faces, she continued in her mock serious way, "Oh come on, there must be a centurion or two. This officer wants to know who is in charge." This caused a great deal of laughter and a tide of shouts claiming various titles and ranks accompanied by much saluting.

Marcus was beginning to get well annoyed. It seemed that every woman in the world, starting with Amalaswinth, going through Rebecca to Arantxa and now this lot, felt they had the right to bully him.

"All you, stop what you are doing! Get here now."

"Ohhhhh, the officer is getting a bit..." A huge slap just to the left of her mouth took away the rest of her words as she looked at her attacker in horror and more respect. Marcus immediately regretted what he had done, his first instinct was to apologise and try to make up for his actions. Putting these feelings aside, he controlled himself, looked the woman in her hurt surprised eyes and growled, "I said get here now, all of you!!!"

In a meek, but defiant way, they obeyed slowly. "Now!" Their speed increased ever so slightly.

"I want to know what is going on with the Vasconis girl."

"She's a witch and shouldn't be here among good folk." The woman rubbing her face spat out and immediately flinched as Marcus raised his hand again.

"And you *good* woman, tell me who is your man among my troop?" Another woman stood beside the spitter giving physical and moral defence, "She, like me, doesn't have one, we are appreciated by a larger audience than just one."

"So, you're whores, and from this lofty social status you choose to judge my friend, the woman who saved a fair proportion of this command from certain death at the hands of her kinfolk and in doing isolated herself from her people. This is the thanks she gets from you *good folk*."

"She's a witch and not even the wagon wants to carry her."

Marcus moved menacingly closer, then in a slow deliberate calm voice explained what the head of the repair team had told him, inviting his attentive audience to check with the man if they wanted. "So, clearly it wasn't her fault. She is ill, and must be looked after. I am making you," he pointed at the slapee, " responsible for her physical well being. If she doesn't recover quickly, then when we arrive in Tarraco, I will ensure that you are publicly whipped, and if, by some misfortune she dies, then you will suffer the same fate but in a much slower and painful way, have I made myself clear?" with this salvo Marcus marched off trying not to show how surprised and shaken he felt at his completely out of character performance.

In the following days the men treated him not with respect, but they were certainly more wary of him. Also, news filtered forward that Arantxa was recovering well, even if her standing among the other women had not improved. His actions, though effective in the short term, now making it impossible for her to ever have a decent relationship with them. This was the main reason, he told himself, why he felt so much concern and responsibility for her.

"You look troubled, Marcus."

Startled from his musing, he looked up to find his commanding officer standing next to him.

"I do hope you are not contemplating hitting any more of the women folk. Centurion Milo has chewed my ear off about your brutality. You must have had your reasons for doing it, I must say that I found it hard to believe when I first heard. I just hope that a repeat performance won't be necessary."

Marcus jumped to his feet and saluted in his crispest fashion.

"Yes sir, sorry sir."

"Don't go all military on me. All this saluting and sir-ing I know that there must be something wrong. Sit back down, and if I may, I'll use the other chair, then if you think it's necessary you can tell me what it's all about."

Marcus desperately needed to unburden himself, and as he had no one else, he spilled all the beans, talking nonstop and uninterrupted for ten minutes, the longest monologue of his life.

"Ummm, I see. I understand your position, however, it was all most predictable and one of the reasons I opposed her coming on this trip. She's very attractive, a lot like her sister, which makes her appealing to men and rejected by women, especially the sort of women who follow a troop. On the other hand, I do agree with you, we owe the girl a debt. None of us would be alive, if it weren't for her. Perhaps the situation could be put to everyone's advantage. I know you told me as we were arriving, but what's the name of this place."

"Els Munts, sir."

"And you say that your family owns this mighty fine building."

"Yes. We use it as a sort of summer home when the city gets too unbearably hot."

"Sir."

"What?"

"You forgot the *sir*."

"Oh sorry, sir!"

"Only playing with you Marcus. It's a beautiful place. In its Roman day it must have been truly spectacular. Anyway, how long would it take you to go into Tarraco?"

"Less than an hour on a horse, about three walking."

"Ok, take Arantxa, absence will cool the situation, and this is what I want you to do there…...."

*

The knocking was loud, persistent and authoritative, making Amalaswinth scurry to answer it as soon as possible.

"I am here to see the duke."

As bold as brass, just like that, without a bye your leave, or good afternoon, was how she related it to Maria later.

"You are? And who are you, and more to the point who the hell do you think you are?" That's what I said to him. The dirty Jew all full of airs and graces.

"Well done you, calling him a dirty Jew. I met him in the market strutting around as if he owned the place, he was. I gave him what for but I didn't call him a dirty Jew, wish I had."

In reality Amalaswinth was too shocked to say anything other than she'd go to see if the duke was receiving visitors, she shut the door on him though, not wanting his kind to infest her house any more than they already were. She suspected that a horde of them would arrive at any moment, in fact she'd spied a cheekily waving Rebecca standing the other side of the street to the main entrance waiting to pounce.

Fuming, Rebecca did stand close enough to the house to be seen. She had been *ordered* by Hillel to wait there, which she had done with little protest as she had solemnly sworn to her father to behave in her errand of taking Hillel, well, walking two paces behind, to the duke's Palace. She had presumed that she would be used as the go-between, and at least allowed across the threshold, only to be unequivocally told to wait where she was. Not wanting to disobey her father, nor to show any hurt in front of Mr Arrogant, she meekly submitted to his more than request. She did allow herself a little fun though by giving Amalaswinth a cheery old buddy friendly type wave.

To Amalaswinth's horror, she was instructed to show the Jew in, whereupon he strode through the house without showing the slightest deference to his betters.

"I am Hillel, the new rabbi and leader of the Jewish community in Tarraco. I am here to talk about an alliance that has been undertaken by my fellow Jews to support your venture against King Wamba."

Ranosindus had never been spoken to like this before, and he had no intention of starting any time soon.

"Hillel, you say, well normally I would ask my guest to be seated and order some refreshments. However, as you will not be staying much longer, I will forego that pleasure."

An impassive stone face greeted this statement, so Ranosindus continued, "Up until now negotiations and contact have taken place in an instructive and cordial manner with a most able interlocutor from your community. This is a state of affairs will continue. I suggest, strongly, that you liaise with her."

The left eye twitched denoting an emotional response which wasn't shown in any softening of the tone of the voice.

"The person in question is not authorized to speak on behalf of the community. I am. As spiritual and moral leader, I demand my rightful place. What is more, the person to whom you refer is a *female,* and as such could NEVER be accepted as the official interlocutor of the Jewish community, not here, not anywhere."

"That just leaves me the pleasurable task of bidding you farewell as she is the only one of *your* community who is welcome in this house.

Furthermore, if you are looking to liaise with an equal of your spiritual level, might I suggest you going to see the bishop? I'm sure he would be delighted to exchange opinions with you. Amalaswinth, this gentleman is leaving, show him to the door, could you please?"

"As I said, Maria, the duke gave that repugnant Jew short shrift, threw him out almost immediately. Good job too. Don't know what the world is coming to with this sort of scum brazenly walking the streets and into good folk's house as if they were equals."

*

Purple was the predominant colour, the hot air inside had surpassed the balmy sunny weather outside in intensity and duration, six bishops, six talkers and no listeners. It was, had been, and would continue to be, chaotic, in a word. Cyprianus was trying to boss the show with little or no effect. A hand raising system of turn taking was proposed and it soon evolved into the strange sight of six elderly men holding a hand up, normally the right, and then everyone talking in parallel. The proverbial henhouse would have appeared to be a silent hermitage in comparison. An awful lot had been said, repeated, and said again by the same person or different ones. Bishop Guteric, Ilerda, was haranguing Bishop Domum Dei, Emporiae, for his over complicit subservient attitude towards the Narbonese. In fact this was the dominant split in the room; those willing to cede the leadership to Count Hilderic in Nemausus, and those who thought that Tarraco was the natural seat of power implying the leadership of Duke Ranosindus. It was two for, two against, and two wavering. On a superficial level it was a geographical divide with, Tajón Gerunda, and Domum Dei of Emporiae being closer to Nemausus on one side, and Cyprianus and Guteric on the other. The middle ground was held by Georico of Ausona, and Serando of Egara.

This long winded tactical dispute didn't affect the fundamentals on which they were all agreed; the need to reassert themselves. All six had been present at the Ecumenical Council of 653, all six were getting on in years, and none of the six wanted to follow Cecilius to the grave without the rightful restoration of their area to its proper place in the world, and with it, their participatory function of bishops whose opinions and council was sought at meetings in general and councils in particular. Twenty years since their invitation wasn't just a slight, it was a total exclusion and rejection. Their united venom and hatred was reserved for two people in particular, Quirico, in fact it never was just Quirico, it always had a derogatory prefix, the favourite being *that toady*, and Julian, the devil incarnate, the architect of their demise and the concentration of power in Toletum.

Wamba himself excited no real animosity. What they knew of him was that he wasn't a bad chap, just too weak for the job, too weak to stand up to the power of Julian. Perhaps if there was someone with more personality, they could curtail the centralisation and the natural equilibrium would be restored. However, the time for reform, in everyone's opinion, had passed, it was time to separate.

The problem remained, who would be the visible head of the push to break up. As no overall majority could be found, the meeting petered to an end, more through exhaustion rather than conclusion, with the willingness to try again in the very near future.

*

"I have to ride that? I don't ride. I have never ridden. Our tribe don't hold with…"

"Do shut up and just sit on the bloody thing. I don't suppose it wants someone so ungratefully unpleasant to sit on him either. We need to get in and out of Tarraco. On horse is the best way. Do you want me to get the woman who was looking after you to come to help you get on?"

The glare which went way beyond a threat, boarding on the point of a promise of retribution, didn't deter him, nor affect his hand cupping motion next to the beast. A small crowd of onlookers was beginning to swell, so feeling that her shame and embarrassment could not increase too much, she put her muddied right foot into his cradled hands and immediately felt it hit the ground again jarring her back.

"I thought you.."

"Wrong foot. Use your left, otherwise you'll be facing backwards."

The crowd, especially the men, showed their appreciation at this part of the entertainment by laughing loudly and calling out any number of unhelpful contradictory pieces of advice. The women kept their response to tuts. Arantxa flushed scarlet, lifted her left foot, stamped it down into the proffered lift and launched herself upwards with such power that she all but came off the other side of the horse. The loudest laugh this time came from Marcus, though there was quite a cacophony behind him and even the horse looked round with a nay of disapproval, regaining her equilibrium she managed to land her heel hard into Marcus' right shoulder. "Oh, terribly *sorry*." To his surprised, now non laughing face, she sweetly voiced, "I was aiming for your stomach not your ..." The rest was lost as the horse, evidently tired of playing with these amateurs, lurched forward forcing Arantxa to grab the animal around the neck in an attempt to hang on screaming *etenaldi*. It did the opposite of what it was requested, eventually reaching a full gallop.

As there were no home stables to head to, the horse sought the comfort of what passed for the herd, which was peacefully grazing on a piece of scrub land no too far from the sea. The whole of this area didn't do lush green, so the animals had to make do with what they could find. The arrival, at speed, of one of their own with a woman clinging on its back, caused a few raised heads in idle curiosity rather than any major interest among these seasoned beasts. In contrast, the young lad, who was charged with watching over the herd so that they didn't wander off too far, was startled from his tree supported sea view slumber into immediate action, dashing to the aid of the damsel in distress. Quickly he managed to sooth both horse and rider as he was a known and liked element to both.

Holding the reins tightly, with his head pressed into the neck of the beast he murmured reassuring calming words, while Arantxa tried her best to catch her breath and calm herself down.

"The Romans used to have horse racing sports in the circus in Tarraco. It hasn't been used for years, however, after that performance, I think I might be able to persuade my father to re-open it for a day. The local people need entertainment. And that, without a doubt, was most enjoyable, the whole of the camp that saw it are still laughing and I'm sure those misfortunate to have missed it, will be regaled with the story for many a moon." Marcus had trotted his horse to a measured distance alongside, out of kicking or slapping range, something which didn't stop Arantxa from trying both almost simultaneously and in the process re-frightening the animal. Thankfully the boy's tight grip prevented the attempted bolt, though not the overbalance the exertion entailed, she landed left shoulder first heavily on the ground. Neither boy nor man laughed, the fall was too serious for that, instead both moved to her aid. Hell hath no fury like a woman unseated from her horse and bereft of dignity in the dirt. As she was in no condition to lash out with her arms, her tongue took up the challenge. Thankfully most of it was in her language, so precise meanings were lost. There was no mistaking the passion though nor the direction, Marcus was the main target with the horse and boy receiving some collateral damage. Kaka zaharra (shit), Sasiko (bastard) were a couple of the words that seemed to take priority in the vent.

"What a charming scene. Marcus, I thought I ordered you to leave for Tarraco."

"Sir, I .."

Paulus reviewed the sight again, cowered boy, solicitous officer, non pulsed horse and a dirty injured furious woman. Perhaps he didn't need, nor want to be involved any further, he had come down from the house to find out what all the commotion was about.

"If you would be so kind as to remount. I will ensure that Arantxa is seated behind you. I believe that those people are not keen on riding. Well, that's what Aitziber once told me."

While Marcus went back to his horse, which wore a look of total disinterested disdain for all this unusual activity, Paulus turned on all his charms, firstly by physically helping the girl to dust off, then by talking quickly and quietly trying to smooth the ruffled feathers by asking whether Arantxa could do him the great favour of going into Tarraco with Marcus to help with a particularly difficult and tricky diplomatic mission which would be made considerably easier by her presence.

Arantxa hadn't been made to feel valued in such a long time that she allowed herself to be persuaded, even if it meant sitting on a horse. At least this time she wouldn't be alone up there.

*

"What do you make of the duke, my darling?"

The question was delivered with such over the shoulder casualness that Lady Chlodoswintha was immediately on her guard.

"Oh I don't know, he seems a nice enough chap."

"Most affable and in his own way quite handsome, wouldn't you say?"

Her suspicions were confirmed; suspecting her visit to Ranosindus's bedroom had been observed and reported. Having never had the need to lie to her husband about anything similar before, she stuck to her usual policy with him; sailing close to the truth without ever saying it.

"Not at all bad. Certainly better to look at than those uncouth ugly Franks and fat friars you are always bringing into the house. I commend you on your choice. From now on, could we have more like him?"

The count felt himself smiling despite himself. The woman amused him. He did like her, she was clever, sharp and fun. Also, still an attractive woman with her long blonde hair and fullness of figure, he could see why most men who came into contact with her fell under spell. He certainly had all those years ago. Their bedroom life wasn't that much of a success due to her lack of interest. She had always given the impression that she was doing a duty rather than a pleasure, quite unlike all the other women he was having sexual relationships with, and as he got his fill elsewhere these days, it seemed just too much hassle to bother with going through the motions with her. They had managed to sire a child and it was after the second that was conceived and miscarried that their infrequent amorous encounters dwindled to an absolute halt. These days there was a tacit agreement that nothing was said about his *activities* and no pressure was applied for her participation. Through mutual consent they slept in separate rooms.

All of this didn't mean to say that he didn't feel jealous when she flirted quite so openly with nearly all the men who she proclaimed to be *not so bad*. Ranosindus was a case in point. Her coquettishness with him bordered on the extreme, invariably, she diminished its importance by justifications involving the need to charm the man, for her husband's sake, of course, in order to get him to come along with THE plan. However, when one of the servants rather embarrassedly, mentioned that the Lady had taken food and drink to the duke's room and had stayed there a considerable time, his jealousy started eating away at him.

"He's also a most reasonable man." Chlodoswintha continued as nonchalantly as she could, "Did I tell you that I went to have a chat with him about the impasse at dinner? Poor man was totally upset at the way in which the Franks had behaved themselves, and who could blame him, dreadful, awful brutes."

"No, you seem to have neglected to inform me of this. Where and when did this meeting take place? I thought he had left at first light the morning after the dinner."

"As he did. No, I went to see him in his room."

"Chlodoswintha!"

"Don't *Chlodoswintha* me. The plan can NOT succeed without him, and more importantly, his army's assistance. So, I took him some food and drink in an effort to bring him back on board, or least, to prevent him from jumping ship."

"So, you offered yourself as a sacrificial lamb, did you?"

"Oh, you silly man, no, I didn't offer myself on the altar of your vanity to become king. What we did do was talk around his legitimate concerns of the capital of the kingdom being so close to the Frankish kingdom. He does NOT dispute your right to be king, he has no designs on that."

"What does he have *designs* on then?"

"I think I will ignore that remark. We talked about possible solutions."

*

Conflicted and contradictory, without a doubt that is how Arantxa felt as some impressively big stone buildings started to appear on the horizon. Not only were they huge, they also shone giving off a golden hue.

Being on a horse was really a most unpleasant experience, being both uncomfortable and dangerous. Having fallen off once back in the camp, she was most wary whenever the horse stumbled slightly on the loose slabs of the Via Augusta. She thought that was what Marcus had called it, also, saying something like it was hundreds of years old and actually went all the way to Rome, wherever that was.

On the plus side, each unsure step meant that she had to hold on tighter to Marcus. At the beginning of the journey she announced that she would rather die than hold on, as she had been told to do. This stance and willingness to give up her mortal state lasted less than ten minutes. In her repositioning, mentally and physically, she found, well, pleasure was the only word for it. Marcus did not have the most manly body in the world, in fact it was still boy-like with underdeveloped shoulders and torso, but it felt warm and still more surprisingly, it smelt really good. Each excuse to hold tighter, gave her a delightful tingly feeling inside.

"We are entering Tarraco, once the second capital of the Roman Empire and capital of Hispanias." The pride in his voice was clear to hear.

"And that's supposed to impress me, is it?"

They were entering the city properly now and the truth was, she was mega impressed having never seen a big building, here, there were LOTS of them and they were truly massive. How was it possible to build so high and strong. Clearly there was an air of neglect around them, nevertheless, there was no denying their size. Unsure as to whether her eyes or mouth were open the widest, she couldn't stop herself from being agog. The only thing saving her pride this time, was the fact that Marcus was in front of her and thus couldn't see her face.

"What's that?" She blurted out in awe before she could stop herself.

"That's the amphitheatre. It's not much used these days."

In for a penny, she may as well ask all her questions now, she thought.

"And why have they built something new in the middle of it?"

"Arhh, it actually looks as if it's finished. It wasn't when I left. They have been working on it forever. It's a church dedicated to the first martyrs who were killed there by the Romans."

"It looks silly stuck there in the middle. You Christians do have a way of destroying things, don't you?"

It was Marcus's turn to be shocked. She wasn't a Christian!

He'd never given it any thought before now. It was a presumption. Obviously he knew that not everybody was. Rebecca, as he had been warned often enough, was Jewish, but Arantxa wasn't Jewish, so, she had to be Christian his unconscious thought pattern went.

As far as he was concerned, Christians came in a number of varieties; there were devout, and less devout, he counted himself among the latter, and then there were Catholics and others, like the old bishop from Dertosa, Cecilius, nice old chap, and a regular house guest, who still harked back, at any, and every opportunity – *"we're losing our identity and our faith."* To him the "true" Goth form of Christianity, was Arian. They were all Christians though, as were the Vasconis Bishops they had met in Pampaelo. His reasoning, if there had ever been such a thing on this matter, something which he doubted, went along the lines of; if there were bishops, then, the "flock" had to be Christian.

"You're not Christian?" Try as he might, turning to see her face was made impossible by the firmness of her grip, something which he didn't want loosened as he had been enjoying the soft pressure of her breast joggling in rhythm to the horse's movement up and down his back.

"Can we get off this animal and walk as we seem to have arrived?"

Oh shame, end of the ride, thought Marcus.

Pulling up in front of yet another incredibly large building, he adeptly slid off the horse's back and stood offering assistance. Arantxa toyed with the idea of not accepting until a twinge pain in her arm reminded her of her previous descent, so she condescended to allowing herself to be lowered gently to the ground.

"What's this place?"

"The Circus. It's where the chariot races used to be held. Again, it doesn't get a lot of use these days."

Her musing as to why these impressive structures were so under-used and badly kept was interrupted by a number of women who, upon spying Marcus, came running all of a fluster.

"Marcus, Marcus, Marcus." they screamed. "You're back."

As Marcus moved off to meet them, Arantxa was left to wonder both at the buildings and at this female frenzy. Without a shadow of a doubt, she was out of her depth in this place and with this man.

After a few minutes of high pitched chatter, the women went back to wherever they had been going before all their *Marcusing* and sheepishly he returned to her.

"Their fathers or brothers are in the troop that went off to fight the barbar…, the enemy."

The look of sheer hatred told him that he hadn't managed to cover his loose language.

"This particular barbarian, who now has a very sore arse, would like to know why she has been brought here, and where we are going, and …"

"Marcus!"

Arantxa stopped midsentence as an extremely exotic and impressively beautiful woman had tapped Marcus on the shoulder and then hugged him most affectionately.

"So good that you are back, I didn't think that a useless little pipsqueak like you would be able to go to war AND come back."

Marcus coloured.

"Those tribes you were fighting must be slow and inept, if they weren't able to catch someone like you."

Marcus coloured even more.

It was then that Rebecca noticed Arantxa. "or perhaps they *did* catch you." Rebecca stepped forward to deliver a kisses greeting, only to have Arantxa step back into the flank of the horse. Unperturbed, Rebecca shot out a hand, "I'm Rebecca. This little boy used to run in the same group as me, though I have to tell you, he was always the last. I'm very pleased to meet you."

Unable to move any farther back, Arantxa had moved to the side, slightly behind Marcus and instinctively, as if for protection, she held onto the back of his elbow.

This caused Rebecca's eyebrow to rise. Marcus had always admired her ability to do this, raise one eyebrow. Having spent hours at home practising, he had finally come to the conclusion that she was just more talented than him.

"Sorry, I didn't mean to frighten you." Rebecca enunciated very slowly as if talking to a not particularly bright child with hearing difficulties. "Does she not speak Latin, Marcus?"

Flustered Marcus tried to regain control of the situation like a proper military official before it got completely out of hand. "Being part of King Wamba's advanced guard, we are going to my father's house to liaise on certain matters. We are based out at Els Munts, so, doubtless we will see each other around."

Rebecca realised that the war-going-little-boy, who was always desperate to show his authority, was still, very much the little boy who had come back.

"Yes, doubtlessly." With that she crossed back to whence she had come, that being the company of a striking young man, who was obviously of her faith, standing at a discreet distance. Marcus's eyes followed her with interest; who was he?

Arantxa, realising she was still holding Marcus' elbow, removed her hand. "Who was *she*?"

"Arh nobody important. Just a local Jew."

"A Jew? One of those people that do terrible things like eat babies?" Marcus let out a laugh which was both of relief that the encounter was over and genuine amusement, "Where did you hear that?"

"The women of the camp were always talking about it."

"Well, I think you should have learned not to listen to that lot. You don't have to imagine all the things they say about you. Come on, we need to get to my father's house."

*

Count Hilderic was back to his stomping pacing around.

"Do all men have to do that?"

"What?" The question came quite out of the blue. Lady Chlodoswintha was sewing something that required great attention to detail and had been quiet for a considerable time since declaring that she would ignore him and his innuendo. Meanwhile, her husband walked the equivalent of a forced march well into Frankish territory, hands tightly clasped behind his back and head lower much in the same way as his wife's attention to stitching detail. The inside of his head was in turmoil. Not knowing was the worst thing to him, and it was quite evident that knowledge was wanting in a whole number of areas.

Firstly, what his wife had *actually* been up to in the duke's bedroom. She was his property whose job it was to please and obey him, why did it never *feel* that way? She did allow him to *feel* as if he had sway. In reality though, ALL the major decisions were made by her, not in any imposing authoritative manner, she was too subtle for that, it was always a case of when there were differing voiced opinions, she would concede early and then, later, somehow or other, the final decision made was extremely close to her initial position. Quite how she did it, he was at a loss to say and the worst part was that these decisions, which were attributed to him, naturally, almost invariably turned out to be the best ones.

Secondly, what was going on in Tarraco with the force Wamba had sent? If there had been an armed clash then he felt sure that he would have heard something.

"Pacing. Practically every man I have ever known when faced with some sort of quandary, feels the need to go from one side of the room to the other as if they were ploughing furrows in a particularly difficult field."

"Every man.."

"Here we go again. Hilderic! I was thinking specifically of my father and brothers, not the army of lovers I have been keeping in tow all these years and, for now, have stowed in a spare bedroom for use when necessary!. I really think.."

There was a loud knock on the door followed quickly by a servant's head popping around it. "Bishop Gunhild has arrived and asks for an audience, Sire."

Pleased that the strained- going-to–an-abyss conversation had been interrupted; he almost gleefully granted the request. Chlodoswintha re-bowed her head to concentrate on the stitch in hand.

"Count, Your Ladyship," The Bishop strolled in. "I have received some news from Tarraco, I thought you would like to hear."

"Good to see you bishop, do have a seat, and tell all."

Hilderic's expectations weren't met. No great battle, no skirmish, nothing, just that the soldiers had set up camp just outside the city and gave off anything but the appearance of a aggressive fighting force, being more interested in sea bathing and catching up on their domestic chores than preparing battle formations.

"Zachary sends word that the son, Marcus, has been dispatched as some sort of ambassador to set up a formal meeting with The duke and General Paulus."

"Who's Zachary?" Her head hadn't lifted from her embroidery.

"A Jew, Your Ladyship. He's our major source of information down there. He dispatches regular information to the Rabbi in Narbo. "

"Very effective. Those Jews are quite an insidious little group, aren't they?"

"That they are. Anyway, it looks very much like inaction for the foreseeable future, unless we actually move ahead with the coronation unilaterally."

Chlodoswintha's head was now fully erect and attentive.

"That's a good idea, however, sadly not really practical without totally splitting our precarious alliance. If only…." There was a momentary pause for a fleeting thought, "It would most certainly force their hand somewhat, wouldn't it? I can't tell you how tired of all this waiting around I am. We do really need to get things going."

"Admirable sentiments, dearest husband, action is what is needed, perhaps though, we could influence matters in these meetings towards that end. I don't imagine the Jew will be in attendance at these gatherings, so what we really need is someone to represent our view there. Hilderic, you can't go, as you have to be seen and based where the Franks can cause no trouble. However, Gunhild here, would be the perfect candidate."

Gunhild looked anything but enthusiastic. Confident in his oratory and persuasive skills, as he was, this felt just a little like the old sport in Tarraco of feeding bishops to the lions. Before being able to object, the count came to his rescue. "He can't leave either. He is training and preparing our forces through my commanders, he's too integral to all our needs here."

"Perhaps I ought to go then…."

*

The sea. What a novelty. Being from small villages inland, or a couple of the more sophisticated ones, from Toletum itself, the sight of the vast mass of water was awe- inspiring and more than a little daunting for the forces based in Els Munts. They'd all seen, washed and fished in big lakes, but this unending blueness was new. Waves practically didn't exist, making it less frightening to approach, then gradually enter. Once that barrier had been surmounted, it was most difficult to stay out of.

The weather was still hot and the sea was wonderfully cooling, though the new sensation of salty skin was thought to be a little unpleasant. Nevertheless, the sand, sea and rocks had an irresistible pull on all those from the camp.

The camp chores were relatively simple. Els Munts was situated next to a forest which provided game, fruits, berries and firewood in abundance. Also, rudimentary nets were crafted which allowed them to pull out some of the teeming abundant fish that came to play with the splashers.

Milo tried to maintain some semblance of discipline by making the men drill daily in full battle dress. Flavius had insisted on this, however, it rarely lasted more than a couple of hours. Then it was off to the beach with the women, everyone in a state of undress.

Leaving the man she was lying on the sand with, Marta made a beeline to intercept Milo, who had just made an appearance. It wasn't exactly running with open armed enthusiasm, it was just one notch slightly further down that scale, walking very fast with her large breasts bouncing and an open mouth smile leaving the receiver in no doubt about her emotional, and physical, state.

"Finally, you've decided to join us Mr. Important Centurion."

"Marta, some people have responsibilities."

"Come on, Milo, we're not in the land of the enemy here. This is our country, not some foreign land." She took him by the hand and led him to a little cove which was momentarily uninhabited. He acquiesced, giving off feint resistance. "You have to remember that these people could be in open rebellion wanting their own country."

"Wouldn't you, if you lived here? It's magnificent. I'm not that keen on leaving. I have never seen a better place."

Milo frowned, inside though he felt something similar. He came from a small village in the south where eking out a living wasn't easy, the determining factor in his *career choice*, soldiering. Being the third son of a poor family didn't give a plethora of options in life. Cold in winter, baking hot in summer meant that crops were scarce and precarious in his village and all the others around. As a-wet- behind–the-ears yokel being marched into Toletum for the first time, he was awed by its opulence, size and wealth, a sight that he would forever associate with pain, as his head turned to take in this magnificence, his marching step found itself out of time to the rest of the troop, hence the stinging sensation of a whip on his calves.

Housing for him pre-army meant mud, thatch and wood with the very basic necessities, all shared with a multitude of kin. Military life suited him, a step in the right direction, now, despite the relative happiness and comfort of all these years of experience and all the distance travelled, he knew his head was being turned again. A reconnaissance mission that morning was his labour and although he didn't actually enter the heart of Tarraco, what appeared in front of him put Toletum into the shade. The size, the *height*, the opulence of the buildings was a sight to behold. He returned to Els Munts truly impressed.

"Look at this house." She interrupted her undressing of him, to point up to the building above them. "Can you imagine living somewhere like that? They say that it belongs to the family of that useless officer, the one who's besotted with that

Vasconis witch, what's his name?"

"Marcus, and it does. Actually, I overheard the commander speaking to him about it. Apparently, it's their summer home!"

"What! You mean that they have another one in town? Shit! I should have tried to treat him *nicer*." She delivered this with a sly creeping smile as she resumed her disrobing.

Not everyone in the camp was quite so ecstatic with their positioning. The contingent from Tarraco were thoroughly pissed off, so close to home and loved ones, yet they had been told that they were not allowed to break camp to go into the city. There was genuine discontent and murmurings of desertion, which for the moment was on hold, but rife. Before Marcus getting saddled, he had promised to take their grievances to the commander upon his return, once that is was assured that Tarraco wasn't a hostile territory to them. How weird had that sounded, the city of their birth, the place where their families lived, behind enemy lines, or worse still, the enemy. They allowed themselves to be momentarily mollified in front of him, however, once he was off on his way, they got together to discuss the very perplexing issues raised by just this thought. Where were their loyalties? They had fought with Wamba's army, sort of, might be more accurate to say they were with Wamba's men while some fighting existed, the men they marched here with, were comrades in arms, despite a wary start, true bonds of friendship had been made. What would happen if armed conflict between them became a reality? Undoubtedly, they would put hearth home and family first, but this would mean killing or being killed by men who had become genuine friends. The immediate results of this could be seen on the beach with their group occupying the southern sector and the *others* in the north. Neither group had done this deliberately as a conscious reaction to their present dilemma, instead it was natural happening.

*

Rebecca watched as Marcus led horse and woman uptown laughing conspiratorially together. Hillel was still smarting from his treatment at the hands of the gentile, the blame for which laid squarely at doorstep of this woman next to him. Not explaining what had happened in the palace, nor why it was so brief, despite being plied with questions on their descent from uptown, he wanted to change the conversation and he wanted to strike out.

"Was that the little boy you told me that you used to *play* with?"

"Play, with that innuendo? Please, Hillel, get a grip. Not so long ago we were kids, since then a lot of water has gone under the bridge, and sadly, it would appear none of us shall ever play childish games again. The time of innocence and innocents is over. Were you ever young, Hillel? You can't be more than twenty-five now, yet you give off the atmosphere of Methuselah."

"I'll take that as a compliment. As one takes on the responsibility of rabbi, I believe that the wisdom it bestows actually gives one an appearance of age."

"*Actually*, it was not meant as a compliment. You give off the air of someone who has never had fun in their life. You know what, I'm not sure I would confuse dullness with wisdom."

Rebecca had been forced into the company of this man for days now. As the go-between of the local Jewish community and the Christians, she was obliged to report to him all the details of the previous meeting and put up with his insufferable way of speaking and endless questions trying to prize out the tiniest detail, accompanied with words of world wise wisdom, by relating matters to scripture, or implying that there was much more to Rebecca's relationship than she was saying.

The nub of the problem was clear to Rebecca; the fact that she was a woman. This Rabbi was of the school of thought, prevalent in all societies, but especially in some of the stricter interpretations of Judaism, that women should not be involved in any important matters; hearth and home was their territory not state politics. Fundamentally, they were viewed as inferior and taught they were unclean due in no small part to their monthly bleedings. A chicken and egg thing, you are unclean because you bleed monthly, you bleed monthly because you're a woman and therefore unclean. What was clear to see, was that it offended him, and his pride, and probably the whole of the Jewish faith that he had to conduct his affairs with a female. She, in turn, loathed him. He was smug, arrogant, opinionated and invariably wrong and she'd bitten her tongue so often on her father's advice that to actually say a little of what she felt, came as quite a relief.

Hillel was shocked that anyone, even less a woman, would dare to speak to him in this way. He promised himself vengeance. Trying to remove her had met with opposition from the local Jewish community, which, to him, showed how corrupted and degraded the Jews of Tarraco had become, and now, surprisingly from the Christian authorities as well. The collusion between the groups had become so strong that he felt that he must be the instrument of God's will to save these people from themselves. They weren't actually anusim, the forced converts, but they acted in a similar matter to the point of being so absorbed into the local community that their identity was in serious doubt.

Being brought up in the south of Hispalis, the line between the two communities was well defined. Most of the Goth ecumenical edicts were enthusiastically enforced by the Christians down there. Two separate entities, which if it weren't for the repression that accompanied it, he found himself in agreement with. No inter-marriage was logical and desirable. Banning the Jews ownership of slaves had had the beneficial unintentional boom of driving the Jews off the land into commerce. So successful had they become in this field that the law prohibiting trade between the communities was introduced, which again had the silver lining forcing them to become self reliant and almost independent. The ban on religious practises made life, especially as rabbi, somewhat difficult, though in most cases they could duck and weave their way around it by pretending to convert or clandestine religious ceremonies. However, forced conversion with punishment, which was meted out by other convert Jews, for all those found wanting in their true adherence to Christianity, plus the removal of their children to be brought up as Christians were steps far too far. All of this made this rebellion not only desirable, but totally necessary, even if it meant dealing with another set of less bad Christians. It was a case of your enemy and my enemy makes us allies, if not friends.

Needing to change the topic and not show his pain and desire to attack, he moved onto a theme which might hurt her a little, he casually inclined his head towards the moving away horse and two people saying, "That must be his Vasconis whore?"

"Vasconis whore?"

"Yes. And quite a sordid tale it is."

Rebecca didn't want to show that she was interested so she tried, and failed, to look as nonchalant as she possibly could. Hillel, realising this was an opportunity, ladled on the gory details as much as possible. How both the army officials now based at Els Munts, the general and Marcus, had had sex with some local women causing Wamba's army a minor defeat at the hands of the local tribes, and how that defeat could have become major, if it hadn't been for the betrayal of her own people by this whore who was now being escorted through the streets of Tarraco.

"Can you imagine betraying your own people?" He looked pointedly at Rebecca, "perhaps you can, women are so weak."

Rebecca had punched people before for less, the only thing that stopped her now was the consequences that her family would have to pay within the community.

"For me, there is nothing worse than betraying your community, religion, history, in short, who you actually are. Women seem to find it easy, usually blaming their weakness of character on some spurious concept of *love*; impetuous, irrational, emotional creatures who need guidance throughout their lives."

Rebecca decided to prove his point, a right cross to the chin made him stagger and fall. She didn't look back as she moved away, but the commotion and noise did make Marcus turn, and, in awe, give a lopsided smile.

*

"Arrh, my little boy!"

The words were unexpected from the wizened crow-like woman who opened the door and her arms, clearly though Arantxa observed, they were only words, her eyes betrayed other emotions.

"Most kind of you, Amalaswinth. Where is my father to be found?"

"*Most kind* indeed! The little boy has become a soldier man now, has he? No longer needs his nursemaid, does he? Is all grown up, is he?"

Marcus never ever having liked this woman, found her overt display of false emotion decidedly uncomfortable.

"And who may I ask is this?" A scrawny finger was jabbed disrespectfully.

"Not that it's any of your business, but this lady is Arantxa, and we are here to see my father, so if you could be so kind as not to point at my guest, and instead point me in the direction of my father, I would be most grateful."

" *Most grateful, my guest,* my little boy has certainly acquired some airs and graces, hasn't he? Arantxa, what sort of name is that? Not another Jewess. I do hope not, we have had quite enough trouble from that other one."

Arantxa bristled with indignation by the bucket load; a Jewess, a foreign name, *another* one, and all delivered in such a spiteful undertone.

Opening her mouth to speak, she unexpectedly found a hand in the small of her back not so gently pushing her past the woman, moving deeper into the opulence of this incredible building.

"If you won't tell, I'll find him myself. Meanwhile prepare some refreshments for me and my guest."

"Ooooo.."

The rest of the words were lost as Marcus set off at a brisk pace, softly now, shoving Arantxa. Turning to glare and at the point of slapping either his arm or face, she heard him whisper with feeling, "Sorry, ignore her. My father believes she means well."

Pottery, statues, artwork in abundance littered their path through the entrance way. Open mouthed, she couldn't help but be impressed. "You live here?"

"When I don't have to go out fighting nasty barbarians, yes." His own laughter saved him from the second almost slap in succession. "Lighten up. Enjoy yourself. You are not being hounded by vicious women and you are in the company of a very important person....in this house, at least" He chuckled again. Leaving Arantxa silent to contemplate a number of things, why was *she* here, who Marcus actually *was*, and what role this beauty Jewess played in his life.

"So you are here, about time, I hear you've been camping out in the summer house for days."

Duke Ranosindus, in a garb that gave off the appearance of a gardener rather than nobility, was making his distracted way down a long marble spiral staircase. Goths had become Latinized in most of their habits, however, there were some things they hadn't managed to take on board, one of which was male embracing, be it friends, comrades, or father/ son relationship. The back slapping hugging approach of the Romans, was frowned upon as not becoming of a real man, instead firm elbow holding was preferred to any effeminate show affection. So, despite the real pleasure father and son felt at seeing each other again, only elbows were held after hands were shaken.

"And this must be the famous girl from Vasconia I've heard about."

"What!" exclaimed the visitors in unison.

"Come on through and be seated, I'll get Amalaswinth to bring us something to drink."

"Father, that's already taken care of, we had the unfortunate and dubious pleasure to be met by her. But, how do you know about Arantxa?"

"Arantxa, is it? I didn't know the name, and a very pretty one it is, as you are, my dear, very pretty. Terribly sorry if you had the misfortune to get an Amalaswinth greeting, she gets worse every year, I have had to have serious words with her recently. Actually, I was on the point of letting her go. No secret is safe in this house, so do be careful what you say out loud. Also, she was infamously rude to your Jewish friend, Rebecca, spits blood and fury upon the sight of her. Not that it bothers Rebecca much, water off a duck's back. Not worried about that one, she can give as good as she gets."

The vision of the sprawling Jew and Rebecca walking completely nonplussed away, came flooding into Marcus' mind and he had to nod his agreement.

" A very interesting woman, that one. Sorry, I am forgetting myself," slowing down his speed of delivery and enunciating as much as possible he continued, "do you speak some of our language, dear?"

Marcus's head was spinning, an almost sacked Amalaswinth, his father and Rebecca, as thick as thieves, evidently an awful lot had happened in his absence.

"I …. think…I might be…able to ….understand you, if .." there was a long pause in which it looked as if Arantxa was searching for the right mote. "if you spoke at a normal speed and stop treating me like some half-witted backward child!"

Ranosindus spluttered with laughter which lasted so long that refreshments were brought and left with Amalaswinth scowling throughout without a word being exchanged by the servant or its recipients, before the duke managed to dry his eyes and regain his upright posture.

"Marcus, you seem to have chosen *another* witty one. I'm sorry, my dear, my intention wasn't to insult nor belittle, forgive please."

Shock upon shock, upon shock; the city, the house, the Jewess, the *other* one, and now a duke apologising to her. Marcus had done it, which shocked her, but he was just a boy, although it appeared that he was an extremely wealthy boy, and now his father, the owner of all this, asking for her forgiveness. These Roman/Goths were certainly strange people. A man from her country would never apologise to an inferior woman. It led her into quite a quandary, Should she say that she *forgives* him, or, accept his apologies or, what? Thankfully Marcus came to her rescue, "Vascon is her first language, every word is incomprehensible."

"Sasiko!"

"See! My point exactly. From context when she used this at both the horse and me, I presume that this is not a compliment."

"Actually, as your father is seated here, I suppose the word has no validity."

There was silence for a minute while the sentence was processed and suddenly it was met by another burst of duke-ish laughter.

Marcus didn't find this funny, he coloured at being upstaged.

"Perhaps, father, you could stop laughing and tell me," a quick look at Arantxa, "us, how you knew about my arrival here with *a girl from Vasconia*. Was it one of the Tarraco men from my troop? I know Pere has been sending you some information."

"No, what? Pere? No, his one report was so long ago that I could be a grandfather now," a slight smirk in Arantxa's direction, "No, I heard it in Narbo."

"Narbo?"

*

The ride back was quiet, very quiet. The horses hooves on the well worn out Roman road was the only sound besides the faint watery noise of waves hitting to shore with the same amount of strengthen as Arantxa's two fingertip grip on Marcus' waist.

Both lost in their own thoughts, processing exactly what had happened in Tarraco, neither had had any clear vision of what they thought would happen before they left, and neither could have imagined what had actually happened.

It was not too much of an exaggeration to say that Arantxa's view on and of the world had been totally changed. A young village woman, whose family had been slaughtered by friend and foe, facing life on her own, had been entertained and treated kindly by some of the most important people in the land; her ex, were they still?, enemies. Both father and son had treated her like an equal; no ordering, no condescending, no abuse. Never ever before in her village life had she been listened to and appreciated by men, any men; from the lowest to the highest, she was dismissed as just a woman. It was a new feeling and she liked it. However, she was more than a little wary of it. Would it, could it, last? Something she did know, without much doubt, was that she *really* liked Marcus. This was something that she had been reluctant to show throughout their journey, now, she felt that she would never be able to show it. How could someone THAT important be interested in her except for a little sport? If it was a game, well, she didn't want to play. From everything she saw in the village she associated men with pain, physical pain, beatings for doing this wrong or not doing that, was a norm. The only woman she ever knew who experienced emotional pleasure, was her sister, Aitziber, and look how that ended. She couldn't allow herself to fall any further under the spell of this boy / man. Hence her fingertip hold; wanting the physical touch, at the same time knowing that she could not hold on.

Marcus' thoughts were less personal and more geo-political, although he did, briefly, wonder what Rebecca was up to as a regular visitor of his father, and, just who was that man she was with outside the Circus? What worried him more was his piggy in the middle position. His father's statement, left little room for doubt, the "rebellion" did exist. Being led by Narbo, the intention was to break away from the present Goth kingdom under Wamba, to set up their own, covering the whole of Tarraconensis/ Gallia Gothica, giving the rather fanciful notion that this could be achieved peacefully by showing force on their side, and at the same time paying a certain amount of taxation to Toletum. They would become a sort of vassal state for a short period of time, before becoming a totally independent ally.

Marcus knew better. Having seen Wamba fighting to expand the territory and subject all and sundry to Toletum rule, he was sure that there would be no way that the king, or any king, would accept secession of part of his kingdom without a fight.

The situation at the moment dictated that General Flavius couldn't challenge Tarraco / Narbo with the forces at his disposal. He could though, provide a useful vanguard for the invading Wamba army. His father, Duke Ranosindus, in what a loving son could only describe as naivety, believed in the power of persuasion, and to that end had proposed a meeting with the general in Tarraco at his earliest convenience, with himself as the messenger and honest broker; piggy in the middle.

The speed of the journey to Els Munts was a surprise to both, having only just set off, they could spy a welcoming party awaiting.

"Shall I help you down, Miss?"

More politeness from a Roman/ Goth. Arantxa permitted herself to be lowered by this big man whose name she knew was Pere, Marcus's right-hand man.

As she was walking back into the camp proper, she heard the exchange;

"Marcus, we really need to have a chat."

"Not now, I have to report to the commander."

"Marcus, now!"

"Pere, shouldn't you be saluting and calling me sir, instead of giving me orders?" Marcus' voice had taken on an air of authority.

"Marcus, don't give me that shit, I've known you since you were knee high to a grasshopper, and everything you know about playing soldier, you have learnt from me!"

"I will not be talked to ..."

"Yes you will. Come, I really need to talk to you before you see the general, it's in your own interest."

Pere's considerable bulk guided a slightly reluctant and at the same time intrigued Marcus towards the sea, to a sheltered inlet, whereupon he was told, in no uncertain terms, about the intention of his men to leave camp, probably when night fell.

"Desertion?"

"No, going home. They have done what was asked of them. They went to war, now they are a couple of hours walk from their families, who they haven't seen in months, bivouacked in a threatening army. Understandably, in my opinion, they believe that it was not your father's intention to send them away to be brought back to fight against Tarraco itself, and they are determined not to do it. So, their intention is just to melt away in the hours of darkness."

"They shall be stopped."

"If they are, they are prepared to fight their way out against men who have become their friends and who, by the way, have every sympathy with their plight."

Piggy in the middle.

"Thank you, Pere. Could you ask the men to delay their final decision until I have spoken to the general? I promise that if the general puts up any opposition, I, personally, will lead the camp exit."

*

"Why did you do it?" Isaac's head moved sideways in the family's familiar soft profound lament.

"But why? Such an affable chap and SO knowledgeable, forever quoting the Torah in such exquisite Hebrew, a genuine intellectual, we should be proud to have among us as our spiritual leader."

"Poppycock!"

"Rebecca! Show some respect to your uncle at least."

"Oh, papa, I don't mean to disrespect your opinions, dearest uncle, but that man is nothing but a grade one humbug, so puffed up with his own self importance he'd put any peacock feather show to shame. And he squawks like one too! Wonderful Hebrew? How would we know? His pronunciation is different to that of rabbi Saul, I'll give you that, it's also different from all the others we have heard when trading with foreigners, so, at what point does that make his *better*?"

"He's an intellectual, a rabbi and –"

"And what?"

"Daughter, daughter, daughter, calm down. We are only saying that by hitting him you showed a lack of control and respect. You need to apologise, publicly and remorsefully."

"I won't!"

It was at this moment that Hillel chose to walk through Jacob's wide open front door. A small red mark gave the only slightest hint of his ordeal.

"Ah, dear rabbi, we were just talking about you. I believe Rebecca has something to say."

A killing glance struck her father's eyeline, however, before she could open her mouth to compound whatever mess she had caused, Hillel interrupted smartly, "Rebecca, I'm sorry I didn't escort you back home, the problem was that I slipped, having had some serious problems with my sandal. I really need to get this strap fixed. I never seem to find the time, what with meetings, studying and services. Today is the day though, before I do myself real injury."

With that short statement he turned on his heel, evidently the soundest part of his footwear, and smartly marched out with a cheery, "See you all later at Shabbat services."

Eyes and mouths wide open, nobody even uttered a goodbye reply.

"What the ?" Isaac was first to find a couple of words before Rebecca interrupted him with a short sharp snort of laughter.

"No need for me to apologise because it never happened! The peacock is too proud to admit he was decked by a woman, so it didn't happen. Incredible!"

It was Jacob's head's turn, surprisingly the family never seemed to have a synchronised shake, preferring instead individual performances, the perceptively slow motion, denoting the depth of concern, "Daughter dear, you have made yourself a very dangerous enemy."

*

"The little bitch is back."

"Oh Miss High and Mighty."

"Not that high, she fell off the horse!"

More comments and raucous laughter accompanied Arantxa back to the women's area. As custom would have it, the female section was set apart from the main camp, usually in a vastly inferior area to pitch a camp. Here though, the concept of a *bad* area, didn't exist, there were only less good ones. It was a magnificent spot, not high up on the rock where the house was placed, lower down, at the end of a gentle stream, closer to the sea. The women had made themselves most comfortable, rudimentary huts provided daytime shelter from the still hot sun and night time sleeping arrangements. Most women found it more convenient to wear little or no clothes, something which encouraged skin darkening and men, both of which were welcomed.

As Arantxa had no one to share with, there was no shelter for her. Having no desire to hear more ridicule; she headed for the shade of a scrubby excuse of a tree which was far enough away to be out of earshot. Her "welcome" was making her review her previous anti- men stance. This lot here treated her as badly as the village men, the concept of female solidarity was conspicuous by its absence.

When she had first entered the women's camp with the Wamba army, she'd felt accepted, not just tolerated, never rejected, but accepted for who she was. The general feeling was all the women were in more or less the same boat, and it made sense for everyone to row in the same direction. Ezte being there helped greatly, she often found herself wondering how her friend was doing, and whether she should have made the same decision to stay.

One thing was certain, she could not stay with this lot for much longer, she had to make a decision sooner rather than later, to get out. The problem was, to where. Having heard the beginning of Pere's words to Marcus, and knowing the rumours around camp before her trip to Tarraco, she felt sure that the local men were about to return home, which would leave her in a much worse position. Perhaps her best option was to tag along with them. This led to the worrying thought of how she would be treated by the local Tarraco women, if she turned up with their men. Out of the frying pan, into the fire?

"Ah Marcus, do come and be seated." The general was a-glow; good health, rest, sea sun and good food would do that for you, and it had done for him. As they moved through an opulent dining room to a terrace with a spectacular view over the bay, silence of two differing varieties reigned; nervous tension versus relaxed serenity.

"How strange must it feel to be welcomed into your own house. You people certainly know how to live well. It's not at all surprising that Roman Emperors used to hang out here."

It did feel strange, not to the point of offence or anger, but he was peeved that this man was playing host in *his* summer house.

"You're looking very much at home, General. I only go away for a day and this house now gives off the impression of being more yours than mine."

Paulus' antennae were buzzing, the last thing he could afford to do in this "enemy" land was upset his local contact, who was also the best chance of resolving the upcoming conflict peacefully.

"I thank you, and your most generous family greatly for extending their hospitality, it is most appreciated. I promise I won't lose sight of just whose house this is."

Feathers smoothed, a more mollified Marcus reported back on his trip, reiterating his father's invitation to Tarraco for talks as soon as possible. While Flavius mulled, Marcus thought the time right to mention his men's grievances.

"That is desertion!" The move from pensive to indignant anger, was a swift one.

"Technically, I am not sure that it is, as they were enrolled to fight one campaign not to become a permanent part of Wamba's army."

"**King** Wamba, and call me sir."

Marcus was thoroughly fed up with army life and being subordinate to a stranger in his own house and this was the final straw. He remained seated but his voice took on a steely edge he'd never used to anyone older or *superior* to him.

"General, you are a foreigner in my country, and in my house, as far as I am concerned, my commission and position in your army is over, so, I will no longer call you *sir*, nor will I, or my men, take your orders. This evening I will march them out of the camp back to their families and if you decide to try to stop us, then there will be a fight, which given your superior numbers you are almost bound to win, but know that you will be pitching friend against friend as the two groups have become entwined over the last few weeks. Furthermore, your victory will be hollow as my father's forces would track you down soon enough."

Completely taken aback by the cold determined way in which these threats, or promises, were made, Paulus knew he had no choice but to make some sort of compromise.

"Let's not be hasty here."

"Haste there is, my men will leave with or without me. They have had enough. I don't think you will be able to stop them in any way. What I suggest, would be something orderly and which gives off the appearance of part of the plan which was always going to be implemented. The choice is limited, but it's yours."

Marcus made to stand only to find a restraining hand on his wrist.

"Sit,… please."

The general found himself impressed, and appalled in equal measure, at the situation. Impressed by the no-longer cowering boy, and appalled by his lack of real options. His command was falling apart. He could stop them from leaving, the arithmetic, as mentioned, was overwhelmingly in his favour, the price for this clash though, be it minorly or majorly bloody, would deal a devastating blow to camp morale. His men would understand the Tarraco men's position. In fact, they would demand the same, if they were anywhere near their home. What's more, his men were exceptionally happy in this spot and wouldn't miss the Tarraco crowd in any way, the logical thing to do would be to agree to the ultimatum. The fact that it was an ultimatum was what really galled him. If they had talked about it, then perhaps he wouldn't be in this position of losing face.

"Your proposition Marcus is a good one. However, to make it work I, as commander, need to look as if I am involved somehow. I know that you do not want to harm me."

He arched an eyebrow causing Marcus to momentarily stop listening; here's another one who can do that, why wasn't he able to it?

"…in Tarraco, what do you think?"

"Sorry, General I missed that, would you mind repeating it?"

Thinking this a clever ploy for Marcus to formulate a response, the general happily repeated, " we arrange that when I come into Tarraco, the day after tomorrow, your men form an honour guard outside the city's main gate to welcome me in."

"No."

Hackles rising, the general was about to go for the bloody option when Marcus added, "It would have to be tomorrow. If I give them a couple of days free, I will never be able to find them all again as some are from outlying villages and …"

Flavius nodded agreement and restored some more of his authority by commanding Marcus to instruct the scribe to write a letter of acceptance to the duke.

"Shabbat shalom." Chorused around the room, the meeting was being held in a sort of backroom in what passed for the town's synagogue, Jews could not afford, in political rather financial terms, to be ostentatious. A small three roomed building in the heart of uptown, closer to the duke's palace than Jacob's or Isaac's houses down near the port. Some of the wealthier Jewish merchants, the guebirim, owned houses in this section of town, and between them they leased this building.

There were two main rooms for praying, one for the men and another for women. This backroom was a communal space used for meetings, changing and storage, however, by most it was still considered part of the synagogue, so the gender separation was respected, meaning that Rebecca was not allowed to attend, something which chaffed greatly.

"You know you are not permitted there, so why are you arguing."

"Because it isn't fair."

"Five thousand year history has to be changed because my niece thinks that she's hard done to? My God; Rebecca, you really are full of your own self importance."

"Uncle, it is not that, and you know it! However, I am important to the success of this meeting with the duke. Yet I am excluded from its preparatory session because I am a woman. All the other meetings have been held at our house, why does this one have to be held in the synagogue?"

"Hillel stated clearly, and the elders agreed, that this was a matter of life and death to us, and, more importantly, to our faith, therefore we needed to be as close to the presence of God as possible so that we should be spiritually guided by Him."

"What a heap of…claptrap. Hillel just wants to exclude me."

"There she goes again with her self- importance."

"Isaac, you may be correct that my favourite little daughter here, has an inflated opinion of herself,"

"I'm your only daughter and I'm not *little*."

"But, actually, I think she is right. From my understanding of scriptures, God is everywhere, so why he'd prefer us to be in a cramped airless little cupboard rather than a light-filled living room or courtyard, is beyond me and my understanding. I suspect the choice of venue has a great deal to do with a certain *blow* against Hillel's authority. My darling, still favourite, daughter, I believe it's payback time. You are and have been excluded, I suspect Hillel will do his best to marginalise you as much as he can. Apparently the duke has made it clear that you should be there, your role is not so clear. Being a khakhamim, a rabbi and intellectual, and I don't think that even you, Rebecca can dispute that! Hillel stressed how wrong it was that you should be there, scripture being quoted at GREAT length. However, he was powerless to prevent it. Surprisingly, he took his grievances to the bishop and they were well received! Though it would appear that all the real clout in this story lies in the hands of the duke."

"I am sorry to say to you, dear niece, that Hillel was most convincing in his arguments. Not just according to scripture, look at it dispassionately, it would be most strange to have a meeting where there was ONE woman present and that one woman was a Jew."

"Start getting used to the idea, daughter, that your presence will be required for introductions and warming up chit chat, then Hillel will move to have you removed in order that serious negotiations can take place."

"He wouldn't dare!" Rebecca's voice was assured and strident not betraying any of the qualms that her father's words raised in her, she knew that he was right. Perhaps she should have controlled herself and not punched him, still, the feeling brought about, a warm glow of satisfaction, and the sight of him sprawled on the floor was worth it.

*

The shade provided by the excuse for a tree had totally disappeared after midday and she was being roasted alive. It hardly ever got this hot where she was from. Sometimes it would be pretty warm for a couple of days, then a refreshing storm would blow through. Here, it was always hot, or very hot. Since arriving back, she'd be sitting indecisively, weighing up her options, coming to a decision which then wouldn't stand up to a little more thought, going back to the beginning, discarding, rectifying, and all the time melting in the heat as she was incapable of even making a move into the shade decision. Suddenly, feeling a little cooler she realised that someone's shadow was covering part of her. Squinting up into the sun, the smiling face of Pere was looking down on her.

"You're so sweaty that I think you'd be drier going into the sea. Are you coming in?"

Lowering her painfully sun-squinting eyes, she realised that she was actually on eye line of his penis.

"I don't think…"

"Arantxa, this not an attempt at a pick up or anything, we all know that you are sweet on our commanding officer, it's just I am going into the sea and I think you ought to. I don't need any complications as I'm really looking forward to going back to my wife today or tomorrow. Come and cool down."

What the hell..? Arantxa jumped up out of the penis level, shed her clothes and sprinted for the sea. After the inaction of the morning it felt great to be doing something. Skipping a couple of ripples that masqueraded as waves, she dived into the shallow water, it was warm and salty, new sensations for her. The lakes were always cold or colder and never salty. A large splash indicated Pere's arrival.

"Much better, thank you, Pere." Neck deep they were able to stand. "Has it been decided then, that you're going back home?"

"We've decided. Marcus is communicating that decision to the general now."

"What if he says no?"

"Then it'll get… messy. We're going one way or another. It really wouldn't be in their interest to stop us."

"I wish I could come with you."

"There's nobody even trying to stop you. That lot," he indicated to the main part of the women's camp, "wouldn't miss you, and I dare say you wouldn't be too upset to leave them behind. Vicious bunch. The men in the troop are on the whole very nice people, especially Milo, but them!"

"Where would I go? What would I do?"

"There's Marcus."

"Pere, be serious. Have you seen his home?" The man nodded and clicked his fingers while letting out a low whistle.

"I didn't realise that anyone could be that rich. I just thought he was a sweet lost little boy playing man."

"He is. Actually, I have known him all his life nearly. He's a good lad and he's grown a lot on the trip."

"Yeah, that's as may be. Still, he's out of my league."

"Probably. His father would expect his only son to make a good marriage, still, there's no harm in trying, in reality, and sorry for being so blunt, you haven't got a great deal to lose."

"Thanks ! Succinctly put. Should I stay or should I go? Obviously the latter is a better option if there was something to go to. I can't return home."

Pere looked at her, possibly for the first time, until now she had been the target of coarse comments and expressions of desire among his men, who liked her and appreciated what she had done for them. Nevertheless, she was seen as just a fine piece of work that Marcus was lucky to have the chance to play with. Seeing her suffering, lonely and future-less tugged at the old soldier's heart strings.

"Why don't you come back to my house? My wife is a good woman, I'm sure she'll have some ideas of what to do."

"Really?" The hope was clearly heard as both wondered just how the "wife" was going to react. Was this one of those Basajaun moments? Basajuan was the Lord of the forest whose job it was to help. However, he had an equally important role and that was to antagonise humans. Was he playing with her now? Leading her on to her eventual demise?

*

"Amalaswinth, tomorrow I am expecting guests. I doubt greatly that they'll stay for supper. However, just in case the meeting drags on, I want you to be prepared. It doesn't have to be fish, the bishop will not be in attendance. What my guests will need is refreshments - ale, good wine and something to pick at, make sure we have plenty of everything."

"For about how many?"

"Not sure. I suppose about six."

"It will be done. Are you expecting any overnight guests either today or tomorrow?"

"Very much doubt any will be staying the night, with the possible exception of Marcus."

Amalaswinth knew she could not afford to lose this job, so refraining from asking any details and trying to pull a face which showed as little interest in her master's affairs as possible, even though her eavesdropping had provided her more than an inkling of the attendees; Marcus, his commanding officer and a couple of Jews, probably that arrogant bitch Rebecca among them.

"And the woman who pulled up in the courtyard a few moments ago with a military escort, will she be not needing her own bedroom tonight?"

"Woman, courtyard, own bedroom, what the devil are you talking about?"

"Ranosindus! What a magnificent house; I should say palace. You look shocked, I'm sorry, as the door was open, I let myself in without announcement. I dearly wanted to see your happily surprised face, now, I'm not so sure it was the best idea." Chlodoswintha cast her cloak onto the back of the nearest chair, "Delight is not being shown. Also, I do think you are much more handsome with your mouth closed."

"Chlodoswintha…"

"Well, that's a positive start; at least you remembered my name."

"What..?"

"Oh good, some things haven't changed. Forever with the *what* question." Looking now at Amalaswinth smiling sweetly, "Do you find that he's always asking questions with "what"? I presume you are the housekeeper. Pleased to meet you. I am Lady Chlodoswintha from Nemausus, I shall be staying for a few days, if you wouldn't mind making up a bedroom for me, I should be most grateful." Then she added conspiratorially, "Men, good with the *what* questions, never think of these things, do they? My husband would have everyone out in the

(246)

stables or at the local inn. I imagine this one is the same. Lucky he has you, isn't he?"

Amalaswinth was a mess of emotions; indignation at the woman's effrontery at just marching in her house taking over, and pride in that she had be finally recognised for her true value. Picking up the cloak she all but bowed when saying, "Yes, Your Ladyship." Then preened her way out.

"Chlodoswintha, what..?"

"Do stop the "whats", Ranosindus. Also, I do think that you should refer to me by my title in front of servants. You really don't look at all pleased to see me, most upsetting, especially after all I had to do to wangle myself back into your company!" Walking determinedly across the room, a kiss was planted full on the lips.

"Perhaps that goes some way to answering the main *"what"*. The cover story is that I am representing Nemausus /Narbo as nobody else could be spared from the war preparations."

"War? I really hope it doesn't come to that. I believe negotiations backed by force will suffice."

"Forever the innocent, both in love and war, I shall see what can be done to rectify the situation in the two fields. Let's retire to somewhere less public to plan strategies for the meeting, I'm sure your palace is the same as mine in that the walls tend to have ears, by the way, when is it?"

"Tomorrow."

"Then we have no time to lose." She held his hand firmly, "Lead me where you will."

It was quite a sight, the like Tarraco hadn't seen for decades or longer. Pere had marshalled his forces, with Marcus nominally at their head, both sides of the Via Augusta. In full dress uniform they shone in the sunlight, the reflected glory of the kingdom was theirs. Spears, breastplates and helmets returned the rays of the sun in a blinding display, the morning's effort and elbow grease had its reward. The men felt proud. Proud of who they were, what they had done, and how they were to greet their brothers in arms who at this moment could be viewed in the distance by the most eagle eyed, and heard by all but the deaf. Their boots and marching rhythm was unmistakable, for weeks they had been part of the same sound.

All of Tarraco had turned out. The crowds behind the shining soldiers were dense and full of anticipation.

The Tarraco troop had returned the previous night a lot more inauspiciously, there was no fanfare, no waiting throngs, nobody knew they were coming. Rather than be allowed to go back to their homes just minutes away, they had had to pitch a temporary camp in the middle of the amphitheatre around the newly constructed church dedicated to the first Christian martyrs: Fructuous and his deacons Augurius and Eulogius. If truth be told, they were most displeased by the situation and even more disparaging of the construction. Some of them had spent their whole lives watching the building rise and couldn't believe that it had taken such a long time to produce so little.

They had been persuaded and mollified by Pere's voice of authority explaining that they had to do things properly, not just slink off tails between their legs, back to their place between their wives legs. No, this would be like times of old when returning armies would be given a Triumph.

Wives and families had tried to enter the amphitheatre, only to be shooed away by the two leading soldiers, Marcus and Pere. In no uncertain terms they were told that the men would be on duty until midday the following day, and anyone breaking that rule would be sentenced to forty lashes in public.

Flavius Paulus looked re-splendid a top of his white stallion in full dress uniform. Head held high, looking at nobody - just the middle distance, he seemed impervious to the noise, and what a noise it was, any non battled-hardened horses would have been skittish and nervous at the din, his had faced and heard a lot worse, took it in his stride, much as its rider.

"General Flavius Paulus, Tarraco greets the presence of you and your men!" Marcus boomed.

It had been decided that a duke should not welcome a military force, instead leaving that to his military, in the person of his son.

Slightly farther back up the hill, hugging the walls of the Circus there were two groups of non cheerers. The larger surrounded the rabbi. Its conspicuous silence was broken by Jeremiah the naysayer, who had taken to following their new leader everywhere, earning him the nickname of Hillel's puppy, "Who are the goodies and who are the baddies?"

"All Christians are the enemy."

"Yeah, but I thought that they were supposed to be fighting each other and us backing one of them. Which one?"

Hillel looked down his nose to the puppy, struggling to remain calm, "The entering force is Wamba's, the greeters are the duke's. Now, Jeremiah, which do you think we are, in theory, supporting?" This was delivered with such sarcasm that even the puppy realised just how stupid his original question was. Silence was resumed.

The other knot, a little to the left, were Jacob surrounders. Here silence never existed as Trudy was in full swing veering from passive factual commentary, "Now that's a big horse and SO white," to dire depictions of gloom, "There are times when I am glad I don't have a daughter. Danger for all women in the next few days, do you hear me, Rebecca? You mind your step and don't leave the house by yourself."

Rebecca didn't feel trepidation, not about her personal welfare, she was well able to take care of herself. The fears she did have were about what could happen in the upcoming meeting. At the moment the only feeling she had was pain; her head really hurt and looking into the bright sunshine and listening to Trudi, which was akin to the ceaseless pounding of a blacksmith's hammer on an unyielding lump of metal, wasn't helping.

*

"I think we are being followed."

The heat of the day had gone and the sun was beginning to follow suit as the Tarraco forces were led out of camp. It wasn't a big farewell, nor was it a slink, everyone knew what was happening and why. The general, still smarting at the almost rebellion, stayed in the big house watching in a darkened part of the balcony; he could see them, they couldn't see him. He had to admit that Marcus had learned, this was an orderly well-executed manoeuvre, nothing like their debacle leaving Wamba's camp, something which seemed like a long, long time ago. Three abreast, wheeling to the right of the trees up the dirt path in the direction of the Via, nice. Miffed at seeing them go, and go so well, he had to accept it as the only possible solution, the part that still rankled was that it wasn't *his* idea, the lament being the fact that he should have thought about the situation more instead of enjoying his pampered lifestyle in this wonderful house. As a general that was his job; to think. The house was distracting. It was full of interesting things; ancient charts, Roman artefacts and a cellar full of wine, some local and some imported, all things that could be dwelt upon and thoroughly appreciated. It was a lifestyle he would like to get used to.

His family weren't poor, more middle merchant class. Their move to Hispanias happened a couple of generations ago, hence his tagged name, the Greek. Not having any personal memories of the place, and his father only saw Greece as a child, it seemed somewhat unfair to be saddled with this name. Any of the traditions of his grandparents' homeland, and the greatness of his ancestors had been well lost on him and his siblings, though the language had still been present when he was young. Starting with a trading firm on the coast, his family gradually bettered themselves eventually moving to the centre of power- making in Toletum. Despite their relative wealth, they were never totally accepted, always considered the outsiders, something he encountered wherever he went, even in the army. Hermenguild never thought of him as one of theirs, and Kunimund treated him as the new kid on the block.

His commission was only obtained through connections. Being the second brother and little interested by the excitement of commerce, an army career was thought the most appropriate option, at least for a while. An old commercial alliance between his father and the father of someone who was to become an important bishop, Julian, had proved most advantageous, and once in the army, his dash daring and skill pushed him up the ranks faster than others. Also, he had an important trait, people liked him. Wamba had inexplicably taken to him, much to the annoyance of all the top brass, almost immediately, bestowing smiles, audiences and favours like his present position.

This weakness for opulence had led directly to his lack of military insight. The well-being of the men is, and should always be his number one priority, and he had been found wanting. Making a vow to himself, he resolved not to think of civilian matters while he still wore the uniform. As the dust cloud of marching men was dissipated, he contemplated which wine he should have with supper.

"Who do you think is following us?" Pere tried to sound innocent.
"One person by themself from what I can make out. I'm not sure who it could be. "As I have the horse, I'll double back behind those trees and come up on them from behind."
"Good plan, Marcus, but I don't think that will be necessary, I know who it is."
"You do? Tell."
"Arantxa"
"Arantxa?"
"Arantxa, I said. I told her to follow at a discreet distance"
"You did what? Why the devil would you do that?"
"Because you didn't! You know, probably better than me, she can't stay in that camp with those women. If they don't eat her alive, they'll make her life even more of a misery than it is now."
"But.."
"No buts. I didn't tell you because I thought that you didn't need to know, and worse still, may have done something to stop it. Marcus, please don't look at me like that. Yes, I know you are my commanding officer and I shouldn't make decisions off my own bat." One more glance up at him on the horse. "No, no, before you say whatever you are going to say. I actually think that you would have done the same, if you hadn't got the constrictions of your office. The girl is lonely and miserable and you owe her your life, a debt that I think you should never tire of repaying. So, I

told her to tag along and once in Tarraco, I would find her somewhere to stay."

Whatever Marcus was going to say had disappeared in the slight refreshing evening breeze. Staying quiet, he mulled. Pere, as usual, was right in everything he'd said. Marcus had given thought to the situation before leaving and came to the conclusion that he couldn't do anything about her, without seeming to show far too much favour, until the main troop appeared in Tarraco, and he had wondered what the hell he could do with her then.

"Thank you, Pere."

*

"I hope that your Ladyship slept well."

"A most satisfactory night it was, thank you, Amalaswinth."

"I just wondered cos your bed don't look as if it's been slept in at all. I thought perhaps, what with you being in strange surroundings that you couldn't sleep."

"Slept the sleep of the good and just. My maid, Bertrada probably made the bed. Most efficient she is, can't put anything down for a minute without it being tidied away."

"That is the girl who hardly speaks any Christian?"

"Yes, her Latin isn't the best, she's from deepest Frankia, apparently called after the recent Queen. An awful guttural thing they speak up there, and when they do speak our language it has such a strong accent that it's difficult to work out which language they are speaking. Nice girl though and sooo efficient, and such a hard worker, my life would be chaos without her. While I am here, you do not have to worry about my personal needs, or the bedroom, as Bertrada will take good care of it."

"Oh it's no bother, your Ladyship.."

"No, Amalaswinth, Bertrada will save you some work, I really do not want to be of the slightest bother. Have you seen your master?"

"Yes, your Ladyship, if that's what you want, though bother, it isn't." A stern stare showed without doubt that part of the conversation was terminated. "The duke is at the table awaiting you, and breakfast, which shall be brought along immediately, Your Ladyship."

"Ranosindus, there you are." He was sat at the top of the table lost in deep thought. She moved very close to him, touched his hand delicately before taking the chair next to his while whispering, "That servant of yours is quite the busybody, isn't she? I think she'll have to go."

"Already making household improvements for me? Don't tell me that you've made the decision to move in."

"Don't be silly. That won't ever happen, and you know it won't ever be possible. It doesn't rule out frequent long stays though, which naturally, would have to be discreet. Your servant seems anything but that."

"I believe you are totally correct. However, she's been in the family for, well, forever, and letting her go, much desirable as it is , especially from one day to the next isn't really possible."

"Actually, you are a duke and her employer. Thus, you are able to do these sorts of things. Tactically though, it would be a bit unseemly, especially as it coincides with these planned frequent long visits. You'll just have to do it bit by bit, gradually easing her out. It is time she was put out to pasture anyway, she's ancient."

"She only looks and acts that way. She's actually just a bit older than I"

"That's what I said, ancient."

This produced amusement and a desire to physicality only stopped by the hurried entrance of first the servant, followed by the soon to be pasturing Amalaswinth, bearing breakfast.

While they were being served, conversation remained spasmodic referencing the weather mainly.

*

"Papa, papa,papa!"

Three smallish kids came hurtling towards Pere's open arms, there being insufficient arms the littlest made do by holding onto one of his large thighs.

Hearing the commotion, a woman with unkempt hair in her late twenties wearing a working smock appeared in the doorway.

"Finally decided to come 'ome, 'ave you? I 'eard you've been holidaying out at Els Munts. And who the 'ell is that? What 'ave you brought home from your travels this time!" An inclination of the head indicated the wary, worried woman by Pere's side.

"Antonia, love of my life, my sweet, mother of my children, woman like no other."

"Don't give me that shit. Try again. I am Antonia, the one you impregnated three times and ran off to play soldiers while I struggled to bring 'em up and put food on the table. The question is simple, what 'ave you brought with you?"

"Papa, papa, lift me up" The thigh-grabber was as insistent in her requests as the mother. Unleashing, momentarily, the other two, he scooped her up, "Arhh little Maria."

More or less this was exactly what Arantxa had been dreading. Her insides squirmed, her most fervent wish was to be elsewhere, anywhere, back in the rejecting camp, at home to face the wrath of family, anything seemed preferable.

"Let's all go inside and have a pot of ale."

"Your war whore is not coming across this threshold and you can stay outside with 'er as well."

Quite a little crowd had gathered, the port area wasn't a big place, everyone knew everyone, and everyone knew everyone's business. Initially they were all excited to see Pere, a popular neighbour, return, now they were intrigued to see the outcome of this standoff.

"Antonia, be reasonable, let's talk about this in private, inside, please."

"You've become deaf as well as stupid, 'ave you? She ain't coming in MY house."

Arantxa stepped forward about to speak. "Don't open your mouth! I don't want to even 'ear your voice." Changing direction, Arantxa tilted towards Pere, "Thank you for trying. This is what I expected."

Eyes full of tears she headed out through the small space left in the crowd only to bump full frontal into Rebecca. Not quite falling to the ground, both women were winded by the blow and stood bent over trying to catch their breath. Pere moved quickly to help Arantxa.

"That's it, go to your whore's assistance. Never mind that you've left us 'ere alone for months upon end."

Being the least hurt, Rebecca was the first to recover. Having only just arrived, she'd missed the whole encounter and had no idea what was going on except that Pere, a neighbour and long time tutor of her childhood playmate, Marcus, was back in town.

"Pere!"

Busy being solicitous, without actually touching Arantxa, he didn't register who was speaking to him.

Eyes watering now for two reasons, Arantxa was totally disorientated. She knew she had to leave, and leave as soon as possible. Un-doubling herself she slowly tried to set off again, only to find a firm restraining arm.

"You're the foreign girl that Marcus was with the other day."

Through her tears, Arantxa could make out her arm holder, it was the exotic beauty, the Jew, the potential baby eater. This made her desire to leave even greater. The grip remained firm.

"She's my 'usband's war trophy, that's who she is and she's NOT coming into my 'ouse."

Rebecca looked in the direction of the snarling almost spitting Antonia. Despite living but a street away, they had no real contact, the worlds in which they moved in were parallel, occasionally touching in market queues or street passing, nowhere else.

"Antonia, I think you are mistaken."

"And 'ow would you know, Miss 'igh and mighty Jew!"

Pere now knew that it was time for him to intervene and be a man.

"Wife, shut the fuck up! This woman, her name is Arantxa, is NOT mine, never has been and never will be. It's thanks to her that men from Tarraco, who volunteered to go into a battle with Marcus, me included, have come back. She saved Marcus and part of our force. They'd all be dead if it were not for her. We owe her a great deal. I brought her back here to receive some Tarraco hospitality, in a show of gratitude for what she'd done for us and what does she get? This.." he slowly moved his arm indicating the scene.

A light came into Rebecca's eyes, "Oh I heard of you! You were held up as an example of why women should never be trusted by a dreadful pig of a man." Releasing the arm hold, Rebecca took her into both of her arms, "I welcome you and thank you from the bottom of my heart for saving Marcus and all the others. You are a very brave woman."

Unable to control her emotions any longer, Arantxa completely broke down holding onto the baby eater for dear life and sobbing her heart out. Pere encompassed both women and the three children joined in making it a big huddle.

"Perhaps I've been a bit quick to jump to conclusions," Antonia, doing her best to put the unruly hair back to where she thought it should be, turned house-wards, "Come on in."

It wasn't really a table, it was more like an over-sized plank of wood, they sat round it with pots of ale in front of each.

Pere knocked his back in one. "I can't stay. Nobody is allowed out of camp unless they want forty lashes and I am supposed to be that order's enforcer along with Marcus."

"I'm sure *officer* Marcus can manage for a bit longer by himself." Rebecca playfully remarked

"As you know him very well, you also know, I can't leave him any longer by himself. No, got to go." Indicating Arantxa with an incline of his head, "Antonia, may I leave her here?"

Dithering ensued. "I'm sure we'll be able to work out something between us." Rebecca happily chirped.

Off went the big man only to return a couple of seconds later to plant a peck on Antonia's head and say, "See you tomorrow."

The sound of kids running and questioning faded with him into the distance.

"Men! That's what I get after months of nothing but 'ard work and no money. 'e better be back tomorrow and with 'is severance pay as well, I've about exhausted my tick with all the traders. You would think 'e'd show a bit more interest and concern, but no, we are all 'ere, well and 'appy at 'is return. It's like we've been in a bubble of suspended animation waiting for the return of the *master*. Who'd be a woman."

"All three of us here at the table anyway. Arantxa, that's your name, isn't it?" A nod. "Lovely name, too. May I ask you a question?" A second less sure nod. "I have noticed that you keep on looking at me out of the side of your eyes as if you were frightened of me. Have I done anything to upset you?"

Not knowing how to respond she blurted out the truth, "Do you really eat babies?"

Initially shocked, Rebecca started to laugh almost uncontrollably, spluttering, "Only very tender ones for VERY special occasions!"

Two sets of eyes widened. Rebecca realising that her joke hadn't been taken as such, stopped her laughing. "No, we don't! Jews are not cannibals. We do not eat people of any size, nor for your information, do we eat pig. We do have some dietary restrictions which are not easy to explain but I can assure you that babies are never on the bill of fare."

There was a silence while this information was digested, "I like a bit of pig, me, couldn't do without me bacon. More ale, anyone?"

Pots were replenished and the uncomfortable silence resumed.

"My 'usband spoke mighty 'ighly of you, said you saved them all, what did you do?"

Wariness set in again, she didn't like telling the story.

"The man I mentioned earlier said that you betrayed your people for love, is that true?"

"No, it isn't, if anything, it was for hate."

"Tell us.....if you want."

Arantxa didn't want. It was part of her past, a past she wanted to forget. However, she felt that *a* story about her would be doing the rounds soon enough, it may as well start as the truth, whatever it spawned into later, as all stories do, she had no control, so, she related all; her sister's death at her family's hands, the destruction of her village, her near death fight with Caius and the escape.

"What a story."

"Men are disgusting things. Good for fighting and fucking, little else. They seem to be the same all over."

"You say that your sister was in love?"

"Blissfully. I'd never seen her so happy. I don't think I could ever feel that way about a man."

"I certainly ain't. A peck on the 'ead is the nearest mine gets to giving me bliss! 'ell of a price for your sister to pay though. Perhaps I am better off with the peck."

The following laughter and the effects of the second ale, relaxed the atmosphere.

"Can I ask a question now?"

It was a mulling on the concept of love, blissful or otherwise, Rebecca who nodded.

"One of you is a Christian and the other is a Jew, what's the difference?"

"OH sweet Jesus! I have a Jew and a Heathen under my roof. May the Lord save my soul."

*

"Too old for you and your needs, am I?"

The servants had gone out of earshot at least; with Amalaswinth given clear instructions to make sure that the door was completely closed thus avoiding that annoying early morning draft.

"*Too* old? Well, perhaps not. Last night was certainly a significant improvement on Narbo. Still there's work to be done, and luckily for you, I'm prepared to dedicate myself to the task in hand." While looking innocently around the furnishings of the room she slid her left hand up his thigh.

The before breakfast Ranosindus was in a whirl. Instead of concentrating on the important upcoming meeting, he found himself thinking of the woman who was now attempting to touch parts that had never been touched at a dining table.

Confused he was. Sex was just SO different and he wasn't sure whether it was an improvement or not.

With his wife, Heva, sex had been simple, functional and usually quick. Heva was always delighted to comply. Her participation couldn't be described as active. She seemed quite happy about the outcome and never complained, nor demanded anything different, all of which suited Ranosindus to the ground. This was how it was, and should be.

Chlodoswintha was a completely different kettle of fish. It was more like a performance directed by her. A string of comparatives was the order of the night- slower, harder, faster, more gentle, along with instructions of where and when to touch various parts. Doing his best to comply at the time left no mental space to contemplate, those reflections hit much later. Never having been ordered around in his adult life, in or out of bed, this new experience was… disturbing.

Removing her hand forcefully, much to her wide eyed surprise, he stated "We need to prepare for this meeting, they'll be here soon. .

"I'm still confused." Arantxa was struggling to deal with all the strange words and concepts that the two other had talked and contradicted each other about. Antonia was no scholar and limited herself to saying things like; "it's natural", "right, it is", "the way things should be", whereas Rebecca sought through thousands of years of history to show that they were actually the chosen people. "You both believe in the same god, and only one of them?"

"Actually, we 'ave three, God, his son, Jesus, and the 'oly Spirit."

"But the same chief god?"

"Yes, and Jesus was Jewish."

"What? Enough, I don't understand. The only one that I can identify with is the Holy Spirit one, he's like one of ours, there but not there. I think I'll stick with our lot, not perfect but you can pick and choose favourites, they do the same with us, as well." Her voice dropped to a whisper, "I don't think that Odei likes me and if the truth be known I particularly dislike him."

"Odei!?"

"Shh, he's the god of thunder, don't want to cross him. Mari, she my favourite, she's chief female god."

"You've got a female god, and more than one?"

"Of course."

*

Cyprianus had made his way back to Tarraco unaware that THE meeting was planned. His first suspicions were raised by Maria.

"Tarraco is all of flutter, Your Grace, what with Marcus' men camped in the amphitheatre."

"Camped in the amphitheatre? How strange. I thought that they had set up base in Els Munts. Why would anyone, especially Tarraco soldiers, want to do that?"

"That's what everyone is asking. Something is afoot and if you want my opinion, nothing good is going to come of it."

The Bishop made a mental note to pop around to the palace tomorrow to find out what Ranosindus knew. It couldn't be anything too urgent or important otherwise he would have been told.

Later that evening after supper, Cyprianus was to be found, sweet wine in hand, comfortably seated in his favourite chair, thinking about the success of the bishops' meeting. True that they had come to no conclusion, that was a norm on these occasions. What was particularly pleasing was the way in which everyone had looked to him to control events. Something else, which was also abundantly clear, was with this uncertainty of leadership with the grasping hands of the count everywhere, this fact made for a strong possibility of failure in the venture, which, undoubtedly, would unleash a frightening backlash. Feeling that some insurance would be worth having, he called in on Quirico on the way home.

He really despised that little toady - forever willing to do any dirty work Toletum sent his way, never questioning, or willing to accept that Julian and company could possibly be wrong in anything; a repellent spineless little man.

They spent a hypocritical hour telling half truths and outright lies to each other. Cyprianus explained nothing about the meeting he'd just come from, and Quirico didn't ask even though he had already been informed of the outcome. Personal health issues were mentioned and best wishes for future collaboration were expressed with considerable false enthusiasm.

Cyprianus felt perfectly content with the outcome, friendly relations were maintained in case of future necessity.

"Your Grace, I know it's late and you don't like being disturbed at this hour, but there is a strange and most insistent man at the door. I did tell him to leave and come back tomorrow but he said his business was urgent."

"Life in the service of the Lord is constant," he signed, "I suppose you ought to show him in."

"Your Grace, he's one of *them*."

"*Them?*"

"You know, Jews, Christ killers."

"Then perhaps we ought to meet in my office. Don't want the best room contaminated, do we?"

*

"Papa, let me introduce Arantxa."

"Pleased to meet you. Exotic name, you don't look at all Jewish."

"That's because she's not, she's a heathen, as the Christians would call her , and believes in lots of gods, some of whom are female."

"Rebecca!"

Antonia, after the third pot of ale and considerable enjoyment, had offered a place in her house to sleep, which was accepted with enthusiasm by Arantxa, who hadn't had this much fun in, well, possibly ever. Three women with lots to say and developing chemistry could have gone on as long as the ale kept flowing. Sadly, the reality of whining hungry clamouring children became impossible to ignore.

"I'll have to get home. Papa will wonder where I have got to."

"You live in the big house around the corner, don't you?"

"I wouldn't call it big."

Antonia in a dramatic gesture swept her arms around, indicating the four walls that were the house; living, cooking and sleeping space. "Compared to what?"

"Ok, it's bigger than here."

"Considerably! And you only live with your father , don't you?"

Rebecca acknowledged the truth of the statement.

"Then perhaps this little 'eathen would be more comfortable staying with you."

A familiar feeling was beginning to well in Arantxa, rejection - polite, pleasant, nevertheless, rejection. Seeing this, Antonia continued, "No, no, you are VERY welcome 'ere, and if this one," she indicated Rebecca, "even threatens to serve you babies, then you get your 'eathen arse back here smartly. I just think that you will be more comfortable there and you won't have to listen to this lot." The insistence of the children was getting louder. "You'll 'ave your own to put up with soon enough. Tonight go and 'ave some peace and quiet in Jewish luxury."

Nothing compared to Marcus's palace, Rebecca's house though, was much more impressive than anything Arantxa had seen before the palace. Big, well-decorated, with archways. Archways! and all sorts of lovely items scattered about and hanging from walls. The "papa" who met them, in the inner courtyard, had a stooped back and a kindly face.

"Two minutes into the house and already you are Rebecca-ing. I do wish you'd expand your vocabulary."

Arantxa was shocked. This was no way to speak to an elder, a man, not to mention your father. She would have received, at minimum, a slap for uttering anything half as bad. However, instead of the awaited blow, Rebecca was rewarded with an indulgent half smile and a lamenting, half head shake.

"Do you see what a poor father has to put up with? I do hope that you treat your own father with a great deal more respect."

Not knowing how to reply to this, Arantxa dithered trying to think of a neutral way to say something. She needn't have bothered.

"I don't think so. He murdered her sister and tried to kill her."

"Oh dear, oh dear, oh dear. Killing one's daughter is a bit excessive, though I have considered it at times."

"Papa, this is NO joking matter, it's true!"

"Really? I thought this was just another of your bad taste jokes. I do apologise, my dear. I am terribly sorry. Do stay here as long as you want." And with that he scurried off to his "office" not wanting to hear any more of the unsavoury details and realising he'd made an awful faux pas. To the hurrying back, Rebecca shouted, "We will make supper. Sorry no babies tonight. The heathen doesn't care for them!"

In mid flight, stopped in his track by this, and turned a little, "Babies?" Realising it was a diffusing problem type joke, his head went back to its familiar Rebecca accepting movements as he walked more serenely on. Arantxa watched spellbound by what she'd seen - daughter / father banter, added to the fact that yet another man apologised to her. She was beginning to get used to it, not expect it but not be so surprised when it happened.

*

"My name, as you may already know, is Rabbi Hillel and I am here to talk to you as a fellow leader of a faith."

The bishop was struck by the self assurance of this young man.

"Hillel? Well, I have absolutely no idea who you are, nor anything else about who might represent your community. It is not my wont, in general, to deal with the Jews, my belief being that, if we do have to share an area, then it should be on parallel lines with few, if any, points of convergence."

"My opinion is exactly the same. However, we do seem to have some matters in hand, especially one in which *your* community has sought *our* help, namely, the potential rebellion against power in Toletum."

"I believe that *help* is being sought from Narbo, certainly not here."

This made Hillel stop and contemplate. Are all these Christians on the same page? Is there a scission among them? Trying to decide how much more he knew and whether it would be better to leave the pompous cleric in the dark, his vanity got the better off him as he blurted out, "Then the proposed meeting makes no sense."

Cyprianus, believing that he was the man with his finger on the pulse of events, was taken aback. What meeting? When? With whom? Why hadn't he been informed?

Not wanting to show the slightest bit of ignorance in front of this *Jew*, a straight face and straight bat had to be maintained.

"Yes, it's true that we need to talk. However, that doesn't imply any plea for help. Your people may be invited to participate as a matter of shared interest."

Hillel saw clearly that the man was winging it, still he needed allies, so he continued, "As a man of God, how do you see the participation of a woman in this proposed meeting?"

"Totally against. It is NOT the role of women nor should it be. I don't imagine that will happen."

"Actually, it will. The duke is insisting that the daughter of Jacob should be present."

"What! That saucy little Miss! Dreadful girl, no respect for anyone. You must prevent it, after all, it is your community."
"I am trying, which is why I am here."

*

"Does your religion have any dietary restrictions?"
"What do you mean?"
"Are there things that you are not allowed to eat?"
"No, why should there be?
"You know, things that your religion says you can't eat, or put together with other things like milk and meat."
"What a silly idea. Our gods wouldn't tell what to eat or not to eat. Eating and drinking are good things, to be enjoyed. I thought that you were joking earlier about not eating pig, like the baby thing."
"Oh no, there are a whole pile of things we can't eat. It's an important part of the religion, it's called caixrut."
"What a daft idea."
Conversation over the meal was a trifle stilted. Jacob didn't want to put his foot in it again, so, restricted himself to comments on the food. Rebecca informed her father that they'd seen Pere, and he and the rest of the Tarraco troop were bivouacked in the amphitheatre.
"That must be unpleasant for them, especially being so close to home. You would think that they'd let them spend the night with their families."
"They don't want them all to disappear before they provide an honour guard reception for the rest of the troops who are coming in tomorrow." It was Arantxa who provided this information, it was the first time she had spoken besides answering direct questions, usually, monosyllabically.
"Interesting. I wonder whether Hillel knows this. I'll go and tell him as soon as we are finished here."
"We are finished, there's nothing else."
"I'll be off then." Jacob stood, he was keen to leave and even seeing Hillel was more appealing than sitting with two women with liberal type views.
"Do give him kisses and best wishes from me!"
"Re ..bec..ca!!"

*

"Another one" Rebecca was pouring more wine. "This is the second and all that ale earlier. I have never drunk so much."
"I don't suppose I ever have either. Good feeling, isn't it?"
"Oh yeah, it's a bit like floating. I have seen men in the village drink lots, they usually get very unpleasant wanting to screw any woman, or pick a

fight with any man. Then at some point they end up face down in the dirt snoring dust up their nose; quite disgusting. I really never understood why people drank. Now though, I see it a little differently."

Arantxa liked the woman who was plying her with alcohol, she could see why Marcus found her *interesting* and there was a definite niggling sensation of jealousy.

"When we were talking about Aitziber earlier, you seemed very interested in her feeling of love."

"I was. Who was she in love with?"

"The General, Flavius Paulus, the one leading the troops in tomorrow. Decent enough bloke, not my type though, far too austere, never seen him smile, never mind laugh - very serious." Now seemed as good a moment as any, "Have you ever been in love?"

Rebecca sipped and shook. "Not even with Marcus?"

"MARCUS! Oh no, no, no! You didn't think... You can't have. Marcus? He's a boy. We used to play in the same group. Marcus? Oh no. Also, he's a goy. A very rich important goy."

"Goy?"

"Non Jew."

"You're not allowed to ..., you know with *goys*? "

"You're certainly not supposed to marry them. Not as bad as a Jewish man marrying a goya though. The thing is that our Jewishness is passed through the mother not the father. Anyway, contrary to what Marcus's housekeeper and other Christians may have said, I have never had the slightest bit of interest in him. And I doubt very much that he knows anything about love or women in general."

"He doesn't. He's a virgin"

"What!"

"Shit, I didn't mean to tell you that. Too much drink."

"Don't worry. I have known Marcus all his life and it would have surprised me even more, if he weren't. However, while he was playing soldier, I've heard that things like this happen when women get *used*. And I was told that you and him..."

"Where, when, by who?"

Rebecca shrugged.

Using the same logic as earlier in Antonia's house, Arantxa thought she may as well tell all, so she embellished her previous tale explaining how the Goth troops had raped all the women in the village, and how she'd been set apart by Marcus and protected by him, and it was then that he revealed his virginal state as a way of explaining that he didn't want his first time to be one of force. He was seeking a willing partner.

"Well done, Marcus! He always did have an open mind. That he played here on the docks with the "poor" and Jews was very much to his credit. I can see by your eyes that it would no longer be a case of unwillingness, if you had the opportunity again."

Thinking that she'd kept her secret well up to this point, she was surprised by the statement and the alcohol having unleashed her tongue she agreed to it.

"I certainly did consider that it might be possible. That was until I saw his house and met his father. He's out of my league. I could never be anything but an enjoyable pastime now."

"There's nothing wrong with pleasure."

"True, but there would be no happy ending. He would have to marry someone of his own social status. What am I supposed to do, have a bastard baby by him and live a life in regret?"

*

"Been bloody bitten again! Always go for the arse, these mosquitoes have got to be all male! They are more annoying than men as well. I spend my life scratching like some flea ridden mongrel."

"That's not a bad description of you. Actually I heard you called worse."

The banter around the women's camp was always fairly close to the knuckle, rarely though was offence taken, even though most of the insults contained more than a grain of truth in them.

"I hate the bloody things as well. Pain in the arse. Sorry Marta."

"Don't worry, it's the truth. I suppose everywhere has got to have some bad points. The mosquitoes are the only bad I can see here. I wouldn't swap it for any other place I've ever been."

Life had settled into an easy routine where nothing was difficult and there was always time for fun. All the normal chores of camp life were quickly and easily fulfilled. There was an abundance of practically everything they needed on hand. The kids that had been dragged across the country were in seventh heaven, or at least some body of water, the river or the sea, all day.

"What do you suppose is going to happen, Marta? Will there be fighting? You are forever showing your mosquito bites to Milo. What does he say?"

"He's as much in the dark as we are. Nobody knows. They went off to the big town, some sort of capital, just to show that they are here. Milo reckoned they would be back very soon. Then? Well, depends on the meetings."

"I hope we can stay here for MUCH longer."

"I think we all agree on that. "

*

Having never slept in such a luxurious bed, Arantxa had presumed that sleep would be easy. It wasn't. The two causes came not from the clean smelling comfort, but from her head. Cause one; every time she closed her eyes this paradisiacal bed span, it wouldn't keep still, producing a dizziness which made her stomach want to empty. It was truly very unpleasant and unsettling. Keeping her eyes open and anchoring herself with a foot on the floor was a sort of respite. Having eyes open means being awake, being awake means thinking, the second cause of her inability to sleep.

Today had been a very good day. The best for a very, very long time and who would have thought it? With a Christian who had hated her on first sight and continually called her a heathen, and an exotic Jewess. The three of them couldn't have been more different, yet they had had fun and talked more intimately than she had with anyone besides her sister. Perhaps she might be able to make a life here. Rebecca, after all that drink, had mentioned that her family had business contacts and she would see what could be found, which may have been just been the alcohol talking, still, it was nice of her and the alcohol to try to help. Not wanting to get her future hopes up to high, she tried to deal with her immediate problem; the spinning bed.

*

"Centurion, sir, the men want to know how long we are going to be here in this amphitheatre. It's not ideal as camps go, should we start making it a bit better?"

Milo wasn't completely sure, his conversation with the General had been brief and distracted. There was an air of nervous uncertainty around him, unusual in this flamboyant laid back man.

"We can use what the Tarraco boys have left, they have all but cleared out. Don't make yourselves too comfortable. It's my belief that we won't be staying long." Another part of his reasoning was that the general had ordered him to instruct, one could never order, the women's camp to remain where it was. Usually an uppity lot only too eager to argue and rebel against any and every authority, they were delighted to stay in what Marta described as this "Enchanted little spot".

After their triumphant entrance to the city and official greeting by Marcus, the men stood in perfect formation with the Tarraco force either side of them. It was all very formal with only a conspiratorial wink or two exchanged between the friends of the "opposing" forces to show that it was nought but a performance. Marcus then mounted his horse, pulled up beside the General, and preceded to march the men around the upper part of the city showing themselves and their perfect alignment to the masses of locals. It was like a guided tour without commentary.

The Wamba force was duly impressed. Most of the boys that joined the army weren't from wealthy families, a few of them were from Toletum, most had never seen a city. Tarraco, even in its decaying unkempt decadence was incredible. Such building! The wide open eyes in the heads of many of the marchers swivelled in awe at what they were seeing. This had been Marcus's intention, he was, rightly, exceedingly proud of his city and the fact that his family was the most important in it, would increase his standing with the men which was already ascending, after they found out that Els Munts was his family home. Having sold the whole concept of street marching to the general the other way around; saying how the locals needed to see how impressive the army was, everyone in the troop preened through the streets.

The reception from the locals was, in general, silent or low mutterings. There was no cheering as the intentions of the force were not clear, nor, for the same reason was there any outright display of rejection.

*

This was looking completely different to the Narbo meetings that her husband expected her to go to. The norm being, her dining room stuffed with pompous boring, usually fat, older men from which she did her best to cry off as much as possible or stay the minimum protocol would allow. This though, was a room with a view in comparison. Surprisingly, she wasn't the only female. There was a rather beautiful exotic scantily, in her opinion, for a formal meeting, dressed creature that Ranosindus was most flirty with when he was showing everyone in. Clearly *something* had been going on between them in the past, what it was, to be investigated later. The beauty was sat next to a strikingly good looking man. What a handsome pair these made. Without a doubt they were together representing their community, the Jews. Also, it was impressively obvious that they loathed each other. The body language and the lack of complicity was there to be observed by anyone who cared to look. Furthermore, at one point she thought that she saw the beauty almost hit him. Marcus sat on the beauty's other side, in sharp contrast, here the tone, the way they looked directly at each other without any hint of shyness, screamed former complicity. A great deal of banter was going on between them, they knew each other well, while the best the handsome man got was her back. Surprising that both father and son should have such a good relationship with her, as a Jewess, she couldn't possibly be a family friend, or even a frequent house visitor. The mystery of the exotic woman deepened. The flirty nature shown in the father's attitude wasn't there with the son. They gave off the unlikely appearance of buddies. Marcus hadn't taken on many manly traits yet. He was a big boy. Emitting an atmosphere of harmlessness and innocence, she liked what she saw. He would do nicely for her daughter. Ranosindus was next to his son, both vied for the beauty's attention. Mulling on long past days, she thought about how she used to have this effect on men, well, if truth be told, she did, but with an older, less interesting variety of the male species. A pang of envy shot through her, not against the beauty, more in lament of what she had once had. Next to her, and not at all interested in her, was a young man, late twenties perhaps, in full military uniform which gave his good looks an austere appearance with that exciting hint of ruggedness provided by the significant scar running down his face and he seemed to be missing a finger. Relaxed he was not, responding with minimum answers to her attempts at social chit chat. Perhaps if she had been ten years younger... no, who was she kidding? It would have to be more like fifteen, then he'd have been more responsive.

*

Marcus felt most strange, nothing was right. Sitting in his own dining room, feeling like a guest, being laughed at and generally chastised by a girl who used to run faster than he around the docks, but who would never have been allowed to come through the front, and who was one of the main reasons he was forced to go to join Wamba's armed forces. A decision which had turned out to be for the good as he now felt more mature and self assured than before going. Well, he did until Rebecca started talking at him. She treated him as she had always done, with disdain, and when he tried to be aloof, too superior to react to her jibes, she always found another way to get to him. Making matters worse was the fact that his father was listening and occasionally joining in to support her, either with a comment, or chortle at his expense. When he did try to play the military prowess card, she trumped him totally by *accidentally* letting slip that she knew his bacon had been saved by Arantxa. How could she have known that? He loathed her. No, he didn't, he really liked and admired her, but just one day he desperately wanted to beat her at something.

*

Hillel sat in silence, watching, observing, weighing up the others around the table. He was not impressed. The only one who seemed slightly serious was the military commander. The others; what a shower! His biggest surprise upon entering the room was to see another woman besides the dreadful thing he had in tow. Noting the depth of the malaise in Tarraconensis/Gallia Gothica before, he shouldn't have been so surprised. He just didn't realise that they were still digging, how far could they go? With allies like this the future was NOT bright. It was then, when he caught the military man's eye, he was conscious that he was at fault as well and must look weak. Jacob's daughter did not know how to behave nor dress. Instead of sitting meekly and serenely as would befit a woman, she was holding court, outrageously chatting, perhaps even flirting, with both father and son. This was unacceptable. Having had all his reminding little nudges and pokes in the back ignored, he tried leaning over to whisper in her ear only to receive a forceful backhanded almost nonchalant shove in the throat. From experience, he knew she was capable of extreme violence, and as it wouldn't look at all good if she punched him in front of the others, so, he desisted his physically persuasive efforts. Sadly, he thought that the other woman had spotted this violent handoff and there was a gleam in her eye that must have been something akin to female solidarity. Undoubtedly a regal looking lady she, at least, knew her place, not making a show of herself, instead spending her time, much as he was, checking out the opposition. The only point not in her favour was her proximity to the duke, far too close, denoting either that the alliance between Nemausus and Tarraco was fissure-less, or a personal affinity which shouldn't exist, something that may prove useful to exploit later. The meeting needed to start so that he could implement the first part of his plan.

*

Ranosindus was in no hurry to begin the formal proceedings, he was enjoying himself. This little Jewess was exceptional; sharp, witty and flirtatious as well extraordinarily attractive to look at. They didn't produce them like that back in his day. The way in which she tied Marcus around in knots was a joy to observe, and occasionally lend a helping hand. What she was up to, could in no way, be described as malicious; it was fun, frustrating fun for Marcus but fun nevertheless. He was like a puppy sharpening his teeth; improving with time. The fact that her tunic was relatively low cut also improved the situation. She leant forward regularly showing, he was sure Chlodoswintha thought, too much, though in his opinion it was enough to be tantalising without being immodest. When she'd first come to the palace and had been accused of trying to ensnare Marcus, she'd replied something to the effect that he was nought but a boy. This was abundantly clear now in the way she treated him, almost like a appreciated, slightly trying, little brother. They obviously enjoyed each other's company, however, Marcus had a considerable way to go to get to her level. Hill-something, Ranosindus vaguely remembered a name like that, was exactly as he had come to the palace, straight backed, austere, self- righteous and smug. He gave off the sense that he was far too good to be with the others in the room, he was there under sufferance, for the sake of, what? His religion? His strategy? His people? His god? It was plain that his was to endure whatever had to happen. Marcus's military commander was also quiet, however, instead of an air of superiority his was more of uncertainty; not quite sure of his role, or the cards he was going to play, or be played. His partner in crime, Chlodoswintha, was close, a bit too close for his liking. In some ways it was good to feel her physical support, what he had some trepidation about, was her sense of fun, which might involve a roving under-the–table-hand.

*

Never having been involved in anything but military command meetings, Flavius found himself feeling awkward and unsure of his role and manner in which it should be dispatched. Army meetings were easy, whether in a subordinate position, or a commanding one. The roles were well defined with hierarchy dictating what you said, how you said it, how long, and with which tone. This situation was totally different, no pecking order was pre-established, along with the fact that there was no definitive end solution. His remit was to prevent the rebellion from gaining traction, something easier said than done with his meagre force not offering an obvious dissuasive presence. Furthermore, not being quite sure exactly what the grievances were, it would be hard to address them, especially as he hadn't been given any power to offer some sort of compromise. All in all, he wasn't comfortable. Taking in the other participants, the only other that gave off the appearance of discomfort was the Jewish chap. Rather than trepidation, he oozed annoyance with everyone and everything, champing at the bit to be off and running. Clearly he had things to say and he wanted to say them soon. His displeasure was incremented considerably by the woman showing her back to him, chatting animatedly with Marcus. Given her posture, it was difficult to see what she looked like, though it did surprise him that such a young woman would have a seat at such an important meeting - he couldn't imagine what her role might be. If she were serving rather than seated, he would have been able to understand it more. The elder woman looked more at home, in her correct place, it was obvious she'd played this game before. Her face had gone past pretty, though it must have been at one time, now, the word handsome was more appropriate. Her shrewd eyes were being judgemental on all. He was hit by an unexpected emotion, he cared, he cared what she thought about him. This thought confused and clouded his outlook on the meeting yet further. The host seemed an affable sort of chap, much like his son and neither gave the appearance of being the slightest bit phased at what was about to happen, too busy chatting with the back.

*

Rebecca was all of a jitter, her head felt like it was going to do an uncle Isaac and start wobbling uncontrollably. She kept her sweaty hands moving as she feared that they would begin to shake, if they were kept still. A total mess of nerves, she knew she was out of place just being seated in this room, and just in case she hadn't been completely sure of her out-of-placeness, Amalaswinth's death desiring stare, and snide asides at the door made her fully aware. Hillel hadn't uttered a word to her on their way to the palace. The community had decided that it wasn't ideal that Rebecca should be there but as the Christians were insistent, then the two representatives should arrive and sit together. This decision pleased neither representative. Hillel's rejection of it manifested itself in silence and a demeanour of her non-existence. Once past the death wishing door "greeter", she felt the need for some semblance of safety. Thankfully it was provided by the duke himself; his expressions of delight at her presence sounded sincere and heartfelt, he even took her arm guiding her to the meeting room. Once there, she saw Marcus already seated, she made a beeline to take the chair next to his.
Marcus, Marcus, Marcus. She could never feel nervous in his presence. He hadn't seen her coming until a gentle cuff announced her arrival. She launched into him, asking every question she could think of, then proceeding to make fun of him. She hadn't meant to mention the fact that she knew Arantxa's role in his military escapades until it slipped out ,when he was trying to be a pompous arse claiming military accolades. It really knocked him sidewards, and left him bemused as to how she knew. This made her quiet for a while not wanting to let on about the revelations of the drunken night. Again, the Duke came to her rescue joining in on the fun at his son's expense. She was beginning to relax despite the constant sharp digs in her back by the taciturn Hillel. At one point he broke his monastic silence trying to whisper a reprimand in her ear, her *accidental* throat push put a stop to his objections.
Throughout the banter with son and father, she could feel eyes boring into her, turning her head she caught the other woman's eyes appraising her. Not having taken in the others around the table, it was with considerable relief and satisfaction to see one who was female. The penetrating eyes weren't reapproving, nor were they overtly friendly, more like an examination, the passing of which was in serious doubt. The previous

unease returned. Automatically presuming that this was a kindred spirit; another female in a male's world, she was now doubting just how much of an ally she would
prove.

*

A strong squeeze on the top inner part of Ranosindus's thigh told him that Chlodoswintha needed immediate attention. Turning to her she whispered "I believe you should stop playing with little girls and start the meeting; people are waiting." There was a playful steel in her statement.

"SO," his voice raised to get attention, when in reality, it was only the group he had been involved in that was making any noise. "As we are all here, I think it would be appropriate if everyone introduced themselves to the others."

It was at that moment one of the large doors was pushed forcefully open, causing it to bang loudly making Rebecca, among others, jump. In marched the robust figure they all knew so well.

"I do hope that I am not too late."

Ranosindus was surprised on two counts, firstly he had deliberately not invited this loud repellent attention seeker and secondly, he thought him not in Tarraco.

"My dear Cyprianus, I had no idea that you were back in town. I thought that you were representing our interests in the ecclesiastical council in the north."

"Got back last night. Luckily for us all, I found out about this meeting in time."

"I'll ask Amalaswinth to bring in another chair."

"That won't be necessary." Hillel stood, "The chair next to me is to be vacated immediately." This not being totally unexpected Rebecca began to raise her objections, only for Hillel to raise his voice louder, "It is my opinion, and I believe that of the metropolitan bishop as well, that a woman should not be present at this meeting. She holds NO official role in my community, and therefore cannot speak with ANY authority. If she is here for decoration, I do not think it appropriate."

The standing, sweating church clad Bishop nodded his head throughout and joined in the moment that there was a slight pause. "I could not agree more. The role of women is not to decide but to be informed. The Church has always worked on those principles and I see no reason why they should change now. Furthermore," quickly adding, stopping anyone else from voicing their opinions, and there were a number attempting to do so. "I have had dealings with this woman in the past and found her moral character… wanting, not a person to be trusted. Thus, I will take up Rabbi Hillel's offer of the seat next to him."

Crestfallen, fight seeped from every pore of Rebecca's being. Hillel she could attempt to fight, but with the bishop in league there was no way, especially given this public destruction of her character.

An unexpected chair, not Rebecca's, scrapped backwards and the standing of its previous occupant caused its intended commotion. "The Bishop and the Rabbi are perfectly correct. Women should not be involved in the *natural* affairs of men, so, I find it necessary to exclude myself on both the grounds mentioned about this girl; I am a woman AND my character is, I am sure, at least as blemished as hers."

A totally flustered Cyprianus realised he had made a mistake. However, before he could attempt to rectify, Hillel's voice was heard. "I believe, you, lady, are making the correct decision and as soon as…"

No more words were heard as it was now the host's turn to stand nosily. "YOU," he pointed at Hillel, "sit yourself down, I'm not sure it'll be for long as I believe you will be leaving. Bishop you were NOT invited to this meeting in the first place, so shortly I will ask you to go back from whence you came. This meeting was called by me. Its primary function being a first contact between the representative of King Wamba," he indicted an astounded Flavius, military meetings were definitely not like this, "and the forces of Tarraconensis/Gallia Gothica, which consist of my men, and those under the command of this lady's husband, Count Hilderic of Nemausus. The count has sent Lady Chlodoswintha as his trusted representative; I don't think it's our role to call into question the judgement of the count. Anyone else here, is present due to *my* courtesy, not by any right on their part. Bishop, besides your personal guard, you have no military might, though your opinions may be valued at times, they are NOT necessary here. And you rabbi, your people throughout the region have embraced the concept of the possibility of a new country, certainly a new approach, and have offered assistance. Again, militarily, your presence is all but null, in terms of bulk and legitimacy it is important. You personally though, have NO importance. We need someone from your community we can trust, and I do not trust you with your preening vanity. Please remove yourself from my house once I have finished. Rebecca, for that is *her* name," now his pointing arm indicated an ever decreasing in size shrivelled woman, "on the other hand, has proved herself a most efficient and reliable intermediary of the two peoples of Tarraco. It would be my wish that you continue in that role, despite, not because of, your gender."

Hillel rose slowly with as much dignity as someone ejected from a meeting could have and, as he pushed his chair back silently and elegantly, he spoke loudly enough for only Rebecca to hear, "You, goy lover, have not heard the last of this, I promise," then considerably louder for the others, "As I mentioned earlier, this woman, regardless of her name, and the influence of the Christian powers, does not, and can never represent the Jews of Tarraco. You may keep her, but any information she may bring will not be heard."

Still standing, her upset chair hadn't been righted, Chlodoswintha in a level, almost regal tone spoke again, "Sorry, I didn't catch your name, young man."

"Hillel."

"Interesting name, well, Hillel, I arrived from Nemausus a couple of days ago. My last act before leaving was to attend a meeting called by my husband, the count, where there was an metropolitan bishop, a few bishops and a couple of rabbis. One of whom introduced himself as Abraham, I believe, the leading member of the rabbinical council, or something similar. The other was Ariel, the rabbi from Narbo, a well known and appreciated visitor to the palace. Funnily enough, neither objected to my presence due to my gender, and both were enthusiastic participants in all the plans for a new country, promising unconditional Jewish support from Dertosa to Nemausus. Now if you are proposing to withdraw Tarraco Jewish support, I believe the rest of us should be informed immediately as it may cause some variance in plans already agreed on. Let me get this quite clear, this is what you are, threatening might be a trifle harsh, promising, may be a better word, so are you *promising* us this?"

For the first time ever in Rebecca's experience of Hillel, he was showing insecurity in his face. She'd seen fear and surprise when she thumped him, disgust when she'd mentioned her period, but he'd always maintained the air of invincibility and superiority. This had evaporated, his silence continued, he had no immediate answer and was losing face by the second.

Eventually, after what seemed like an eternity and ignoring Chlodoswintha completely, he addressed the duke, "You will hear from us presently." And with that he slowly removed his stiffened back from the room passing close to a pondering bishop.

"Ranosindus, maybe I was a little too.. rash earlier. Of course I didn't mean ALL women, some, when delegated, as is the case of the esteemed Lady Chlodoswintha, could be included, as I believe was the case in early instances in the history of the Church when women took the place of indisposed men. However, I do believe that lines should be drawn and my opposition to this person," a more upright Rebecca was again pointed to "remains. She does not represent her community, nor will she, as the rabbi said, be listened to. Therefore her presence is superfluous." With this he moved towards the table to take up a vacated seat.

"Cyprianus, I think I stated in no uncertain terms earlier that you are NOT invited to this meeting."

"Don't be preposterous, Ranosindus, the Church must be represented."

"My decision stands."

"Duke! The Church through my presence demands to be included. Surely you wouldn't risk ex-communication for disobeying the Church." The bishop had played the most feared ace possible.

General Paulus uncertain what to do or say, thought that at least he could be a little chivalrous, set about restoring the verticality of the lady's chair and inviting her to resume her position, something she was not quite ready to do.

"Bishop Cyprianus, I fear that you are confusing two totally different concepts; the Church and your personage. Perhaps you would like me to inform all present why *Metropolitan Bishop* Argebaud and Bishop Gunhild also desired that you *not* be present at this meeting?"

This stopped this metropolitan bishop in his tracks. He was now in the same position physically and emotionally as Hillel had found himself a few minutes earlier.

"I, er, don't believe that will be necessary, I can only presume that because of my lack of military knowledge, they feel that my role may be more pastoral and secondary, which I must say is a sound approach. I, myself, had my doubts about just how useful I would be in this particular meeting." His slowed stuttered march to the table continued with more vigour, "I will bestow my blessings upon you all individually and allow the meeting to continue." With no delay, as if this had been his intention from the very beginning, he went around the table grasping the hands of all, barring the Jew, in his two, letting the hands go after a few moments in order to mark the sign of the cross on each forehead. Labour complete, he exited wishing every success now God would be even more present.

Later, in bed, both Chlodoswintha and Ranosindus expressed their admiration on just how well he'd managed to turn a disastrous defeat into a dignified retreat, pointing out the stark difference of youth, represented by the rabbi, and experience of the bishop, in how to deal with an adverse situation.

And then there were five.

*

Hillel had sauntered nonchalantly to the door ignoring the barbed comments of an ecstatic housekeeper, who delighted in her role of Jew expeller. Once back in the street he set a course to the synagogue in the upper part of town, which he had made his base. A cherem, that was what was needed, it had to be planned meticulously and would include daughter and father. Of ancient lineage, cherems were first described in the second century CE, in the Mishnah, the earliest written compilation of oral rabbinical tradition. It was true there was no agreed list of offences that would warrant a cherem, some having a more restricted view than others, but few would deny the total disrespect, especially in front of, and for the benefit of, gentiles, should be on any list. A cherem ranged in severity from public rebukes to the shunning of the culprit for a period of time; weeks or months, even possibly years. Reinstatement to the community was always possible, if the individual was willing to repent and accept the prescribed penalty. An exemplary cherem was called for, especially in the case of the woman.

What a beginning to a meeting. Certainly never experiencing anything like it before, Flavius was unsure how things could or would proceed. The Bishop's exit was masterful, hot air moving seamlessly from humiliation to benevolent blesser, whereas the Jew had lost all credibility, the sort of enemy, if you had to have one, you'd want- slow, predictable and ineffective. The duke's performance in control was tardy, if it hadn't been for the elder woman, he may not have taken the day. She would be a formidable opponent in any game. Thankfully, he could only presume that she'd never be given control of an army. As an ear-whisper and behind the scenes strategist though, she was one to watch. Marcus, his trusty ex-second in command, on the other hand, hadn't moved throughout the whole shebang, preferring to keep his head down, like some auxiliary reserve force that wouldn't be pitched into the fray unless the ebb of the battle was far out-weighing the flow. Flavius noticed that Marcus's concern wasn't for his father, evidently he must have felt confident on that front, instead reserving his worry for the young lady next to him. His concerned eyes had followed her public disgrace and subsequent retreat into her shell. Flavius having had his vision of the woman blocked throughout the meeting, was only now, thanks to the departing clerical bodies getting a clear view of her. What a sight! Her fallen frightened face gave off an air of fragility within the undeniable beauty. She was spectacular. Why hadn't he noticed earlier? Was she the reason that Marcus was playing so hard to get with Arantxa? Was he holding a candle for her? Feeling that he should get himself noticed, he spoke for the first time.
"You really know how to hold a meeting here in Tarraco. Do they all start so excitingly? I do believe we were just getting to the introduction stages, and it seems to me that you all, those who are left, know each other fairly, or extremely well, the onus is on me to say who I am, and then perhaps you can tell me who you are. After that, you might be able to explain something that I heard a in the preceding melee which disturbed me

greatly; the new country idea that was referred to at various points." He stood to be seen in his military splendour. "I am *Dux* Flavius Paulus, general in the army of King Wamba." Dismissively he turned "Marcus, you needn't bother saying who you are as we all know."

Chlodoswintha immediately knew what was happening; beauty strikes again! "Welcome Dux, although this is not my house to welcome you into, I do. Actually, I believe that it was made clear in what you called the *melee* who I am, Lady Chlodoswintha of Nemausus, and who the duke is, well, father of your comrade Marcus is among a great number of titles he possesses. The only person who really needs to introduce herself to you and I, Dux, the father and the son apparently know her well, is the cause of most of the commotion."

Rebecca hadn't been expecting this, her mind was still reeling from the encounter. The very real threat to her and her family that was the parting Hillel shot, disturbed her greatly. He was a proud vengeful man who had been publicly humiliated, a counter attack was to be expected, the only doubt would be its severity and who would be involved as collateral damage. She worried greatly for both her father and uncle. The bishop was another source of concern, the instalments on the agreed loan had dried, after this, he was sure to insist on them immediately which would just be the beginning of his revenge. Being capable of wreaking much more than financial havoc, he had to be worried about. Furthermore, it had been shown that there was an unholy alliance formed with the sole aim of the destruction of Rebecca. The future didn't look bright making the enjoyment of this temporary victory impossible to savour.

"What? Sorry, I .."

"Calm yourself, girl, your enemies, from this room, at least, have been removed, now you are among *fans* and strangers and I, for one," here Chlodoswintha shot a meaningful glance at the dux, "would like to know something about you, and, how you manage to divide the people who know you, into two opposing camps."

Unsure what this elegant woman was saying, Rebecca felt she ought to answer but didn't know how. If she said something in her own favour, she would be blowing her own trumpet, if she said something against, then she'd be throwing stones at herself.

"I really don't know what to say." She opted for the mundane, "My name is Rebecca, daughter of Jacob, we live in the port area and have an import / export business."

"And.."

"I don't know what to say, really I don't. I am a Jew, so is Hillel, but he's just an arrogant prick who wants to belittle everyone around him, especially women."

"Prick!" Chlodoswintha gave off a gasp of shocked amusement.

"Oh, I didn't say that, did I? I meant to say, *man*. Sorry, it's just that with all.."

"I am beginning to see why there are two camps on the Rebecca question."

"No, I really didn't mean that, he's our new rabbi and he has had problems adjusting to the way we do things in Tarraco, he's from a much stricter version of our religion."

"And so, a *prick* who doesn't like women."

"Ohh, I really didn't mean to.."

"Excellent. Now enlighten us on why the bishop disparaged you so... he really was most uncomplimentary towards you and your character?"

"He's just an old.." Rebecca bit her tongue literally.

Chlodoswintha hadn't enjoyed herself so much for years. This young woman really had character. "Would you like me to suggest words to finish the sentence, my dear? I know the man to some extent and I can think of a couple of corkers"

"Corkers?"

"Choice adjectives."

"Oh no, I didn't actually say anything this time, did I?"

"Not this time dear, no."

" It's just that he doesn't like me, or perhaps he does, I don't know. I don't really know him, how could I? He's an important Christian bishop. All I do is take him the instalments on the loan that my father is giving him."

Seeing the hole she was digging getting ever deeper, Ranosindus took pity on the girl and decided to lend a helping hand, "Once I walked in on one of these meetings, the bishop seemed to believe that he was due some *interest* even though the loan was being given to him."

"Really! This gets better. It really is quite a shame that we have to talk business after all this."

*

Arantxa was by herself, nothing new in that, she'd been tempted to go to watch the parade, she knew both groups; the welcomed and the welcoming, she was bound to see people who would smile at her, but she sought quiet in the hustle of this massive place. Never having seen so many people and so many buildings of all shapes and sizes, her head was dizzy. An unblocked horizon was needed to put things into perspective. Eventually, after an awful lot of walking in the now deserted streets, as everyone had gone up town for the show, she found a quiet jetty where a couple of securely tied fishing boats were bobbing rhythmically in the gentle movement of the water. The sea was vast, even more so than in Els

Munts. On her right there was coastline that stretched until it disappeared behind a headland way in the distance, and on her left, Tarraco itself jutted into the waves otherwise blocking a clear view to Els Munts somewhere in the distance. In front of her was just blue, and more blue. Breakfast this morning was a quiet affair. The embarrassed father ate and ran claiming pressing business, leaving the "girls" to pick at goat's cheese and olives. Neither had an appetite and neither felt inclined to chat. Arantxa's head hurt, her mouth was totally dry and her stomach was in full rebellion. She suspected that Rebecca was much the same as her slow gait and pale complexion screamed anything but chirpiness. Stating that she had to attend a meeting near the uptown synagogue first, and it wasn't sure how long that would take, Rebecca suggested going to the parade together whenever that meeting finished. Wanting to continue yesterdays' good vibrations, Arantxa was tempted, however, the thought of just hanging around by herself killing time uptown until the meeting was over made her feel insecure and vulnerable.

It was better to choose to be by yourself than be dependently waiting on someone else. So, she sat contentedly reflecting.

Coming to Tarraco felt like an upturn in her fortunes. Since leaving her village, time was something that had to be got through; a morning was a start, a day an achievement, gradually days had become weeks and now months. With time came distance. She was so far away from the village now that nothing could be seen except this blue, and beyond that... who knew. Getting used to living in a city was going to be a challenge, but one she was willing to take if Rebecca was serious about finding her some work. Her mind was spinning, it was not the alcohol this time, instead it was the possibility of a more permanent situation that made her dizzy.

"Looks as if you've been here a long time. Antonia said she thought she saw you wandering up this way ages ago. Did you not come to the show?" The dying sun was being blocked out by the large frame of Pere. "No, needed to do some thinking."

"Must have a lot on your plate, I've never spent a whole day thinking. Wouldn't know what to think about for that long. Good place to do it though. I always come down here when I want to get away from the kids or Antonia's talking."

"I like your wife."

"So do I, that doesn't mean that she doesn't talk too much."

Pere lowered himself pulling a net with him, he then removed a needle hook type instrument and searched the net for snags to be repaired. "See that boat down there?"

She could hardly miss it, being one of the two tied to the jetty. "I reckon I can make it out, just"

Pere smiled, "It's my family's - fishing family us."

"Thought you were a military man, teacher of Marcus and stuff like that."
"I am. A boat can only hold so many. The third son needed to find other employment. Always enjoyed going out on the sea, the challenge against the elements and finding a catch was a magic feeling. Much better than trying to stop people killing you, or having to kill them."
"There are many jobs, why soldiering, if you don't like it?"
"Part of the problem is my name."
"Pere? It's not that bad. I'd never heard it before you."
"No, my family are Hispano-Roman who have a long history of fighting to keep the empire safe from foreigners. Originally, we were based down in Dertosa and my parents named me after the famous Pere from Dertosa who fought the Visigoths last century, quite a hero, he was. So my fate was sealed especially when they found out that I was more than a bit handy with a sword."
A comfortable silence ensued each lost in their own thoughts in time, one projecting forward and the other reflecting past.

*

Rebecca had enthralled and entertained everyone. Father and son, both confirmed fans, thoroughly enjoyed a vintage Rebecca performance, her sincere spontaneity aligned perfectly with her passionate innocence was what they had come to expect from her. Lady Chlodoswintha was catching up with her admiration of this plain speaker, she wasn't sure that she had a bright future as a diplomat though.
"So, dux, let's on to real business. As you heard said, we feel that there is a need for a serious change in direction of the kingdom, or, with reluctance, we are prepared to secede from it."
Flavius spent some time contemplating an answer, "As you all know, I am here leading not a military but a diplomatic mission. What I have been mandated to find out, is why. Why you are prepared to take this radical step, which, as you well know, may well involve considerable bloodshed."
The duke spoke eloquently for a considerable period of time without interruption, laying bare the grievances that the region had with the centralised power in Toletum "and after years of silence to our demands, we feel that we have no alternative but to take this, as you rightly pointed out, radical step."
Rebecca, who had been half listening still marvelling in her own ability to mess things up, felt she needed to speak again, gingerly, she raised her hand this time. It was Chlodoswintha, acting as a sort of master of ceremonies, who noticed. "You would like to add something, young lady?"

"Actually, yes. The duke outlined the reasons from the Christian point of view and neglected to mention the horrendous situation faced by the Jews, which is understandable, him not being a Jew. But as I am, I think I ought to say something, if that's ok with everyone else here, because in reality, I am the only Jewish person left, and even though it's been made clear that I don't and can't speak for the Jewish community, there's nobody else here to do it, so.."

"Yes, yes, dear, you have made your role clear enough. Do speak."

What followed was nearly as long as the duke's contribution, without the free flowing sequential order, instead, it was packed with reactions to information which went backward and forward chronologically, delivered with immense feeling.

"Let me get this clear, you are joining this, rebellion is too strong a word as of yet, disagreement, shall we say, in the hope of overturning one hundred and fifty years of Concilia decisions?"

"Yes, because they are not fair. We just want to live in peace and harmony alongside the Christians as we had done for years, centuries, before."

At this point, Lady Chlodoswintha felt that she had to become a contributor, not just the moderator, "I am not sure that we want to reverse ALL the decisions. What we do want is a re-interpretation of our relationship with the Jewish community."

Blood was rising fast to Rebecca's head, her light olive skin was taking on a pinkish hue. Observing this, the duke jumped in fast.

"I believe that now that the positions have been made clear, there's little else we can expect of the dux, I do not imagine that he has the power to even come close to granting any of our requests, or even to start any negotiations on them. We would hope that he would relay our position, faithfully and in detail, to the King, in the hope that armed conflict can be avoided. However, he should also make abundantly clear to the Toletum powers that we are prepared to resort to violence, if a satisfactory outcome cannot be achieved by dialogue. I declare this first encounter over."

Rebecca was still bursting to speak, opened her mouth to, and seeing the don't-look on Marcus' face, she decided not to. Marcus, having received clear instructions from his father's eyes, came to life, "Rebecca, I will show you out."

Once they were well out of earshot, the duke asked everyone to remain seated just a while longer.

"I didn't want to say this in front of the Jewish representative, such as she was, but I want to speak with absolute clarity to you, dux, that we are not fighting for Jewish rights and we are certainly not prepared to break up the kingdom on such a trivial issue. Some control over that community is necessary, however, we believe the repression may have gone too far and actually become counterproductive, which is why many of the newer edits are not enforced in Tarraconensis/Gallia Gothica. So please do not portray us as something we are not."

*

Marcus was perfectly charming and even tried to make a joke about her performance as they made their way to the door, none of which detracted from the feeling she was being ushered out with undue haste. Knowing that they had backed her over Hillel, she knew the reason for this chivvying wasn't because of her or anything indiscreet that she'd said. Most of her indiscretions were against her own, though admittedly complimentary to the bishop she hadn't been, even if there was a palpable and pretty universal dislike of him. What she smelt was a rat; a Christians re-united rat.

Out of the house and in head down deep fast walking thought mode colliding full tilt into her father was inevitable once he had decided that his daughter would surely stop. The result being a massively winded elderly man and a greatly surprised thinker, "Papa, what are you doing there?" Bent double, it was abundantly clear what he was doing; trying to catch his breath, a glare very much told Rebecca this. Holding his arm and trying to be solicitous about his well-being took over from her inane enquiries. Guiding him to a small stone wall she managed to make him sit.

"Shall I fetch you some water? There's a fountain a little farther up the street."

"Give me a moment, then we are heading home. I really need to know just **what** you have done this time. The whole community is …" A spluttering coughing fit took away his last words.

*

"Let me help you, is he alright?"

Rebecca was supporting the left side of a shuffling Jacob. Arantxa didn't wait for an answer, instead providing equilibrium on the right side. Between them they took the bulk of weight and effort of moving, it was a case of all but carrying him. Both were struck by the same silent thought, how little he weighed. There were curious Christian onlookers who dismissed this sight as yet another of these strange Jewish traditions. Their progress was slow with numerous grunts of pain until they finally managed to plonk Jacob in his favourite seat. While Rebecca fussed, Arantxa went for water.

While he was sipping tentatively, Arantxa was afforded the opportunity of asking what had happened. Beating Rebecca to an answer and with remarkable perkiness, Jacob spluttered, "She tried to kill me, this time physically as well as spiritually!"

"Oh Papa! You do exaggerate. We bumped into each other."

"With all her sails unrolled she bashed into me at full speed. I thought that she would stop but oh no, straight into the midriff she hurtled, piling physical pain on top of all the other."

"Papa, you really do go over the top, you were winded not mortally wounded, relax a moment, drink the water and get over it. And just what are you referring to with "all the other" comments?"

"Sympathy, the sympathy I get from my daughter is boundless. I hope you treat…" looking at Arantxa in the hope of support for the correct daughterly role, he suddenly remembered what he had been told of her family history. "*people* better. What I really want to know Rebecca, is what did you do in THE meeting. Hillel is spouting to anyone and everyone who will listen that you sided with the Christians against him, to the point when you actually insulted him, when he was trying, legitimately, to defend the interests and honour of the Jewish community."

"The little lying prick!"

"REBECCA!"

"He is. That's not what happened. He tried to get me thrown out of the meeting because I was a woman, not taking into account there was another, very powerful, woman from Nemausus in the room. She defended me and my rights. I didn't insult him. Well I did, but he was no longer in the room. That fat slug of a bishop, who I did insult, must have told Hillel."

"You insulted a rabbi and a bishop!"

"Everyone was insulting the bishop, I just sort of joined in, and I may have let slip a comment about Hillel, but as I said, he'd already been ejected from the meeting for being a total arse by upsetting and annoying all the Christians. If he thinks that's the way to defend the community, then it's no surprise that we are persecuted throughout the land. We need to build bridges not burn them."

"You insulted a bishop and a rabbi!"

"Papa, you're repeating yourself."

The head had started its familiar movement. "Have you any idea what you have done? This is a catastrophe."

Isaac had entered the room during the last part of the conversation. "So it's true! I thought it was another one of Trudi's tales spun out of control. Apparently, there is an official meeting called for tonight to decide whether a cherem should be put into force."

For the first time Rebecca began to look worried, "A cherem? Against who?"

Arantxa, noting the concern on her new *friend's* face ventured to ask what was this word they were all using. "It could mean the possible expulsion or isolation from the rest of the community," was Rebecca's controlled measured response. "Uncle Isaac, we are going to need help. Your help."

"Me? What can I do?"

"That meeting you attended in the north, was it attended by a man called Ariel from Narbo?"

"I really can't remember all the names…"

"Think, please. And was Abraham there?"

"Oh yes, I remember him, he was in charge of the meeting and I think I do remember a rabbi called Ariel. Why?"

"We need to get a message to him as soon as possible and we need to delay tonight's meeting somehow."

*

"I really ought to get back to camp. We didn't come prepared to spend much time. The march back to Els Munts has to completed before darkness."

"We can take a short cut going around the city to the Amphitheatre, if we cut across the port area."

Flavius, as was hoped and expected, most impressed by the sights of the city and the history guide provided by Marcus. "It's most understandable why you are so proud of the city and its history. Toletum doesn't compare. Marcus, you have to realise that power doesn't need big buildings and illustrious history, it needs will, and the Church and the Monarchy have decided that should reside away from here. Sometimes you just have to accept change and move with the times."

"I believe what my father is saying is that you shouldn't turn your back on history, embrace it, don't ignore it."

The feeling between the two men was convivial. The slight tensions that existed in Els Munts had evaporated.

"Slumming it, are you? Or just showing how people who don't live in palaces live?"

Rebecca and Arantxa had been sitting together on the quayside for some time. Minutely THE meeting had been re-told with both women marvelling on the power and influence wielded by the Lady from the north. Also, the seriousness of a cherem had been explained. Eventually, they had moved on to lighter, but no less pressing, problems like, what Arantxa could do if she decided to remain in Tarraco. The choices were not extensive. The skills that Arantxa did possess, with animal husbandry and the like, were not in demand in a city. Asked whether she could read, write or do some numbers was met by the expected blank face. Apparently, the written word was not valued even among men in her culture. Rebecca resolved to embark on the time and effort consuming task of teaching her, as long as nobody else found out, she was sure that would get her into yet more trouble if anybody did. None of this helped the lack of employment in the short term. For the immediate future she could work in the house, taking over some of Rebecca's chores, leaving her more time to dedicate to the business tasks which her father was beginning to struggle with.

It was at this point when they met with a sight never seen in the fishing area; two important military clad tofts wandering by.

The sun being directly in front of the men, they hadn't noticed anyone in particular and now shielding their eyes they could make out the two female forms.

"Yes, we have lowered ourselves to frequent your neighbourhood briefly. Ah, Arantxa, I didn't notice you there. What are you doing down here and in such bad company?"

"She's looking for a job with good folk. Do you know any good people who live uptown that have a job to offer?"

"Well.."

"Thought not."

"So have you decided to…?"

"What she has, or hasn't, decided has nothing to do with you, Marcus." Flavius watched this exchange realising this girl was even more, what would be the word? Dominant, confident, forthright, in her own area than she had been in the duke's house. Arantxa looked better than he had seen her of late, almost relaxed. It was clear that these unlikely women had become buddies. Arantxa already had quite a character, similar to her sister's, Flavius recalled. Now though, under the tutelage of this one, her personality could only increase.

"I thought your performance this morning was most interesting."

"It wasn't a *performance,* nor was I there to please you and any of your kind. My job was to tell those who don't want to see how difficult it is being a Jew these days." Flavius's comment had been delivered in a pleasant tone, her response was not. For some reason feeling the need to show more empathy he continued, "Which I thought you did admirably."

"Don't patronise and condescend to me, just because.."

"Stop, stop, stop. Please, *stop.* You are getting angry with me for no reason. I seek not to cause any offence. I truly believe that your intervention was both informative and moving. You represented your people well, very well."

Rebecca visibly deflated her righteous anger and adopted a more conciliatory tone.

"Sorry. It's just that I am receiving a considerable amount of negative reaction."

"Can't see why, you were much more effective than that other arrogant chap."

"Hillel, that prick."

Realising she'd done it again, she looked around to see if there was anyone of her community who could have overheard. Thankfully, there wasn't.

Being used to coarse army language her words didn't shock, the fact that a woman said it, did. "I think that was the consensus opinion of him, though I rather think that if you keep repeating it, your troubles, both, with him, and the community, may increase rather than disappear."

Rebecca looked at this man squinting into the sun at her. He was actually attractive, very attractive, a good strong face, despite the scar, slim, big shouldered and directly in front of her, a fine pair of legs in that army garb; shapely, powerful and not overly hairy.

"Marcus, why can't you learn from this officer? He's very pleasant to talk to whereas you.."

"Whereas I treat you exactly as you should be treated otherwise you'd get too uppity. That poor rabbi, what's he done to be treated so harshly by you? And as if that weren't enough, the way you treated the highest representative of the Church in Tarraco was scandalous."

Rebecca jumped to her feet as if ready to hit Marcus. Flavius stepped in between.

"'ello Jew and 'eathen, what have you dragged down here now? These two ponces, I suppose are with you. Not the normal sort we get. Not saying they ain't nice to look at, with being all dressed up like, but they definitely got nowhere to go if they strutting about down 'ere. Who the 'ell are they, and why are they here?"

This had a collective stunning effect which Arantxa was the first to react from.

"Antonia, good to see you."

"See you, *schee* you, who are they?"

"Surely you recognise Marcus, Pere's pupil."

"Bugger me. Last time I saw 'im he was running after 'er," nodding in the direction of Rebecca, "and getting absolutely nowhere near 'er. Oh my lord, ain't he grown. Looks MUCH better now. Will you be wanting to see Pere? Left 'im at 'ome trying to work out which kid is which. Well, come on then, it's really close."

"Actually, I don't think.."

Arantxa jumped in, "Probably very true, you don't think, still I am *sure* that you recognise Pere's wife and you'd love to see Pere in his home."

"Recognise me, 'im? No way. Those folk for uptown don't 'ave time for us down 'ere, certainly not the women folk."

Accepting the fact that he wasn't going to get out of this well unless he acquiesced to the invitation, "I'd be delighted to accompany you to see Pere. Are you coming along general?"

"General, is it? Well I never…"

"This, I believe, is a Tarraco mission which doesn't involve me. I really must get back to the camp. The scribe should have finished the message and Milo should have got everyone ready for the march back to Els Munts. If you just point me in the right direction of the amphitheatre, I should think that I will find it."

Antonia had sussed the way in which the wind was blowing, "Not sure about that *general,* you look a bit of a lost sheep to me. Rebecca, why don't you accompany 'im?"

"I'm sure I wouldn't want to trouble…"

"I reckon it'd be no trouble, eh Rebecca? And general, I'm sure that you'll appreciate the view!" with a wink at Rebecca, she turned linking her arm through Marcus's, "And you 'eathen, grab the other one," indicating Marcus' right side, "so 'e don't run away."

Enthusiastically joining in the fun that Antonia had brought to the situation, and revelling in the embarrassment that Marcus was obviously feeling, she forcefully intertwined her arm tightly through his.

*

Chlodoswintha and Ranosindus were seated comfortably close without being scandalously so, a sort of shell-shocked silence had prevailed since they moved from the meeting/ dining room. Furbished with drinks; a refreshing ale and something a trifle stronger, they sipped.

"Dear duke, I really must congratulate you, you really do know how to hold a meeting down here, don't suppose you've seen the like of it since the lions were let loose on the devout. And for a Jewess to steal the show, quite, shall we say, *novel.*"

As his thoughts had been running along similar lines, he heard no warning of danger in Chloda's words. From his point of view, Rebecca was a remarkable person, not just a beautiful woman with character, there was far more to her than that, she was bright, sharp, witty and fun. If only he were twenty, what was he saying twenty-five years younger and she weren't a Jew.

"She does it regularly, it wasn't a one off."

"Does she now?" Danger signals were now unmistakeable. "I had the impression that you and her were, shall we say, acquainted."

Danger, danger, danger, damage limitation or avoidance necessary, he drained his cup.

"Would you care for another drink, Chloda? Mine is empty. Thirsty business talking so much."

"No, thank you, I still have plenty."

"Amalaswinth!" Her almost immediate entrance looking sheepish gave away the fact that they both had suspected, she was on station trying to catch as much as she could.

"That was quick. Excellent service. Could you bring another ale?" Thinking she'd got away with it, the servant turned to go only to be stopped in her tracks,

"As you were probably listening, you know the topic of conversation."

"NO, no Your Ladyship, I ..."

Brushing aside the feeble lies, Chlodoswintha continued, "The Jewess. I suppose you get to see her a great deal here at the house, could you give me your honest opinion of her?"

"Here, far too often for my likings, don't see why good folk allow that sort in."

"Is this because she's a Jew or because of her character?"

"Both, milady. An arrogant one, full of herself she be, well above her station she thinks she is."

"Thank you, Amalaswinth, most informative. Please do fetch your master's ale."

Silence prevailed until the ale was delivered and the servant told to leave the room completely on pain of dismissal, if she were caught listening at the door.

"Care to explain?"

"Not really. I am not going to be interrogated in my own house. What I do OR don't, is totally my business and nobody else's. However, for your information, I will tell you that I find Rebecca a charming fascinating *girl*, who deserves more in life than she'll probably get."

Chlodoswintha, not expecting nor seeing this outburst of dominant behaviour was, well, she wasn't sure what she was besides being extremely surprised. Initially, she felt she should flounce out of the house in a mega huff at being spoken to in this manner, then upon a slight reflection, she realised he was probably right, and if truth be told, she liked this spirited side of the duke, her own husband not daring to cross her in years on any manner of substance.

"Bring her up in the world, marry her off to Marcus, why don't you?"

"Marcus and Rebecca? Don't be silly. First and foremost, she's a Jew, and, dukes, nor sons of dukes, marry Jews, even if they convert, which I very much doubt she would ever consider. Furthermore, they are not the slightest bit interested in each other in *that* way."

"This all goes to show that we need to get Marcus away from temptation as soon as possible. The marriage to Avina needs to take place before Christ's Mass."

*

"Sire, we've had word that the reinforcements from Toletum will arrive shortly."

"Excellent news, General Alaric, it's time to do *something*, since General Paulus left we've had no real action, I feel as if I am wasting my royal time here. We need to go on the offensive with a decent sized battle, not these pathetic little skirmishes."

"Sire, as General Kunimund is forever pointing out, we can't risk an all out battle with the numbers we have, if we lost a small percentage of our merge force then the whole venture would become untenable."

"I believe it already is. This is little more than an unpleasant holiday away from the back-stabbing politics that is Toletum. Talking of which, who have they sent as leader of the reinforcements?"

"Your nephew Egica, sire."

"GOOOD. For once they take notice of my orders, makes one feel almost like a king."

At the beginning after Paulus had left, Alaric found it unusual, and a bit scary, that a king would bellyache about his lack of power to a subordinate. In theory, if he spoke to anyone about these things, it should have been the role of the most important general, Kunimund in this case. However, the King didn't try to hide his disdain for the man and his caution. Flavius Paulus had always been the favourite, his charm, swagger and good company had swayed the king from the beginning of the campaign. As now he was bereft of this support, Alaric had been turned to, not in the position of confidant, more akin to a sounding board for his complaints about his lack of authority.

"Sire, I wonder whether I might be bold enough to suggest a plan."

"Oh, my Lord! Initiative! What is my army coming to? You'll be suggesting going on the offensive next with some wild all out attack."

"Actually Sire, that's exactly what I propose."

Wamba stared at an increasing in confidence officer, "Go on. I suppose you've neglected to mention this *idea* to your superior officer."

"Well, Sire, umm, the idea, as you call it, only occurred to me once the message had arrived from your nephew. He states where he is now, and having looked at the most reliable map we have, he has but one way to get here."

"Nothing spectacularly earth shattering in that."

"No Sire, agreed. But it does mean that he would have to pass close to this valley." Unrolling the parchment he was holding, his slightly unsteady finger indicated the said pass.

"Alaric, do continue and stop pausing so much looking for reassurance or comfort. If you're wrong, I will tell you, and then praise you for trying to think, if you are right, you may well be our ticket out of this place, for which, you'll have my undying gratitude. So, it's win-win. Do get on with whatever it is."

Emboldened, a smaller piece of parchment with more much rudimentary squiggles indicating topological features was unfurled. "This is Flavius's reconnaissance report."

"I thought her name was something like Aitziber."

"As it was. He must have combined both, as this map, in my opinion, is much more accurate than the *official* one. Here is the same valley, it's where we know there is a significant concentration of the Vascones, probably in the region of a couple of thousand. They feel relatively safe there given their numbers and the narrowness of the northern entrance closest to our position here, plus there is a possible escape route to the south. Due to the fact that we haven't got the numbers to split our force and attack from both ends, they continue living in what they believe is a secure haven."

Wamba's face began to radiate light, "So, you are proposing that Egica doesn't join us at all, thus giving away our new strength, and instead attacks the valley from the south while we do the same from the north.

"Exactly, Sire."

*

Silence reigned, neither knowing how to start a conversation nor what to say. It wasn't a comfortable silence of two people at peace with each other finding words superfluous, it was tense and fraught. Flavius found himself wanting to impress and be liked, could think of nothing that would do the job. Rebecca, always determined never to be in awe of anyone no matter how important or frightened they made her feel, was reluctant to leave a bad impression on this one, and of late she was very aware that her words had done that. Silence then was perhaps the best option.

Having left the fishing dock, they were well into the area reserved for the bigger trading vessels. Tarraco wasn't a patch on what people said it used to be when there were ships from every part of the Mediterranean queuing to be unloaded, and then reloaded. Still, it was one of the busiest ports in the Visigoth kingdom, accounting for the bulk of the ever diminishing trade. Docked, and being emptied as they passed, was a foreign vessel Rebecca didn't recognise.

"I wonder where that one is from." This would be a neutral way to break the quiet.

"By the shouts of the sailors, I would imagine that it's Greek."

Never having considered herself a short woman, actually she was significantly taller than most of the others in the market, she had to look up as he was at least a head taller, into his dark brown eyes, which he noted for the first time, were decorated with eyelids that gave the appearance of having been coloured or shaded in some way.

She was unsure whether this way of showing knowledge in such a blasé manner impressed her or not. She spent a considerable amount of time delivering manifests for ships departing with Tarraco goods, or coming to the harbour master to claim their part of a shipment. Most of her interaction was in the international language of the Jews; written Hebrew and some spoken Latin. Sometimes, the accents in Latin were so strong, that they were difficult to comprehend, almost like another language, making the use of a written exchange compulsory. Despite all this time, and miscommunication, she wouldn't have been able to work out where the people were from just by listening to them.

"The ship is Greek then, eh?"

"Difficult to say. The sailors are communicating in Greek but that doesn't mean to say that they are Greek or the ship is from there. At the other end of the Mediterranean Greek is still used in commerce and shipping as a lingua franca."

She noticed that he didn't say this in any show-offie type way, just a matter of fact, which he was sharing. While she was still contemplating whether she thought this a good or bad trait the thud of something big landing just behind them, made them jump.

Flavius spun hand on the hilt of his sword, only to be confronted with a now split package, which had obviously dropped off a rudimentary crane device that was being used to unload the ship. Visibly he became considerably less tense, but none the less angry shouting "Próseche" at the person operating the machine.

"Sygnómi" came a meek reply once the culprit realised he was talking to a large armed military uniform.

"What was that, don't tell me you speak their language!"

"I can get by in it. My family is originally from Macedonia and my grandmother spoke to me in nothing else. I don't get to use it much, so it's getting rusty."

"Just enough to insult someone in it."

"No, it wasn't an insult, I was just telling him to be careful."

The dilemma of whether she was impressed by this approach deepened. Any other man, and probably her as well, would have shouted something choice at the dropper, calling into doubt his parentage, or occupation of his mother. This military man though, showed controlled restraint backed by willingness to action.

Silence was re-established. They continued their unhurried walk along the beach heading towards the temporary encampment which was looming into view.

Wracking his brains for something interesting to say, finally Flavius gave up, choosing the mundane in a desperate attempt of saying something.

"Have you always lived in Tarraco?"

"Yes, for generations."

"Generations of Jews in Tarraco?"

Warily she eyed him, "Yes, what's wrong with that? This was once known as THE Jewish town."

Realising he may have said the wrong thing, he set about trying to rectify. "NO, I didn't mean, well, it's just that, it's, well, I've never really met a Jew before."

Rebecca's swelling in indignation showed that her response wasn't going to be in the tone of a friendly don't-worry- there's-a–first-time-for everything, necessitating another stumbling words interjection.

"Obviously you see Jews around, but social interaction never takes place. In Toletum they keep themselves to themselves in a quarter of the city where others don't really go, and when you see one outside they are always in a hurry, scurrying lest they be stopped or, well, I don't know. So, I, well, you, are the first one I have talked to, *properly*."

"Scurrying? You mean rat like? And half a dozen inconsequential words while walking along the dock is proper talking to you?"

"No, clearly not, I didn't want to imply rats at all, you are misconstruing my *few* words. Also, I did hear you talk for a good while in that meeting this morning."

"Are you saying that I spoke too much?"

Like a bait worm squirming on the end of a hook, it didn't matter how much he wriggled it wasn't making the situation any better. "I didn't say that."

"It was the implication, though."

Flavius stopped walking, Rebecca, made to continue, gently he held her arm to stop her. Her immediate reaction was to shrug it off, stopping herself from doing so, she turned to face him.

The brave soldier didn't look her in the eyes, instead keeping his vision slightly over her head taking in the wide expanse of sea, "I seem to be getting this all wrong. Let me try again." She gave her assent with her head. "I have never spoken at any length to a Jew, and I had never heard things from a Jewish perspective either. I know that Jews are considered a problem, but I have never stopped to question why, nor what should be done about it. Your talk this morning, and you as a person, has changed my stance to one of wanting to know more of why it is happening and whether it is actually correct."

His eyes lowered to a beaming face which said "So you'll have to do a lot more listening."

*

Despite playing down in the port area all of his life, Marcus had never actually been into *any* of the buildings. He was noticing, for the first time, there were quite a variety. The warehouses along the dock front were large airy and not what you'd called solidly constructed. Marvelling at one, he wondered how long it had been there, or perhaps more poignantly, as they were passing right through it, how long it would remain standing. There were some fairly elegant buildings, one which he recognised as a safe refuge of Rebecca, which she must call home; like so many buildings in Tarraco, it had seen better days. The majority had never had a period of glory, a case in point was the rudimentary fisherman's ... hovel, was the only word that sprang to mind to describe these basic constructions.

The women hadn't stopped chattering all the way, he thought they were saying things for his benefit; Antonia pointing out the sights and Arantxa providing the interested audience. If he ever had been listening, he's stopped a long time ago. His eyes were concentrated upon seeing for the first time, added to the fact that his tactile senses were alive. In theory, and to outward appearances, both women were doing the same thing, holding onto one of his arms. The Antonia side was numb, no feelings were emitted despite an occasional pinch to try to attract his attention to something she was particularly insistent on pointing out. The Arantxa side was alive to every slight change of hand movement farther up or down his arm or to any increase, decrease in pressure. At one point when she was laughing at one of Antonia's bawdy remarks, she pushed gently into his body and he felt the softness of her breast flatten against him. Heavenly.

Suddenly Antonia released him, "This is us." Standing outside a particularly derelict "cottage", she spoke with some pride. "Not a palace like you're used to, and a bit run down cos my man's been playing soldier for a while, but it's ours."

Marcus managed to voice a "it's lovely" before he was literally pushed across the threshold, "Won't go to 'eaven, if you lie!"

Inside was dark and difficult to see anything until the pupils adjusted from the bright sunshine outside, so, he felt the movement rather than saw it; a man standing to attention barking the word "Sir!"

"Sit down, you soft 'ap'orth, you ain't in the army no longer and 'e ain't no sir. 'e's our prisoner and we brought 'im to see you."

The eyes had done their job and Marcus was faced with a dishevelled looking man who always used to look so perfect in his well kept uniform. "Plonk your posh bum down, I'll get the ale. 'elp me, 'eathen."

Pere was very conscious of what Marcus was used to, having taught him in the palace gardens for years, he was embarrassed about his own circumstances. "Perhaps we could have our ale outside, it being such a lovely day and all."

As his subordinate's discomfort was easily detectable, Marcus immediately agreed by reinforcing the splendour of the day that shouldn't be wasted indoors. Pere carried two rickety chairs outside on which they sat finding that they had no conversation whatsoever. Idle chit-chat had never been in their repertoire, it was more a relationship of instructions and directions, for many years given by Pere, and over the last few months the roles had been reversed, the narrative remaining the same; imperatives.

It suddenly hit Marcus that he had never even wondered whether Pere had a home, wife, family and things like that, he was just Pere; the teacher, or, Pere; the trusty second in command.

"'aving a great chinwag about old times, I see." Antonia carried two mugs of ale followed by a shadow doing exactly the same, "And where be our chairs?"

"Antonia, you know we've only got two."

"I do, and I also fully understand that the guest is seated on one of them, what puzzles me is why I ain't seated on the other."

Marcus made to stand, "Stay where you are you, and drink this." Ale was used as a weapon to reseat him.

"But Arantxa needs to sit as well."

"'er? She ain't nothing but a 'eathen savage, a chair would be wasted on her."

Marcus was genuinely shocked at this treatment and then confused as Arantxa laughed heartily adding "My bum isn't Christian enough to sit on one of Antonia's chairs."

Pere, now standing, stated that he'd bring the bench out, only to be told that she was quite happy to sit on the flagstone next to Marcus's chair. She asked him to hold her ale while she made herself comfortable, a comfort that made him slightly uncomfortable, as their legs were touching.

"For being such a gentleman, you can 'ave the privilege of sitting next to me."

"Antonia, you're pushing your luck. I'm not one of the kids." He mock sternly said taking his place next to the chair.

"Talking of kids, where are they? You were supposed to be taking care of them."

"They're off playing with some other kids."

"Whose? What's their names? Where have they gone?"

"How should I know?"

"Cos you were supposed to be in charge. Don't tell me Maria has gone as well."

"No, she's too little, she's asleep. What sort of father do you take me for?"

"Not a very good one. I 'ope 'e were a better soldier."

Marcus, back in tactile heaven, realised that he was being included in this scene of domestic bliss which he sought to leave as soon as he decently could. "Excellent. The best."

Arantxa liked Pere, she'd more or less managed to block out memories of his connection to the massacre of her village by not ever dwelling on them. This reference to him being an excellent soldier brought some unwanted visions back. She moved into herself, and physically as far away as she could from Marcus's chair, causing what he thought would be a temporary interruption of this pressing pleasure.

Pere was the only one to notice Arantxa's face. "No longer, hopefully a soldier no more. If the Lord is kind, I'd like to return to fishing, it's easier to sleep at night and, it's time to get this house fixed up a bit."

Arantxa timidly smiled her appreciation of his words and Marcus saw his opening, "Which I shall leave you to do, I thank you kindly for your hospitality and I do hope we can repeat it again soon."

"Your place in 'eaven is in serious doubt if you keep on lying all the time. Anyway, if you're off, do something useful afore you go, walk the 'eathen back to the Jews' 'ouse while I get this lump to work now he's said publicly that 'e'll do it.

*

"Rebecca, what are you doing hanging around here? It doesn't look good a woman, a Jewish woman … a Jewish woman who is about to have a cherem order against her, just loitering in the streets not going anywhere or doing anything from what I can see."

"Uncle Isaac, I.." she really didn't know what to say. Having agreed, she didn't know why she'd done it - to wait for Flavius while he sorted out a couple of things so that, as he said, he could continue his education. She hadn't known where to wait nor what to do, so she wandered aimlessly along the side of the Circus and back as if she were somehow slovenly guarding it.

"Oh, I AM sorry, niece," he thought he had detected real discomfort and distress in her eyes, "I know you must be worried about my mission to delay this evening's meeting. Really though, there was no need to follow me and wait for me uptown, I would have reported directly back. Let's walk back together and I'll explain all."

Shit! This wasn't what she wanted. Actually the whole cherem thing, which had worried her so deeply this morning, had disappeared from her head while she'd been with Flavius. Linking her arm through his and walking as slowly as she could, her mind raced trying to find a way out. As conspiratorially as she could, she asked,

"Tell me, were you successful in your mission?"

Glowing with pride at a job well done, a smirk told its own story.

"Oh well done! You're the best! How did you manage it?"

Still aglow he all but whispered, "I may not be the brightest in the family…"

"Uncle!"

"It's true. However, I do have my ways and I'm not giving away all my secrets to you. It'll suffice to say that the meeting has been put off until after Shabbat. This gives almost a week, ample time for the message I sent to Abraham to arrive and may be even enough time for a reply."

"I don't care what you say; you are the cleverest uncle I have."

Isaac stopped their slow progress to take in his niece, "I'm your only uncle."

"See! Proved without doubt."

"Rebecca,"

"That's me. Now you are beginning to sound like my favourite father. And I think you should hurry along and give him the good news. I will only slow you down as I promised Marcus that while I was uptown *waiting* for you, I would deliver a message to his house as he's been delayed down in port area in Pere's house."

With that salvo she turned and headed apace back to whence they had come.

"Message? Pere? Marcus? Rebecca, I don't understand…"

"See you later, you really are the best!"

Feeble, it was the best she could come up with.

*

"All packed up and ready to go I see, Centurion Milo."

A crisp salute accompanied the "Yes, sir."

"Get the men into marching formation; I'll be with you in a moment. You haven't seen my scribe anywhere, have you?"

"In the church, sir."

"The church?"

"Yes, sir, said he couldn't concentrate with all the shouting and banging that packing up brought. The only place with a bit of quiet was the church."

Paulus headed in that direction and found the little man using the altar as writing table.

"A bit sacrilegious, that, isn't it?"

A face looked up, "Nearly finished, general. I did ask Jesus' permission and there was no loud objection. I remember a sermon where it said something like; the Lord helps those that help themselves, so I thought…"

"Most resourceful of you, though I'm not quite sure that you remember that sermon accurately. Still, nearly finished, you say."

"Drying as we speak. You'll need to sign it, and stamp it, and then Bob's your uncle."

"What? Who's Bob?"

"Just an army expression that the lower ranks use, means everything is alright."

"Ohh, you don't happen to know whether this *Bob* brought the stamp along, do you?"

"Bob didn't, I did. Never travel without it."

The stamping and signing done, the scribe was told to find the messenger who was due to leave with the reports that were regularly sent.

"Now, here, we have a slight problem, sir, He remained in Els Munts, we can give it to him as soon as we arrive though."

"No, it's urgent. Aren't there any horses with us?"

"Only yours, sir."

Annoyance was written all over Paulus. His intention was to set the troop off marching while he extended his little talk with the pretty girl, then catch them up on his horse before they reached Els Munts. Wamba really needed to receive the information as soon as possible, which meant that he had to ride ahead himself.

"Do you ride?"

"Me? Actually yes, extremely well, my father used to be head of the stables in…"

Cut off from his pleasant parental memories, he was told to take the only horse and exercise it well, as it hadn't galloped for a long time. An almost whooping with glee little man shot out of the church only to stick his head back in, "Where's it tied up?"

"Ask Milo."

One problem solved brought others hard on its heels. How would he get back and what excuse did he have for not leaving with the others? Coming out of the dark church into the bright sunlight he was met with ranks of gleaming soldiers eager to be moving.

"Centurion, I still have a couple of things to do here in Tarraco."

Milo and the front rank that were in earshot sagged with disappointment, they were bored and restless doing nothing in this amphitheatre, keen as mustard to get back to the good life with the women on the beach.

"I will not keep you, carry on without me."

"Sir, I will leave you four men as a personal guard."

"We are not in enemy territory, well, at least not yet, so, I don't think that will be necessary." "If you could send a rider back with another horse when you arrive, that would be helpful."

The perfect formation noisily, iron tipped sandals crashing down onto the flagstones, marched away.

*

"Don't know why Antonia said that, I don't need protection nor do I need walking anywhere, as if I were some sort of animal. Besides, you don't know where we're going, I do."

"I would wager a bet that our destination is that large house up there on the right."

"I thought you didn't know port area."

"I don't really."

"But you do know Rebecca's house..interesting."

They had reached the entrance and as always the front door wasn't just slightly ajar, it was wide open, dithering as to whether they should enter together, or wait at the doorstep, as they were both reluctant to bid their farewells. Their vacillation was cut short.

"And who might you be? And what do you want at my brother's house."

For a man who had rarely been known to say boo to a goose, it had taken considerable courage on the part of Isaac to come out with the words to anyone, let alone a military man in full ceremonial uniform. In fact, it was the uniform and its ceremonial nature that had tipped the balance towards bravery. The man looked familiar and not in the slightest bit threatening - surely, if it were something serious there would be a whole posse of them here.

Marcus straightened his back to raise himself to his true height and stature, "Do I have the honour of addressing the father of Rebecca, the owner of this house?"

Before a slightly surprised Isaac became a totally surprised one, Arantxa butted in, "No, that's not Rebecca's dad."

"How do you know that, and who the devil are you, young lady?"

"I'm the heathen who is temporarily living here."

"What!"

The commotion had brought Jacob out of his study and it was at this point he felt that he should intervene. "Good Morning to you all. Perhaps, as I know most of you, I should do the introductions."

After presenting himself, his brother and Arantxa, he turned, "And you I presume must be General Marcus, the son of Duke Ranosindus. We've never met, however, I did see you this morning receiving King Wamba's forces on your father's behalf."

"That's where I have seen you!" light suddenly shone into Isaac's brain. "Also, I have seen you scampering around the port area, usually trying, unsuccessfully, to catch my daughter."

Marcus took an immediate liking to this formal-looking austere, undoubtedly Jewish figure before him. "That's me. Not a general though. I do wish you hadn't taught your daughter to run so fast!"

Ice completely shattered, everyone accepted the offer of a drink which Arantxa knowing where things were kept, offered to fetch.

"Brother, who the hell is that? She introduced herself as a heathen and more to the point, why does she know where the ale and cups are kept in this house?"

"*That* as you call her, is Rebecca's latest addition to her friendship circle, and she calls herself a heathen because I believe that she actually is."

"Arantxa is her name." Marcus added helpfully.

"Oh, sweet Jehovah! As if we don't have enough problems with the rabbi and the cherem. She's gone and made our situation considerably worse; sharing a house with a goya. How could she? She could have told me, I've just spoken to her, wandering around by herself uptown, she was."

"By herself?" A confused Marcus joined in the conversation.

"Yes. Some cock and bull story, saying she was going to take a message to your family from you?"

The furrows on Marcus' brow deepened to plantable proportions.

"Yes, you remember you asked her to tell your family that you'd be late as you were visiting Pere" Arantxa had half heard the conversation rushed in slopping three mugs of ale.

"Slow down girl. I honestly prefer my ale in the cup rather than on the floor. You've only brought three, where's yours?"

Arantxa started off saying that she wasn't thirsty then admitting, after many prying questions that she wasn't used to so much ale and she'd woken with a huge headache today.

"Oh, it gets worse; drunken women! Did anyone see my niece inebriated?"

"She wasn't, and no, we were here."

"Damage limitation; at least no more fuel will be added to the cherem fire."

Grateful at Arantxa's intervention, he would have dropped Rebecca even deeper in the pigshit, if he'd mentioned that she was walking with Wamba's general. Being still confused, he ventured to ask the meaning of the word *cherem* which was being used constantly. It wasn't a long explanation; even so, it transmitted fear and foreboding. Not understanding what she could have done to deserve such a fate, he thought about listing her virtues, and then thought better of that, instead asking the simple question - why.

Isaac reluctantly, after all he was a goy, explained that rabbi Hillel was accusing her of siding with the Christians undermining her faith and disrespecting Judaism in general and him in particular by insults.

"The little prick!"

"Those are the exact words that my daughter used."

"Well she's not wrong; I was there in the meeting." Marcus went to explain exactly what had happened and it dove tailed totally to Rebecca's version of earlier.

"At least I know for certain that my daughter doesn't lie, well, at least not about this. Sadly though, we won't be able to use you, nor your information as you are not of our faith. I do thank you. Would you care for another, this time full, cup of ale or.."

"No, thank you, I really must get back to the duke."

They all stood and shook hands warmly. "Even though you are not of our faith, you are always welcome in this house. Please remember that especially the next time that you are chasing Rebecca and she thinks she's safe here! Arantxa, would you see our guest out. Brother, shall we go to the office…"

Back to doorstep dithering, neither knew what to say. Finally Marcus blurted out, "I doubt I will be chasing Rebecca along these streets anymore, we're too old for that, but I'd quite like to come back to see how you are getting along."

"Only *quite?*"

*

Communication lines were immensely difficult. It was going to be hell to try to coordinate this attack. Egica had been instructed to leave his forces about half a day's march from the southern end of the valley so that if the locals twigged their presence, they wouldn't have assumed anything resembling an attack. The presumption would have been that as the reinforcements to the main force, the only passage north to Wamba's main camp would be following the river in the adjacent valley to where they were based.

With a great deal of skill, stealth and darkness, the reluctant Kunimund had manoeuvred Wamba and ALL his available men to a striking distance of the northern end. It was due to the use of *all* the forces that Kunimund had significant objections.

"Sire, it does NOT make any military sense to risk everything on one throw of the dice. A rearguard has to be kept for any possible contingency. What if they get wind of us and bring another army behind us, we'd be fish in a barrel! Furthermore, breaking through that valley will be costly both in time and lives. If anything happens to Egica's forces and we are left to fight alone, it'll be carnage. What if …?"

"Enough general! We've been whatifing for months now with NO success whatsoever. With your plans, we could all die here… of old age! I am tired of waiting."

"Patience is an important aspect of war. The Vascones are steadily losing men and soon they'll be suing for a peace treaty, mark my words."

"Ok, they are marked. We are attacking."

No cooking fire had been lit, silence was maintained throughout the day march and chilly night vigil. Despite the absence of noise, a noticeable buzz of keen anticipation permeated the camp; like Wamba, the soldiers were heartily fed up with this campaign of no interest, no excitement, no fighting nor booty. They had been informed that it would a two-pronged attack which had a high probability of success and could mean the beginning of the end of this war. The sooner the better was the general sentiment.

Kunimund had scouts everywhere fearing any surprise move. Reports so far had shown no significant movement of forces from any other area. Left without excuses, there was no reason he could delay or stop this mission; it had to go on.

"Centurions, form the men!"

The plan, Kunimund thought that it didn't even warrant the word, was to try to break through the narrow pass by force and attrition. The defenders would have the heights, so spears, rocks and other projectiles would rain down on them without respite. Two groups of the most agile had been dispatched to try to climb the rocks, one from the left, and other the right, in the hope of reaching the defenders before the death toll became too unsustainable. It was most unlikely that the ground force would be able to break through, especially as the massed hoards would be waiting at the end of the bottleneck to pick them off as they dribbed and drabbed their way through the torrent of missiles. This *plan* dictated that, if they could resist for long enough, then the Vascones might realise that there was a more serious threat coming from the southern entrance, withdraw troops to meet it, leaving Wamba's forces with a chance of progress.

"Shields!"

A perfectly synchronised clash showed a much practised elegant manoeuvre where the half a centurion cover their heads and sides and slowly shuffle forth. All hell broke loose as soon as they entered the gorge. Spears thudded into the wood of the shields or bounced of the metal rims without too much damage, rebounding back like springs as the sturdy forearms recoiled. The sound and impact of large rolled boulders was a different story; they wreaked havoc, smashing holes throughout the tightly packed formation and no amount of forearm strength and reforming was compensating. Screams of crushed men rang out. The delight of the defenders was heard as well seen, as they celebrated yet another crushing blow, standing bare-chested, yelling, they presented easy targets for the archers who had sneaked as forward as possible by hugging the side and the overhangs. A hail of arrows took their toll, with falling bodies being added to the stones and spears.

"We've lost three squares already. Time to call a halt to this waste of life. Sire, react."

Wamba had been in the field before where death and confusion reigned, the scale of this unfolding before him was something else. He was literally opened mouthed watching blood, bone, broken bodies to the soundtrack of immense agony; he was wavering.

"No, not yet. The climbers are almost there. I'll lead the next square and try to organise pockets of shield walls to cover archers on both sides up to the point where we have established ourselves in the valley." Alaric didn't want his plan to fail.

"One hundred and fifty men sent in so far and we have gained only about hundred and fifty paces. Do you really think that the day can be saved without a total massacre?"

"I do Sire, which is why I will lead it."

Wamba said nothing else, Kunimund tried to object until a silencing royal gesture made him bide his time. "On your head be it, Alaric." He did manage to mutter loud enough for the king to hear.

"Literally it will be!" was the almost jaunty reply "Next square, form around me, archers follow and taper off as we move in."

Their pace wasn't so much a shuffle any longer as a stride, while still managing to keep the tightest of formations. As they walked over dead or dying, Alaric called to the survivors who were staying as close to the rockface as possible, "Form small shield walls to protect the archers I will lead you."

Knowing what was expected of them, groups of about ten gave shield cover to two or three archers at ten pace intervals. Then their training kicked in - moving in perfect time they covered, and opened, to allow the archers to do their job, it was like a well oiled door opening and closing. This caused the hurlers to take cover more often, resulting in the decreasing size and quantities of rocks. The bravado of standing and chucking had become hidden legs kicking down shale, the storm diminishing in intensity to something more like a shower. The agile hill climbers were now doing their work as well, causing a retreat by the previous occupants. "Send the next square!" Alaric screamed back at the waiting troops as his men were making reasonable progress without being holed too often.

It was then an army horn could be heard from the southern part of the valley. It was only a matter of time, this day was won.

*

The blistering heat of summer was a thing of the past. That's not to say the days were cool and pleasant, they weren't, it was bearable heat that could be ventured out into, not one that had to be shied away from. The days were long, this day Rebecca thought was the longest of her life by far and the sun was yet to set. Hangover, what hangover? That can't have been this week, or month, it must have been eons ago, when in reality it was this morning, an auspicious way to start to be sure.

The meeting, oh dear. That didn't bear reflecting upon, then the cherem, with all the fear and trepidation that brought with it. The lies to her uncle, how awful, especially as he'd been fighting on her behalf. The anxious waiting, the stumbling non-conversation, all this in one day. And she'd actually left out the most momentous part, the late afternoon, early evening.

Flavius had apologised profusely for taking more time than he had anticipated, explaining that there was one point where he thought he wouldn't be able to make it at all, and how worried about he'd been. If he hadn't been able to let her know it was circumstances beyond his control, not a lack of desire. She wanted to replicate everything he'd said by telling the Uncle Isaac story. Choosing a cooler approach, she demurely thanked him for his consideration. Part of his story involved his horse and the sending of it without him, which he apologised again for, as they would now have to walk. This detail somewhat shocked Rebecca. What did he imagine, she would jump on the horse behind him? Thankfully, he'd changed out of his dress uniform, favouring something a great deal more informal, and they would ride away somewhere? The scandal would have been all around Tarraco before they reached the Via Augusta. When asked where they should go, and what he should see, mentioning in passing that he'd had his fill of Roman architecture, she'd suggested the beach path, partly because there would be nobody down there, and she wanted to take him to one of her favourite places which she didn't get to visit as often as she would like as it took quite a bit of time to get there, and obviously the same amount of time to get back!

It was a small cove - two beaches, and some rocks farther north. It had been an accidental discovery, the first time about a year or so ago. Being angry with everyone and everything, her father in particular, she'd set off at pace *somewhere*, yelling at her father not to expect her back for lunch and if he wanted something, he'd have to do it himself. Her head filled with righteous indignation, by far the best indignation for striding angrily not noticing where you are going, she found herself in a beautiful secluded cove. There wasn't any vast expanse of sand, just enough to make it not completely rocky. The waves, if there were any, broke on the rocks at either side of the cove leaving the blue, blue water still and totally invitingly transparent. Having never learnt to swim, water was a frightening concept, here it was shallow enough to wade into without any fear, giving a cooling and adventurous feel to any non mermaid.

Not telling him their destination, nor how long it would take, she mentioned that the beach might be nice. The scenery and weather made up for their sparse conversation as they walked. It wasn't as stilted and sticky as the getting to the amphitheatre jaunt. By both agreeing to take this time and stroll together, a psychological barrier had been overcome, a declaration of intent to deepen their contact had been made, thus making their presence together less strained. The trouble was that as their worlds were so far apart, no idle chit-chat sprang to mind. Footwear helped for a while, having taken off her sandals to splash through the shallows of the incoming piddling breaking waves, she suggested he do the same, only to be met with a stubborn insistence that a soldier never takes off his sandals except, and not always then, when going to bed. Thinking that he was joking, she'd laughed at him mercilessly, drawing up all sorts of ridiculous scenarios where the shod soldier would be in a disadvantage or the subject of ridicule. It was well onto the second beach when it finally dawned that he was being serious. This was the first point against him, it didn't counter balance the many she accrued in her head in his favour. Still, a sense of humour about sandals was found sorely lacking.

"See, you had to put your sandals back on."

"To cross sharp rocks, I would say that is a sensible thing to do. Here in this lovely little cove, by the way I think we've walked far enough, the sandals referred to will be removed again. Amazing, isn't it? Off, on, off, it's as if this little strap was designed to help in this radical action."

"I know you're laughing at me, but us soldiers.."

"Do and say silly things." She ran into the water deep enough to be able to kick water at him.

"Stop.."

She stopped, took on a serious tone "General, I believe you will have to retreat or face the prospect of having wet sandals," and started kicking with abandonment. The retreat was swift.

"Another great Jewish victory to go down in the annals of history." Realising that he wasn't having as much fun as she'd hoped, she came out of the water and plonked herself on the edge of the dry and wet sand so the gentle ripple-like waves would occasionally wet her feet.

Flavius wanted to play, play the way he used to with Aitziber, but something stopped him. Unsure whether it was the pain of a re-lived experience, or not wanting to open himself up again, he felt he couldn't participate. Memories of their brief time by and in the lake, flooded back. Not wanting to sink into the melancholy that he forever carried with him, and very conscious he was making a terrible impression, when he so dearly wanted to do the opposite, he moved to her side and removed his sandals. Offering them to her, "Spoils for the victor." Her anticipated snatching move was fast enough only to grasp the air as he moved them out of reach. "The trophy has to be earned."

"Your price, oh-defeated Goth?"

"I would like you to tell me more about your people. I was deadly serious earlier when I said I wanted to hear more and now seems the perfect time."

This request really did catch her off guard, when they'd set off, just the two of them, she wasn't sure what would transpire with this walk in the sand accompanied by no prying eyes. Numerous possibilities had passed through her head in the silent trudging moments, none of which came remotely close to the present situation.

"As it most certainly is, I would be stretched to think of a better time and place!"

She sounded serious but he wasn't sure whether she was being sarcastic or not. Anyway, she launched into the history of the Jews in Roman times, passing through the Arian Goth period, arriving at the present day Christian Goth life.

Brief is wasn't, every Jew knew the story to some degree, Rebecca's depth of knowledge was profound - details, concilia were embedded in her brain and were dying to come out. Her presentation wasn't boringly confined to dates, she gave them colour, which, may or may not, have been strictly true, it didn't matter as there was nobody to contradict her. The general wasn't *playing* good listener, he was actually extremely interested. Having little base knowledge to come from, he often interrupted with clarification questions which kept him concentrated when he found his mind wandering, spending more time on the deliverer not the delivered.

She was incredible to look at, such beauty, augmented, whenever she got passionate. The moments her deep brown eyes shone with anger he felt she was looking into him, sending a quiver throughout his body. Unlike those who glaze by fixing their vision to the middle distance to relate events, her unrelenting stare made him feel part of the story.

"Why did they change so radically once they had given up Arianism?"

"They? You mean *you, your people?*"

He'd been made to feel so much part of the story that this undeniable fact hadn't really sunk in; this had all been done in his name, so, therefore by default, by him. Not being completely stupid, he knew that Jews were persecuted and not ever questioning it, he'd always accepted the line that stated that they weren't like *us*. It went something like; *they* were an abomination, responsible for the death of the Lord Jesus and practiced all manner of strange rituals meaning that they had no place in a good Christian country; their very presence was a corruption of society.

"I suppose I do, I'm part of that repressing Goth machine. Still, it's all a bit much for me to take in. I need a break." With that he stood and disrobed, having many fewer problems taking his clothes off than his sandals, it seemed.

"I'm going for a swim. Coming?"

A pair of firm male buttocks was moving athletically away from her at speed. Another moment, another shock. Having not expected to be the provider of a potted history of five centuries of Jewish life on a beach, she certainly didn't expect its near conclusion to be met with a call for male nudity. She didn't know what to think, how to judge the situation, never mind how to react. Truth be told, she'd never seen a naked male body before, so value laden comparative judgements could not be made, however, it had to be said that she did like what she was seeing.

After his sprint and wave hurdling into the water, he dived to emerge much farther out than she'd imagined and then he kept going, out, swimming quickly, and to a non swimmer's eye, expertly. Not knowing what she should do, nor what was expected of her to do, her mind raced. One option, that of going to join him, had been removed. There was no way, even given all the will in the world that she'd be able to go out there, he must be half way to Rome by now. Choosing to stay seated as if nothing out of the normal had happened was her final decision, so she waited, watching the distant flailing of arms in some sort of swimming motion..

Flavius hadn't really given any thought to taking off his clothes to go swimming; you can't swim with clothes, so they had to be taken off. The fact that a little known female was sitting with him, didn't really come into his calculations either. He was hot, the water was cool, it didn't require a great deal of thought, unlike all the other stuff he'd been hearing. As he struck out for open sea, he reflected on how, not quite stupid, but certainly unthinking, he'd been throughout his life. He'd swallowed the *us* and *them* argument hook, line and sinker. So much so, that he'd crossed the street when he'd seen any Jews on his side of the road, what was worse, and he'd even considered telling them to cross the road as he was already on this side! Truly awful.

Feeling guilty and angry with himself, it was clear he didn't have time or space in his brain to question whether he should or should not be naked. The coming out of the water posed another problem for Rebecca, should she look away or not? Choosing the latter option, she was more intrigued than excited by what she saw. Imagine having a thing like that dangling down there, it must be awkward and uncomfortable, was her overriding thought. "You seem to be totally naked, general, would you like your sandals?"

"Not necessary at the moment." Landing heavily, he layered himself and sprayed Rebecca with sand. While brushing the odious stuff off her clothes, Rebecca reflected that irony didn't seem to be Flavius' strongest suit, whereas sand certainly was. He positively rolled in it.

"It's great when it sticks to you and then gradually drops off."

"Wonderful, I agree, so you end up in the state you were before putting the sand on. Have you ever thought that if you don't put sand on in the first place, then you'd actually save time and energy?"

Lying face down looking away from the sea, she was talking to the once running, now very still, but nonetheless alluring, buttocks.

"You're missing the fun and adventure. Don't you like sand? I'd never seen any until we arrived at Els Munts. Now I love it, as I say, especially after coming out of the water."

"It's the thing I hate most about the sea; the stuff gets everywhere, it's crunchy and unpleasant."

He turned his head to look at her, "See, it doesn't matter that you are Jewish, the thing that separates us most is our irreconcilable attitude to sand, oh Aitziber."

"Aitziber?!"

Totally flustered, he turned his sand caked form to hold her hand, "I mean, Rebecca."

She let his hand go as if it contained leprosy rather than sand.

"I told you, I hate sand. Tell me about her."

"Well I'm not sure that.."

"After mixing up our names, it's the least you can do. I know who she is, and I know a little of your relationship. Arantxa and I were drinking last night, her sister had a starring role in the conversation. Arantxa is still very much affected."

"As are we both."

A case of the proverbial flood gates, it wasn't. It was the first time that Flavius had been given the opportunity to talk about Aitziber to anyone in a real sense. The king knew her name and used it to make fun of him. Marcus knew a great deal more, and obviously, had had a significant role in the end, her end, but one doesn't talk emotion to another man, especially not a man who is your subordinate in the army. Wanting to speak wasn't his problem, instead the how and what was. How do you embark on a tale about one beautiful woman that you'd had a passionate relationship with, and who died tragically, to another beautiful woman, who you'd like to have a relationship with. Just what can you say?

As Flavius' brain worked overtime, his voice remained mute. The last thought now took precedence over all others; *another woman he'd like to have a relationship with*. He knew that he'd been captivated by her charm and incredible looks. Who wouldn't be? A whole number of women had interested him with those two facets, there was nothing new in that. In those affairs, he liked to believe, a good time was generally had by both parties. It had never meant that he wanted a relationship with them, or them with him, and that modus operandi was interrupted by the appearance of Aitziber, (who knows where that would have led? if it hadn't been cut, the operative word, short,) and it would be resumed once memories began to fade.

However, since this morning he'd felt his life had changed. Yeah, trite shit, isn't it? Generals don't fall in love in a morning, not a love that could or would last, yet here it was, he felt TOTALLY different with Rebecca than any other woman ever! Now his problem was telling her about Aitziber.

"She meant a great deal to me. Her murder was ..wrong."

"What a strange word, wrong. Aren't all murders by definition, wrong?"

"Yes, no, it's just that, it shouldn't have happened, it shouldn't have happened the way it did... it was...wrong."

The silence returned. In one day these two had gone through so many different types of silences that the gamut was just about exhausted. This one was pregnant with possibilities.

Both feared saying the *incorrect* thing. Rebecca's intrigue was more than piqued though she didn't want to make the man suffer, or worse, feel that she was forcing him into revelations he wasn't ready to make. Flavius didn't want to scare off this woman by expressing his feeling for another. The silence continued.

"It's getting late, everyone will be wondering what has happened to me. My excuse of delivering a message to Marcus's house is a bit lame now, don't you think?"

Exceedingly grateful to be given a way out of this impasse, he jumped up a bit too enthusiastically showering sand all over Rebecca.

"Oh! You great lump! You've covered me in the stuff." She rose, not quite so quickly, and started brushing sand off her clothes.

"Oh, I'm SO sorry, it's just…" A most contrite general began to assist in the sand removal.

"Stop!"

He did.

In measured tones not wanting to offend or reject his honest endeavours she said, "I'm not sure a naked Goth general should be putting his hands all over a young unaccompanied Jewish girl."

"Oh, I'm sorry, I didn't think." He took two steps back bringing him into the correct focus of the complainant; she definitely liked what she saw. Now in a fumbling, apologetic state he was more vulnerable than the arrogant self assured nude of before. Although the body was the same, the attitude was much more *appealing*. Covering the two step distance quickly, she planted a kiss on his cheek, "Thank you for trying." Turning she picked up both her and his sandals, leaving him to find his dispersed clothes. She was onto the rocks before he caught her up, more or less clothed. Her sandals were in their appropriate place for sharp rock walking. Climbing up to, and walking to where she was, he was obviously in pain, his foot recoiling on every non flat piece of rock.

"What would you like for them?" He pointed to his sandals in her hands. "I can offer fame and fortune."

It was then that they heard the sound of horses coming along the beach they were headed to. Worried, Rebecca immediately gave up her hostages, "Who could it be?"

Slipping on the sandals and squinting, Flavius laughed, "I think it's my scribe."

"Your scribe?"

"With two horses. Splendid. Now you won't have to walk home."

Rebecca's tone changed from playful flirt to something akin to fear. "I can't possibly be seen here with you, and I certainly won't get on a horse with you either. What do you think people would say? I'm hiding down here in the cove while you go to meet your *scribe*. Do NOT mention me, please."

Reacting to her concern, he understood the situation immediately. He'd made mistakes with Aitziber, not wishing to repeat them again, he quickly asked a final question, "What would have been your price for the sandals?"

"To repeat this experience tomorrow."

"That's no price, that's the best reason I have heard for tomorrow to come and quickly." He stooped down, kissed her cheek gently, "until tomorrow."

Then scampering across the rocks in the other direction, she could hear the hooves getting closer. She crouched feeling the glow which had started in her cheek spread to all parts, she muttered to herself "Oh dear."

*

A triumvirate of bishops sat in a small room in a large palace, their trust in their fellow man didn't extend very far for these senior clergymen. When they did develop their policies, it was hard not to hear them, as they made sure they were delivered from every pulpit in the land. However, while they were hatching and refining their thoughts, they wanted no one else to participate. Quiricus, Julian and Taio were likeminded on nearly all questions of doctrine and theology. Being from Caesaragusta, Taio was slightly more sensitive on the Vasconis front, believing a stronger hand was needed. His line invariably started with a variation on the theme; these heathens needed to be dealt a serve blow, driven to the other side of the mountains back into Frankia where they belong, expelled permanently from *our* God-fearing land.
The others didn't disagree, their objection was one of timing. For them, the Jewish question was paramount.
The reason for this particular meeting was a combination of Vascones and Jews, plus a potentially explosive element uniting them, which may prove a Godsend to solving both at the same time. Concretely, this came in the form of a note from the Bishop Quirico of Barcino, outlining all sorts of details about the rebellion. Rumours of unrest in that part of the country had been swirling around the capital for quite some time, nothing new in that. With the baronial system that the Goths had always used, there was always one baron trying to get a jump on the others by flexing his muscles in some way. The beginning of the previous king, Recceswinth, had been particularly bloody. That was almost a generation ago, however, since then, they, the bishops, had gained more power. The fact that the Church's anointment of anyone wanting to accede to the leading power position of the state was now obligatory, had had the positive effect of quietening down baronial aspirations considerably, and increasing the influence of those wielding that precondition, the instrument of God's earthly power, the leading bishops.
To the group in conference, what was particularly shocking about the objective of this rebellion was that it was not to install yet another king, raising yourself above your peers, and being able to exercise central power in favour of you and yours, something perfectly legitimate, Goth history being littered with such history changing events. Instead, what was being contemplated this time was to break away from the kingdom

completely, with the aim of forming a new state with the toleration of Jews as one of its central planks.

"We have all read the letter; the question is what shall we do about it?" Quiricus started the ball rolling.

"Does the king know to what depth and extent the rebellion runs?" Julian's intelligent beady eyes were screwing themselves into thought mode.

"I shouldn't think so. He doesn't have our *network*. Dux Paulus has only just arrived according to Quirico's source, which believe it or not I think is that old fat fool, Cyprianus."

"Cyprianus? He's a Tarraco man through and through, always bellyaching on the tragic loss of importance of Tarraconensis, his beloved Tarraco in particular. God, that man can talk! Once I had the misfortune to be sat by him at a .."

"Taio, let's stick to the point, shall we? Cyprianus's tongue is infamous, I'm sure we all have tales to tell. What interests me, is, why Cyprianus has become a tell-tale. Is it a reflection of a deeper schism within the group? We've always known that the main movers and shakers come from Nemausus and Narbo. The addition of Tarraconensis is recent, and makes things both more serious, and perhaps infinitely easier to exploit." The other two waited for Julian to continue. "I've known Paulus nearly all of my life, comes from a good, immigrant-family, almost a neighbour, intelligent man, utterly loyal. If anyone can talk the traitors down, it'd be him. His force is meagre so he can't threaten in anyway, Wamba must be hoping that a small dissuasive gesture and Paulus's persuasive manner will be enough. Let's hope he fails."

"Fails!" They chorused.

"Yes. This could be a wonderful opportunity. The barons will all rally to the call to arms to stop this break-away kingdom, we could have a massive army within a very short period of time, look how long it took us to turn promises into bodies in that relatively small army we've just sent to Wamba. A horde added to that newly reinforced Wamba army could add up to significant numbers, more than have been gathered for generations. The rebels would not be able to stand against us, we'd be able to put them in their place once and for all. Also, as Quirico's letter states, they are looking for allies, relying on the Jews and even talking to the Franks and Vascones. Wonderful! We'll be able to finally deal with the Jews for their insurrection, cower the Franks and smash the Vascones. A full set!"

"Does it have to be in that order? As we already have forces in Vasconia fighting them, we could really do a job on them and then turn our attention to the north-east. With such a force in the field,

Tarraconensis/Gallia Gothica would probably surrender before any blood was shed."

"Taio, that is exactly, what we don't want. No fudge surrender where everyone can hold their head up. No, we need a pulverising victory that will be remembered for a generation at least. They have to be smashed!"

"I agree entirely, Brother Julian. The only problem that I can foresee is leadership. Everyone will want to make a name for themselves leading such a force."

"True, Quiricus, true. Any suggestions? We can't have anyone who is remotely soft on Jews Once battles have been won, this is a big opportunity to rid ourselves of the vermin once and for all."

"Wamba is already there, so he can lead the newly united army. Egica would then be free to lead the force from here. We can't have one of the dukes lording it over the others. No, that would not do, no matter how anti-Jewish they are. Egica would be a much better option"

*

"Oh, Uncle, just what have you been messing around at for all these months up here? That was so easy, like scattering the birds in the plaza."

"General Alaric, could you kindly cuff my nephew around any ear you chose, and the force of the blow is up to you, though I would personally recommend extreme."

Looking from one to the other, Alaric was in a real quandary. To hit or not to hit? General Kunimund's forceful entrance to the royal tent saved the day.

"Sire, that was a close thing. If the Vascones had.."

"Oh no, General, don't tell me that we are now going to get a pile of post battle *what ifs*. Surely we had enough of those pre-battle? Let's just celebrate a job well done. Firstly, allow me to introduce my nephew General Egica."

"Pleased to meet you, general, I have seen you around Toletum, however, until now I have not had the opportunity to speak to you directly."

"The pleasure is mine at meeting such a renowned general."

"Thank you. Sire, before celebrating perhaps, you'd like to know the number of casualties."

"Arh, yes."

"67 dead or dying, dozens badly injured who won't fight again in this campaign and ought to be taken out of camp. General Egica, how did your force fare?"

"We lost about a dozen. As I said, it was a relatively easy fight."

Kunimund had not entered the tent a happy man, and his unhappiness increased. A general's first concern should always be his men. No war is won without them. They must not only feel valued but also be so. Dead and wounded, in his book, always took precedence over celebrations of victory. Those left standing had every right to show elation that they had survived, they also had the duty to show concern and proper deference to the fallen. For this young dandy calling himself a general, not to even know the exact number, or show concern was too much.

"Easy it may have been from your side as you were left with nothing but women and children in the camps to frighten away. I am surprised that you managed to lose such a high number, those women must be as ferocious as they say."

Egica bristled and moved a step closer to Kunimund who replicated the gesture. "General Egica, you may be related to the crown, as many people are. Here though we maintain ARMY discipline and I am your senior officer as long as your *uncle* maintains me in this post. Do you wish me to stay, Sire?"

Wamba's reaction wasn't instantaneous, a fact noted by all, "Of course, I do, general, and I am sure that General Egica will have no problems with the hierarchical system. What are the estimates of their death toll?"

Tension decreased slightly, but it was still at boiling point with the possibility of spilling over at any moment.

"The best part of a couple of hundred. If we had been slightly better coordinated then it could have been the massacre we need to end this conflict."

"General, there you go again. You are whatifing."

Conscious that he was doing his cause no good by speaking in these terms, he needed to redirect the conversation.

"We do have some prisoners, one of whom has airs of importance and most vocally and insistently demands the right to talk to *our chief.*"

"Splendid, I am a king and a chief, do bring him in."

Kunimund left to fetch the prisoner giving the other two time to speak in lowered tones. "Gentlemen, Kunimund may not be the most adventurous general there has ever been, but he is our most experienced and we need him, please maintain respect."

A long-haired powerfully-build sparsely-clad man was led in, taking in the surroundings with quick glances to his left and right. His penetrating brown eyed stare rested on Wamba. His Latin was more than reasonable. "You must be the chief."

"I am King Wamba. And who might you be?"

"Who I am has no importance. What I am, has. I am one of Zorion's sons, he has a number."

"And who may this Zorion be?

"Incredible, you are fighting us, destroying villages, killing women and children and you don't know who we are! My father is the chief of the chiefs in this area, from here to the coast."

"So you can negotiate a surrender of all of these forces?"

"Surrender? There is no way we will ever surrender. Some sort of pact respecting each other's rights might be feasible. One was recently negotiated with the Franks in our territory on the other side of the high mountains."

"This is certainly an interesting proposal. Guards, please remove the prisoner."

His dismissal in such terms earned Wamba a glare of pure hatred as the proud hostage shook off the restrainers to walk head held high to the exit flap.

*

It was beginning to get dark, the sun was well and truly setting on what had been, without doubt, the longest day of Rebecca's life, when she stepped back into port area. Soon a new day would start, Jews, unlike Christians counted their days from sunset rather than sunrise. Mentally and physically, she was totally exhausted. Waiting for her was something she neither wanted nor expected. Thinking that she'd be able to sneak in, find Arantxa and cook up supper and a believable story at the same time, and no one would be the wiser was a colossal miscalculation.

"Where do you think that you have been, young lady? Worried? Were we worried? Your father, god praise his patience and love, may actually be dying of a heart failure in his office, breathing heavily, he is, I can hear him through the door, he won't let anyone in. And your uncle, my poor Isaac is pulling his hair, what little he has left, out, witless with worry, blaming himself for leaving you alone uptown with all those dreadful Christians that you like to befriend. And me? Poor me."

"Hello, Aunt Trudi."

Having to push her aunt slightly with her hip to get past in the narrow entrance hall, she headed straight for her father's sanctuary. Without knocking she entered to find her father slumped in his favourite chair.

"Why's she here again?"

Jacob's head came up to register that it wasn't an enemy invasion, "Because everyone had just about given up on you being alive."

"Sorry to disappoint."

The door crashed open and Isaac, to say that he dashed in, would be an exaggeration on anything except a snail's scale of dash, he did move as fast as he possibly could, embracing Rebecca as if she were the biblical prodigal son. No words were spoken just a strong hug. A well squeezed Rebecca expected talk of a fatted calf at any moment.

"Uncle Isaac, it's alright. I'm fine."

"Jehovah be praised."

"See what you've done Rebecca, a marauding Trudi and an emotionally distraught brother. Spit it out, where have you been? And, please, try to respect our, I know in your opinion, limited, intelligence with at least a credible story."

"Nowhere in particular." A look from her father told her more was needed.

"The meeting this morning was very stressful for me, you know better than anyone, I have never been in a situation like it. Then to hear that that prick Hillel was trying to issue a cherem on the basis of what I'd said was so unfair that I just didn't want to see anyone, so I walked along the beach and sort of lost track of time. Look!" she shook off some sand which was still stuck to her dress. Well it was close to the truth and not an outright lie.

"Oh Rebecca, Rebecca, Rebecca, you will be the death of me." The lamenting head was back in action. Isaac had finally let go and was studying her eyes as he believed himself a great one in business for judging the honesty of the other party. "And you'll be the death of us all if you keep calling the rabbi a little, whatever it is you say."

"I'm sorry that I caused so much trouble, I had no idea, sorry."

"Initially we weren't too worried as Marcus was here and said that you'd gone to his house, corroborating what you'd told Isaac, but that was at lunch time, since then well.."

"Marcus? Here? In this house?"

"Yes, and very pleasant chap he seemed too. He walked back your friend, who, by the way, is in the kitchen preparing something to eat. She's been very helpful and asked all sorts of questions about caixer and said she'd do her best not to break any rules or cups. Nice girl, can't imagine why her father would want to kill her, imagine if he had to put up with what I've got."

"PAPA!!"

*

After their frosty post-meeting reality check, Ranosindus and Chlodoswintha had gone their separate ways to attend the various needs of their staff. When a late lunch was called, they appeared without much desire either to eat or converse. As a guest and with no rights or jurisdiction in this house, or over this man, Chlodoswintha knew she was in the wrong, a fact that she would never admit as it would make her weak in his eyes. Never having been weak nor seeming to be, she was not going to start any time soon.

Ranosindus, on the other hand, was reviewing the situation. He'd spent what was left of the morning with his estate "manager", the man who actually made his lands and houses work, balancing budgets, cutting this, discarding that, and taking on new commitments, all of minor importance, nevertheless essential. In front of him, actually seated to his left, was another balancing problem that needed weighing for its pro and cons. The woman was attractive, entertaining, interesting in bed if somewhat too dominant, and most of the time, fun. She was also extremely wilful and used to having everything her own way. Did the former outweigh the latter? He valued his peace and quiet, his simple uncomplicated way of life, something which he'd have precious little of if she became any sort of permanent feature in his life.

Lunch in this house was always something simple, especially in the summer months as nobody really wanted or needed to eat heavily at midday. Cured ham, cheese, bread and wine with olives was today's, and most days', fare.

"Sorry I am late. I thought you'd have lunch without me. I do hope that I haven't kept you waiting."

"Our guest was dying of starvation but I told her that we had to wait for my unfailingly punctual son to arrive. It wasn't until she'd fainted for the umpteenth time that I insisted that we start without you."

Marcus faced the happily champing Chloda, "I really am SO sorry, I"

"Don't listen to him. We didn't even consider whether you'd be here or not. Amalaswinth, could you bring another plate and cup please?"

More weight on the negative side. Why did she think it was her job to demand a place to be set at their table when his son, himself, or the servant, would have just taken it for granted that with his arrival, all the eating implements would be provided.

Marcus sat. "Quite a meeting, wasn't it? Flavius said that he'd never seen the like of it."

It was the guest, who again was quicker than the host to respond, even though the statement wasn't directed at her.

"I don't think any of us has. What else did the general say?"

Marcus explained Flavius's opinions, dislike for the rabbi, interest in the Jewish cause and sympathy for the political position of Tarraco. In fact, he was so impressed that he'd sent off a note to King Wamba suggesting a meeting and a compromise of some sort.

"Excellent news, hopefully this whole thing can be solved amicably."

"Don't be naïve. The general is a no-one who will take whatever orders he is given. Actually, I would go so far as to say that Wamba himself doesn't count for much, so, even if in the unlikely case that the general manages to get Wamba's sympathetic ear, they'll both be overruled by the real power in Toletum, the bishops."

There she goes again, showing him up in front of his own son, calling him naïve.

"To have hope of it not coming to bloodshed may be, in your words, naïve, but it is what I would like and dearly pray for."

"I agree with father. The avoidance of war should be sought. I doubt you, Lady Chlodoswintha, have ever seen the reality of battle. I now have, and let me tell you, it's not the stuff of glory and song, it's gore and pain and should only be a last resort and never something to be hoped for."

"Well and truly I have been put in my place, haven't I? I bow to your superior experience in the matter, and I apologise for coming over as some sort of warmonger. However, what I have had, is experience with the bishops, Quiricus and Julian, and I can assure you that they don't do olive branches. When push comes to shove, Marcus, where will you stand?"

"Lady Chlodoswintha, are you really asking me that question in my own house in front of my father? I find it most offensive and hope that you are not inferring that I may take sides against my family."

"No, no Marcus, I was not inferring that at all. It's just that you've been fighting *with* Wamba's forces and now you may be fighting against old comrades."

"I was fighting *with* Wamba, as you say, at my father's behest."

"Marcus, I apologise again. I don't want you to get the impression that I am attacking you, it's just that time will come, sooner than we think, when we will all be asked to make big sacrifices for the successful completion of our endeavour."

Marcus asserted in no uncertain terms that he stood ready to make those sacrifices for the sake of his family. Ranosindus saw where the countess was going and thought that the timing was completely wrong. The question was, how to stop her. "I think…"

"Sorry for interrupting you, dear duke, I have a couple more things I'd like to explain to your son."

Marcus didn't like the content of what she was saying nor did he like the tone of its delivery.

Chlodoswintha went on to outline the problems the coalition were having, specifically those of leadership and how they were desperately searching for a compromise, which was the main reason for her presence in Tarraco. Marcus, listening less negatively and considerably more warily, digested what she was saying, venturing what he believed was a logical solution. "So, have a leader in the north, your husband, and, one in the south, my father."

"I must say that you have good grasp on matters, it took you minutes to come to this conclusion, whereas it's taken us weeks to come to more or less the same one."

The ship has sailed, too late to stop it, may as well join in, thought Ranosindus.

"Which is where your sacrifice will come in, Marcus."

"Sacrifice? Would we call it that? I don't think so. I think it's a wonderful opportunity."

"WHAT?"

"Your marriage to my daughter, Avina. A truly lovely girl."

"My marriage.."

"You see the idea of a northern and southern power is feasible, even desirable, in times of conflict against a common enemy. However, when peace comes, which we all pray will be quickly, there might be a temptation for one of the parties to feel that he has done more, or deserves more, thus assuring an internal conflict. The best way of avoiding this scenario.. is.. if the two parts are united in some way, and what better way than marriage?"

*

"Do sit, nephew, it has been a morning of messages, I think they will interest you greatly."

"And where is my *superior* officer?"

"Shall we call this a family get together rather than a meeting of the High Command? Don't be too harsh on Kunimund; his skills are as considerable as his caution is annoying. One fact that can't be denied is that he is well loved by his men; they know that he cares for them. It doesn't matter how good a general may be, if he's not followed, and followed enthusiastically, then the day is easily lost."

Egica didn't try to speak, he knew what he knew. Disputing facts would get him nowhere.

Brandishing two scrolls, "I received and read this one first, it didn't make a great deal of sense until I read this other one. So, I'll give you them in logical rather than chronological order."

"The nub of this one, is that General Paulus seems to have gone native."

Pausing for effect and getting none, he went to explain how he'd dispatched a smallish force under the command of Paulus to Tarraco, in order to point out the error of the ways of those once loyal subjects. What transpired though, was that instead of convincing the usurpers to come meekly back into the fold after being given a couple of minor concessions, Paulus has written a message supporting the legitimacy of their grievances with the suggestion of the acceptance of most. This, in his opinion, would help avoid the resulting independence that non acquiescence would result in.

"In all but declaration, he has sided with them, even suggesting more comprehension on the application of the laws against Jews. This news shocked me as I both trusted and liked Paulus, certainly the best leader of men I have seen on this campaign. I can't imagine what has turned his head so dramatically. He signs it *your humble servant* so perhaps not all is lost, still….."

"This rebellion was all the talk of the town before I left Toletum. As if they could consider declaring a new state just because they don't feel valued enough! Then to add insult to injury, to provoke, rile and agitate those vermin, the Jews against the power of the state, how low can you get? I tell you, the bishops were hopping mad. Excommunication and annihilation were two words bounded about."

"Interesting. That fully explains the content of this message from those bishops."

Most of the content was old hat to Egica, having heard practically nothing but in the corridors of power. He wasn't important enough to hear any of it directly as he was doing now, but court exists on gossip and conspiracy talks. This one had the lot, tales of intrigue involving dukes, counts and bishops, all conspiring with the Frankish enemy, to eventually destroy the kingdom with the help of the Jews. Feeling against Tarraconensis/Gallia Gothica, which rarely was positive, as it was believed that the people of that area were trying to live on the past glories of the Roman age by always sneering and looking down their noses at the *new* centre of power, was now at a fever pitch of hatred.

"This is the part that concerns you; *General Egica is to return to Toletum immediately to take charge of a force that is being gathered here.*"

Wamba went on to explain that the new forces that Egica had brought with him, were to remain and be integrated into the army already present. "You know what, Egica, it's great being king. Everyone, it seems, makes all the decisions for you. It's really easy, you ought to try it one day."

Wamba, in his usual affable self, started a lament that was to last quite some time. Actually agreeing with all of the content of the bishops' message, his main problem was his lack of involvement in the process. He would have proposed Egica as well, as it kept family above the squabbles of the barons, all of whom believed for one reason or another, they were superior to the others. What chaffed, was that he'd been denied any input. Knowing that he was a new king and his ascendancy to this position was a direct result of the intervention of the bishops, he wasn't strong enough to oppose their collective might. Never having sought this exulted role, he needed time to adapt. Once settled, he was determined to wrest power from the clergy and bring it back to the monarchy, the traditional Goth leadership way; the first among equals, until then he would bide his time and bite his tongue. Once back in Toletum at the head of a massive victorious army, the people would see him in a different light, giving him the power and backing to start to take on the bishops.

"And I expect you to be by my side in that fight."

"Uncle, you know you can count on me."

Egica was pleased to get out of the tent, needing time to reflect, this privilege being bestowed on him by all the powers that be, boded well for his future. Not wanting to get back too soon to Toletum, the petty positioning and re-positioning of the barons would take some time, he really did not want to be involved in that playground dispute, it'd be better to float in once the hierarchy among them had been decided. His thoughts ran to having a bit of fun, he'd take a few trusted men and have a nice time getting back via many a tavern.

Kunimund was next to appear in the command tent, "You sent for me, sir."

Wamba outlined the situation to his senior general.

"We need to speed up negotiations with the prisoner's family. Release him to get in touch with his father and arrange a meeting as soon as possible."

The tent flap let out the second general of the morning and let in the third. The same information was relayed to Alaric with the additional fact that Wamba hadn't told Kunimund, "I shall be leading the troops from here and I expect you to accompany me. General Kunimund is important to the peace process, so shall remain here with some forces to make sure of compliance. I have yet to inform him, I would be grateful if you didn't."

Alaric promised to be as silent as the tomb and thanked the king for his trust in him.

"One thing that really bugs me though, is why Paulus would take up their cause so easily. You were more or less friends, can you think of anything that would turn him against us?"

"None, Sire, I always thought him a most loyal character."

"Do you think that boy, what was his name, the disaster of a soldier that was sent to us from Tarraco?"

"Marcus."

"Yes, that's it. Do you think he has had a persuasive influence on Paulus?"

"I doubt that very much, Sire, he didn't have what you might call a dominant character. Rumour has it that he was not even able to fuck that slave girl he got from the fighting."

"I wonder what it is. I really did like Paulus."

"As did I, Sire."

"A most diverting fellow."

*

"What are you making?"

"I wish I knew. Your father told me some of the things I couldn't use, so I went down to the market and bought some of those you could."

"I don't think we've ever had it the way you are doing it. It looks, errm, lovely and very different."

Arantxa wasn't sure if this was a compliment or not, still, she was doing her best. What was of more interest, was where Rebecca had been and *what* she'd been doing .

"I was getting really worried. I couldn't tell your father that you'd gone off with the general cos he's a goy, isn't he?

"Who's been teaching you this vocabulary?"

"Never you mind, quick learner, me. Anyway, what worried me was that he was a man, a military man, and I've seen how they are with women, and with you being gone so long, I had to ask someone for help."

"Oh no," premonition of disaster looming, "who?"

"I wasn't spoilt for choice, was I? In the end, about a couple of hours ago I sent one of the little kids at the end of the street with a message to Marcus."

"Oh shit, you wrote a message to Marcus?"

"You know I can't write, it was oral, just saying; *don't know where Rebecca is, do you*?"

Within the whole concept of disaster possibilities, this wasn't so bad, presuming Marcus had enough sense not to ask the wrong people, which was a lot to presume with Marcus though.

"Show me which kid, so I can tell him to tell Marcus, I'm back."

Leaving things cooking, they popped out of the front of the house to find the street, and the whole area devoid of children. There were not even children's noises coming from anywhere.

"There were loads earlier."

"I'll have to go myself"

"You can't, it'd make things worse. Leave it a while, we'll keep checking the street, one will turn up soon, unless they are all in cooking pots. I promise I haven't gone completely Jewish by cooking one."

Rebecca smiled for the first time since arriving home. Arantxa linked arms setting them on a path back to the kitchen. "Now, will you tell me what happened?"

Sparing few details, besides her feelings, which she wasn't sure of herself, she did.

"You have that look on your face."

(319)

"What look?"

"The Aitziber's look! You are falling or have fallen for him."

"No, no, no."

"I wouldn't mistake that look anywhere. Oh, Rebecca, please be careful." These last words were heartfelt and followed by a meaningful emotional hug.

"So this is the way things are! I trudge the streets looking for a lost Jewess only to find her hugging another woman in her own kitchen." Marcus had wandered around uptown, down by the amphitheatre and even along the beach, then back through the docks, before finally coming back into port area in order to report his lack of success.

Actually being pleased to get the note, he was sure nothing untoward would have happened to Rebecca, not in the company of Flavius, it gave him an excuse to get out and think about what he'd been told, and as yet had been unable to react or respond to.

After Chlodoswintha had delivered the blow, he felt he could say nothing, leaving the table he picked up his sword, headed into the backyard, where he used to practise with Pere, to continue his training by himself.

Cutting, thrusting, jabbing and above all hitting, made him feel, if not better, at least numb.

If a charging lion had come full tilt around a corner with every intention in the world of devouring him, he may have noticed. Otherwise, he saw, noticed very little, he may have passed right next to Rebecca seventy-two times, or none, his head was awhirl and his eyes unseeing. What was he to do? There wasn't one line of thought worth pursuing, they all led to the inevitable; his marriage to a *truly lovely* girl. Never having given the idea any thought whatsoever, marriage seemed a frightening and most unwelcome prospect. Being the sole heir to the duchy of Tarraco was something he's always lived with, it having its advantages and disadvantages, but marriage when so young and inexperienced, was never even an idle future speculation. Now, it was a reality.

"Ohh Marcus, you're here. I was just about to send you a note." Unclasping herself from Arantxa she saw instead of just hearing her childhood playmate. "God, you're so pale, you look awful, are you well? Come, sit. What's the matter?"

He allowed himself to be shepherded to one of the kitchen chairs where he sat blank faced.

"I'm going to have to get married."

*

The smell of cooking greeted the two horse riders as they pulled into the Els Munts area.

The scribe, true to his word, had demonstrated fine horsemanship on the way back. Conversation is always difficult at a canter, and the general appreciated that the scribe didn't try, nor had questioned the fact that his superior office was in a dishevelled state on a beach far from anywhere. Upon arriving in Tarraco, he'd asked around as to the whereabouts of the general, only to be met with blank faces. Finally, an elderly woman carrying a significant amount of washing said she saw two people wandering up the beach; a big broad man and a young woman. Not having other clues, the big broad man was the best he'd heard, he thought the horses might as well have a gallop across the sands. He was about to give up when upon nearing the rocks of the second beaches, when the general, in his state, appeared. The only thing he said was "It wasn't easy to find you sir."

To which he received the reply that he had and it was a job well done. There was no sign of the said young woman though.

"Supper must have started without us, sir."

"Evidently."

Upon entering the house he was met by Milo, "Thought we'd lost you, sir."

"Thought or hoped?"

"Sir! That wish would never cross the lips or go through the mind of any soldier here. Truth be told sir, everyone is exceptionally happy with this sojourn by the sea. There is some unease however as to what our role is here, and how long it may last."

"Men keen to get back home, are they?"

"Not at all, sir. Home is a relative concept for most of the men here, they are professional solders, home is where the sword and shield is."

"What is it then?"

"They really like it here, and would like to stay longer."

"Well, you may inform the men that their wish is a reality for the foreseeable future. I have asked the king to clarify our position, also mentioning that I believe some of the grievances of this region are legitimate. Let's see how he reacts."

*

"What!"

The two females reacted with the same word, there the similarity stopped, it was one word said with two distinctly differing emotions. Arantxa collapsed into a chair as if winded by a goat moving at high speed hitting her in the midriff. Rebecca moved towards Marcus, full of concern and *wh* questions; who, where, when and finally the most important why.

While he related what had been told to him by the countess, and to a lesser extent his father, Arantxa didn't look up, not having recovered from the blow - tough things these hurtling goats, whereas Rebecca had drawn up a chair very close to his so that they were almost touching and played the role of active concerned listener. The thing was, she wasn't *playing*, genuinely she was concerned.

"So, as son and heir, I am expected to do my filial duty."

"I always thought men had it good, it was only girls who had their husbands chosen for them. Evidently you rich have different rules. Do you know anything about her besides that her mother says that she's *a truly lovely girl*?"

"I know she's thirteen. Really, it doesn't matter what I know, nor what she's like, I have to do what is expected of me."

Rebecca took his hand, a gesture that surprised and embarrassed them both, "I don't suppose you want to go back yet to your house to see the countess and your father. Stay here for supper. We'll send a note, Arantxa has already set up a direct messenger service to your house."

"What, stay here to eat, in a Jewish house?"

Rather than be offended, Rebecca realised this was not a normal thing to do, it was going to be difficult for her father to understand as well. Theirs had the reputation of being a most hospitable house among the Jewish community; it wasn't unusual to have people, besides family, eating there, but the son of the duke, this would be a first.

"Strange, isn't it? And it gets weirder, a heathen is cooking!"

The drained pallid face rose to see a smiling encouraging Rebecca awkwardly holding the hand of the man she…would never have.

*

Chlodoswintha was politely late for supper, and made no apologies for being so, to the already waiting, not so patient Duke.

"I see the table is set for two, Marcus not joining us?"

"Apparently not, I've just received a note from him saying that he'd be dining out this evening."

"Dining out, in your own city, what a strange concept. I suppose he must be with that general. I do hope he's not divulging too many of our secrets."

The annoyance was there to see as Ranosindus strove to keep a level amicable tone, "I am not sure what *secrets* we have that my son could, or would, want to give away to the enemy. Furthermore, I don't think he's with Paulus, the note came from a child from port area according to Amalaswinth."

"Port area? What's that?"

"The port area. I believe that Rebecca's family lives down there."

"Oh, intrigue upon intrigue, consorting with our allies not our enemies." Chlodoswintha wasn't a completely insensitive woman, although it paid to appear that way at times. She could see that Ranosindus was no longer doting on her and her words, she was just more than a little reluctant to accept the situation because she really did like the man and found him impressively attractive. It was true that he wasn't much use in bed, those things though, could be taught if the pupil is willing to learn, and it must be said that the duke was showing inclination to wanting to be top of the class.

"Consorting. You do choose some strange words. It's much more probable that he needs some sort of consolation after what you said at lunch."

"My dear duke, it needed to be said at some time."

"I agree, but you didn't have to blurt it out like that. We could have spent some time building up to it."

"Blurted out! You make it sound as if it was something terrible he has to do. It isn't, my daughter is.."

"*A truly lovely girl.* We all know. My son though, was not contemplating marriage to anyone, truly lovely or not. It has come as a shock. Even you must see that it is life changing. It'll take him time to get used to the idea, and if that means talking it through with an intelligent girl who he has known all his life, then so be it."

"It seems to me, dear Ranosindus, that whatever I do or say, causes displeasure, Perhaps I ought to go back to Nemausus in the morning." At that moment the food was brought to the table thus enforcing a ceasefire between two people who had said more than either of them wanted to. Ranosindus was wondering whether her going was a good or a bad thing; if the woman weren't quite so bossy, he would like her much more. Chlodoswintha had made the threat expecting it to be rejected and compromise deal of a day or two more would be agreed. To her chagrin the enforced silence continued well after the servant had withdrawn.

"That's settled then, I'll leave in the morning."

*

"Alright, say it."

"Say what?"

"The food wasn't the greatest you've ever tasted."

"The food wasn't the greatest I have ever tasted."

"I knew, I knew, you were being polite at the table saying it was lovely."

"Can't both statements be true? It was lovely, but not the greatest I have ever tasted. I have been living off army rations for god knows how long, and I can assure you it was MUCH better than I tasted there."

Arantxa and Marcus had gone for a post supper stroll.

Politeness and surprise were the two words that could have summed up the meal. Jacob being the leading exponent of both. Surprise in that he had no idea what the thing he was eating was, even though he was told that he had suggested it, and politeness to find his table populated with an assortment of people he could never have imagined there; a non god believing foreigner, and the son of the duke. His initial worry was what they would talk about; at first glance they did not appear to have a great deal in common. He need not have worried as his first born took it upon herself to talk ceaselessly about very little or nothing, not excluded from the conversation, nor requiring him to participate with much more than affirmatives or facial grimaces, was fine by him. The poor boy at the other end of the table had even less to do. The females just talked over him, leaving him to pick his way through the thing on his plate which clearly he was not enjoying. All in all, it wasn't a chirpy fun culinary pleasure, relief being felt once it was over.

His ever practical daughter more or less threw the two guests out, telling them to go for a walk while she cleaned up the kitchen, despite the protestations of the other woman. Jacob made a beeline to his office not caring to know what was going on.

The night was getting lighter as a nearly full moon was beginning to make its appearance to compete with the unmistakable redness of Mars sitting just above the horizon.

"That's Llazki."

"No it isn't, it's the moon."

"She's the daughter of mother earth and before sunrise, she usually returns to her mother."

The conversation then moved onto disagreements about what the early, first to be visible, constellations were called. It was a playful fight with comments like "How could you see a bear in that combination?", "You must be blind or have a vivid imagination," or "That's plainly ridiculous." In the end they agreed to disagree as they both claimed victory.

The atmosphere was relaxed and fun, even when the topic of her cooking was broached and successfully navigated.

Having passed the sparsely populated port area, they were heading for the totally deserted beach. Arantxa felt relaxed and confident in his company, so much so, that she linked her arm through his the way she used to with her sister. This comfortable feeling didn't detract from her overriding emotion; sadness. Knowing that it was ludicrous to feel this way, she tried to keep it in check with reasoning. Her conversation with Rebecca had brought into the verbal what she had already thought. She knew and re-knew that a relationship with Marcus would never happen, more than would never, could never. Their social status had made that abundantly clear. Reason and emotion are like oil and water, they don't mix, as she'd heard said, the problem with the two was that you can't reason yourself out of something you didn't reason yourself into in the first place.

"Want to talk about it?"

"The truth is, I don't even want to think about it, never mind talk about it."

Squeezing his arm a little, she kept a respectful silence.

"It's just so unfair. I'm too young to be pushed into something like this."

"My sister was fourteen when my father gave her to one of his buddies who was unpleasant, old, fat, and fairly impotent. At least you are getting *a truly lovely girl*. Actually, thinking about it, she's a year younger than Aitziber was, so I don't imagine she's that keen on the whole business either." There was enough light to see her head tilted in his direction with a broad smile.

"Do you think that I am all of those things you said about your sister's husband. What were they again; unpleasant, old, fat and impotent?"

Her head still tilted, her smile changed to a pensive pose, "I know you are not two of them. You are the same age as me, so you can't be old, and evidently you are not fat."

Stopping, unlinking their arms, he gently held her shoulders turning her to face him.

"So, you think I am a horrible person and impotent, do you?" The tone of playful flirtiness with which the conversation had started was pushed up another notch as she delayed her response. "Well, at times you are not awfully pleasant to me, and as for the other, by your own admission, nobody knows whether that is true or not."

She had miscalculated, thinking that he'd find this funny and part of the banter; his deflation into almost a saggy person was immediate. "I suppose you're right. I'm sorry if I have been unpleasant to you, it has not been my intention."

Another sorry from another man of rank and importance to an *inferior* female. This strange phenomenon had reached epidemic proportions.

"As to the other *thing*, I suppose I will find out on my wedding night."

"That would be a disaster. Two people not knowing what they are doing. At thirteen, I don't imagine she will have had any experience."

"Are you suggesting that I go and avail myself of the offers of the ladies of the night?"

"That would be one way to learn and it wouldn't be forcing anyone, something you have eloquently expressed revulsion in doing, and something I respect you greatly for not doing."

"So, I need classes, do I? Pere taught me the arts of war, various tutors have attempted to open the world of letters and numbers to me, and now I need a prostitute to open a completely new world. Interesting. Forever the student, me."

"Look, Marcus, the first time, it's going to be bloody and she'll probably be in a great deal of pain, if you are not calm, she may panic."

"How do you know so much?"

"Oh, Marcus, don't be so naïve, I am sixteen. I was brought up in a rural village where animals are doing it all the time, don't you think that I ...., do you?"

The pause screamed that he did think that she was still a virgin.

"I vaguely remember you saying that you'd been promised in marriage but.."

A shadow crossed her face and all the lightness of the conversation evaporated, "Yes, I was promised first to an elderly relative, then to my cousin Iñaki, as reward for restoring the family pride by murdering my sister. I never did anything with him, the dirty cowardly scumbag."

"I've never heard that expression before; I suppose it's a translation of something you say in your language."

"Look Marcus, if you want to know whether I have had sex with other men, then the answer is no, but boys, well, there were a few experiments. And I can tell you that the first is bloody horrible, well, it was in my case. I bled for the whole of two days and was sore for much longer."

"And you did it again after that negative experience."

"Of course. It's also very pleasurable and the feeling is better when you are with the right person. If I'd been a virgin, there was no way I would have even attempted the *ordeal* with that shit Caius."

Marcus was having problems absorbing this new information. "Lighten up, Marcus. Sex can be fun. My poor sister didn't find out until she met the general. Her husband was a total disaster and it wasn't for lack of experience, he was over twice her age."

"So what do you have to do to be *good*?"

"Like the person you are with, and be interested in the pleasure for both. Well, that's the way I see it, which admittedly is a woman's point of view. From what I heard from the other women in the village, most of their men were just interested in shooting their load and then sleeping. The boys I played with tended not to last long but were usually willing to try again, and it was better the second time. It also helped when they had good *equipment*."

"Good equipment!"

"Yes, you can't shear a sheep with a blunt knife, can you?"

"Blunt knife!"

"Stop repeating what I say, you know what I mean. You don't need to worry though."

"What!"

"Your tools looked fine to me that day you tried to kill me by throwing me against the rocks down by the river. Thankfully the general came to save me and my honour."

"I didn't try to kill you or take your honour!"

"The more's the pity, I think."

If the words weren't clear enough, there was no mistaking the look.

*

Rabbi Hillel left THE meeting absolutely seething. It couldn't have gone worse if he'd planned it to, however, as he often remarked; every cloud... The silver lining in this case was he would be able to destroy that woman, who didn't know nor accept her place in society. He would make sure that she did, and would make an example of her that would make any woman thinking of following in her footsteps, think twice. It wasn't just her, it was bigger than her, the whole alignment of Jewish society in Tarraco was wrong. From what he had gleaned from other Tarraco Jews, the father was as much, if not more, to blame, having not given the child the correct education, and instead, doting on her, some rumours had it, going so far as to treat her like a boy by teaching her to read from the Torah. Others might be tempted to see this as a rotten apple; his belief was that it was symptomatic of a rotten barrel of apples which needed some radical cleansing before Judaism in Tarraco was completely corrupted. This was his new mission in life.

"Rabbi, Rabbi, I have news that may interest you." This was delivered by a shrivelled little man, "My wife says that Jacob has employed a non-believer, who has no idea about caixer, as a cook, and this evening the duke's son is having supper there."

Hillel thanked the man and while showing him the door demanded that if his wife should have any more information or details to please facilitate them to him.

This cloud's lining was not silver, it was gold. Gentiles, infidels, no attempt at keeping caixer, all added ammunition, it may be possible to include the whole family in the cherem.

*

A new routine had been established in Jacob's house without him noticing nor wanting to notice, too much. The only annoyance, as far as he was concerned, was the house, despite clear evidence of the two women sweeping, never seemed as clean as it used to, with the presence of sand forever present. The crunchy underfoot sound and feel was one that he particularly despised and not knowing its source and the efforts to rectify the situation that were ongoing, he supposed he'd have to get used to it, at least until the wind from the sea stopped blowing.

The new girl was really very pleasant, solicitous to his needs, and was even beginning to make passable food. In the division of labour between her and Rebecca, Arantxa was in charge of supper and Rebecca controlled the other two meals. Both girls were lively, bubbly and looked very happy with life, which made eating together fun, if somewhat draining from his point of view, especially when they started to chortle, which they did regularly, at some in-joke between them. Being left out of their conspiratorial relationship didn't perturb him in the least, in fact, he was extremely happy that Rebecca was so distracted. The cherem was set for post Shabbat which was tomorrow; he'd spent the last three days with considerable foreboding and brooding on the matter, hidden away in his office. The only person he'd spoken to, business was slow at this time of the year, was his brother, and that was a mistake, he made everything feel worse rather than better.. Poor Isaac, even as a little child he was a worrier, and now having his ear chewed off daily by Trudi, his worrying reached stratospheric proportions.

Initially he wasn't particularly in favour of the foreign girl staying, her not being Jewish, he thought would bring problems nevertheless quite the contrary was true, her adaption to every part of their lives and her close relationship with his daughter was a boon. Whatever happened tomorrow, these few days had been happy, except for the amount of sand.

Rebecca placed blame on Arantxa, whereas Arantxa believed it was inevitable, and Rebecca was as much to blame. Sand came back with them. These fights usually took place while preparing lunch, their time to exchange intimacies and accusations.

The day after her night walk with Marcus, Arantxa had said little. Rebecca, who shared her room with her, had heard her come in; it was late, very late, in fact it was so late it could have been described as early. Not asking for any explications, she was offered none, just the usual chit-chat and instructions about how to use ingredients filled the kitchen.

On her walk to meet Flavius for the second time, her head was a mix of thoughts. What had Arantxa done / what would she do? She was given plenty of time for these thoughts to come to fruition, be discarded and started again, over and over, as it was a fair distance to *their* beach. As they had set no particular time, she'd set off as soon as she decently could without drawing too much attention to herself, and had had to wait, and wait, and wait. Toying with the idea of leaving, he had finally turned up.

Apparently the great military mind had confused the beaches and had been waiting on one much farther up the coast closer to Els Munts than Tarraco. He lived to regret giving her this information, as she tortured him mercilessly with irony and jibes. A lot of the irony he didn't quite understand, the jibes though hit their target with great accuracy. How he wished he'd lied and said he'd been delayed at the camp.

Once off his horse, he'd started with the apologies and an almost careless kiss on the cheek. This was the same action as they had finished on, one which caused her a poor night's sleep, and it felt NOTHING like the one she'd just been given. The first was full of exciting promise, this was, punctuation among the apologies. It was her disappointment that had made her quite so sharp in her mocking of his mistaken beach.

With the horse tied to a scrub type bush, they sat in the same place as they had done the previous day and after her chastisement, yesterday's initial embarrassed silence also returned. Having both made a considerable effort to be there, it felt as if neither did really want to be sitting on the sand with the far away horizon offering the same as their conversation, everything and nothing.

Rebecca shrieked, a noise that might have been heard for hundreds of miles and managed to frighten both the general and the causer of the shriek, the horse. The bush offering little interest or resistance, the animal had easily pulled it out by its roots and had wandered over to nuzzle into the neck of this stranger sitting next to the master. Not expecting this reaction the horse galloped away, and didn't stop until it reached the rocks at the far end of the beach, where it was debating whether to jump up on them to continue its escape, or take notice of the calming calling of its master. The rocks, not being the ones it had arrived over, lost their allure; it waited patiently for its cooing master to come closer.

Bringing the horse back, talking reassuringly to it all the way to the seated beach section, he called out to Rebecca, "You frightened him."

"I frightened him! He frightened me!"

" Come and make friends."

Reluctantly and fearfully Rebecca made her way across to the animal and its holder. "He's not going to bite or kick, is he?"

"Improbable unless you do first."

This statement got a derisory scowl as she reached out to touch the space between the ears. In reaction the horse shook its head making Rebecca almost jump backwards.

"If you show fear, he'll notice. Be confident." Flavius was slapping the side of its neck affectionately. Rebecca's second approach was done more confidently; she joined in the neck slapping motion which didn't seem to displease the animal.

"That was a hell of a squeal. This horse is trained for battle and has never shied away even when men have been screaming, stabbing and slashing at him. You evidently are one frightening woman."

"You'd better believe it. Take note from your horse!"

Tied back to a sturdier looking bush, the horse was happy to no longer be in the limelight. The humans resumed their sitting; the ice well and truly broken, conversation came much easier.

"Was it in one of these battles, when the horse wasn't scared, that you got that scar on your face?"

"That addition to my good looks is a recent acquisition, from a skirmish with the Vascones, as was the loss of this finger." Holding up the maimed hand.

Conversation began to flow, her, angling towards the part that involved Arantxa's sister, him saying firmly on the fighting front. Flavius answered some questions, avoided others by answering something completely different.

"So, who won?"

"When I left it was very much of a stalemate. Victory for the Vascones would be if we left, they could never win an outright battle against us. Victory for us, I don't know, some sort of peace treaty where the locals paid a money tribute as a sort of vassal state that we would allow to exist."

"Do you think that's the best case scenario for our situation?"

"I really don't know. By gathering so many, especially your people,"

"Our people?"

"The Jews. Many would see this as weakness rather than strength, which is how I view it, and I imagine the powers that be in Toletum would strive for an all out war as THE solution. If that happens, there will be only one victor. The numbers are weighed too heavily against Tarraconensis/Gallia Gothica."

Conversation continued along these politico-historical lines all afternoon until it was clear that it was getting late and Rebecca said that she HAD TO get back for supper.

Reluctantly, Flavius agreed and having his offer of a ride back on the horse well and truly rejected, they stood to say their goodbyes.

The embrace felt right and as they pulled away with great reluctance, she held her hand out to trace the scar on his face, "You must have been handsome once!"

Playfully he grasped her finger tracing arm and at the same time gave her a peck of a kiss, not on the cheek this time, but on the lips, "Still am."

Stepping back, more in a coquettish manner than rejection, she said, "Not bad."

before turning away, then hitching up her tunic to clamber across the rocks.

*

Marcus was still fast asleep when Chlodoswintha's carriage rolled out of the courtyard. Ranosindus nearly missed it as well. He'd had a fitful sleepless night, knowing that he could still change events if he wanted to. He was sure that a little excursion along the corridor would be well received by the occupant of the other room. His problem was, he had no desire to go crawling to her, having to apologise in an effort to make up. Feeling that he'd not done anything wrong, and being more than a little tired of being bullied, his inclination was to do nothing and see if she would come to him as she had back in Narbo. His ear perpetually cocked, sleep was hard to come by and when it did, not long lasting. One fairly loud noise in the very early hours made him wake totally, turn onto his other side so he could see the door, close his eyes tightly and pretend to be asleep. The door handle didn't turn and the creaking of an opening door came from the opposite direction to his hopes. Where had Marcus been until this time, was his last thought when he did finally fall asleep. The next sound that woke him was a great deal of banging downstairs. It was light. Jumping out of bed, throwing on some clothes he managed to reach the courtyard as Chlodoswintha was entering the carriage.
"Oh, Ranosindus, I really didn't want to disturb you however, these military men can be so noisy when getting ready. It's all the metal they have to wear I suppose."
"I thought you'd stay for breakfast at least."
"As I was awake and could see the sky darkening, I thought it'd be a good idea to get away before the downpour."
"You woke early."
"Actually, some of us didn't sleep. I heard you snoring. Marcus came in extremely late, I hope my future son-in-law wasn't up to any mischief." She almost winked, which surprised the duke. "Anyway, I'm sorry that you don't want me around, we could have had a bit more fun. Still, that's life. Doubtless we'll meet again to finalise all the marriage arrangements. I hope by that time you will have sorted out your interests and priorities. Until then, farewell, dearest duke." She gently dragged her left hand down his face before entering the carriage. True to form, he did nothing. The clouds of pre-rain dust from the accelerating wheels was the last he saw of her and he felt, well, he wasn't sure what he felt; sadness was one emotion, relief was another.
Marcus eventually came down late and offered no explanation for his tardy nocturnal arrival despite being asked by an almost conspiratorial

duke asking, who was trying in some way to regain the confidence he thought he used to have with his only child.

 The rest of the day they spent doing what they thought was most appropriate; control of finances in Ranosindus's case, spear and sword practice for Marcus. They met again at supper. Marcus was late coming to the table.

"Forgotten your manners in that army, you." Amalaswinth was bringing in the first course as he entered.

Stopping before his chair, glowering in her direction which was having no effect whatsoever as she was concentrating on not spilling the soup, he restored to a verbal approach.

"And you, Amalaswinth, need to learn your place, you are a servant and nothing else. I will no longer tolerate you speaking to me in that tone."

"Which tone may that be, Master Marcus?"

"As if I were five years old. I am not!"

"I'm terribly sorry, I am sure. You have come back from the wars all grown up, have you? Well, as I have always done *everything* for you since you were a baby, it might take me a little while to adjust."

Placing the soup on the table she struck a pose of false contriteness mixed with a secure defiance. To her surprise, the next attack came not from her baby boy, but from the duke himself.

"I find myself in total accord with my son. He is a man, taking on the responsibility of a man, and so, should be treated as such. If this adaption proves too difficult, then an alternative arrangement may be found for you."

For Amalaswinth this was a body blow and the second time in not so many days that she'd been threatened with the sack. She'd have to change tack by treading more softly in the house as she could not afford to lose this position.

"I apologise to you both and will endeavour to mend my ways." Trying to keep what pride she had left, she exited.

An almost formal expression of gratitude followed, "Thank you, father, for your support."

"Marcus, I am sorry. I am sorry for so many things, it's difficult to know where to start. The marriage thing was not my idea, nor was telling you so…abruptly."

"Father, I know it makes sense. I am not blind or stupid, just give me time to adjust, that's all."

Ranosindus saw the pain on the boy's face align itself with the determination of duty, causing a genuine feeling of pity for him.

Marcus was keen to get supper over and done with. Understanding his father's position, he didn't blame him. However, he did feel somewhat betrayed by him in that none of the BIG decisions ever required any input from him until it was too late to change anything. Firstly, this rebellion, call it what they will, that's what it was, had been brewed, meshed and served while he'd been sent to fight with the soon- to-be enemy forces. Where was the joined up thinking in that? From what he could work out, his banishment came about when these seditious ideas were in their infancy and thanks to Amalaswinth's malicious tongue spreading unfounded rumours about him and Rebecca, his father had had a rush of blood to the head. Furthermore, he doubted greatly that the marriage concept came from any of his father's thinking on the matter. The Lady Chlodoswintha showed her mettle in the meeting, giving the impression that she was the power. There was no throne yet, so she couldn't be behind it, without a doubt though, it was the future role she had mapped out for herself.

All these ideas were fighting for a place inside his head which was already completely full of thoughts and now memories.

Being the off-spring, more especially the male and only son of a duke, meant a life of learning, forever being taught something that would, you were told, prove useful or invaluable in adult life. Some of the teachers were excellent, as was the case with Pere. A little too harsh at times, excellent nevertheless, as he had found out in his campaigning experience. The procession of numbers and letters teachers showed that none of them had the talent or patience to stay. The frustration of a couple was so patent that they could not continue regardless of the amount of money they were offered. They could not understand how, or why, he couldn't understand, and despite chastisement and sometimes beatings, the light didn't shine through. Eventually, one poor cleric managed to make some headway. The price was high, it nearly cost him his vocation and belief in God. Marcus could now say that he was competent with both numbers and letters, better the former than the latter.

His latest teacher was superb. After just one session he thought that he was getting the hang of it and keen to continue classes in a short while down on the beach once it got sufficiently dark. Admittedly, his first attempt didn't go too well, as the teacher said; he showed a little too much enthusiasm. The second was described as "an improvement", the third and final, just before it started getting light, was given the comparatively glowing report of "almost acceptable." His aim tonight was to rid himself of the almost.

Arantxa had been mega patient and encouraging. Patently, she had quite a bit of knowledge and experience to share. Between bouts, they lay looking at the stars avoiding conversation about anything connected to feelings or future arrangements; no straying into the unknown territories of politico-history was called for, so they talked around their childhoods. Arantxa's seemed pretty awful - beatings, duty and work were the order of the years, with all there being present in differing quantities at different stages. There was no mention of tutors. The only high point, the rest wasn't said with any poor-me tone, it was what it was, no different to anyone else, was her relationship with her big sister. Knowing how that story ended, and not wanting to give too much contrast to his pampered existence, he tried to move conversation onto firmer ground; Rebecca. With this he hit the jackpot. Having known Rebecca for just a few days, she was already under that spell that Rebecca weaved, talking about her in terms that echoed some of those used about her elder sister. When it was his turn to talk about the Jewess, he spoke about his admiration for her, and reluctant as he was to admit it, he was caught in her web as well. Arantxa's short monosyllabic replies showed that there was something wrong. This point hadn't been on tonight's lesson plan. Nevertheless it was an invaluable learning experience; never talk in glowing terms about another woman when you are lying next to a naked one. Trying to row back by saying things like she could never be considered as sexual etc., really didn't help his cause much. His anguished attempts of rectification were finally brought to an end by Arantxa initiating the third bout.

*

Clambering onto the last set of rocks before arriving at *their* beach, Rebecca couldn't yet see the horse although its naying was audible, meaning that Flavius was already there. This surprised her as she thought that by arriving early, she'd have time and space to settle and get her thoughts straight. Throughout her walk here she turned over and over in her head what the afternoon might bring besides rain, the clouds were threatening. This would be their third time together and possibly their last. Tomorrow it would prove impossible to leave the house; the family Shabbat meal had to be prepared, with Isaac, Trudi and David present, which would lead to the probability of Trudi appearing at some point with an extra dish, or some *essential* advice on how to cook something. There would be no leaving the house the whole day of Shabbat, and then it was the night that her future may be changed forever, the meeting, which she would be excluded from, to decide on a cherem against her.
Try as she might, she couldn't get those thoughts of dire consequences out of her brain. Needless to say, this entire future imperfect, affected the present. How should she approach the horse's owner, with the tenderness that the last one finished on, or with caution?
If it weren't for the possible consequences of the cherem, she'd be clear, allow this, whatever it was, *relationship* perhaps, to grow slowly. Then the elephant in the room would appear, how could there be *any* relationship, fast or slow, he's a goy!

Seeing her coming, he moved to the edge of the rocks, to help her down he took her firmly around the waist and lifted her onto the sand. Quite expecting some protestation or a push away once she was safely grounded, he was as surprised as she was, when her arms moved around his neck and their faces were brought together. It was the kiss of the starving. Her experience in this field was precisely nil, his considerable, however, only one person dominated, controlling the rhythm and pressure. Insufficient air was the main culprit in the cessation of proceedings. Physical space made visibility of each other possible.
"Hello."
"Hello, Scarface."

*

"My darling, you've decided to return, I see."
"Oh, Hilderic, don't tell me you've come down to greet my carriage just to chastise me? I have been travelling for two days and had to spend a god-awful night in a dreadful inn. The least you could do is kiss and embrace a woman you once said you loved and is now to-ing and fro-ing for you."
Doing as requested, he apologised in such a believable way that she had no choice but to forgive him.
"If you invite Argebaud and Gunhild for supper, I will give my report back then. Now, I am totally exhausted and intend to rest for what is left of the afternoon."
With that announcement, which brooked little discussion, she wearily made her way to her bedroom. Before falling into a quasi comatose state, she spent some seconds pondering; were all men weak, or was she too strong for her own good. The result was the same; she wasn't happy.
The table was set for five, she wondered who the fifth was. She didn't have to wait too long to see the ex-abbot, now bishop, strut in. It hadn't taken him long to grow into his role.
During the meal everyone was polite and solicitous concerning her welfare and the tiresome journey she must have had. They gave her the scant gossip and happenings in Nemausus since her departure. The Franks had sent representatives giving their wholehearted support, promising men and supplies whenever they were needed.
"We see this as a dual edge sword. If they arrive too soon, then it'll be all out war between the two kingdoms on our territory, with us as the major sufferers, if they come in late, then they could just absorb us the way that Toletum is doing now." Her husband explained.
With everyone explaining things to her and using her as a reference, she felt compelled to compare it to the way she'd been treated by a Jew in

Tarraco who wanted her removed from the meeting because of her gender. Her story-telling provoked different reactions. The most surprising, by far, was metropolitan bishop Argebaud, all but shouting after some face scrunching, "Hillel. Hillel, that's his name."

Chlodoswintha was agog, "You're correct. How did you know that?"

"The Church blesses some of us with extraordinary powers."

"Horse shit!" The count's expletive was both loud and rude.

"My dear count, the ways of the Lord are mysterious to some, but to others.."

"Ariel! I saw Rabbi Abraham here yesterday. It surprised me, him travelling up from Gerunda. He told me he'd dispatched Rabbi Ariel to Tarraco on an important mission." Gunhild, who had been quiet throughout, as if he had more important matters on his mind, which perhaps he did, as it was his portfolio to negotiate with the Franks, suddenly and dramatically joined the conversation.

"As I said the ways of the Lord are.."

Chlodoswintha's interest was piqued, "I'm sure they are, metropolitan bishop, but what did Abraham say?"

"Only that there was a new Rabbi in Tarraco called Hillel, who was a little on the problematic side. The story of his demanding your expulsion from the meeting was one of the highlights. In point of fact, he said that you were not the target of his attack, you were more collateral damage as it were."

"That's true. The main attack was against a pretty little girl who Ranosindus has taken a shine to and appointed as the official interlocutor of the Jewish community."

"A girl to represent the Jewish community! Well she must be VERY pretty, Never heard the like of it. Is Ranosindus being led by his dick?" The count scoffed, he was enjoying every second of this, thinking that his wife had designs on the duke, only to see his interests lay decades younger.

"It seems not just the duke. Abraham also informed me that Bishop Cyprianus was well and truly enamoured as well, but was totally anti this girl as she had spurned his advances."

"Oh, this gets better. What an incredible temptress she must be. We really need to meet her. Is there any way.."

"I have met her and she is a beauty as I mentioned earlier, but she's also exceptionally intelligent and speaks impressively well, much better than a lot of the men I have had the misfortune to suffer." Poignantly, she took in all the others in the room.

Gunhild thought this was the right moment to ask Lady Chlodoswintha whether she'd made any progress on the main problem - Tarraco accepting that Count Hilderic should be proclaimed king as soon as possible.

"The answer to your question Bishop is, *yes* and *no*. Yes, in that the leadership should without doubt come from Nemausus, no, in that it should permanently be placed here."

This caused everyone to start speaking at the same time with nobody listening. Chlodoswintha bade her time, allowing them to talk themselves out, as there was no dialogue, only statements varying from annoyance to potential declarations of war; it wasn't long before they became silent.

"The compromised deal we considered the best, is that for the duration of the conflict ALL military decisions should come through one unified command, under the leadership of Count Hilderic. Once peace has been gained and consolidated, then we shall crown a king who combines both houses. Ranosindus's son will marry our daughter Avina. We also agreed that this marriage should take place as soon as possible, certainly before Christ Mass."

*

"You're later than yesterday, I'm not sure how to cook this, can I..? Are you alright? Have you got your period?"

Rebecca was wiping her legs and the smell of blood was definitely present. "Doesn't your religion say that you are *unclean*, and you shouldn't touch food or something ridiculous like that? Don't worry; I'll finish supper, just tell me what I shouldn't, or can't do with this chicken."

"No, I haven't got my period."

The two women looked at each other for a very short time then Arantxa squealed with delight grabbing her friend by the arms and pulling her in for a bone breaking hug. "Congratulations!"

"I'm not sure."

"Well, you'd better be, cos it's too late now to go back!"

"I didn't intend it to happen. It hurt."

"I hope it happened more than once, and I bet the second time didn't hurt as much."

"No, it was quite pleasurable."

"Only quite! Girl, you need to practise more."

"So it does get better then?"

"Ohhh, yes! Well I never, you and Marcus both being de-flowered in the same week and surprisingly not together."

"You haven't been, have you?

"Where do you think I go to every night?"

"I thought you went to look at stars."

"They do get seen. Horizontal is a good position to see them."

"Arantxa!"

"What? Don't tell me you did it standing up or doggy style?"

"Arantxa!"

In this house it was usually her name that was used as an expression of shock or surprise and by her father. The daughter seemed to have inherited the trait.

"I don't suppose that there are that many stars to see in the afternoon."

The women laughed and hugged again. Arantxa explained that the bleeding usually stopped quite quickly, but she, herself, had bled for two days.

"I won't be able to see him again at least for two, possibly never."

"He can't be so callous, getting what he wanted and…"

"No, no, it's me, well, my religion as you call it. Tomorrow is Shabbat. Nobody leaves the house that day. Then when that's over, the cherem will take place."

"Oh dear. Not sure what all that means, but, oh dear."

"It'll affect you as well." Rebecca explained the impossibility of having a non believer and her Aunt all on Shabbat in one house, "It means we'll have to find another place for you for a day or so. We'll go to talk to, or better said, be talked at, by Antonia after supper."

Arantxa's bright fire of happiness had been doused in one short sentence, and it showed.

"You'll be able to come back after Shabbat, don't worry"

"It's not that, it's.."

Rebecca realised what was happening. "He won't have to wait too long. We'll make some sort of excuse to Antonia for you, anyway, waiting is a good thing. Make him fret a bit, then he'll appreciate what he's getting!"

Jacob was really struggling to understand any part of these conversations around the supper table. Perfectly innocuous words like sand or stars set the girls off into peals of laughter and other strange comments. It wasn't disagreeable; he just wished that he understood. Yet again, thinking about it, it was probably better he didn't understand. The only thing that he did know was that Rebecca was happy, and at least not overtly, worrying too much about what might happen.

*

"Oh dear Lord, Pere, shut the children away, a Jewess and a 'eathen are coming down the street." Antonia, who was sitting outside their house with her husband enjoying the cool night air, something nearly everyone did in the warm months, said this loud enough for the two women to hear.

"Sounds as if you are really pleased to see us."

"Get the bench out, dearest 'usband so these women of the night can be sat down."

"No, don't bother, I'll perch on this stone and Arantxa is not staying long."

"She off to see 'er fancy man down on the beach again, is she?"

"What!" came the chorus from both women in unison.

"Every night she go by about this time, and I never seed 'er come back. There's only one thing that would keep you on a beach at night for hours."

"I like looking at the stars."

"Don't we all, lovey? Some of us dreamt about them when we was young as well, and then the first child comes and there's not so such time for *star dreaming*. What is it you'd be wanting with me anyway?"

Rebecca explained the whole story and asked if they would be willing to take in Arantxa for one night. Pere, realising that none of this conversation concerned him returned into the house to re-fill his mug.

"You Jews do some strange things; still, I'd be neglecting my Christian duty if I didn't take this 'eathen in." She turned her head to Arantxa, "You 'ave to keep good Christian hours in this 'ouse, though. No star gazing."

"I will, I promise." With mock servility Arantxa answered and curtseyed at the same time.

"You'd better be off with you now, the brightness in those stars do go out most quickly. One minute you are blinded by it, and then you don't even notice if it's there or not. What do you say, Pere?" she turned to where he should have been, "see, come and gone" The women smiled together as Pere came out bearing mugs of ale for the two guests. "And come again!" Offering the refreshment, a familiar admonishment came from his wife, "Weren't you listening? The 'eathen's off to play with heavenly stars."

"She might want a drink afore she goes, I hear it's thirsty business that." The women were all surprised, thinking Pere understood nothing; they had to review their theories. Arantxa gladly accepted her mug and drained it in one. "It certainly can be, let's hope so." Handing the mug back, she waved goodbye to all and set off in the direction of the beach.

"Certainly settled in quickly that one, do you know who it is?"

"I really couldn't say. Quite the mystery it is."

"My foot!" holding Arantxa's empty mug brought realisation that he'd left his own empty inside, another barrel trip called.

*

Cyprianus had spent a conflicted few days. Not sure that he'd done the right thing contacting Quirico, and having nobody he could confide or share his doubts with, he'd spent days marching around this palace playing out differing possible scenarios in his head. The odds on favourite outcome was that some sort of compromise would be reached before any clash of swords. If that were to happen, and the old foes became new found friends, then his duplicitous role could well be discovered. If it came to a fight, that wouldn't be so bad, as he had to have a foot in both camps. Toletum certainly had overwhelming force, if they wanted to use it. His appeasement with them through Quirico was more or less covered. If Tarraconensis/Gallia Gothica could mobilise the Jews, and rumours abounded that both the Franks and the Vascones were prepared to lend support by opening new fronts. Then was Toletum prepared for the sacrifices that a long bloody war would entail? On and on went his inconclusive wanderings.

"Would your Grace care for some refreshments?" Maria's concerned voice asked. She knew that her employer was extremely worried about something. He hardly ate, was always pacing around, and thankfully, as far as she was concerned, for quite some time, it hadn't been deemed necessary for her to receive any Christian blessing bent over the table. Cyprianus was often short and unpleasant to his housekeeper, maligning her in public as well as private; it was a case of familiarity breeding contempt. She'd been playing this role for decades, this was her life, a fact compounded by not having any close family left. Sadly, and in relatively quick succession, they'd all succumbed to various illnesses. The *attentions* and *blessings* bestowed on her were initially well received, as they were both reasonably young, and he wasn't quite so whale-like. These days, it was just another chore that had to be done. His increasing disgruntled attacks on her and her way of doing things, she put down to age and his disruptive digestive system. She bore them as any other Christian martyr would.

"Refreshments?" the Bishop was about to launch into a tirade about how could anyone think of food or drink in such times of crisis when he stopped himself, noticing the way his housekeeper held herself. The once, not attractive, but not ugly woman, was cringing like a beaten mongrel expecting another beating. "No, thank you. Would you sit with me a while, tell me what's happening in the town?"

Maria provided a triple function - housekeeper, a relief valve and a weather vane. He couldn't and didn't want to wander through the streets chatting with the local populace. Finding out their grievances and woes was not his style. Besides, who wants to hear the constant whinging of the poor. Instead, he grilled Maria for anything and everything she knew. Grilled is the wrong word, as the woman needed little coaxing, it was more like opening the sluice gates, the information came rushing out. "What are people saying?"

Maria gushed out how the whole town was alive to the possibilities of war, the troops marching in, albeit peacefully, had made an impression. Women were worried that their sons and husbands were going to be involved. Nobody really understood what the problem was, they agreed that the area had lost influence and they no longer lived in a thriving important town. Every year there were fewer business opportunities because there were fewer people, but this wasn't a good enough reason to go to war. The idea of a new state meant not a great deal as it wouldn't affect their lives too much, one way or another. What was worrying were the possible alliances that would need to be forged. Arming and fighting with and for Jews, didn't seem right. Nor was the prospect of external forces like the dreaded Franks or even the Vascones, whoever they were, being on *our* side against fellow Hispano-Romanic- Goths.

"Interesting, so you'd say there is no real appetite…"

"No, your Grace. The exception might be the duke's son, I've heard say that he's struck up a more private alliance with the Vasconis girl who people say is a heathen, God forbid! And him supposed to be marrying a nice Christian girl as well."

The arched eyebrows showed that the bishop was out of the loop on the marriage front as well. Rapidly changing that situation she related all, well, nearly all, she left out Amalaswinth's speculation on the house sleeping arrangements when the countess was in residence.

"Very interesting, to join the two families by marriage. Clever, a good solution. Do tell me who this *other* girl is. Before doing that though, if you could bring something to drink, it'd be good, then later we could say a few prayers together."

*

Marcus was already in the water swimming more horizontally parallel to the beach rather than striking away from shore. Quickly shedding her clothes, she paddled out to him. Seeing her coming, he swam back to the shallows diving under the water as they got closer. Swimming between her legs, he emerged with her sat on his shoulders, this unexpected action caused a squeal of delight. Being no longer a land virgin, it wasn't long before he broke his water virginity as well.

Back on the beach they caked themselves in the still warm sand. She told him of the day's happenings and how she'd be moving house temporarily.

"Come and stay in my house, there are loads of rooms."

"Marcus, get real. You know that can't happen, especially as your future mother in law is there."

"She's gone. Left first thing this morning. I think that my father was annoyed with her for something, probably announcing my future wedding plans so precipitously."

Whoops, there it was; the cat out of the bag, the big topic that they'd been avoiding as if by not mentioning it, it didn't exist. Despite them lying in each other's arms, a wall had suddenly been erected between them and the temperature dropped.

Eventually and timidly she whispered "When is it going to happen?"

"Never, if I can.."

"Marcus."

"They said something about it being done before Christ Mass."

"When the hell is that?" the annoyance and hurt that she felt crept into her voice.

"Mid winter time. Sorry, I forgot that you are not one of us."

Knowing he'd said the wrong word as soon as he'd said it, he lifted himself up onto one elbow, "I mean not .."

"I know exactly what you mean," she turned slightly away from him. "It's the main problem, isn't it? I'm not one of you in any way, not a Christian, not a Roman- Goth, not from a rich family. It would be difficult to be less one of *you*."

The atmosphere was well and truly broken, their protective shield no longer covered them, all manner of disagreeable disaster could now seep in. Every part was physically shrivelling in the silence that followed.

Surprisingly, Marcus began sniggering. This really annoyed Arantxa, as she felt that she was being laughed at, as well as humiliated, by the rich boy.

Her glowering angry face turned to face him ready to unleash a lot of abuse that she didn't feel, but wanting to hurt as much as she's been hurt, when he said, "It could be worse."

Before her onslaught started she felt compelled to ask, "HOW?"

"You could be Jewish!"

Stunned she didn't know how to react, so, he continued, "Imagine if it was Rebecca instead of you."

"Rebecca is prettier. Everyone loves Rebecca."

"Not me! Imagine having to put up with her bossy sharp tongue every day. I think I would go off and start wars just to get some peace and quiet."

In spite of herself, Arantxa did find this amusing. Even liking Rebecca the massive amount and the way she did, it had to be admitted that she was VERY bossy and some of her comments were extremely close to the knuckle. The number of times that she'd felt sorry for Jacob in the last couple of days couldn't be counted.

Seeing the thaw, Marcus allowed his elbow to buckle, landing on top of her, closing the distance between their faces enough to start softly kissing her cheek, and not being rejected, moved onto the lips.

*

The Shabbat meal was simple and quiet. Everyone was lost in their own thoughts about future happenings to actually enjoy either the food or the company. Even Trudi was morose and taciturn, a most unusual situation as she always had a great deal to say about nothing. Besides telling Rebecca what she'd done wrong with the food, little except the constant flow of negative or positive imperatives to David passed her lips.
The gay girlie banter with Arantxa was missing, making the food and prayers session dour at best. Even Jacob, who thought he didn't like the inane female chatter, preferred it to this wake-like atmosphere. It was a relief when it was all over and everyone could go their separate ways; the brothers to the office to plan, Rebecca to the kitchen to tidy up and Trudi decided that home was a better place to be, making David "escort" her.
"It's so difficult to plan a defence when you don't know what the attack is going to be. We can expect the *crime* of disrespecting a rabbi."
"Certainly can, and I suspect there is not a lot we can do to defend that one. Probably, it's just better to pay the fine and be done with it."
"True, Isaac. No one can deny that my daughter is forever calling him *a little prick.* However, I don't think there are any Jewish witnesses besides us in the family. What worries me more is, that there's no denying that she assaulted him. Again, it's only his word and he chose to say nothing at the time so.."
"It's the word of a rabbi against a female!"
"True again, Isaac. Did anything come of that message you sent to Rabbi Abraham?"
"No, no sign or signal. I had hoped..."
"The best we can hope for now is damage limitation, and a not so hefty fine."

*

It was late afternoon, Marcus was slashing and jabbing in the yard and his father, with a wont to do nothing in particular, was watching. His son had gained a great deal in technique and in strength. He was no longer the weedy specimen that Pere was forever cajoling and shouting at. Actually, he'd go so far as to say that the boy was pretty formidable.
Amalaswinth interrupted the family appreciation moment to announce the arrival of a visitor.
"Who is it?"

"The bishop, Sire."

"Tell him that.."

"Oh my dear Ranosindus, it's good to see you. I thought we could have a chat about preparations; what you'd like me to do and where, you know that sort of thing." Spotting that it was Marcus who was deftly swinging a sword, "Impressive. The boy is no longer a boy. Quite the man now, isn't he?"

"It would seem."

"Good for him. I hear that he's getting some *practice* in before his proposed marriage."

"How did you know about the marriage, and what are you talking about *practice*?"

"Ordinarily I would call it for what it is, a sin. However, I am led to believe that she, the female in question, hasn't even been baptised. Even so, I can't condone it. The girl should be offered the salvation of the Lord."

Ranosindus waited; there was no point in making the bishop's triumphant piece of gossip more important than it was.

"Surely you know, dear duke."

Silence, just a bit longer and all would be revealed. Suddenly, the duke didn't want to hear what this fat obnoxious man so desperately wanted to tell him. Recently his contacts had told him a potentially explosive rumour, which he'd been keeping up his sleeve. It was now time to play his ace.

"There are many things I know, some I don't and others I don't want to know at all. Don't you find this the case being a man of the Church? Talking of which, how is Bishop Quirico? It's sooo long since he visited Tarraco; I've almost forgotten what he looks like."

This bolt came completely out of the blue. Cyprianus was totally blindsided. He'd come to re-build bridges with the rebel authorities, and, it had to be said, gloat somewhat on the information Maria had given him. Usually so good at getting out of these situations, this time he was all of a fluster, his reply was practically a stammer, "Well, very well. Popped in to see him as I was passing. You know, a couple of ecumenical issues that needed resolving."

"Good to hear, I've always thought Quirico a honest straight forward sort, not one who would stab you in the back. Do give him my best ,if you are to see him again soon."

"Unlikely," getting back to firmer ground despite all the barbed innuendo, "we generally move in different circles."

"Shame. What was it you were talking about earlier? I was somewhat confused… something about my son, marriage and baptism."

"Just wanted to congratulate you on the upcoming wedding, joining the two strongest houses is a shrewd move. Well, must be off, no rest for the wicked as they say."

"Surely not wicked, you?"

"Just an expression. I'll pop in another day when I have more time. Farewell."

His exit reminded the Duke of an on-land duck in a hurry.

"He didn't stay long. I don't want to sound too disrespectful, but I'm much better pleased when I see him going and not coming."

"You and me both, probably a good thing for you too, because I'm not sure if he wanted to talk to you, or about you, waffling on about *practice, a girl, and baptism.* Couldn't make head nor tail of it."

Marcus' face was bright red, more than likely the result of too much training this afternoon.

*

According to custom for cherem, a practice that had existed since the earliest rabbinical traditions were committed to the written word, the synagogue was lit by candles of black wax, seven in a large hanging chandelier and another twelve around the walls. At the front were only two people, the self appointed *nasri*, the intellectual leader, Hillel himself, and one other, *parnas*, Jeremiah, Hillel's adopted puppy.

"ONLY two for this *parnassim*, that's ridiculously few," Isaac whispered as the congregation was beginning to settle in an expectant hush. A cherem was not a regular event in Tarraco, they had happened before, though never on such a formal basis, and because of this everyone knew that the consequences could be severe, hence the extremely large turnout. The usual procedure was that the result of the cherem was read out, there was no discussion as to the guilt or not, that had been previously decided by the *parnassim*.

Trudi, nodding at the other women known and unknown in the women's section, was Rebecca's only support. They sat together, with Trudi trying to ensure that the maximum physical distance possible when seated next to another person was respected. She needed to show that although they shared the same gender and were family, they were not of like minds and attitudes. No words passed between them. Nobody greeted Rebecca at all. She was alone and very frightened.

Jeremiah stood and cleared his throat as a way of commanding silence. For the most part, it worked, and those who hadn't noticed were soon hushed by others.

"Rabbi Hillel would like to start the proceedings by giving a brief introduction in order to give the case a framework."

"As you all know, I arrived here recently to replace the lately deceased and much appreciated Rabbi Saul. I have to say that I was greatly taken aback by the lax way in which our religious commitments were adhered to. There were a whole number of areas of neglect and digression from the norm. However, none more shocking than.."

There was a slight kafuffle at the back of the room as a pair of latecomers made their way into the room, one was the respected elder, Zachary, close friend of the departed Saul, and the other was a stranger. Eventually, they found a place by persuading an already full bench to become yet fuller, then gradually, after much shuffling, the quiet was restored.

"As I was saying, none is more shocking than the permissive attitude of the community to allow a female to represent it in the most important negotiations we have had with the gentiles in a generation. An untrained, unschooled *girl* whose only attributes seem to be a pretty face and an ability to be liked by our opponents in this discussion. SHOCKING! I repeat this is, SHOCKING! Tarraco, how low have you stooped? Furthermore, it was this unscholared *girl* who engineered with her Christian cohorts to have the true representative of the community, your Rabbi, removed from the decision making meeting, claiming that it was she, not he, who should be present."

Rebecca went to stand up to contest this lie, only to be pulled sharply down by Trudi, who angrily whispered, "You can't speak. It'll only make things worse. For once follow the rules!"

"Not content with her victory, this *girl* with her Christian collaborators, went on to insult the Jewish religion and its representative, by using foul and disrespective language, which I am too ashamed, as there are women present, to even use as a quote here."

There was a significant murmuring and tutting throughout the whole synagogue, but more especially in the women's section.

"Since my arrival, this *girl* has sought to challenge and undermine me in the eyes of the Christians at every possible turn, and for the crimes of disrespecting a rabbi and engaging in theological discussions with Gentiles, I demand that.."

The stranger stood and in a loud voice, clearly a voice quite used addressing crowds of people, demanded attention, "I apologise for interrupting, Rabbi Hillel, I know it's most unusual, but I think that before you pass sentence, perhaps we should have a talk, privately."

"And who are you to demand such a thing?"

"I would not dare to demand anything. However, I would like to be able to discuss these matters a little more profoundly, especially, as you so correctly pointed out, we stand on the precipice of one the biggest decisions the Jewish community, not only in Tarraconensis/Gallia Gothica, but also in the Hispanias , has ever made."

Jeremiah imparted some information in Hillel's left ear, "I repeat, who are you and in whose name do you speak? I have been informed that you are not part of the Tarraco community."

"That is true. As I mentioned earlier, the decisions made here can and do affect so much more than the legitimate, or otherwise, punishment of the girl in question. I have asked to be here today at the behest of the spiritual leader of the whole of Tarraconensis/Gallia Gothica, Rabbi Abraham. I, by the way, am Rabbi Ariel of Narbo."

Low chatter filled the air with this revelation. This certainly was shaping up to be no ordinary cherem resulting in a minor fine, or a week's shunning.

Hillel, who had been in full sail flowing with a strong following wind, quite suddenly found himself becalmed. His only option was to tack.

"You are most welcome, Rabbi Ariel, you are a long way from home, and as you said you have no authority here. I feel no need to review the case in private, as the facts are blatant and flagrant. There only remains the reading of the cherem which shall be enacted upon forthwith."

The newly arrived rabbi didn't change his standing stance, his face, though, did lose some of the lightness that it had possessed.

"I really regret doing this, but you leave me no choice, I challenge the validity of the cherem. A *parnassim* of two does not count as the collective will of the community. According to my information," here he looked down on Zachary, "no consultations were made among the elders of Tarraco. This *event*, I am afraid to say, smacks more of a vendetta, not a cherem. This is not to say there aren't grounds for such a course of action to take place. I am not taking the part of the person accused, instead, I am challenging the procedure. We can, as suggested earlier, meet and discuss the wider ramifications, and any suitable outcome in private."

The ground below Hillel had been removed. If he continued, the cherem would forever be questioned, as would he, and his actions; the word vendetta had really hit home. His audience, who had been lukewarm from the beginning, might turn against him, his rapport with them had yet to be established. It was the appearance of Zachary by the side of the northern rabbi which was determinant in the their eyes.

"I formally dissolve this meeting."

*

Els Munts was as beautiful as ever, the view, the house, the weather, everything was perfect except for Flavius. Not knowing what to do with himself he'd tried to join in the morning exercise drills. Fairly quickly it was made clear that his presence was a hindrance rather than a help to the smooth workings of the routine that Milo was running.

Going swimming just brought back vivid beach memories he was trying not to relive *too* often, he didn't want to wear them out! They were wonderful. As he didn't come from a close knit family, they all, siblings and parents, more or less, got along without any major hassles, he didn't miss them when he left for his soldiering career. Being away from home was different, most of the time, less pleasant, but he couldn't say that he yearned for the sight of any family member.

It was two days since last being with Rebecca on *their* beach, and he *really* did miss her. Thoughts of her filled his mind; the way she held herself, the way she moved, her smile and scowl, her voice and her body, that magnificent black hair. These two days felt like an eternity, and the worst part was that he didn't know when he'd get to see her again. Desperately wanting a date and time to look forward to, he'd pestered her incessantly on that afternoon, only to be told that it was out of her hands; she'd be in touch whenever she could. What did that mean? The mechanics of the question were daunting; how could she, a woman from Tarraco, get in touch with him, a general stationed in Els Munts? He had suggested that it'd be much easier, logistically, for him to get in touch with her. She wouldn't have any of that, saying it would be far too dangerous, nobody could know of their relationship, ever! Her life and her family's reputation, would be ruined. Flavius, with the memory of Aitziber still fresh, acquiesced.

On the face of it, this relationship was a lot like the one with Aitziber, cross-cultural, clandestine, with a potential enemy. However, this was where the comparisons stopped. Aitziber had been, it'd been something immensely enjoyable being with her, he'd looked forward to seeing her on the way to their trysts, and he'd revelled in the afterglow on the way back. What he hadn't done was spend his time away from her, constantly thinking about her. This occupation of the brain by one person was an entirely new sensation. He'd had quite a number of intimate encounters. Fact, women found him attractive and he'd never found it difficult to acquire a willing partner. In nearly every case he hadn't needed to play hunter, stalking his prey for periods of time, no, the women he'd been involved with, knew what they were looking for, all experienced in the field, most married, they took what they needed and left a sweet taste in his mouth.

What was clear from the beach was that Rebecca had never had any experience before. She was a virgin. It was her first time, and he wasn't sure that *he* liked it. He'd just presumed that she'd be like all the rest, but the pain and difficulty involved showed that not to be the case. Feeling guilty at causing her pain, he'd moved away from her, only to be physically dragged back, have his face cradled in her hands and her saying, "This is my choice. It's what I want. Let's try again."

It wasn't good sex, he'd experienced much better, It was, though, an absolutely incredible experience when they lay on the sand together. It didn't matter that she was constantly complaining that sand was getting everywhere, even though they were on his cloak. In a strange way, it actually made the moment more real.

Everything just felt *right;* the way they held each other, talking to her - in reality, she did most of the talking, the way their lips moved perfectly in unison when they kissed, and all this despite the afternoon heat, the stickiness of the salted sea wetness of their bodies, and being aware that they were in a race against both time and destiny. Flavius knew he'd entered a new world, a world he could not control, a place where he hurt, a world whose future was at very best uncertain.

His sweet and bitter revelry was interrupted by the apparition of a messenger coming up the steps in a considerable hurry.

"General, sir. A message, sir. From the king, sir!"

Three *sirs* in one sentence, this must be important. Flavius' mind fleeted momentarily back to the time not so long ago, when he'd tried to teach Marcus to use *sir* and salute properly. Unrolling the scroll, he sat down to read it. Just as well he had, as he may have fallen down if not. The contents were as surprising as they were shocking.

Not only were Flavius's compromise proposals rejected, but it also accused him of siding with the enemy to the point where it could be considered a treasonable act.

Treason? Him? How could he have been so misinterpreted? Furthermore, he was ordered to abandon wherever he was, make for Ilerda forthwith, where he was to join, in a subordinate role, a large force coming from Toletum being led by General Egica which should arrive by the end of the month.

This inevitably meant that all out war was the chosen option and it was imminent.

*

The back, one time store-room, had seen more meetings since the arrival of the new rabbi than ever in its life. So much so, that the faithful were in the process of officially changing its name to the small meeting room. Moreover, if the number of participants in these meetings continued to grow, it wouldn't be long before a mid-sized meeting room would be needed.

One rabbi and support at each end of the table, Hillel plus Jeremiah, in front of Ariel and Zachary. Whether there should be anyone else present was the first dispute. Zachary argued that there should be more men from Tarraco present, Hillel didn't oppose this as a concept, but fervently objected to the two names put forward; Jacob and Isaac, as they were directly implicated in the case and may even be culpable in some ways. The first compromise saw Jacob excluded, Isaac included, and a friend of Jeremiah's, whose standing in the community was not questioned even if his backbone was, returned equilibrium to the proceedings.

Hillel was playing at home and wanted everyone to be aware this was *his* synagogue, started by reiterating almost word for word what he had said earlier, eventually he was stopped by Ariel, "We understand, and to some extent, accept what you are saying; a female should not be representing the community. Our, by that I mean, the rabbis from the north, point is, that these are unusual circumstances which may mean different non-conventional methods may have to be, temporarily, invoked."

Hillel reacted with a resort to scripture quotes to back his position with the warning that if some important parts of doctrine are ignored at will, then what other fundamental pillar would be next. The whole essence of their religion would be called into question.

"The fact is, though, we are standing on the cusp of one of the most important moments in the history of Jews since our expulsion from the Holy Land, we can't let a relatively small detail like this destroy this opportunity."

"Let me get this clear, Rabbi Ariel. You are proposing ignoring tradition and scripture, you are allowing the enemy to choose who should represent us, *and* you are condoning the actions of a *girl* who insulted a rabbi in front of Christians, all in hope of an alliance with one group of Christian oppressors against another."

"The fact of the matter is that the Christians do not want to deal with you, Rabbi Hillel. The account that Lady Chlodoswintha gave of the meeting was radically different to yours. I am not saying that I accept the word of a Christian over a fellow rabbi, but she was most insistent that it was you who wanted all women removed from the meeting, including her own person. They, the Christians, felt it was you who was trying to make yourself the arbiter of who *they* should have as a representative. Over the last few months I have spent many hours in the company of the count and countess in the planning of this possible uprising, and I have found both very pleasant and courteous. However, despite trying, on various occasions, to make them understand the righteousness of our grievances, I always felt that there was a lack of real comprehension. Nevertheless, this time, Lady Chlodoswintha was most vocal on the validity of our complaints and necessity of a radical change of direction in the new state. This sea change was brought about by Rebecca's, that's her name, isn't it?" Her uncle was nodding enthusiastically, "intervention in the said meeting."

"This doesn't detract from the fact that they are Christians, and Christians can only be seen as our persecutors. Making an alliance with them is akin to making alliances with the devil."

It was Zachary's turn to refute. "Rabbi, I don't mean to be disrespectful and fully understand your point of view, but what I don't understand is what other options do we have besides just accepting the slow strangling of our religion by one more vicious law after another."

"We need to make it known to the authorities, the bishops in Toletum that we are not a threat and we can live as two totally separate societies that never have to interact; complete segregation, is the answer, in walled communities if necessary."

A collective "WHAT!" came from four people.

"It's the only way. We need to keep ourselves pure."

Ariel was considered by most as a man of extreme patience, his demeanour was beginning to show that even his, was wearing thin.

"You're missing something fundamental here, why should they accept us in *their* country? This is not the Holy land where we are defending our way of life in our own land against some invading force, like in the days of the Roman Empire. This is their land, the dominant religion is Christianity, and it's becoming almost an exclusive faith. This was a place that used to tolerate and accept us, and others like the non believers. It is no longer, ever since King Reccared's conversion from Arianism, there has been this inextirpable slide to becoming a mono- religious theocracy."

"All the more reason we should not collaborate with ANY group of Christians."

"You almost sound as if you are willing them to expel us."

"A mass return to the Holy Land would have its advantages. The Byzantine Christians are no longer in control there. The new religion of the Mohamedans has been allowing Jews to return to the Holy Land for quite a number of years. Perhaps it's time for all of us to return to a place where we are not so rejected, and if we did it en masse, then we'd have some power."

"Back to Zion? I suggest you gather your followers, if you have any, and make your move back to Jerusalem."

"It's what we all should be doing. Not squirming and grovelling to Christians for the honour of staying in their country. If we are going to spill blood, ours as well as theirs, it needs to be in a just cause in our land, fighting for our rights. The spirit of Masada needs to be rekindled; their brave sacrifice should be our example."

"Are you suggesting that we all kill ourselves, contrary to scripture by the way, in some sort of mass suicide pact here or back in the Holy Land?"

"Wherever we can actually fight to make a separate Jewish identity."

" You poor deluded man; Masada was not a victory, over 900 people, men, women and children, died and not one Roman attacker."

"The glory of Masada was that they wouldn't die by the invaders' sword."

"There's no glory in death. The Sicarii, who were not adverse to killing fellow Jews, never understood that. If that is your aim, then I'm afraid with that attitude we cannot have you as the interlocutor of the Jewish community whose intention it is to try to make a better life here."

"You do not have the power to stop me from being Rabbi here."

"I don't think that you were listening, Rabbi Hillel. Nobody is removing you from anything. You may continue as rabbi here, that choice is yours and the community's. What I am saying is that you will NOT represent us Jews that want to stay in Tarraconensis/Gallia Gothica, in any of the joint meetings with our allies, the Christians."

"You are supporting a *girl* instead of a rabbi?"

"No. We accept your legitimate point of view on this question, it's not correct that a female holds this position. We will negotiate with the Christians to find someone suitable to both parties as a replacement."

*

"What is that noise?"

"Inside the building or out?"

"There's nothing new about the outside, it's been going on for days and gradually increases in volume. It's getting to the point that even thinking is becoming a problem."

"My dear Julian, as the saying goes, you can't make an omelette without breaking eggs. Having so many men in and around Toletum is bound to be a little noisy."

"I thought they'd all been allotted different fields around the town to assemble."

"They have, you ought to go out there, the number of banners and the multitude is seriously impressive. I have never seen the like of it."

"That doesn't explain all the men and noise inside the city."

"These are just a few officers who have permission to be here. They are the responsible quiet ones!"

"The sooner they are on their way, the better."

"That won't happen until the noise inside; the barons discussing logistics and hierarchy, comes to some sort of conclusion. My suggestion is stay away from the banqueting hall; most of them are there, they're collaring anyone looking vaguely important or influential, desperately seeking allies to further their particular cause. Personally, I only use the back stairways and passages and I try not to wear the robes of office."

"Surely Quiricus, we as the highest clerics in the land can impose some order on this uncouth rabble."

"Every king has been trying to do that for the last one hundred years. You weren't here in the 40s, were you? No, too young. That was the last time that order was imposed. King Chindaswinth carried out what he called house cleaning. It was bloody, very bloody. The old nobility was decimated; up to seven hundred murdered was the figure that was bounded around. Bloodletting in extreme, which, as you can hear, came to nought as the barons bounced back with more rather than less power vis-à-vis the crown."

"We will just have to be patient. Nothing is worth trying until Egica arrives, which doesn't seem to be any day soon as he sends messages from various places saying he's on his way, only he never gets any closer. I would wager that he wants to stay out to the squabbling until the dust begins to settle; a sensible tactic, which leaves us to grin and bear the noise for a few days more at least."

The two men agreed on most matters of doctrine and state, which made for a harmonious relationship. Before the noise had become too unbearable, they were plotting how it was possible to impose their policies from afar. Julian, being the younger man, was tempted to accompany the force to the front to ensure the will of the bishops was followed. It was only fear of others in the copular of bishops, who would take advantage of his protracted absence, that dissuaded him. There was a need for someone that they could trust entirely, that is to say malleable enough. Also, that person had to be of a rank that would be respected by the dukes. There were very few who fitted all of the categories. Their number one choice, way out in front of the others, was Bishop Iulianus of Hispalis. His credentials were impeccable; not only did he give vocal support to all the anti- Jewish measures passed in concilia, he also, imposed these policies with fervour in his city. He was no waiverer. As to his malleability, they had both thought that this wouldn't prove too problematic as he had aspirations to more power than he already had in Hispalis, and to have success in the capital, you needed a mentor, protector, or perhaps a rightly coined phrase, a godfather. Sadly though, he had either not replied to messages, or fobbed off the summons to come to the capital, with some lame excuse or other.

"The bait we are offering has to be more explicit, I believe. So far, we have invited or ordered him to come without explaining why. Legitimately, he might fear a trap of some sort. Let's put it into words; the appointment of a special envoy with absolute control in the suppression of the rebels with special reference to the final solution to the Jewish question."

"Julian, I like it, *the final solution;* sounds perfect,"

*

The store-room felt empty with only two inhabitants and neither spoke. Jeremiah was frightened lest an uttered word would upset the Rabbi yet more; the Rabbi was deep in contemplation of his future. This awkward stance was maintained for quite some time. It was Jeremiah who cracked first, "Shall I set a new date for the cherem?"

Looking up as if woken from a deep trance, Hillel spoke in a manner denoting profound resignation, "There will be no cherem."

"Rabbi Ariel agreed with you, the girl shouldn't represent us. It will be relatively easy to gather a decent sized *parnassim.*"

"I tell you there will be no cherem. Tarraco, in fact, the whole of Tarraconensis has demonstrated that they are not worthy of my talents. The battle between the Christians either will or won't take place with the result of Tarraconensis/Gallia Gothica capitulating. The real losers in both scenarios will be the Jewish community. *You* will be made to pay for your disloyalty to the crown. I pray that this will not involve mass murder."

"Surely not."

"Someone has to try to stop the catastrophe. I will be leaving for Toletum in the morning. If you'd like to accompany me, you may."

"What will we do there?"

"Talk to the bishops to find a solution that is acceptable to both us and them. They want us out of their Christian kingdom, so do I. Expulsion would be the perfect fit. However, it'd be so much better if it were done in an orderly controlled way, not as an impulsive post victorious collective punishment. We need an exodus without a following army and the need for the partition of the Red Sea."

Meanwhile, three of the other store-room participants huddled in a corner of the now empty synagogue.

"That man is exceptionally dangerous. Your information, Zachary, was timely and invaluable. I am sure the whole community, if it knew, would join me in giving you a heart-felt thank-you. I believe we have averted a complete catastrophe. That man makes the Zealots look like liberal collaborators."

The non verbal communication of Isaac and Zachary showed that they whole- heartedly concurred.

"The question is how do we proceed, who shall we appoint as the replacement for your niece, Isaac?"

Surprised at being asked, Isaac hesitated long enough for Zachary to intervene.

"After my close and much missed friend Rabbi Saul died, we were some time bereft of true leadership, yet we managed admirably until he was replaced. It transpires that that replacement is considerably worse than the void. I would suggest that we return to that state for the time being."

"Sounds like a plan. I actually don't believe that Hillel will stay much longer in Tarraco. He's a proud man and his pride has been hurt badly and in public. I imagine that you'll be searching for a new rabbi very shortly. A return to your bridging in-between state would appear to be the most sensible option."

Isaac, at the mention of Rebecca had gone on to think elatedly that his niece, and the family, would get out of this potentially dreadful situation, relatively unscathed.

"Who was it that performed those functions?"

Zachary pointed at Isaac.

"What?"

*

"How did it go?" Arantxa was seated on a stone at the port area at the end of the road that she thought that Rebecca would have to use coming back from the synagogue, she'd been waiting and waiting as she hadn't known its starting time, nor when it might finish. It wasn't one of those anxious waits, even though Rebecca had explained its possible dire consequences, it was more relaxed for no reason that she could fathom. She believed that nothing too bad was going to happen. Lots of people passed by, some she recognised, others she didn't, none greeted her in any way, it was as if she wasn't really there.

Eventually, Rebecca, arm in arm with Jacob, not looking too disturbed, arrived at her stone. To her surprise it was Jacob who answered, "You've been waiting here? That is most kind of you." He looked down on his new *daughter* dotingly, " I suppose you are desperate for news, perhaps I would venture to say that the result was *inconclusive*; however, I'll leave Rebecca to fill you in on all the details. I do hope you make it back to our house soon. It's much cleaner when you are there."

Unlocking her arm, Rebecca playfully slapped her father as he was beginning to walk away. "You could always clean it yourself."

Jacob stopped, turned, "Rebecca, that's exactly the sort of comment that gets you into trouble. Please try to behave, at least in public. My health won't stand too many more problems with the authorities."

"Don't worry. I'll be back tomorrow to try to help you order all the contents of your house, including your daughter."

This made Jacob smile, she really was a very nice girl, that Arantxa, he couldn't imagine why she had been so rejected by her family and people.

"What a creep!" Rebecca had waited until her father was out of earshot. "Backing my father against your saviour in Tarraco. What you wouldn't do.."

"Honestly, Rebecca, I do think he's right, sometimes, you do go over the top."

"What! You are lecturing me now, are you?"

"NO, no, no. It's just that you have an ideal father and you treat him pretty badly at times."

Rebecca's annoyance dissipated as quickly as it had arrived.

"Thank you, Arantxa, I need someone to tell me at times. I appreciate it." They hugged. Rebecca had never been one of these touchy, feely women who has the need for constant physical contact. Sitting at her father's feet leaning onto his legs was as far as it used to go. These days, things were different. Jacob had been pleasantly surprised when she linked her arm into his upon leaving the synagogue. And it was her that initiated the present clasp.

"Tell me what happened."

As they walked, Rebecca explained how Hillel had laid out his stall lying and exaggerating without fear of contradiction, the way in which she was mercilessly criticised and how bleak everything looked until a surprise intervention by another rabbi.

"So, what's the result?"

"Pending. The important people are meeting, Uncle Isaac is among them, so there's hope that whatever it is, it won't be as harsh as it would have been."

More hugging, this time the instigator was Arantxa.

Finding themselves at the end of the port, they gravitated naturally towards the beach.

"Is this where..?"

"This beach, yes, but a little farther down, not this close to the ships. It's been two days and I am beginning to miss him. When we last… met, I told him about your predicament, Holy days and Antonia, so, we arranged a fall back meeting for tomorrow night. Shit, I am looking forward to it."

"Lucky you! My problem is, I don't know how to get a message to Flavius, we weren't so organised as you. That bloody cherem could have been really severe, meaning that we might not have been able to meet again, ever. I'm jealous of you! I'd love to see him. It's just that I have no idea how to get in touch with him."

"I could ask Marcus."

"NO! he can't know, Nobody can."

"Then, tomorrow I will walk out there and back, - shouldn't take much more than a morning."

"You'd do that for me? No wonder you are my father's favourite. Perhaps I could come with you, not all the way to the camp, there's no way that I can be seen there, but I could wait somewhere close by."

*

Hearing conversation from the office, she headed there. Opening the door she was met with a glum looking Uncle.

"Come in, favourite daughter. Don't knock! You know that you are always welcome in my one place of privacy in this, my, house."

Rebecca immediately turned around, went back out, closed the door and knocked softly.

"Go away, we are busy."

She came in anyway. "See father, you'd just try to exclude me, if I followed the rules, so, really there is no point. Uncle, you look awful, do you have bad news for me?"

Isaac didn't speak, her father did, "He's in a major pickle, and I believe it's your fault. He does as well, but he's probably too nice to say so."

Rebecca slumped to her floor knee-hugging position, "Uncle, I am so sorry, whatever it is, I am sorry. You should not be involved; it should not be you that pays for whatever people think I have done wrong, even though I am totally innocent of doing anything wrong."

"You may yet. The cherem has been left in the hands of Hillel though if it does continue; it won't be as severe as it would have been."

"That's great news. Why the long face?"

"The two major decisions that the northern have insisted on, are; one, that neither, you, as a female, nor Hillel, as a radical zealot and unacceptable to the Christians, can represent the Jews of Tarraco, and, two, that representative honour should be given to my brother."

"I can't do it; I don't want to do it. I loathe meetings, speaking in public and being in any way *important*. I want a quiet life."

"Brother, you don't have a quiet life. You're married to Trudi!"

Never having heard her father say anything quite so bold, Rebecca laughed, "Come on Uncle Isaac, it'll be fun. I will help you."

"Brilliant! That's exactly what I need, isn't it?"

*

"You've come back to us, have you? I knew you would. Marta predicted it as well, said you'd come back tail between your legs asking to be taken in by us again. I, personally, don't have an opinion one way or the other, for me, it has to be the decision of the women. You walked out, without

(357)

any by-your- leave, or a word of gratitude, after all they had done for you; taken you in, treated you as one of their own, true Christian values, and what did they get in return? I'm not sure they will accept you back."

"Have you finished, centurion?"

Milo, who was secretly pleased that she was back and would be more humble in her ways, was shocked by the brazen way in which she spoke to him showing absolutely no respect.

"See, this is how you got into trouble with the women in the first place, you need to be less arrogant, more respectful."

"Evidently you haven't got to show any respect to me! I don't have all day to listen to your *advice*, I am here to speak to the general on a matter of importance."

Milo's disposition was hardening, this girl was pretty, there was no denying that, but she had a mouth on her, she really needed breaking.

"Appealing to the general won't.."

"Nobody is appealing to anyone. I don't want to be back in that nest of vipers that you call the women's camp; I'd rather be torn apart by wild horses. I said I have a message for the general, are you going to take me to him or shall I find my own way?"

The slap that was coming to this girl had to be delayed as in his peripheral vision he could see the general coming down the steps of the mansion.

"Arantxa, I thought that was you. Do come in."

As always with this woman, Milo was left with unfulfilled desire. One day things would change.

Having seen both of Marcus's houses, she thought that she preferred this one. It wasn't quite so ostentatious, it looked as if it was possible to live in, whereas the other was just too much, nobody could ever be comfortable there.

"You look hot, I'll send for drinks." He called the orderly.

"Thank you, I walked from Tarraco."

"That must have taken you a long time. Is this a social visit or is it, as Milo was shouting about, your possible return to the viper pit?"

"So you heard... No, I don't want to come back, nor is there anyone I would want to visit socially."

Flavius sat forward about to ask for exception from the blanket social visiting. "No, not even you, general. Your relationship was with my sister, not me. I am told you have redeeming qualities, and must accept that my sister thought a great deal of you, but for me, you will always be the man who instigated the destruction of my village and the murder of my friends and family."

Flavius had started this conversation in a happy almost flirty way trying to be charming. This last statement put a stop to that.

"So, what is this message you have for me? Deliver it and you will have no more reason to suffer my company." The refreshments arrived.

Arantxa took her mug and began to sip slowly. After the harsh words this imperious sipping infuriated Flavius.

"Get on with it, woman, I haven't got all day."

Arantxa continued to sip and spoke just before Flavius exploded, "I didn't think you'd want your orderly to hear the contents of the message, that's why I am delaying. It's not to spend any more quality private time with you."

Realising she was totally correct, he did his best to deflate his anger.

"There's no need to wait outside the door, soldier, I don't think I will need protecting from this woman." Noisy sandals were heard moving down the corridor.

"As I said earlier, you seem to have some other qualities besides killing, because there is another woman who is prepared to risk everything to be with you."

Flavius hadn't known what sort of message Arantxa could have been carrying, he'd suspected it was something from Pere, as he'd heard that she'd taken up residence in the dock area. His heart leapt when he realised it was Rebecca she was talking about.

Arantxa pulled out a note she had hidden in her sleeve.

Snatching and reading the few words avidly, he looked at the bearer, "Thank you for coming. I honestly do appreciate it."

For the first time she looked him directly in the eyes, "Please be careful. I lost one best friend, I don't want to lose another."

"Rebecca is very, very, important to me. I will do anything to avoid having her hurt in any way whatsoever. Where is she now?"

"She walked with me part of the way, she stopped on what she called *your* beach."

"The note says to meet tomorrow, but I think that I will surprise her and ride there now. You can come on the back on the horse with me, save you walking so much."

She tilted her head with a look of almost pity on her face, "For a general, your planning is rubbish. I admire your enthusiasm, you're certainly keen, but how do you think it would appear to the rest of the camp if we rode away together?"

Crestfallen and admonished, he had to accept the validity of her observation.

Feeling sorry for him she said, "Ride off now, as if the message requires your urgent attention, I will follow walking." Elation covered his face.

"Just remember, I have to go across that beach to return to Tarraco, I don't want to stumble on any *unexpected* sights."

Taking her hand in his, she immediately pulled away as if she were handling a slimy fish. He managed to say before she wiped it on her clothing, "I really do want to thank you, Arantxa."

With that he rushed to the stables, yelling at people to get his horse ready, while she slowly wandered down the steps. Her presence had caused a stir in the usual boring routine in camp life, and towards the end of the path she'd have to take to go back to Tarraco was a waiting group of women.

As nonchalantly as possible, she walked towards them, and had managed to get halfway through the mob when the name-calling started. She continued unperturbed; this had the effect of an increase in venom and volume. It was then the sound of a galloping horse was heard.

"One more word from any one of you, I'll have you publicly whipped." Marta stepped forward saying "But..", only to receive a riding crop on her back. She yelped in pain. "I think my order was clear."

Sullenly the other women stepped back. Arantxa walked on and the horse moved away at speed.

*

 Having lived her whole life next to the sea, Rebecca didn't think much about it, it was there, and it would always be there. They gained their living by importing and exporting, the sea was essential, as were the ships it brought. The worrying trend was that every year fewer of them floated in. The captains and notes sent from Jewish traders all lamented the same situation of diminishing markets, dropping demand and the general drying up of international trade. It wasn't just Tarraco that was suffering, it was a Mediterranean phenomenon, and nobody had any explanation as to the whys. It was true that the Byzantine Empire was shrinking, losing power, land and importance as the new religion expanded, which by itself though, wasn't sufficient to explain the huge drop in demand at the western end of the sea.

Rebecca reflected that the sea had meant life, trade, good views and wealth to her, not a play thing to be splashed around in for fun as she was doing at the precise moment. Arantxa had been gone for quite some time; she was bored and tired of thinking again and again about the same problems connected to Hillel, so she'd decided to go into the water. It provided a nice, warm and refreshing relief from the excess thinking, heat and boredom. Splashing about in the shallows, she realised she was actually enjoying the sensation, so she decided to be more adventurous, removing what was left of her clothes. She went in much deeper, nearly up to her neck. For her, this was scary stuff, especially fearing the idea of her face getting wet, she hated that, every wave hit brought its danger.

Trying to control this irrational panic, she knew she had to overcome this stupidity. In her mind's eye, she had the vision of Flavius, quickly skipping over the waves. What delightful memory; his attractive naked body! Trying not to think of that, she attempted to concentrate on remembering what he did in the water; this swimming lark. Screwing up all her courage, she launched herself into the sea, her face got wet and she panicked, spluttering back to her upright position. First attempt, not successful but still alive, she needed to try again. Deciding she was too deep, she waded a bit farther back towards the shore to try again, only to get similar results. Determined not to give up, she repeated and repeated the same action, it wasn't fun, without a doubt there was a steady incremental loss of fear. To any neutral observer the word sinking rather than swimming would spring to mind as a description of her maritime messing. After a good while, she felt tired and frustrated and made her way to the rocks. Because she was all wet, the last thing she wanted to do was sit on sand; it would stick to every part of her body, horrible. Why did God invent sand?

Soaking up the sun she'd become completely dry and pretty uncomfortable. No matter what position there was always sharp bits of rock to worm their way into her soft flesh. Wanting to head home with or without Arantxa, she was beginning to despair when she saw a familiar horse galloping towards her. He was certainly going very fast. Wondering why, she quickly put some clothes on. Her note specifically stated that they'd meet the next day so why all the rush to come. She hoped that nothing bad had happened to Arantxa.

There were no preliminaries, no hello, how-do-you-dos, it was straight off the horse into an embrace and long, long kiss. Eventually they came up for air.

"I've missed you!"

"As I see. It's only been two days."

"Two very long days."

"You're not supposed to be here. Where's Arantxa?"

"She'll be along shortly, she wouldn't allow me to give her a ride."

"I should hope not! The girl's got to have some moral standards. Anyway, she has all the man she wants to handle."

Another kiss and a move onto the rocks after Rebecca made it very clear she had no desire to sit in/ on the sand.

"Marcus has finally made his move then."

"Oh, yes. He's getting married."

"What? To Arantxa?"

"Don't be daft, he's the son and heir of a duke. He'd never be allowed to marry her. No, they are coupling him up with the daughter of the Count of Nemausus."

"Good strategic move, not good for Marcus or Arantxa, I imagine."
They continued exchanging bits of information sandwiched between bouts of kissing. They both wanted more but the imminent arrival of Arantxa acted as an irritatingly annoying frustrating brake.
Rebecca was expansively eloquent in her damming of Hillel.
"That's the man you call a *little prick*, isn't it? The arrogant one from the meeting?"
She confirmed, then explained that at the moment everything was on hold, which was the best that could be hoped for but at any given time though, this could change for the worse. The only really negative thing was that she'd lost her liaison job.
"Not such a bad thing. I must admit that it was more than a little strange seeing a woman representing the Jews."
"Meaning what, oh general? That women can't do this type of work or what?"
Seeing which way the wind was blowing, Flavius became super conciliatory,
"No, no, no, you did an excellent job; it's just that it is not a *normal* thing."
To some extent mollified, she carried on, "My uncle has been pushed into the role even though he hates it, and knows he won't do it well. I would do it so much better. Still, him being a man, and not a *girl*, everyone, except him, is convinced that he will be able to do it MUCH better."
They talked around this situation until a tiny figure could be seen in the distance. Realising he hadn't much time, he rather blurted out, "There's definitely going to be war. Wamba has rejected all my suggestions of compromise. Various armies are being assembled."
Rebecca moved slightly away from him so she could see his face properly, "Why are you telling me this? Surely, I now rate as one of the enemy."
"Technically, I suppose you do. It's just that I want to keep you safe. I am beginning to think that you are really very important to me, Rebecca."
Stunned into silence, they waited for the figure to grow in size and proximity. Before her outline became truly sharp, Rebecca crossed the space between them again, took his face in her hands, kissed him gently and passionately, pulling away to say, "As you are to me, Scarface.....I really need someone to teach me how to swim."

*

As generals go, General Kunimund didn't fall into any happy general fold, nor could it be said that he was in any way a happy person. Having never been described as the latter, it didn't bother him much that people thought him miserable and morose; however, he'd always got great pleasure out of his job from the lower ranks all the way through his steady sure rise to the top. He wasn't one of these Generals that sought or strove for action to try to justify his pay and position. No, inaction was totally fine. Hermenguild taught him well in this aspect with his constant mantra - *when there was no action it showed they were doing their job well, when there was strife, killing and bloodletting, then, it was due to a failure of some sort.* The inaction around the peace process with the Vascones was proving too much even for his most patient disposition. They were stalling.

What he couldn't work out was why they would want to do such a thing as it was in their interest to get his forces off their land and for their lives to go back to normal, even if this was under a new vassal state type relationship which would be considerably more costly than their previous pre-war status.

Finally, this morning he'd got an inkling as to what was going on. His men had apprehended a suspicious sort of character a couple of days ago and eventually they had *persuaded* him to talk. It turned out that he was part of a go between group that was in negotiations with the King of Aquitaine, Lupus. They all being or feeling part of the greater Vasconis family, they were trying to find a way of opening a new front to challenge the Goth forces. The aim was to keep as many of the present occupying Goth troops here in this area by stalling or re-kindling this war. Their thinking being that the worst case scenario of this would be a minor defeat on both fronts with an evident and increased threat, therefore, enabling them to sue for much better cessation of hostilities conditions. The best, as significant victory.

Receiving this information spurred him into action. Today he would send out various horse parties whose sole objective would be to wreak as much havoc as possible. Killing people was not a priority, burning crops was. He would turn the whole area into one late summer bonfire.

*

"Sorry, Papa, but it's a cold supper after the soup tonight, we've both been exceptionally busy today and haven't had time to prepare anything elaborate."

Jacob knew better than to ask where they had been all day, they'd set off reasonably early after announcing that they wouldn't be in for lunch, armed with some cock and bull story about helping Pere's wife Antonia. That they had trailed in a quantity of sand which would merit the proportions that Moses could get lost in, didn't bear mentioning, he accepted. What was really strange was the lack of chatter. Both girls were lost in their own thoughts and barely attempted anything like polite table conversation. Not thinking he'd ever miss such innate chirping, it was left to him to try failsafe topics such as the weather, which got affirmations rather than expansion. Something was afoot and at the risk of mixing body parts metaphors, he couldn't put his finger on it.

Besides joking comments on the eagerness and enthusiasm that Flavius had shown to see Rebecca, the walk back was a reasonably quiet affair. Arantxa's enthralling, not a detail missed, tale of the camp women and how they were put in their place was only half-listened to due to the one sentence, its tone of delivery, and the depth of emotion expressed on the face, was playing on a loop inside Rebecca's head -*I am beginning to think that you are really very important to me*. This was producing a similar feeling to being out of her depth in the water trying to learn to swim - uncontrollable panic. What had she done? What was she doing? What was clear was that the shells were broken, the eggs couldn't be put back in, and it was now a question of what she was going to do with the eggs - make something fun, interesting and memorable, or,.. not. The loop came in a form they usually did, there was no ending; it just continued to go around and around. Occasionally, it was paused when considering what to do with the other shell-shock information delivered by Flavius; the imminence of war. Without betraying herself and her *meetings* with him, how could she tell Uncle Isaac and the rest of the allies that a massive army was heading their way?

*

Sitting on the sand, Arantxa felt she'd spent the whole day on the stuff. Used to hill and solid ground walking, the trudge through or sinking deep into this soft surface was much more tiring. She really was exceptionally tired. Darkness had been beginning to fall as she left Rebecca's. Her route of choice was much longer because it deliberately circumvented most of the inhabited areas, a sensible precaution as the majority of people were outside their houses enjoying the most refreshing part of the day. The fact that there was no moon helped, tonight she really did not want to be noticed. With her stiff aching legs and the detour, she'd imagined he'd be waiting for her. He wasn't. Plonking her weary body down, she began her vigil. Sitting alone in the near pitch dark, time dragged by much slower than it does in the light, doubts started to fill the void, doubts about Marcus, which was a hark back to the past sensation. Until this doubting she believed that he was not only enjoying the physical part, learning a lot, she also had the strong impression that he was having a good time with her and her company, they laughed and had fun. Until now it had never crossed her mind that he might not turn up. The wait continued and she was beginning to get upset, not angry, just upset, perhaps more so with herself than him, after all, when all was said and done, he was only a man, a young one, what can you expect from them? She thought that she'd accepted that this *relationship* could have no future; it was his fling before him doing his duty and getting married. Trying to convince herself that for her it was the same as other fun fucks from the village, she'd managed to avoid thinking too much about its real effect on her. This uncertain wait was showing that deep down there were other feelings, feelings she wasn't comfortable with

Tired of thinking and being stupid, she stood brushed the sand off and headed back.

"No stars out tonight, 'eathen?"

Lost in her thoughts, she had forgotten to avoid Antonia's house on her return journey.

Not wanting laughter to be plied onto her disappointment, she explained that she'd had to walk out to Els Munts and she was falling down with tiredness.

"Stick your little arse next to me, 'ave and ale and tell me."

Reluctant to do any of the requested things, she reiterated her desire for bed.

"Pere is off somewhere, one of those man about a dog stories, sit yourself down, I'll get the ale. I need a bit of company."

Taking a deep draft, she realised that she was actually very thirsty.

"Thanks, Antonia."

"You are going to get 'urt, you know that, don't you?"

Arantxa tried putting on a show of no emotion, just the quizzical rising of eyebrows.

"'e's well out of your league, luvy. It's only a matter of time afore they marry 'im off to some breeding mare with class."

"I know, he's got to get married before Christ mass, whenever that is."

"Bugger me, that's quick, and it explains the face on you, seen 'appier pigs going to slaughter."

In a quandary whether to open up to this woman who was without doubt always good to her, who gave the impression of being genuine, but at the same time having the knowledge that she did have a very loud mouth, Arantxa quaffed what was left of her drink.

"Thirsty business, being in love, ain't it? I'll get you another."

As Antonia made her way back inside, it left the mugless one to wonder whether she was or not, in love. If anyone, including her new best friend, Rebecca, had asked, she would have virulently denied it. Antonia didn't ask a question, it was a statement of fact.

"Oh, here you are. I thought you'd stood me up. I was late, sorry, father problems. I was hoping I'd find you."

"Well, look what the cat's dragged down to port area, Prince Charming. Will you be wanting one of these or are you too posh to drink with the likes of me?"

"Good evening, most beautiful wife of my ex sword instructor, I would be delighted to partake in one your fine ales."

"Don't come snotty on me, I remember your arse 'anging out of your britches chasing the Jewess. Is that a yes, or no?"

Well and truly put in his place, Marcus agreed it was a yes, as Antonia turned to go back in, he took Arantxa by the hand. "I really am sorry." He looked contrite Arantxa was thinking as her hand was suddenly dropped as if it were red hot.

"Don't mind me, you can 'old 'ands as much as you like as far as I'm concerned, I won't be telling no one, well no rich folk anyway. Most others down 'ere 'ave a good idea what's going on anyhow."

"As I found out this evening from my father, the bishop came to taunt him about it."

"That'd be that Maria, the bishop's 'ousekeeper. Always an open mouth that one, and open legs, if rumours be right. So, you ain't got nothing to lose, 'old 'er 'and, she be right glum, look at the face on 'er."

Retrieving a more reluctantly given hand, he tried to make out her face on this dark night, he couldn't see anything amiss. The situation for him was awkward, publicly holding hands with a female was strange, talking about it and drinking ale in port area made it even stranger.

"I 'ear that congratulations are in order, as you're getting spliced afore the yuletide and it ain't to the one you're 'olding 'ands with neither."

"More's the pity." He squeezed. "I dearly wish it were."

"Bullshit! You're just saying that now cos she's 'ere and you got a right case of puppy love. Given a while you'd be tiring of 'er cos she ain't your class and looking anew anyways."

Antonia's brutal honesty was surprising, he should have been due some respect for who he was. Clearly, he wasn't going to get it. Amalaswinth used to talk to him like this when he was a misbehaving boy, he wouldn't take it from her now. Should he take it from this woman?

"Antonia, that's your name isn't it? I don't think .."

"That's part of the problem, ain't it? You don't think. I suppose you were going on to say that it ain't none of my business, and you're dead right, it ain't. But as you're both sitting outside my 'ouse supping my ale, I'll say what I like. If you don't like it, then sling your 'ook."

Admonished, Marcus was in one of those should I stay or should I go moments.

"Did you mean what you just said about wishing it were me and not the countess' child?"

Staying would mean him saying things that he wasn't ready to say, "If the girl is anything like the mother, I do. What a frightening prospect that would be. You haven't met her, she's *tough*."

"So, you meant it if the girl is frighteningly horrible, if not, you didn't."

Being flippant and funny was not going to get him out of the situation, if anything it has just made things worse.

"I didn't mean that and you know I didn't. The truth is," a draft of ale and a big sigh were called for, "I don't know. It may be a case of what you call *puppy love*, I don't know. See, I don't know what *love* is, I have never been in love. What I do know, is that over the weeks of being in Arantxa's company I have grown fonder of her every day. If that's love, lust or familiarity, I don't know."

"Don't know much, do you?"

"Don't suppose I do."

The darkness was made more complete with the long silence that followed.

"Oww!"

"Sounds like the Jewess 'as come avisiting. Mind your step, love."

"Great advice after someone's just fallen over. I'll be really careful not to fall over that stone again. Why's it so dark?"

"'appens at night time."

"You're on form tonight, Antonia. Don't you have candles? Who's that sitting there with you, Arantxa?"

"And 'er lover boy."

"Sorry, I didn't realise. Am I interrupting? I just came out to get some air and to be talked at by Antonia for a while."

"Nah, not interrupting nothing important, just everyone, not me, saying 'ow much they love the other, but none of it got any future, the usual sort of thing. I'll go and get an ale and a candle for 'er ladyship."

Rebecca found a space on a stone facing the couple. Her eyes were beginning to get used to the darkness, it looked as if they were holding hands!

Bringing the lit candle and the beer, it was now clear they were holding hands. A pang of jealousy shot through her, if only she could hold Flavius's hand in public. Taking a longer look her pang was put well and truly into perspective, this wasn't the hand holding of a joyous couple, it was more like the grip of people hanging on to life that was about to end.

"Apparently the duke 'as caught on to what everyone else knows; his son 'as a new playmate in the port area and he's gone from Jewess to 'eathen. 'e got sent to war with my Pere, for chasing you around. What do you think they'll do to 'im now?"

"They won't have to send him to war, it'll be here soon enough." It was out before she realised what she'd said.

"Perhaps it won't come to that. I have it on the highest authority that negotiations will take place."

"Marcus, listen to her. She knows what she's talking about."

Slow on the uptake, Marcus was about to dispute Rebecca's ability to predict the future, when he remembered Rebecca and Flavius walking away together the last time they were down in this area.

"Oh! Any other details I could pretend I gleamed from Els Munts and not from you?"

"Only that a massive army is being gathered in Toletum and they are in no mood to make any compromises."

"Only! I will be discreet, I promise."

*

Defining the pecking order of this massive army was proving even more difficult than was contemplated. The squabbling was invariably loud and occasionally violent, scuffles broke among the barons themselves, sword fights with fatalities between differing groupings of the restless camps were not uncommon in the shared areas, like taverns.

As Egica rode in taking in the sight of the unfurled proudly flying flags and pennants, he thanked his wisdom of staying out of what must have been going on. The hostility in the air was palpable. It also put into perspective his task; to mould these camps into one cohesive fighting force. It wasn't going to be easy.

"Eventually! We are most pleased that you have finally decided to join us, general." Quiricus had known Egica since he was a child and still had a slight tendency to treat him as one, much to the general's annoyance.

"I came as fast as I could without killing my steed. Besides, I wasn't overly perturbed with a wise, authoritative figure in charge."

"Why do I have the feeling that you are making fun at my expense, young man? I do hope that is not the case. As you know, I am but a poor cleric with little understanding of the military way of seeing things, which is why you are here, and, also, of course, because you are the king's nephew, and as such, may be seen as a neutral arbiter of the rival claims of superiority that have been ringing in our ears for days. Why don't you get cleaned up? Over supper we will outline our plan for this campaign."

Isaac knocked timidly at the side door entrance.

"At least one Jew knows his right place to enter this house. Not like that arrogant bitch. I suppose you're her replacement. I heard she got the big heave-ho."

The mildness in Isaac snapped. "You, servant, take me to the duke, I am expected. I was not called here to listen to the twaddle that some menial, unimportant loud- mouthed housekeeper has to spout."

"So, you're getting uppity now, I'll take you when I am good and ready." Briskly turning around and banging the door behind him, Isaac walked out and back to where Rebecca was. As he was feeling very nervous concerning this out of the blue summons, he'd gone to see his brother for support. Rebecca, seemingly full of knowledge, explained that it was probably just an informative update, not to worry and she'd walk uptown with him to lend support. Once there he'd refused her insistence that he use the front door, knowing full well that wasn't the correct entrance for Jews. However, he was not going to be treated like some piece of dog shit that had got stuck to a servant's sandal.

"Come!" Rebecca who had heard rather than seen the whole exchange, held firmly onto her uncle's upper arm. She marched him to the main door and, as loud as possible, she banged on the door.

Amalaswinth opened the door in rush fearing that something terrible had happened only to be faced with two Jews, "I told you…"

Still with her uncle in tow she pushed past and headed deep into the house. Before Amalaswinth could stop her, they bumped into the duke.

"Hello duke, I'm sure you've heard that I am no longer allowed to represent my people, my uncle here has replaced me. The only thing is that your servant will not permit him to enter, after you'd actually sent word that you wanted to see the Jewish representative."

"It's lovely to see you, Rebecca. A controversy is never far away when you're around. Yes, I had heard of your removal and that of that man you eloquently called, what was it? Something like *that little prick*. Dreadful man, glad to be shot of him. So, this is your uncle. Very pleased to meet you."

He held his hand out and Isaac, recovering from their entrance, his daughter's familiarity, and the description of the rabbi, was slow on the uptake.

"Don't want to shake hands? I suppose you are too offended at your reception, I understand. Perhaps if Amalaswinth apologised it would make it better." He glowered at the housekeeper, who realising her job was already hanging on one string, and that wasn't the strongest thread in the world, ate humble pie expressing her deepest regret.

"Now, will you shake my hand?"

Disentangling himself from his niece he did so eagerly without managing to say a word, he was so awestruck.

"He'll get around to telling you his name is Isaac, sooner or later. I'm not supposed to be here and will get in terrible trouble if I stay. So, bye." As she headed to the door, her getting-a -great -deal -of -practice –these-days wink was aimed at a fuming Amalaswinth.

"Remarkable girl that. You must be very proud of her and more than a little frightened of what she might do next." Ranosindus took over the arm-holding and guided his guest to a comfortable seat in a resplendent room, calling behind him to Amalaswinth to bring refreshments.

Getting straight to the point, he relayed the information that Marcus had given him via a source in Els Munts. As the drinks arrived, so did Marcus and the general.

"I didn't think that you'd actually come. Well done, Marcus!"

"No merit on my part, he was most enthusiastic, also, very lucky as his horse beat mine. I don't know how, but he seems to know the short cuts, which personally I would call cheating."

"Every officer's obligation is to know the terrain he is fighting on. Pay the wager."

Isaac watched in amazement, never having mixed with the rich and famous. Like his niece's previously held opinions, he'd always thought them an austere aloof bunch, that's how they appeared at all the official ceremonies anyway. This lot were anything but. Their treatment of Rebecca, and by default, him, and now this, the potential enemy coming in full of friendliness and good humour.

"You are Rebecca's uncle. We met, very briefly in port area."

Flavius's head shot around at the mention of her name to see a frightened man looking as if he wished he were anywhere else.

"Sorry, I didn't do the introductions. As my son appears to be acquainted with you, no introduction will be necessary there. The other chap, the better horse rider, is our potent adversary in war, General Paulus."

All equipped with a drink in hand, they moved to the table.

"General, a little birdie has told us that the king has rejected any notion of any sort of compromise"

"I'm not sure where you get your information from, and I don't care to confirm or deny it."

"Most understandable."

Isaac swallowing some of his fear managed to speak. "This morning Rabbi Ariel told me that all the barons were sending men to Toletum in the hope of forming a massive army. He wasn't sure whether it was there just as a threat, or an inevitable instrument of war."

"I heard about this Jewish network of yours when I was in Nemausus, most impressive, thank you. Confirmed then. I called you here today general to inform you that you will be given safe passage out of the area before any hostilities start. Talking to Marcus earlier, he was most adamant that your mission was some sort of an attempt at peace, not to be the spearhead of an attacking force. It is not your fault, and I'm quite sure that when you came to negotiate, it was in good faith. I wish you the best of luck but would require you to vacate my property as soon as possible."

"Most generous, duke. Before leaving I would like to say that I do understand your grievances, and I think them not unfounded. That also goes for the Jewish community. While here, I have been made aware of how badly treated you are and I dearly wish it were different. I thank you again for your hospitality, let's hope this dispute doesn't snowball."

Standing, he moved around the table clockwise shaking hands, leaving Marcus to last, who he felt merited a short manly embrace, "You still owe that wager." Then marched out of the room.

"Nice chap, shame he's on the wrong side."

Isaac was speechless, a gentile who is a general in Wamba's army saying that he'd come to understand how badly Jews are treated and would like to change it. How was that possible?"

"Time I left as well. It's been a pleasure and honour meeting you, duke and, you, ..., *your son*. I must inform the community."

"The name's Marcus."

"Yes, pleasure meeting you, again, *Marcus*." A well and truly flustered Isaac headed the wrong way out of the building only to be corrected and guided by the momentarily forgotten name.

"Rebecca is not easily replaced."

"Certainly isn't. Still, seems a decent enough bloke. What we need to do now is inform the count, and start to make serious preparations. To that end I propose that you go to Nemausus immediately. It'd also be a good opportunity for you to meet your future wife."

"Father, I can't."

"Can't? Whatever is so important here that you can't leave it, or should say her?"

"As I think you well know, it's her."

"Yes, I remember her well when she came here with you. Very pretty and spritely lass but not, alas, marriageable material."

"Father, we are both conscious of that. It's just that war is coming, anything might happen, I promise that after the dust has settled, I will go to the altar with whoever you deem pertinent. Until then, please allow us some time together."

Ranosindus thought about this doing the classic chin-stroking gesture. His first thought was that he needed a shave, the second was, why not? He was correct, war meant death, and that could be any, or all, of them. Let him be happy for a while, he'd have the rest of his life to do his duty.

"That doesn't detract from the fact that the message has to be sent. I will need all my officers here, so none of them can go. If you can find a

suitable replacement before the end of the morning, I will agree to your request, if you can't, then you'll have to go. Deal?"
"Yes, deal."

*

Egica strolled carelessly into the dining room, the massive table was set for three, screaming intimacy; none of the competing barons invited spoke volumes for the trust between the war instigators and those that would carry out their will.

Julian was the first of the clerics to enter. Knowing who he was, yet not knowing the man except by reputation, Egica waited for the more senior man to speak.

"I am Bishop Julian, I must assume that you are General Egica."

Except for the slightly high pitch less-than-manly voice, this was how Julian had been portrayed; aloof and arrogant. Ruthless was another adjective associated with the man. This though, was a bit more difficult to ascertain in an introduction of so few words.

"Sorry I am late. Good, you seem to have introduced yourselves. The reason for my delay is that we shall be joined by another guest for supper. He has recently arrived, and at this moment is readying himself to eat with us. I suggest a glass of this sweet wine from the south which I find most agreeable as an aperitif."

They whiled away the waiting time sipping the wine, sitting in the more comfortable chairs, talking of Egica's journey, the weather, and the king's health. Not long conversations, summed up as long, dull, too humid and robust in that chronological order.

"I am so sorry to have kept you waiting. I did propose leaving our meeting until after supper, however, Bishop Quiricus insisted that I be present."

Bishop Iulianus of Hispalis, who looked as if he missed very few meals, was a big man with a big voice. No one in his congregation, even in the final pews, would miss a word said.

"You know, Julian, I fear that you have yet to have the pleasure of meeting General Egica. Shall we be seated?" Hands were shaken and heads inclined.

A succulent superb meal was served in many courses, Egica picked at this rich food which wasn't really to his taste, preferring instead a more basic fare. His attitude and approach were in sharp contrast to the other three, who devoured the table, especially the southerner. Quiricus and Iulianus came built for the role with large stomachs to fill. Julian was more of a surprise as he had a thin wizened body with a spiteful face and an overly large nose. Perhaps that was where he stored all that he was tucking away, mused Egica.

Quiricus held court explaining the details of the Tarraconense /Gallia Gothica problem to Iulianus and concluded by saying "They are arrogant, have notions of grandeur from their historical past, they challenge central authority and are most lax on the Jewish problem. They are in the process of proclaiming a new state which would recognise Jewish rights, undoing decades of good work by all our concilia. I suppose they will call it a kingdom, once they have decided who shall take that role; I believe there are internal disputes about this. Furthermore, we are told that they have entered into an alliance with the Franks and may be negotiating a similar alliance with the Vascones. All in all, it is the biggest threat we have faced since the Byzantine invasion. It'll be the job of you two, Egica militarily and you, Iulianus, civilly, to restore some order."

"I don't like to interrupt your flow, Quiricus, but aren't you forgetting someone quite important? Namely, King Wamba. When I left him, he was gathering all his forces ready to strike from the north."

Slightly wrong footed Quiricus rectified, "Of course the king will be in overall nominal charge. It's just that we feel that he will need some expert guidance to ensure that we do not see another rebellion of its kind in a generation. This is no time for leniency, we must make an example of the leaders of the rebellion and especially the Jews, who need to be cleansed from this Christian Kingdom."

"Finally! I whole–heartedly agree with your sentiments. I have tried my best in Hispalis with measures to discourage, isolate, convert, and even encouragements for them to leave, but like infestations of vermin, they are always there. It's time to pull out the problem by the roots so that it'll never grow again."

*

Head down, brimming with different thoughts and scenarios, Flavius moved at top speed to where his horse was tied up in the outer courtyard. As a result, he didn't notice anyone near the horse, and if he had, he'd have presumed it was a groom brushing it down after the sweaty race with Marcus. One foot in the stirrup he was about to mount.

"I don't even merit a hello anymore?"

Half way up and half way down, he stopped, this voice was the protagonist of most of his thoughts and all of the scenarios. "What are you doing here?"

"Nice greeting! Your horse was happier to see me."

"I meant, well, it doesn't matter what I meant. I am exceptionally happy to see you."

"Better, close to convincing."

"So you told them, did you?"

"Of course, I couldn't not tell them. Don't worry. Only one person suspects the source and he won't tell anyone."

"We really need to talk. Not here. On the beach as soon as you can?"

"You're talking as if you were issuing orders, stop!"

"Could you please meet me on the beach later?"

"On the beach? Are you sure it's talk that you want?"

"Among other things, yes. I really need to talk some things through with you."

"I couldn't possibly get there until after lunch."

"Rebecca, it's really important. I'm going there now and I'll wait. I need some thinking time anyway. Please come as soon as you can."

Jumping slightly at the noise of the main palace door opening and quickly closing, she said she would try before speeding back to the waiting point for her uncle. He was already there when she arrived; she took his arm both through affection and also because of his unsteadiness.

"Oh niece, I am not designed for these sorts of things, why do people keep pushing me into them? You are so much better. The way in which the duke treated and talked about you, he has respect and admiration for you. Amazing. You, a Jew and a girl. Well done. Sadly, I don't believe he thinks so highly of me."

"I'm sure he does, perhaps, more so."

"No. I couldn't even remember the name of his son! You know I am terrible with names, it was so embarrassing."

"Marcus? That's funny. Don't worry, nobody remembers *Marcus'* name."

"OH yes they do! Rebecca, stop putting me down."

Rebecca had the decency to blush a deep shade of puce.

"Where did you come from?"

"That's a stupid question, little Miss Smarty-pants. We all came from the same place. Didn't you hear me running after you?"

"Evidently not, otherwise I would have said even more horrible things about you. What's the hurry, and why do you want to speak to us lowly Jews?" The arm that wasn't supporting her uncle was now linked in Marcus', making him very uncomfortable. Knowing and befriending Jews is one thing, having your arm linked to an extremely attractive one, even if the uncle is hanging off the other side, was more like a statement. Noticing his squirm and less than comfortable posture, she held on for just a bit longer before releasing him.

"Actually, it's not you that I want to speak to Rebecca, it's your uncle." She swapped arms, leaving a confused Isaac in the middle. "How can I help you, *Marcus*?"

"Congratulations, uncle!"

"Ignore her, the rest of us do. It's just that you said something in that meeting that interested me greatly about the rabbi from Narbo."

"Narbo. David. No, that was the other one umm."

"Try Ariel, uncle."

"Ariel. Yes, that's the one."

"When is he leaving?"

"He may have already left. I know he wanted to get away sharpish this morning."

"Would you mind taking me to where he's staying? I would dearly like to talk to him."

They changed direction, heading back up town to where Zachary lived. Nobody spoke. Isaac had nothing to say lest he'd immerse himself deeper in this quagmire he was slowly sinking into. Wanting desperately to stay near Arantxa, Marcus had to find a way to persuade the rabbi to take the message in his stead. Rebecca was keen to get away as soon as possible, this detour was not appreciated as it would delay her beach arrival. She wanted to see him as she was most inquisitive about what Flavius had to say. However, no matter what it was, there was no way she could just suddenly abandon her uncle.

In a hope that matters would be resolved quicker without her, she waited outside. Surprisingly, it was a very short wait, and it was Marcus who came out by himself.

"Your uncle says not to wait for him as he's got to report back to the others about the meeting."

Relief appeared all over Rebecca's face.

"May I escort you, if you are going back to port area?"

"I don't need escorting anywhere, thank you. If you'd like to keep me company, then you may, as long as you tell me what this is all about."

Marcus detailed his success in getting rabbi Ariel to take a message to Nemausus.

"A most accommodating bloke. In fact all the Jews I've met have been really good people. That is, besides *the little prick* and you."

"What! I'm lovely. Ask your father."

"He doesn't know you like I do. You're always mean to me. Anyway, he has terrible taste in women."

"That's not true, I.." Actually she couldn't think of a time she'd ever been nice to Marcus. "Why did you want Ariel to take the message?"

He explained.

"So, your father is turning an official blind eye to Arantxa while hostilities last?"

"From what I understand, that's about the measure of it."

Stopping them both in their tracks not far from her home, she kissed Marcus tenderly on the cheek. "Who says I am not nice to you?"

*

After a couple of days touring the different encampments to talk to each baron individually, Egica realised two things. The first was that they needed to get onto the road as soon as possible, if not, the regular petty skirmishes would be upgraded to uncontrollable battles among the groupings. The only thing preventing this so far was the lack of any major natural alliances. Besides family bonds, everyone hated everyone; the only differentiating factor was the amount of hatred involved. The second was that he could trust nobody. Nearly every baron had an axe to grind with one or two others. If and when it came to battle, he'd be hard pressed to keep one force as a reserve for another as it may be in the long term interest of the reserve baron, *not* to enter the fray until the first had been severely weakened or destroyed, if they entered the field at all.

It got to a point where he had to keep a written account of who he thought hated who more than they would hate a supposedly common enemy. It was like a jigsaw where some parts fitted, others didn't belong and there was no overall picture to make up. This was no way to run an army.

"Quiricus, you've known me all my life. You were very good friends with my father, why is it that you hate me so much?"

The bishop was somewhat taken aback by the question, "What makes you think I have any animosity for you, Egica?"

"Because I believe it was you who volunteered me for this role of general of this disparate group of noble back stabbers."

"They are a trifle unruly, I'll give you that. However, I am sure that when push comes to shove, they will all be pushing or shoving in the same direction."

" A man of great faith! I need your help. I know, don't bother denying it, that you run an effective secret spy network with connections within the camps of all the major players."

"My son, you overestimate…"

"No, I don't. I said; don't negate this fact I know to be true. What I need from you, to stop this venture from being a total disaster, is information. I have been trying to keep a list, but it's woefully inadequate. On the battlefield I have to know who I can rely on, who hasn't got previous with someone else, and would want it to become payback time."

"Well, I don't think that I can help you."

"If you don't, I will refuse to lead this squabbling rabble anywhere. If we were going to put down a local bun fight, I am sure it could be done without your information. If however, we are faced by these insurrectionists backed by an organised Frank force, we will be obliterated, which may mean, not only the loss of a region but perhaps the whole kingdom as the Franks would see no reason to stop if this, the largest army we could field, loses."

"I will see what I can find. I will send a person to your rooms later who may be able to help."

"There's another thing I need."

"More?"

"This one is easier. I would like you and Julian, either together or separately, depending on your logistics, to go around to each campsite in the next day or so, to rally them to the cause, and, more importantly, threaten any baron with excommunication if they do not follow my orders. They may think twice before attacking a friendly force, if they know that heaven will be denied them."

Quiricus agreed that this would be a smart move and would be done even though it may take more than a day.

*

"Where is he? You said you went with Isaac to protect him and you come back without him. What have you done to him?" Jacob had only noticed his daughter, he didn't realise there was someone in her wake. "Oh, hello young man. We meet again. If you are here for supper, I do hope that it's better than last time."

"Sorry, I did try my best with these strange ingredients."

"Arantxa! I didn't see you there, either. I didn't mean that it wasn't good, it just could have been better considering we had the son of the duke at the table."

"Thank you for trying to make amends, Jacob. I know it was awful, and Marcus, the polite guest, already told me."

"I did not! I think I said that I had better."

Seeing the poor boy floundering as was he, Jacob decided to return to his opening question. "Talking about food is all well and good, but where is my brother?"

"Uncle is reporting back to Ariel and Zachary. War is imminent."

"What!"

"It's been confirmed that Toletum is amassing a huge army."

"This is terrible news. I had hoped that negotiations might solve the problem."

"As did we all. My father was convinced it wouldn't come to this, especially after talking to General Paulus."

"I've heard that he's a terribly nice chap, well, as far as an enemy commander goes. Do excuse me, with this news; I really need to attend to some business matters."

"Papa, they aren't at the city gates, they won't be here for weeks."

"Still, a stitch in time and all that" with that he all but ran towards his office.

The three of them watched him with mild amusement, unsure whether he was more worried about the massed enemy forces, or the talk returning to the merits of Arantxa's cooking.

"He's like that, always preparing for the worst, talking of which, I think Marcus wants a conversation with the cook of the year. Do not cater for me for lunch, I have to… make some plans as well. Will be back in time for supper."

With that she moved at what looked like a set family-fast speed- mode in the other direction to her father.

*

Left alone in a house that belonged to neither, they felt strange and out of place.

"Shall we walk?"

They did, in an awkward silence and a prudent gap between them. Not needing to agree on where they were going, their feet took them in the only plausible direction even though it felt strange. For Arantxa, the fact that it was light, and for Marcus, because he was going towards the same destination from a completely different angle.

"Thought you two only lived in the dark. Everyone'll see ya. Tongues will be wagging, I can tell you."

Antonia was much more efficient and dedicated to her role than any sentry post in the army. Nothing and nobody got past her. This time she had the three kids and a bundle of washing in a basket, whether it was clean or dirty really didn't bother the walkers too much.

"Let them."

Marcus's statement surprised the women. The imminent call to arms was the talk of the town and Antonia knew that Marcus would have a leading position in the fighting, so she presumed it was a devil take attitude that had caused his words. Whereas Arantxa thought this is what he'd come to talk about, THE goodbye.

"Like your attitude, boy. Fuck 'em. Come on you three, this way." She shouted a cheery bye as she headed towards the wash-houses. So the clothes were dirty, thought Arantxa.

On the face of it normal services were resumed with the gap and the lack of words. Inside, though, Arantxa was a mess. She knew that this moment would come and she'd been preparing herself for it in a number of ways; daily telling herself of its inevitability, and ring-fencing her emotions by continually repeating that he was nothing more than any other fling. She'd really liked one boy back in the village, he'd hurt her when he started going with another girl at the same time, claiming it was all good fun. For days, even weeks, she'd felt that the sun wouldn't ever shine again. It didn't help that it was a bleak mid winter with lots of fog. What she was experiencing now wasn't in the same universe. This was real pain; her stomach hurt, her legs were weary and her mouth was bone dry. Having gone through the port with its lone ship still standing idle waiting for a cargo, they were still a fair way from the beach.

"We don't have to go to the beach, we could just say goodbye here, nobody's looking, I'll give you a final kiss, it wouldn't be so far to walk back."

"What? Who's saying goodbye?"

*

Bishop Iulianus was trying to get a feel of how things were in the camps, and like Egica, was doing a tour introducing himself and interviewing the most important, those with the largest number of troops, barons. What a disparate lot. No two were there for the same reason, well, at least, they didn't voice the same reason. Lots of meaningless rubbish like; "to defend the kingdom" was spouted. He suspected that the Jewish problem was not anywhere near the top of their agenda; his work would be cut out. The solid backing of the Church's highest echelons needed to be turned into practical reality on the ground. In an effort to shore up the top of the military pyramid, he knocked and entered Egica's chambers only to find another man deep in conversation with the general.

"Oh Bishop, if you wouldn't mind waiting a few minutes, I need to conclude this conversation."

Iulianus was not used to being made to wait by anyone.

"I'm sure this man wouldn't mind returning later, I would like to converse with you immediately."

If Iulianus didn't like waiting, Egica hated being ordered around by someone who was not, and could not be, his superior. The man in question stood to take his leave.

"Sit. Bishop, I told you, I would be with you momentarily."

Iulianus held his massive frame in its most upright position for a short while, then decided not to make an issue of this lack of respect. Payback time would come, turning and without another word left the room.

"I think you've just complicated your task yet further, that's not a man to be affronted."

"Perhaps when you've finished telling me about the barons, you ought to give me the low down on him."

Iulianus smouldered downs the tairs to bump into Bishop Julian greeting a man who was unequivocally Jewish.

"Ohh, Bishop Iulianus, I wonder whether you'd like to join us, we are going into the meeting room to talk."

"Talk to a Jew?"

"I understand your distaste," the Jew answered," I have no desire to be in the company of a gentile either; however, it may be of mutual benefit."

Julian led the way with the reluctant pair in his wake. Once seated, Julian who placed himself at the head of the table, started, "I believe you have travelled from Tarraco."

"That is correct. My name is Rabbi Hillel, the former leader of the Jewish community there."

"Former?"

"Yes, I have serious disagreements with our community taking sides in what I see as an inter-Christian conflict."

"It may be the objective of the conflict to rid ourselves of this so called Jewish community," Iulianus almost spat the words.

"Then, if that is the case, we may have an interest in common."

A bevy of baffled bishops were stunned into silence.

"I believe, and I think we are of like-mind on this matter, there should be little or no, interaction between the Jewish and Gentile communities. We are, and should remain two distinct groups and like oil and water, cannot mix. I would like to propose that the Jews be kept in completely separate segregated areas, which would ensure that there is no accidental mingling."

"Why should we tolerate you in this country, a Christian country, at all?"

"Historically we have been here as long, if not longer than the country has been Christian, so there are some accrued rights. If, however, simply by our presence we cause so much offence, then I believe we should be encouraged and helped to leave with the natural home of the Jews as our destination."

Julian sat back in his chair. This was most certainly an unexpected turn of events, not one that should be dismissed out of hand. Severe draconian measures had been in force for quite some time without any major reduction in the influence and size of the Jew population. A collaborative element to the final solution may yet prove invaluable to the overall goal.

"I think that you ought to accompany our forces. On your way out, tell the servant where you are staying and we'll be in touch."

Hillel took his leave without bidding anyone farewell.

"Julian, you can't be serious."

"Think with your head, not your heart Iulianus. How many years have you been trying to rid Hispalis of Jews?" The other bishops made no attempt to answer. "Has it worked to any significant level?", still no response. "I don't imagine it's for any lack of effort on your part. With one of *them* arguing the same thing, we may be able to reach those inaccessible areas; the so-called converts."

"But you won't have to be with him on this journey, I will."

"I'm sure you will find a system where you'll be able to avoid each other, except for essential meetings. After all, he hates you as much as you hate him."

*

Coming over the last rocks, she could make out the horse peacefully munching on tough dune grass. Something from its demeanour and evident lack of enthusiasm showed its unhappiness with the fare, whereas the barely clothed general was doing something between pacing and marching, hands clasped behind his back, with the same head down pose similar to the outer courtyard mode when he hadn't noticed her stroking the reluctant chomper. This must be his thinking pose - the man, not the horse - and given the level of concentration, not a brilliant one for a general, as anyone could sneak up on him, forcing him to revaluate whatever he was thinking with a more immediate problem. Knowing that she wouldn't be observed by this non- attentive soldier, she stood admiring the view. He really was an attractive sight; big broad shoulders, a large slightly hairy chest, tapering waist, massive thighs and a cute- well formed bum. She certainly could have done worse. A happy few minutes were spent enjoying the sight until her curiosity got the better of spectator sport. Climbing down, she tried to make a noise so that he wouldn't be startled.

"You're here, you're early."

"You really have to work on your happy greeting repertoire. You don't make a girl ecstatic with words like that!"

"Sorry, I was thinking and I.."

"Have no real excuses. Do I at least get a welcoming kiss?"

"Er, yes." Quickly covering the distance, he placed a per functionary kiss on her lips.

"Excellent, that was really worth trekking all this way in the sun for. Should I go, and come back later when you've thought all your thoughts?"

"No, I don't think so."

"Flavius!"

"It's not easy, the same ones keep coming into my head and they are wrong, so, I go for the other option, only to find out it is worse, then, the process starts again."

Stopping her pretend hurt, she could see that the man was in a right quandary. "Perhaps if you said them aloud to me, it'd make more sense."

"The thing is that you're part of the problem and I'm not sure that you are part of the solution."

Pretend pain became real hurt. For once not worrying about how much it would irritate, she lowered herself onto and into the soft sand. Following her lead he thumped himself down causing a slight sand spray, which at any other moment would have warranted telling off material. This time in a careful caring way she took his hand.

"I really don't know what to do. Whatever decision I make now, it'll change my life forever, and there would be no going back. "

Her hurt was nothing compared to what he was suffering, wanting to share, wanting to help, but knowing it was better that she remained quiet, all she could do was squeeze his hand a little tighter.

It came out slowly with considerable effort like prising a determinedly unwilling to leave mussel from the where it was happily stuck on the rocks. Wamba had all but accused him of treason for suggesting a compromise, and saying that some of the rebels' concerns were legitimate. This had offended him greatly as he'd always believed himself to be loyal to the crown and to Wamba in particular; a man he both liked and respected. Upon reflection, he wondered whether it could be true as he was questioning some of the foundations the kingdom was built on, fundamental pillars such as the centralised unquestioning power of the king and his bishops to impose their will on everyone.

Tarraconensis/Gallia Gothica had been told to obey, and should do just that. Then, there was his discovery, through Rebecca, of what it meant to be Jewish in this state, something which he found grossly unfair and unjustified by any of his understandings of his religion or the previous Arian history of the Goths. The final factor was his inability to contemplate fighting for these values in general and, specifically, fighting against the woman he loved.

The air was heavy. This was as profound as it was unexpected. No wonder the poor man was in a distracted pacing pickle. She needed to lighten it.

"I may be a bit presumptuous here, but I suspect this woman you say you love is sitting beside you, and would dearly delight in a kiss from the man she truly does love." .

If his admission of love for her was a surprise, her own voicing of something that she hadn't even dared think, was immensely shocking.

When they finally came up for air, she pushed him back slightly so she could see his conflicted face. Written in capital letters was "a traitor in love."

"The decision is made, isn't it? You are going to betray your country. Well, I think it's the least I can do to betray my people by declaring myself for a gentile."

*

Whoever lives in the future is a prize idiot was Arantxa's way of justifying her delirious delight. Marcus could never, through no fault of his own, make a future commitment to her/ them. He had though, fought for a present. It made her feel something she'd probably never felt in her life; valued. This happiness couldn't last, so it had to be enjoyed for what is was. They spent hours making love, resting, swimming, telling each other totally uninteresting stories from their very different formative years, laughing. It was heavenly.

This wasn't a one sided voyage into pleasures unknown, Marcus had never experienced anything like it either. It was bliss. Doing his best to block out anything except the present, thoughts of combat, blood and death did intrude. Fighting, the unknown at the time, Vasconis tribes, had caused some fear, not any anguish. This time it'd be both, as he'd be fighting people like Milo or Flavius, people who spoke the same language, shared the same culture, it'd be fighting *us* not *them*. At one point, when Arantxa was exhaustedly snoozing, he looked down on her features. Six months ago she could not have been anything but, *them*, now what is she, *us*? His north, his certainties, had been lost, or at least mislaid, he needed to think through this more, then looking farther down than the face, he knew thinking was going to do no good.

"What, again?" she said sleepily as she began to realise what was happening.

It couldn't be said that they walked back, it was more like they dragged their bodies back to port area. The physical gap between them was still present, if a great deal smaller than the outward journey.

"Bugger me. You two are going to die of exhaustion. You've been *star gazing* all this time?"

"It's a beautiful night, Antonia."

"It may yet be when it gets dark! We'll 'ear the patter of tiny feet within the year I'd wager."

This interposed a future real into Arantxa's mind set, which she quickly dismissed with all the other possibilities.

"Who knows what will happen in the next year, a lot of terrible things I imagine, and a baby wouldn't be among the worst of them."

"Girl, I've got to admire your thinking. Do all 'eathens have the same outlook?"

Before she could answer, Pere came out of the house with the smallest child in his arms.

"Thought I heard other voices aside, my darling wife. Marcus, I saw the duke today. The call to arms is going out tomorrow. Every man will be expected to do their duty"

*

In the not so distant past, the Hispano-Romans were not allowed to serve in the Goth- led armies, so the fighting forces were relatively small.

These days everyone had to fight for the liege lord. When he said "fight", everyone called, had to stop whatever they were doing; fishing, harvesting, or whatever to respond to their master's call.

The centuries old traditions of the migrant peoples from the Baltic shores had changed, especially since the Goth elite had moved into the field of landowning vast tracks of the countryside. The Germanic tribe values of more or less equality had been lost with the acquired Roman approach of elitism being adopted, in which the norm was master and vassals, the latter continually in debt and owing anything and everything to their *betters*. A feudal system had emerged for the first time.

After all these years on the Iberian Peninsula, the Goths had in all but name disappeared. Literally in name, as for taxation purposes, it was still better to be seen as a Goth landowner rather than a Hispano-Roman one. Those below the elite had had to change as well. This new status quo was that all the people within the estates belonged by tithes to the lord. Nominally, most remained within the concept of freemen not slaves. The distinction, once sharp in the brotherhood communities fostered historically by the Goths, was becoming more and more blurred as the few amassed great wealth. This new elite protected their property or expanded it with the help of the number of men they could call to arms. Some of these private armies were vast. Central power was always beholden to and wary of these large forces.

Duke Ranosindus could personally call on a significant number and oblige a number of minor or medium landowners to follow suit. And this is what he'd done.

"Light training in the mornings with everyone allowed home to harvest in the afternoons is the order that has gone out. You and I have been assigned the same group."

"I didn't .."

"No, your father didn't know where you were, and when I offered to find you, he told me not to bother as he said you'd be back soon enough. Just thought you ought to know."

"Thanks, Pere."

Future present, thought Arantxa.

*

There were differing emotions ranging from annoyance to disappointment and passing through relief within the Tarraco Jewish community at the fact that Rabbi Hillel had upped and left after the his failed cherem. Jeremiah was particularly vocal in his defence, blaming people for not being sufficiently devout to keep such an excellent visionary. As a result, and yet again, they were rudderless in this insecure time of upheaval. The Jewish men hadn't received an official summons to come to the training sessions, it wasn't a legal obligation they were under, nor was it necessary as the vast of the majority of the youth attended spontaneously. Pere had been impressed by their enthusiasm, if not their ability.

It was the norm that people hung around to chew the fat post services. Friends too busy to see each other during the week, gathered together. Today the huddles were distinct in the air they were giving off. There was an excited buzz of the younger ones, each eager to recount their triumphs, and the failures of others in their days of combat training. This was matched by the sombre reality of what all this would mean to their off-spring by the older generations, none of whom had experienced the likes of war, but had enough sense and perspective to realise this was not going to be *fun*,

Rebecca stayed apart, partly because she didn't naturally fall into any group, and partly due to the fact that she felt, justifiably or not, she wasn't sure, excluded. A sensation exacerbated by Jeremiah spitting on the ground as he was walking by, an action, she chose to ignore. She knew this was the best it was ever going to get once the news of her relationship with a gentile was discovered.

At this moment the only people who did know were Arantxa, probably Marcus, and Antonia, the only one of whom, who was trustworthy enough not to breathe a word, was Arantxa, the others were leaky at best. Her father needed to be told before he inadvertently found out from one of these leaks. It would break his heart, she knew, still it was better coming from her, not some helpful friend. In the last couple of days, there had been various times when she could have broached the subject without going into detail, but she'd chickened out, thinking the man deserved his happiness a little longer.

Seeing her father standing with his brother, the pair of them gave the appearance that they were shouldering all the problems of everyone present. Who was she kidding? Preserving what happiness a bit longer?

*

Marcus, covered in sweat, was dismounting as Flavius entered the courtyard in the most basic uniform he'd ever seen the general wear. In fact, if he hadn't been wearing a sword, Marcus would have struggled to differentiate it from his casual house clothes.

"A bit underdressed to visit a duke, aren't you?"

"Whereas you smell as if you desperately need to bathe. How's the training going? I hear they are somewhat raw and you have a big job on your hands."

"A general of the opposing army really can't be asking questions like that. When will you be packed up and off? I am told that there has been no movement in that direction."

"Actually, that's what I am here to talk to your father about. Will you join us?"

"As you said, I am not fit for polite company.

"If you stand upwind, it won't be so bad. Please come with me, I want you to hear what I have to say."

They sauntered with purpose in together. Marcus noticed that Flavius wasn't his relaxed confident self. His movements, usually striding with head held high daring the world to challenge him type approach, was now small-stepped hesitant even polite, holding the door for Marcus to enter first. Something was amiss, regardless of his smelly grubby state, he needed to know what, for the life of him he couldn't imagine what could have caused such a change.

"Arh Marcus , I thought I could smell you. I really wish you'd …"

"Father, General Paulus is here and he wanted my presence, so please excuse my inappropriate odour."

"General, do come in, have a seat. Would you like something to drink?"

"No thank you, duke."

Marcus noted that his tone was different as well, more like the insecure uncle of Rebecca than the general he knew and respected.

"My house-servants tell me that there are no preparations to leave Els Munts, well, nothing visible to them. I thought we had an agreement of a few days ago that you'd vacate the premises as soon as possible."

"It's true that I have given no orders to strike camp. In fact, I haven't told the men of the information that was given to you the other day."

A little tension crept into the air. Was the general going to fight using Els Munts as his base until the main force arrived? Surely not? That would be almost suicidal.

"I'm sure you must have your reasons,"

"Which is why I am here."

Eye contact between two men rarely took place in any walk of life. There is a difference though, not gazing into another's eyes, and avoiding them altogether, which was what had happened until the moment that Paulus raised his head and looked straight ahead.

"There's no easy way of saying this. I am about to do something that I would not have imagined I could have until a few days ago. I am *not* going to fight for Wamba while he continues this unjust campaign against Tarraconensis/Gallia Gothica and his persecution of the Jews. There. I have said it."

The standing upwind, as instructed , Marcus nearly fell as he sought stability from the closest chair. The duke, momentarily speechless, was the first to recover. "Well, this has come as a bolt out of the blue, a very welcome one, I must say. I celebrate your words and admire your courage, it could not have been easy for you to come to this decision. Would it be too much to ask the hows and whys of this incredible change?"

"You may ask, as I ask myself. The problem is that I doubt I am able to answer you any better than I have answered myself."

"I believe I know at least part of the answer; Rebecca."

Flavius remained quiet. The duke nearly leapt out of his chair.

"Really! Oh, my god! Well, I never! You can knock me down with a feather!"

Flavius was beginning to show his annoyance with these theatricals.

"Sorry, general. It's just that, well, I am surprised. Actually, thinking about it, I am not surprised. Rebecca is probably the most impressive female I have ever met and I don't really know her. If anyone could turn a man's head and heart, she's the one."

"I don't think so. She's a pain in the arse."

"Ignore him. My dear Flavius, may I call you Flavius? general seems somewhat inappropriate now, you really have complicated your future. Putting aside your military career, and how Wamba will react, she's Jewish. That'll be a difficult sell to both her and your people."

"Which is why I would ask that this information doesn't leave this room, I took the liberty of making sure that your housekeeper was nowhere near the door when we came in."

"We will not breathe a word." A quick glance at Marcus received an exaggerated nod. "Even though I feel it's a decision we should celebrate."

"I need to tell my men first; it's my first obligation."

"Indeed you must. I do realise the turmoil that must be in your head. However, may I ask another question?"

The head had returned to its downward floor observing state, "Go on." was said most wearily.

"As I understand it, you have decided not to fight with Wamba. Does that mean that you have decided to fight against him by coming on to our side? We could certainly use someone of your military experience and know-how."

"I am still not sure I am able to make that step. I really need to spend some more time thinking this through, I'm sure you understand."

"We most certainly do. We will respect your wish and not mention any of what you've said to our allies and friends until you have made your final decisions. I thank you greatly for the courtesy of you informing us before others. I look forward to counting you among our number soon."

An elated Marcus offered to accompany Flavius to the door, expressing his relief and happiness that they wouldn't be facing each other on a field of battle.

"Marcus, I really need to see Rebecca. It's too late in the day to go to our usual place, I wonder whether you know anywhere that we could meet that's discreet."

"The simple answer to that is no. A general and a Jew meeting anywhere will cause talk, which neither of you want nor can afford."

"There must be somewhere. It's important."

Marcus thought and could only think of one place where the general wouldn't be out of place and Rebecca wouldn't either. They would have to arrive separately and under the cover of darkness. Suggesting that Flavius leave his horse in the courtyard and go to have some supper in a tavern near the port which catered for sailors and travellers, Marcus would come and collect him later. First, he'd go to see if he could contact Rebecca.

*

Sat in his office in the comfortable chair, hands clasped in front of him, not at the table poring over numbers as was his wont in his privacy, he was trying to decide what should worry him the most.

Business had been in steady decline for years, no markets for exports, and nobody was buying imports. There were a whole number of factors in play, all of them out of his control. So, logically, pondering and worrying was going to do no good. Still, here he was. The lack of physical money was one of the biggest problems. True, there were a great number of gold coins in circulation. No, that was the wrong word, they didn't circulate, they were kept, hidden, buried, squirreled away for a rainy day. As nobody could spend them it didn't make too much difference. Smaller denomination coins didn't exist; therefore no change could be given if someone wanted to purchase something small, and relatively inexpensive items like the ceramics in which he dealt. The beautifully crafted imports from the east were in demand, but couldn't be paid for. People had almost returned to a barter system where some locally handmade, not wheel turned, article, was exchanged for something else, without the need for currency. The fact that these pottery plates and cups were shoddy leaked and lasted not a long time, didn't matter, they were the only things available.

This was the lot of the ever dwindling urban population, his market. The big estates, where an ever increasing number of folk was migrating to, were more or less self sufficient for all their basic needs. The workers forwent any idea of independence, their labour power was exchanged for food. Times were tough and options were few. The land owners accrued wealth, power and importance, and eschewed the beautiful quality items that used to set them apart, resulting in the bottom dropping out of that market as well. The future of trade in general, and his business in particular, was bleak.

His instalment loan to the Bishop was one less worrying point as it had moved, well, to all appearances anyway, to the backburner.

The looming war was a more immediate worry. It was hard to ever be positive about an armed conflict unless you were a blacksmith. The bulk of the suffering was always the lot of the little man, be you a combatant or not. Understanding that they, as Jews, had to be involved in this inter-Christian conflict, otherwise slow strangulation was their only future, it still felt too risky to put all your money on just one throw of the dice.

The only slightly bright point on the horizon was Rebecca's avoidance of a cherem. It had been an extremely close call. Thanks to Isaac's connections, they may well have heard the last of this, especially, as Hillel had deserted ship.

"Papa, there you are. May I join you?"

Rebecca asking politely and not just barging in, this was new. "What's the matter? You never ask."

She plonked herself down in her little girl safe position next to his knees. "Don't you think you are a bit old to do that? You're a grown woman; it's not sightly for anyone. It wasn't for a little girl never mind..."

"You're right, I am a grown woman, but there are times when it feels much better to be a little girl."

Heightened awareness; there was something seriously wrong... this timid approach was not his daughter's style unless something dreadful had happened, or was going to happen.

"Papa,"

"*Yes*, I think that my role has been established, though I'm not sure how well I have played it. You are not what anyone would call a conventional daughter and I suppose I am to blame for that."

"I don't think so, papa. If you think about what you've just said, you are rather denying me my own personality by saying it. It's true that you have been a contributing factor, it shouldn't be denied, though, I am who I am because I want to be that person, and it's part of that process I need to talk to you about."

His stomach tensed and knotted. This was going to be bad. When she knew she was in the right and everyone else was in the wrong, which was fairly often, her approach was always bluster, loud self-righteous bluster. This softly, softly manner spoke of something mega, bordering on the catastrophic. Unsure as to whether he wanted her to stop speaking or get on with it, he remained totally still, and quite thankful that from her position she could not see the worry lines that were already there, slowly deepening to become furrows.

"I really don't know how to tell you this. I suppose I should just come out with it and then it's done."

His mind racing through various possibilities, he was beginning to panic.

"I'm in love."

An initial sense of relief hit him, quickly followed by a massive sense of foreboding as the inevitable *who with* question was asked.

"This is the part that you are not going to like."

"Not that Marcus?"

"What? No, he's a boy."

"Who then?"

"General Paulus."

"Who? The enemy commander? How? Why? You don't even know him."

"I do, certainly enough to know that we love each other."

"But he's the enemy. He's a gentile. He's ….inappropriate. Rebecca!!!"

"I don't think he's going to be the enemy commander much longer. As to the fact that he's both inappropriate and a gentile, I'm afraid they are true."

Jacob buried his face in his hands.

*

Supper had been sombre. Food was pushed around the plates without much being eaten. Rebecca didn't want to say anything, Jacob couldn't trust himself to say anything that he would later regret, and Arantxa felt she shouldn't say a word.

"I'm going to my office, please do not disturb me there." Imparting this information Jacob shuffled away, leaving Rebecca to reflect that the last time he'd said and done this, in contrast to this slow moving shadow, it'd almost been a sprint. Guilt invaded her every pore.

"So, you told him about Flavius."

There was a nod of agreement.

"In my village, firstly the girl would NEVER have said anything. If she'd been found out, then, if she was lucky, she'd be beaten soundly and chained to a post until her future was resolved. If she weren't, then, well, look what happened to my sister. You have no idea how fortunate you are."

"I don't know. In some ways I think I would prefer that."

Indignant swelling began to appear in Arantxa's face.

"No, don't! listen to me. I'm not belittling your sister, nor praising the reaction of your family, which was awful and inexcusable, even if it was the norm. What I am saying is that I have profoundly hurt the person I love and respect most in the world and I would dearly like things to be different. If he opposed me, got angry, it would something to fight against; a position I am used to. Something that I'd prefer compared to this immense guilt that I feel. I would like to think that he will come round and accept it, although I know that there is no way he can. His only child with a gentile! It's not what the community will say and think, he'd live with that, as he did with the cherem. It's a more fundamental betrayal of him and everything he has taught me."

"He loves you more than his religion or even his life, if he sees that you are happy he may come to accept it."

"With the path I've chosen, can I ever be happy?"

"YES! Look at me. I rejected and *betrayed* my people and was totally alone. Now I have found a happiness here in Tarraco I have never known at any point in my life. Who would have thought that was possible? Rebecca, this is easy to say but hard to do. You have to be true to yourself regardless of the consequences."

Rebecca thought about this remarkable statement. Women were not allowed to think this way in any culture - not in Arantxa's nor the Christian and certainly not the Jewish. They were expected to always put men first; father, husband and sons, all had prior rights on their lives. The best a woman could aspire to was to live their lives through these men, influencing them behind the scenes. By stating something so incredible this girl was showing that she had certainly travelled a long way, and not just in distance.

"I feel totally guilty. If he was horrible, nasty and violent, it would be easier. He's not. He's gentle, considerate and loving. The only slight possibility of winning him over is that I am not a son."

"What?"

"In our religion, Jewishness is passed on through the mother, not the father."

"Logically."

"Meaning that if I ever have children then they would still be Jewish. It would be my job to educate them as such, something I intend to do. I may love a gentile that doesn't mean to say I am converting to his religion."

A shadow appeared in the ever open door, it was Marcus. Shyly he checked the area before stepping over the threshold to plant a peck on Arantxa's cheek.

"Pathetic!"

"Actually, I'm not even here to see you, Arantxa."

"Nice!"

"It's not like that! It's Rebecca I have a message for."

"Me?"

"Yes, you. You've really put the cat among the pigeons this time, haven't you? Flavius has just talked to my father, telling him that he no longer intends to fight for / with Wamba's forces. He's sent me to find you as he feels the need to talk to you, and can't wait for the *usual time and place*, wherever that might be. The only place I could think of that you might be able to meet discreetly would be in Pere's house."

Arantxa snorted, "Discreet, with Antonia?"

"It's the best I could think of. At the moment he's in a tavern having supper. I'll go to see Pere now and arrange it. Will you be able to be there shortly?"

Rebecca agreed and thanked Marcus for his effort. He puffed up with importance and in a dominant manly tone addressed Arantxa, "And I'll be back for you later."

"Good, because I may or may not be here."

*

Pere was standing in the doorway watching for movement in the not quite pitch dark, a tiny amount of light was provided by the exceptionally new moon. He immediately stood to attention when he saw a cloaked figured moving slowly hugging the shadows.

"Sir!"

"SShhh, Pere! He's no longer your commanding officer. Move your big body and let us in before everyone realises we are here." Marcus shoved the large frame to one side to allow the general in.

It was difficult for Antonia to show respect for anyone. Her usual attitude went along the lines of *"his shit smells as well, doesn't it?"*. This time though she was more than a bit apprehensive about having a, *no the*, general in her house. She'd even spent some time tidying and sweeping. "Good evening. This is most kind of you. I truly thank you for your hospitality."

She preened with the compliment. In fact, she'd been given no choice in the matter, Marcus had told Pere, and for once, perhaps the first time of their life together, Pere had ordered her, as if she were just an enlisted man in the army, to follow instructions. Rarely had she seen her husband so nervous and anxious. Thinking it better to comply, she was contaminated with the same feelings.

Being sat behind the stub of a candle, it was easier for her to make out his features than he, hers. A fine specimen he was. The Jewess had caught herself a looker who sounded polite as well.

"You're most welcome in our 'umble 'ouse. I've sent the kids to me sister's and I'm off to join them there. So, make yourself at home. That lump of a 'usband will wait outside in case you need something and to make sure you ain't disturbed. And yeah, I know, it's super secret and Pere has promised to rip me limb from limb if I says a word about, well, anything."

"I truly hope that you come to no physical harm. I would, though be extremely grateful for your silence about what's happening here."

"Like a tomb, me, not a word, asides, Pere says that you might be coming over to our side in this fight thing. Says you're one of the best generals there is, so we'd be lucky to 'ave you. So, all in all, if that Jewess, pretty one 'er, ain't she? Can persuade you, I say welcome."

"Antonia, you've said enough."

"Yes, *dearest* 'usband, I'm off now, ain't I?"

Walking out, she heard Pere apologising. He'd pay for that later.

Once delivered, Marcus had left the general to go back to see Arantxa. Inevitably he met Rebecca coming the other way, they stopped in front of each other with lots and nothing to say. They just stared, then surprisingly, she hugged him and thanked him again.

Rebecca didn't hide in the shadows, it was her norm to walk these streets. She sauntered by, nodding at or greeting those she knew, who were, as usual this time of the evening, enjoying the cool breeze, which tonight was blowing stiffly off the sea.

Knowing that this meeting had to be hush-hush, she thought the best policy of stealth was to pretend nothing was happening. This approach clashed considerably with Pere's it would seem, as he was standing outside his own house on guard as if he were protecting the crown jewels. "Pere, get a chair, sit down. You look nervous and conspicuous. Anyone passing will wonder what you're hiding."

Once inside the betrayers embraced hungrily and tenderly. While still pressed together, not daring to pull away, with intermittent face caresses and neck kisses, they exchanged their stories and the pain they both felt. Rebecca broke down in almost silent sobbing when she told him about her father. It was not Rebecca's style to cry, she rarely did, usually she was able to control herself. This time, though, the flood gates opened. Unsure as to his role, crying women was something he had absolutely no experience of, he kept quiet, held tighter with one hand and tried to stroke her unruly curly hair with the other. Eventually, she slowed and stopped, much to his relief.

"Sorry, I don't usually do that. It's just.." And she started crying again. "Let's sit."

Thinking that a change of position might help, he found himself with a logistical dilemma; there was only one chair. Being the decisive general he was, he took the only logical action. Sitting on it, he dragged her across his lap to sit on him. Feeling proud as it had had the desired stemming tears effect, he set about drying the ones still falling with his fingers.

The loud crack and thump brought the ever vigilant guard bursting through the doorway to find two people in a heap on the floor with remnants of a chair around them. The light from the candle stub, which was flickering in a dying dance, was enough to see two very shocked faces. Rebecca's creased as she started to laugh almost uncontrollably, whereas the best the two men could do was laugh politely along with her. Pere tried to help her to her feet, no mean feat as an upright posture was difficult due to the need to bend over laughing.

Flavius was dusting himself off as Pere was whittling on about the chairs not being sturdy. All of a sudden she stopped and undoubled herself, "I do hope that that is not a portent of what is going to happen to us."

*

The Els Munts camp had been rife with every sort of rumour. They were going back to Toletum, or to fight the Vascones, they were surrounded by rebel forces who wouldn't allow them to leave so they were in effect, hostages … all fuelled by the repeated and elongated periods of absence of their leader. So, it wasn't a massive surprise when all centuriae were ordered to attend a meeting in the villa.

Being asked to be seated and relax around the table made all six men immediately suspicious; this was not normal, not even under the slightly unorthodox approach of General Paulus.

"Gentlemen, I have asked you here today because I have something of the utmost importance to tell you." Instead of relaxing, every experienced soldier's back became rigidly upright.

Flavius had spent time planning this talk. He wanted to sound, not arrogant, more secure and confident in that what he was saying was the correct, and the natural course of action given the situation they found themselves in. He related the exchange of letter with the king, the latter's accusation which he denied strenuously. However, since that moment his world had changed. Explaining how he now found himself unable to continue fighting for something he believed was wrong. In his opinion, the people here had a legitimate complaint, and that grievance should be addressed without resort to an armed conflict. The logical conclusion of which was that he no longer considered himself a general in the *exercitus* (the permanent army).

"Where does that leave us?"

Looking the enquiring centurion in the eye, Paulus explained that he had arranged with Duke Ranosindus their safe conduct to Ilerda where, apparently, the royal forces would be gathering.

"Personally, I find my loyalty is to *MY* general first, and the kingdom second. If my commanding officer believes this war to be unjust, then I accept that and back him totally." Milo's measured tone found agreement around the table. "Furthermore, if we return without our general, our cohort would be disgraced, some of us disciplined. Those not dishonourably discharged, would be scattered into other parts of the army never to be trusted again."

"There's no chance of me receiving my *praemia* for long service. I agree with Milo, we must stick together."

"General, sir. May I ask whether you are considering, or have agreed to join the rebel forces?"

"Centurion Milo, I believe you have every right to ask that. The short answer is that I haven't made a decision yet. What is sure, is that from this point on I shall be considered a rebel whatever I do. My thinking at the moment is that I may as well be hanged for a sheep as a lamb."

This sentiment received universal agreement.

"Again, hoping that this doesn't sound too bold, general, may I suggest that you return to Tarraco and negotiate our entry into their forces with the most favourable conditions possible? Like the increase in our salaries, and a promise of fulfilling the praemia years of service we already have with a view to receiving a piece of land around this area."

*

The personnel involved and the attitude had changed completely, Kunimund was pleased to observe. Although heads were held high and the strut remained, there was an air of almost humility around the latest group of peace negotiators. The extensive field burning had yielded a crop that they hadn't expected. With the looming prospect of a hungry winter with empty larders, there was a new interest in the negotiations. It was Kunimund who was no longer in any rush, dallying, stalling and quibbling over any and everything to show who was now in control.

It took a few days more, and a whole number of fields more, before a deal was actually struck. The Vascones acquiesced to nearly all of Kunimund's Wamba limited demands. The king's instructions were clear; a peace treaty that was reasonably fair to both sides without the defeated feeling humiliation. The reason proffered by the head of the realm being that a peaceful vassal state that could pay a tribute well within its means would be less inclined to want to start fighting again. The general did not adhere nor sympathise with these aims. His opinion was that if you go to war, which they evidently had, then you must win at all cost and that means defeating the enemy to the point when they are not capable of raising arms against you, if not ever again, certainly not for a very long time.

It took great restraint on his part not to force home the advantage that the scorched earth policy had given them, especially when the long haired youth started mouthing off; an action which cost a two day delay with a great deal more smoke in the air.

Finally, the amount of tribute was agreed, and the burning stopped. Kunimund had received orders that he was to stay put for at least a month to ensure that there was no temptation to backtrack on the part of the losers, something he was most reluctant to do as all the real army work was taking place without him, a loss most keenly felt causing a significant anti-Wamba feeling to take root in him.

*

"Back again, General? I am always pleased to see you and by the look on your face, for once, you are not bringing bad news."

"Bad? That is open to interpretation, it's better described as dramatic and, for some of us, traumatic."

Once Marcus was called, greeted and seated, Paulus laid the conditions of his men on the table. "If you agree to these, then the whole cohort is prepared to serve under the colours of … by the way what colours do you have?"

"This is really good news to have a battle hardened core to add to our inexperienced enthusiasm. As to the colours, there's no agreement. We will have a southern command under my leadership, and a northern lead by Count Hilderic, with overall control ceded to the count."

"Father, that's a mess. From my limited experience, it's better to have a clear concise chain of command."

"Marcus! That's sounds quite astute and most military; you can't be that boy who was unable to say sir or salute."

Marcus coloured, mumbling that paraphernalia and clarity were two totally distinct concepts.

"The truth be told, son, I agree with you. The trouble is that we couldn't accept the count's authority down here, and they would not accept mine up there. Hence the compromise and your proposed nuptials."

"Why don't you suggest to Lady Chlodoswintha, she appears to be the real power, a better compromise at least for the duration of the conflict; appoint General Paulus as overall army commander?"

"It would make sense as he's got the experience. I would accept his views better than the count's, or come to that, my own. It would be a difficult sell. For us, we know the man and his views as to why he's changed sides and we trust him. Nemausus, on the other hand, doesn't know him, nor his reasoning. They may just suspect he's taking advantage of the situation for his own gain."

"It's good to hear all of this. However, I do wish you'd to talk to me and not about me as if I weren't here."

Ranosindus apologised whereas Marcus carried on with his train of thought. "But they do know him, at least Lady Chlodoswintha does, and from what I saw, she really did wield a great deal of sway. Send her that message, and propose a meeting as soon as possible somewhere halfway, like Gerunda. I think it's important that he take the troop as well, not as a show of force, more like this is what I have to put into the pot."

"You are quite the strategist today, aren't you, son? I must say that I agree with every word, and time is of the essence. I'll send a swift messenger now with a proposal for a meeting on Saturday in Gerunda. Do you agree, general?"

"Finally consulted! I think it's a sound proposal, especially taking the cohort. I'm just surprised that it came from Marcus!"

Stuck between real and pretend offence, he opened his mouth to say something, only to be beaten to it by his father.

"I believe he sees a way out of getting married. Sorry, to disappoint you, son, but that is the permanent cement we will need after the separation. general, can you stay for supper? I will need to bring you up to date on what and why things are happening. We have a couple of hours or so."

The ex-General's face fell slightly, "Err, yes. It's just that, no, you are right; I need all the background information that you can give me."

"Father, I think that our new general was hoping to fit in another meeting."

"Another meeting? But there's nobody who knows, arh, *another* meeting! Marcus, go down to port area and invite her for supper. If that's alright by you, general? If you invited the uncle as well, we can pass it off as another planning meeting. I'd like to see her as well, and I am SURE that Amalaswinth would be delighted to cook for her."

"Can't be pig, though."

"Why ever not, no, don't explain. Tell Amalaswinth to get some mutton, everyone eats that, don't they? "

Having informed the housekeeper there would be about six for supper and refusing to answer her enquiries as to who, Marcus happily set off down town. His demeanour and step were bordering on jaunty. Having Flavius and his men on their side considerably increased the possibility of winning an armed conflict, considerably diminished his role as a leading military figure, and despite what his father had said, made his upcoming marriage more remote and less urgent. Win, win, win was how he viewed it, and was keen to pass on the good news to Arantxa.

"I am what?"

"You, and your Uncle."

"How can I go for supper in your house? Sometimes, Marcus, I think you are as daft as a brush, and others, I don't think you are very bright at all. We are trying to keep a low profile with no-one knowing, and you think that having a cosy gentile supper would be the perfect cover?"

"It's my father's idea and Flavius didn't disagree."

"So these will be the planning military brains that will win this war! My God. We haven't got a hope, unless the others are worse."

"You're not coming then?"

Rebecca picked up a heavy doorstop ready to hurl when Arantxa came through the said door. "Let me help you with that." She removed it from Rebecca's hands and replaced it back to do its true function in life.

"Besides you trying to kill my friend, what's going on?"

Marcus thanked her while filling in the missing information.

"What a stupid idea!"

"At least someone else has a functioning brain in this town. Tell Flavius I will meet him tomorrow, he knows where and when."

"We'll be two short for dinner, Amalaswinth will complain about all her effort for nothing."

"Good, the old bitch."

"I'll come."

Marcus who'd been enjoying Rebecca's discomfort now looked aghast.

"That's solved it then, thanks, Arantxa."

Egica was pleased to be away from Toletum, its poisonous atmosphere, the back stabbing and above all the bishops, who repeatedly stated that they would not interfere with any of the preparations, and then, did, daily, and most unhelpfully. What had been of use was both their pep talk to all the dukes outlining the consequences of disobedience in the eyes of the Lord - namely, that ex-communication would be their fate if they strayed from the path laid before them by their commander on this most Holy of missions, and, the information provided by the spy network, which was outstandingly detailed and extremely useful. He now knew who had a beef with whom, why, *and* how deep the sore ran. For days and nights before their leaving, he had spent hours studying these documents. The crisscross of hatred was worse to sort out than the most mixed up fishing net, and more likely to snag. When the day of the march to Ilerda arrived, he was sure that he had the column organised in such a way that the minimum conflict could happen. Still, every time they camped for the night, disputes rang out as to which group would get the prized pitching spots. It was exhausting and truly petty.

Another thorn in his side was that he had to ride with the two who didn't have their own forces to lead, a bishop and a rabbi to boot. Hillel was totally repellent, arrogance personified, and what was amazing was that he was Jewish, which therefore meant that he had absolutely nothing to be arrogant about, something which the Bishop of Hispalis, Iulianus, never tired of telling him, all to no avail. The only good thing about this hatred was that neither ever chose to talk to the other, resulting in silence for most of the riding time at least.

*

"Her again. You brought her once before, didn't you? Let me look properly this time. Is she the one everyone is talking about? The foreigner? I've heard tell that she's not even a proper Christian. That's better than being a Jew, isn't it?"

"Amalaswinth, for once, could you just do your job and not ask impertinent questions of my guest?"

"They say she don't speak Christian neither, so, don't worry your head none cos she won't understand me."

"I really wish I didn't." Turning to Marcus, "I think this wasn't a good idea. Sorry I mentioned it. I ought to leave."

"You will not! This malicious old crow will learn to hold her tongue or I'll make sure she's put out of the house this very second."

"*Old crow*, is it now! To me, the woman who's been more of a mother to you than any other on God's earth."

"What is going on? What's all the shouting? Arh Marcus. That's not Rebecca."

Close to tears Arantxa was doubly insulted, for being who she was, and, for not being someone else. "I'm sorry to disappoint."

"Don't worry, dear. I was looking forward to seeing Rebecca; we usually get fireworks when she's around. Still, not your fault. You came here before, didn't you? Hang on, I think I remember your name, very pretty name it was. Bianca, was that it?"

"Arantxa."

"That's it, lovely sound to that word."

It was hard to get annoyed with this man who just said what he was thinking. He meant no harm, it wasn't until the general came in, with his face of disappointment almost hitting the floor that she really started to get angry. Her temper had always been a problem, it was quick to come, often quite virulent, and normally, fairly fast to disappear. Her hands hit her hips as she took her stance.

"Right, I think I have made a mistake by coming here as you all were expecting Rebecca and are evidently all disappointed that I am not her. If though, anyone of you intelligent men had actually thought about the situation, you would have realised that there was no way that she could come here to supper, either with, or without her Uncle. A plainly stupid plan, whosoever it was."

She didn't wait for anyone to argue or contradict her. She flounced out of the room in full sail with a following wind.

The men stood looking at each other until the loud bang of the slamming closed front door disturbed their trance–like state.

Marcus made a move to go after her, only to be restrained forcefully by the wrist.

"Don't! If you run after a woman in that state, you can only lose. Leave her, let her stew, she'll realise that she's made a mistake and will apologise, eventually."

Marcus didn't struggle against the restraint, so Flavius let go.

"I tell you what, I don't envy either of you. This one, and Rebecca …you've chosen characters! In my day, women were much simpler. Let's go and eat, I'm hungry."

*

The palace of Lupus wasn't opulent or splendid, it was more comfortable and functional as seats of kings went. This didn't stop him thinking and planning big. The news he was hearing displeased him and his possible plans greatly. His cousins, the western part of the Vasconis family had concluded a peace treaty with the Wamba regime, this after him agreeing

to their recent suit asking for help in opening a new front against the
Goths. If only they had been able to hang on a bit longer. All manner of
interesting happenings were taking place not far to the south of him.
Tarraconensis/Gallia Gothica up in arms with the help of the king's
favourite General. Surely this was too good an opportunity to miss.
He would dispatch his son, Odo, with a sizeable force to go to find out
what was happening and to assess the opportunity that might arise from
this squabble. His sources told him that the Franks, that useless shower,
were already sniffing around Nemausus.
After hearing the full report of the capitulation and sending a stinging
message accusing the western Vascones of having no balls and little
spirit, signing in what was his Vasconis name, Otsoa, he sent for his son.
Odo was a powerfully build lad with flowing locks who caused a stir
wherever he went just with his physical presence.
"You sent for me?"
Lupus brought him up to speed telling him about the defeat, the Goths in-
fighting and the Franks.
"Who's leading them?"
"We're not quite sure. They haven't had a proper leader since Clovis
died. I suppose it's those two good for nothing brothers; Chlothar and
Theuderic."
"I bet the Goths are really frightened now. Those two together would find
it difficult to slaughter a tethered calf. I would be more frightened of the
mother."
"So would anyone, Balthid, what a woman! Anyway, your job will be to
find out what we can gain from this tiff. Don't join the fight unless there
is a clear possibility of victory, and if you think it's necessary and to our
advantage, don't hesitate to ask for reinforcements. I'm sure with just a
little bit of push, we'll be able to gain a considerable amount. "

*

Horses lathered in sweat were lined up not far from the stables, a young
man was unsaddling and wiping the heavy breathing animals down. It
was the quiet after the pandemonium.
Inside, another servant, this one with more experience and a significantly
higher social standing within the household, was doing his best to
organise and calm the clattering, hard booted, sword carrying men.
"Gentlemen, gentlemen, if you could all come into this room the count
will be with you in a moment."
Being frequent visitors, the two established bishops, Argebaud and
Gunhild, led the way followed by General Wittimir and the two men who
had ridden the farthest; Bishop Jacinto, and nobleman Arangiscle from

Castrum Libiae and bringing up the rear, sauntering in no hurry, as if in a world of his own, was the newly appointed bishop, ex-abbot, Ranimiro. Gradually, they all took seats, leaving the top of the table and the chair immediately to its right free. Noisily they quizzed each other about the need and urgency of the meeting with everyone having a theory, but nobody able to furnish any evidence based reason.

The count and countess came regally in, her hand hanging demurely onto his arm as custom would require. A most unusual sight in this palace as old lags like Gunhild and Argebaud well knew. Something had gone awry and it was being announced by this display of formality.

"Gentlemen, forgive the haste in calling this meeting, it is due to the fact that we have received significant news, which I feel should be shared with you." No words were needed, the exchanged glance between the regulars screamed that something was amiss, perhaps of calamitous proportions.

"I sent a message last week informing you of Wamba's predictable negative reaction to his own general's suggestions of a negotiated settlement. This general, I think you all know him by reputation rather than personally, Lady Chlodoswintha is, I believe, the only person to have met the man, whose name is Dux Paulus, has made quite an astounding decision; he, and the cohort he leads, have joined our cause against the injustices of Toletum."

There was quite a unified expelling of air from every guest, followed by positive sounding words; *excellent, splendid, terrific news* and the like, filled the room. The only person to look warily was the General Wittimir. "What's his price?" he growled.

"This is the point I find most confusing as well, Wittimir. He seems to be demanding nought for himself, instead only insisting that his men will be well treated, specifically, that their *praemia* should be respected along with a slight increase in their wages."

"Most noble of him! I don't trust the man, nor his offer. It was well known within the Regis Fidelis that he was a favourite of the king. Why would such a man swap, all of a sudden and with no obvious benefit, sides, to a considerably weaker position? It's the action of an idiot, and from what I know of the man, he's anything but that."

The positive noises were instantly replaced by conspiracy theories, the loudest words were in the ilk of *long game, stab in the back* and *Judas*. Again it was Wittimir's voice that quietened the others. "Count, don't tell me that we have been called here at great haste, to take this rather ridiculous offer seriously."

All heads turned to the top of the table where the count was beginning to colour, either through embarrassment, or anger. They were about to find out which as he was starting to move to his feet, only to stop halfway as he felt a restraining hand on his wrist. It was Lady Chlodoswintha's voice that was heard.

"The general makes a most valid point, however, I am somewhat surprised that he might suggest that we would be so naïve as to not consider and discard this before calling this meeting. What is he implying? Stupidity? As a matter of fact, we do have further information which might make this apparently illogical move somewhat more plausible."

The silence was absolute. Wittimir hadn't intended to offend, and was somewhat abashed that his words had been taken in that light by the most powerful Lady of the land. He needed to make amends without actually apologising, an act which would only compound his words by making them appear all the more premeditated; silent dithering resulted. Chlodoswintha, as the impressively consummate speaker that she was, knew how to use moments without words. Nobody, except her, was comfortable. At the same time, nobody wanted to add salt to an open wound by supporting Wittimir's remarks or demanding further information from the countess.

When she felt that they had squirmed enough, she continued, "We all know that betrayal and side swapping happens ALL the time within this Goth nation. We only have to look at the procession of *kings* that have been ousted from power by one plot or another during this century. No one has had a long, happy reign, dying of old age in his bed. Sadly, it has become endemic and something not in the true vein of what our great nation once was. Men, in their lust for power, have abandoned the higher morals that have bound us throughout our history; our trek south, our uncomfortable relationship with the Romans, our defeats and victories over the Franks. We had a code, a set of values which was the rock of who we were."

A purposeful sweeping glance around the room showed that there was an audience of avid listeners.

" What we are intending to do, does not, I hope, fall into this mould of self- aggrandising power seeking of the petty people I mentioned before, no, we want to make our own state where different values, not different people, reign, the values that have been lost, the values that make us Goth.. If any further proof of this were needed, look at our inability to name a king to replace Wamba. We are not rallying around the standard of one power crazed man, instead, we are going to build a new society."

This statement of intentions didn't get a standing ovation with shouts of "Long live!", It didn't even get a ripple of applause, instead, it got barely audible murmurings of words with rising intonations, indicating a question form.

Not getting the adulation she'd hoped for, and fearing the rumbling of confused discontent, she continued, "It is in that vein that General Paulus has joined us, I believe. I met the man in Tarraco, his honesty and integrity impressed me and the others present."

"Surely, that isn't enough to warrant such blatant betrayal?"

"Betrayal, Bishop Argebaud? Could or should we be using such words? Surely you don't believe that is a word that can be used to describe our endeavour?"

"Most definitely not, it's just that we have been through the decades of marginalisation, humiliation and false values imposed on us by Toletum, whereas this Paulus man was a fervent supporter of them until a couple of months ago. Is it possible to turn so completely in such a short period of time?"

"Bishop, like General Wittimir earlier, your point is valid and well made. Allow me to add some other information to my belief that the man finds sympathy with the values of our cause. It has come to my knowledge that the man is in love."

"Love? With whom?"

"Do you remember our conversation a while ago when Abraham gave you the report from the Tarraco meeting?"

"Yes, there were problems with some overzealous rabbi, can't remember his name?"

"Hillel."

"That's the chap. What of it?"

"Do you remember that there was talk of a Jewess? I think you, dear husband, mentioned that the duke was being led around by his dick, and it was also pointed out that Bishop Cyprianus had tried his luck as well."

There was a chorus of yeses from three of the attendees.

"Well, it seems that this much sought after commodity has plumped for the general, who has followed the suit of the other *dick-led* men. The word is that they are both deeply in love."

Wittimir and Bishop Jacinto had become spectators, interested ones, in this meeting where incredulity reigned supreme, three different voices mouthing them.

"Would love to meet this bewitching woman."

"She's a Jew."

"Difficult to believe that love is *that* powerful?"

The last remark earned the count a deep scowl causing him to move the conversation on.

"Ranosindus is proposing a meeting with Paulus in Gerunda in a few days, hence the haste of this meeting. I suggest that we all attend."

This caused considerable discussion as to who could be available at such short notice, and how much inconvenience this would cause. However, in the end it was agreed that they would all attend, including a most reluctant Lady Chlodoswintha.

*

Milo received the news of their imminent departure with relief and gratitude. The training sessions he'd insisted upon since their arrival in Els Munts were becoming shoddier by the day. Nobody took anything seriously, the men knew that serious, being lashed, punishment was off the agenda while they were here. Any other reprimand or chastisement was easily taken. The result was that soldiers turned up late, badly dressed and disinterested in the three hour activity. The other centurions were proposing the suspension of these sessions as they thought them detrimental to discipline rather than helpful.

Milo's reaction stood apart from all the others. Nobody else wanted to leave, even if it was only for a few days. There was great lethargy and sullenness throughout the camp in the preparations. The men were told not to carry lots of equipment and the women were instructed to stay where they were, as this was an exercise, not a change of location. Milo was actually seen whistling, he was happy, believing that two or three forced pace marches would do a great deal for discipline and sharpness.

*

Meal times dragged by. To outside appearances everything would seem the same- the food, the times, and the seating arrangements. Not looking at each other, pushing food from one side of the plate to the other, rarely conversing, nothing was the same. It was the only time of the day that they had to see each other, and neither wanted to lose or miss this opportunity, this one point of contact, the bridge back. They were alone, together, as they had been throughout their lives. Arantxa was spending more and more of her time, officially, based at Antonia's house, though when Rebecca bumped into her this morning, she did nothing but complain about Arantxa's absence. It was much easier to imagine who Arantxa was spending her days and nights with, rather than where. Rebecca missed sharing the little intimate chats with Arantxa. They understood each other's, different though similar, predicaments. She was also jealous of her comparative freedom with the ability to see the source of her problem. Rebecca hadn't set eyes on Flavius since the tears, broken chair and dust of their disastrous meeting in Antonia's house. Logistically, it was a nightmare; she couldn't go to Els Munts, and he

(405)

certainly couldn't be seen here. The situation was compounded by the absence of Arantxa and, by default Marcus. One afternoon she had walked out to the training ground, which was based about an hour out of town on the road to Dertosa. Once there, she kept to the trees in the hills behind the flat stretch of land. It was possible to make out both Marcus and Pere, and at times to hear their shouted instructions of frustration with some wrong manoeuvre. Having no excuse to get closer, she could but watch. Her mind raced with various possibilities, without solutions. Biding her time uncomfortably, she did all the things a dutiful daughter was supposed to do around the house hoping her father might react in some way. Even getting angry and shouting at her would be better than his mournful silent body dragging from his office to the table and back. Once she resolved to go into the office and, well, she wasn't sure what she would do, only to be thwarted by the door being blocked on the inside. There were no locks inside the house, her father evidently had found something big and heavy to impede entrance.

After two full days and nights, she was getting desperate. Deciding that something had to be done to alleviate her dire mood, she decided to walk to *their* beach to re-live some sweet memories.

Her heart jumped upon reaching the top of the last rock, the horse was there. Its owner's head could be seen well out to sea bobbing up and down in the waves. After greeting the horse with great affection, off came her clothes and into the sea she went. When she was about waist deep, she realised she'd been spotted as the bobber was racing towards her in that difficult stroke that he could do, and she'd failed to learn. Salmon-like he leapt at her, knocking her under water. Coming up for much needed breath she found herself cradled in his arms, him standing and covering her face with little kisses.

"God, I've missed you. I couldn't .."

Unsure whether she wanted to be in this subservient position, which, truth be known, she was actually enjoying tremendously, she managed to wriggle out of his grasp only to go back under water. Not noticing the first time, with utter disbelief it registered while emerging, there was no panic. Being underwater wasn't quite so terrible anymore. Fear lost. This time being determined to come up on her own two feet, she "swam" slightly away from his body. Emerging triumphantly while brushing the hair from her face and water from her eyes with one hand, she sought his hand with her other, taking him determinedly to shore. On the point where land met sea and the water petered out, she initiated their love making.

Spent, they caressed, her wet straggly hair plastered across his chest. Not wanting to give the impression of being clingy and dependent, she chose not to tell him how two days without him seemed an eternity.

Instead, she tried to keep her conversation to the pleasure of here and now, only timidly venturing into the uncertainty of their future. It was then that he told her that he'd be leaving for a meeting in Gerunda with the Nemausus group.

Noticing her disappointment, which in some weird way felt even worse without words, he blurted out, "Why don't you come as well? Actually, I am taking the whole of my force."

Her angry head rose from his chest, "Why do you say things like this, when you know I can't come?"

"I'd like.."

"There are lots of things I'd like, but I know I can't have. By you saying things like this, it makes it sound and feel like it's me that is putting obstacles in the way. You know that I can't leave. Why do you think that we've been unable to see each other these days? And it's not just for me. Do you think that your men would follow you quite so readily if they knew you were in the grips of some Jewish lover?"

"I'm sorry, it's just that I would really like you to be there."

"Please, concentrate on what we can do, while we can do it. Until then we must remain a secret."

*

Their march wasn't quite a march, it wasn't sloppy, nor was it crisp, they showed that they were in no great hurry to get to the meeting point in Ilerda. The king had reasoned to General Alaric that logistically, and for appearance sake, it would be better to lead in their much smaller force, rather than host the reception of a much more powerful one led by others that weren't the king's, so they ambled, determined not to be the first to arrive.

Wamba, despite all the pressing matters on his mind - the peace negotiations with the Vascones, the challenge, no, the open usurping of his supposed leadership role by the bishops, the rebellion of the oldest sector of the kingdom, and the betrayal of his favourite general - was in a splendid mood, enjoying the ride, the scenery and the company of Alaric, who, admittedly, wasn't one of the most entertaining of people, was at least respectful and knowledgeable about the area they were passing through. Not hailing from this area himself, Alaric had spent time here campaigning under the late Hermenguild, who was originally from Caesaragusta, and quite a little fountain of knowledge he proved to be while riding along side by side.

They dined together every evening, which proved more challenging to maintain a conversation not having the scenery, or the history of a village or town as a starting point. Almost inevitably, they returned to the same topic, Paulus. Neither had a bad word for him. Even at his most impetuous, he was seen as fun. Many anecdotes of his escapades were recounted and relived, despite them both knowing the story the other was telling.

"Why has he betrayed us?"

Although it looked and sounded like a question, it wasn't, it was much closer to a lament.

"He had such a bright future in front of him, the head of the Regis Fidelis, was his for the asking and as the best general of his generation, the head of the exercitus was well within his grasp."

Alaric said nothing, it was only when Wamba looked in his direction wondering about the silence, he saw the pained expression on the man's face.

"Oh, sorry Alaric. I do respect you and your abilities, it's just that Paulus had.."

"Sire, I don't disagree. What is difficult to hear is something that I already know. Paulus had a flair and style that the rest of us lack. He was a natural, whereas we work hard at our chosen profession. Undoubtedly, this must be the reason that the forces in Tarraconensis/Gallia Gothica have appointed him military commander. However, it doesn't answer the question of why he accepted it."

This, or a version of this, was the standard fare with whatever was provided to eat every evening.

*

"We have a thief! Things are going missing from the pantry. I skinned a rabbit yesterday and left it to hang. This morning it was no longer hanging or anywhere else to be seen, and I really don't believe it got down and walked off by itself. Also, there are other smaller things that have disappeared. I have asked all the other serving staff who could possibly enter the house, they all deny any involvement."

"Amalaswinth, I'm sure there is some simple explanation. Be more vigilant."

"I just don't want you to think that I have any involvement."

"Thank you for bringing it to my attention. I will make sure that the household budget is increased to make up for these losses. Tomorrow I am leaving early in the morning. While I am away, see if the mystery can be solved."

Ranosindus knew full well, as did Amalaswinth, who was responsible for these disappearances, it was the same person who hadn't eaten at the house for more than two days. Quite where his son and woman were shacked up, he wasn't positively sure. He suspected that it was a cottage along the coast road which was temporarily empty as the tenant, an elderly man, had died recently and his steward was yet to decide who was to get this very poor living. The land being useless for any crop, the man had eked out a living from sea without a boat. God knows how he paid his rent, not an easy life.

Having heard Marcus chatting about various properties with the steward the other day, he deduced that this would have been a good option - good views, isolated, and not too far from the improvised training ground. He had seen Marcus come bustling in the other day to change clothes. Claiming he had no time to chat as he had work, Ranosindus only managed to inform him when the trip to Gerunda was planned before he shot out the door calling that he'd be there at the appointed time.

Having heard the women in the camp talking about some place called *heaven*, and what a desirable place it was, how they shouldn't do terrible things, otherwise they might be excluded from this everlasting happiness, Arantxa thought she had achieved heaven on earth in her time in Tarraco. Now, in *her* cottage, the only remaining doubt about heaven on earth was how many levels it had. Being with Rebecca and Antonia had been glorious, the best time of her life. However, since the uncomfortable horse ride, she didn't like these animals, even holding on tight to Marcus' waist wasn't enough compensation for sitting on them, to this cottage, with its marvellous views of the coast and best of all, no neighbours. She believed that she'd ascended to another level of delirium.

More than two days of bliss. While he was playing soldier during the morning, she went into the small wood at the back of the property to pick berries, leaves and roots to add to the meat that Marcus had brought back from Tarraco. This morning she'd disturbed a small roe deer grazing, without fear it had looked at her with those massive eyes before slowly moving onto another more succulent patch. It was a reflection of the undisturbed harmony she was living in.

The cooking was proper cooking, unlike the strange combinations she'd had to put together in the Jewish house. This was more like things she would have eaten at *home*. Her preparing food for them, to eat together, felt real and timeless, as did the way they spent the afternoons and evening playing with each other's bodies and talking. In reality, he didn't say too much, she did the lion's share, which again, was something new in her life. In all her other close relationships - her sister, Rebecca, they had been the dominant speakers, being the more experienced and having more to say it was natural for her to take the listener role.

Once when she'd resorted to this role, so he could actually say something, the illusion of heaven had to come to an end. Marcus casually, ever so timidly, mentioned that the following morning he'd have to leave early as he had to be in Tarraco to meet his father and Flavius to go to Gerunda.

The bubble burst. She was more than a little upset, not that it was happening, it had to at some point, the issue was, that it was quite so soon.

*

The encampments of the different barons took up little or larger areas as far as the eye could see - an impressive sight, depending on who you were it could be viewed as frightening, definitely, the like of which, this area hadn't seen since the Romans first took the town and surrounding areas from the Ilergets, hundreds of years before. The settlement of the Ilergets, their crown jewel, was replaced by a Roman walled city which was to enjoy centuries of prosperity being the centre of the commerce of an area of fertile plains. As the empire began to crumble, so did the city, walls, and all semblance of thriving urban life. What Egica saw was what was left after another invading force, the Sueus, had been driven out by the re-conquering Visigoth forces a couple of hundred years ago, a tumbled down wreck of a place, with not even a shadow or hint of its former glorious self.

The Episcopal palace of the Bishop Guteric, who was conspicuous by his absence, had become the centre of operations and home for Egica and Bishop Iulianus. Hillel had presumed it would be his place of residence as well, until the Bishop of Hispalis absolutely refused to share a roof with a Jew, forcing the rabbi to squat in a barely standing *house* that was close by.

The Episcopal palace was in a constant flux of comings and goings with Egica having to play arbiter in many a, until now, minor dispute. It was a role that the military commander despised because it made him feel like a mother who has far too many important matters to worry about, to be separating and pacifying bickering children throughout the day and night. Thankfully, he had his criss-cross scheme of who hates who committed to memory. This provided the basis of a successful resolution in nearly all the cases, thus achieving his objective of, if not making things better, at least not making them much worse. Neither was this intertwined plan of inter-family rivalries a static picture, it continually shifted, sometimes in totally unexpected ways with all sorts of, perhaps temporary, alliances being formed between the most unlikely of candidates. An example of this, was the bonhomie that had sprung up between two exceptionally powerful barons, Ervigius, a constant mover, shaker and consummate meddler of Toletum, and the powerful, well connected though not central figure of the Betica baron, Teodofred.

Before setting off on this jaunt, Egica had been warned that this was the big one to watch as their animosity was no secret and stretched back over gencrations. In the last couple of days however, they had taken to coming to the palace together with a shared grievance or just on a social call, something which was as unbelievable as it was real. And it got *better*. The previous evening they had even invited themselves to supper, bringing choice pieces from their larder with them and, surprisingly, a good time was had by all after an initial sticky start involving something connected to a recent birth of another daughter, who at the moment was nameless but would be a much younger sister to the eldest child, Cixilona, to Evrigius.

These two powerful men helped Egica's peace keeping tasks considerably, as together they outweighed any one other baron, with no other *natural* alliances springing up to challenge them yet. The result was that while they waited, impatiently, for the king's arrival, there was a considerable reduction of tension around the camp. When the fact that Hillel was positively encouraged not to step into the palace was added, Egica began to relax, and if not actually enjoy himself, at least rest easier. Also, he was acquiring skills that didn't know he had. Still a young man with young hedonistic ways, he hadn't devoted any time and energy to scheming, planning and deception; personality facets that had never been required or desirable in his relatively short life and lowly position at Court. Having generally taken a person, whatever that had to say, and their demeanour towards him, as being a true representation of their opinions, he hadn't needed to dedicate time in reflection afterwards as to what was *actually* meant by this comment or that. Oh, the good old days, he reflected after the last meal with the powerful pair. Their attitude towards each other and him was sickeningly smooth and false, with heaps of tentative fishing type statements to try to gauge his, or the other baron's reaction to a totally oblique view, something which would have caught him off guard just a couple of months ago. His learning curve had been impressively steep, and up until now, blemish free. He had learnt to play, and at times, excel at these petty, but so important little games. So much so, that he was beginning to be able to identify a problem before it became one, and read between lines possibly better than he could read normal Latin.

What wasn't said was so much more important than what was, and it was abundantly clear that neither man had the slightest bit of respect for Wamba as king, instead believing that one of their family, namely their own personage, or at a pinch their off-spring, should occupy that position by right. This was the basis of their initial almost-spat about yet another daughter, again something immensely clear to anyone who didn't listen to the words spoken.

The length of his uncle's sojourn in the top job promised to be anything but long and trouble free if these two had anything to do with it. Egica believed that he had to box clever as nephew, and military commander, to keep these two from undermining the campaign in an effort to present themselves as an alternative to the king in the eyes of the leaders of the realm, the making or breaking bishops. At the moment, he was extremely closely aligned to Wamba and thus had to make a success of putting down this rebellion without either of these barons playing a leading role. Later if needs be, he would put daylight between his uncle and himself.

*

A small, walled pretty town, Gerunda had little to boast about. It existed without ever shining in the Roman period, and little else had happened since then. It had been chosen for the meeting mainly because it was about midway between Tarraco and Nemausus.

Half of the Gallia Gothica group took up residence in the Bishop's palace, a fitting place as they were all bishops themselves. The other half stayed with the nobleman Arangiscle, who though being from Castrum Libiae, had family who were willing to play host to such important visitors. The Tarraco delegation was hardly slumming it in the residence of gardingo Hildigiso.

"Did you watch the troops, Wittimir?"

"Most impressive, count, most impressive, beautifully manoeuvred, sharp, précis, a flawless performance! I wish I could get my men to that sort of level. Until this morning I thought my lot did a pretty competent job. Now, I see we have a way to go to reach these professional standards."

"Why do you think that he brought them? Is it a threat, a show of force, or just a peacock tail's display?"

"Who can say, it could be all of those things."

The men were heading towards the meeting room where the four bishops were already chatting. It had been agreed previously, that the meeting would be chaired by the most neutral person; Hildigiso. The seating arrangements had been a source of considerable controversy until Lady Chlodoswintha insisted that the other end be occupied by all the bishops, with Nemausus; Count Hilderic, nobleman Arangiscle and General Wittimir on the left and Tarraco; Duke Ranosindus and General Paulus on the right. Marcus and Lady Chlodoswintha had been excluded.

It was never going to be a short meeting, not with so many bishops attending. However, it seemed interminable to the Tarraco pair. It was one of those meetings where there was a great deal of speaking with precious little said. Positions and policy that everyone knew and accepted were said, and then re-stated. After about three hours of arse and brain numbing nonsense, the real questions were starting to be asked, and nearly all of them directed at Paulus. Questions about why he'd joined the rebellion, what were his future intentions, all of which were well fielded by the confident competent general. The love angle conversion to the cause; everyone knew about, nobody mentioned it. By the time they broke for separate lunches, everyone was satisfied that progress was being made, it was the speed of this progress that was a bone of contention.

Marcus had joined the other two to eat a frugal meal and listened attentively as his father expressed his frustration at the pace of progress. "It's all these bishops! I thought Cyprianus was unique in his windiness. How wrong one can be! It seems a prerequisite to become a bishop to be able to talk forever without saying absolutely anything."

"You're lucky," Lady Chlodoswintha breezed in and without any invitation or acceptance, pulled out a chair and sat next to the Duke, "all meetings in Nemausus and Narbo are like that: totally insufferable. So, am I to presume that nothing concrete was agreed?"

"Yep! Nothing. Seems as if the general here made a good impression and it's universally accepted that he's actually on our side, but precious little else."

"Do come in, Ariel." The countess called over her shoulder. "Take a seat. Bread cheese and wine, you can eat that, can't you?"

"Thank you countess, I'd rather not sit, or eat, as I will be wanted back in Narbo immediately. If I could just make my report, and I'll be gone."

"As you please. You know everyone except General Paulus."

"Yes, only by reputation. It's a pleasure to meet you, general. I have heard that you speak well of my people's just cause."

Flavius nodded, not wanting this conversation to go much further. "What is your report?"

"Through our network, we now have confirmation that all the state forces are heading for and using Ilerda as their assembly point. Wamba is bringing the bulk of the force from Vasconia, Egica is leading an enormous force of dukes and their men, numbering, they say, about seventy thousand. The information we have received is that their intention is to split into a three - pronged attack."

"So many? I didn't imagine that they would have been able to mobilise so many so quickly. We really need to get organised."

"Which is why I brought Ariel to you, and not to the windbags. After lunch, I will attend the meeting to see if we can push it along a bit faster. I have spoken to Duke Ranosindus," both Marcus and Flavius looked puzzled as to when she could have done this. Having not left his side since leaving Tarraco, they hadn't seen him and the woman together, "and we are in agreement that you should lead the unified force and be in overall military command. I doubt whether my husband will oppose the idea as he's realising that he might be a little out of his depth, not being a very experienced military man."

"I don't know what to say.."

"Yes, is the correct response. Marcus, could you pass me a cup of wine?" Spellbound by the efficiency of the woman, Marcus was slow to react, Flavius filled the void.

"Thank you, general. Marcus, I do hope that when it comes to fulfilling my daughter's needs you are a little more attentive!"

*

Lonely, worried, depressed, and heartily fed up with the guilt she was suffering every time she saw her father, Rebecca decided she had to get out of the house. Where would she go was the problem. Discounting anything involving sand, sea, the beach of her place of refuge pre-Flavius, didn't leave her with too many choices. Also, there were other "female" issues that she needed to talk to someone, another woman, about. Setting out on what had become a well-trodden path, the only option, not the best or wisest, was Antonia.

When Rebecca spied a woman with a bundle of washing and her own troop of squabbling children, she felt that perhaps she ought to reconsider her only option.

Too late. "Jewess, come and 'elp me, will you?"

Rebecca covered the distance between them quickly with a false show of enthusiastic eagerness. "How?"

"I'll give you a choice. Either carry this basket of clean clothes, or grab the kids by the 'ands and march them in the right direction. If I try to do both, the clothes will fall and one or both of the kids will die as a result."

Rebecca placed herself in the middle of the fighting children, taking one in each hand. This didn't stop their dispute; instead it just made it a little more difficult to hit each other as Rebecca became the barrier and the recipient of swaying, flaying hands.

Antonia's voice lowered menacingly, "One of you touch the Jewess, then woe betide you. When we get 'ome, you'll feel real pain!"

The effect was amazing. Arms were stilled, as were squealing voices after one last slap was delivered by the elder to the younger, establishing the natural order.

The remaining distance was covered in total silence respected by all.

Once the washing was safely placed in the house, Antonia took the children, who were now holding Rebecca's hands tighter than ever, into the house and shouts and cries were audible to Rebecca, who planted herself on the rock near the door.

"Sorry about that," Antonia emerged, her hair more dishevelled than normal. "Sometimes they get a bit out of control. Pere's never 'ere neither. Now Marcus 'as gone off somewhere, then, Pere's been left with all the work and responsibility. 'e spends all 'is time training out there on the Dertosa road; worse than when 'e's away playing soldier somewhere else."

Rebecca reflected on the position that women were forced into, waiting, suffering, maintaining the semblance of normality while their men were away "adventuring". Which role was the worst, she wondered.

"Anyway, you ain't come 'ere to 'ear my woes, what's up?"

"Just wanted a bit of company that's all."

"'No, you didn't. Spit it out, someat's eating you, besides your fancy man being away."

Perhaps her transparency was clearer than she had thought. Rebecca imagined that she'd been doing a good job of hiding her worries. This opened a new line of thought; had her father noticed?

The pause lasted while Antonia watched the in-turmoil face. There were times when she knew how to remain quiet.

"I'm late."

"Bound to 'appen, weren't it? All that frolicking. That's the way of the world, lovey. Our Lord has decided that you should be blessed. Should really offer you congratulations, but you don't look at all 'appy."

"Antonia, it couldn't be worse. He's a gentile, a general, a war is about to happen and.."

Whatever the *and* was, nobody found out as Rebecca broke down sobbing.

Antonia moved to the seated sobb-er and pushed the tear streaked face into her stomach in show of female solidarity. "Come on dear, it could be worse."

Looking up in surprise, Rebecca incredulously mouthed, "How?"

In best thinking pose Antonia looked down, "Suppose you're right, difficult to be much worse." And started laughing almost uncontrollably.

*

Chlodoswintha, now present, allowed her husband to start the meeting with the recent report from Ariel's network. It was greeted with shock and fear. The pre-lunch bravado was cooled considerably by the stark reality.

The bevy of bishops were first to recover, with lots of inane chatter about the need to organise and pray. Thankfully for all the rest of the participants, they were quietened by the still nominally in charge and host, gardingo Hildigiso. He'd been pre- meeting briefed as to the content and direction the meeting should take.

"I thank the count for the information and the impressively efficient way in which it was gathered."

"I can take no credit for that. We have to thank the Jews and their network for this intelligence."

"From the Jews? Can we trust them?" Bishop Jacinto spoke, not with any malice the way in which Cyprianus might ask the question, more in genuine concern about validity.

"Without a doubt. Their reports have all proved totally reliable thus far." Gardingo Hildigiso, again rested control by stating the urgency of coming to conclusions so everyone could go to prepare. "The thorny question of overall leadership needs to be resolved here and now. Having spoken with the parties involved, we have ascertained that neither the northern forces under Count Hilderic nor the southern forces under Duke Ranosindus would be totally comfortable in a united body with just one of those men taking control, and as a joint approach would lead, inevitably, to misunderstandings, we have agreed that for the duration of the conflict we accept the military supremacy of General Paulus."

Those not party to this cobbled-together lunchtime agreement, namely, the bishops, and General Wittimir, were aghast at such a bold and unexpected turn of events.

"He's an outsider. Not known to anyone outside this room. Before lunch we had had serious doubts as to his conviction towards our cause and now; we are offering him total control!" Wittimir was on his feet "This seems rash, unethical and sorry, general," he looked directly at Paulus, "I don't know you enough to trust you. Again, may I point out that you were the right-hand man of the king until very recently."

"I agree with you entirely, general, I do not seek this role and don't want it foisted upon me either. I would happily serve under the command of the duke, the count or even yourself. As to trusting me, well, there's nothing I can do to assuage your apprehension or fear on that point. All I can say is that I am who I say I am, and only time and perhaps blood will prove that point."

Chlodoswintha didn't like the course that the meeting was taking. Once this topic was open for discussion, again the bishops would sail in with their unending noise. "General Wittimir, do we need to allay your suspicions, or are you proposing a completely different course of action? Maybe, you are pushing your own candidature of overall commander?"

"Lady Chlodoswintha, you do me a grave injustice. I care not for self advancement. The count is my Lord and Master, and I serve him. If he tells me that the duke of Tarraco is to take charge, then I would serve him with the same diligence."

Ranosindus had been drifting in his thoughts wondering whether he should leave this squabbling to head back to Tarraco to organise the defences, when he heard his name mentioned.

"I have not enough experience in leading men in battle and I whole-heartedly cede this position to the man who is a professional in this field with recent experience, General Paulus."

The count chirped up as well, "I concur. If we are entertaining any military victory, we need a military man to lead this stage of the separation process."

Chlodoswintha, conscious that a woman shouldn't be seen as leading this meeting looked at Bishop Gunhild, her usual go to reliable cleric, to help out, who saw the invitation.

"General Wittimir, do you accept that everyone is prepared to cede power to General Paulus and that you will serve under his command as well?"

"Well, I suppose if everyone…."

"That's agreed then. Now, I would like to take matters a step further. Without too much imagination I can see that General Paulus's right and validity will inevitably be called into question by many more than just General Wittimir here. I believe," he paused not for dramatic effect, more through fear and temerity of the statement he was about to deliver, one that he and Lady Chlodoswintha had talked about and agreed on during the lunch break, "yes, I believe that for the duration of the conflict we should actually elect General Paulus as king, with the proviso that he relinquish power, once the armed conflict is over to the eventual rulers of the kingdom, the children of the Count of Nemausus and the Duke of Tarraco."

The cacophony of noise was impressive. Lots of people were up on their feet objecting in some way except, curiously; the count, countess and the duke.

Ranosindus hadn't been informed of this development and was unsure about whether he thought it a good or bad thing. Giving Paulus the military power was logical and even desirable, actually making him king though, well, that was radical in the extreme.

The loudest voice of opposition was coming from Bishop Argebaud who could be heard mixing his nos with words like sacrilege and abomination. Flavius had stood to object only to be yanked back down by the elbow by the countess. He was now seated looking desperately unhappy and completely dumbfounded. He did NOT want to be king.

Eventually the uproar died down to a reasonable level of indignant spluttering. It was the count who sought to restore order.

"This is a most *surprising* development and I, personally, need time to consider my position and the wider ramifications of such an action, so I propose another break until supper time when we can reconvene and discuss this in a more sedate manner."

The duke's voice was the next to be heard. "I think the count's proposal is most reasonable, however, I really need to get back to Tarraco to organise the defence of the city, something which has become imperative given the information of the proximity of Wamba's forces."

Chlodoswintha, who was trying to maintain her low profile, could not allow this to happen. The decision of making a king HAD to be decided by the two main parties.

"A most understandable concern, duke. Your presence here, though, is paramount. I suggest you send your son ahead of you to start the preparations. It is my understanding he has proved most adept at military matters of late. I am sure he will do a fine job."

Seeing the logic of him staying, and Marcus going, Ranosindus permitted himself to be persuaded.

*

Imagining that the walk wouldn't be much longer than her, until recently, daily wander to *their* beach, Rebecca was surprised and sweaty after what had seemed an awfully long time of plodding along the sand. Antonia had advised staying off the main road south as it was transited by all sorts of lowlifes, plus it was the main drag to the military training ground where her husband spent most of his time these days, so full of testosterone filled potential fighters. Sand walking was always more arduous than road, prettier to see the sea and splash in the piddly little waves that did anything but crash onto the beach, but much harder work especially as there were outcrops of rocks to be climbed over between the coves, or long stretches of sand where the end couldn't be seen.

The instructions she'd received were less than precise, ensuring that this sand trudge wasn't carefree as she wasn't sure whether she'd gone past her destination or not. It seemed an age since she'd spotted the easily identifiable lighthouse from where Antonia said it was impossible not to find the cottage as there were no others in the vicinity, a fact that was without a shadow of a doubt, undeniable. There wasn't a cottage, or any other construction to be seen. Feeling sure that she must have gone past it and about to double back, she spotted a lone almost naked figure walking in the water taking an avid interest in some rocks.

"What's so interesting?"

Arantxa literally jumped in shock and fear, one hand going to her mouth and the other behind her back. "Shit! Rebecca, you scared the life out of me!" Doing her best to breathe normally, she took in the welcome sight of her *friend*.

"You look awful! A sweaty mess."

"Thanks, I am pleased to see you as well. I can't say that you look particularly well dressed either."

"You may have noticed, I am in the water. Clothes aren't necessary here."

"What are you doing?"

"In reality, I don't think I am doing anything but I can tell you what I am supposed to be doing... finding shellfish."

"Oh, we used to do that a lot when we were kids. Not supposed to eat them, as they aren't caixer but I love them. Let me help."

In less than a jiffy, Rebecca was unclothed and in the water. Together they moved a little farther around the headland and quickly stumbled on a crop of mussels stuck to the rocks. Arantxa produced a dagger from behind her back, so, this was where her hand had gone when she was startled. This caused eyebrows to be raised.

"Marcus, left it. Said he'd worry less if I was *armed.* He reckoned that after my *performance,* his word, with Caius, he would sleep easier as nobody would better me."

Even with the help of this significant instrument, it was hard work prising the rock muscles off, so they took it in turns, speaking about nothing but their prey.

After a while they had quite a little haul in the cloth that Arantxa had brought for carrying purposes. "Enough?"

"Enough."

The path back to the cottage was definitely a path that would not have been found by anyone who didn't know it was there. It wasn't very far, but the rundown excuse for a cottage was exceptionally well hidden by untamed nature.

"The last resident didn't want to be found, did he? Also, he didn't care much for repairs, either."

"No, but it's lovely, isn't it?"

"A bit different to Marcus's other houses."

"It's not really his, well, actually, suppose it is, but, not really."

Going inside was a relative concept as there was a massive hole in the roof.

"It's great, I can see the stars from the bed."

A bundle of cloth on the floor must have been what she was calling the bed. Rebecca, hadn't seen such poverty in the city, yes, there were exceptionally poor and falling down houses, but nothing on this scale. Yet, Arantxa gave off the appearance of being genuinely house proud.

"Alright, tell all. To what do I owe this social call, it's not as if you were just passing and decided to drop in."

With initial reluctance, Rebecca explained her general worries, especially about her father, moving onto the specific, her late period.

Arantxa, the much more tactile of the two, reached out and held a hand while all the time a smile crept across her face until it almost extended from one ear to the other. This caused the stirrings of annoyance, another woman not taking her, not to put it too dramatically, tragic dilemma, seriously.

"I really don't think this should amuse you. As I said to Antonia, it couldn't be worse, and she just laughed. Neither of you take it seriously enough. Imagine if it had happened to you!"

This caused another hand to be grasped and teeth being shown in the most open of smiles possible, "It has."

*

The honour guard that was mounted to meet the entering king's forces was, at best, paltry, well turned out, sharply dressed and controlled it was, though numbers were lacking. This, Wamba took in without his countenance registering any outward emotion of his bubbling anger at this slight. His nephew and overall military command until this moment was there to greet him. A crisp salute, which was answered by no more than a slight inclination of the head, expressed everything without words; the receiver was embarrassed, and the arrivee was fuming, both knew better than to air their varying displeasures in public under the, not overt or obvious but nevertheless present, eye of the most powerful barons. Wordlessly, Egica led the King, once unhorsed, to the palace of his residence. Noisily, with their clattering of armour, they made their way to the main room with its fire well ablaze, it was becoming that time of year when it was considerably colder indoors than out. The vocal silence was maintained while servants made a considerable racket removing the bulky protection the King wore, and the best parade attire that Egica possessed. Once they had finished, cleared the metal and themselves out of sight, Wamba looked his family member directly in the eye, "Well?"

"I know and I am sorry. We didn't get the information about your arrival until very late, the scouts belong to Baron Evrigius, reported to him and not to me. It was only after sitting on this for some time that he decided to tell me, his excuse being that he believed the force not to be hostile and no more than Baron Teodofred bringing his troops back from an exercise. I mustered what I could of the exercitus in a very short time. I know, it's not good enough."

"Deliberate snub or an honest mistake?"

Egica's eyebrows lifted in genuine horror that the king would ask such a naïve question. "Just checking that you realise what is going on as well.

The real point of issue here, young nephew, is what am I going to do about it?"

"I fear that there's little that can be done, certainly in the near future." Wamba started his well known thinking pacing after instructing his host to order some refreshments. By the time the ale arrived, the king had probably covered the equivalent distance between Ilerda and Tarraco. Dumping himself in a chair opposite the uncomfortably sat military chief, he took a long draft. "Give me the update on the position and readiness of the enemy."

"Uncle, that's not an easy question to answer as the term *enemy* could apply to anyone."

Wamba looked up, suddenly taking in the creased face of the astute man opposite.

"So right, no clear outside enemy, just differing inside ones. We are all Goths, and not a one to be trusted. What a state of affairs. Though, in reality, not much different to at any other time this century. Let's look at the declared insurrectionists first, shall we?"

Egica gave what intel they had, which wasn't extensive nor particularly updated as the main source was the Church's tentacles, which reported directly to the bishops in Toletum, who filtered and sent on what they wanted the army to hear. The nub of the information he had to give was that various meetings of the different players were still taking place with no real call to arms yet."

"So, if we attacked quickly we would have a pretty easy time of things."

"I believe so. They have internal leadership disputes and there is a considerable lack of will to actually fight. There seems to be a general belief that they may be able to achieve their, or some of their objectives, without resort to actually fighting, believing instead the threat will be enough."

"Oh dear! And you think I am naïve. These people obviously do not know what the bishops have become. There is no way they would allow anything like this to happen, and I, as the nominal head of state, have to be seen as the victor in this fight so as not to lose any more ground in my battle with them."

Egica was totally shocked. "You mean without the prodding of the bishops you would consider allowing them to break away?"

"My dear nephew, there are many ways of skinning a cat. The die, however, has been cast and fight we shall, and win we shall, without any one baron taking too much credit. How we achieve that, is the next point to be talked about."

This was all said in such hushed tones that both men had to strain to hear all the words the other voiced as they were more than well aware that these, and every other wall, had ears.

A map was unfurled onto the table by the military commander, as the king joined him muttering, "I do hope this wasn't bought in Toletum." After a considerable amount of time, more ale and quite an amount of decision re-making, they decided that the best approach was to split the force to make a three pronged attack. The logic of this was undeniable. What was considerably more difficult to decide was how the army should be split and who should lead these sections.

*

Marcus was saddled and ready to go, the deep furrowed worry-lined face of his father stood holding the bridle.

"So, don't engage until I get back. The information from the Jews says that all the forces are squabbling in the presence of the king, still in Ilerda, trying to divide themselves into three pronged assault apparently. How we know this I really don't know. Anyway, this means they shouldn't arrive in Tarraco any time soon, and certainly not in any major numbers. If, however, they do, don't engage them until I get back."

"Father, this is the fourth time that you've given me the same instructions and if you say *don't engage them* again, I will ride directly to Ilerda to fight the whole lot by myself."

Still looking extremely troubled, he added a slightly contrite air to his appearance.

"Sorry, Marcus. It's just that I should be going with you. Instead, I have to stay here to ..., well, I don't know what we are going to do, except probably crown your old friend the new king."

"King Paulus of Tarraconensis/Gallia Gothica! Doesn't roll off the tongue, does it?"

"No, not really."

"What makes me feel sad about having to ride away now is that I didn't get to meet my future bride."

The furrows became shallower as his father came close to smiling.

"I bet you are."

"It's true! Going to Tarraco to engage with Wamba's forces is much worse than meeting *a truly lovely girl*."

"NOT to engage."

The horse moved away as the duke's hands let go to remonstrate. Marcus increased the speed to a fast trot, looked over his shoulder, shouting; "Oh yes, I forgot. Were those instructions for the girl or the army?"

Back in the main room there were knots of conspiratorial conversations. After the period of enforced reflection, the proposal had not received universal acclaim. The reality was that there was not one person who was enthusiastic about the idea. Paulus was part of the group led by

Chlodoswintha, which saw the necessity of the action not because it had merit in itself, it was more of a case of any other alternative being considerably worse.

The opposers weren't violently against either, their feeling was that it didn't seem quite right. The only person who was virulently against, was the *other* general, Wittimir. His view being more self-interested in that he couldn't see the need for a king at all, and if there had to be a military man in overall control, then that role should be his, something he found difficult admitting to himself and would never voice.

The duke's re-entrance refocused everyone's attention.

"Gentlemen, shall we be seated?" The count wasn't his usual jovial self, the reality of what they were doing and its potential dire consequences played heavily on his mind.

"I think we all accept that we need to have this overall leader and that role should go to General Paulus. However, there is less agreement on whether we should crown him for the duration of the conflict. As the people with most to lose in this *schism* and the most vested interest in the way the power is distributed, Duke Ranosindus and I, have decided that we should go ahead with this coronation as soon as possible. Paulus has solemnly sworn on the Bible that he will relinquish all rights to the thrones as soon as an amicable arrangement with the Wamba forces is reached. Further and to this end, we are in the process of drafting a letter to Wamba proposing the division of the kingdom as it now is, along the borders that existed in times of King Leovigild a century or so ago, in 569."

"What? What are you talking about?" Wittimir could contain his anger no longer.

It was Bishop Gunhild, in his best soft spoken priest-like voice, who gave the required history lesson, without saying, nor hinting, that as a general of the Goth nation, Wittimir should know their shared glorious past. This passive put down was enough to unruffle most of the protruding feathers of the less than submissive general, who realised he'd done little to further his cause by showing such ignorance.

Paulus got to his feet and made, for him, quite a long heartfelt speech in which he detailed his journey from Wamba enforcer to potential candidate for royalty in such a short period. He emphasised how much he didn't want this role and to the same depth of emotion, his belief in their legitimate aspirations of change, while making clear, he'd do everything possible, bar surrender, to avoid bloodshed within the Goth family. "We need to point out in the most uncertain terms to King Wamba, who I know to be a most reasonable and intelligent man, that there is no threat to the kingdom, it will be like two brothers sharing the inheritance. Making it abundantly clear that we know that we are the younger brother, who is willing to take any, and all, the advice of the elder brother, as long as it doesn't interfere with the running of our part of the estate."

Not expecting a round of applause, and being prepared for more than a few raised voices, Paulus was pleasantly surprised by the low muttering that filled the air.

The count allowed this to continue for a while until he perceived a slight increase in the decibel range, "Gentlemen, I will ask this for the last time. Is there anyone who disagrees so strongly that they feel they can no longer give their all to our just cause?"

Silence reigned.

"Then I will pass over control of this meeting to Bishop Gunhild to outline the logistics."

This announcement took most by surprise as nobody had realised to what extent Gunhild had been in league with the main movers and shakers, none more so than his direct superior, the Metropolitan Bishop Argebaud, who turned to look at the man at his side as if he were taking the man in for the first time in his life.

Gunhild explained that the church of the martyr Saint Feliu would be used for the coronation with the Bishop of Gerunda, Amador, playing a significant supporting role to the lead of Metropolitan Bishop Argebaud. The already dumbstruck cleric almost fell off his seat, not just by the content of what he'd just heard, but also by the offhand but not off cuff delivery, as if everything had been done and dusted prior to the meeting. "Arh, interesting. And, when, may I ask, was I to be consulted on these arrangements?"

Gunhild, realising he'd made a major error not counting on the Metropolitan Bishop's pride, started to stutter an answer, only to be cut off by the now pulpit tone and volume voice.

"I want to make clear that I was not party to any previous agreement. Furthermore, I have severe reservations as to as the legitimacy of this coronation, though I can find myself agreeing with its expediency. However, I most certainly will not allow my office and person to be used as the primary instrument of this dubious action. And, if I may ask another question, with what do you intend to *crown* this new king?"

The mutterings were no longer low.

Gunhild's normal poise was nowhere to be seen, he was visibly floundering at the broadside from the man once seated, now stood, next to him. His silence and inability to act showed that he'd obviously taken too much for granted.

It was Bishop Jacinto of Castrum Libiae, who sprang to his rescue. "I was not party to any preparations either. However, I believe it was clear which way the wind was blowing, and thus I am not at all surprised that some contingency plans have been discussed and are on the point of being put into place. In fact, I have had this very conversation with a number of people here present, plus a few of the most involved who are not physically in this room, for example, Bishop Amador, in whose fair city we sit. He has come up with a way in which we can temporarily solve the problem of the crown; an idea which is in line with the whole concept of this coronation, in that it would be a non-permanent state." A drum roll type pause, "The suggestion being, that we could borrow a crown and return it forthwith once its use is deemed no longer necessary."

"From whom? Do you know many people who have a spare crown to lend, Jacinto?" was the scathing question.

"To tell you the truth dear Metropolitan Bishop, I did not. Bishop Amador, on the other hand does. King Reccared, when he was celebrating his, and our nation's conversion from Arianism, gave a crown to the martyr Feliu's memory, which is stored in his church, the place of the proposed coronation. It is our belief that Feliu would not be averse to lending this object for a short duration."

Spluttering to his feet the Metropolitan Bishop yelled as if he'd been stung by a wasp, "This is blasphemy!"

*

"I have brought you a few things that you might find useful."

Rebecca laid out some of this year's dried and preserved harvest and a jar of olive oil.

"I'm not an invalid, I'm sure that I can find..."

"Do shut up. By the second month of the new year, there will be precious little to scavenge. Also, you'll be huge and bending will no longer be so easy. If you won't accept it for you, then take it for the baby."

This was Rebecca's third trip since they'd shared the information of their shared state. Despite carrying a heavy load, the journey seemed shorter each time, even if she never really found her way, it sort of found her. She supposed that this was because she was truly looking forward to seeing Arantxa to swap the little intimacies she could share with nobody else. Fortunately, she hadn't been, unlike Arantxa, affected by any vomiting stage. Trying to explain that away in the still frosty all but silent atmosphere of the house would have tested her powers of storytelling. Her father's way of dealing with the situation, the part he knew about, was to ignore it, not to the extent that it didn't exist or had never happened, but to ignore the results of it by keeping conversation to the minimum. Meals were quiet affairs with comments on food taking up most of the agenda. Never asking where she was going, or where she had been, she didn't find it necessary to lie or say anything about her trips to Arantxa. The last two Shabbat family meals had been cancelled for some reason, once by Isaac and once by her father, it was as if they'd made a pact not to put Trudi and Rebecca in the same room.

All in all then, making the long trek, laden with provisions, to this ramshackled house was a pleasure. It was also something that Arantxa looked forward to. Her freedom enjoyment was a little lonely, and during some strange noises nights, frightening, at times, still, she was relishing this period, in spite of how dreadful she felt each morning. It was a weird and exhilarating feeling that once she'd emptied her stomach, she could decide how she would spend the hours. There was nobody to order her around, nobody she had to please, such freedom was heady stuff.

Although her life back in the village had been the opposite, she found herself thinking more and more of those days, trying hard to remember. Not suffering an attack of sweet reminiscing, instead, she was trying to recall how the men had done the *manly* things. The berry picking, fire wood gathering and even some of the basic house repairs were relatively simple, but she knew she had to be more resourceful. Having found and repaired an old net, it was now anchored by the nearest rocks. To her surprise, most days it yielded something that was edible. And on the days there was more than a daily meal she set about preserving the extra with salt that Rebecca had delivered on her second trip. She even had set traps in the woods, this was where her memory was stretched to the limit, as she was yet to snare anything.

Even though she really was grateful for everything that Rebecca was bringing, she felt guilt and dependent, her pride though would have to be swallowed as she the realisation of the truth of Rebecca's mid-winter predictions were logical and inevitable. Where she was from, the winters were long, dark and very cold, her big hope was that the climate here would be a little kinder.

"Thanks. I know you are right. If you could put the things in that area, I've found it's the driest and most protected, I am using it as a sort of pantry. Let me just get some water and we will make a hot honeyed water."

With that, and a welcoming embrace, the proud host set off to a fresh water mine which she'd found not too far into the woods behind the house.

This left Rebecca to look around and reflect. She was at a loss to see why Arantxa was so happy here, as she was forever saying, it really was a pitiful existence, certainly not a life that she would revel in; lonely, basic and frightening. The final item came even more sharply focused as her hearing picked up the sound of a horse being ridden at speed in the direction of the cottage. Looking around for something to defend herself with, there was nothing. Arantxa wore the dagger at all time, usually strapped to her thigh or the base of her spine, giving a warrior appearance to her dishevelled dirtiness. Hiding seemed the second best option, if there had only been somewhere to hide! The third and only realistic choice was to flee to the woods. Just as she got out of the cottage the horse skidded to a halt and a man leapt off, landing in front of her and totally enveloped her.

It was to this scene that Arantxa returned dagger drawn.

"Would you mind unhanding my friend and giving me a cuddle!" Marcus obeyed and added profuse and profound kisses to the order.

Looking on, Rebecca was racked with conflicting emotions, happiness at their evident delight in seeing each other, and regret and jealousy that she couldn't experience the same. After giving them a bit of time, she then cleared her throat, "Perhaps I should be heading back as you two seem to have a lot of catching up to do."

To her surprise, it was Marcus who insisted that she stay a while longer as he had all sorts of news that she needed to hear.

"I think we've got some news for you as well."

*

The crowning ceremony would not go down in history as one of the most grandiose nor auspicious. It was teeming it down, the heavens had opened early morning and it was getting to the point of torrential with deafeningly loud thunder and far too many bolts of lightning to actually count, when the small wet, bedraggled group entered the church in dribs and drabs, having given up on the idea of a royal parade through the streets of Gerunda full of pomp and circumstance.

There had never been any enthusiasm for the event by anyone; a deemed necessity, accepted by all parties, was as far as positivity went.

The final yell of Metropolitan Bishop Argebaud, who was conspicuous by his absence, of "Blasphemy!" rang louder than the thunder in everyone's ears. Perhaps God was showing His displeasure by this atmospheric display.

Removing their sodden outer garments to reveal some of their finery of best clothing made the scene a trifle more special, though far from the royal splendour they had hoped and briefly planned for. The fact that their never overly large group had dwindled yet further didn't help matters either. Excluding serving staff and unimportant hangers on, they were pitifully few; four bishops - Jacinto, Gunhild, Amador and Ranimiro, a count and countess - Hilderic and Chlodoswintha, a duke - Ranosindus, a nobleman - Arangiscle, a general - Wittimir and of course, one future king, Flavius. Pathetic in the eyes of all.

The ceremony itself was brief and performed by the hometown bishop with the guiding hand and voice of Bishop Gunhild. God was beseeched to bestow His blessing on this newest royal of the Goth nation, who, by the way, was a non Goth by birth, as the borrowed crown of Saint Feliu was placed on his head. It was answered with an almighty clap of thunder which those present afterwards joked to each other was a resounding sign of approval from the Higher Being, whereas they all saw and heard it individually as a roaring thump of disapproval.

"I don't want to sound churlish, dearest uncle, but you have not long arrived and I have had to put up with them in Toletum and all the way here as well."

"Perhaps I ought to propose you for beatification? Saint Egica. Has a nice ring to it, don't you think? Died, martyred on the vanity and self-empowerment of the enemies of the Church and State."

The two men were dining alone after a day of intense negotiations with the barons. Both being exhausted and exasperated by the tediously slow pace of developments, it seemed that every time they managed to get a plan where nobody was too upset there always came a last minute hitch that forced a re-think.

Making sure that there were no servants around, and keeping his voice very low, the king all but whispered, "When we've won this war and we are back in Toletum, I think I will be in a position to impose my will. Never again will a Goth army have to go through these interminable negotiations. Imagine if we were faced by a real force that was organised, No! This is the last time that these pumped up power crazed men will slow the progress of an armed force."

"How will you be able to stop it? They have the money, their armies and the power."

"For a while now I have been working on the idea of a military law. In fact, it was the idea of General Paulus, our present enemy. I actually do miss him. A good man, intelligent, good company and used to have his head and heart in the correct place. I really do wonder what made him rebel, it doesn't make any sense to me. Anyway, we used to have interesting chats when he wasn't traipsing off around the countryside fucking all the local girls and calling them reconnaissance missions."

Wamba chuckled to himself in fond reminiscence, "Good chap, shame he wasn't loyal. Still, it was in one of these conversations we came up with the idea of a military law."

"A what?"

"A military law. It would force *all* the nobles and the Church to send troops without leaders, to be absorbed into a national force under the single control of the exercitus, whenever there was an invasion or rebellion."

"Good luck with passing that."

"That's why I need to win this war quickly, and well, without any baron shinning too brightly. The law, to be effective, would have to have teeth. Paulus proposed a mandatory death sentence with the confiscation of all properties of those not complying, with the remaining members of their families being sent into exile. His argument was that we'd only have to make an example of one baron, neither the most powerful nor the weakest, then others would all fall into place."

"It may work. It can't be worse than the shambles we are dealing with."

"I am relying on you, as military commander, to provide the gory details of this pathetic excuse for a fighting force."

Egica, while agreeing tried not to show the disquiet that this idea provoked in him, it would necessarily mean sticking his head out a trifle too far as he knew just how weak Wamba was at the moment, and how any move like this would, quite probably, mean him losing his position and life. Still, there was no denying that the idea was both attractive and necessary.

There was a discreet knock, followed by the entrance of a servant to announce the request of an audience from Bishop Iulianus and a Jew.

"Oh, no, just when you think that the day can't get any worse. I can't do this tonight."

They all looked at each other expectantly, Marcus and Rebecca brimming with their undisclosed information, Arantxa, quite a way behind in the enthusiasm stakes looking decidedly sheepish. Fortunately, Marcus didn't notice as he only had eyes for Rebecca. Evidently his news was primarily for her rather than his lover. Realising this, she began to feel a cold chill rising from the place where the warm glow of the baby usually was, the news could not possibly be good, the best she could hope for was less bad. So, she decided to revert to type and started to make fun of the duke's son.

"Did you get to meet your future wife, the truly lovely girl?"

Initially he was taken aback by the question and began to stumble until he saw that familiar teasing Rebecca look that he had suffered so many times before. This required a skilfully laid ambush response.

"No, sadly she was not in attendance. However, as I left they were about to crown the future king."

Spurred into action by Rebecca's nasty little comment about the future wife, Arantxa decided to join in the fun, "Well, our favourite little Jewess here is about to increase the number of subjects that this new king will have."

It took a while for Marcus to work out what he was being told. "What! You are.? Well, I never. That makes my news even better!"

The girls, now extremely interested in the new information, waited impatiently while Marcus savouring the moment, took his time by choosing his words carefully, "What a busy month he's having, to become a king, and a father."

The joint *what*, didn't come like a loud howling wind, it was more a low gust of severe intensity.

"Are you trying to say?"

"I'm not trying to say anything, I AM saying, we will have, actually, probably already have, a King Paulus, who it seems has set about securing his lineage."

This house didn't boast any chairs just a poorly constructed bench type thing and a sawn down tree trunk, Rebecca chose the former to plonk herself down on. Her complex world that she didn't think could get any more so, had.

Marcus delighted in both his handling of the situation and the effect; for once he had trumped Rebecca and left her speechless. His glee was written all over his face for any and all to see. Wanting to persevere with his triumph he continued, "Just think about it, you are carrying a potential little Prince or Princess!"

Arantxa, couldn't join in the fun as she was conscious of how much more difficult a terrible situation had become, squatted next to her friend and took her hand, which made Marcus finally realise that this wasn't quite the gloating victory he had hoped. She glowered at him, and spoke, "You evidently think that becoming a parent despite any adverse conditions is a good thing. That makes me happy."

Noticing that she looked anything but happy, Marcus ventured a quizzical look asking why.

"Because you will be a father in the new year."

It was Marcus's turn to slump, as Rebecca had the only good sitting place, he sought support from the door frame which crumbled in his hand. Not finding the physical prop he needed, his eyes searched for an emotional bulwark, she had her back firmly turned towards him and had moved to stoke a fire which was already blazing.

Arantxa had never wanted to tell him. Obviously, she realised that at some point this would become unavoidable if they went on seeing each other, but she was not certain about that, nor her feelings towards the whole situation concerning him and her child. She had no doubts that she wanted the baby, what wasn't so clear was how much role he could play, or that she wanted him to play, especially with his upcoming nuptials.

Still holding the rotten piece of wood that had broken off, he went towards the determined back and tried to spin her around to face him. She was an immoveable object refusing to turn. Momentarily defeated, he held her shoulders and kissed the top of her head. Being totally unsure about his feelings, he desperately wanted someone else to take charge emotionally. It hadn't crossed his mind at any point in their sexual exploits that she could become pregnant. It wasn't that he didn't know the consequences, it was just, he didn't expect it would happen to them. What could or should he do?

"You are supposed to say *something.*" Rebecca unhelpfully chivvied from the chair. She desperately wanted them to talk, fight, do anything to distract her from her own thoughts; her Flavius, gentile, father of her baby, king!

Along with two of the people, the silence in the room was pregnant. Nobody knew what to say.

*

"Incredible!" Wamba's pacing wasn't pensive mode, it was stridently fuming.

Egica, who had been in attendance listening to his royal uncle complain bitterly about the awful evening he'd had listening to and keeping peace between an arrogant Jew and a bishop whose spite had no limits. His sympathy wasn't brimming as it was he who'd had to put up with this pair all the way, day and night, from Toletum. The mood from pained sufferer to indignant parchment slapping marauder was precipitated by a messenger and the said, now much abused, piece of correspondence.

"How is this even possible?"

"Dearest Uncle, if you'd like me to join in this conversation, and perhaps answer your question, if it wasn't rhetorical, then you need to enlighten me somewhat with further information."

"Our once loyal general has been kind enough to write to me proposing that we share the K

kingdom. Graciously, he leaves me with the larger part and the role of *elder brother.*"

"Decent of him."

"Egica we need to march. Today, now, quickly to resolve this situation immediately!"

The younger man did his best to calm the king–in-a-hurry down by pointing out some basic necessities of who marches where, plus the thorny issue, which they had been trying to resolve the last few days, of who is to lead the three parts of the attack.

They returned to the forever open map spread across the less than sturdy table.

"I will take the main force directly to Tarraco and then work my way up the coast via Barcino and Gerunda. That leaves the second grouping, with Alaric as the head, to go along this road here, the Strata Ceretanis, which will cross the mountains here," using his rolled up kingdom sharing document as an indicator, "heading towards Castrum Libiae. There will be some resistance there, nothing major I suspect unless the Vascones decide to join in. We have had reports that Lupus has sent envoys that made wild promises, which I am sure he would like to keep. However, since the victories and peace treaty that Kunimund has obtained, I suspect their ardour for more bloodshed has diminished. Then, if he follows the river Tet, in no time Narbo will be within striking distance. He will be instructed to wait for me outside the city, we'll all attack together, not as separate forces."

A deep intake of breath pause, "That leaves you, the third prong of attack. You'll have the relatively simple task of passing this way," pointing along another pass via Ausona through the mountains. "Initially, yours should meet the least resistance at least until you get to Clausurae, so I propose that you take the most conflictive of our barons, also, the one seeking to cover himself in the most glory, Ervigius."

The logic in this was undeniable to the listener.

"You do realise that you will be saddled with your preferred pair, the Jew and the bishop?"

Wamba had spent half the night thinking about a way in which he wouldn't be lumbered with them and had come to the conclusion that he had to take the pain. If he didn't and passed through Jew dominated urban centres like Tarraco without them, he'd be opening himself up to attack from the likes of Julian and company back in the capital for any perceived leniency, be it true or not. Taking them with him meant he was covering his back with a couple of Toletum appointed fall guys. It was just that he did not relish travelling with them nor having to be a spectator in the vile retribution against the Jews. Still, prices have to be paid.

"Who is going to take Teodofred?"

Although this baron from Betica didn't give off the appearance of being as power- obsessed as Evrigius, he was certainly a threat with the size of his force and his family connections. Being a son of the former king Reccesvinth, his claim to the throne was real and evident.

"Perhaps I should keep him close to me, he may do less harm there. Also, he's well acquainted to Bishop Iulianus so perhaps I could fob one off with the other."

General Alaric and the other interested parties were called in individually and told their part in the scheme and given instructions to be ready to march the day after tomorrow at first light.

*

Formalities over, nobody wanted to hang around in the church. The deluge outside impeded their immediate departure, so they huddled around the front two pews to have the first Council of State of the new kingdom. The king, in name, was exactly that after returning the borrowed crown, limited his interventions to technical military matters. If anyone from the outside with the information that a new monarch had been crowned had stumbled upon this scene, and were asked to guess who the person was who had been appointed regal, they would have struggled to get it in three. Any betting man looking at how the meeting progressed, and seeing who everyone looked to for approval or advice, though that person spoke very little, would have wagered his estate on the only female present, Chlodoswintha. Her presence dominated while she maintained her womanly role of silence. Her only verbal intervention was to suggest moving farther down the church as rain was beginning to more than drip through the roof above where they were sitting.

Realigned at the back, their interrupted meeting received another impediment to its unofficial non-existent agenda, a messenger, whose insistence at the door was loud and disrespectful to the guard manning it.

"Let him in," called the yet to be re-seated count.

The completely sodden man, who squelched up the aisle, looking fit to bursting with his new information, was unsure who to deliver it to. Taking in the assembled nobility trying to decide who was the pack leading top dog, going through his head was the thought that men's lives had been forfeited upon mistakes like these. His quandary was intensified by the very obvious fact that he was a Jew in a hive of important Christians.

"I was told by rabbi Ariel to report to …" The now frightened confused man ground to a halt as the splendidly clad grouping was all glaring at him.

"You've come from Narbo? Do tell the king what our friend has to say." It was Chlodoswintha who came to his aid by pointing in the direction of Paulus.

The man redirected his vision and gave a short report to the now standing figure. Paulus, feeling more secure than he had since entering the church, asked only one question, dismissing the man before anyone else had time to react. It wasn't a moment too soon as the muted pandemonium of dam breaking curiosity was in the mouths of a number of the dignitaries.

(433)

Paulus held his hand up while he stared Wittimir into silence. "This changes matters considerably."

The Jewish network, which had previously assured them of a royal / baronial impasse, had now provided the unwelcome news of a three pronged army on the move.

"Tarraco will be first hit." Paulus looked at the duke, "I'm afraid that we won't have time to get there to save the city. Furthermore, I think that if Marcus puts up any sort of serious fight, he will be pulverised along with all those southern forces which we desperately need intact."

"If I set off now, at least I will be there to help."

"No, duke. We need Marcus to put up some sort of delaying action while sending the bulk of your forces up here to make a stand."

"Suicide?"

"No, bog them down in a stalemate of negotiations. Wamba will not want to lose too many of his force too early. I imagine he'd prefer to talk, at least for a while, rather than face depletion. Could you get a message to him forthwith giving him those instructions?"

"I still think.."

"Duke Ranosindus," for the first time Paulus played the role of commanding officer king, "you, along with the others, put me into this role of overall commander. Please do as I say. We need you here to command any troops that Marcus manages to salvage from down there." Seeing the logic in what he was being told though not agreeing with his participation, Ranosindus accepted the order and set off into the rain to organise a letter and deliverer.

"That leaves the north to be organised. Again, I believe the best that Barcino can do is delay the advance, so I'll make sure that happens. I think that our preferred place to engage this coastal army, which is probably the bulk of their forces, may be slightly north of here. From my reading of the map, which I have been studying greatly, I suggest Clausurae provides us with a good opportunity and it's easily reinforced from the north. I'm sure that those of you who know the terrain much better than I could provide me with any pertinent details directly after this meeting." A quick scan gave him a number of agreeing heads. "General Wittimir, I need you to go to Narbo to ready the forces there. Bishop Gunhild, it is you who has conducted the negotiations with the Franks, I would like you to go to Frankia to see if their promise of troops is a reality. If it is, bring them no farther than Nemausus, we don't want a foreign army maundering deep into Gallia Gothica."

Both men accepted their missions without comment. Paulus then turned his attention to Bishop Jacinto and nobleman Arangiscle, "You two need to get back as soon as possible. The second column will have to pass through Castrum Libiae. If you hold them there, we will get reinforcements to you and we should be able to inflict a defeat on them, freeing up your men to come back to Narbo to form a second line of defence. The Vascones indicated that they would lend assistance there, however, their envoy was more than a little shifty when I spoke to him. I don't trust Lupus to get involved unless he sees that we have a serious chance of victory. Wamba has already inflicted too many heavy defeats on the Vasconis nation. Don't rely on any help from that quarter."

Everyone scuttled off as instructed, leaving just the count, countess and the local bishop, Amador. Chlodoswintha eyed the new King her thoughts were written on her face, we have the right person for the job. "I presume, *Sire*, you'd like us to return to Nemausus, send down as many troops as possible while maintaining a dissuasive force so the Franks don't get the idea that we are allowing them in the back door to do as they please."

Paulus looked the handsome woman in the eyes, she really would make a great leader of men, having grasped the situation much quicker and more astutely than her husband could ever do.

"If you wouldn't mind. Bishop Amador, could you see to the defences of Gerunda. Again, the fight will not be here, just slow them down as much as possible."

*

To everybody's surprise, the voice that broke the long pregnant silence came from a completely unexpected source, a recently arrived dripping in sweat, exhausted figure that was in the doorframe recently vacated by Marcus.

"You look a happy bunch!"

All eyes took in the less than elegant figure of Pere.

"I only found this place because of the hoofmarks from your horse, certainly chosen a place literally off the beaten track. Marcus, I have run, as you can see, from the training ground. One of our outposts has reported in that the royal forces have been spotted but a day's march away."

"That's not possible!"

"Yes, it is. We must leave, and start preparing the defensive position."

This spurred a looking-over-her-shoulder Arantxa into action, she turned completely embracing Marcus with as much force as she could muster. He responded in kind.

This scene was becoming too intimate for Pere so he went to turn away only to be stopped by Rebecca's sensible military question, "How big is the force?"

"The outpost says it was difficult to estimate but at least twenty cohorts with supporting cavalry of significant numbers, and he says that he definitely saw the king's standard flying."

This stopped Marcus mid kiss. "That's incredible. They were not supposed to be here in such numbers for at least a couple of weeks. This won't give time for reinforcements to be sent from the north. Dispatch a messenger straight away."

"Already done, I took the liberty.."

"Well done. How many can we get together?"

"If we are lucky, about half their numbers and nowhere near the amount of cavalry. Don't like to interrupt but we really need to leave now"

Arantxa withdrew her restraining arms only to immediately replace them around his neck to yank him close enough to her face for a last kiss. Not wanting to pull away, ever, she broke the hold, "Go and do your duty you son of baron."

"I'm heading back to Tarraco to see my father. You ought to come with me." Rebecca's advice was given to the forlorn looking girl.

"No, I'm staying in *my* house."

"I think you would be safer doing as Rebecca suggests."

"And I think you'd be safer not going out to fight a battle with the king." There was a standoff which Pere interrupted again, "I think Arantxa is right."

"What? I should stay here like some coward."

"No, not on that part, you have no choice, you must lead the men. What I think she's right about is staying here. It's very difficult to see, nobody will be looking for you, if you clean the path of hoof marks, pull a bit of brush over the beginning, the part closest to the beach, and stop using a fire in three or four days' time. Then, even if we lose, you'll be safer here than in Tarraco."

Losing, hiding, being safe these words said out loud made everything so much more real, it was if a sudden exceptionally cold wind had blown through the door.

"Perhaps you ought to stay as well, Rebecca."

"Marcus, you may have the obligation and right to order troops about, you may not do the same to me."

"I only said *ought*."

"I stated my intention of going back to my father." With that she moved Marcus out of the way to embrace her friend. It was longer and more tender than either had anticipated it would be. "Stay safe. I'll come back if I can, when all this has blown over. You just make sure that you win!" The last remark was aimed at her ex- playmate from her youth.

Speedily exiting the house, she only paused to stroke Pere's stubbly face, "Don't you get hurt either, you have a wife and children to take care of." Without looking back she hastened down the path.

"Pere, go back to the training ground, prepare the men to march to our agreed point. I presume the king's forces are staying to the road."

"Yes, sir."

"Then I'll gather what I can in Tarraco. Send out messengers to all the nobility to send whatever forces they have, and we'll meet there as soon as possible."

He turned to Arantxa who stopped him by saying, "We've said our goodbyes, not necessary to repeat the action. Go!"

Initially taken aback by her hard tone he realised this was her self-defence technique as it was clear that she was doing her level best to maintain a composed front even with her eyes beginning to well up.

"I'll be back."

As Marcus went for his horse, Pere lingered, he honestly believed that Arantxa would be safer here than in town, it was just that he didn't like the idea of abandoning her, nor what he imagined Antonia would have to say on the topic. "You know you're always welcome at ours, if anything goes wrong here."

"Thank you, Pere, that is most kind of you. Let's hope that nobody finds me. I think you are in considerably more danger, and I reiterate what Rebecca said; do take care, and if you can, keep that one," she indicated the horse mounting figure, "out of trouble."

She then repeated the face stroke of the last woman, leaving Pere wondering what it was about his face that it needed stroking so often.

Marcus quickly and easily caught Rebecca up before the beach.

"I know you are going to say no, but I believe it would be quicker if you got on the back of the horse."

"With you?" She was about to reject his offer with a considerable amount of scorn, when she checked herself. For once she ought to swallow her pride if she were to get back to her father as quickly as possible.

"If you drop me well before we get in sight of the city walls."

*

The leaving of the encampment near Ilerda was anything but orderly. As they had never been pitched and organised in the way in which they would be divided, it necessarily meant that one group had to cross the path of another, and the other was never too keen to have their area invaded by another. Blood wasn't spilled, though it was a close run thing on a number of occasions. The king had observed at a safe distance on an adjacent hill. Utter dismay was his reaction and a deep sadness that this was the best that the once great Goth nation, backbone of the Roman Empire had descended to. Thankfully, they wouldn't be facing a massive well-organised invading force as their chances of victory would be close to nil. It was imperative that this rabble and antiquated form of army gathering be changed as soon as possible.

Not knowing who to ride with, he had spurned all offers, instead opting for splendid isolation with the Regis Fidelis surrounding him, dissuading any who sought to ride close to the sovereign. Allowing Teodofred, with his most numerous contingent, to actually lead the procession through the countryside was an unusual approach, which would have been rejected as weak by most other kings. However, Wamba was quite happy to seed this role to the southern Baron for two reasons, one that there would be no one to witness the event, any and every able bodied person had more sense than to hang around to watch an army march past, and two, when it came to the fighting he would like to actually reduce the Baron's numbers by using them as the frontline shock troops in the first battle.

They had made very good time and camped for the night near an insignificant settlement which nestled in the shadow of the hills almost guarding the pass which as yet, had no formal name, though apparently, some locals referred to it as Montblanc.

*

Riding into the camped forces, his mind shot back to the time he'd done the same thing with the king's encampment not so long ago. Then he'd been impressed, so many men, so much armour, pennants and flags flying all over the place This time what Marcus was observing on his slow trot was anything but impressive. Partially clad, scruffy knots of milling men with little in the way of serious armament who gave off the appearance of fish well out of water. This was going to be a slaughter.

Pere was waiting for him outside the only pitched tent, "I thought you'd like your own command headquarters."

Eyes met and they both started laughing. Marcus managed to splutter, "Thank you, *general*, most thoughtful."

Going inside, Marcus was met by an empty space and not quite enough room to stand upright.

"There wasn't time to get any furnishings. Actually, I was lucky to find a tent at all."

This reality seemed most poignant, they had something resembling an army, possibly up to ten thousand men, however, in reality they had nothing. Few of these *soldiers* would stand their ground when the swords began to smash into their shield wall, they would break and run, leaving certain death to all the others.

"Pere, what are we going to do?"

Offering two rolled up parchments, "These arrived. They might help us. One is from your father and the other from General, I mean, King, Flavius."

Reading them both quickly he realised that they were both saying the same thing; he was on his own, he shouldn't sacrifice too many good men as they were needed for the real fight later but he had to slow the process of Wamba to give those in the north more time to organise.

"Pere, where should we make our stand?"

Explaining that he'd spent the morning with a local lad, they had decided that the best place was just before the hills that the main road crossed. There was a narrow opening which the army had to follow because the hills were steep with no paths, and going around them would mean the large force would have to be broken up and come across in small groups, something which no general worth his salt would even contemplate. Furthermore, as Wamba's was vastly superior in every way, numbers, experience and cavalry, they wouldn't avoid a direct clash, they would look forward to and delight at it.

By blocking this path, it would reduce the number of experienced men they would need in the shield wall, making it more possible to avoid a rout. The majority could just be gathered behind to look like a mass of reserves.

"Well done, Pere. I think if we hold the line for the first assault, they might want to try to negotiate. Wamba would realise that he would win at a cost which might be too high for him to pay."

*

"Papa, Uncle Isaac, I've got news."

Rebecca burst into the house after a most unpleasant journey on an animal she did not like. By trying not to fall off and at the same time not holding on too tightly to Marcus, she ended up doing both, it was an ordeal never to be repeated no matter what the emergency. The two brothers were to be found in the hall way, her uncle was either arriving or leaving.

"Wamba's forces are only a day's ride away."

"We know."

"All the men are being sent to fight them on the road to Ilerda."

"We know."

There are lots of them, possibly twenty or thirty thousand."

This caused them to take in her dishevelled appearance and agitated state.

"So many?"

"With the king leading them, that's the king from Toletum, not our new king."

"New King, we have our own king now, do we? May I ask where you have been and how did you come by all this information? All we know is that all able bodied men have been called to arms"

"Pere told us."

"Who's Pere and who is *us*?"

Mistake. She'd have to add this to giving no more regal information and circumvent both. "Antonia's husband."

"And who's Antonia?"

"Practically your neighbour here in port area." An arched eyebrow told her that more information would be needed, so she explained who Pere and Antonia were. "And he's in charge of the Tarraco forces Well, in name it's actually Marcus, but in reality it'll be Pere as Marcus is fairly useless at everything."

"Marcus, I know him, nice chap, the duke's son, came here a few times, seemed smitten with Arantxa. By the way, where is she these days? I haven't seen her for quite a while. Nice girl, Arantxa."

"Papa, you don't seem at all bothered that we are about to be attacked."

"Rebecca, I really don't know what we can do about it. We're too old to fight and we've taken precautions to ensure our gold is hidden. The rest is in the hands of God."

"If it's any consolation to you, niece, I am panicking. I knew this is what would happen. The whole idea was stupid, we should never have got involved and now it'll be us, the Jews, who will have to pay the highest price."

"It's true, Uncle, that we may lose this battle, but that doesn't mean to say that the whole war is lost."

"My daughter has become a general! Pray, do tell why you think we are going to lose this battle? There must a goodly number of men on our side, for days men have been arriving from all over the province. Then, we will be reinforced by the armies from the north, I presume."

"I think that you may presume too much. It was said that they wouldn't be able to get here in time."

"Oh, my god! Sweet Moses, we are doomed! It'll be us that will be sacrificed; we are lambs awaiting the slaughter!"

While his brother walked wringing his hands calling down the assistance of any number of biblical characters, Jacob deflated into the chair the bishop had occupied on his first visit, a time, not so long ago, when Jacob feared losing his fortune. Now, matters were considerably worse. If Wamba's troops entered the city nobody was safe, especially women, and young attractive women would be at a premium.

"Rebecca, you've got to get out of the city today. Go north to where that man you say that you love is. What's he doing there anyway? He's supposed to be a general and defending our city!"

"Man she loves, a General?" Isaac stopped his lamenting. "What? You and .."

"Yes. Apparently they are in love. I know, Isaac," Jacob held a fit to explode brother at bay for a moment with a hand gesture, "he's a gentile, totally inappropriate. I was hoping that it would all blow over and given time and space, they would both come to their senses. We no longer have that luxury. With an occupying army here in Tarraco you must leave. Do you still feel the same way about each other?" Meekly Rebecca nodded. "Then prepare to leave today. Go and join your general."

"Actually, he's now become king."

*

Baron Teodofred walked past the guard without a second thought of either asking permission to enter, or being stopped, and was mightily surprised when the two men belatedly reacted to block his path. Glaring at the larger man, not deigning to utter a sound to this lowlife, he expected the man to wilt like a drying autumn flower. Instead looking straight ahead at nothing in particular while keeping his sword crossed with his partner, the soldier maintained his poise. Realising the futility of glaring at someone who wasn't even looking at you, the baron found his voice.

"I am here to see King Wamba. Let me pass!"

There was no reaction from the two well-armed men.

"I have vital news. I demand entry immediately."

Just as the scene was about to take an ugly, perhaps violent turn, a smallish unarmed man of the ilk of a scribe appeared.

"Arh, baron, can I be of assistance?"

"Tell the king that I am here and wish to see him immediately."

"Regrettably, the King is indisposed and will not be receiving visitors for a while. I am sure that as soon as he is, he will send for you."

"I demand to see him now, it's of the uttermost importance."

"I will relay this information, if you would be so good as to wait for a while until I have an answer."

Steam wasn't actually coming out of the baron's ears but otherwise his head resembled an overheated kettle, red and exceptionally hot.

"Wait! There's a battle to be fought, man. Let me in immediately!"

He pushed against the crossed javelins to no avail, except forcing their bearers to take a step closer to each other in order to maintain their collective blocking force.

This tense impasse was broken by Wamba's voice, "Is that Baron Teodofred? Do come in."

Wamba had been observing this standoff at a discreet unobserved distance. In the last few days he'd felt the need to show his power through little significant gestures as he felt he was not being given due respect from some of the barons, who made up the majority of the force he was nominally leading.

Flustered and knocked out of his arrogant step, the baron entered the dimmer light of the tent. "Do have a seat and pray tell me of your urgency."

Dismissing the chair, the man launched into his *report*. "My men have spotted the enemy lining up for battle about half a day's march from here."

"Yes, I know." Wamba, who had been using his scouts in parallel to the leading forces of Teodofred, had been informed some time earlier that morning.

Surprised, the baron stumbled in his haste, momentarily being lost for words. "We believe there are anything up to five thousand."

"Actually the number seems closer to ten thousand and they are led by one of our ex-officers from the engagement in Vasconia, Baron Ranosindus's son."

Teodofred's surprise had moved up a notch to bordering on being flabbergasted, how did he know all this information? Determined not to show his shock he blustered on. "Still no match for our forces, we should be able to clear them out completely in no time."

"I am sure that is true, baron, however, they do seem to have chosen an interesting and effective defensive position. It may actually be better to hold some sort of talks first."

"Talks? My God, now is the time for action, not words! We should smash through them and move on to Tarraco."

Wamba strode about in an attempt at showing himself to be indecisively confused , whereas, in reality, he was most exceptionally pleased with the way the conversation was going. "So, as commander of the leading force you will be prepared to make this attack tomorrow with the view to a swift victory."

"Without a doubt." The baron for a brief moment thought about adding a respectful title like *sire*. Dismissing this, he poignantly left the space blank.

Wamba noticed this show of disrespect, as he was meant to, without any outward sign. "Splendid. I will leave the initial assault in your hands and under your sole command. I will be waiting farther back with the Regis fidelis."

The baron continued to be taken aback by the King's hands off approach to military leadership. This was the third time in a such a short space of time he had just ceded the dominant role; no true leader of men could, should or would do such a thing and hope to remain in power. Internally smirkingly joyous, Teodofred took his leave.

Wamba thought about sitting after this tense affair and found he couldn't. Despite the fish taking the line hook and sinker, he was still a little wary playing this dangerous game.

He had been told by his scouts that the Tarraco forces had chosen a superb defensive position in which no cavalry could possibly be used, archers would have limited value as well, and thus it would be shield wall against shield wall, which is always a matter of attrition and training. Knowing that the baron's forces had not been involved in any serious fighting ever and that Marcus had at least a rump of a force which had been bloodied by the Vascones, then, despite being fewer in number, he felt that the Tarraco force could at least hold the line. The Baron's soldiers would eventually win due to sheer numbers, but the cost for him, and his bigger aspiration, would be significant, thus reinforcing his, the king's, rightful role.

A small sturdy squat man entered the tent without any problem from the guards. In fact, they showed due deference.

"General Badwila, as you were standing so close to the side of the tent, your outline was clear with the sun blazing behind you. However, I don't think the Baron noticed, you obviously heard every word, so I don't have to inform you, what do you think? Are your scouts totally correct both in their estimation of numbers and the position of the enemy?"

"Without a doubt, Sire. Also, they have been manoeuvred expertly into position by an old comrade, Pere." The King's face registered no recognition of the name. "He was Marcus's right hand man, exceptionally competent leader at centurion level, well loved as well. He will have them extremely well trained for sure."

*

It was a loud and most distinct sound; horses. She was quite a way from her cottage. Having found a clump of blackberry bushes she was harvesting as many as she could to build up stocks. The noise though, froze her in mid pick. At least four horses. This wasn't anyone she knew nor was she expecting anyone. This was the clear and evident danger she had been warned of. Not really believing the depth of Pere's worries for her, she had taken most of the precautions he had advised - hoof marks had been swept away, the entrance to the track she'd covered with brush.

However, she'd not doused the fire completely; reduced its size, yes, but she needed a kettle with warmed if not boiling water.

The animals and their riders pulled up relatively close to where she was.

"I told you I really did see smoke coming from this direction."

"But there's nothing here. No farm, no homestead, no small village... nothing!"

"Perhaps it's farther in the wood."

"With NO paths towards it? We've been on the sea side, there was nothing and here, I see thick bushes. I am not taking my horse through that for... what? A hermit boiling vegetables?"

Another voice, "I agree. I'm sure if we head inland we will find both food and women."

With that they cantered away in a south westerly direction.

The relief that Arantxa felt was immense. Evidently, she hadn't taken the warnings seriously enough, overestimating her ability to defend herself. There would have been no way she could have fought off a group of armed men looking for plunder and rape. Touching her belly she promised herself, and whatever was in there, to take more care as she made her way quickly and quietly back to put out the embers.

*

All three were beautiful horses, stallions for the king and the baron, and slightly to the left, diagonally on an opposing hill, a mare supported the weight of Marcus. The two shield walls could not be very long as the width of the pass forbade it with its steep rocky inclines on either side. The air was filled with the smell of tension and sweat. The exalting had been brief and rather tentative as these things went. The loud bravado and display of individual heroics and challenges barely happened. This was clearly not a case of two seasoned armies squaring up for yet another battle. Instead, they resembled two virgins attempting sex for the first time fearing any pain or ridicule that their attempts might bring.

The Tarraco force knew its job was not to move, either forward or backward, under any circumstances, unless ordered to. Pere had drilled them for hours every day, when they weren't harvesting in the afternoon, doing the same thing again and again and yet again. When the less than straight wall of the royal forces advanced causing an almighty clash, everyone reacted as if it were second nature. Their first line was made up of their most experienced soldiers and they moved as one; superbly tightly, bringing their shields to cover and their long daggers and short swords to jab and maim. The second line, having slightly longer weapons poked and slashed depending on the movement and requirements of their comrades. Necks and legs were the two main targets and each hit produced a variable fountain of spraying blood. The Tarraco men who fell were quickly replaced and their bodies, dying or injured, were pulled back behind the lines so that they didn't cause any impediment or something to stumble over.

"They are good." Wamba was truly impressed. It was a slightly unfair fight as the soldiers of the now worried looking bloodless faced Baron, unquestionably had not the skill and training. Enthusiasm they didn't lack and continued their onslaught each time the Tarraco forces took a step back, in unison, to avoid being embroiled in the melee of bleeding dying forms being left on the ground.

Teodofred was absolutely livid, his forces were taking a beating and looked as if they would continue to do so. If this unremitting slaughter carried on for much longer his troop would be seriously depleted as would his influence. His anger was getting in the way of his clear thinking, he needed some face saving way out of this mess before it was too late.

"It looks as if my forces have softened up their enemy line, perhaps now is the time to replace them with the fresh men of the exercitus."

"I see little evidence of *softening*. What I see is something resembling a very one-sided battle. I do believe that if we continue this attack, you, and ultimately, us, will lose far too many men in this one encounter when we will need them for much tougher combat to come. I would suggest a slight retreat; see if their line breaks to continue the chase, if it does, then we will make short work of this day. If, and I believe this to be more likely, they hold their ground, we offer them the possibility of talks."

"*Talks*?!"

"Yes, talks. They are not stupid. They know they will lose, it's just a matter of time, and deaths on our side. I think that with negotiations, and the fact that we will be sending troops towards Dertosa, who I trust, within a few days will appear to their rear, they will see the logic of a negotiated surrender."

What Wamba had predicted came to pass with the superbly disciplined Tarraco troops not taking the bait of a disorderly retreat to pursue, instead maintaining an excellent text book shape. The shouted offer of negotiations was accepted with General Badwila and Pere meeting in no man's land in order to talk over the details.

*

Relief, exhaustion and total elation were the emotions felt by the Tarraco forces once it was clear that they were being stood down for the duration. Searching for friends and comrades with effusive back slapping was the order of the day. The rear guard, who were immensely relieved that they hadn't been called into action, greeted the warriors as something they clearly were in their eyes; *heroes*. This euphoric mood was dampened when the scouts began to trickle back into the camp. A large force was skirting its way around the mountains in the direction of Dertosa with the evident intent of attacking from a south westerly direction, Also, and of more immediate importance to this motley crew of farmers, Jews and semi professional soldiers, was what was happening throughout the scattered villages to their homes that they were ostensibly fighting to protect. Rumour had it that scavenging parties were running riot, not only stealing their hard earned harvested food, but also adding rape to their pillaging. When Marcus heard, he was incensed . Realising this could have a galvanising or dissolving effect on his troop, he shouted loudly so that everyone knew what he was doing, ordering ALL the horses, their so called cavalry, to leave the camp immediately, to split into groups to chase, apprehend or kill any of these looters. Explaining that this would be a quicker and more effective way of countering these groups than the men returning home, he pleaded with his men to stay firm at least for the time being, pointing out that *if* they did break now, instead of just a few riders, there would be a victorious army going through their villages, with all the consequences that would bring.

Having assured the loyalty of his force, he moved to the place of the suggested meeting. High level hostages had been exchanged to ensure that there was no trickery on either side.

The meeting point had been chosen well by the king, wanting to make Marcus feel secure, not threatened, or surrounded by hostile forces, the tent had been pitched close to both camps relatively high up on the mountainside. It was the view that he wanted Marcus to see, not of the faint stripe of blue in the distance which could be imagined to be the sea but the vast expanse of men and horses that encompassed the royal force. Duly, Marcus was impressed.

The sight of the men and the sun shining off gleaming armour extended as far as the eye could see, and horses, there were fields full of them, dented his confidence, putting into perspective the measly little battle that they had just won.

The *welcoming* guard, unarmed and unsmiling, were men he had known from the Vasconis venture. If they were pleased about this reunion, they didn't let it be known, guiding him silently to the venue was their task. Upon entering the tent, he was met by a group of faces, some familiar, some not. There was a table set up with two men seated, a baron and a bishop, he would have guessed by their garb. Behind to the right lurking in the shadows, much to his surprise was that arrogant Jew, Hillel, was that his name? Marcus only really remembered him as the *little prick*. Sat, less than majestically more uncomfortably, was King Wamba on a raised platform, the throne? It was all he could do not to bow or salute as he had been taught to do so many times in the past when looking upon his former monarch. It would have been most inappropriate to show any subservience to the *enemy* Marcus had been telling himself on the journey here, so, he limited himself to a controlled nod of the head which wasn't reciprocated in any way.

"I am Baron Teodofred and this is Bishop Iulianus of Hispalis." The voice hovered between neutral and disdain as the hand of the speaker indicated the one seat in front of them. This was another thing that Marcus had pre-thought. How would he introduce himself if it were necessary; son of a duke, didn't really cut the mustard. Choosing instead not to say anything, he took the proffered seat.

"We demand your unconditional surrender, complete access to Tarraco, supplies for our forces and this man" pointing in the direction of Hillel, "access to the Jews."

Marcus made an effort to look as if he were considering this proposal. "Interesting. With an opening phrase like that anyone would have thought that you had won, or least weren't totally mauled by my forces in the battle. Very interesting indeed. As we don't seem to have too much to actually talk about, I will take my leave and we will see each other later on the battle field. Goodbye, gentlemen."

With that and immensely proud that his voice hadn't quivered, he pushed his chair back and headed for the exit, leaving all present with a dilemma, or feeling total anger. The dilemma was the baron and the bishop's, they couldn't call him back to explain that this was just the opening gambit. In effect that they didn't mean what they were saying and were prepared to negotiate, and anger felt by the king at this remarkably stupid way of starting a negotiation. Neither party felt they could stop the exiting young man so they didn't.

Marcus left the tent and rode with less than cheerful guard back to his camp.

Wamba broke the silence that remained in the aftermath of the departure, "That went very well didn't it, Teodofred? Quite brilliantly handled. I am so pleased that you two persuaded me to stay out of the negotiation as you forcefully mentioned that it would have been demeaning for a king to talk to a lowly son of a baron. I would be feeling a proper idiot now, if that had happened to me."

"It matters not. He now knows that we mean business."

"What it actually means, my dear baron, is that YOU must win this next battle, otherwise our next negotiating point will have to be much lower, as we agree that we can NOT afford to lose too many men here, nor waste too much time doing it."

"You did what?"

"Walked out without saying too much."

Pere was actually impressed; his little prodigy was becoming a man. A better answer could not have been given. This, he knew, meant that another attack was imminent, and the tactics would be different this time. This was something that they were prepared for, even though this time they would have to defend with some of their less experienced men as he had been spiriting away some of the more experienced fighters north to help Ranosindus in the real battles up there, once that their delaying measures were finally put to a stop. He felt sure that the new men, especially the young Jews, who were itching to get into the action, would give a good account of themselves, especially if it was against that shambles of a force they had fought the first time.

They didn't have long to find out.

Against all military logic, the attack started mid-evening without any shenanigans previous to the engagement. They must be in a hurry thought Pere. It couldn't be described as a surprise attack as everyone was waiting for it; sooner or later it had to happen, it was a bit sooner than expected. As well as the inevitable confrontation, Pere wasn't in the least surprised by the tactics employed. Gone was the straight-ish wall to wall approach, in its stead were a couple of wedges, there was no room for more than two. For this to be an effective way of smashing through a solid deep shield wall, the wedges had to hit the line at the same time sowing doubt, confusion and turmoil in the defensive line. Whoever was in control of this charge fluffed his lines, almost literally. The gap between the first and second one hitting was determinant in the way the battle would go. Pere's well drilled front lines parted akin to a biblical Red Sea, as the first ill-conceived and poorly-constructed wedge hit, allowing enough of the point of the attackers to be absorbed and set upon by the waiting forces behind, When Pere shouted the expected order, the wall reunited like a well oiled door hinge. The enemy caught behind the lines were cut off from their comrades and set upon with great gusto by the waiting Jewish youths; a massacre ensued. It was a superbly enacted manoeuvre, which was repeated with equal expertise at the other end of the shield wall when the second wave hit.

The watching King wanted to clap, if the dire consequences that would follow weren't a reality, he would have.

"So, it looks like negotiations will have to start again from a considerably less advantageous point. This time I will lead them. Baron, do us all a favour and call off this attack by your inept troop, bring them back to camp, arrest their commander, put them into a strict training regime led by members of MY exercitus."

The distraught baron had to comply; he knew he had lost face, credibility and a heap of men. Coming back from this would be difficult. He would personally make sure that his military commander, Veremundo, would suffer the consequences.

The king's envoy was sent packing after delivering his order of further negotiations that evening, with the instruction to return the following day, not too early with another, more politely framed invitation.

*

It was an improvised raised platform looking none too sturdy under the weight of the eleven men it supported, nevertheless it was the centre of large open area and the attention of the ever-growing crowd looking on. This was the culmination and fruit of the negotiations. It wasn't so much a trial, as all had been declared, not found, guilty, more like a public viewing of the working of the state which was now back in control. The eleven were in three distinct groupings; at one end four royalist troops, in the middle two minor Tarraco noblemen with Marcus at their side and, finally, a distance from the others, three Jews.

In a seated line in front of them were the dignitaries; in the centre, King Wamba, flanked on one side by Baron Teodofred and the other Bishops Hispalis and Cyprianus. In between the two sets were some soldiers, a huge man testing the sharpness of his two implements; a dagger and long sword, and a fire which clearly had been burning for some time as there were no flames, just glowing red coals. Also, off to the right stood Hillel. The second round of negotiations had the same personnel, excepting the baron's military commander, Veremundo, who had been lashed, in front of his men, in a long bloody, pain filled session, as the price of the humiliation suffered by Teodofred. This time there was a different organisational set up. The same table only had two seats; one either side for the two protagonists; Wamba and Marcus, the others were banished to hug the sides of the tent as far away as possible from the talks.

"I must congratulate you on your obvious rapid learning in the military arts. In the Vasconia, you were at best, let's say, green, at worst, useless. However, I see you are capable of performing great deeds on the field of battle. Do I detect the hand of our dear and much missed General Paulus?" Wamba was most affable both in tone and spirit. He had liked this young man and saw no reason to change that opinion even though he had taken up arms against him.

Marcus wore a face of bravado trying its best to hide his awe and nerves at this face to face encounter with the king, well, ex-king. He wanted to point out the newly elevated status of Paulus, then thought the better of it, instead choosing to incline his head in an acknowledgement of the compliment.

"Unlike the last *chat* that was held here," his voice now showed irritation and disdain, "I am not going to demand your immediate unconditional surrender. Your brave defence deserves a more measured approach. However, you do realise that a surrender is what you will have to give? Otherwise, all your troop and the city of Tarraco will be destroyed, something neither of us want."

No sound came from Marcus though it was clear the way his eyes moved down, he was accepting this opening proposal.

"Good. So, the question is what should we agree on to facilitate this course of action. A price has to be paid."

At that moment there was a noise of rustling as the tent flap opened to allow entrance to the sweating corpulent figure of Cyprianus who was all but shouting his apologies for arriving late. His actual words were lost with Marcus's exclamation "You! You traitor, snake in the grass, turn coat."

The king's measured response brought the atmosphere back to *normality*, "Actually, Marcus, that's your name, isn't it? It's *you* that is the traitor. Bishop Cyprianus has been a loyal subject."

"Since when? Since your army arrived?"

"Extremely usefully, he has been providing information to Bishop Quiricus for the last few weeks."

Marcus looking directly at the still and puddling wet mess, "So, you saw the lay of the land was shifting, did you?" Turning back to Wamba, "It may interest you that this man was one of the main movers and shakers from the beginning, egging my father into action as he was Metropolitan Bishop only in an acting capacity because Toletum refused to confirm this position thus insulting the whole of Tarraco."

Wamba looked at the dishevelled blob, who was about to proclaim his innocence, instructing him to take his place at the back of the tent, remain totally silent all delivered with the undercurrent of this new information being that it would be dealt with later, in private.

"Let's get back to the main question, shall we?"

Wamba announced that he did not want his troops to enter Tarraco in any form, declaring that Tarraco should be respected as an import city of his realm. He moved on to say that he would do his best to address some of the grievances voiced by the population as a whole. His mission was to bring the people, humble and great, back into this great Goth kingdom rather than punish everyone for the error of the decisions made by a few.

"If that be true in any way shape or form, why do you allow scavengers to terrorise the smaller villages and isolated homesteads by looting and rape?"

For the first time Wamba began to lose his cool. His face actually coloured as he turned." General Badwila, is this true?"

"I believe not, Sire."

"Perhaps you ought to stop believing, and actually find out!" The general all but ran out of the meeting in his search for the truth.

Wamba's losing-colour-face was back facing Marcus, "The culprits will be found and publicly punished. I gave VERY clear instructions that this sort of action was not to happen. The scavengers do exist, but they were all furnished with a large bag of money to pay for any product they took ,and under no circumstances, bar total resistance, harm any member of the local populace. We are NOT an invading army, we are the army of everyone, and should behave that way. In fact, as there is a dearth of small currency, the soldiers were instructed to pay OVER the accepted price. This system we used most effectively in Ilerda and found that people actually brought the produce to us without us having to send out any requisitioning parties."

Marcus could see the man he'd admired so much; a man of integrity and honesty, and he believed him totally.

*

The instructions were for ALL the adult Jewish population that weren't involved in the fighting to attend the synagogue.

"Papa, it says everyone."

"Just for once in your life I want you to follow my instructions. No, Rebecca! As you are into the military these days, obey my order. Nobody knows what this is about, but it doesn't take a genius, military, or otherwise, to see what is about to happen. The forces your friend Marcus is commanding will either be defeated, or surrender without the help of *your* king. Hopefully, the latter, as it will spare the lives of our youth who went to war so willingly. There will be a price to pay and blame will be attributed. You are far too closely aligned to the failed policy; you will be an obvious and easy target for any and all who want to vent their anger and frustration. I have asked you to leave the city for your benefit, you haven't. I am telling you not to go to this meeting for yourself, AND your wider family. If you won't do things for yourself, please think how this will affect Isaac."

"Uncle Isaac?"

"He replaced you as representative to the gentiles; he will have consequences to face. With you there, those consequences will be more strident and probably more severe."

Rebecca looked how she felt - crushed. Her father was right, she knew it. She was willing to put her own life, and anything she had left of her reputation, on the line by not hiding, showing her face and her defiance, but she couldn't risk Uncle Isaac. She would have to skulk at home while others decided the fate of Tarraco's Jews.

"Jeremiah? I thought he'd left weeks ago." The brothers, flanked by David in the aisle, were in the middle of the congregation, on the male side, trying hard to blend and not do anything to draw attention to themselves.

"Brethren, we are gathered here today to make some difficult decisions. Thankfully, we have a clear light to follow in these times of deep darkness."

"Since when did he get his gravitas and self-importance?" was Isaac's second whispered surprise question. Jacob felt a metaphorical cold shiver run down his spine and then back up again. The clouds of doubt were clearing and what was about to happen boded non too well for him and his.

The introduction finished and a gasp of surprise, in some places horror, filled the air as Hillel took the stage. This wasn't the jubilation of the returned prophet; his demeanour was more the harbinger of doom.

"Fellow Jews of Tarraco, you have been led astray, followed lying, incompetent voices from both inside and outside your community. You refused to listen to those who tried to rectify the situation while there was still time to do so, and now we *all* will have to pay the price!"

In his deepest possible and slowest timbre, he outlined the reality of the battlefield, emphasising the valiant if pointless role the young Jewish men had played. The result of which was a negotiated surrender at which he had been present in his role as representative of their interests.

"Despite calls from the a bishop from Hispalis for the death of every second Jew, and rejecting their usual modus operandi in these situations - forced conversions, I managed to persuade them to allow the community to leave the city into exile."

The noise and commotion this announcement made, was couched not in shouting voices but in loud hushed tones of despair to those seated closest, and extremely worried glances across the gender separated sections anxiously trying to find the eyes of the spouse.

Being a tried and tested speaker and manipulator of crowds, Hillel allowed this to run its course before demanding attention again.

"I hear the word *where* being used a great deal and this IS the salient point. The Goths want us no longer in their kingdom, not here, nor in any other part where the repression against our fellow Jews is significantly worse. After a great deal of effort and coaxing, I have persuaded them to an alternative."

The silence was so profound that a feather would have been heard falling. "We will be given a maximum of two months to put our affairs in order. After that, by the end of the ninth month, of their calendar, we will be expected to have boarded ships taking us away from this land forever."

Not allowing the cries of desperation and dissent to rise, he continued more forcefully and considerably louder. "Where we go is up to us. Well, not exactly, as we will not be welcome in Frankia or other Christian countries around the Mare Nostrum. My intention, and suggestion to you all, is to return to the Holy Land which is no longer occupied by Christians. A new, more tolerant religion holds sway there, and would not be adverse to our returning."

This time the uproar could not be quickly quelled.

"This is what he has wanted from the beginning, this, or some spectacular mass suicide heroic gesture like Masada." Isaac's voice was one of pure resignation. "And sadly, it looks as if we have facilitated it."

Hillel viewed the seated disarray with smug satisfaction, waiting for his moment to continue.

Not having actually heard the word, he knew he had to start with it.

"Price, I hear many of you say. Yes, it will be costly both in terms of the journey and all the wealth, like houses, we will have to leave behind. However, there is another cost that the gentiles demand. They seek public punishment for those of you who have led the community so badly. To this end, there are four soldiers, two from the local Tarraco force and two from Wamba's, a joint force to show how the gentiles unite in the face of the Jews, waiting outside this building to take into custody three people; Zachary, Isaac and probably the worst instigator of our demise as a community in this city, Rebecca, daughter of Jacob."

Gasps of horror mixed with some applause greeted this announcement. Isaac slumped, Trudi's voice could be heard from the women's section "I told him, I did," she repeated loudly.

Jacob gingerly made his way to his feet. "My daughter is not here. I demand to be taken in her stead."

"I agree you are culpable as her father, however, we only want your daughter."

Unseen by most, a figure near the back of the synagogue left quickly and quietly.

*

Rebecca heard the door which was, unusually, closed, a precaution insisted upon by her father before he left, bang loudly open and the heavy panting. Flee, fight or hide, for the second time in such a short period of time were the options running through her brain after this violent entrance, until she heard a familiar voice shout "Rebecca!"

The exertion of just saying this word onto top of his breathless state was almost too much.

"David!" Rebecca all but caught him before he fell. "Breathe, slow down, breathe again, no don't try to speak yet."

Ignoring this advice, David managed to splutter "They are coming to get you."

Helping the boy to a semi upright bent over pose, she stated defiantly, "Well, they will find me here."

Recovering quickly although still doubled over and gasping for breath he managed, "You must. Your father sent me. They have already arrested my father."

"If it's another cherem, we will face it like the last one."

Straightened completely now, and breath returning to normality, "No, it's the Christians. They want those responsible for leading the rebellion."

"Christians?"

"King Wamba's forces, helped by that rat, Hillel."

This changed her confidence but not her resolution.

"Rebecca, please. Your father was most insistent, you must run or hide."

"I will not. If they want me then they know where to find me."

"Well said, girl!" Another totally unexpected shape had joined them in the open doorway.

"But if you want my opinion, bloody stupid. You ain't gonna gain nufing by that, cept probably losing your 'ead. Shame, it being a pretty one."

The young Jews looked at the intruder, one with puzzlement and the other with surprise.

"Antonia, what are you doing here?"

"Same as this young chap, methinks, trying to save your life. I got a message a short while ago from my nearest and dearest and his commander, the duke's son, telling me to hightail it over 'ere as quick as I could to get you away as you are wanted big time."

"Pere? Marcus?"

"Yeah, like I said, worried big time, they be. So you're coming with me whether you like it or not. You, young lad, scarper, and you ain't 'eard nuffing, all right?"

With a concerned look and a parting "Please don't get caught," David left his favourite cousin knowing that the less he knew, the less he could say to anyone who may want to ask. Rebecca touched his trailing hand, "Thanks, David."

On his way back up to the Call, David saw Hillel, Jeremiah, and two soldiers dressed in the Duke's livery heading down town in a quick march. Upon his arrival, he saw his father, uncle, and Zachary being led away by two soldiers in unfamiliar dress. He tried and failed to get close as the crowd was packed tightly around the direction they were not heading. There were shouts of support, and others of condemnation. Trying to push his way through, he'd almost got to the front when a heavy yanking action pulled him back.

"Don't you go anywhere near! Your father has made his bed and he'll have to lie in it. We, on the other hand, will have to pay a bigger price."

A pure look of hatred met Trudi's words, and slapping her arm away he continued forward managing to catch his uncle's eye before he disappeared around the bend in the street. Uncle Jacob's look was of thanks and relief, as he understood what his nephew was silently communicating.

*

The frustration and annoyance felt was there to be seen by anyone who cared to look. Nobody did, as nobody cared how Hillel was feeling, nor was there much of an audience. The lap dog, Jeremiah, was wasting time in a meticulous fruitless house search, *just in case* as he had justified it. That the bird had flown the nest was easy for the onetime Tarraco rabbi to see. Nobody leaves their front door wide open, unlocked or slightly ajar, unless maybe when the master is at home and expecting welcome guests, but completely unashamedly not doing its prohibitive function, no door would be left like this. Standing in the, had-seen-better-days, opulent, entrance hall, he was unconsciously stroking his chin wondering where she could be. The brother's house was next on their to-be-searched list, even though he doubted, given the aunt's loudly voiced opinions, whether that would bear any fruit. Of all the people he most wanted revenge on in Tarraco, Rebecca was the one he would most like to see being publicly shamed and hurt by her Christian friends, especially in front of an on-looking Jewish crowd.

"Hey, Jewman! You looking for that cheeky little Jewish slut, Rebecca?"

Turning and preparing a stream of verbal abuse, Hillel found himself confronted by a familiar, though he couldn't quite place it, face. Swallowing his pride, he answered quite neutrally, "I am."

"Well, you aren't going to find her here."

The baron's housekeeper, that's who she was, the memory of her venomous brittle voice that matched the revoltingly spiteful face came flooding unpleasantly back.

"And if I were to tell you, what would be in it for me? Everyone knows you Jews have all the money."

"I hate to disappoint you, but this Jew is a rabbi, a Holy man who doesn't have two beans to rub together. Though I will mention your public spiritedness to the king because I am on his errand."

Amalaswinth weighed up her options; it was true that this man, even when he came to the palace, was poorly dressed so the holy poverty line could be true. Being on his quest at the behest of the king was also not a lie, as he'd been seen coming through the main gates with an armed escort of both baron and king's men, and having your name mentioned favourably can never be a bad thing. Furthermore, she would be playing a pivotal role in the downfall of that saucy mouthy bitch with ideas well above her station, and a Jew to boot.

"She's hiding in Antonia's house."

"Antonia's house?"

"I'll take you there."

Despite it being very close by and the journey taking no time whatsoever, they had gathered quite a little following of expectant viewers. Rarely had this sight ever been seen on the streets of Tarraco, a Jew in the pursuit of another Jew with two of the baron's soldiers under his command, standing outside a Christian house demanding the right of entry.

"We are on the king's business and demand that you send out the fugitive that you are harbouring!"

This unequivocal announcement was met by mutterings among the on-lookers and silence from the not overly elegant house.

The lack of interior noise was because it had interrupted an animated conversation within where the two women had been disagreeing about Rebecca's immediate future. The host encouraging a swift city exit to the relative safety of Arantxa's hideout, and the guest claiming that laying low for a couple of days, she could reappear and be of help to her family. With a "We're a bit buggered now, ain't we?" Antonia headed out to confront the proclaimer.

"Why are you shouting outside a good Christian 'ouse, Jew?"

This wearily delivered statement was greeted by an undercurrent of agreement from the swelling crowd.

"We believe," Hillel looked to his side expecting to see the baron's servant who was no longer there, instead she was side-footing her way through the bulk of the people. This infuriated Hillel even more, and he was not going to allow this tell-tale to get away with her actions scot free, "This woman," pointing directly at Amalaswinth, "has informed me, good wife, that you are harbouring a person wanted by the authorities."

This had a moving affect, the crowd shifted farther from Amalaswinth and Antonia moved away from her doorway, showing clearly the open door.

"What? You're looking for the harbour? Don't really understand what you're on about, nobody in my 'ouse, not even the kids."

"Then you won't mind if we search the premises."

"Oh, but I would! I ain't 'aving no baby eating Jew in my 'ouse." The getting larger and louder gathering voiced their agreement and understanding.

Feeling that a compromise was needed before he lost control of the situation, Hillel tried "I will not enter your property, but these soldiers will."

Seeing the soldiers in the baron's regalia shift uncomfortably, Antonia pressed home her advantage, "I don't know who they are, but they sure as 'ell know whose 'ouse this is and I doubt that they will take the orders of a Jew to search it."

This fact was born out immediately as the men refused Hillel's order to enter the open door but twenty paces in front of them.

Call it a rush to the head, or just a reaction to his sheer frustration, or whatever else it was, the only real word for his next action was *mistake*. The infuriated and totally frustrated rabbi, set off at speed, his path being blocked by Antonia. The immediacy of his pursuit necessitated bold actions. She was pushed forcefully out of his way, and the reaction to this violent act was immediate. The passive crowd lost its adjective, attacking the foreigner for manhandling one of their own. The realisation of his massive error of judgement came by lifting his line of vision once the woman was sent sprawling to the ground, they were coming menacingly for him . Not trusting that the soldiers would lift a finger to protect him, Hillel ran through a gauntlet of swaying arms.

Victory assured, Antonia, back on her feet, made to go back inside when she did an abrupt about turn and headed in the opposite direction. The hawked phlegm was delivered with power and accuracy into the face of the completely isolated figure without any following words from either party.

*

Rebecca had watched the proceedings, not exactly cowering in the shadows, but certainly well out of sight.

"Thank you, Antonia."

"Been wanting to spit on that crow for years and so 'as everyone else. She'll 'ave lost a lot of 'er power now."

"No, I mean for hiding and defending me."

"I did nothing of the sort, just ain't 'aving any bloody Jew in this good Christian 'ouse. They eat babies, you know?"

This produced a wane smile. Causing her reflect on just how much they had lost in such a short period of time, it had been a while since they laughed and smiled together. Her maudlin memories were interrupted by a large framed man coming through the door.

"You two been having fun? Just seen that snotty Jew sprinting uptown looking a proper mess, torn clothes and the lot."

It was then that Antonia did a most uncharacteristic thing which caused Pere to wonder what exactly was going on. She came across the room and hugged him. "I'm glad you are back, you useless lump."

Given the lack of furniture, everyone being able to be seated inside wasn't too easy, managing the best they could, hey settled to hear Pere's report back on what was happening at the front and the surrender negotiations. Finishing the detail, he finally explained why he was there. "Marcus says that I've got to get you out. Most of our good troops have already been sent north. He says, if we're quick we could catch them up by taking a couple of horses from his stables."

"I'm not going, and certainly not on one of those things."

"That's what I said as well."

Antonia joined in, "You got to go somewhere, we can't keep protecting you here. Next time, they'll be back with the king's soldiers."

"I know. I'll go to Arantxa."

"Marcus says you aren't to go there. There are scavenging parties all over and two women would be easier to find than one. Also, cos of who your boyfriend is, you are valuable property the enemy could take advantage of. You've, no, we've, got to go north. I just don't know how."

"You great lumps of men really are useless at thinking, aren't you"

Hugging time was over, normal service was being resumed, not fast enough Pere thought about denying the charge.

"What's your family job, lump?"

Dawning realisation was about as fast as the rising sun. Eventually, though, light spread out across his face. "The boat, yes! We can take the boat and head up the coast to join Paulus there. Why didn't I think about that? It's so obvious. I'm sure Marcus would provide my brother with some monetary compensation. It'll be easy."

"Because you are a man."

"Sorry, but I am still not going. I can't leave my father."

"Apparently, Marcus insisted that your father wouldn't be arrested and much to that arrogant Jew's disgust, the King agreed. So, he should be safe."

"My uncle?"

Pere shifted uncomfortably, "That's a different kettle of fish as the king said that apart from the one exception of your father, the rest of the Jewish problem would be solved by the Jews themselves. Otherwise, the Bishop of Hispalis, a renowned Jew-hater, would be allowed free reign. You were top of the list, and when Marcus tried to get you removed but the Jew wouldn't budge, you were his number one priority, and responsible, as he told it to the king, for the Jews supporting or even instigating the rebellion. That's why you *have* to leave."

"But.."

"No buts. If you stay you will be endangering yourself, your father, Paulus as well as my family."

*

The scavengers knew why they were there. The Jews were clear about their status on the "stage", however, the two noblemen were at a loss to their presence. They had done nothing more, or less, than any of the other dozens of landholders; comply with a direct order from their Lord of the area in a call to arms. They had not had any leading role in the fighting, nor the rebellion, they just answered the call.

Marcus knew why they were there and had insisted on being there with them. The reason was a turn in the negotiations he couldn't rectify. While discussing the terms of surrender, Wamba stated that there had to be a public price for the attempted rebellion and that should be borne by the duke, who though not present, had to be condemned in front of the population of Tarraco, all of which could be delayed. It was then that Cyprianus tentatively moved forward to say that he had received instructions about this matter from Quiricus and Julian, his proposal was followed and supported by the Bishop of Hispalis, Iulianus, claiming he had the exact same instructions. The bishops of Toletum, through their bishops on the ground, stated that the protagonists of the rebellion had to be executed and their lands be forfeited to the Church.

Wamba's insides churned with anger at this display of power and arrogance, he was king and he would decide. The problem was that the forces with him at the moment had been recruited and sent in the name of the bishops and would certainly enjoy the chance of trying to overrule him with their collective power. Fortunately, the only baron of note left with him at the moment was Teodofred whose stock had diminished considerably due to the fighting and was in no position to mount any challenge. Still, he had to be seen to be a little harsher than he had intended, to prevent any blow back on this point later.

"And your proposal is, bishop?"

A little flustered, Cyprianus looking constantly at the parchment in his hands for physical and moral support and authority, stated that the all the baron's and twelve other minor noblemen's land should become Church property. This caused Marcus to stir, standing then moving closer to the getting more nervous Bishop, "If this is the case, then there seems no sense in surrendering. We will fight and lose the same but we will take a lot of you with us!"

"Please sit, Marcus. This will not happen. I believe the bishop mis-read. In fact. it says that the Baron Ranosindus will donate no more than a quarter of his land to the charitable institution, and there shall be at most two noblemen among the main instigators of the rebellion, who should forfeit their lands to the Church."

Cyprianus looked at the paper again, and was about to speak when he thought better of it.

"They shall be punished physically as well." Bishop Iulianus knew when he was defeated, but wanted to make a statement expressing his disapproval.

"Of course. I believe the Metropolitan Bishop of Tarraco even has the names of the two."

Cyprianus looked as if he were re-reading what was in his hands knowing full well that there were no names mentioned, but giving him enough time to think of two people. He gave the names as if they were on the document.

Marcus again shouted his disagreement. He knew the two men fairly well and he knew one had time and again showed his lack of respect for the person holding the highest clerical position in Tarraco, and the other had a sizeable property next to land already owned by the Church.

"I believe that these names have been insisted on by the power of the Church, so I cannot interfere with that." The king was telling Marcus that this was the best he could do under the circumstances and it was an offer he ought to accept.

"Then, I insist on standing with them and receiving the same physical punishment. I cannot leave them alone!"

*

Ten bare chested men and one completely naked one, with their hands tied behind their backs, offered a spectacularly unusual sight to the public, who surrounded them in banked masses. The Camp gave generous space for those looking on, though it wasn't difficult to find a place to view as it wasn't overly full. Not knowing what to expect, nor having seen the like of it in at least a generation, the locals were a divided bunch, baying for blood for those occupying the extremes of the stage, and hoping for clemency for the middle group. One in ten of the royalist forces had been chosen by lots and commanded to attend, separated from the others, occupying a space at the back left. Their sympathies lay with just one grouping; the most numerous, their fellow soldiers. There weren't many Jews in attendance. Hillel, in an effort to curry lost favour in the Tarraco community, had recommended that everyone stay away from this Christian farce that they had no control over. A minor grouping, including Isaac's family, stood huddled together apart from both of the Christian blocks.

Behind the dignitaries was another distinct ordered cluster of well dressed men; the local nobles with their eyes firmly set on the two missing from their number who were being displayed. The message conveyed was not so much of sympathy or empathy, it was more; *there but for the Grace of God go I.*

As General Badwila read the charges against the soldiers the huge man moved onto the stage. "For stealing from fellow citizens of the realm, you will lose a hand. Due to the mercy of King Wamba, he has decreed that it should be the left, not the right."

The first shaking man was lead to the previously placed tree trunk in front of them. He was whimpering, barely audibly expressing his innocence as his left arm was untied and placed on the block. With almost no backlift and little effort the arm became handless and quickly cauterized by a second man holding a flat red hot iron. The now stumped man collapsed unconscious after an ear splitting yell of pain.

This procedure, including more or less noise, was repeated to the next two men. The silence in the soldiers' section was profound, and didn't contrast too much with the lack of noise from the locals, who seemed too shocked to express their pleasure. This changed somewhat with considerable baying when the naked man was pushed forward with his left hand unshackled.

"Your crime, rape of a number of local women," intoned the general, "is even worse and warrants no clemency." Before the last word was out of the general's mouth the dagger had been used. Starting low and in an upwards direction its ultra sharp edge removed, without much difficulty, the man's testicles and penis. The man looked down in horror instinctively moving his free hand to cover what once had been there and now was a veritable fountain of blood as he collapsed into a heap, left to bleed to death.

One section of the crowd cheered loudly at this display of knife skill and slow death while the huge dagger wielder moved off the stage momentarily to clean and re-sharpen his instruments.

The two tethered noblemen were now visibly quaking and shaking as the general read out their crimes, "Rebellion against the lawful king is a treasonable offence and is punishable by death." One of the noblemen's bowls emptied, much to the merriment of the sober soldiers. "Again though, King Wamba has felt that leniency should be applied. All your lands will be forfeited to the Church." He paused as the big man edged near the first noblemen, slightly to the left to avoid treading in the liquid and excrement. He was holding his genital removing dagger, which he used with a lightening quick flick of the wrist, removing one eyeball, then moving to the other side slicing the other eye while it remained in its socket. This manoeuvre was repeated on the second nobleman, and the screaming men were led off stage by the onetime glowing red hot iron holder.

Marcus was next; he was well past beginning to wish he hadn't opened his mouth with such foolish bravado saying he would stand with the other two. What a stupid person he was. Rebecca had always maintained that this fact was true and he would now have to agree with her. It's all well and good playing the role of concerned lord of the manor when it comes to minor matters, but losing an eye, a hand, or God forbid a part he'd only just found pleasure with, was, well, foolishly stupid.

General Badwila mounted the stage, taking care not to stand in too many blood pools and stepping over the still emptying dying figure of the rapist.

"This man is the son of one of the rebellion's leaders. He followed his father's lead, as every true son should. However, he has also served King Wamba in the campaign against the Vascones and showed great courage wanting to stand next to his noblemen. If it weren't for him, you" the General pointed at the assembled finely clad gentlemen, "would all have suffered the same fate as your two colleagues."

Baron Teodofred now stood taking over the speaking mantle, "If Marcus, son of Ranosindus, is prepared to swear allegiance to King Wamba, here, publicly, he will be made the rightful Duke of Tarraco. If not, his life is forfeit."

This came as a bolt out of the blue to all those present, not least Marcus. What should he do? Not wanting to die nor wanting to betray his father. He was in a real quandary, while his thought silence reigned. "What do you say?" The impatient voice of Teodofred demanded.

"You are young, I'm sure your father would understand, I would. Choose life." It was Jacob who uttered these thoughts not very loudly, enough to be heard only on stage. Most surprised Marcus had even forgotten he was there. They looked each other in the eye, Marcus saw clearly where Rebecca got her attitudes and steel from, silently he mouthed a thank you. "I will swear to King Wamba."

"And to cement this fidelity, my daughter will be given in marriage to you as soon as conditions allow."

Another shock, not quite as mortal or imminent, but shocking, nevertheless.

"But I am already promised to another."

"The daughter of Count Hilderic, we know." Marcus quite expected her to be described as a lovely girl. "However, that is annulled, as the count will no longer be a count of anything much longer."

The second surprisingly trivial thought given the circumstance he found himself contemplating, shot through his head; how am I going explain this to Arantxa?

Leaving the future duke mulling over what he'd just done and all these women that kept on getting thrust at him, the general moved to the end of the platform.

"Jews are an abomination at any time, and when they rise against a good Christian hand there can be little mercy shown. However, at the instigation of their rabbi," Hillel was moving from the shadows to be visible, "we have, magnanimously allowed the Jewish population to move out of Tarraco to a place of their choosing, away from this Christian Kingdom. They will have the period of one week to complete this move. Any Jew remaining after this period will be fair game to be killed, in a manner of choice of the perpetrator, without any fear of retribution from the law. All the property of these leaving Jews will be requisitioned for the use of the Holy Church." He left a pause to allow this to sink in, then turning to the three men to his left. "These men, however, have been identified by their rabbi as the main instigators in the rebellion against the lawful forces and as such shall receive a punishment fitting their crime."

The big man was back, ready to perform once the talking stopped. Tossing the dagger in one hand, showing remarkable skill, he walked up to and then past Zachary, upon reaching Isaac he turned to retrace his steps This time, though, he plunged his knife halfway into the man's gut, dragging it along with the considerable strength needed for such a feat. It was yet another surprise in this man's endless sack of tricks. Initially, nobody, besides the recipient, noticed and it was only when the man's guts began to spill out that it became clear what he had done. Along with the intestines, Zachary let out a long low moan as he collapsed to the floor. The public's gasp was their acknowledgement of this killer's skill. It was plain there would be no immediate death for this Jew; the agony was designed to be acute and long-lasting as well as fatal.

Isaac was a complete jelly, he couldn't stay still. The executor approached only to hear Hillel's shouted words, "Stop! This is NOT what we agreed. We said punishment, not death."

The executor seemed to acknowledge and accept what was being yelled at him moving his bloodied dagger towards Isaac's left eye, much as he had done with the noblemen, only at the last moment to thrust in with great force through the eye, well into the head, where it stayed. This time death was immediate, the body falling with the knife still protruding from the face, causing the killer to tut with annoyance as he had to lean down, push the body onto its side in order to retrieve his prized possession before cleaning it on the cloth covering the dead body's lower half.

Hillel was apoplectic, screaming at the king and other dignitaries that this was a betrayal of trust, only to find himself being held firmly by two guards who then proceeded to ensure that his mouth was forced wide open. The relatively undirtied knife was quickly slid across the end, removing quite a chunk, but not all.

"Nobody, least of all a Jew, speaks to the king like that."

Jacob was the last man standing along with Marcus, he was in total shock. Zachary was still dying, his brother dead, he no longer cared what would happen to him. However, what was happening came as a surprise, the important people were beginning to leave their seats knowing that the *show* was over.

"I demand death. I have no reason to live. Don't spare me. You killed my brother when it was I who was more guilty." Jacob was kneeling next to the lifeless form of what used to be Isaac.

"It was agreed that you should not be executed."

"I demand death!"

"Jacob, please leave, Rebecca will need you." Marcus, who was no longer on the stage was still close enough to be able to talk without shouting.

"I cannot live with the shame and guilt of my brother's death. I can live no longer. Life will no longer have a meaning."

"But, Jacob, you are going to be a grandfather.."

The swish of the long sword was only heard by those close by, but everyone saw the head loll to one side, held on by only a thread of neck tissue with the perfectly formed exclamation "*what?*" on the open mouth.

*

Having left Gerunda, after giving the same instructions, "Put up a token delaying defence, don't lose too many men and send the main force north", he'd sent to Tarraco, to Hunulf, for his return to Barcino, the new King Paulus set up residence in Clausurae. It hadn't been a long or arduous journey, yet upon entering the keep, they all looked weary and tired.

"Is that word from Nemausus?"

"Chlodoswintha sends her regards" Count Hilderic was reading, "says the Frank leadership is beginning to arrive in Nemausus in dribs and drabs. She sounds none too happy about playing host to these uncouth men."

"She made good time getting back there so quickly. Once we have consolidated here, I think it would be wise for you to go home and entertain the Franks."

"I do agree. She also says, Bishop Gunhild, who is in Frankia, reports a large mobilisation of troops their side of the border, so perhaps they are actually going to put into action what was agreed. You can never trust anything they say or do. A big part of this lack of reliability is not that they don't keep to their word, it's that nobody is quite sure who really is in charge. They may promise all in good faith until push comes to shove, then the promiser, realises he can't fulfil his word and becomes most remorseful in an opaque sort of way, though never admitting that his power has been trumped by someone else. They really are the most frustrating ally and enemy."

Paulus could see the concern in the count's countenance and felt the same way; it was a dangerous game they were playing, holding the door wide open for the traditional enemy to walk through.

"We can't win without them. It'll be a question of controlling them."

"Well, that shouldn't be a problem then, should it?" Both men smiled. "I will leave tomorrow and check that General Wittimir in Narbo has prepared the defences."

Another *king* might have been offended by this controlling statement not asking what he should do, rather telling his *commander* what he was doing without consultation. Paulus realised what was happening; a reassertion of power, and didn't overly object as he knew himself to be a figurehead rather than the real king. If truth be known, he'd be much happier once he was allowed to stop playing this unwanted role.

Ranosindus, who had gone out to check the increasingly large sprawling camp of soldiers on the slopes heading up to the fort, entered with a broad smile, "Quite a number of my men have already arrived and they say that there are plenty more on the way. Apparently, they were sent away after the first battle in which they gave Wamba's troops a right royal bloody nose, so much so that Wamba sued for negotiations which Marcus was stalling on."

"That's very good news; knew that boy had the makings of a military leader."

A quizzical brow was asking the validity of this statement, so Paulus continued, "Though I imagine that he was ably aided by that Pere chap. Still, it's great news and buys us some more time."

Paulus's thoughts were split between this report and how this would be affecting Rebecca. In fact his head, when not trying hard to concentrate on military matters, was always full of visions and reminiscences of her.

Not being given time to dwell on his memories, another dispatch was brought to him. This was from Castrum Libiae, penned in the beautiful hand of Bishop Jacinto. It gave off a confident air, boldly stating their readiness and ability to stave off the second Toletum column which was heading their way. Their defensive position was good and would hold despite their lack of numbers. The negative note was tagged onto the end. All the hot wind and big promises sent through the rather impressive character of Aquitaine Vasconis "king" Lupus's son, Odo, seemed to have come to nought, with complete silence being the response to the messages sent.

Castrum Clausurae was set in a magnificently wonderful defensive position high on a hill. Not on the highest, if it had been placed there, it would have been difficult to supply and less controlling of the only winding path through these not quiet mountains. The Roman architects that started this structure hundreds of years previously had, as with nearly all Roman structures, known what they were doing. Smaller lookouts were placed on the highest points, which offered a view that stretched as far as the eye could see both north and south. Furthermore, they could communicate directly with the main fort by sight.

"Good position to stop them, I think this must be our most strategic point. If this is held, there are only two ways round, Castrum Libiae, which sounds as if it's in good hands, and sailing an army around the headland to land farther up the coast. I really don't think that they are that well-prepared to do that. They could commandeer enough vessels to act as a sort of supply chain, not move great numbers of men."

The sun was rising on another late summer day when Hilderic saddled up with his personal guard ready to head back home to play host to the Frank allies. The king and duke came to see him off, wishing him all the diplomatic patience he could muster.

"I reckon they won't take a blind bit of notice of me, probably won't even notice I am there. Chlodoswintha will have them under control I am sure. Still, I feel I ought to be there."

Both Ranosindus and Paulus dutifully laughed at the joke that all three men knew to be true. If there were a power in Nemausus, it was wielded by the countess. Without a doubt she was one of the most impressive women either man had met in their lives, a fact they commented upon once out of the earshot of the count.

"That girl, who you are smitten by, seems to be made of the same stuff. Give her time and I am sure that she will outdo even the countess, though how she'll be able to express that being a Jewess, god only knows."

Flavius remained silent thinking about this fact. It was so blatantly true, she had that inner power and also, there was no way she'd ever be able to express it on a macro scale, unless, of course, he could find a way of making her legitimate.

"I am sure she'll find a way. When we win this spat and the Jews are a little less oppressed may be she'll…"

"That is not going to happen. The Jews will never be truly accepted by us, you know that as well as I do."

"I don't know.."

"My dear *king*, they don't want to be like us, they don't want to mix with us. They believe themselves to be different, special, superior even, how can they mingle with us? It'll be impossible on both sides. The very best we can hope for is some sort of peaceful co-existence of parallel living."

This was an idea that Flavius had never stopped to contemplate. He'd heard Rebecca talk at length of the oppression of the Jews. He'd also heard her talk about the gentiles and how they were viewed from within the Jewish society. When the two were put together it would make their relationship nigh on impossible. Would their undoubted love for each other be able to survive these external forces?

His thoughts were interrupted by Ranosindus talking military tactics. Evidently he had been for a while, and by the expectant look on his face he was waiting for an answer to a question that Flavius hadn't heard.

"Sorry, I was.."

"Thinking about your perky woman, can't blame you, better than what we are facing here. Still, my question was, where do you want to place my men?"

Startled back into reality, Paulus changed into military commander mode. "I believe the battle here to be vital. I am confident that Bishop Jacinto and Arangiscle will do a fine job of holding Castrum Libiae. What I need to ensure is our defences along the coast. There's a place, Castrum de Caucoliberi, which on the map looks a good disembarking point, from where Wamba could attack our rear. I would like to take a force there to ensure the fidelity of the warden of the keep. Meanwhile, if you would do me the honour of commanding the forces here, I would be most grateful. Wittimir should be able to supply you with more men from Narbo once the Franks move on from Nemausus. As I said earlier, I really don't want them to come too far into the kingdom as they may have another agenda, and the local population may see them, not Wamba, as the enemy."

"You do me an honour, general, I mean king." This caused another shared sly grin.

"I will leave you all my cohort except for a few men I may need to enforce my views on the coast. You will find Milo a most able centurion."

Leaving Tarraco pacified, King Wamba felt that only a token force needed to remain in order to ensure their continued loyalty, and ensure the edicts against the Jews were complied with. This left the massed army to enjoy a peaceful ride up the coast. Word had spread that the king was paying well over the odds for almost any product that the locals could provide. The result was that the column was inundated with farmers, and merchants selling their wares.

This hearts and minds policy, as Wamba had christened it, was working to a level of perfection that no one could call into question, not even the biggest and most vocal opponent, Teodofred, who advocated exemplary punishment, believing this to be the most dissuasive factor for a generation to come. Their ride north was more peaceful than a Sunday trot to Mass on his estate, a fact that peeved the dignitary greatly. Having had his troops so bruised and battered, so publicly, with all the subsequent loss of prestige, he was itchy to redress this imbalance. Barcino had been his best hope of military redemption. It wasn't to be. The first and only "battle", which was little more than a skirmish, was led by the exercitus, not the vilified and ridiculed baron's contingent, and consisted of a bit of posing, some noise and then the locals running away or surrendering en masse. On every hunt he'd been on in his life, the wild boar had put up more resistance. Truly pathetic it was. At least the public trials provided a little more in the way of punishment, unlike the leniency showed in Tarraco. The only good part of that show trial was the public commitment of his daughter to the future Duke. Despite seeing Marcus as a rebel, his thinking was that the Duke of Tarraco had been, and would always be, important. Especially if they played by the central government rules. Moreover an alliance with his estates in the south would be a powerful tool when it came to choosing a new ruler, which given Wamba's clear and evident weakness, couldn't be too far away. He needed to start manoeuvring soon. Furthermore, he really disliked this particular daughter, Gelvira, his eldest. She had a mouth on her, and way, which was loud and infuriating, he'd be glad to be shot of her.

The Barcino leaders had been paraded through the streets, heads shaven, led out to a place of public execution where Eured, Pompedio, Gundefred, Neufred and the deacon Hunulf were swiftly and mercifully dispatched. The only rebel who was made to suffer for hours in his death was the gardingo, Hildigiso. Wamba had had intelligence, from the bishops' network of spies, that this was one of the main instigators of the rebellion, a fact the gardingo didn't attempt to deny, instead proclaiming the sovereignty and right to the independence until his last breath. This public defiance, despite his evident pain and throes of death, particularly annoyed Wamba. It flew in the face of his hearts and minds policy. If someone was prepared to suffer SO much and still hang onto the concept of separation, then that could inspire others to do so. The last thing he wanted was to create martyrs for this cause. Resolving to ignore those who insisted on exemplary bloody deaths of the rebels, he would endeavour to ensure that the future executions wouldn't give a platform to further their cause.

The other disappointed bloodhound who was baying for blood aired *his* views regularly. Wamba did whatever he could to avoid the company of the Bishop of Hispalis, at times though, meals especially, when they stopped in a town, it was impossible. Trying to fob him off with Teodofred while playing a more than slightly deaf mute who cared greatly about the local cuisine, he managed to keep outright disagreements to a minimum. Struggling to see why the bishop felt so rabidly vindictive against the Jews, he found it difficult to swallow when he vented his spleen, especially as the policy of de-Jewing the kingdom, his kingdom, was working so well, with so little loss of blood. When Iulianus found that the, admittedly, small Barcino Jewish population had high-tailed it before their arrival, he was incensed. When it was pointed out that this was the objective, he would sit and glower with pent up resentful rage.

Grudgingly, he had agreed to the public shaming of the three Jewish Tarraco leaders, even making a pact with that slimy disgusting toad, who he'd had to suffer for days, that the lives of these men would be spared - an agreement he'd had no intention of ever keeping. It was on his orders, not the king's, that these men were shown true justice through the sword, not just slightly maimed, as previously agreed. It was not enough, not even when Hillel's tongue was split, more blood should have been spilt in a public display of power and might of the one true religion. In his opinion, the time given to this vermin to leave Tarraco peacefully was also excessive, it was his unilateral decision to reduce it so dramatically to a week. During the negotiations, his weakened military position was insufficient to oppose this historical mistake so he had to look as if he was accepting it. Once on the punishment platform; Wamba couldn't contradict him. All these facts would be reported to Julian, to show the depths of laxity that this so called ruler would stoop to, Jew saving; this verged almost on treasonable indulgence as far as he was concerned.

*

Having found three nosily squawking laying hens and one even nosier cock tied to a branch near the beginning of the path from the beach, a couple of days previous, Arantxa knew that her presence was known, and given that it was a gift , an extremely thoughtful and useful one at that, she had to assume friendly intentions. These were most certainly not the actions of a hostile raiding party, nevertheless, she was wary while she was out and about, always sticking to the shadows and still not daring to light a fire, not that it was needed for anything but cooking, as the weather was scorching most days. Late summers, early autumns were never like this where she was from.

She heard fallen twigs breaking underfoot before she could make out the shape which was struggling, tugging something that didn't want to be pulled. Creeping silently closer with her large dagger in hand, she could make out the back of what looked and sounded like a most frustrated man, now swearing, quietly, at whatever he was trying to coax or drag with him. It was a set of shoulders she knew well, and often spent time dwelling on.

"What are you doing?"

"Oh shit! Double shit! This was supposed to be a surprise."

"Well, I certainly didn't expect you."

Moving closer, she could see the cause of his sweat, a most reluctant to move brown goat with a pretty white face, who was happily tearing bark off the tree next to it and saw little advantage to its life by being moved on from this place of food and contentedness. Arantxa squatted and made a strange clicking noise with the back of her mouth which caused the goat to stop its de-barking, and reconsider its until now firmly held outlook. Another strange sound saw the goat walk, almost happily, towards it and the noise maker. Arantxa scratched the animal's neck as soon as it was close enough, something which indeed did complete its happiness by its expression.

"She's lovely. For me?"

"No, we've become the best of friends and were just out for a stroll."

Much to the goat's displeasure, Arantxa gave up her scratching and moved enthusiastically to Marcus with her arms wide open. Rather ungoat like, more sheepishly, he accepted her embrace.

"What's the matter? Why aren't you happy to see me? Were you just going to ditch the goat and leave, the way, I presume, you did with the hens? Are you trying to allay your conscience about me with animal gifts?"

So many questions, and so near the mark, without him actually saying a word. He dreaded what would happen when he actually spoke.

"Let's go back to the cottage. You bring your new friend; she doesn't seem to like me too much."

"Not surprising. So tell me…"

Marcus played all the questions with the straightest bat possible, determined to say little, or nothing, until they were in a confined area.

"Nice and cool in here."

"You mean cold?"

He had actually meant cool, it was good to be out of the stifling goat pulling heat.

"I haven't had a fire since I heard some soldiers quite a few days ago now."

Marcus, standing awkwardly near her, explained that those precautions would no longer be necessary as the enemy had moved on.

"Leaving you here, untouched."

The next explanation, which he tried to keep as short as possible, involved the battles and the surrender.

"So, as far as Wamba is concerned you are the new Duke?"

"Yes, until we finally drive them back. Flavius has concentrated most of our troops in the north. I am hopeful that the counter attack may start soon."

"Duke, eh?! I suppose Wamba's not too keen on you marrying the Count of Nemausus's daughter despite her being such a lovely girl."

"No, that's been officially cancelled."

This caused a beaming Arantxa to reduce the distance between them to nothing, stroke his face and express her sorrow at this *terrible* news.

"So, you are no longer engaged."

"Well, no and yes."

"Don't tell me that you feel some sort of obligation towards her?"

"No, not her."

"Who then?"

"You see, as part of the agreement," Arantxa stepped back one pace. "I have been promised to.."

The slap was significant.

"I didn't have a choice."

The second slap restored the balance of pain to both sides of the face. Deciding that if he was going to be hit every time he spoke, it was probably better not to speak, he dedicated himself to face rubbing.

"Whose daughter is this one? And how lovely is she? You impregnate me and become a serial engager to anyone and everyone else." Arantxa was showing anger that she didn't know she had. Not having ever expected anything from this relationship, she couldn't fathom quite why she was reacting this way.

Marcus was definitely out of his depth and was floundering for something to either say or do.

Arantxa lowered herself onto a tree trunk she used as a chair. "I'm sorry, that's completely unfair, it's just.."

"Don't worry." He knelt beside her, "I am sorry that it has to be this way but, I don't feel that hard done to."

A steely look entered Arantxa's eyes and her arm twitched as if she were about to continue her assault when Marcus found his voice again. "Let me tell what has happened."

Although he kept the details to the minimum, he had to tell her about Jacob. She began to sob within the confines of controllability, but only just. When Marcus reached out to hold her, she buried her face in his chest, mutterings words like "What a lovely man" "Why him? Wouldn't hurt a fly."

It was only after some considerable time, many shoulder shuddering outbursts of tears as she recalled and named other facets of that lovely man's character that she suddenly lifted her head as if she'd forgotten some very important thing. "Rebecca, how, where is she?"

*

"Sire, your most humble servant would like to present you with the keys to the city." Amador's head was so low that the only possible part of the king he could make out with any clarity was his boot clad feet.

The royal forces had arrived with the setting sun the previous evening, pitching camp not far from the city walls. No ambassadors nor envoys were sent, though one was received from the sitting bishop, Amador, requesting in the politest, most grovelling terms possible an audience at the earliest convenience of the royal party.

Wamba had spent yet another unpleasant suppertime in the company of the bloodthirsty brothers, his new nickname for them, which sadly he had no one to share with. These were the moments when he missed the company of Paulus, he would have laughed and joined in the merriment. True to form, and their new name, these dining partners sought more exemplary punishment on the lines of Barcino, or more stringent, as this was the place of the rebel's coronation. Wamba had allowed them free reign to express their views without offering any himself, which added to the frustration and high blood pressure levels of the two men. At one point the Hispalis Bishop was literally spitting feathers, a product of insufficient plucking, which Wamba was sure some cook would pay dearly for.

"Bishop Amador, before I allow the Bishop of Hispalis, the highest representative of the Church with full powers given to him by the hierarchy in Toletum, to speak, I would like to ask you one question. Why was it thought necessary to make Flavius a king? Surely commander in chief was enough?"

Not raising his head any higher than knee level, the supplicant, in an unsteady voice, explained the problem of north and south and how there was no one both parts would follow. They needed a compromise and had to make that person look authoritative in the eyes of all.

"Interesting, and I believe you officiated at this ceremony, is that true?"

"I but helped, the main role was performed by Bishop Gunhild."

The King nodded at Iulianus, whose manner and line of questioning was more aggressive and accusative, with a great part of it centred on the blasphemous plundering act of stealing the crown donated by King Leovigild to the sacred memory of Saint Feliu.

Amador was a quaking mess, pleading innocence and fidelity to King Wamba which, he wasn't to know, was actually, the correct approach. Left to the tender mercies of the Church's inquisitor, the bishop would have been flayed alive and his carcass nailed to the city gates.

"As the crime is heinous and against both Church and State, I believe we should send this one-time bishop back to Toletum to face the highest Church authorities in the land. Baron, could two of your men provide an *escort?*"

This statement took the wind out of Iulianus's sails as he was building up to his crescendo of righteous justice, but left him with no alternative other than to agree as he could not be seen to, publicly, contradict the king and belittle the Church's power in the capital. His glowering indignant state needed another avenue to vent itself, "And the Jews, where are they?"

The cowering remorseful figure somewhat relieved that punishment was not to be applied immediately, and knowing that in Toletum he could call on his old friend Quiricus, one time neighbouring bishop in Barcino, to intercede on his behalf, was more than happy to supply the answer to this query. "The population here has never been very large, and upon receiving news of what was happening in the south, they upped and left taking little with them some days ago."

"Before you are taken to Toletum, I expect you to furnish me with a list of all their belongings and wealth left behind, it has all been allocated to the Church."

*

"I really can't tell you just how pleased I am to see you!"

"Perhaps I should go away more often." Count Hilderic had literally just dismounted when his uncharacteristically flustered wife appeared with a greeting of such emotion, unheard in many years, if ever.

Taking him by the hand, she led him passed the main dining room, which had closed doors but still emitted a cacophony of loud male voices, to a minor room, which, in the past, she'd used as her getaway peaceful sewing room.

"They are impossible to deal with. They won't listen to me. I am supposed to be the host yet they tell me where I should go and what I should do."

"Successfully?"

"Well, successfully *tell me,* yes, but what I do is a different matter."

A grin showed the pleasure Hilderic felt. He could imagine the situation all too clearly and was thankful that he wouldn't have to submit to wife controlling classes by any Frank. Leaving Chlodoswintha trailing in his wake, he headed back to his dining room banging the door open with considerable force, causing a lull in the noise levels.

"Right, everyone out! If you have someone in charge, he may stay, the rest of you, remove yourselves from MY house."

A sullen silence greeted his order, not the meek compliance which he'd hoped though not expected. A heavily built bearded figure left the pack and sauntered towards him. Unlike the order giver, this man was wearing a sword.

"Who the devil are you?" Hilderic's voice remained more stable than he actually felt.

"My name is Chlothar. I lead the Franks who have come to help you against Wamba."

"I welcome you, and your men, but NOT in my house. Get them and their muddy feet out. You, I will talk to over supper tonight, which will be held in this room."

Not allowing any time for response the count headed out of the room hoping rather than believing that they would adhere to his requests. Looking at a discreet distance was a most impressed Chlodoswintha. She'd never seen this masterful side of her husband before. Hurrying she sought to catch him up to wherever he was going, which neither of them actually knew. They ended up in the kitchen, from where they could hear, and just about see, the Franks traipsing out not very quietly.

*

Odo's forces sat on an adjacent hill watching the total pig's ear that the defensive forces were making of this battle, clearly no man of experience was leading them. They should never have even tried to leave the castrum, and why they thought it necessary the line up in that formation would remain a secret in history. They were cut down easily, effectively and quickly by the attackers, who in reality should have been bogged down in a long siege with an uncertain outcome. If this was the mettle of the so called rebels, he positively didn't want to nail his colours to the mast of that sinking ship. His father's instructions brooked little interpretation; *join the fight if the rebels will undoubtedly win.*

Bishop Jacinto was reluctant, counselling caution, only to be over-ruled by Nobleman Arangiscle whose men made up the bulk of the defenders. Seeing a gap in the attackers line which could easily be driven through, he sent out what cavalry he had, supported by a great wad of men on the trot behind them. They were cock a hoop, thinking that they would make light work of these obviously inexperienced troops. Arangiscle was so confident of victory that he led the charge himself.

General Alaric had left the gap just in case; he never really thought that anyone would fall for that old trick. When he saw it unfolding, or in this case, folding like the pastry around a pie, he felt genuinely sorry for the demise of men so poorly led. It was a slaughter. Never in his military life had he seen such a well built easily defendable position fall so quickly and almost without cost to his army.

What was left of the defenders sued for peace immediately, something he did not accept. With the bit between their teeth and the defenders in complete disarray, Castrum Libiae fell within one day of the battle commencing. A rout.

Two days of looting, pillaging and raping followed, there were not many women and the fights over them probably cost more of his men's lives than had been lost in battle, these fights continued until the drunken, exhausted men finally collapsed. General Alaric's orders were complied with; no prisoners were taken.

*

Not thinking that life could get any worse, it was a surprise when it did. After three vomit filled days of coast hugging, Pere refused to accept that this counted as sailing. Two nights feeling incredibly cold on beaches later, they arrived in Clausurae Caucoliberi only to be arrested and bound before being dragged before the headman of this Keep. Throughout the journey Pere had waxed lyrically about the beauty of the coastline, giving special reference to the magnificently attractive coves. Sadly, there was still no stopping him, pointing out the splendour of the natural harbour within a harbour, even asking the arresting officer about some of the more strategically wonderful defence location facets the place boasted. Rebecca had always had the impression that Pere was taciturn, rarely saying anything unnecessary. This evaluation was under serious review. She was sure that he'd meant well with his endless prattling while the contents of her stomach, and so much more, emptied into the sea. Perhaps it was his way of trying to distract her from her self pitying wretchedness. It hadn't worked and it wasn't working now as they were not quite dragged, more prodded, along the quay towards the imposing structure overlooking the harbour.

"It's normal, they are just doing their job. Don't worry, it'll all be sorted soon enough."

Unable to reply to such cheerfulness as they were unceremoniously pushed into a sprawling pose at the feet of a corpulent rather smelly man, Rebecca's reservation went unsaid, while the lead guards uttered one word, "spies."

Pere tried to rise to refute this accusation, only to be kicked back into position by the speaker.

As their heads were more or less pinned to the floor, literally under foot, they couldn't see the fat man approach but they could feel and smell him. "Let him tell me who he is, and what his business here is."

Pere was allowed into a near kneeling pose, "We are from Tarraco. I am Duke Ranosindus's lead guard, and I am escorting this lady to see General, no, King Paulus."

"And why did you come by sea?"

"Neither of us like horses and we were in a hurry after Tarraco fell to Wamba."

Allowing the pressure to ease on Rebecca's neck, she immediately sat up and demanded to know who was treating them so badly.

"She has a mouth on her, this one! Are you a Jew? You look Jewish." Rebecca nodded assertively with an outward show of bravery she was not feeling.

"We've had a few boatloads of Jews trying to land here, running from the fighting, the cowards. They were given short shrift, we don't want their like infesting us here. I must say that you're a prettier prospect. Pull her to her feet and rip that tunic off, let's have a look to see if she's worth keeping before we toss her back into the water."

Enthusiastically the guard moved to comply with orders only to find the large, still shackled form of Pere barring his path.

"I wouldn't do that." It wasn't said in any agitated way, more like a real threat.

"I am Leofred, I give the orders here."

Pere was pushed aside unable to maintain his balance due to his bonds he landed in a heap. The guard needed a few tugs to rip the sturdy material, leaving Rebecca completely exposed.

"Nice!"

"Leofred, you will die for this. This lady is VERY important to the king."

"I imagine she is. Let's see if she feels as good as she looks."

At that moment a heavy breathing soldier entered, took in the sight, and then managed to blurt out that a troop of heavily armed soldiers was approaching at speed.

"Oh, pleasure delayed!" After appraising his future delight, he noticed that the woman was not cowering, nor whimpering, nor did she look in the least bit frightened of him. "This is definitely a saucy one who needs taming before being ridden." He headed out to find out what, or who, was approaching and whether they were a threat of any kind, something he very much doubted, instead suspecting they were some reinforcements send from Narbo.

Not able to cover any part with her hands that were still firmly fixed behind her back, Rebecca crumpled herself as much as possible in a crouching type pose.

Having his view destroyed, the guard barked orders instructing her to stand, which she ignored. Sure that Leofred would concur, he moved over to pull her to her feet leaving his sword and shield to the side, as he would need both hands to pull her up and cop the feel he believed was his due. When his face was smashed by the impact of the rapidly rising head, it emitted a howl of pain, allowing Rebecca to stand and kick him in his state of arousal, causing a low pitched sound of expelling breath. The other guard rushed into action with his sword leading the way, only to be tripped over by Pere. Unlike his partner, there was no noise after a significantly well placed kick to the head was delivered.

"I'll hold the sword, you rub the rope along its edge as best you can." It was this sight of Pere clasping the weapon behind his back with Rebecca, her back to it, pulling her bounded arms back and forth in her naked state with her much larger than normal pregnant breasts rhythmically swaying that met Leofred and following along slightly behind, the recently crowned King of Tarraconensis/Gallia Gothica.

*

Three days, three whole days, which included two evening meals, it took for the heavy assault machinery parts to catch up with King Wamba. Despite finding Gerunda not an unpleasant place to be, he really wanted shot of the Bishop of Hispalis and Duke Teodofred's company, or at the very least, have them diluted by the presence of others. His only regret in packing Bishop Amador off so quickly to Toletum was this. Saving, or at least elongating his life by taking it out of the blood thirsty clutches of Iulianus, it was he who now had to pay the price of having to listen, well, hear… he did his best to pay as little attention as possible, during the set meals, to the constant, and annoying, voice.

The bishop was a frustrated man as all the things that he felt were his by rights were somehow being removed from his hands. An example of Amador should have been made in front of the people of Gerunda. Sadly, the Jews were no longer there to be tortured and displayed. Moreover, to heap clemency upon indignity, the local dignitaries who had sided with the rebels were all pardoned by Wamba with their only punishment being an amount of their future wealth to be paid to the Church, something he knew would be extremely difficult to collect. Furthermore, the forfeited wealth of the departed Jews amounted to almost nothing. Contrary to popular belief, it seemed that not all Jews were rich. This lot here were not poor, they were involved in trade and money lending but on such a small scale that it was exceptionally difficult for the Church to accrue much in property or gold. All of which made him bitter, annoyed and reluctant to be superficially pleasant to this weak man, who apparently had hearing problems, calling himself king. His conversation with Teodofred was also limited by the presence of the monarch as their major point of agreement and topic of conversation was how inappropriate Wamba was for the office he held.

The hours had dragged by for all, important people, the soldiers, and their wary hosts. The Wamba policy of hearts and minds was working for the local population but not for the armed forces; spoils, riches, sacking, looting and rape were the standard fare for a successful army. It was true that they hadn't done much in the way of actually fighting, still, they were victorious and due their part. Instead they were kept under control by officers, and anyone who got a little too drunk and over enthusiastic with a local woman was punished. Unlike their counterparts in Tarraco, they didn't lose their manhood then left to die. This time the penalty was a crude form of circumcision which left them bloody, sore and unable to use their instrument for anything other than pissing.

All in all, everyone was pleased when the order came to march out.

*

"Guards, take them!"

"Rebecca!"

"Rebecca?"

Seeing two of their fellow soldiers lying sprawled on the floor, the two that were escorting Leofred warily made their way forward weapons to the fore.

"Stop!"

Looking from their master to this newcomer, who was being treated with the utmost respect, they were in a total quandary as whether to precede or not.

"I said stop." Then turning to Leofred, "What is the meaning of this?"

"They are spies we apprehended…"

The rest of what was going to be said was lost as Paulus smashed the man in the face with his gloved fist. Then quickly extracting his sword from its scabbard, he jabbed it into the midriff of his host causing the cloth to part, allowing a trickle of blood to be seen.

This stirred the guards into action who turned to face this armed threatening stranger. Ignoring his "don't", they moved to their master's aid, only for one of them to receive a thrust, not a jab this time, in his leg, a clear attempt to wound not kill.

"The next will be more serious. Put down your weapons!"

They both complied without much hesitation and their eyes averted from the stare they were receiving from their injured Lord.

Moving quickly past them Flavius removed his riding cloak to wrap the nearly unbound naked figure in. Unable to fling her welcoming arms around him she settled for a nuzzling against his chest.

Hearing the clatter of a number of boots, he moved away to face a group of men led by someone who looked and dressed like a sergeant of arms who was clearly bewildered by the whole scene. Addressing his master, he sought clarification.

Leofred, feeling the warm blood but little pain, was weighing up his options, this battle could be easily won, but he would be taking on the might of the newly crowned head, which would be suicide. However, at the same time he knew that his life was in serious danger as this woman he had stripped and humiliated, a Jewess, was obviously close to the new King's heart, figuratively as well as her at present pose.

"Halt! It appears that we have a misunderstanding here, which we can solve amicably. Do you agree, Sire?"

Everyone, friend and foe, noticed the emphasis on the last word.

Paulus, forever the calm reasonable man, was inclined to accept until a vivid flashing memory of another naked woman, who had been threatened and eventually taken from him, came into mind. His blood boiling he tried not to show his emotional state as he sauntered without malice and with a reassuring smile, back to Leofred, before sticking his still unsheathed sword into the man's throat.

*

Milo was a little unsure just how he should approach his role in Castrum Clausurae. The overall commander was Ranosindus, but the sum of his military knowledge would barely fill the hole in the tooth that had been troubling the Centurion for the last few days. Having dealt with the son, Marcus, he hadn't expected much. However, what was shown was shockingly poor. The only saving grace of the duke, was that he knew how much he was lacking. This at least was refreshing, not a norm from Milo's past experiences. Many a time had he been responsible for enforcing a particularly stupid strategy dreamt up by one his *betters,* only to later get the blame for its failure.

"Sir, it appears that the last of the stragglers from Tarraco has arrived."

Ranosindus, who was behind a huge wooden table with a map spread out in front of him, sat up and asked for whoever it was to be brought in immediately.

A two man delegation was ushered through the door, Ranosindus vaguely recognised one of the men as being part of Pere's group of trainers. The man, clearly very pleased to be in the presence of his Lord, gave an extensive report back of the first battle. This one Ranosindus had already heard about, but allowed the recounting to see if there was any substantial difference from the first time around. There wasn't. The second battle was new information, and its telling, and outcome, made a father feel immensely proud of his son; besting the outnumbering Royal army twice was quite a feat. The details of the peace accords were to be expected and most lenient; no sacking of Tarraco and no public executions, except for Jews, which would be popular, was welcome, if disturbing news. This Wamba approach would not galvanise the population to fight against the invaders, their, at best, lukewarm enthusiasm for the new separate state would diminish further if they saw how reasonable the old state could be. That Marcus was safe, and named the new duke, was of enormous relief. Once this conflict was over, Marcus would have all the responsibility and he could enjoy his latter years.

Cyprianus's role was less of a shock than something to be expected from the fat slug of a man. However, what was upsetting was that it was clear that the vengeful pig had chosen the landowners to be blinded. One had been an outspoken critic of the Bishop and the other had a sizeable valuable piece of land next to Church property. Ranosindus found new depths of contempt for Cyprianus and promised himself that the man would be made to pay.

The news bearer wasn't sure who the Jews were, his attitude being that they all looked the same, but was sure that all of them were elderly, and two were brothers. This information would have to be relayed to Paulus, as it sounded as if they were the family of Rebecca. Remembering the shy man, an uncle, who looked totally uncomfortable in the role thrust upon him from the meetings, he felt a pang of sympathy.

Thanking and dismissing the men, his focus was brought back to the present by Milo, who hadn't left the room, stating that the other and more *important* information the men had brought was that an enemy column was only hours away. So concerned with matters in Tarraco, Ranosindus, much to Milo's impatient disgust, had forgotten to ask.

*

The prospect of being in the company of Evrigius was not one that Egica had savoured. In fact, feeling somewhat aggrieved and peeved at his uncle's division of forces, it was a most sullen general who had led his forces north. However, contrary to all expectations the two men got along extremely well finding that they had things in common and their views on the Goth world weren't too dissimilar either. One area that Egica was in almost total agreement with the baron, but something a nephew couldn't be seen to be agreeing with, and was forever half-heartedly curtailing, was his opinions on the king. It was difficult to not see that his uncle was weak, ineffective and blatantly the wrong man for the job, and liking his family member as much as he actually did, didn't detract from these facts. In contrast to Wamba's forces pushing up from the coast, they had cut a swath through the countryside leaving death and destruction in their wake. It mattered not that they had met absolutely no opposition. They were there to punish and to make their passage through the territory a thing that the children's children would retell with fear and horror so that they would never again think about rebellion. Those were the instructions from the bishops. The significant, though inconsequential facts like most people they made suffer didn't even know there was a rebellion, never mind what it was all about, nor were there any Jews in this area, again, mattered nought.

"Finally, it looks as if we have some serious opposition. Nicely placed that fort, if you want to collect taxes or control the flow along the road, but it'll not be easy to defend once we have taken the heights over there." The two men sat on their horses behind the heavy cavalry which had yet to be used since coming up from Toletum. It seemed unlikely that they would be bloodied in this conflict either, as the defenders wouldn't be stupid enough to leave their walled fort. Still, lined up just out of arrow range, they did make a most imposing and impressive sight.

Milo had pointed out this flaw of the heights to Ranosindus days ago and the duke had sent up a significant, but nevertheless token, force, to defend them, arguing that more could and would be sent when necessary, which given their present numbers, meant when they were reinforced from Castrum Libiae, or Wittimir in Narbo.

A harmony between Egica and Evrigius had been struck very early on in their march forward. Although the vast majority of troop belonged to, and were loyal to, Evrigius, he allowed Egica to look as if he were in control, issuing orders, instructions, deciding where to go, whether to delay for plundering or sport, and generally be the visible point of control. This state of affairs wasn't lost on the king's nephew, he was astute enough to realise what was happening and how to play the game, always consulting the wise counsel of the older man. It was in one of these consultations that the baron suggested their attack strategy.

Baron Evrigius was a large man who rode well and enjoyed a hunt as much as any landowner of the nation. However, that wasn't his passion, archery was. Often his use of a horse in a hunt was little more than the transportation to the required area; from that moment on, stealth was the order of the day. Finding the standard issue Roman /Goth bow lacking in accuracy, range and piercing power, he, his blacksmiths, and bow makers had spend a great deal of time and effort redesigning and perfecting this instrument to the point that he now believed that what his bowmen carried was unequalled in the modern world. Seeking experts from the East, adding that to the knowledge accrued by the Germanic tribes, his men had a significantly elongated range and provided a selection of shafts and heads for every occasion, and this was one such situation of which he'd dreamed.

When the fort was built and throughout its history there was little that anyone could do by taking the surrounding hills. Yes, it was a weak and vulnerable point as mentioned by Milo, but it wasn't *that* significant as any projectile throwing machine would have to be dragged up those sheer slopes, which would be no mean feat. Furthermore, arrows fired from such a distance would have little strength on impact as they were so far away. The baron believed that this day would change history.

*

Seeing the heavy cavalry lined up outside the gates didn't worry Ranosindus as much as the parchment in his hand. General Wittimir had written with the most perturbing news. Four words; *Castrum Libiae has fallen*, was the reason why there would be no reinforcements.

"Centurion Milo, it looks as if we are on our own, at least for the foreseeable future. How long do you think we can hold out for?"

"We have two wells, the food stocks are high after the harvest, the moral is good. I would say that we are equipped to withstand a siege of a few months, possibly the whole winter."

It was at that precise moment that an arrow landed not too far away from where they were standing, at the edge of the open space just behind the main gates.

"How the hell..?"

"That's impossible. No archer is close enough."

The two men headed up the ladder to the ramparts to see if there was an infantry protected group of archers in sight, only to be forced to take cover as a hail of burning arrows streaked across the sky landing at different points beyond the walls.

No longer looking in front of the fort, Milo's eye line moved to an adjacent hill which was, surely, too far away to be the origin of the attack, only to observe another hail of burning arrows heading their way.

Even with the, admittedly strong, wind behind them, it shouldn't be possible to fire an accurate shot that distance. Yet, here they were, landing in ever increasing numbers causing little fires all over the fort. "Clear all combustible material to the back of the fort." Milo yelled at a group of his men who were cowering behind a wagon. "You lot, dowse those fires! Start a water chain!" Turning to his nominally commanding officer he tried to sound reassuring, "If we can avoid any major fire breaking out, then they'll run out of arrows soon enough and we should be alright."

Barrage after barrage of fire arrows rained down for what seemed like an age. Milo's men moved relentlessly round trying to keep ahead of the situation which they were doing with considerable success and few injuries, it was then that the rain of arrows changed into a torment, the sky actually darkening with the number involved. Suddenly the panorama changed from scurrying men to sprawling ones. Bodies were everywhere. Ranosindus looked on with horror only to have his attention drawn to the outside of the fort as shield protected infantry squares scuttled their way to the gates with all the material necessary to scale walls. The majority of defenders were staying as close to the wall as possible for protection, not daring to show their heads over the parapet.

Ranosindus stood bellowing orders only to be hit by two arrows, one in the chest and one in the head. Death was instantaneous and the rest of the battle didn't last that much longer. Milo's body, which was near the main gates, resembled a pin cushion.

Once these two were gone, leaderless, the surrender was swift with the gates being opened allowing the attackers to enter.

"Take prisoners. No killing!!" All the centurions were repeating the same order again and again, which was obeyed on the whole. As the attackers had lost nobody in the fight, there was little appetite for blood lust revenge and as everyone spoke the same language there was little in the way of mis-communication.

The baron and the general rode in with their personal guards to survey the damage done.

"Impressive, Baron, I believe you have changed the face of warfare for a generation."

Evrigius was smugly pleased; this would put his name on the lips of every fighting man and noble in the land. "I believe you are correct."

Having followed a policy of no prisoners against the non resisting population so far, it was both a surprise and a complete U turn in tactics when Egica ordered that there should be no mass slaughter. Knowing that a lot of these soldiers were the ones that Paulus had taken from the Vasconia, he reasoned that they would be more useful turned than dead.

From his horse he shouted that leniency would be granted to all those who wanted to be reincorporated with the royal forces. Each man though, would be branded on the neck with a T so that everyone would know of their treachery.

*

Rebecca squealed in horror, she'd never seen anyone die before, never mind being murdered so viciously.

"Who's next?" Paulus wielded his sword towards the sergeant, who dropped his sword immediately followed by the rest of his group.

"This woman is important to me and NO man shall ever threaten her again as long as I live."

Moving back over to the still tied one time prisoners, he used his sword in a chopping motion to release them. The sword, still bloody, made Rebecca cringe and begin to sob, with what emotion she wasn't sure. She was majorly conflicted, relieved at being freed and no longer in danger of being raped or worse. She was horrified as she had just seen the man she thought she loved, murder an unarmed person. Unsure whether she was grateful or repulsed by the person in front of her, she didn't know how to react.

"That's torn it," It was Pere rubbing his wrists who was speaking quietly to Paulus, "you realise that was a mistake, don't you?"

Paulus was about to demand the respect he wasn't being shown when Pere continued, "I reckon that had a lot to do with what happened in the Vasconia, still it was a mistake."

"What?"

"We all heard tell about that girl you was sweet on, I must have heard ten different versions of it around the camp, but they all had two things in common; a naked girl with her throat slit and your inability to stop it."

It was Rebecca's turn to *what*. Pere continued, "I'm not saying what you've done here is wrong, but it's bloody bad timing. That pig would have raped a pregnant woman and most likely killed us both afterwards. Still, you'll need someone to defend this Keep as Wamba will surely be sending supplies and reinforcements by sea."

"How do you know that?"

"It's logical, ain't it?"

Flavius mind was processing these thoughts. This man, Pere, his name, he seemed to recall, was totally right, with Leofred dead, killed by him, he would not get loyalty from his men no matter how much he threatened or cajoled, nor would they obey anyone he left here, even if he did have anyone of sufficient rank and stature, which he didn't. Slowly realising that he may have jeopardised the whole rebellion with this one hot-blooded action, he sought for a solution.

"Sergeant, who is the next in command here?"

"The brother, Dag."

"Find him, NOW!"

Rebecca remained dumbfounded and confused. She recalled both what Arantxa had said and what Flavius hadn't said on the beach about the sister, Aitziber, a name and a person she'd thought a great deal about, while the new king did something he often saw the other king do, pace around in chin stroking thought.

"Pregnant!" He instinctively moved to Rebecca who all but ran away to hide behind Pere as he'd forgotten that he was still holding his bloodied sword. Letting the sword fall in realisation of what was happening, he moved again to the cloaked figure, muttering a question, "Am I going to be a father?"

Back on more solid ground where she could control the situation, Rebecca moved away from both her protector and her pursuer. "I'm not sure I want the father of my baby to be a murderer. You didn't have to kill him"

"I was doing it to protect you."

"No, you weren't. You were doing it to cleanse your guilt and memory of Aitziber."

Initially taken aback by the name being spoken by Rebecca, he recovered, "I didn't save her to my guilt and shame, I agree, and I can't ever bring her back nor can I change what happened. It's just not possible."

The less than noble appearance of Dag came in at this point to see for himself what he'd been told. "You must be the slayer of my brother. Can't say I'm too upset to see him dead, arrogant pig. Still, he's family and I must revenge his death. I'm not sure who you are but I can assure you that you will not be leaving here with your life. The rest of your escort has been taken prisoner, which just leaves you two and the woman."

Bending to retrieve his sword, Flavius was joined by the bulk of Pere who was first to speak. "I totally accept that honour requires this course of action, it is what is expected of blood. I just want to point out that by taking this step, you do realise that sooner rather than later you are condemning yourself and ALL your relatives to slow very painful deaths."

"Brave talk."

"Not at all, just stating a fact. Do you have any idea who you are threatening?" Waiting for enlightenment the new warden of the Keep began to take an interest, so Pere continued. "This is the newly crowned king."

"Well I'm sure that King Wamba will reward me greatly when he arrives. Take them."

The six men including the sergeant inched forward most hesitantly. Having seen the death of their Lord, they were in no hurry to catch him up.

Pere had borrowed a weapon from one of the dead bodies and stood menacingly at Paulus's side. There was stalemate with neither side willing to take the decisive step forward. Surprisingly, there was suddenly a whirl of sound and movement as Rebecca dashed forward to retrieve the other fallen sword. Tying the cloak tightly around her waist leaving her breasts free she looked directly at the father of her child, "What! I used to beat Marcus all the time when we were kids and played sword fighting."

"Dressed like that I am sure you did!"

"We need to get to the horses in the courtyard. I suggest me first and you defend the rear."

"No, you lead, it's.."

Rebecca strode to the front slashing the first man's legs, making the second lunge in, only to be deflected by a crosscut front Pere. The ex-general then joined in the fray by taking out two soldiers who were warily watching the formidable half naked lady.

The kafuffle was heard from the courtyard where the king's escort of ten were corralled into a corner watched over by about the same number of armed men, none of whom expected the sight of an armed bouncing pair of breasts come hurtling through the door followed by the man they called the new king plus another big chap. The guards turned to face the oncoming threat only to be attacked from behind by the escort who had finally got around to doing the job they were employed for. As the "invading" party was obviously hell bent on leaving, there was no real enthusiasm from the defenders to join the fight, feeling it was their job to see them off the premises rather than risk life and limb to apprehend them.

The horses, which hadn't been unsaddled, were disturbed from their drinking to be forced into a speedy exit with Pere doubled up on a rather large stallion and Rebecca firmly grabbing Flavius from behind on his mount.

They hadn't gone far when they realised there was no pursuit. Slowing down to a gentle trot instead of the gallop was favoured greatly by the insufficiently rested animals .

"My arse is killing me; I've got to find some clothes. And I hate horses, even if I do like holding you."

*

Supper was a great deal more polite and ordered than Chlodoswintha had expected. Having seen nothing but brutish behaviour from her guests, she was surprised to see that their leader, Chlothar, was quite civilised, tending to chivalrous, around a dining table. His manners to her and the situation, were exemplary. Believing that she should be seen in her secondary role as wife to her newly returned masterful husband, she uttered not a word unless she was asked a direct question. She found the situation most frustrating as she believed that she could add a considerable amount to their talk on tactics. Still, it was important that she didn't undermine the count's authority in front of these foreigners. It was easy to see the role that Chlothar was playing; benevolent saviour with no ulterior agenda, when in fact he was a wolf waiting for the right moment to pounce. Despite the Hilderic asking various times what the Franks would like in return for their *invaluable* assistance, the man was vague, only mentioning that a stable friendly neighbour was more than enough compensation for the little they were providing.

Chlodoswintha thought, and, almost, said that was probably the only true word that the man had spoken all evening; *little*. Although when seen inside the confines of a smallish city like Nemausus, or her even smaller dining room, the Franks gave the impression of being numerous, they were, in fact, pitiful in number compared with what Wamba was bringing to the field. Perhaps Chlothar had noticed, or was sensitive enough to feel the scepticism emanating from her because he addressed the number question immediately, claiming that he had brought the rapidly assembled advanced force which would be followed by a vast horde his brother, Theuderic, was assembling back in Frankia. This, again, only provided the hostess with contradictory emotions; with this *horde* they could actually defeat Wamba and then lose everything by being swallowed up, dominated, and perhaps even annexed by Frankia.

Once their guest had left, the countess aired her fears to her husband who concurred with every word. The trouble was, as his shrug and deflated voice showed, there was little choice in the matter. There were no other options.

*

Still not sure whether they were on the best track to find their way to the main road to Narbo, the only thing they did know was that they were heading in the right direction. Until smoke was spotted in the near distance, they hadn't seen any sign of life whatsoever, no traffic, houses, and people working the fields were conspicuous by their absence.

Despite the leader of the escort group, Frideger, one of Wittimir's trusted officers, urging speed in case they were being followed, Rebecca's sore behind was the determining factor in the decision making process. They had to stop.

It was a decent sized house with well cared for fields, the property of a fairly prosperous and influential man. Standing in front of it, armed with a large kitchen chopping implement was a woman in her forties, who had what looked like an elderly retainer protecting her right flank with a pitch fork. Not a formidable defence force against a dozen armed men, still, her attitude was confident. In a fearless voice she demanded to know what they were doing on her property. Frideger, as the most local took the lead, requested, not in the politest terms, to speak immediately to the man of the house as they had no time to waste on idle chatter. The woman remained silent while tightening her grip on her weapon. Frideger was clearly agitated and getting more so by the second. The woman's resolve faltered somewhat when she realised that one of these men had an attractive woman wrapped in little more than a rough cloak sat behind him.

"Get off my property!" The order was given more in hope than conviction. Frideger's sword was withdrawn, which caused Rebecca sigh in exasperation, muttering audibly, "Stupid man," as she slid off the back of the horse, confirming the woman's suspicion of nakedness.

Moving in an unthreatening way, she slowly got to almost touching distance.

"These men rescued me from...well," indicating her state of undress, " you can imagine, and we were wondering whether you had any spare clothes that I could buy off you." Rebecca had no money but hoped that Flavius did. "We are on our way to Narbo and I can't tell you just how uncomfortable it is sitting on that bloody horse."

After taking in this honest exceptionally pretty face's words, their recipient reacted by laughing, "I *can* imagine." The tension in the air dissipated, much to the relief of the elderly man who was so close to Rebecca that she had been able to feel the vibrations of his quaking.

"My husband and all our men are in Narbo with General Wittimir. There's some sort of problem, I think with the Franks. Come with me. They," nodding at the mounted men, "can stay outside. Unwén," she indicated the calming pitch fork holder, "will show them where they can water their horses. And you, young man, put away that sword before you cut yourself."

The inside was well furnished with sturdy useful pieces whose use was more utilitarian than decorative, giving off the feeling of hard work providing a comfortable living.

"Are you alright? Would you like to sit, have something to eat?"

Rebecca was slightly taken aback by the sudden change in this woman's attitude towards strangers. "No, I'm fine, and certainly do not want to sit anywhere, thank you."

"I don't have many clothes and I'm not sure any of them would fit a tiny little thing like you. Perhaps it might be best, safer, if we dressed you as a boy. My teenage boy, who died last year, was about your size, slightly bigger, but that will be a good thing as you are going to need bigger clothes as you expand."

Although a whirlwind of thoughts dashed through Rebecca's mind about this woman, she managed only a perfunctionary standardised phrase regretting the death of her child before echoing the word *expand*.

"You're pregnant."

"How ..?"

"You've got that glow. Is the father any of that lot outside?"

Still struggling to recover, Rebecca affirmed with a huge grin that the one she was sitting behind was the guilty party.

"Handsome him, despite that scar down his face; looks as if you've done alright there, he was right concerned about you when you got off the horse."

Chatting as if they had been buddies forever, they made their way into the back room to sort through boy's clothes.

"We really should be on our way. You do think that you could ask that woman to hurry?" Frideger, not realising the relationship between Flavius and Rebecca, was showing, though politely, how irritated he was by the wait. "Caucoliberi could have sent men after us."

"What was your name again? I don't remember."

"Frideger, sire."

"Well, Frideger, if this force from Caucoliberi arrives, then we'll have to fight them, something you failed to do when we were there. And when we do get to Narbo, I want a full report from you telling me how you and my *escort*, were taken prisoner without any struggle whatsoever. So, I suggest you spend your time waiting for the lady to get dressed inventing a story which might save your neck!"

The two women did eventually come out, Rebecca with her hair hidden in a hat, dressed quite convincingly as a boy.

Flavius laughed, "I sent in a naked woman and I'm sent out a young man, interesting. How much do I owe you, woman?"

"The clothes are free but I want money for that mare. Rebecca here says that she doesn't want a horse of her own but there's some chap called Pere who's too big to be riding double and so, does need a horse."

Pere hearing his name appeared from behind a scrum of men and was introduced to his new mount; it was mutual hatred at first sight.

Rebecca kissed the woman tenderly on the cheek, thanked her giving her a considerable amount of money that she requested from Flavius. "Thank you. Goodbye."

"Goodbye, Rebecca." She gave a last hug, and changed direction to take in Flavius, "You take care of them both!" then turned and headed back into her house.

General Wittimir headed the welcoming party as the *king* and his escort arrived through the city gates. "Welcome, your *Majesty*." There was more than a slight hint of irony on the emphatic use of the title.

Flavius decided to take no issue with that or the inquisitive eyebrow at the *boy* sharing the horse. "Thank you. general. Once you have clapped this man in irons, I would like a full report of what's happening and a review of your defences."

"Frideger?"

"I believe that's his name; a coward who neglects his duty."

While this greeting ceremony was taking place, into the city came the last straggler, swearing and cajoling on a mount that clearly only worked at one pace, a slow trot, despite any and every encouragement to an incremental increase in speed.

"Nice of you to join us Pere, I'd quite forgotten you were among our party. Find food, lodgings for the horses, men, and this boy. General, shall we go?"

Delighted to dismount, Pere rubbed his arse, and grabbed the reins of the horse to drag it. The mare though had other ideas. Thoroughly fed up with her mistreatment, she refused to budge and strong though Pere was, he couldn't move her. Eventually, a groom came to his rescue and with a couple of pats and some words the mare trotted happily off with him.

"I hate those bloody things, I hope I never have to get on one ever again. Come on, *boy*, let's see where you can stay the night."

Rebecca meekly accepting her role as previously agreed on the back of Flavius's horse, followed him in the same direction as a loudly proclaiming-innocence Frideger.

The news that General Wittimir imparted was much worse than Paulus could ever have imagined. Not only the loss of both Castrum Libiae and Clausurae, but also the fact that they had fallen so easily in such a short amount of time, hardly slowing the Toletum advance, was devastating.

"How would you describe our situation, general?"

"In a word, dire. "

"I have to concur. It would seem that we are well and truly in the hands of the Franks."

"I'm sure that I can hold Narbo for some a goodly amount of time. I believe that once you are rested, you ought to continue on to Nemausus to galvanise thcir resolve and bring a considerable force here to drive Wamba back. The walls are sturdy, we have enough of everything; men, ammunition, food and water but the sooner we were relieved the better."

"Again, general, I can't disagree with you."

Having, against her wishes, and with her evident, though silent, reluctant disaccord, deposited Rebecca in a safe place behind the stables, Pere went a wandering to see what he could find out, and lo and behold the first man he bumped into was one of the men he had trained back in Tarraco. There proceeded a great amount of back slapping and manly elbow holding as they swapped stories of events. Well, swap is the wrong word, as Pere kept down the information he gave to an absolute minimum while receiving with relief what had happened in Tarraco. Wamba had kept his word and there was no sack of the city with life proceeding very much as normal. The show trials and executions seemed moderate and within the whole scheme of things, appropriate; two maimings of Wamba's troops, a couple of nobles blinded and a castration to death for rape. Reasonable.

"And there was some Jews who were executed as well."

Pere suddenly became more interested, "Who?"

"I don't know, Jews is Jews, there was three of them, ringleaders they was called. It was curious though as the punishments had been demanded by one of their own, who then had second thoughts, he lost his tongue for changing his mind and objecting, that was fun to watch."

Hillel came into Pere's mind quickly followed by Rebecca's family. With more force than he intended, he re-gripped the man's elbow, "Can you describe them?"

"No, not really," the man shook off the hold and began to rub it, "there was three old men. I think two of them were brothers."

Unbeknown to Pere, the *boy* had appeared behind them.

"Can you describe them?"

"Nah, as I said Jews be Jews. The last one wasn't supposed to be executed but insisted as his brother had already been topped. A clever stab through the eye, nobody saw that coming, least of all him!" the man began to chortle at his own joke only to receive a thump in the side of the head, which nearly knocked him over completely, from his ex- trainer.

"What was that for?" he whined as Pere led the *boy* away back to his seclusion zone.

Rebecca sat with her head in her hands, muttering.

"It may not have been him."

Bringing her head up slowly, "You and I know that it was. *Him* and Isaac were taken away, you said so yourself when you came to rescue me"

"But.."

"And only my father would demand death after seeing his brother killed. Pere, what have I done?"

"You? Why is it your fault?"

"I believed in this rebellion. I pushed Uncle Isaac into his role of leader. God knows, it wasn't something he wanted. Now he's dead and so is papa."

She broke down sobbing uncontrollably with her whole body shaking. Pere looked on not knowing what to do. Antonia didn't cry, well, certainly not like this, and if she did, she rejected any physical approach at comfort or sympathy. He tentatively closed the distance and offered his arms to help pull her up. No effort was needed as she stood and then buried herself into his chest blubbering.

It was this disconsolate scene that Flavius walked in on. His request for enlightenment was most un-general like. His voice, barely audible tiptoed its way to the clinging pair. This was no loving embrace; Pere's incredibly uncomfortable confused face showed that his body was being used as a support for Rebecca's emotions.

Removing her sodden face from the enormous chest, a lament came from deep within her, "Flavius, what have we done?"

*

General Wittimir's opinion of his *king*, never being high, descended further when he saw an obviously distraught boy being all but dragged to the private apartment where the ex-general would be resting before setting off to Nemausus. Each to his own, but still…at least he was doing it furtively, constantly checking that he wasn't being observed. Wittimir's unblocked aerial viewpoint from an upper window afforded him vision in many ways. Taking in the walls, defences and men at his disposal he was convinced that his defensive position was strong. They could resist for quite some time. His belief in this revolt was measurably weaker, and now, it seemed that the outcome was, at best unsure. His doubts extended to whether military victory would actually bring about a better state than the one they already had. It was true that Toletum had ignored and abused them for far too long and something had to change. Given the way things were panning out, it appeared that their fate lay in the hands of the Franks, something he seriously doubted that would bring about any improvement in their lot. He spied the bustling figure of the Jewish leader here in Narbo, Ariel. Forever busy was that man. Having never had much truck with Jews, he'd had all the stereotypical prejudices, only to have them overturned, one by one, by the attitude of this man and the people he led. They were serious, hardworking, seemed honest and without a doubt the most enthusiastic troops he commanded, not necessarily the best, but with an undoubted belief in the cause. They certainly knew what they were fighting against, if not, like everyone else, what lay at the end of this struggle.

Once inside, Flavius placed Rebecca on the one beautifully upholstered chair, choosing a kneeling, squatting type position in front of her while holding her hands with a direct view into her contorted face.

Biding his time, he impatiently waited, purposefully not uttering a word, mainly because he had no idea what to say, not being sure quite *why* she was so upset. Many possibilities of this most uncharacteristic behaviour spun through his head. She was such a strong woman that she wouldn't break down so totally about something trifling, he felt sure that it had something to do with her pregnancy, perhaps that horse ride had dislodged the child, perhaps…

"It's my fault that he died."

"No, don't worry these things happen."

Rebecca's head shot up at this overly callous remark, she glared with intense hatred at the man she thought she loved. Alright, it was a given that he was a military man, and death was all in a day's work, but this was her father they were talking about.

"Arantxa said that you could be cruel, but I didn't realise that you could be quite so uncaring."

"What!"

"He," there was a pause while she strove to choose the right tense, "*is* everything to me."

Completely confused, Flavius was all at sea grasping for straws. He had no idea what he'd said wrong to cause such a vehement reaction, in the end he plumped for something, he thought, relatively neutral. "So, it was a boy, was it?"

A tentative knock on the door stymied anything Rebecca was about to let forth, allowing Flavius an excuse to change his physical position with a hope of changing the emotional one as well. Springing up, he strode to the door and yanked it open to find the face of a Jew.

Ariel looked more than a bit sheepish, he'd been informed that the general /king had been seen entering these rooms with a boy. This information, which had been given to him with an enormous smirk, didn't fit any of his perceptions and previous knowledge of the man. For a fact, he knew that the man's participation in this rebellion was due to his sympathy for the Jewish position which had been instilled in him by his love and affection for a Jewish woman. The whole boy concept didn't make sense. As he had urgent information that the military man needed, he thought he'd test the validity of the *boy* question.

"General, I mean Sire, I err," Ariel's vision shot past the large figure in the frame of the door to someone who was quite clearly a boy sitting in an obviously distraught position behind him.

"What do you want?"

"I have information about Tarraco; I think that you ought to hear as soon as possible."

Rebecca's ears pricked up at the word Tarraco. She couldn't see who Flavius was talking to and before thinking that she was supposed to be playing the role of a boy, she blurted out, "Tarraco? What do you know? Come on in."

It only took a couple of steps into the room for Rebecca to realise he was a Jew and for Ariel to reverse his assumptions of gender and religious persuasion of the other occupant of the room.

Ariel had met the general before, although Paulus didn't remember who he was, so, he felt it necessary to re-introduce himself, "My name is Ariel, I am the rabbi here."

It was the female voice who answered, "I know your name, my uncle spoke highly of you."

"Your uncle?"

"Yes, Isaac, brother of Jacob, I am his daughter, Rebecca."

The scales from his eyes fell in unison with the rest of his face. He had not been expecting this.

"What's this information?" Flavius was anxious to get on with whatever was the matter in hand, Ariel though, showed a greater reluctance to speak. "Come on, spit it out, man."

Rebecca stood for the first time and moved closer, "I think I know what you are going to say; it's about my father and uncle, isn't it?"

Ariel nodded.

"I have already been told."

As relief appeared on Ariel's face, he closed the gap between them, taking both her hands and saying something in Hebrew (*May God console you among the other mourners of Zion and Jerusalem.*)

"Could someone tell me what is going on?"

Rebecca looked over the shoulder of her spiritual supporter, "You didn't know? What the hell were you talking about a few minutes ago when you said *don't worry, these things happen?*"

"I thought you'd lost the baby."

Such an array of emotions hit Rebecca that she came close to physically staggering; he wasn't callous, he was worried about her. The death of her father and uncle confirmed. Ariel being the closer, steadied her with a firm grip on the arm.

"Sit, child, sit."

Willingly she complied while beseeching the spiritual leader to provide her with all the details. Initially, he showed reluctance fearing the pain and distress that it would involve, only to be persuaded by both her words and eyes; she needed to know everything to be able to process it.

When he finished, he was no longer looking at the distraught face, instead choosing the far distant wall as a safer place. So it was with some surprise when he heard the next angry words,

"That little shit, Hillel. If I ever catch up with him he will lose a lot more than his tongue."

"I agree, child. The fact that one of our own instigated and called for these punishments is totally abhorrent. We are used to suffering at the hands of the Christians. This just feels so much worse when it's one of our own. The back to the Promised Land movement is so ridiculous, there's nothing left there for us."

"There doesn't seem much here either, especially if Wamba wins. How likely is that, Flavius?"

Paulus had remained still throughout the conversation not wanting to be seen or heard. His reaction to the question was less personal and more calculating. Wamba was playing an exceptionally clever game, taking the minimum of revenge and only against easy targets. Undoubtedly the Jewish auto-expulsion was popular, as was leaving the infrastructure of the local state relatively intact. People in general, and landowners in particular, would see no reason to risk their lives, family and property for no clear and overt reason. His cohort had been decimated along with the majority of the Tarraco force, the troops available in Narbo and Nemausus were considerably fewer than Wamba had. So, if the Franks decided to back the rebellion, who would be seen as the invading force, the Goth army under Wamba or the traditional well-hated enemy of the Franks? The future of this war was clear. The only thing to do would be to sue for peace. This would have to be done quietly without anyone knowing, otherwise, the force that they did have would crumble to nothing immediately.

"Well, things do look a great deal more difficult than a few weeks ago, but wars always have ebbs and flows." Opening the door he'd been propping up to allow Ariel through, he bade the rabbi farewell at the same time as offering him heartfelt gratitude and promises of a meeting with general Wittimir shortly. Turning back to Rebecca, he resumed his subservient position at her feet while holding her hands. This time he expressed the depth of his sorrow for the loss of her father, the stupid confusion and his concern for her immediate welfare suggesting that she no longer accompany him.

"What! You are saying I have to leave you, the only person I have left to care about in this world? No, is the answer."

Taking his hands out of hers, he held the sides of her face gently, and at the same time, firmly. "Rebecca," wary of the depth of meaning put into this one word, she lowered her belligerent stance, "I honestly believe this war is lost. Our only hope of saving lives is by suing for peace and hoping that Wamba's policy of leniency continues." She tried to speak but was prevented from doing so by his increased grip. "I do not know if that mercy shown will extend to me as I will be seen as even more of a traitor than the visible heads of the rebellion, especially now that Duke Ranosindus is dead."

"Marcus' father as well? Oh no. I really liked that man."

"Rebecca," There was that word again bringing her back to what he was saying, "as I said, I don't know what will happen to me, but I do know that I would not be able to protect you and our child in any way."

She removed his hands from her face slowly while trying to think of what she could say. She knew her place was by his side in whatever was to come. "I'm staying, get used to the idea."

"Rebecca,"

"Stop using my name, I know who I am."

"It's not that I don't want you by my side, I do."

"That's settled then."

"No, by worrying about you, I will not be able to do my job properly and many more people will die than would otherwise."

"Are you saying that I am a problematic liability to you?"

"I am saying that I love you dearly."

"So I am."

Looking into his pained face, she realised that he was doing what was best, not what he wanted. She may have to follow suit.

"Where would I go? Nowhere is safe."

"If we could get you back to Tarraco, Marcus is now the new duke, I am sure he could find you a safe hiding place until we see what happens." Rebecca's mind shot to the tumbled down cottage that Arantxa called home.

*

Peace, if not harmony and tranquillity, had returned to the residency of the Count of Nemausus. The streets, though, were a different story, with numerous incidents involving the Franks and the local population who viewed these foreigners with fear and loathing. It was clear that Chlothar was actually trying to control his men and restricted them to only one part of the town. It was also abundantly obvious that he was failing in his objective as incidents increased both in number and severity. Mutual recriminations had become the staple diet of the many meetings between the leaders of these forces. These in their turn, were held in an ever incrementally negative atmosphere.

The dour determinedly defensive face of the Frank General was sat in his usual position waiting for the litany of complaints, when the highly disturbed count made his appearance.

Without any of the initial cordial greeting that usually prefaced these events, Hilderic launched into his statement.

"We have received bad news. It seems that Wamba's force is making much quicker progress than we had anticipated. Our last report has them camped outside the gates of Narbo."

"Really?" Chlothar was genuinely surprised and shocked at this news. "What happened to your defensive positions at Castrum Libiae and Clausurae?"

"It appears that they have been overrun."

"Over run? It was but the day before yesterday that you were bragging about how solid those defences were, and how we should ride out to relieve them from attack."

Hilderic was at a loss as to what to say. He had been convinced that both of those places were fortresses and although would not be able to defeat the advancing forces, would be able to slow them down considerably to the point where a stalemate siege would be in place. That both places had fallen so quickly and with such a huge loss of men, including the Duke of Tarraco, was as baffling as it was worrying. It also had the effect of changing the power relations in this room, he was now totally dependent on the Franks, Chlothar would go from a contributing voice to the dominant one, as without his forces, the defeat was a certainty in a very short period of time, and even with his help, their destruction may only be a question of delaying the inevitable.

"General Wittimir will hold Narbo, and as soon as your main force arrives then we will be able to relieve him and enjoin the battle there." The twitching of the count's left eye, a new nervous tick, was duly noted by the Frank as he agreed with his host in what they both knew was a bare faced lie.

*

General Egica had decided, with extensive consultation with the new hero of the forces, Baron Evrigius, on a campsite within view, but not striking distance of the Narbo walls.

"There will be no repetition of your arrow feat here, Baron, no surrounding overlooking hills and look at those walls."

"Sturdy stuff, aren't they? I suppose we will have to settle in for a siege here. So, we may as well make ourselves comfortable while we wait for Wamba. Would you like me to send my men out on scavenging raids?"

"I think that would be appropriate. If you wouldn't mind, I would be most grateful."

The relationship between the two men had blossomed. They now gave off the appearance of having been bosom buddies since childhood. They chatted and agreed on nearly everything. Wamba being a bone of some contention, all and every comment or reference to him was avoided except for speculation as to his arrival.

After living, frankly, pretty well, for two days, the scouts interrupted a lavish evening meal, to report that a large military column was moving very slowly in their direction about three days' journey away.

"That gives us a bit of time to organise a hunt. My men tell me that there's a lush forest teeming with boar quite close. Would you care to join me tomorrow?"

"Most kind of you, Baron, I do love a good hunt. However, I feel it is my duty to be here if you are not."

"Very dutiful. I suppose you are right. I can't see Wittimir sending out an attacking force, still, better safe than sorry." The baron paused to take a really good look at this younger man. He had to admit that he liked what he saw. Having heard nothing but snide comments about this well connected youth, who had been raised to a status well beyond his years, he had actually found almost everything about the boy agreeable, especially the fact that he listened to, and, on many an occasion, deferred to his views on the conduct of the campaign. It was clear that the boy had a bright future and it would be no error of judgement to get him onside.

"Egica, I was wondering whether you have considered your future after this venture is over."

Taken aback, this comment had a sobering effect with Egica immediately on his guard. Trying his best to sound nonchalant between bites of chicken he said something like, that bridge could and would be crossed when it appeared.

Ervigius was not to be deterred from his path, "Have you thought of marriage?"

Bits of the bird found flight again as they were projected out with a splutter.

"Calm down. It's just that I have a daughter who will be of a suitable age in a couple of years. Cixilona is a very attractive lively girl who would make a wonderful wife, I'm sure. She is my only daughter, so, would come with a considerable dowry. I know this has come as a bit of a surprise and we don't need to talk about it seriously for quite some time, but I would like you to consider the proposition. It would do your future prospects absolutely no harm by being related to one of the oldest and most influential families in the kingdom."

*

Flavius, with an escort of seven and the *boy*, left the side gate of Narbo at dusk. Despite the enemy forces being in sight, it was thought that the *king* would have a better chance of getting away if he didn't draw too much attention to himself. Also, the attackers were definitely not in any battle-like status. Their only attempt at military awareness was keeping a healthy scouting system going. The majority had settled in to wait and spent their time in boisterous party mode, which included lots of drinking and singing So much so, that Paulus and Wittimir had seriously considered a sortie to attack, in the end erring on the side of caution as their numbers would not stand any depletion.

Once clear of the area and in a fork in the road, the little party stopped. The *king* and the boy moved slightly ahead.

"Flavius, I really don't want to leave you."

"Neither I, you."

"Then.."

"Rebecca, you know as do I that it's the ONLY way."

Dismounting with her defiant waning, "Well, if I do have to go, I am not going on that bloody thing." Slapping the side of horse, which was totally unconcerned about the opinions of the inexperienced rider that had been hanging off its neck since leaving Narbo.

"It'd be much quicker with a horse,"

"Not any safer. Pere is as useless as I am. We'd be more discreet if we walked."

Flavius had to agree as Pere had shown himself to be even more incompetent than Rebecca abreast an animal.

*

It was quite a sight; the massed slowly marching main force followed by a whole array of wooden constructions being dragged along by teams of oxen.

"So, that's why it's taken him so long to get here. Baron, I don't think we'll be needing your arrow innovative approach for this battle. I wonder where he acquired that lot. We certainly didn't have them back in Ilerda or in Vasconia, nor was there any word that they would be sent on from Toletum at any point."

Having never seen anything of its like before, the baron looked on trying not to show just how impressed he was by the amount, size and type of military hardware on show.

The guard of honour set out for the King's entrance to the camp was perfect, the right size, state of pristine dress, and the precision displayed. "Good day, General Egica, Baron Evrigius." The greeted men showed the due deference. "Formidable walls," Wamba took in the sight of Narbo in the distance, " that'll test how good this stuff I've brought is."

"Sire, where did you get it all from?"

"It was sent up from Toletum by ship. Some very helpful captain of the guard in a place called Castrum de Caucoliberi, who'd had an unpleasant time with Paulus, was only too happy to allow the ships to dock and provide men to unload them."

As he had been entering the camp, Wamba had seen signs of things that caused him more than a little disquiet. Knowing full well that the situation would be better dealt with in private but wanting it to cease as soon as possible, he took a calculated undiplomatic stance.

"I couldn't help noticing the abundance of food and some pretty unhappy females in the camp as I was riding through. Could you tell me from whence they came?"

The Baron Ervigius, wanting to show himself as a leader to be reckoned with, voiced with pride, "My men have been going out every day *collecting* from the surrounding villages and homesteads."

"Did you pay for the things you took?"

"Of course not. We are at war!"

The controlled anger in Wamba's voice was there for all to hear. "That practice will desist forthwith, the women will be returned to their villages, paid compensation, and any food that has been stolen will be paid for as well. All of that expense will come out of your purse, baron."

A spluttering with no discernible words interrupted the flow, without stopping it.

"These are OUR subjects, not the enemy, and will be treated as such. If some of their leaders are somewhat misguided, it is not the fault of the local population. They will not view *their* king as an invader. Set about rectifying this wrong as soon as possible." Looking directly into the puce face of the man opposite, he continued, "If you disagree with this policy, I shall ask you, and your troops to leave the field of battle immediately and take yourselves back to your lands."

"I refuse to order my men to do as you ask."

"Baron, please ready your force for an exit before dark. Now, remove yourself from my presence before this unpleasant scene and your disobedience to the crown gets worse. When I have put down this rebellion, we will have further words on this matter."

Baron Ervigius was now in a real quandary; to lose face, or to start a civil war at that moment. His force was sizeable, and would make a good fist of a fight, but ultimately they would lose, something which was made clear by the glee on the face of the man with the largest force, Teodofred, who had joined the little grouping as the king was speaking. A third option might be to join the rebels, he was sure that Paulus would welcome him with open arms.

"We will be gone by dark. This, though, will not be the end of this matter." Having made his decision by delivering that dark warning and with as much pride as he could muster, he left the gathering.

"Perhaps you ought to come into the tent, Sire." An alarmed Egica held out a shepherding arm for guidance. Once inside, slightly away from the others, he showed his concern, "Uncle, what was that all about? The baron is not an enemy that you want, and all over such a little thing."

"Since we are talking in family terms, *nephew*, I believe you have a few things to learn about statecraft. Firstly, that man is an enemy whether he's by my side or in open opposition. Personally, I prefer him in the latter position as it makes it clearer to everyone. Second, this war / rebellion, or whatever you want to call it, has a basis in something. It is not just the discontent of a few. It's a generalised feeling caused by us in Toletum not taking care of this area the way in which we should have. One approach would be to behave like a foreign invading force, the way in which the rebels want to betray us, in which case, even when we win, the rebellion will happen again in the not too distant future. The alternative approach is to show the people that we are all together, and their interests are, in reality, the same as ours and far from any alliance with the real enemy, the Franks. The way to do that, *nephew*, is by treating the locals with courtesy and respect, not rape and pillage."

A new-found respect and admiration came upon the younger man.

"I will make sure that the women are returned and the any food taken, paid for."

*

Their final embrace was tender and wordless. There were no words that could express their shared hatred and the deep emotion they felt at the arrival of the moment. The conscious unvoiced knowledge that this wasn't a farewell, it was more than probably a goodbye forever, made them cling together for as long as they could. It was a distant discreet throat clearing from Pere that produced their last face stroking followed by an almost military about face as Flavius headed back to the horses.

"General, about this horse, I really don't want.."

"Don't worry, Pere, Rebecca's already made that decision for you; you're walking."

There was a massive sign of relief, "I honestly believe it will be safer. Also, if we head to the coast we might be able to find my brother's boat."

Startled, Flavius exploded, "You can't go back there!"

"With Rebecca as a girl and in daylight, I agree. General, I promise, if there's any danger; I won't risk it, but, I reckon that there's too much happening for anyone to be worried about a poor father and son." Taking in the evident concern, he continued, "I promise, I will look after her. She will get back to Tarraco safe and sound. General, I mean king, I can't get used to that you just ensure that you win this bloody war and come back to join us. It'd be nice to have the queen staying with us for a while."

A firm handshake and a manly clash of shoulders was their final goodbye.

*

The walls took three days of pounding before a significant crack, a bit of a crumble, then all of a sudden a smallish breech occurred.

With the enemy forces camped outside and Paulus gone, Wittimir felt quite at ease. The walls were massively strong, their supplies of food and water more than enough for a long, long siege and his men were loyal, disciplined and in good morale. All in all, it had been a time of seeing the world through a half full cup. Fretting set in when he saw the extent of the firepower that had been assembled on the hill to the right of the main gates. Those wooden structures dominated the skyline and although the first few shots were wayward and loudly jeered by the defenders, the cup moved to half empty status upon the first stone's impact, it sent a shudder through the walls and up the spine of the general.

Three days of relentless daytime pounding with a few night time fireballs, which resembled meteorites, to keep them awake and alert, were taking its toll on the spirit of all those within the walls. Wittimir's plans had been based on the belief that they would be able to hold the city for weeks or months until the new Franko- Nemausus army would relieve them. The cracks that were appearing both in the walls and optimism within Narbo made Wittimir review his strategy.

The first peace envoy had been sent away with a flea in his ear and much scoffing. The second, just after Wamba's hilltop display of force, was treated more respectfully but still given short shrift. The third, who had arrived that morning, was afforded a full interview with the General where his unconditional surrender was sought in exchange for the promise of no retribution but for the punishment of a few of the main ringleaders, the general's name appearing among them. Preferring to die sword in hand like a true warrior rather than be executed at the hands of another in some gruesome public display, Wittimir rebuffed the third and last attempt at a peaceful resolution.

Later that very afternoon and a number of well placed stone thumps later, the size of the breach finally signified the emptying of any liquid Wittimir had left in his cup.

*

After two full days of walking and as the sun was beginning to lose its strength, they were actively on the lookout for somewhere a little more comfortable to sleep than the previous night. Although it hadn't got to the time of year when the nights were very cold, waking up in a dew soaked state was less than pleasant. Today it had taken hours of walking in the bright sunshine, something which made Pere most anxious, to dry out. His policy had been to hug the forest, using the tracks which afforded easy quick protection if needed, was being flouted, making him spin his head regularly like a worried deer.

"Rebecca, move quickly to that copse over there on the right."

She knew better than to argue or question and sprinted nimbly to the indicated place despite the fairly heavy bag she was carrying. Huffing and puffing Pere finally caught her up in a densely shaded green canopy with a view of the road they had just left. From this position, she could see the dust cloud.

"Who do you think they are?"

Getting his breath back, Pere squinted into the low sun, "I really don't know. One thing for certain is that there are a shit of a lot of them. With that amount of dust, and that's only the front part, I would imagine that there are thousands of them."

"Could it be Flavius or Wittimir?"

"I can't see how that'd be possible. It doesn't make sense that it's Wamba's forces, they're going in the wrong direction. I think we have to assume that they are hostile and try to find the deepest part of this wood to retreat to in case they have an active scouting system."

An old badger set near the bottom of an oak tree afforded enough space to squeeze into. Rebecca, not liking being told what to do was reluctant to obey Pere's instructions to get in and stay put, while he went to spy on the ever getting closer column, but stayed she did.

"Who are they?" Not wanting to give up on hope, the intonation in her voice was rising.

"Some baron or nobleman. Perhaps one of those from the south, I reckon. All the pennants and flags don't mean a thing to me, but, I did see something similar to them when I was with Marcus in the fight around Tarraco."

"Meaning?"

"I ain't got a clue. It don't make no sense. They can't have taken Narbo. Why a significant chunk of Wamba's forces would be heading home, I have no idea. All I do know is that we got to stay out of their way. We'll hold up here for a couple of days until they are well gone, and then head in the same direction."

"No."

"What do you mean, no? You don't want to go back to the general, king or whatever he is, do you? Cos if you do, he won't thank you for it, nor me, come to that."

"No."

"There you go again with the nos…"

"Pere, let me speak, please."

The dominant male trying hard to play his role went quiet, and started to look a little sulky. The realisation that he wasn't talking to a bunch of raw recruits was dawning on him, this was more like those Antonia type conversations he did so loath.

As delicately as possible Rebecca spoke attempting not to undermine his *authority*, "I think we should tag along at the end of the column."

"You can't be serious.."

"Pere, please let me finish. Arantxa told me many stories of her trip to Tarraco."

"I know, I was on the same *trip*."

"Yes, but you were with the head of the army not at the back. You were an organised marching force. Did you know what was following you?"

"Well, not.."

"Precisely. Arantxa said there were all sorts of people who strung along behind the camp following women. Mostly people tagged along for some sort of protection from any bandits or outlaws who roam the roads making them unsafe for lone travellers. We could be a father and son looking for the same safety in numbers. We wouldn't have to mingle with any one, we'd keep ourselves to ourselves, you could even say that I was ill. That would discourage anyone from approaching us."

Pere's silence and face was clear evidence that he was not dismissing the idea.

"It'd only be for a couple of days until we got close to Castrum de Caucoliberi. Also, it would make our entrance to the town even more inconspicuous than we had intended."

*

Wittimir and Ranimiro, the onetime abbot, now proud and extremely worried bishop of Narbo, stood near the breech watching men piling debris, stone and wooden structures high to fill the gap, listening and feeling the constant thuds of massive stone balls crashing into the nearby, still resisting, walls.

"That's not going to hold them up for long."

"Thank you, bishop, for that sage warning, I'm sure it would have taken me a great deal of time to come to that conclusion."

"There's no need for sarcasm, my dear general. I know I am stating the obvious. It's just that our predicament feels stark and real. Should we consider the surrender proposals?"

"Your name was on that list of those wanted for exemplary punishment as well. Do you really want to die trussed and bound in front of a jeering baying crowd? I certainly do not. It is my intention to die a soldier's death."

"Being a soldier that seems appropriate and right. My dilemma is that I am a man of the cloth, not the sword. We need reinforcements and quickly. Perhaps if I left under the cover of darkness tonight with just one servant, they wouldn't notice. I'm sure I could bring my influence to bear on those tardy Nemausus forces."

"So, you're proposing to run away?"

"Of course not! Even you must accept that without help we are doomed, it's just a question of time."

"And how long do you think it would take you to get to Nemausus to use your *influence*? I'll tell you; too long."

The new bishop didn't want to look the coward that he felt. However, at the same time he didn't want to die, a hero's, or any other death, in the near future. His was a long a glorious life to live, especially now that he'd ascended to the purple cloth.

"There is a force at Beterris, I could certainly get there and back in no time."

"Who's going where?"

With the noise of the rubble shifting, they hadn't heard the approach of the third man.

"Ah, Rabbi Ariel. The leader of the Christians here in Narbo is suggesting that he courageously, and singlehandedly, should go to get reinforcements. I suppose you, as the leader of the Jews, would like to join him?"

The rabbi's hands were clasped behind his back. His face, which had been a picture of confusion and worry, changed abruptly to one of anger.

"General, I find your suggestion offensive and impertinent. We Jews joined your Christian in-fighting with a clear objective; to fight for a better state within which we would be treated fairly and with respect. So, fight we will, have no doubt about that, and I request that you give us the respect we deserve."

Wittimir had never been a fan of the Jews, thinking them little better than vermin, however, all the dispatches received from all the places that had seen fighting had emphasised the bravery of the Jews.

"I apologise, Ariel." The general's shoulders visibly shrunk. "It's just that .."

"Don't worry, general. Actually, I think that the bishop's proposition is a good one, he should prepare for his journey as quickly as possible. If there is anyone with enough influence to encourage others to ride to our assistance, then I believe that Bishop Ranimiro is the man."

Ranimiro's face shone, reflecting the powerful sun's rays and his inner delight.

*

Castrum de Caucoliberi seemed a totally different place to their last visit. The pretty little village with an oversized Keep and as many dogs as people, had converted itself into a bustling port town thronged with men doing *manly* things; carrying loads to and fro, shouting, drinking and looking threatening with weapons. Rebecca had never seen Tarraco, one of the most important ports in the kingdom, ever look so busy. She was most grateful for her wrapped-up-ill-boy look, which had served them so well on the two day journey and was now keeping her out of the eye line of these uncouth and partially out of control men. Noticing with grim foreboding that there were NO women under grandmother age to be seen anywhere, she shambled lamely along trailing in the wake of her *father* in her hooded sack like garments which didn't betray any of her gender. Pere, whose only line to others on the journey had been, stay away, *my son is ill*, stopped to talk to people and had ascertained that the troops belonged to a Baron Evrigius, who had had a falling out with Wamba, and was heading home. The immense array of sail power had been the transport of Wamba firepower from the south and, apparently, the Baron was trying to buy the services of a couple of ships to transport himself and some of his most important men back home more speedily. Actually, the group of men that Pere had spoken to were hoping that they wouldn't be included in the seagoing group as none of them could abide ships, and they'd miss out on all the fun of an army's retreat through *enemy* territory.

While Pere was relating all this to Rebecca, her vision had strayed from his face and the important news to a distance behind his head.

"Bend down, move closer to me. No! don't look around! Take care of your ill son quietly."

Pere did as he was told, feeling and hearing a group of men, not boisterous nor out of control, more authoritative and dominant, brush past him none too gently, almost making him lose his balance.

"It's the brother of the man who tried to rape me, Dag, was it? If he wouldn't recognise me dressed like this, he might you. Pere, we've got to get out of here."

*

The Royal forces couldn't stream in, the breech wasn't large enough - it was more a case of filing through to be picked off one by one by the defenders. However, there comes a point when the defenders literally couldn't chop, maim or kill so many bodies and the file quickly became a stream, which progressed into a flood.

The clashes were disorganised, fierce and often individual. Egica's orders of no quarter, had been relayed to the defenders not by word of mouth, instead by clarity of sight as an unenthusiastic group tried to surrender by dropping their swords to the ground, only to be brutally dispatched. This vision of butchery steeled the defenders into a desperate, if not overly effective, fighting force.

In the streets, in the houses, on the walls were knots of men evenly or unevenly balanced, sweating, panting defending and attacking and leaving bodies, whole or in bits, strewn all over the places. Once the defenders realised that they were literally fighting for their lives, they gave an extremely good account of themselves, winning most of the early conflicts. Inevitably tiredness set in. After the first hour, Wittimir organised a strategic retreat to one of the main plazas. Here, for the first time, they were able to form a shield wall which held the attackers at bay for some considerable time. Egica's more important officers were slow to catch the vanguard, leaving their men relatively leaderless. The strength and effectiveness of a shield wall was known by all, which meant that nobody was stupid enough to try to attack it single-handedly. A standoff eschewed with milling individuals, sizing up their former compatriots until the tardy arrival of Egica with some heavy cavalry. The ability of horses to break a well organised wall was exceptionally limited, and using them here in these narrow streets would mean a mass of dead horse meat and triumphant defenders. The inexperienced general was about to order the cavalry forward when he was stopped by the wise words of Baron Teodofred, who had cantered up on his light pony, "Not the best idea, methinks. Any dead horses will give them another protective barrier."

The rush of battle blood that had gone to the younger man's head was cooled as he sagely took in the logistical situation of the forthcoming battle, "I believe you are right, baron. As time is on our side, we'll form our own wall to face them and sooner rather than later the archers will arrive to give us some protection by softening up their wall. Do you agree?"

"It's exactly what I.."

As the baron was speaking, Wittimir's defensive line moved quickly into an attacking stance, moving slowly and surely forward with incredible precision and organisation considering it was not a pre-planned nor practised move, instead being just a group of men, some with more, some with less, experience who happened to be in the same place at the same time with the same will to survive. Roles reversed, the attackers didn't form up quickly enough and some of the horsemen saw this as their time to shine by leading a totally ineffective and not overly aesthetic charge which barely dented the advancing line, although it did stop the forward progress as the dead horses, predicted by Teodofred, blocked their way providing a barrier which ironically saved Egica's men.

His attack frustrated by this unexpected event, Wittimir realised that his moment had come and gone. The only result of this restored stalemate would be a bloodbath as soon as Egica's reinforcements arrived. He slowly started his plan b. Actually, it was his final move. Peeling off troops from the back of the line they were sent to the one last defensible position, the church, to make their final stand.

The setting sun gave off enough light even in the comparative darkness of the church for Egica and Teodofred to make out the carnage of dead and dying.

"I'm sure Our Lord will not approve of this in His house."

"I never met Wittimir alive," Teodofred gently turned the head of the armoured very dead body with his feet, " his reputation went before him and will live on after him. A good soldier, who led his men bravely. However, making his last stand in a church can only be seen as blasphemy and as such he will be condemned to the fires of hell. And look at the company he has chosen to take with him on his journey to Hades; a Jew!" He none too gently kicked the un-armoured, maimed and almost unrecognisable body of Ariel.

"Don't get me wrong, I'm no Jew lover and am of the opinion that they need to be removed from our kingdom, but if I had to fight against the odds the way that Wittimir did, then I would like quite a few Jews, actually, the more the better, to stand by my side. If it hadn't been for them, we would have won so much sooner and wouldn't have had to pay this," he indicated the sheer number of bodies, "heavy price in our men. Perhaps because they are, they fight like demons."

"All the more reason to cleanse the kingdom of their presence. Scum!" A second more powerful kick was aimed at what had been Ariel's head.

The fighting had been fierce, bloody and long. All afternoon long the defenders held off attack after attack until blunted swords and weary arms could slash and chop no more. A surrender would never have been offered after the death of so many of their own, but the fact was that none was ever asked for, they literally fought to the last man.

"Whatever Wamba says, we are not leaving here for a couple of days. Let the men sack, pillage and rape to their hearts' content. Then, when they are exhausted, we will try to bring them back in line. They deserve their fun."

*

Speechless with anger, Wamba viewed the mayhem of streets full of dead bodies. All the enemy he'd been informed, their men had already been removed and disposed of with some dignity and little ceremony. Dotted among the carcasses were screaming, sprawled, mainly naked women, knots of huddled crying children and drunken men humping or drinking.

"Shall I impose some order, Sire?" Alaric ventured.

"No, general," shaking his head in sorrow and disbelief, "it's gone too far for that. I do not intend to wait here until this lot are spent. Could you inform my nephew of my extreme displeasure, and tell him that I will take the main force that hasn't already entered the town along to Beterris? He is to report to me there within two days, with a full explanation of what happened here, and above all, why."

*

It was a sad bedraggled bishop who wearily rather than triumphantly headed hopefully towards Beterris. The journey had been dreadful. Firstly, not long out of Narbo, his elegant steed had tripped, thrown him, and gone lame. Once recovered and brushed off, the choice was to return to get a replacement animal to continue their flight, or to make do with the less than elegant animal that his trusted servant was astride. The sun was rising, and with it came the significant roar of battle. The decision was made for them, well, them, by him. Clearly, the scrawny horse would not be able to carry two men, so the once invaluable servant became excess baggage to be left with the crippled beast. Stoically, without sound or look of reproach, the servant accepted his fate, being last seen standing quite forlornly in an over the shoulder glance by the one-time abbot, who was attempting to persuade his replacement horse to move from a cantering mode into something resembling a gallop. Beyond the solitary figure, a group of riders came into the cleric's line of vision, meriting a furious amount of thrashing of the unhappy mare.

Ranimiro didn't know this area, and there was nobody abroad to ask. Therefore, he regularly got lost, horribly so at times, turning a day's ride, into a three day and two night ordeal. Having to sleep rough, having nothing to eat, being in constant fear of being followed, he hoped he was riding in the right direction.

"Hey boys, look what we've got here!"

Dressed in a uniform he'd never encountered before, the bishop's way was blocked by a group of four on horses much more powerful than his.

"I demand to be allowed through, I am Ranimiro, Bishop of Narbo!"

"Narbo? Isn't that where we left the rest of the army? The place with the big walls? I get mixed up."

"I think so. Lots of strange names up here. Beterris? Where's that? Is that where the battle was going to be?"

"No, there's where we're going, I think. So, does that make him one of ours or theirs?"

It would appear that these confused scouts had little idea of the bigger picture either geographically or politically.

"Don't know. There are bishops on both sides. I reckon, though, if we take him back to Baron Teodofred, we'll get rewarded. If he's one of ours... "

Although Ranimiro had problems understanding their accent, what he did comprehend of the content filled him with dismay. "I am a bishop. Let me through or you will burn in Hell." With this forthright statement the cleric spurred his horse off the path to go as fast as it could, which in reality wasn't that quick, after all the beating and riding it had endured the last few days.

Ranimiro was a proud man, believing that he was superior to most men in most things and destined for greatness. One thing he certainly prided himself on was his horsemanship, so he felt relatively confident that leading this, admittedly undersized, undernourished mount, through the trees he would be able to lose the better horses. For the second time in so many days and through absolutely no fault of his own, he was thrown from a horse.

"There goes our reward from the Baron."

The scouting party looked down on a bishop with a broken neck.

*

"I am King Flavius Paulus, I demand entry." Given how he looked after days of riding and with his paltry escort, it was easy for Flavius to see the point of view of the guard barring his entrance from the top of the wall near the main gate. "Tell Count Hilderic that I am here, immediately!" With the steady stream of embellished stories of defeats, the atmosphere, tension and conviviality of the forced sharing of one city by two different armies became daily more strained until it had, inevitably, cracked and then snapped.

Upon receiving the news of the death of Duke Ranosindus, Lady Chlodoswintha was devastated and totally distraught. Forgetting her newly acquired role of meek acquiescent wife, she stormed into the meeting room where husband and the leader of the Franks, Chlothar, tried to contain and minimise the daily grievances of both parties. She directed her err at the Frank, "YOU! For weeks now you've been here, eating our food, drinking our wine, your men causing mayhem both day and night while the war is being fought and LOST. Just where is this large army being led by your brother? And when might it arrive here, if in fact, it does actually exist?"

Having never been spoken to like this by a woman, Chlothar was fuming, his anger being increased yet further by the fact that her suspicions were correct. His brother had sent word that the promised masses would not be coming as he'd decided that the fight was already lost and not worth sacrificing one Frank life for, all of which left Chlothar in quite a sticky position. An announcement of his imminent departure would inevitably lead to trouble with his hosts, and, as he was considerably outnumbered, may mean a defeat, loss of men and perhaps even his capture and ransom. Silently and menacingly he stood, walked slowly towards the agitated trollop and slapped her with all the force he could manage. She fell shocked and hurting to the floor, causing her husband to come rushing to her aid. A drawn sword brought Hilderic's chivalrous dash to an abrupt halt.

"It's about time that this woman learnt her place. You, *count*, are not up to the task, so it'll be me who will be forced to teach her." Bending slightly, while keeping his eyes firmly on Hilderic, he grabbed a chunk of Chlodoswintha hair and pulled her screamingly upright. The room filled with more armed men, divided equally between the two groups as had the previously agreed norm for all their meetings. The standoff was brief as Chlothar drew blood from Chlodoswintha's neck with the tip of his sword, "Anyone who comes any closer will be responsible for her death. Take her as well." The last instruction was to his men by the door where, Avina, the daughter, once promised in marriage to Marcus, stood open mouthed in front of them.

Huddled together with their leader and the females in the middle, the Franks beat a retreat to *their* part of town.

Back safely with the bulk of the Franks, who were totally surrounded and outnumbered by the Nemausus forces, Chlothar didn't feel too disturbed. In fact, this was probably the best way he would have of leaving the city with his force intact. Furthermore, his room in the quarter had suddenly developed a view, - he'd had Chlodoswintha stripped naked. Surprisingly, though much to his pleasure, she'd done it herself after being given the choice of doing it, or having it done to her daughter.

"If you didn't have that mouth on you, I would consider taking you with me."

"To do what? I am used to real men who don't have to capture women and girls to protect themselves."

This earned her a forceful punch and yell of fear and pain from Avina rather than the sullen recipient, "I may yet show you what a real man's cock feels like."

*

It was Bishop Gunhild who appeared at the gates to *greet* the King. Seeing and feeling the tension of sword drawn men everywhere, Paulus was most confused. "What's happening?"

"The Franks have taken hostages and are demanding safe passage from the city."

"So, there will be no saving Frank force?"

"It would seem not."

"I suspected as much."

"I didn't. Actually, I truly believe it's more of a reaction to events rather than a pre-planned move. If it were preconceived, then nobody told Chlothar about it, otherwise he'd have not let himself be sucked into his present predicament."

As they walked together farther into the town, Paulus could see a few quite severely mutilated dead bodies.

"Franks who were in the wrong place at the wrong time. They were, let's say, not overly popular guests." was the given explanation.

"Where are the rest?"

"In their quarter, negotiating with Count Hilderic."

"Why hasn't he attacked them? He must have twenty or more times the number of men."

"True, but as I said they are holding hostages. Perhaps I neglected to say that the two principal detainees are the countess and the daughter."

"Oh dear. That complicates things."

A shield wall and archers lined up in front of a group of houses which were flimsily barricaded with carts and barrels. A few decapitated bodies strewn about lay in a gruesome replica of the previously seen dead Franks.

"Count."

"General, King, I mean.."

The leader of the home force was visibly vexed and not his calm affable self.

"Given the state of affairs, I think just Flavius will do."

"Nothing looks too bright, does it? This situation, or the war, Gunhild, here, suggested a peace mission to Wamba, so we've dispatched our never overly enthusiastic rebel Bishop Aregio to Beterris to negotiate."

"Beterris?"

"Narbo fell."

"Narbo as well! Things are worse than…" At that moment a naked lady came into his eye line, "Really?"

"Every so often, he parades her for all to see." There was no fight, anger or even indignation in the voice, instead a dull monotone.

"This is not acceptable." With this Paulus marched towards the barricade. A spear like projectile landed close by reassuring Paulus rather than frightening him; it meant they had no archers. "Frank! Stop hiding behind women and get out here and talk to me!!" His voice was loud, sure and most authoritative.

Chlothar appeared in the doorway.

"And who the fuck are you?"

" The King."

This brought a snort of derision. "Not for too much longer."

"Perhaps not, but if I die, it'll be fighting like a man not hiding behind naked women."

"Pretty though, isn't she?"

Increasing his volume to maximum he shouted, "You Franks still believe and accept the concept of an individual challenge to solve a conflict. I, Flavius Paulus, challenge you!"

Chlothar had always acquitted himself well on the field of battle, having proved himself time and again more than adept as a military leader. He knew though, he was not the best at individual conflicts, it was for this reason that he kept a champion. Sadly, however, his champion had been in another part of town whoring when this little spat broke out, and had not returned, so, was presumed dead. This *king* was evidently a fighting man, he'd heard tell of the exploits of General Paulus, and didn't fancy pitting himself against him.

Ignoring the challenge, he boldly stated, "If you have come to negotiate then allow us to leave and we will return the women once we are out of the gates."

"So you are a coward. Fight me, and once you are dead I will promise that your men will be allowed to leave."

"I don't trust you, Goth. Lying thieving scum that you are, it's impossible to trust a Goth's promise. My last offer, choose, mother or daughter, I will release one now and the other once we are clear of the gates."

Knowing there was little more to be gained by insulting the manhood of this individual, he was evidently too frightened to fight, Paulus returned to the husband and father. "I'm not sure we'll get a better deal. If we attack, we will win, losing many much needed men and all your family. If we accept, there is the possibility of saving both females."

Chlodoswintha had been in a constant state of fear since the first slap, but there was no way she'd ever show that to her captors, especially since Avina was with her. The daughter had inherited much more of her father than her mother, being quite weak in character, and not what anyone would describe as a beauty, both of which made her a delight as a person who was constantly described as a *lovely girl*. Literally quaking next to her mother, it was all she could do to maintain her equilibrium.

Thankfully, her mother transmitted calm assurance constantly. Each time Chlodoswintha was sent out to be paraded naked, she made it clear to her daughter that she was more than content to show just how beautiful she was to everyone. Escorted through the door, her head was held high, her shoulders back in an attempt to give her breasts some of the firmness they once possessed. She struck a pose of pride personified, she didn't cross the line into glowing or gloating when all the jeering lewd comments were shouted out; just supreme serenity, not attempting to cover anything, much to the annoyance of Chlothar who dearly wished to see her cowed, submissive, embarrassed as well as embarrassing.

Hilderic's face showed the major quandary he was in, knowing what Paulus said was the stark reality of the situation. After a few seconds of thought, he sprang to life. "Tell him to set my daughter free, and clothe my wife before they are permitted to leave."

*

 Beterris had opened its gates without putting up any attempt at a fight or trying to negotiate any peaceful surrender. The approach was more reminiscent of a dog rolling over in front of its master, hoping not to get punished after doing something wrong, than two warring parties. Wamba, the benevolent master, duly complied, not quite going so far as to scratch the belly of the supplicant animal. His thinking was that it was as good a place as any to wait for his nephew and Baron Teodofred's army to catch up. His men were afforded the run of the town as long as they didn't take anyone or thing by force. Wamba himself set up shop in the house of the town's most important resident, who, as a strong supporter of the rebellion, had found it prudent not to be in residence when King Wamba came acalling.

After being told that a bishop had died falling off his horse while trying to evade some of the baron's scouts, the body had been brought in.

"I wonder which one you are?"

It was while looking down on the body, he was told that he had a visitor, another bishop, this one, though, alive and breathing.

"Sire, I am the former Bishop of Nemausus, Aregio and I have come.."

"Who's this?"

The newcomer sidled respectfully and humbly up to the king's side, though one step lower down to take in the almost peaceful appearance of the man who'd replaced him, "Abad, or Bishop, depending on your point of view, of Nemausus, Ranimiro."

"Your replacement, once you refused to go along with the rebellion?"

"That's the one. We both were in favour of the aims of the rebellion, as you call it, though not the ways in which it should be achieved."

Wamba took in the honest face of this huge man who would pass for a centurion, stone mason or anyone who wasn't a man of the cloth. "Oh yes, I remember, we received some correspondence from you. So, you stand there telling that I am in the wrong. I must say that seems either very brave, or extremely stupid."

"Perhaps a bit of both, Sire. I did not and do not believe that we should take up arms against the rightful, lawful and God chosen king. However, it is my opinion that Tarraconensis/Gallia Gothica has been, and is, treated most unfairly by the central government, both ecclesiastical and civil."

"Both brave and stupid you seem to be, you are also undoubtedly an honest man. We need more of them. Be seated and tell me why you are here."

Aregio launched into an impassioned plea for cessation of all hostility with the rebel powers, offering surrender, if certain conditions, like clemency for all those involved were on offer.

Wamba listened carefully, then outlined his desire that no more lives should be lost nor destruction caused. He found it impossible to agree to the clemency plea though, as he, and the barons, felt that a price had to be paid.

"I would though like to be fair and not punish more than necessary, just the main ringleaders. You could prove a useful ally in this, if you agree to be my advisor on this matter then I imagine quite a few lives could be spared. If not, I would have to allow the leaders of my forces to round up and punish all those involved, and, I warn you, these men are not in the business of grading involvement. As you may have heard, at this moment, in Narbo, there is exactly the sort of destruction I am seeking to avoid, going on."

Aregio sat back in his chair impressed by the statesmanship approach of this regal power. His position would be ugly and difficult condemning some and sparing others but it would undoubtedly save a number of reasonably innocent lives. Also, may God forgive him for the sin, it would give him the chance of rightful revenge on those who had pushed him and his counsel aside in their headlong foolish rush to war. Sadly, Ranimiro was already dead, others like Gunhild, deserved the same fate.

"Without enthusiasm or malice, I will agree to help you, Sire."

"I will make sure that the Church here will be the recipient of any forfeited property. Sadly, the Jews, thanks to my predecessors' foresight no longer possess land; there will be gold and urban property though. The Bishop of Hispalis is cleaning up in the towns we have already taken, I'm sure that you and him will see eye to eye on all these matters. I just have one further question to ask you."

"Anything, Sire"

"General, or the self styled king, Paulus… What do you think of the man and why do you think that he joined the rebellion?"

"Sire, I hardly know him. Actually, I have barely met him in person. From what I have heard, he seems to be an honest genuine man who fell into the whole plot by being bewitched by a Jewess rather than any personal desire for power."

"Interesting!"

"It is said, though the truth of it I cannot own to, that while in Tarraco he met and was put under the spell of a Jewess, who wielded extraordinary powers, influencing Count Hilderic and Duke Ranosindus as well."

It was the king's turn to lean back and exhale loudly, "A woman, eh? Now that does sound like the Paulus I knew."

*

The smallish group of horses stood in a circle just out of arrow range with a good view of the main gates. In their centre was their hostage strapped to her horse. Chlothar was rather pleased with himself and his successful extraction of his men from what could have been an extremely difficult and bloody situation. His Frank force had marched away towards the safety of Frankia, which was relatively close, quite a while ago. Chlothar, and his personal guard, waited in sight of Nemausus to ensure that the Goths wouldn't renegade on the agreement. Being totally aware of the vulnerable situation she was in, Chlodoswintha had been mute throughout the whole exit process, and this was a stance she maintained still. There was nothing she, or anyone else, could do, except trust this uncouth foreigner. She was pleased that her daughter was safe. For once, her husband had made the correct decision.

"I believe our forces are far enough away now. Be prepared to gallop." Chlothar manoeuvred his horse slightly behind his hostage. "My choice would have been to pierce you in a different way but…" with those words he thrust a long dagger into the back of Lady Chlodoswintha, causing an expulsion of breath as the only noise. She slumped slightly forward but was held firmly to the horse by the straps.

"Let's go."

*

Tarraco felt and smelled different though to all intents and purposes it looked the same.

The sea voyage back had taken much more time than the outward trip, and far longer than they'd expected or hoped. A dreadful journey which involved them either being becalmed by absolutely no wind, or being battered and buffeted by unexpected short sharp squalls which forced them to take shelter in many a cove.

Back in the streets of Tarraco, Rebecca gave thanks to the showery, seasonable falling rain which gave her the legitimate excuse to have her hood pulled up. Pere, a few paces ahead, felt no reason to hide his face. He was back and wanted all to see and know it. His lapping up the attention role acted as a lightening rod with any recognition and excitement being levelled at him, not the covered woman behind, who was evidently not walking with him anyway.

They were back in port area heading towards their respective houses, a route they could follow together / apart. Shuffling around the little mob of Pere greeters, she veered to the left, her house was very close.

Open mouthed she took in the unexpected, deeply upsetting sight. The main door was hanging off its hinges affording a view of the destruction which lay within, and noises emanating from inside. Sidling up, she got closer, and with the decreased distance came the increased clarity of the words.

"This is my house now! Get out! Leave that! it's mine!" shouted a familiar voice.

"Who said it's yours?"

"If you don't get out, I'll make sure that the duke will make you leave your own house. Now skedaddle, scum!"

A woman left quickly through what was left of the door, clutching one of Rebecca's pots.

Unable to bear any more, and without the strength, or the stupidity to confront the squatter, Rebecca turned while trying to maintain her anonymity. The relatively short depressing leaden trudge to Antonia's afforded her the new normal sight, all the houses of the Jews had been ransacked with anything of value, or use, removed. Shells, empty shells with all life prized out. Just how the residents must have been eked out and disposed of didn't bear thinking about.

"Ain't pretty, is it, girl?" Arms open, Antonia's face was a mixture of pleasure and pain. Led quickly inside, she found herself back on the precarious unstable stool she'd used in happier times with a mug of ale in hand. Despite the rockiness caused by the dodgy leg, Rebecca felt safe, and relatively secure for the first time since they'd docked.

"You're still looking pretty discreet, when I was at your stage with the last one there was no hiding it, I was like a 'ouse end, me. Got some colour in your cheeks…"

"Antonia, what happened?"

"Suppose you gotta 'ear it sooner or later, may as well get it over and done with. Prepare yourself love, it ain't nice."

Trying not to interrupt or show too much emotion, Rebecca listened with deepening sorrow of the "voluntary" exodus. Now there was a familiar word for Jews, of her neighbours; her people. What made it worse was that the whole uprooting was directed by, from the description; *one man unable to talk but giving orders with another subserviently doing all that was requested*, Hillel and his sidekick Jeremiah. Initially, there was some opposition, especially from the older members of the community refusing to leave their houses, businesses, and lives behind to be forced to pay to board chartered ships bound for nobody knew where. This *rebellion* was beginning to flourish until the Bishop of Hispalis came to lend a *helping* hand in the name of efficiency and speed. The turning point came abruptly after the first summary public executions, which finally persuaded even the most intransigent. Houses were locked and the keys were taken and guarded along with all the other precious things the expelled Jews could carry. The ships were barely out of the harbour when the sacking started. It was a free for all with the strongest, or the ones with the most influence having first choice, leaving the others to squabble and grab whatever they could.

"Wanna know 'ho's in your 'ouse?"

"I think I already do. How did she get it?"

"She was down 'ere, screaming and jeering at all the Jews as they were packing up, and lording it over anyone else. People were frightened of 'er cos of 'er connections. She made a beeline directly for your place, shouting about it being her due being given to 'er by the new duke for 'er years of faithful service. It were only after she were installed that we found that she'd been sacked and thrown out by your friend Marcus, but it were too late then."

The fate of her father, she knew, Antonia knew she knew, and nobody wanted to talk about it.

"So, there are no Jews left?"

"Yeah, one, you! And if anyone knows your 'ere, you're dead, and it won't be too good for us neither. Don't suppose you remember the old bloke who lived in that broken down hovel near the lower forum. Nah, no reason why you would, still, he 'ad friendship with an old Jew woman and tried to 'ide 'er in 'is 'ouse. That bishop made a right royal mess of the two of 'em, together. Not nice. And he made everyone watch. We got to get you out of town, perhaps that 'eathen's place down the coast would be the best spot, least for a while."

Despite trying to be as calm as possible, the underlying fear that was in Antonia's voice was relatively easy for Rebecca to detect.

"I just need to do one more thing. Then, I'm off, I promise."

*

The dark, cloudy non-visible moon night, had helped her incident free trek up town. Nobody was out on the streets tonight, there was no call to be outside enjoying the fresh air after a long hot late summer's day as it was unseasonably chilly. So much so, that her first sight of the new duke was with his back to a small hearth fire.

"Rebecca." It was clear that the new man of authority didn't know how to react, a state of uncertainty shared by Rebecca. She mock curtsied. "Your Grace."

They both managed to smile, then closing the distance shared an awkward embrace, possibly, no probably, the first time they had touched each other emotionally in their relatively long shared life.

"I tried to stop him. I'd arranged that he would not be punished but he…" pulling away enough he burst into his unprepared explanation.

"*Insisted.* Yes, Marcus, I've been told. So typical of my father, ridden with guilt about his brother that he forgot about himself and me."

Knowing that not to be the case as he himself on that fateful day, sharing that bloody platform, had clearly reminded him of his daughter. This information Marcus decided not to share.

"A most brave and principled man. You have my deepest condolences. The world is a worse place without him."

Struggling to hold back the tears, she did not want to cry here, and not in front of him, she moved quickly onto the topic of another death, "And I was very sad to hear about your father. I really liked him."

Marcus drew a massive sigh, "And inexplicably, he really liked you, too." Taking her by the elbow, he guided her to the same two chairs where she'd had her first chat with his father.

"Both fatherless now."

"I never really believed in this rebellion, it could never have worked, and the price we have paid, and are yet to pay, is far too high. The expulsion of your people, I do hope you know that I had nothing to do with that! I couldn't stop it. Wamba left that vindictive Bishop Iulianus in charge, and he was ably abetted by your *friend* Hillel. It was dreadful, I'm glad you and your father were spared that sight."

"Do you know where the ships went to? The only family I have left, my cousin and aunt, would have been aboard."

"I don't. I know that the Holy Land was promised, but I think it's more likely they were sent to Frankia or one of the islands."

A heavy silence descended. Never having been good at small talk in any circumstances, and this really wasn't just any circumstance, Marcus scoured his mind for something neutral to say while Rebecca was lost in the horrors of the execution of her family. Her father's gesture of solidarity to his brother *was* noble though it didn't compensate for his lack of consideration, thought and care for her well-being. She felt in some ways betrayed and undervalued, when she'd always considered herself to be the centre of his life.

"How are you feeling?"

Initially, Rebecca thought that her maudlin state had been picked up on by her notoriously insensitive former playmate, until she saw him pointing at her slightly protruding belly.

"Not so bad and should be much better now that I don't have to go back to sea. Not sure which I hate more; horses or boats. How's Arantxa?"

"She's tough, says she notices little difference."

Seeing that he had a strange almost apologetic sheepish look on his face, she knew he'd done something wrong. She'd never seen a sheep looking sorry for itself, though this frightened and contrite at the same time appearance of Marcus is how she'd imagined it, if her thoughts ever went that way, which they hadn't. Nevertheless, it was how she saw the situation.

"What have you done wrong?"

"Nothing, what do you mean? Why do you presume that it's me that's in the wrong? Anyway, it's not my fault."

"What isn't your fault?"

The sheep had moved from an apologetic to a repentant stance, "I'm engaged."

"We all know that, to a *lovely* girl."

"Actually, it's no longer her...." In fits and bursts of vaguely linked snippets of sentences, Marcus nearly explained his new promised matrimonial state.

"That wasn't easy to understand. From what I can gather you are presuming that defeat is assured and you are now making your bed, literally, with someone else."

"That's not the way I'd put it, nor did I explain it that way."

"No wonder Arantxa's angry. The father of her child engaged to two other women."

"Not at the same time!"

"Does the *lovely* girl know?"

"Well.."

"I thought not. Anyway, that you are a serial engager doesn't make it much better. What's this one like? And who the hell is she?"

"I told you, Baron Teodofred's daughter, Gelvira, I think is her name, and I have absolutely no idea what she's like! You talk as if I get some sort of choice in these matters. I don't. I'm little better than a stud horse."

"That's a new thought, you as a stud! Changing the topic, have you any news from the north?"

"Nothing good. Apparently Narbo fell fairly quickly and Wamba is now camped outside Nemausus. Defeat is certain, especially as the Franks have deserted the cause."

"Flavius said they would. Do you think that Wamba would accept surrender?"

"Given his approach until now, I would say so, but what price would he demand?"

"So, you're telling me I should get used to the idea of being a widow before even getting married?

"No, no, I didn't say.."

"You did. Probably the saddest part is that, for once, you are right. I suppose the only thing I can do now is join the mother of your child in the forest. There is one last favour I'd like to ask of the new duke."

"Don't call me that, please. What is it?"

"I want you to get Amalaswinth out of my house. I can't abide the thought of that old crow living there."

"I didn't know she was. It will be done, I promise."

*

Once all the royal forces were reunited, the journey to Nemausus was filled with tensions and no military action. The row was yet to happen, a pre-storm like heavy atmosphere prevailed in the vanguard where uncle and nephew had been reunited physically, if not emotionally. Baron Teodofred had lost his place at the top table, being relegated to the second tier, something which rankled greatly as he provided a significant number of soldiers and was still present, unlike the other baron. Evrigius, the dangerous coward had decided to jump ship on a similar principle, that being; how this war was to be won, and how their soldiers should be treated. Wamba's hearts and minds policy was all well and good for those in control. Their lives outside war had its fill of wealth and sport, a little more or less made not a jot of difference. The common folk who were occasionally forced into being soldiers needed to be given some compensation, the time honoured tradition was the spoils of war; rape and pillage. If the men were not rewarded, then why would they leave home and family to risk live and limb? Teodofred understood this, Wamba most definitely didn't. Thus, Teodofred's dislike, distrust and desire to remove Wamba grew daily, and, although he found Egica naïve and immature, he didn't lump him in the same dangerously useless bracket, instead seeing him as just a privileged well-connected child. Rumour had it that Baron Evrigius eyed the boy as a sort of prodigy, a long outside bet for future power which he'd decided to shorten the odds on by promising his daughter, Cixilona to. This caused the momentarily relegated baron to reflect on whether he'd been too hasty giving away his daughter, Gelvira, to the new Duke of Tarraco. Consoling himself in his relative ostracism, he knew his strength was the short game not the long convoluted idea that his offspring would eventually gain power. No, it would be his, and in the near future.

*

The streets of Nemausus had lost that ghetto-like atmosphere with trouble possible or even probable in almost any and every street once the Franks had departed. The visible real and on-going danger of walking the streets had been replaced with the foreboding of total and complete destruction. Refugees full of horror stories trickled, then flooded through the gates and local residents were stuck in the cleft stick dilemma of what to do; to leave and risk individual suicide, or to stay to accept mass suicide. The dwindling hope was that some sort of peace treaty could be negotiated to save them and their city. News of the destruction of Narbo was balanced against the fact that most of the cities in south; Tarraco, Barcino and Gerunda had been left relatively unscathed. On which side of the balance lay their fate, was the topic of all conversations. There was nobody who held out any hope that this fight could be won, the hated departed Franks had seen to that, especially with their final act of cowardice; the holed lifeless form of Lady Chlodoswintha. Her slumped bleeding body, still strapped to the horse was led to the palace through streets of horror struck residents, who had observed the procession with open mouths or teary eyes. She had been a genuinely loved person in Nemausus, seen as more approachable and closer to the ordinary folk than her distant, somewhat aloof husband. Without a doubt this sight signalled the beginning of the inevitable end in many a local.

Hilderic had spent the three days between the murder of his wife and the arrival of Wamba's forces shut up in the palace seeing nobody and eating little. The door was opened to nobody, no matter how loudly, or insistently, they knocked. Anyone near would have heard the almost door splitting banging that Paulus subjected the wooden barrier to on a regular basis.

The now nominally man in charge, the so called king, could get nothing done as nobody would listen to him. His authority was not so much spurned, as just ignored, with everyone who did deign to answer referencing their loyalty to the count, not to him. At his wits ends, he drew blank after blank of inaction. Furthermore, no word came from the peace emissary that had been sent to Beterris.

On the third day, the door opened and Flavius was guided through the shuttered rooms to meet a dishevelled shell of a man almost unrecognisable from the one who used to be so carefree and dapper.

"Hilderic, come on, man. We need to make preparations."

"It's finished. Over. Don't you understand?"

"I understand that you got me into YOUR dispute with Wamba. I understand that I have lost everything in this quest. I understand that if we don't show some sort of resilience there will be no reason why that lot outside the gates would want to negotiate with us and the whole of this town will be massacred. At the moment you are mourning for one, soon there may not even be one to mourn for everyone. If you don't.."

"Enough! The truth is that I no longer care."

"That's a luxury you cannot afford, or should have thought about before getting the rest of us involved. Get yourself cleaned up, we need to try to save at least a few of these people. I can almost guarantee that the likes of you and me will NOT survive, whether we fight or surrender, so, you won't be doing it for yourself. Think man. Your daughter is still alive and doesn't deserve rape and death because you have given up."

A spark appeared behind the eyes of the wreck of count at the potential demise of his daughter as he began to sit up straight.

*

"General Alaric, you are the only true professional here, what strategy do you propose?"

The command tent on the top of a hill overlooking the impressively sturdy walls of Nemausus, held four men; the king, his nephew, Baron Teodofred and the addressed general.

"There are a few factors to take into consideration. Firstly, it is most unlikely they would consider surrendering especially as news of the sack of Narbo, will have reached them."

This earned the nephew a scathing look from Wamba. "So, they will be set for a fight and / or siege. Given the reports we've had from inside the city, there are masses of people, mainly refugees running from us, the marauding *foreign* army," Wamba's reprimanding stare was accompanied by a snort at Egica. "This will make it more difficult for them to withstand a siege for long, as food supplies won't be *that* plentiful, added to the fact that there are, apparently, deep divisions within the population over how to defend. Undoubtedly, the Franks' departure affected the morale of the city badly in two ways; the fact their only allies ran, and the way in which they did it, by using hostages and murdering the much loved Countess Chlodoswintha. Given these facts, normally I would advise pounding the walls until they are forced to sue for peace, for an unconditional surrender."

"The waiting game again!" Baron Teodofred exploded.

"Baron, I do not believe that your opinion has been sought yet. Could you kindly wait until I request it?" The put down from the king was brutal, resulting in a severe case of frustrated, bristling silence. "I suspect that you have more to say general, pray continue."

"Thank you, Sire. I was just about to add that there is another factor in play now. Two columns of soldiers have been spotted heading this way."

"What? Who?" The baron's silence was broken again. Wamba's repertoire of withering looks was being tasted to the full today. "Sorry, but.."

"The fact of the matter is that we really don't know. It's the wrong direction for the Franks, so we suspect it's not them. But as to whether they are friend or foe, we, as yet, do not know. The one thing that is for certain, is that they are totally different armies, each about ten thousand strong. The farthest away will reach Narbo within a couple of days. The other could arrive here tomorrow or the day after. Scouts have been dispatched to find out more and should be reporting back anytime soon. All in all then, my advice would change from a waiting game to an attack, as soon as possible, with constant bombardments day and night."

The Baron began to applaud.

"I concur and I suspect that the noise coming from the baron means that he agrees as well. Would you like your forces to lead the attack, baron?" The poisoned chalice of accepting the first and most casualties was offered and Teodofred knew he had to take it. "We most happily will." The meeting was breaking up rather than down, which Egica suspected it may have done at various points, when an out-of-breath-sweating-profusely man appeared requesting General Alaric.

Taking the slightly sodden with perspiration wretch aside outside the tent's flap, the commanding officer listened attentively for a couple of minutes while none of the once leaving meeting participants moved. "Well, one mystery has been solved. The closest army are friendly and come to *help* us. It is being led by Dux Wandemir, a name and person not familiar to me."

"To me it is." Teodofred spoke without asking permission. "He's from the far south, below Hispalis. More than likely he's heard the war is all but won and now wants to say that he participated, and is due some of the credit and spoils. It would be typical of the man's character."

*

Paulus was genuinely bemused. The attack, when it came, was a complete surprise, not in that it caught them unawares. No, they were primed for any sort of movement, it was that there was no logic in it, the way it was performed, which would have been laughable if it weren't for the dire circumstances. Military logic, of even the most rudimentary kind, would dictate that sending in ground troops after a short battering of the walls with the artillery was a pointless waste of men. If, however, these troops were mega specialised with a particular target in mind, say, to isolate one of the towers, then it might be acceptable. This was absolutely not the case of what he saw today; they were a rabble. Initially, they gave the appearance of some professionalism, well formed ordered squares that approached in a wave formation, only to break up into groups of brave reckless men trying to storm the walls or, as was the case of the majority, just turning and running. It was pathetic. After seeing this performance, two questions spent their time vying for protagonism in Paulus's mind. How the hell did this lot beat the well marshalled forces in Clausurae / Narbo? and who was the inept commander?

Hilderic had performed well today showing himself to his men, being loud and authoritative whenever he knew what he should be doing, which wasn't that often. He'd never experienced a battle before, but he had the sense to ask for advice, quietly, from Paulus. The attack was so useless that it didn't require too much skill on the part of the defenders, and also had the added benefit of improving the rock bottom morale to a level very slightly higher. Perhaps it was only bottom now without the rock.

"What was all that about?"

"To tell you the truth, count, I really don't know. It just didn't make any sense whatsoever. They should never have attacked and certainly not like that. I presume that there are various barons out there with Wamba, who are all trying to impress, but overall control has to be in the hands of Alaric, a General I know, like, and appreciate. A good man whose traits do not include rash attacks. There must be some deep divisions in their ranks.

"Which offers some hope?"

"Sadly, not much. Still, if they are so divided, and we can put up a good fist of defending for a while, then you never know. We may well be able to sue for some sort of peace."

*

"I really didn't think that they would do it again, though I did warn that it was a possibility." General Badwila's voice was one of resignation not anger, "The Regis Fidelis has been training their leadership throughout the whole trip after that debacle outside Tarraco. Sorry Sire, but, I, we, thought that they would be better this time, especially as Veremundo, their commander, was publicly flogged and broken down the ranks. Apparently, the brave, or stupid, in my opinion, now, in everyone's opinion, very dead ones, who stormed the walls, were those who we had trained. Veremundo was among them."

General Alaric's head shook from side to side, "I would never have allowed this, if I'd believed that they were that bad. Yes, General Badwila had explained what had happened in Tarraco but that was, from what I understand, a very specific circumstance where the defenders were strategically placed and well organised. This is such a waste!"

"That, general, beggars the belief that you think that this time the defenders are NOT strategically placed nor well organised." Wamba was in the same state of mind as in Tarraco, annoyed that his forces had shown themselves up, and pleased that Baron Teodofred had received yet another thumping on the field of battle. At least he won't be so vocal in the near future, certainly not today, as he'd been deliberately excluded from this present meeting, an action that usually produced apoplectic entreaties of his rights as the man providing a great deal of the present fighting force to be automatically included in any decision making process. This time though, there had been a deafening silence.

The one metaphorically thumping on the door to be allowed to participate came in a request for inclusion from the newly arrived army of Dux Wandemir. He too though had been excluded and relegated to a previous summit, not with the king, which he had expected, but with General Alaric.

"Tell us about our latest arrival, please, general."

"Well, from what I can ascertain, Baron Teodofred's analysis of the man and his intention appear to be spot on. He's here for a share of the spoils of victory. Despite his claims of unavoidable delays in gathering his force, the massive distances involved, incredible forced march on his part, and his desire to come to his monarch's rescue from a reported huge Frank army, it's clear to see that he has brought his men on little more than a training exercise with the promise of loot to boot."

"General, after this war we really need to put those ideas of a national army in place. This state of affairs cannot continue. Inform Dux Wandemir that he may have an audience later this evening."

"Yes, Sire. For tomorrow I have ordered a minor attack in order to keep the defenders awake and to show that we are still intent on hitting them hard despite today's losses."

"Thank you, general. By the way, do we know any more about the other army that was reported being seen?"

"Yes and no, Sire. We know more of what they are not, rather than who they are, and what their intentions are."

"Continue."

"They're not Frank, nor are they Goth, which leads me to suspect they are probably Vascones."

"Vascones? But ..."

"Not the ones we were fighting a few weeks ago, but the lot that's based on this side of the mountains, more than likely from the area controlled by Lupus. As to their intentions, again, I am only guessing, but given their numbers, we estimate to be about ten thousand, I suspect that it was their intention to join the rebels and Franks against us. However, as the rebels have about collapsed and the Franks are not showing their hand, they are limiting themselves to *cleaning* areas which we left relatively untouched."

"This is monstrous! They must be chased out of our land immediately."

"Sire, given the task at hand here, that it not so easily done. We'd have to send a considerable force as they are a formidable foe, which would seriously deplete our options here. Furthermore, Frank scouts have been watching, which again, we believe with a considerable amount of certainty, that an army is gathered on their side of the border ready to take advantage of any perceived weakness on our part, which is considerable since the departure of Duke Evrigius . The fact of the matter is, if we do split our army, we may end up fighting on three different fronts; the Vascones, the Franks and the rebels."

This caused the renowned pacing of the monarch to start in earnest while the others, used to this reaction, waited patiently. The delay was much shorter than on previous occasions.

"We'll send a small delegation; General Badwila, I would like you to head it so it is seen to have some gravitas, with a message saying that if the they do not leave our kingdom forthwith, then, once the rebels here in Nemausus have been defeated, we will take ALL our armies to this part of Vasconia, or whatever they call it, to lay waste to the whole area.

Furthermore, if they persist in their *cleansing* activities on their retreat, then the same retribution will be enacted on their land and peoples. It'll be the scorched earth policy of the last campaign, multiplied by ten. Be bold, forthright and above all clear. This is not a threat, this is a promise of inevitable consequences."

*

After a day of being decisive, ordering people around and having the luxury of not dwelling on his profound depression, Hilderic found himself in his favourite chair looking at the seat where she'd spent so many hours sitting near him around the fireplace, dwelling on what might or should have been. Thoughts about the future, something he generally avoided as it no longer really mattered what happened, were forced upon him by the arrival of not one, but two messengers. How they'd got through the masses of the surrounding army was well beyond him. If the contents of the first message were surprising, the second were totally bewildering. Both parchments lay strewn on the table when the sent-for nominal king entered.

"These were delivered to me, when I believe that you should be the true recipient."

Taking in the count's regression to his shrivelled introspective form, Paulus randomly picked up one of the two messages, which, as luck would have it, was the first to arrive chronologically.

"This is good news; a large Vasconis army willing to be of assistance."
Hilderic didn't respond in a vocal way, he merely indicated the second.
"What! How is this possible?"

"It doesn't make a great deal of sense, does it? The Franks cause havoc here, murder my wife and run away, only to offer the help of a huge army which is but a couple of days march away." The Count's words were spat out with the contempt he thought they deserved.

Paulus was sat on the edge, the very edge, of Lady Chlodoswintha's chair.

"With both of these armies, we could actually win," were the words that accompanied, and showed, his changing physical and mental stance.

"What price victory?"

"True. Even if we presume that this brother, Theuderic, knows not what Chlothar did here, it still means that we will be incorporated into the Frank kingdom. There will be no independence. Our lives will be forfeited one way or another as we will not be allowed to live for very long after they take control."

"You speak the truth. Where does that leave us now, though?"

"The same place as we were this morning, in a hopeless position. However, if it were known that we have this option of Franks, it may strengthen our hand in the pursuit of a surrender to Wamba."

"The last bishop we sent, Aregio, didn't come back. Presumably, he has made his own peace with Wamba. This time we could send Argebaud in the hope that he might actually represent us as he's as involved as we are, and thus, has as much to lose as us."

"So, I take it we are disregarding the Frank offer."

"I cannot and will not fight with / for the people who slaughtered my wife."

"Fair enough. The Vascones won't do anything on their own either. So, we carry on as if we'd never received these," he indicated the messages " but inform Wamba that we do have other options if we are forced to use them."

"Correct. How long do you seriously think we can hold out?"

"A couple of weeks. After that sort of time and knowing that we *do* have other options, plus we also know that they are a fractured force, they may be amenable to talks."

*

The talks actually came about two days, not two weeks later, when the circumstances of the defenders could be described as little more than dire; annihilation was their lot.

Day and night massive boulders had crashed into one part of the wall, fire arrows rained constantly, not giving time to put out one area alight before another ignited. A breach in the wall was inevitable. Duly it came about on that second day in a remarkably similar way to what had happened in Narbo, these new massive catapults were making more than their mark. Alaric's variation on the Narbo theme came by not attacking through the newly made gap. In this version, it was a ruse, by sending his most experienced troops to look as if they were about to assault, forcing the defenders to take note and replicate in similarly large numbers to repulse the onslaught. Meanwhile, using the newly arrived and impressively enthusiastic army of Wandemir to attack the walls in a more traditional way on the opposite side of the city where the defensive line had been thinned to the point of non-existence. Paulus's realisation of his distribution error came as attackers appeared behind his orderly lined up troops facing the breach *inside* the city. Mayhem ensued. Not a traditional battle with formations, feints, attacks and bloody shield walls; this was one to one street brawls with only one inevitable winner; the force with the most men.

It was bloody, very bloody, with hundreds of casualties, bodies, bits of bodies, screaming mutilated forms lay everywhere as the defenders tried to hold back the ever increasing tide of invaders. Count Hilderic led from the front and by example. Throwing all caution to the wind; he encouraged his men to counter-attack making great inroads into the not quite so desperate nor ferocious royalists. Such daring couldn't last too long, though it was longer than he had expected. Knowing that he had no chance of surviving the peace, nor seeing any reason to continue living, he actively sought an end to his misery, an end which would befit his ancestral line, dating back, at least, four centuries of Goth warriors. Leading charge after charge, he and his closest men cut swathes into the oncoming lines, time, and time again causing a rush of adrenalin and pride. After what seemed like an eternity of killing, but in fact was no more than a morning, they were so successful that there came a point that they had no one to fight against. Controlling their little area around a well; their present enemy, wearing Baron Teodofred's colours, fearing to take on such an effective group sought easier prey elsewhere.

"Drink lads, we need to move from here and try to join the main group retreating to the amphitheatre."

It was while drinking and congratulating each other on their impressive achievements that the count realised his mistake. There were three roads to the well, he should have kept his retreat line secure, he hadn't. Massed ranks of soldiers filled all three exits, each street was coloured differently, denoting three separate armies. Two of them gave off the appearance of fearful nerves The other, the professional exercitus, was the one which finally led the assault. The order could be heard; "Take the count alive." as the inevitable slaughter of his men took place all around him.

Hilderic's determination not to live came about through what might have been interpreted by some as neglect when he received a sword thrust in the chest where his body armour should have been. Upon seeing his impending fate, he chose not to replace the loosened, while resting and drinking, article. This was his choice. The oncoming blade was met with pride while his thoughts were on a dagger protruding from his wife's back.

Paulus had fared better, conducting an orderly retreat. It wasn't planned, nor was it a rushed affair, it was the inescapable destiny of an overwhelming force against a determined defence that pushed them back, and back, and then back again. The lull in the fighting came as it got dark and neither side had the strength to continue. Through determination and some considerable leadership skill Pauls had managed to get most of his men back to the amphitheatre intact. In truth, it also had a great deal to do with the disparate ineptness of the fragmented attackers, something not lost on the former general, soon to be ex-king. If only they'd had some kind of parity he could have taken the day fairly easily. The fading twilight brought two things; the Wamba emissaries and clarity of his inescapable defeat.

This arena had seen many a gladiator in its long history and this time two opposing bishops came through the arch. Aregio, looking at least in size a prize fighter, wore a smug self satisfied expression which was enhanced by a continual head shaking to show those in any doubt, his disapproval, and Argebaud, wearing the haunted look of a condemned man.

"Well, I didn't expect two bishops. Bishop Argebaud, you look dreadful. Have a seat before you fall down." Paulus took in the other man, "I don't know you personally, though I suspect that you must be Aregio. Count Hilderic told me about you."

"I doubt that would have been too complimentary. However, I am not here to speak ill of the dead."

The now seated bishop interrupted, "His body was brought to King Wamba's tent this lunchtime. It seems as if he loosened his armour in his desire for death rather than capture."

"A brave man who will be sorely missed in these parts."

"I am not so sure of that. Some of us advised against this foolish venture which has brought the people nought but death and destruction. I doubt those who survive will think of him so fondly. However, I am not here to talk about him, I am here to accept your surrender."

"You mean negotiate."

"No, there will be no negotiation; the surrender will be unconditional."

"Why would I want to do that?"

"Because you have lost. The only thing in doubt is when you lose, and how many of *your men*, or as I prefer to see them, *my flock*, have to die due to your stubbornness or vanity."

"I believe we have shown that quite a lot of Wamba's, or whichever useless Baron's forces, will be dispatched to the afterlife along with your *flock*."

Argebaud interrupted again, "Most true. In fact, General Alaric and the King actually praised your well manoeuvred retreat." This earned him a withering look from the ascendant bishop which didn't stop him from speaking. "Wamba has made it clear that some of us will have to be maimed or executed. I believe that I am one of these, but the city will not be destroyed nor will the population in general suffer massively. I am here not to demand like my colleague, but to appeal to your decency, something I know you have, as you never joined this fight for power or prestige. You honestly believed that we were doing the right thing and hoped, as did we all, that no violence would be necessary. Still, it is abundantly obvious that we miscalculated and now have to pay the price, something that ordinary folk could be spared."

*

"This dis-control, as you call it, MUST stop! No, must be stopped by you, immediately!" Aregio's enormous frame was shuddering with anger; his face was puce with indignant emotion, none of which was tempered by the fact that he was addressing the king and victor. "I promised, in *your* name, that there would be no sack of the city."

These words and their manner of delivery caused consternation and equally raised voices on the part of the King's entourage, but not in Wamba himself while he continued his pacing. The fact of the matter was that he'd been trying all day, without success, to remove the *dis* from his description of the situation. Baron Teodofred's men had been corralled by the Regis Fidelis in the quarter once occupied by Franks, only for Wandemir's latecomers to run amok on the other side of the city. No amount of hectoring, threatening or disciplining of the Barons was having the desired effect, houses continued to be looted and women used as the spoils of war. What was more, the disciplined exercitus was raging to the point of rebellion as they were not participating in all the fun. The chaos could, at any moment, turn to anarchy, and there was little or nothing he was able to do about it.

"Now, here is the thing bishop. I am King without power, it pains me to say this but I cannot control this situation without things getting considerably worse. I wish I could. If you could offer any divine inspiration and help, I would be most truly grateful. General Alaric here tells me that if I don't take off the not overly effective shackles that exist, and allow a complete free-for-all, then I am in danger of a second rebellion and / or a civil war between the state forces and the private baron armies. Tell me bishop, what would you do in this situation?"

Yet again Aregio was impressed by the honesty and decency of this man who bore little relation to what most people supposed a monarch to be like. The terrible fact was that there was nothing to be done, the sack had to follow its course until it ran out of drink filled energy.

"Surely, Sire, …" Aregio, for one of the first times in his life, was lost for words.

"I see you see my dilemma. My order will be that we will turn a blind eye for one day and one night. ALL forces, with the exception of the Regis Fidelis, will be allowed free reign." Seeing the pained expression on the bishop's face he quickly continued, "I am sorry, but that is the only way. A considerable amount of money has been promised to the Regis Fidelis to stay sober and not participate, and from dawn tomorrow, impose a harsh curfew on the city. The barons have, reluctantly, agreed and communicated the time limit to their centurions. I suppose that it'll take a few summary executions to restore order, but restored it will be.

Fortunately the rebels have been disarmed and will not be able to leave the amphitheatre. Nevertheless, they will hear what is going on outside, which will cause some resentment. So, I suggest that we start the trials and punishment shortly after dawn to distract their anger somewhat."

*

They could be heard marching steadily through the streets with an ever increasing group of curious onlookers in their wake. An orderly smartly manoeuvred halt was officially yelled as they stomped to serious stillness in the puddles outside Pere's house. The occupants, bar one, were enraptured, intrigued and perturbed. The one, was nothing except extremely worried.

As it had been late when Rebecca returned from the palace, she was easily persuaded, with a mug of ale in hand, to stay the night before setting off down the coast after a decent breakfast. Having taken extreme precaution to arrive in port area unnoticed, a fact helped by the increase in the showery weather of earlier, to almost a torrential downpour, she'd felt relatively secure in her decision to delay her departure. That security was now dust in the wind, or better said, soldiers in the puddles. Escape was impossible, hiding in the tininess of the cottage was equally difficult. So cowering in the corner was her only option.

"What the hell!" Pere, authoritatively yanked open the knocked on door. A rather sheepish looking official who'd been Pere's subordinate at one time, stood parchment in hand, only shaking slightly as he began to read, "The occupants of this house are to be removed, by force if necessary.."

"Who the 'ell are you? And what in God's name are you saying? This is our 'ouse, I, we, pay the rent regularly, and on time, you can't…"

Antonia had snuck up to Pere's side for two reasons, one to offer physical help, and the other to block any possibility of the soldier seeing inside. The kids gathered around her thighs, not knowingly but effectively increasing the blocking.

"Antonia, be quiet!" Pere's tone was harsher than he had intended, something which earned him a vicious look but obedience. "Let the man finish."

Rolling the parchment, the man's voice softened, "If you two could come with me; I'd be most grateful."

"I ain't going nowhere. Send in all that lot, and we'll see who's still standing in ten minutes."

She snarled while extracting a previously unseen meat cleaver from somewhere.

The official's face dropped and took on a pleading look as he addressed Pere.

"I was so hoping that there wouldn't be violence."

"There won't be. Antonia, put that away." A husband and wife standoff ensued, Rebecca, well knew who usually won these. "Please."

Antonia lowered her weapon.

"What should we bring?"

A much relieved officer relaxed visibly, "Nothing at the moment, just you two. We'll return for your things later."

Not daring to move from her darkest corner, Rebecca squatted and weighed up her options again, coming to exactly the same conclusions as she had previously, she had no choice, she had to wait and hope.

Pere quickly got into matching marching step with the soldiers, while Antonia, not so elegantly, scurried her best to try to keep up. The kids, enjoying this game, were skipping happily along in her wake. By deliberately trying not to keep the rhythm, and with an air of nonchalance, she wanted to give the appearance that she'd let this clanking iron sandaled lot clear the way for her through the well overcrowded streets.

Some people called out support, a few others, Antonia's well known enemies, jeered and catcalled. The parade was nearly over when above the marching sound they could hear a strident high pitched almost squealing voice.

"Don't you dare touch me! By who's right? I was given this expressly by the new duke. I said, don't touch..."

Turning the corner, an interesting sight appeared, Amalaswinth being all but carried by two soldiers out of Rebecca's family house.

The onlookers who had been following the marchers, surged forward to see the show of Amalaswinth kicking, screaming and trying to bite her ejectors, who unceremoniously dumped her on the ground in front of the official. Standing up straight while brushing herself down, and doing her best to restore some of her dignity, she addressed the man.

"Finally, a bit of authority! These two ruffians have removed me from my property, have them arrested. And, I will see to it, after I have spoken of this to the duke, that they will be publicly flogged."

With his still not totally stable hands he uncoiled this morning's much used parchment, and in a voice loud enough for all to hear, despite the evident excitement levels, he stated clearly, "This house, which once belonged to the Jew, Jacob, and was forfeited due to his treasonable activities, is now the property of former centurion Pere and his family."

*

The King's pageant through the streets from his temporary lodgings in the ex-count's palace to the amphitheatre was a somewhat surreal affair.

Escorted by his most personal of guards, the rest being occupied in imposing the curfew ending of the *festivities*, the streets were not filled with cheering crowds of soldiers and local folk happy to see their rightful monarch. Instead, the eerie silence was only punctuated with the groaning of the wounded, dying and distraught. Lifeless bodies competed with the barely alive for public sprawling space. The soldiers in the vanguard were literally tossing bodies aside so their presence wouldn't interfere, or get tangled in the hooves of the horses.

Wamba didn't avert his face as Alaric had advised; taking in every detail, his anger seethed inside. His silence was broken only once on the short journey as he turned back to the barons riding directly behind him, who apparently found some of the sights quite jovial.

"Have some respect, these are *OUR* subjects!"

As they were entering the gates of the amphitheatre, a galloping horse caused the escort to unsheathe swords in readiness. It was a lone rider. Both man and horse showed evident signs of fatigue, filth and sweat.

"Thank God. I thought that I'd be too late."

"Nice of you to join us, bishop. The trials are about to start. You are quite a sight! I will certainly not allow you to sit in judgement in that state." Indicating one of his most trusted guards, "Would you mind escorting the Bishop of Hispalis back to the palace, where he can clean up somewhat and change his clothes?"

"But.."

"If you are quick, you won't miss too much. Actually, I am pleased you are here as I would like you to perform one of today's clerical duties. We will wait for you, if you get a move on.."

The lathered horse and sweaty bishop followed the guard at a canter as his mount absolutely refused to go any quicker.

The carpenters had been busy during the night erecting a long platform directly in front of a seated area where the newly arrived dignitaries were to sit.

The king took the most elevated position, flanked by a standing Alaric, and a couple of armed guards. In the row below, and slightly to Wamba's right, sat the significant, in terms of quantity of fighting men, barons, plus his well out of favour nephew, who had the sense to keep a low profile, especially since the only one who had ever taken a shine to him, besides his uncle, Baron Evrigius, had left under such a cloud . Below them, were other minor nobles and Bishop Aregio.

This regal corner of the amphitheatre was relatively quiet and empty, which was in stark contrast to the other end where there was a throng of men emitting a hum of anger. It didn't get any louder than a hum due to an effective noise level management scheme whereby anyone deemed to be making the sound, or perhaps someone close, was speared with the point of a javelin.

*

The sun set late this time of year, and it was finally disappearing behind the western walls when Wamba called a halt to the proceedings. It had been a long, long day and the last day for quite a few.

Insatiable in their blood lust, the two leading barons agreed for one of the first times this day by calling for a proper finale with the three ringleaders judged, humiliated and executed. Strangely, it was the Bishop of Hispalis who jumped in, if not in defence of the king, it was more like a point of order, which would show to all those present just how important he really was.

"Earlier this evening, you may have noticed, I received a message. It was signed by three Bishops; Julian, Taio and Quiricus. In it, they requested that Paulus Flavius be returned to Toletum to stand trial and receive his punishment there."

"*Requested?*"

"Sire, it was more of a suggestion rather than an instruction. Your decision on the matter is final and paramount, obviously. However, given the importance of the rebellion in national terms, they believe its leader warrants a national trial in the capital."

"That actually makes sense."

"They further offer the *suggestion* that this said individual, who claimed to be king, be paraded in the most humiliating of ways through the streets of all the most important urban centres on your return to Toletum."

"They do, do they?"

Wamba stood for the first time in many, many hours, surveying the handiwork of the day, it didn't make him pleased or proud; just something that had had to be done. In front of the improvised stage there was a man struggling to carry a basket full of heads. Speaking quietly to Alaric and indicating the gruesome load, "How many?"

"I been counting throughout the day. I stopped at fifty, Sire."

"Rather than coming back tomorrow, we will finish with one last *big fish*. Bring out Argebaud and Gunhild."

When the two men were escorted onto the raised platform, the behaviour poise and dignity of both, was exemplary. The barons rose to speak only to be told in no uncertain terms by General Alaric to remain seated and quiet, this case would be judged by the King.

"Bishops, or should I say ex-bishops? You have been found guilty of treason against, state and Church. There can be no clemency for you. Without a doubt, you, and those already dead like Abbot Ranimiro, Count

Hilderic and Duke Ranosindus, are responsible for all this death and destruction. The first part of your punishment is *capillos et cutem detrahere*." Wamba nodded to the executioner armed with a long sharp knife. Forcing first Argebaud, then Gunhild to an unsteady kneeling position, their balance being effected by having their hands and feet securely bound, he slowly, with not a great deal of care, scalped each one. Blood streamed down their face, and clotted matted hair lay in clumps in front of them. The men, in obvious extreme agony, remained silent, no screams had accompanied their torment, only a massive expulsion of pained air. Argebaud, unable to withstand anymore, toppled to the side. "Take him away." The bleeding ex-bishop was dragged unceremoniously to the side. "Gunhild, do you have any last words?"

A brave proud man raised his bloody face and in a bold deep voice, belying both his size and state, all but shouted, "We believed, and still believe in a separate state. None of us wanted violence, and none imagined that so much destruction would be our lot. We wanted peaceful co-existence with our brother Goths, not war, not supremacy, just the right to govern our own affairs. Personally, I regret greatly that things have turned out the way they have. However, I DO NOT regret trying to create a better, more just life for our citizens."

"Carry out the sentence."

*

The day had started with many officials and landowners, known rebel supporters, being thrust forward in varying states of disarray. Their fate, it seemed to Wamba, who didn't demean his office by actually participating in their judgement, was quite arbitrary, depending greatly on the rivalry of the senior barons. The first act for all the accused was that Iulianus, the Bishop of Hispalis, gave a speech, which, thankfully, decreased in length as the day wore on, pointing out how they, *the accused*, had caused displeasure to their God by rebelling against His choice of monarch, and as such, they, *the accused*, would be ex-communicated and denied entry into the gates of Heaven. Then, once the charge had been read, the barons argued about the degree of punishment that should be imposed. Generally, the three main options to choose from were, the removal of one eye, blinding totally or execution. At times these discussions got quite heated, which came as a surprise to all the others, the generals and the king especially, as neither baron knew any of the people involved personally. A competition to show who was the most severe was under way, only tempered by constant interruptions for scale and proportionality from a man who actually did know everyone being judged, Bishop Aregio.

"If you continue like this, we will have no one of Goth heritage left in the province." Turning to a trying- to- stay- out- of- the- squabbles monarch, "Sire, we need to rebuild, not leave an empty space that Franks or other foreigners," here he poignantly glared at the southern bishops, " could take advantage of with a weakened border area of the kingdom. We agreed that I, with a heavy heart and absolutely no enthusiasm for the task, would advise of the relative guilt of these people. I am doing so only for my advice to be ignored."

"I concur. Gentlemen, remember the Goth code should be the basis of all your judgements with the recommended advice of Bishop Aregio given the full weight of importance it deserves. Furthermore, if you could find your way to add a liberal degree of realpolitik, the nation, and its future, would be immensely grateful."

Contrary to expectations, the number of executions rose after this intervention due to a surprising turn of events when one exceptionally minor noble, who was condemned to blinding and the confiscation of his land, by prior agreement all confiscated land was to be given to the Church, demanded death, arguing that his life as a blind penniless beggar would be much worse than death itself. Not even Aregio's intercession, pointing out that his everlasting torment of burning in hell, as he had been ex-communicated, would start sooner and therefore last longer, dissuaded him from his choice; death to him was better than the life he was being offered. And so it came about that he became the leader of a fashionable choice.

*

One woman punched squarely in the face was the sum of the violence of the morning, much less than the enthralled public had hoped for, but still, if the total complete and utter humiliation of Amalaswinth was added to the pot, not a bad day's entertainment. The bleeding nosed woman was one of those who had thought they were on safe ground by insulting the arrested Antonia. More would have bled, if Antonia could have found them in the throng, and hadn't been detained, and literally carried back to their former rented residence. Carrying his wife over the threshold, not in any romantic gesture of a newlywed, Pere deposited her in the dark corner next to the clandestine visitor.

"Take your revenge later. We've got to stay calm, not attract too much more attention, for her sake, as well as our own!"

Realising that he was totally right, though not wanting either to show or say it, her only response which could have meant those outside or her husband, was, "revenge will be sweet."

Rebecca was totally confused, having no idea why they had been taken away, or why Pere was playing the strong manly husband when she'd never seen him in this role before.

"What happened?"

Pere thudded his way most noisily to the ale casket to fill his cup, while the pride recovering Antonia filled Rebecca in on all the details, with generous dollops of embellishment.

"So, you now own my house?"

"Well," Antonia hadn't really thought that her upgrade meant that Rebecca was now officially homeless forever, a fact that caused her to stutter and flounder for words. Pere, not for the first time today, came to her assistance.

"Officially, yes, though that's not how we see it, do we?" he shot a stinging look at his temporarily speechless wife.

"We reckon that we'll be your tenants, un-paying of course, looking after your house until you want it back. How does that sound to you?"

"Oh, Pere! Antonia! I couldn't imagine anything better. That is a happy house and has all my fondest memories within those walls. I know my father would be delighted that you are our *tenants*."

Antonia and Pere spied each other. He was looking as pleased as punch, while she had a new found respect for him written all over her creased skin.

*

Having left while it was still dark and the streets totally deserted, Rebecca found herself quite away down the coast by the time a huge sun started to appear on the horizon. She stopped, convinced that she was no longer in danger, as she was, well, she wasn't sure where she was. Despite having made this trip various times, she couldn't quite remember the right way, Arantxa's place had never been easy to find. She hoped that by sticking to the beach, some sort of recall would come back. Sitting on the warming sand to enjoy the sight of the enormous rising sun over the totally mill pond calm sea, she was taking a well-earned break. Swathed in heaps of beautiful beach memories, she felt the pang of longing. It was almost physical pain, thinking about those precious stolen moments, tears started slowly streaming down her cheeks, until she suddenly realised that she had covered herself with far too much of the hateful annoying sand. Jumping to her feet as if she'd been stung by a passing bee, she set about muttering to herself and brushing the disgusting stuff out of every crease and crevice it had wielded its way into.

"If you don't want to get covered in sand, you shouldn't sit in it, you stupid pregnant woman!" Arantxa approached, net in hand, with some creatures wriggling their last breaths inside. "If you are clean enough, I'll take you home and make you breakfast."

Overcome with relief and happiness Rebecca ran at and bundled into her potential host, knocking her and her catch into the sand crying for real now, with happiness, not for bitter sweet memories. Once upright, the women hugged and hugged with no words. Pulling away slightly, speech returned, "Actually, I was hoping for more than breakfast. I am homeless and was wondering…"

As much as their combined bulky midriffs would allow, more crushing embraces resumed.

"Of course!"

Rebecca never having been much of a touchy feely type person found it strange, though not unpleasant to be holding the hand that wasn't carrying a seafood full net. They didn't speak much, it was one of those times when they both had far too much to say to even start.

One thing that Rebecca did realise was that she would never ever have found her way to the cottage by herself. Not having the greatest sense of direction nor one of those visual memories that some have, she would have become the proverbial last wandering Jew. It was also true that Arantxa had made quite a few improvements, one of which was to have the path completely covered, so much so, that anyone who didn't know it was there wouldn't have known. Moving down the path, Arantxa pointed out some traps she'd set, a couple of vicious looking metal things that Marcus had had made to snare an uninvited horses leg, and, closer to the house a big pit.

"You dug that?"

"Mostly, the useless duke did some. He visits whenever he can, not *that* often and when he does come, I prefer he does *other* work."

"Arantxa!"

"Well it's more fun with two, isn't it?"

"ARANTXA!"

The utterer gave a delightfully naughty giggle, leading her new housemate in. A whole number of changes had been made in the interior as well. It was still a run down, almost falling down, building but the roof had been recovered, and everything had been made to look cosier with bits of the forest being reshaped or reformed into either something pretty or useless.

"Lovely!"

"A bit of an exaggeration. Still, I'm getting there."

A couple of big haunches of salted ham were hanging from the roof. "Did Marcus bring those as well?"

"No, that's why the pit was built. Not long after I cleared the land and planted a few things, she came along with half a dozen little ones to dig up and eat my hard work. Into the pit she fell the week after."

"You killed her?"

"No. I didn't have a lance long enough. I had to wait until Marcus's next visit. You should have heard the racket she made for three days and nights. I've got one now though," stacked against the wall was quite an impressive armoury of sharp killing implements for any occasion, "You can kill the next one."

"Can't, I'm pregnant."

"Aren't we all, even the goat, so we'll be swimming in milk come the spring. I may get a new cock again then as well."

"What happened to the old one?"

The pot was indicated, "He made too much noise. Here was I, trying to be secret in the forest and the bloody thing was crowing day and night, he had to go."

"So, we won't have any eggs until the spring."

Arantxa gave her a pitying look, "Oh dear city girl, you have a lot to learn. Hens lay without the help of a cock!"

"Do they? I always thought…"

The days had ticked by in almost total harmony. The daily grind of making forest and sea give up enough for them to live, eat and hoard for the upcoming winter kept them busy from sunrise to sunset, which even in this season, was an awfully long time. Totally knackered, they chatted over food and a sort of berry wine that Arantxa had concocted. It was sweet and gave them a nice fuzzy feeling.

"I wish we had ale."

"And me. It's one of the few things I really miss living out here."

The mellow glow allowed them to lose whatever inhibitions that they had had, giving reign to a different concept of free speech. Starting relatively cautiously, it came to a stage where nothing was out of bounds. There was a great deal that had happened since the last time that they had talked, none of it good, and it needed airing, contemplating and digesting. Tears were shed regularly, especially whenever Rebecca's father was mentioned, "He was far too good for you. I would have loved a father like him."

"I did love him and he well knew it, it's a case of all men need the right training. Talking about training men, when's the new duchess due? Do you know anything about her?"

"I don't know, and nothing. Marcus says he has no information to give as he knows nothing as well, but I'm not sure that I believe him."

"You think that he lies to you?"

"Probably, wouldn't you in his situation?"

The fractious forces that made up the royalist side began their total disintegration with each part going its separate way back to their respective homes. The first to be sent on his way was the one time appreciated and trusted nephew. His behaviour at Narbo, added to the exceptionally close relationship he'd struck up with the expelled Baron, Evrigius, rumour having it that he was betrothed to that dangerous and bothersome baron's daughter, meant that this likeable boy, would have to be kept at arms' length for the foreseeable future. His dispatch was perfunctory rather than ceremonious. Being given a score of an escort, he was told to make his own way back to Toletum, at the pace he chose, and if he wanted to visit every tavern and whorehouse on the way, in a similar fashion to how he returned to Toletum the last time, then, he had the king's blessing.

The other final audiences with the king were brief and could not be described as sweet in any way. No natural alliances had been formed, so they reverted back to their natural enmity as their common foe no longer existed. There was no last supper together, no celebration of a job well done, or a mission completed, just a tense, terse individual meetings of king and baron. Believing that only chaos and mutual recrimination would be the order of the day if they had a joint meeting, Wamba gave the same message to each; gratitude for their support and warnings of dire consequences if the returning armies treated the areas they passed through as enemy conquered lands. The last to arrive was the first to go; Wandemir had had his army packing up to leave all day and despite it becoming dark, had set off immediately after Gunhild's execution and the brief encounter with the king.

"He was keen to go. Why the hurry?"

"Sire, I have no idea. We have no spies or contacts among his men. They didn't mix with anyone else, their late arrival and less than exemplary fighting performance endeared them to no one. We are well shot of them."

"But, general, can we trust them to obey the orders I have just given?"

"Sire, I severely doubt it. My suggestion would be to encourage Baron Teodofred to strike camp at first light. He has to follow the same route south, then, if Wandemir does want to pillage and sack, he won't be given much time with another army on his heels."

"Might they join forces to do a more effective job?"

"In my opinion, Sire, there is absolutely NO possibility of that. They hate each other far, far too much. It would be much more likely that they fight each other than join together."

In the meeting with Teodofred, Wamba's legendary patience was tested to the full. The baron's attitude bordered on contempt, so much so, that the general present, Alaric, kept his hand firmly gripped on his sword hilt throughout.

Upon Teodofred leaving the room the king let out an enormous sigh, "We are going to have to do something about the power of these barons once all this has died down. I don't know what we can do, but we can't continue in this situation where the nominal head of state is in hoc to these private armies."

Unable to hold back any longer Alaric blurted out, "They should be given the same warning Badwila is delivering to the Vascones; submit, behave or be destroyed. Personally, I think that now would be a perfect moment to put that baron in his place. His army is a fighting disaster, it has numbers, but absolutely no leadership or ability, we could take them out in a morning thereby making a statement to all the other nobles!"

Wamba was incredibly surprised at this outburst, having never really heard Alaric express any opinion before, never mind one forcefully and passionately held. No, that wasn't true, Wamba's mind found its way back to the time in Vasconia, when Alaric had given his damming appraisal of General Hermenguild's ability as a military leader.

Conscious of the effect his outburst had made, Alaric moved to his more consolatory tone and apologised for speaking out of turn.

"No, no general, I think that you are not so wrong. However, the optics of this wouldn't be awfully good. A duke comes to help the kingdom, and in the post victory is decimated by the allies he'd joined. No, that would sow seeds of distrust, resulting in more, rather than less, trouble, though I do appreciate your support. I often reflect on our conversation back in the Vasconia when you and General Kunimund gave me your views on the purge committed against the nobility by King Chindaswinth. My understanding of those dreadfully dark days is undergoing something of a sea change. However, on to more pressing matters; logistics. When and how shall we leave. The only thing I have clear is where, back to Narbo."

*

There followed a day of controlled releases of small groups of captured defenders. This policy being designed so that their return to what was left of their homes, families, and lives, allowed for no mass revulsion. The generals having been advised that the feeling in Nemausus was so hostile and inflammatory that their presence, in the most discreet of ways, would be necessary for at least of couple of days longer, informed the monarch of what was, or in this case, wasn't happening. Not having much, if anything, to do, and being confined to the palace for his own safety, because he had been informed that by just being seen and recognised he could provoke unrest, even an attempt on his life by a lone wolf, who felt that because he had nothing left he had nothing else to lose, the king was bored. In the need of distraction, he demanded the kitchens to prepare a banquet for the evening.

It was a glorious affair with lashings of wine from the abundant selection the count kept in the cellar, and so much food that the table would have groaned if it could have. Everything was set for a joyous occasion, until Wamba projected a mental image in his head; him and a pleasant though dour general trying to enjoy a feast. This picture was in need of something, or someone, uplifting. Getting some women there was a possibility, though this wasn't Wamba's style. His appetite in that field was notoriously frugal. Hence, it came to pass that there were to be three people at the table, two expected and one very much not.

When Flavius was extracted from the cell he shared with the still bleeding and puss seeping head that once belonged to a vocal vibrant bishop, who now gave off the impression of being one of those religious monks who impose silence and fasting on themselves, he thought it was probably his turn to be scalped, humiliated or executed despite the fact that early evening wasn't the sort of time of day that he imagined this happening. His intrigue accompanied him to parts of the palace he knew much better than the dungeon. Upon entering a banquet hall with the king and a general, his shock was almost as profound as the said general's.

"I thought it would make things a bit more interesting."

"But Sire, he's …"

"Yes, he is, isn't he? Unshackle him, please, guards, and then you may leave."

Alaric was now on his feet, "The danger! He's a rebel! Your life! We need to.."

"Oh, do sit down, general. Good evening, Flavius. Do you give me your word that you will not attempt to kill your king over dinner?"

Rubbing his now freed wrists and then his chin as if in thought, he slowly and deliberately pronounced, "If the food isn't too bad, then I do solemnly promise."

This brought the first guffaw of laughter from Wamba in a long time.

"Capital. That is why he's here."

Alaric had always liked Flavius - intimate friends, perhaps not, different backgrounds and outlook on life saw to that. Before the Vasconis campaign they hadn't really crossed paths. In the campaign itself, they'd rubbed along pretty well considering they were rivals for similar posts, and Wamba often displayed definite preference for the presently unchained man. Still, he had saved the day and probably his life once, so he wasn't as unhappy that the rebel was at the table. Besides, it might be one of his last meals so there was no reason why he shouldn't enjoy it. Understandably conversation didn't flow like a spring river after the winter thaw, but in a similar mode it began to get more powerful as the event went on, this time being fuelled by wine rather than melt water. The fact that there was a whole herd of elephants in the room, not just the proverbial one, didn't help. Alaric took it upon himself to confront the first elephant, "The reason for your rebellion, what was her name?" Wamba's characteristic explosion of laughter was the first response, followed by words almost choked out, "Excellent, I have been wanting to ask that question for ages."

Throughout the meal, Flavius knowing he was on borrowed time, and in the company of people who didn't dislike him for what he had done, and, who he actually appreciated, had behaved impeccably, not saying anything controversial or out of order. This question changed the rules of the game.

"I'll tell you, if you tell me who was in charge of the army during that pathetic, embarrassing first attack on the walls?"

Wamba's glee deepened as Alaric became more defensive.

"Actually, my generals were quite innocent of that debacle. Duke Teodofred wins all the prizes for being the most incompetent military leader in Goth history. He did something similar outside Tarraco and got trounced by your young protégée, Marcus."

"I heard about that. Unbelievable! Marcus would find it difficult fighting his way out of a latrine without cutting himself shaving. Sire," everyone noted the word and the genuine feeling it was delivered with, "you really need to follow up on that conversation we once had in the Vasconia about a national army. Given something close to equity in numbers, my side would have won this conflict."

The general started to voice his rebuttal loudly, until calmed by smoothing hand motions of the king, which allowed Flavius to continue. "It would have hurt my soul to allow those disgusting brutes of Franks into the kingdom to stay, but if they ever do come, you need to be better prepared."

Before Alaric started again, Wamba, in a quite serious and sober voice asked, "Why did you do it? You knew that you had an assured glorious future with us in the army. You threw it all away ... for what?"

Taking another sip of the splendid wine, Flavius' countenance took on a reflective appearance. "Firstly, I must say that I believe their cause is just."

Alaric again exploded, with words like *monstrous, unbelievable, treasonous,* being shouted only for Wamba to repeat his calming motions,

"I asked a question, I would like to hear ALL of the answer. So, if you could wait to make your comments, I would appreciate it."

"As I was saying, the two parts of this just cause, in my opinion, are, firstly that Tarraconensis/Gallia Gothica has been sidelined by Toletum for too long, their history merits better treatment. Here, this city, Nemausus, could be described as the cradle of us as a nation, and Tarraconensis, the jewel of Roman Iberia and its capital, such an important city with so many impressive buildings and monuments both discarded in favour of a relative backwater. Secondly, I honestly believe that the persecution of the Jews has gone too far. I do not understand why we have to persecute them SO much. Proselytism is not something they practise, nor do they try to control political power, so why are they deemed such an insidious group?"

Alaric's bubbly anger was beginning to show, so Flavius added in a slightly less measured tone in the hope of getting it out before the general's anger burst out, "Neither of which I consider merited a military uprising. These political questions could, and should, have been dealt with peacefully with negotiations. The regnum visigothorum could have solved this dispute by sitting and talking. All that was needed was the will to come to a reasonable, amicable solution on the territorial dispute. The Jews, well, that's a different story. However, once the fighting started it was impossible to stop until your inevitable, given the sizes of the armies not your conduct on the battlefield, victory."

Alaric felt it was his turn to speak but was yet again prevented from doing so by the king, "So, let's go back to the original question of General Alaric, what's her name?"

Wondering whether mentioning her name would put her in more danger than she was, he hesitated before uttering the word; "Rebecca."

"A Jewess then, as we had heard. In my experience of you, Flavius, when you haven't been besotted with one woman, then, it was another. Back in Vasconia, what was the *reconnaissance* woman's name?"

"Aitziber."

"See what I mean, though I don't think you would have committed treason for that one. This Rebecca, I hear that she's quite a beauty who was able to bewitch many men, Duke Ranosindus and Count Hilderic among them. Is her witchcraft the real reason behind the rebellion?"

It wasn't a sip this time, it was a long draft. The territory he was in was a quagmire for Rebecca and her interests, and showing even an inkling of the fury churning through his guts would make matters so much worse.

"I am in love."

This caused a tension decreasing chuckle.

"Sire, your description of my wanderlust past is not untrue. This though, is different. I can honestly say that I have experienced an emotion like no other. You may choose to call it witchcraft, if you will, but I know, and the others you mentioned as well, knew, that this woman is outstandingly brilliant; sharp, bright, charming, opinionated, stubborn and, yes, exceptionally beautiful. If she had been a man, everyone would have proclaimed her a natural leader to be followed almost without question. Fortunately, for me, she is a woman and it has been the highlight of my life meeting her."

"And a Jewess?"

" Yes."

"You have no regrets?"

"Yes, only one, that I won't be able to spend the rest of my life with her at my side."

Neither of the other men had ever experienced anything like what Flavius was passionately proclaiming, nor had they even heard any man say anything similar. It was quite shocking and clearly a case of bewitchment. Alaric saw things clearly; she was a dangerous woman and had to be found and stopped before she did any more damage.

"Do you know where she is now?"

It was the tone that alerted Flavius to the real and imminent danger that he had inadvertently put Rebecca in. "I do not, however, I suspect that she was on the boats that deported the Jews from Tarraco. I know that she won't be the only Jew left in the kingdom once Hispalis and that little prick Hillel have finished their dirty work."

"You know Hillel, then?"

"Yes, a foul toad who takes up far too much space on this earth."

"Can't say we took to him either. Still, he has proved most useful even with half a tongue."

Flavius didn't understand this last reference and hoped that Rebecca was out of danger sailing to… somewhere.

"Let me get this straight, this woman, *Rebecca*, caused you to rebel and you are prepared to die, even happily, for the brief time you spent together."

"That is so. Can you tell when I am to be executed?"

The enjoyable festive moments had been lost once the woman's name had been mentioned, something that Wamba regretted as he had been enjoying the evening until then.

"Not soon is all I can say. Apparently, Julian has requested that you stand trial in Toletum. By the way, how *do* you know him? He appears to have some connection and interest in you that he does not have for anyone else?"

"His family lived fairly close and he knew my father pretty well."

"Ummm, that may explain it, anyway, he wants you alive and well, but totally humiliated back in Toletum. Apparently, you are to receive the *capillos et cutem detrahere* treatment and then be paraded as the King of Tarraconensis/Gallia Gothica in all the towns between here and Toletum."

"Nice! Bishop Argebaud as well?"

"No, his last port of call will be his home town, Narbo. He, being part of the Church hierarchy, is in the tender hands of Iulianus. "

"He's in a pretty poor state, I don't think he'll last much longer. I'm pleased his execution is near, it's better that he's out of his misery. Really, he is a good man, and never wanted this to come to violence."

*

"When did you say, tomorrow? That's impossible. Why didn't we know sooner, this is .."

"Apparently a messenger had been sent quite a while ago, but he got attacked and robbed on the road. He was lucky to get away with his life according to the man I just spoke to. You know that there has been a total breakdown of law and order, travelling by yourself now is a game of chance with the odds stacked against you."

With anger subsiding but impatience increasing Marcus was wondering how the hell he was going to deal with this situation. True, it was expected, and had to happen sooner or later, he just didn't expect it now, or if truth be told, ever.

"Let me get this straight, Teodofred and his army are due the day after tomorrow and the daughter, what was her name?"

"Gelvira"

"Anytime soon?"

"Yes, as the baron said he would be passing, as it were, he thought it would be the perfect opportunity for a family get-together." A vicious glare brought further words, "His description, not mine."

"Alright, prepare the staff, make sure we have enough food etc., and send a messenger to Duke Teodofred telling him that he and his men can have the use of Els Munts. We do NOT want them in the city."·

*

"I don't understand. The house is empty and ready for my stay, but you say that the best camping areas are already occupied. By whom?"

"Women."

"Explain." Teodofred was genuinely puzzled.

"Apparently, when the legitimate forces of the king arrived here to put down the rebellion, they were accompanied by the usual camp followers. After Flavius went rogue, the women stayed rather than join the new

(548)

venture. They say they have the perfect right to be there as they are still part of Wamba's army."

"Just clear them out and be done with it."

"Not so easy. They are well armed and are prepared to fight."

"My God, man, they are women. Surely we can win one battle on this campaign?"

"Without a doubt, sir, but we will lose men, and the women who follow us have taken up common cause with the resident women here. So, our men who have, let's say, relations with our women, show a marked reluctance to fight."

"Unbelievable. History will not remember us as the greatest fighting force ever. Find a new camp farther north."

*

Gelvira had arrived with a small escort the day before her father in quite an amazing coincidence of timing. Marcus had had the briefest of meetings with her as she said that she was exceptionally tired after the long unpleasant journey, needed rest, and would take some refreshment in her room if she could be shown the way.

This statement was delivered in an exhausted tone with a haughty aspect, not that Marcus was listening for details being too captivated by the physical sight of her. There was no doubting her north European Goth heritage with that long, long straight blonde hair and those almost disturbingly penetrating blue eyes.

Knowing that it would be exceptionally unusual for a young aristocratic woman to spend time alone with him, etiquette would dictate the presence of one of her parents, Marcus thought he could take advantage of the rest of the day without being rude or being missed. Furthermore, it may be his last chance to spend some unaccounted for time, for quite a while, by going to see Arantxa.

Leaving his two most trusted men and his horse way back down the beach as per instructed by the mother of his child; she didn't trust anyone to know where the hidden path started, Marcus plodded reflectively to his destination. Being so lost in thought, he almost stood in one of the metal snares he'd set. What is more, he didn't notice that he was being followed either. He was brought back to his senses upon spying the barely clad form of a most definitely pregnant woman chopping wood. The dirty sweaty near naked body was both sensual and a little repelling at the same time, certainly different to the elegant, now sleeping beauty, who was the occupant of his thoughts.

Calling out, as she hadn't seen him yet, she dropped her axe and came bundling towards him like a happy puppy. Finally disentangling himself from her clasping arms, the only thing he managed to say was, "You are incredibly sweaty."

It wasn't the content; it was more the tone that annoyed Arantxa. Turning and moving slowly away from him, she called over her shoulder, "I will wash."

"That wasn't very nice, was it?"

Startled, Marcus himself did some turning, to find Rebecca, a little more clothed, though not much, standing in front of him. "Rebecca!"

"What's on your mind? I've been watching you all the way up the path, you're disturbed by something."

Feeling like a child caught with his hand in the honey jar and being disconcerted by seeing much more of Rebecca's flesh than he ever had, or wanted to, he stumbled for words.

"Spit it out. You've got a few minutes until that person who adores you and is carrying your baby returns."

"It's nothing, just Baron Teodofred is due to arrive this evening, he's setting up camp in Els Munts."

"And?"

Unsure whether he should say anymore; Teodofred's appearance should be enough unsettling news for anyone, he reckoned that he could get away with a bit of bluff.

"Nothing, it's not great having another army pitched on the outskirts of Tarraco. You know that people…"

"What's she like then?"

"Who?"

"You know."

Realising that Rebecca could read him better than she could a book, a quick serving of honesty before a cleaner Arantxa returned seemed the best policy.

"Pretty."

"How pretty?"

"Very. Blonde blue eyed pretty. Sounds as if she's quite a haughty aloof character though."

"And probably has thick ankles."

"What?"

"Never mind."

"Arantxa will never get to hear her character, she'll only see her, which…"

"Is bound to cause trouble."

The new duke nodded his head meekly in agreement.

"And you think it will help by being cool, distant and telling her to go and wash?"

It was a wary cleaner puppy that returned without a spring in her step.

"Better? I see you've met my new house guest. Now, tell me, what the hell's the matter with you?"

Everyone seemed to be able to read him. Making a mental promise to himself that this would have to change, especially as he would necessarily be leading a double life, he didn't stutter this time. "Unbloodywelcome guests. Teodofred has an army camped out at Els Munts. Most troubling, yes, most troubling. Anyway, I thought I'd bring a few things as I don't know when I'll be able to get away again."

Finally putting the heavy sack he still had over his shoulder on the ground, he started to take out all the goodies he'd retrieved from the kitchens of the palace making a big show of useful, or various delicious articles. Once empty, he stepped over them to give Arantxa a crushing embrace accompanied by cheek, neck kissing. "I really have to get back. I'll return here as soon as I possibly can."

"You're going already?"

"Duty calls."

"Go then. I can't imagine what I had to wash for. Next time, if there is a next time, tell me how long you intend staying so I can make an informed decision whether I want to waste my time washing or not!"

"It's just that.."

"No, Marcus, it's just whatever you want to make it, so, *just* go and do your duty."

Knowing that if he stayed he would probably make things worse, he stepped forward to give her a goodbye kiss. She instinctively stepped back giving him a little wave instead.

Feeling deflated and more than a bit dejected, he had no choice but to go, which he did, taking the sensation that he was carrying a much heavier weight than the one he came with.

*

Three people for a meal is never the greatest of numbers, it only ever works when the three like and know each other well. This was most indubitably not the case when father, daughter and prospective son-in-law sat in the great dining hall of the palace. Beyond doubt there was little love lost between the blood relatives; he ordered, she sulked, and conversation flowed as freely as puss from a well-encrusted scabby wound.

Sitting opposite the beauty, Marcus at least had a seat with a view, which was often spoilt by the amount of ugly snarling gestures that sufficed for answers to questions she deemed unworthy of a vocal response. Marcus tried small talk, not his best suit, without any success whatsoever. In the end he gave up, and resigned himself to listening to the baron's monologues of how bravely his troops, with his inspired leadership, fought in all the battles, something which didn't ring true to Marcus as he, well, Pere, as well, had faced and beaten those self same troops and enlightened commander in two battles. Choosing to say nothing and take in the view until the ordeal finished was his option, while he contemplated whether this situation between father and daughter was systemic or punctual. So lost in thought was he, that he didn't realise he was being asked a question that wasn't rhetorical.

"Marcus, the wedding; where and when?"

"Well, I hadn't given it…"

"That settles it then, we'll have it in the south, around Christ Mass time I believe would be best."

Wondering whether his reality accepting face was as transparent as the beauty's look of total disgust, he suspected he may have found the bone of contention which had permeated the whole meal.

*

The triumphal return had started by leaving a smouldering wreck of a city in a profound state of mourning, to entering another, which was full of destruction and empty of people. There was no sign of life in the streets as they rode through and the houses or what was left of them, gave off the appearance of being abandoned, some fairly recently. Word had spread that the southern Goth army was returning to Narbo, which made anyone who was able to move take to the surrounding forest in the hope of avoiding them.

This dismal sight was exactly what Wamba had been striving to avoid, a disaster which would continue to be a problem once a new generation was formed in the hatred their city's sack would have engendered. Thankfully, this gloriously victorious army was to spend but one night there.

Flavius wasn't invited to supper that evening. Though physically present he may not have been, he remained the main topic of conversation. Emotions towards him varied, he was liked, but as to whether he was an absolute dick-led idiot, or just someone to be pitied, there was no consensus. Bishop Aregio, lost in the depths of despair at seeing this beloved city in the state they found it, didn't venture an opinion one way or the other, not caring not a single jot on the topic. Alaric, who had been profoundly affected by Flavius's tale of the previous night was most upset by how a man could be enslaved so easily. Knowing that the Flavius he knew was quite capable of falling for any or every woman he came across, he wondered what sort of power this particular woman had that had driven his colleague to abandon all of his previously held beliefs and even welcome death as the next best option to not spending the rest of his days with this bewitcher.

"Sire, I think it imperative that we find this Jewess. She sounds truly dangerous and left alive, she may be able to entrap yet more vulnerable fools to do her bidding."

"I would certainly like to meet her."

"Who would you like to meet, Sire?" Bishop Hispalis was the supper latecomer, as he hadn't been overtly excluded, he assumed that his presence would be required. His tardiness, apparently, was due to having to personally supervise the preparations for the public execution of Argebaud in the morn. The already seated and eating party felt that they couldn't issue any un-invitation as he was a bishop without playmates. Wamba didn't want to say anything more in front of this man he detested so, but the ever willing Alaric provided the missing information. "The Jewess that bewitched most of the rebels."

"Ah, her! Hillel told me all about her."

"He was besotted as well?"

"No, no, no, he loathed the woman. They hated each other. Some inter-Jewish rivalry. It appears she bettered him on various occasions, not that he actually said that, but by inference it was relatively clear to someone as astute as I am. Did you know her father demanded to be executed because his brother had been? Strange family. Also, apparently she's a childhood friend of the person you've just made the new Duke of Tarraco."

"Really?" Wamba took note of this piece of information, deciding, after supper when Hispalis was not around, to send a message to Marcus telling him to ascertain the whereabouts of this woman.

The rest of the supper was as insufferable as any and every moment spent with this pompous self righteous bishop. Wamba kept it as short as he could.

*

"Get out of this house! I think I made it abundantly clear that, if we are to meet, then it will be ONLY on official business."

"My dear boy, you ought not to treat me in this way, I have known you all your life, watched you grow and mature, I am almost family, I could be described as a sort of godfather to you. Do you remember the time..?"

"I said, get out!"

The demeanour changed from sweaty slimy, creepy, to sweaty haughty, the sweat being the constant with the bulk springing leaks feature, on this scorching late morn, increasing.

"We are the two leading figures of Tarraco and should have a good working relationship. You may be the nominal duke, my power though, comes from a much higher source and I can, and will, make life most uncomfortable for you, both in this world, and the next, if you don't have a civil tongue in your head."

Marcus withdrew the long dagger he always carried from the scabbard tied to his belt. Cyprianus, developing yet more rivulets, neatly stepped behind the closest chair and waved a parchment in the air. "Also, I am here on official business."

Having received a message that morning, Marcus had an inkling what the Bisho was about to impart. Still brandishing the dagger without making a forward movement he issued a one word command. "Speak."

Since the departure of his future bride and her father, he'd been trying to restore some order and pride in his life. Their brief stay had been an ordeal in which he felt as if he had no power, control, or at times, even opinion. He'd been bullied by one or the other, often being little more than collateral damage, or an instrument used in their attempts to better each other. Siding with neither, and disliking both intensely, he was glad to be shot of them. His future promised to be not a happy one. Being married to her was going to be anything but pleasurable, her only redeeming feature was her beauty. She was quite simply stunning, prettier than any picture. Sadly though, this particular picture wasn't inanimate, it talked. And did it talk! The content, delivery and pitch were annoying in the extreme. In the whole time she was in the palace, she didn't say anything nice, except when she wanted him to do something contrary to her father's wishes. Then, she was disgustingly *nice*.

Their stay was three days, the longest three days of his life. His life? That was what he had to look forward to, a lifetime with her? Political marriages weren't expected to be happy affairs, however, in his experience with the ones he'd known, they were tolerant and tolerable relationships, but yet again, all the people he'd seen and met in that position were relatively old, so, perhaps the tolerance and ability to accept comes with the years. All in all though, not an enticing prospect. After they had left, he sought solace out in the forest, only to be told, by Rebecca, that the lady of the house was otherwise occupied and had no time to see him as she was bathing. No amount of cajoling would make Rebecca reveal her whereabouts, so, tail between his legs, he had returned without the needed empathy.

The week after Teodofred's army left, another appeared. It belonged to a Duke Wittimir, someone his future father in law referred to as a jumped up Johnnie-come-lately searching for the spoils of war without getting too involved in the fighting of it. Beginning to get tired of being pushed from pillar to post, Marcus mobilised, with Pere's invaluable help, as many fighting men as possible to sit between the Via Augusta and the entrance to the city, in a warning, with an invitation for the baron to continue on his way. A cordial meeting of dignitaries was arranged and a supper was held in Els Munts, which was still being guarded by the women's camp, in which the passing Baron was encouraged, at the very latest, the next morning, to continue his passing. The threat that Marcus used was never explicit, it didn't have to be, the baron obviously felt that there was easier, if not richer, pickings to be had farther down the coast, especially now as his little diversion had put his army behind that of Teodofred's. Now this foul traitor of a Metropolitan Bishop had come squelching in, wanting to be his friend!

"The Bishop of Hispalis, I am sure you remember him, has written saying that we have to make preparations for a parade in the city."

The message Marcus had received didn't mention any parade, instead focusing on his relationship with Rebecca and the possibility of him finding her whereabouts as the king was most keen, after hearing so much about her, to make her acquaintance. A trap if he'd ever heard one.

"Parade? Wamba agreed that his forces would not enter the city; that was part of our agreement."

"No, I don't think it's going to be a show of military force, KING Wamba has not mentioned anything of the kind. It'll be a small affair where the *King* of Tarraconensis/Gallia Gothica will be shown in all his glory."

Impetuously and without thinking through any adverse consequences, Marcus stated flatly, "I will not be part of that, nor will I help organise it. If Wamba insists that it happens, he may not count on any active participation on the part of Tarraco's civil society."

"But.."

"You may now leave, our business is concluded." Marcus still with his unsheathed weapon moved slightly forward causing quite a scramble from behind the chair to the door.

*

"I told you on your last visit, the lady of the house is bathing."

One of the advantages of living in such secluded isolation was that any visitor, who wasn't coming in great stealth, was easily audible.

"She must be the cleanest woman in the kingdom if not the whole Christendom. I'll make sure that I bring more soap next time as you must be running low." Raising his voice slightly as he felt sure that Arantxa would be close enough to hear everything said. "Actually, I'm pleased that she's not around. The information I have is for you, Rebecca." Indicating two sawn down tree trunks whose new purpose was outside furniture, "Shall we sit?"

Coldness travelled down Rebecca's spine, the tone was serious, and to be invited to sit, all boded ill. Upon hearing the parade news, Marcus had played many different scenarios through his mind of how he would break it to Rebecca, none of which was satisfactory. At one point he contemplated the idea of sending a messenger so he wouldn't have to do it, only to reject that as he would have not been able to live with his cowardice.

There was silence as Marcus sought those first few words and Rebecca looked on in trepidation.

"The duchess is no longer in town, is she?" A clothed woman, not radiantly clean considering all her time and effort in ablution, appeared behind Marcus's back.

"I'm not here to talk about her." It sounded much more dismissive and aggressive than he intended.

"I've heard that she's really pretty, she hasn't left you already, has she? Perhaps she wasn't clean enough."

"Yes, she is pretty, extremely beautiful, I would say. Now, Arantxa, do be quiet, I need to talk to Rebecca."

Flabbergasted, Arantxa was about to explode in verbal or physical violence, or both, when Rebecca in a sad, serious voice said, "Please, Arantxa, I think Marcus is trying to build up the courage to tell me something important."

*

Dawn saw the two prisoners removed from their holding cell to the place of public punishment. Everything had been meticulously prepared, two different imposers of justice stood ready with their respective pieces of equipment; one acting on behalf of the civil authorities, and the other to do God's will through the edicts of the Church in the person of Bishop of Hispalis. There were only a couple of things missing; the king was one, upon being advised as to the content of the day's proceedings, he had excused himself, leaving General Alaric to represent the State. The other absent element was the public. Try as Hispalis might, he could not find many people to attend, only the lame, infirm, or the elderly, basically the ones who, physically, had not been able to leave the city before the column of riders arrived were available. It was quite a sad and pathetic sight even with the numbers being augmented by soldiers who'd been promised quite a spectacle. The contrast in the state of the two prisoners was also stark. Paulus looking relatively spruce and clean, compared to the dishevelled destroyed scabbing puss filled form of the once highest authority of the Church in this city.

"I'm glad nobody is here to see me," were the last words Paulus heard the cleric say before they were separated and given to their new dancing partners.

Paulus's *capillos et cutem detrahere* was first on the bill of fare. What a difference this was to what happened to the bishops in Nemausus, a fair proportion of the head was loped off in the scalping process, whereas this time, it was done, much to the annoyance of the Bishop of Hispalis, with the greatest of care with the sharpest of knives. The man inflicting the punishment was army, he knew Paulus by sight, and even more importantly he had heard the rumour that Paulus had dined with the King and top brass. This indicated that the king might not be fully in favour what was about to happen, a theory reinforced by the king's no show, all of which meant that there was always the possibility that this particular ex-general, in the end may not be executed, as most people presumed to be his lot. Still alive, he may seek some sort of future revenge against anyone who'd done him harm. Despite all these details, a scalping is a scalping, leaving Paulus' head a bloody mess onto which a fishbone, playing the role of crown for the ex-Kingof Tarraconensis/ Gallic Gothica, was fixed.

In contrast, the ex-Metropolitan Bishop's torment was long, very long, and what only could be described as sadistic. Eyes were taken first, as was expected, then other body parts were broken, burnt and eventually removed, and to add insult to these very serious injuries, Hispalis paused to proclaim to all the crimes against God and the Church that this dismemberment warranted, and how it would help this poor man's soul to be cleansed. The soldier part the of crowd thinned as this was not much sport and anyone else who could move did, leaving an almost empty plaza by the time the unfortunate dismembered body let out his last breath.

"Was that *show* really necessary, bishop?" Alaric, who was no stranger to cruelty or rough justice, was a little disturbed by what he had seen. For him, punishment, even of the severest type, was necessary, although from his point of view, the reason for that necessity had to be made clear, be it, an example to others, retribution to right terrible wrongs, or whatever else. There were norms that had to be accepted. This particular ex-bishop didn't fall into any different category to those executed in Nemausus. Why he had to suffer so much more wasn't clear.

"It was my Christian duty to try to save the man's soul. His suffering would have been over, if he'd sought God's forgiveness for his sins. He chose silence which forced me to try even harder to prevent an eternity of pain. I was really doing it for his benefit. Sadly, he did not repent and all my efforts to bring him to God's light was in vain, a non fulfilment of my duties for which I will always suffer . Next time, I must apply yet more leverage."

Alaric did a double take, to try to ascertain whether the man was serious or not. Shockingly, he appeared to be.

"My failure might be assuaged by the fact that I have located the relics of Saint Antolin."

"Who?"

"Oh, my Lord! You are an educated man, a good Christian and you don't know the name, Saint Antolin, son of King Teodoric, one of the first martyrs of our faith?"

"Oh, him."

"King Wamba was most anxious that we find these sacred items and have them removed to Pallentia for safe storage in the new Metropolitan church there."

"Well, I'm glad you've found them, and I *do* hope it helps with your assuaging." Alaric moved away from this most strange man to get back to the company of normal people as quickly as possible. "I'll make sure that Paulus is put back in the cells."

Flavius was in a terrible state after having had to witness Argebaud's slow dismemberment and torture at very close range. The poor man made every human and inhuman sound possible, except pronouncing the words negating the righteousness of the cause he was dying for. How was it possible that someone could endure so much? He knew that when it came to his turn, he would renounce everything, except Rebecca, to speed up his death.

Alaric took him, quite gently in the circumstances, by the arm while whispering, "He's right strange, that one. I thought the army attracted them. Remember that chap, Caius? This one makes him look a pacifist, wouldn't like to get on the wrong side of him."

Paulus looked at his escort with incredulity, "Where do you think I am, in his good books?"

"Oh you'll be alright, Wamba likes you, he'll have you to put to death pretty quickly." *"Thanks."*

*

King Wamba was very pleased about a whole number of things. They were leaving Narbo, the sought for relics of Saint Antolin, had been found, he hadn't been party or witness to, the, by all accounts, dreadful death of Argebaud, and the Bishop of Hispalis wouldn't be travelling with them, as he needed another day or so to *"wrap things up properly"*. On the downside, he felt a little dismayed about no longer being able to invite Flavius to supper, his official punishment regime had begun with the scalping, making it difficult to explain how he could be an honoured guest and a traitorous criminal at the same time therefore his company would have to be foregone. Wamba felt he'd been condemned as well. His sentence; long evenings of dull general chat with dull Generals. The road trip back to Toletum was always going to be a long one, given this evening entertainment night after night, consequently, the journey promised to be much longer. The main reason for prospective duration was that it was envisaged that they would have to pass through every urban centre in order for the local population to see the humiliation of the *king*, complete with his increasingly smelly fishbone crown followed by, and starkly contrasted with, the splendour of the real king. Not wanting to alarm the local populace He never entered a city with more than a minimum escort, the bulk of the army would be camped close to the city to have their presence felt without treading on anyone's toes, his objective being; to look impressive, not threatening or imposing. To a great extent this was working as word spread that these processions usually involved the dispensing of largesse in copious quantities.

This modus operandi was established with very few unpleasant incidents. Individual calls of support to the fish-boned king were ignored in general. If, as happened on a few occasions, this vocal approbation became more generalised, it was dealt with, and swiftly nullified by a specially trained and briefed section of the escort unit whose task was just that.

*

It felt strange, everything was right, no, everything was wrong. It was all familiar, yet, all foreign, it was her house but no longer her home. Expecting her father to appear from the "office", instead she heard the cries of the children playing. Standing looking lost and bemused Arantxa took her hand, "Are you alright?"

Rebecca wanted to bawl, cry the way the two women had found themselves doing various nights after too much of Arantxa's alcoholic berry juice. Despite being on the point of doing so, she felt that an outer serenity had to be maintained, not for her sake, nor for the others present, but for those whose spirits were there.

"I will be." A final squeeze and the hands were left to drift apart.

Pere had escorted them under the cover of darkness. They had told him that his guidance and presence wasn't needed, which in purely logistical terms, it wasn't, he though, insisted, saying that it would be a lot less conspicuous, a man with two women in the dead of night, rather than two women alone. Also, Marcus had given him very specific orders. Antonia had cleared the kids stuff out of Rebecca's old bedroom so she, with

Arantxa, could take up occupancy, a little detail that won Rebecca's appreciation.

Sleep was hard to come by. Being *home* brought back too many memories she'd tried to lock away in the deepest parts of her mind, only to be taken out, recalled and wallowed in, on special occasions. This was the only way she'd found of dealing with what had happened since the spring. So much in such a short period of time; losing home, family, neighbours, friends, finding the love of her life, getting pregnant, now there was a future most uncertain to deal with. On top of all that, today, or possibly tomorrow, she would get to see the man she loved in the most difficult of circumstances.

"Oh girl, you look bloody awful. didn't you sleep?"

"Thanks, Antonia. You've made me feel even better."

"Sit down, 'ave someat to eat and drink, and don't think about saying you're not 'ungry or any other twaddle. You gotta eat, I ain't 'aving you fainting or the like in the streets. Jews ain't supposed to be 'ere, and if we get found out, we'll be in the shit even if you 'ave high and mighty dukes for friends. Also, you 'ave to think about the little one."

Rebecca passively and unenthusiastically did as she was told, sitting at her dining table wearing only underclothes with Antonia serving. This was most definitely a continuation of the theme of everything being both wrong and right.

Arantxa entered, "They are washed, hopefully, they'll be dry for when we want to use them." The "forest women" only had two sets of clothes, one of which was a lot worse for wear, and the other, was less than clean. Arantxa had taken it upon herself to scrub hers and Rebecca's. The latter was about to show her gratitude when all three women froze upon hearing two male voices entering the house.

"Arh, don't worry." The thaw came when the voices became identifiable; Pere and Marcus.

"You! You can wait outside." Pointing at her husband, " I'm not 'aving you in 'ere ogling at two nearly naked young women."

"But I haven't had breakfast and I'm.."

"Waiting outside, is what you're doing. Go on. Get out you big lump."

Marcus, having seen both women in considerably less in their warm weather norm in the forest look, didn't bat an eyelid at their state, being much more perturbed by just how dreadful Rebecca's face looked. It was going to be a difficult day.

"Go on, say it!"

"I didn't say anything!"

"That I look dreadful. My hostess has already told me, and reading your face isn't difficult."

"Ok, you look awful."

"Thanks."

"Stop complaining, Rebecca, at least he looked at you. I don't think he's even noticed I am here, clothed, unclothed, dreadful face or not!"

Marcus, who was about to sit down on the chair opposite Rebecca, stopped mid lowering all of a fluster, changing tack to move in Arantxa's direction, only to be pushed forcefully back, almost making him lose his balance. "Too late! Plonk your arse there! We'll have words later."

Great, Marcus thought, the prospect of a most difficult day has just got worse. Not having been in the role of duke that long, he hadn't acquired all the natural poise and arrogance that came with that position in the social strata. His ordering skills had developed considerably because for once in his life, people, who were in awe of him, actually took notice of what he was saying. This masterful role changed dramatically in the company of these two women, sending him back into the role of a young master – with no possibly of tagging on the full part. Reverting him back to the less than dominant days of his childhood.

"Stop sulking! Tell us what's happening."

Clearing his throat and trying hard to gain back the lost years, he spoke with as much solemnity and gravitas that he could manage without sounding ridiculous.

"As you know, Wamba's forces arrived yesterday. He is camped out at Els Munts. I think every army in Christendom has to spend some time there in any campaign."

"What?"

"It's the third army there in less than a month, and if you add to that, the time that…"

"Marcus, get on with it."

So much for gravitas and solemnity. As instructed he continued. "I have been informed that the *parade* will enter the Via Augusta gate this afternoon. I am expected to encourage all the inhabitants of Tarraco to come out onto the streets to see their kings."

"Kings?"

"As it said in the message; the *king* of Tarraconensis/ Gallia Gothica will lead followed by King Wamba."

"They are going to publicly humiliate Flavius?"

"I have been told that this is the standard procedure that they have followed everywhere from Narbo to Barcino."

"MY *poor* Flavius."

"Apparently, Toletum has insisted that this be part of his punishment."

"Are they going to.."

"Execute him? Not here. He is to be taken back to Toletum and tried there."

"Where they'll.."

"Not necessarily. The fact that he's still alive gives hope. All the other leaders that were caught alive have already been executed. There's hope for Paulus. I know that Wamba liked, and from what I was told last night by General Alaric, still likes, him. Alaric also added that people in high places in Toletum, namely Bishop Julian, is very much a Paulus liker. So, I don't want to give you false hope, but I truly believe there might be some possibility."

What Marcus neglected to tell Rebecca, though he had informed Pere, was that Alaric was most eager to find out where Rebecca was, whether she was alive, in the city or had left. Wamba, apparently, was most desperate to meet the woman who'd had such a profound effect on so many important people. Alaric wanted Marcus to spread the word that a handsome reward would be offered for any information leading to her apprehension. Marcus had every intention of not remembering to tell anyone about this offer.

Pere had to tell someone, he chose his wife whose first and only question was "'ow much?" which earned her such a glare that she quickly added, "just to know 'ow much she's worth, nothing else, 'onest!"

*

The streets thronged. The largesse story had circulated and everyone was anxious to get their share and a bit more. Small coins were to be thrown from one of the carriages. This was quite an anomaly in itself, as small denomination coins hadn't been seen in this part of the kingdom for many a year. The solidus, which was a great deal of money, being the only coin readily seen or accepted. And brought with it many problems as it couldn't be broken down because change couldn't be given. Again the negative knock on effect was that a lot of commerce had either ceased or reverted to barter. These largessed dispensed small currency coins would become like gold dust, worth so much more than the nominal face value. The cavalcade itself was short; a group of spick and span perfectly attired soldiers, followed by the "king" in a grubby tunic with fishbone attached to the scalped head, some more soldiers, King Wamba in all his splendour and then what most people wanted to see, the coin distributing cart whose effect sent everyone scrabbling to the ground, giving the appearance to anyone looking on from the outside that they were showing reverence to their passing legitimate king by throwing themselves to the ground.

As this was a family occasion, it wasn't strange to see three women and three children huddled together behind a group of Tarraco soldiers, whose job it was to line some important streets to make sure that people stayed back when the parade passed. Modesty and an intense afternoon autumn sun ensured that hoods were worn. Arantxa and Antonia flanked a quivering Rebecca, giving her physical and moral support, behind Pere's group of roped- in- against- their- wishes soldiers for the day.

Tension increased as the noise of the parade got closer. Rebecca attempting to take deep breaths as instructed, could manage little better than a nervous pant. The first marching soldiers could be seen coming around the corner towards their position, just before the City's exit gate, a place they had chosen in order to be the last to see the parade leaving the city, which also meant that the crowds were much thinner here because it was assumed that the number of coins to be thrown was finite, and may well have dwindled or diminished totally by the latter stages of the event. They weren't quite alone, but nobody obstructed their view over the shoulders of the day soldiers.

She saw him. Oh my God! What a mess! Tied to a post, the poor man was doing his best to look into the middle distance trying not to see, hear or feel anything, as if he weren't really there. Wanting to scream, cry, trying to make her jellified legs stay rigid, she searched for his eyes. She needed him to see her, to see her love, to see her support, to feel that she was with him. His look though was nowhere; he was lost trying to maintain what little dignity he had.

All of a sudden Pere yelled an order to his group, "Attention!" Pere himself gave a smart salute just as Paulus's carriage appeared in front of him. The noise made Paulus look down, he recognised Pere and smiled, probably the first time he'd done that since supper with the King back in Narbo. Then there was a movement behind Pere, a woman pulled down her hood, they locked eyes and gazed eloquently saying everything and nothing for as long as they could.

HISTORICAL NOTE

This is a work of historical fiction and should be seen as such.

My problem with "history" in general is that most of it can only ever be regarded as fiction. "The father of history" Herodotus is a splendid example being a man much more interested in a good story to let too many inconvenient facts get in his way.

"Facts" are very few and usually open to widely varying interpretations. This is true for all eras and perhaps even more so when considering periods when little was written.

"Historians" in an effort to create their little niche have kidnapped the whole concept of history for their own use and benefit. In their segregated ivory towers they claim ownership of the common past of mankind by "teaching" it through bum and mind numbing boredom. The number of soporific talks given by experts I personally have attended runs into the hundreds. Perhaps they should not be blamed as this is the way academia works, however, the fact remains that most people have not got a clue about what or why things happened in human history.

Before starting this project I, along with nearly everyone in Tarragona, knew precious little of the people named Visigoths. The popular concept of this group went something like – a *Germanic tribe who replaced Roman civilisation with a great deal of nothing thus emptying the once mighty capital of Hispanias of the vast majority of its population.* The people of Tarragona rightly celebrate their glorious Roman past and ignore everything else until the *reconquest* of the Catalan kings. The Visigoths and the Islamic invaders are rather excluded from its history.

My thought lines, initially, were something like; poor things - something ought to be done to glorify their three hundred year stay – they can't have been that bad.

To my surprise, they were *that* bad, but in a different way to how I imagined. Marauding, uncouth brutes were replaced in my head with a systematic dreadful regime which was the forerunner of a feudal economy sustained on a diet of religious persecution, everything the Spanish state became proud of in the middle ages.

In this book some of the characters, according to sources, existed. Their personality and behavioural patterns have been provided by me. Flavius Paulus is a case in point. The *incident* is generally known as the "Paulus Rebellion" and presented as some sort of power grab. Those who write about it fail to address why a successful general, who was well connected in the capital and had the king's favour, would lead a provincial rebellion aimed not at taking over the state, but breaking away from it, when that dux had little or no connection with the area in question. It's presented something like "it's the sort of things people did in those days, rebellions were the norm in Visigoth society". Furthermore, why the power structure in the said provinces should accept him as leader, even to the point of making him a "king", is never addressed in a real substantive way.

The historians, when not quoting each other, use the few written documents of the period, most notably those provided by "Saint Julian". Even if, as they often state, they are reading between the lines, this source use would be akin to using Himmler's diaries as an objective account of the Third Reich. Julian was a repellent racist in both word and deed and should be judged for what he is- a forerunner of mass murder and ethnic cleansing who would/ should be prosecuted in any court of Human Rights rather than canonised and revered by the most populous religion on the planet.

Also, I am guilty of extrapolating this territorial conflict of the seventh century into a still unresolved problem, Catalunya in the state of Spain. There are echoes. It's probably incorrect to draw any direct parallels, especially as all the action happens before any real Catalan identity had been developed, still, I do believe it started to sow the seeds of discontent which have been evident for so many centuries and remains a serious bone of contention today when a nation, defined by language, culture and identity, is not allowed to progress on a path of right to self determination without violence being imposed upon it.

October 2020
John Butler
The Clot Tarragona
Catalunya

ACKNOWLEDGMENTS

Normally I never reach this part of the book as it doesn't interest me greatly. If you are reading, thanks for bothering.

This is a project that has been in the making for many years and a whole number of people have helped to make it a reality.

However, before mentioning those people, I would first like to point out those who have either actively discouraged or have been less than helpful. The number of "experts" I wrote to for help or clarification is considerable, the replies have been close to zero. If anyone would like a list of people not to bother trying to get help from, I would be glad to provide it. It comprises of are mainly academics who are too busy or important to deign to reply. Added to that group are a number of Jewish history organisations, who, again, found their history and persecution at the hands of Christians not significantly interesting to answer any query.

Furthermore, research trips to places such as Nimes (Nemausus), Narbonne (Narbo), Girona (Gerunda) could have been a great deal more fruitful if the local experts had agreed to meet me, or been a little more open and generous with their history. The Jewish museum in Girona is a point in example where they assured me that Jews didn't live in Catalonia until the ninth century!

On the bright side of the street we have a whole group of particularly splendid people.

Helping with the historical narrative were two wonderful women; Meritxell Pérez Martínez and Ma Josepa Estanyol. Truly brilliant historians. They gave their time and knowledge unstintingly. I apologise in advance for distorting, changing, or even disregarding some of their factual corrections – they just didn't fit into the story! Any errors in this area of historical accuracy can be laid quite firmly on my doorstep. Sorry.

My brother, Philip, says he should be in this section as well. I am not sure why but he probably does.

The comma crew were invaluable. You know who you are, thanks.

My daughter, Soph, helped greatly.

Special thanks go out to Anja. Her selfless dedication to the local food and wine on the research trips supported me and the local economies massively.

Printed in Great Britain
by Amazon